Omnibus

The Tutor
Portia Da Costa

The Gift of Shame
Sarah
Hope-Walker

Elena's Conquest
Lisette Allen

Omnibus

The Tutor
Portia Da Costa

The Gift of Shame
Sarah
Hope-Walker

Elena's Conquest
Lisette Allen

Doubleday Book & Music Clubs, Inc.
Garden City, New York

Black Lace novels are sexual fantasies.
In real life, make sure you practice safe sex.

This omnibus edition published 1994 by BCA
by arrangement with Black Lace,
332 Ladbroke Grove, London W10 5AH

The Tutor © Portia da Costa, 1994
The Gift of Shame © Sarah Hope-Walker, 1994
Elena's Conquest © Lisette Allen, 1994

ISBN   1-56865-183-X

Printed in the United States of America

CONTENTS

CONTENTS

The Tutor
Portia Da Costa

Contents

Contents

Chapter 1

The Best of Times?

*I*t was the best of times, it was the worst of times.
   Rosie knew it was a Dickens quote, but for her it always conjured up visions of *Star Trek*. Of Kirk and Spock and a time that had been both good and bad for them. A time like that night, a week ago, when she'd had probably the best sex ever; then the worst of all let-downs afterwards. That night when Geoff had made love to her like a Mills and Boon hero who'd just read *The Joy of Sex*; then told her, five short minutes into the afterglow, that 'it', or more precisely 'they' were finished.

   I should have known it was too good to be true when he brought roses, she thought now, a sad, wry smile on her face.

   'Roses for my Rosie,' she echoed, more in self mockery than genuine bitterness. A canny northern lass like her should have smelt a slippery southern rat from the outset. A smooth, blond, southern rat with a pin-up's face and a strong sexy body to match it. Fool, Rosie! Fool, fool, fool!

   The trouble was, if every trickster and let-down artist could do the things that Geoff could do, then Rosie knew she was going to go on being a fool, putting up with all kinds of chauvinist piggery for the tunes that they – or in this case, he – could play on her nerves and her senses. The way he'd touched her and teased her and brought her alive; tuned her to a pitch of pleasure she'd not thought her body capable of; taught her she was sexy, even though she suspected his motives in doing so and realised now that he'd made little conscious effort to educate her.

Those bloody roses!

'For you,' he'd said, whisking them out of her hands as soon as he'd put them there; just so he could grab hold of her, kiss her and start running his hands over her body. The fact that she was wearing just a thin silky dressing gown made the process all the easier.

'God, you've got a great body on you, northern girl,' he said roughly, sliding the thin, slick stuff over the rounds of her full, fruity buttocks. 'Those supermodels look great in magazines, but there's something to be said for a girl with some flesh on her bones.'

Such observations as those had hurt her when they'd first started seeing each other, but for a while now she'd been more sanguine. She *was* a rounded girl, and there wasn't too much she could do about it without making her life a misery; but she'd noticed of late that a lot of men shared Geoff's viewpoint. She'd seen plenty of hot looks aimed her way, undressing eyes studying her full breasts and her curvy bottom, and she'd started enjoying the feeling.

She certainly enjoyed it when Geoff massaged that curvy bottom and pressed her forward so her pubis massaged his erection. He was stroking the delicate in-slope now, pushing the silk in towards her stickiness, not caring that he'd soil an expensive robe she'd bought especially to please him. She didn't care either, not when he was rubbing her swollen, sensitive folds and getting closer and closer to the core of her. Unaware that she was inciting the process, she began wriggling and shimmying against him.

'Come on, you little sex-pot,' he laughed into her ear, 'let's get you into bed before you come right here in the lounge.'

That sort of thing had also upset her at first. His almost mocking reaction to her sexuality: her easy readiness for him, and the way she couldn't resist even the slightest of his caresses. The way her body showed her arousal so clearly. The hardness of her nipples, the excessive wetness that flowed like sap between legs that slid open without resistance.

The cynic within her noted that he didn't even try to lift her up and carry her. She wasn't *that* heavy, but it would need someone who worked out a tad more than Geoff did to sweep her off her feet and whisk her into the bedroom – and still maintain his Mr Perfect look as he did so.

When he undressed, there was a distinct 'Chippendale' feel to the process. He was most definitely posing, but Rosie wasn't put off by it. His body was so attractive, and what he would soon be doing to hers with it was enough to excuse his airs and graces. She could already taste the smooth fresh warmth of that high-gloss golden-tanned skin; feel those muscles pressed against her softer, feminine body; feel the push of that penis as it forged its way inside her. Oh dear God, the man was so lovely to be loved by he was almost edible!

'This is going to be so good, Rosie,' he said confidently, stepping out of his boxer shorts.

Oh yes, it is! she echoed silently, watching his cock swing up and slap against his flat, sexy belly. Her body rippled involuntarily, already feeling him inside her, and though she should have been used to it by now, her own wantonness still managed to astound her. She licked her lips as her man took himself in hand and began to work the loose suedey skin of his sex over the strong hard core at its centre. He was stiffening himself and readying himself, and she felt a momentary pang, a disappointment that he was planning to penetrate her immediately and forgo the delicious preparations: the strokings and lickings that made her whimper and moan with pleasure, and the chance, and the time, to do some stroking and licking of her own.

13

'Don't worry, kid.' He grinned his film star grin at her. 'I'm going to come quickly . . . then I'll last longer for the second round.'

It made good sense, but somehow the moment was spoiled. As she watched him rubbing his penis, there were two Rosie Howards observing the phenomenon; and while one, the newborn sensualist, thought the sight was extraordinarily beautiful, the other, the cynical Yorkshirewoman, decided that the more desirable a man became, the more his ego inflated.

Stop it, you! she told the hard-eyed realist inside her, and through an effort of will that person was banished. Okay, so Geoff was a bit self-centred, but he was also gorgeous, a wonderful lover, and here with her when he could have been chasing one of the rake-thin achiever-girls from his office. All of whom lusted after him, by his account.

He was building quickly to his climax now, one knee braced on the edge of the bed, hips thrusting forward, his cock hard and reddened in his fingers. She pulled open her robe, baring her pale, waiting body in a mute plea that his semen spurt upon her.

'Please,' she whispered as the cynic turned her back in disgust and walked away.

'Yes, baby, yes!' cried Geoff, his handsome face contorted, his eyes closed. Rosie sensed him to be elsewhere, somehow in a different world, as he pumped his own male flesh and brought himself right to the pinnacle. His slim hips were a blur for a moment, and as her sigh underpinned his groans, his pure white semen shot out of the eye of his penis, arced high, and landed with an unstudied accuracy on the palpitating plain of her belly.

Without conscious thought, she pressed her fingers to her own curved body, paddled in his essence and smoothed it into her skin. It was as if he'd annointed her, and that his erotic white ejaculate contained an aphrodisiac that inflamed her even further. She slid her hot, sticky fingers through the tangle of her pubis and opened up her vulva to caress it.

14

Geoff was lying down beside her now, edging her across the bed, interrupting the very beginnings of her pleasure to make himself a space to lie down in. Rosie felt a momentary flash of annoyance, then forgot it as he propped himself up on his elbow and smiled down at her.

'Your turn now, my horny little Rosie,' he purred, nudging at her wrists to encourage her. 'Bring yourself off for me, darling. You know how I love to see you diddling.'

She wanted to do it. She wanted both the pleasure itself and to please him, but even so twenty-eight years of inhibition made her blush the same colour she was nicknamed. Hot and pink, she closed her eyes and let her fingertips find their own way between the thick puffed-out lips of her sex.

Embarrassed by her own extreme moistness, she parted herself, knowing that her pinkness would be almost crimson down there, slick and gleaming to Geoff's sharp, observant eyes. With a sigh of resignation, then a ragged gasp, she dipped a finger in the well of her juices and drew it up slowly across her clitoris.

'Oh! Mmmm,' she murmured, her thighs slowly moving as she fingered her tiny bud of pleasure. This considered touch, this deliberate self-stimulation, was still quite new to her, and the novelty added extra spice. She flicked herself, then circled, groaning as the flesh itself seemed to grow and re-sensitise in response. Her bottom was lifting from the bed now, her hips swaying, and she was dimly aware that she must be putting on quite a show for her lover. Even as that thought crossed her mind, she felt his fingers slide in next to hers, pushing and pressing to make hers work harder and the tender flesh beneath them leap.

She cried out long and loud, her orgasm flaring wildly, stoked by Geoff's rough touch. Her own fingers had been knocked away by his bigger, stronger ones and he was rubbing her more jerkily than he usually did, as if trying to squeeze her into climax by force alone. There

15

was a faint strand of pain amongst the pleasure, but Rosie was beyond such differentiations now, her body incandescent with sensation.

'I want you, Rosie,' he growled into her ear, his fingers still scrubbing at her sex. 'I want to be in that lush, hot body of yours. I want to screw you so hard that you'll never forget what it feels like.'

In Rosie's more rational moments, an utterance like that would have phased her, set her analytical mind a-pondering. But right now, she had Geoff's fingers between her thighs and analysis and reason wouldn't function. She wanted only what he wanted. To be made love to. To be taken.

With a soft, incoherent cry, she widened her thighs and pulled at him. She urged him to mount her and enjoy the body that was totally his.

'Patience, little sexy,' he taunted, his fingers still moving, still rubbing.

To her shame, Rosie heard herself whine with frustration. Rolling her pelvis, she pulled her legs open wider with her own hands, making her vulva accessible and available.

'Please,' she moaned again, her breath hissing wildly between her teeth as a finger plunged right inside her.

'Please what?'

'Please make love to me.'

'Come on, Rosie, you can do better than that. I want to hear you talk dirty, Miss Prim . . . Miss Librarian with fire in her knickers.'

'Please! I can't!'

'If you don't say it, I won't do it!'

She sobbed, hating herself for being helpless against his ultimate threat. 'Please, Geoff . . . Please will you screw me.'

She hated that word, and could only whisper it so faintly that it was barely audible – but it seemed to suffice.

'Alright, sexy, I'll screw you.'

But something was wrong. The finger stayed inside

16

her and started pumping back and forth, surging in her juices and making a hideous and mortifying squelching sound.

'Geoff!'

'But I'm doing it.' His fingers plumbed her remorselessly, searching crudely for the heart of her shame.

'Please, Geoff. Use your . . . your . . .'

'Say it, Rosie.' His voice was suddenly quite cold. 'Ask me for what you want.'

'Use your cock,' she cried wildly, beside herself with need and frustration – and against her better judgement, with love. 'Put your cock in me, you bastard!' she screamed, almost coming again she felt so desperate.

'That's it, my sexy,' he answered, slipping away his hand as he moved between her quaking, stretched apart thighs. She was trapped by him, pinned by him, caught as much by her own desire as by his rigid body. The head of his cock touched her vulva and she keened like a hound when he wouldn't put it straight inside her. She heard him laughing softly and almost wanted to kill him; then she sighed and gulped in air with relief as he sank down upon her and into her.

And he'd been right. He did last longer. Longer than ever before. So long she lost count of her orgasms and felt revivified by the sheer excesses of pleasure.

In the precious moments afterwards, she'd felt both drained by the exhilarating climaxes and peculiarly dynamised too. She was good at this, she decided, and she liked it; she felt strong and confident, a confidence that she knew could spread out and filter through into the whole of her life.

Half-dreaming, she thought about striking out, trying different things. She'd already tentatively applied for a new job, but now she felt like trying a bit harder. Maybe getting the damn thing. She could be much more the sort of woman Geoff really wanted if she put her mind to it – and right then, flying high on the glow of good sex, she'd felt grateful to him for both the pleasure and the impetus to change.

17

Ah, but wasn't there always a sting?

And God, how that sting had stung, she thought now, after a week of pain and recrimination, and a fury that was directed far more at herself than at him.

As she'd torn up his photograph, it was herself she was cursing for gullibility, not the man in the image for his perfidy.

Even so, she didn't like to think of the details too much. He and she weren't going anywhere, he'd said. They weren't really compatible. He'd met someone else. Someone at his work. She was in PR, she was happening, and on her way to the top.

Rosie had shut off then, knowing that she was none of those things and too much the outsider in his world ever to be able to compete. To her great satisfaction she'd remained calm, composed and almost friendly – until the door had closed firmly behind him and she'd smashed half a dozen dishes in her sorrow and fury, then chastised herself soundly for giving in to it.

Sulking and moping achieved nothing. Weeping and wailing achieved nothing. Breaking things achieved nothing except the expense of buying new things!

The only way forward now was to learn, re-group, start again. And go out and show handsome, self-centred bastards like Geoff that they couldn't get the better of Rosie Howard!

Chapter 2

Mister Hadey's 'Private Case'

*I*f I was still with Geoff, I might not have come here, Rosie reflected as she waited. Fiddling nervously with the deeply revered neckline of her jacket, she surveyed one of the most sumptuous rooms she'd ever seen, and almost thanked her ex for his treachery. Foolishly lost in her dreamworld of sex with 'golden boy', she'd probably have ended up changing her mind after all, backing out of the interview, and missing all this magnificence.

A case-hardened realist now though, she still didn't rate her chances of getting the job all that highly. It was out of her league – well within her technical abilities, granted, but so different from the world she'd always inhabited that it might as well have been on another planet. Nevertheless, a drastic change was what she'd decided she needed. And if she got this job it would mean a *really* drastic change.

Right from the time of getting her degree, Rosie had always taken the safe jobs. The humdrum jobs. The routine jobs. There'd never actually been much excitement in library service anyway, but looking back, the posts she'd taken now seemed the dullest she could have chosen. A wind of change had to blow soon, she realised, or any illusions she'd ever had would disappear. She'd stagnate. She'd be a senior assistant librarian

19

in a medium-sized municipal library forever. A week ago, she'd had only a vague post-orgasmic yen to be bolder for Geoff's sake; but now she needed that 'something new' as much as she needed air to breathe. It was survival now, a shot at self-redemption.

Hence this make-over. The radical re-vamp she still wasn't sure about. The hair, the make-up, the clothes.

Crossing her knees and smoothing down her skirt, she wondered what the girls behind the desk in 'adult loans' would think of her now. This certainly wasn't their Miss Howard with her neatly-bunned hair and her conservative Marks & Spencer outfits. This was a new being entirely, with hair worn loose and swingy right down to her waist, face skilfully made up, and body that was distinctly power-dressed. Rosie had always tried to look attractive – and succeeded, after her own fashion – but she knew that at this moment she looked more like one of those lip-glossed, corporate career-girls than a woman who catalogued books on geraniums and geography for a living. It was all a bit unnerving.

Her slim-skirted pin-stripe suit had cost a fortune, and its hemline was a good six inches shorter than the length she'd always favoured. She'd definitely had a brainstorm when she'd chosen it, she decided, and probably another when she'd bought black patent stilletto-heeled pumps to go with it; but at heart she knew it was simply a figurative thumbed-nose, or more aptly a vee sign, in the direction of Geoff and his betrayal. He'd implied she wasn't 'happening', that she was too parochial. He'd hinted that without him she wasn't sexy. This sharply feminine suit and the cool but challenging look that went with it were a way of telling him he was wrong, and that she didn't need him. What's more, the suit even made her look slim!

Well, not exactly slim, she admitted, primping discreetly at her skirt. What this sexy suit did was make her curves look fashionable, her full breasts fabulous, and her flaring, womanly hips not quite so flaring.

Still trying to adjust to being a brand new creature,

Rosie stared around the beautiful, antique-strewn room and reviewed the peculiar advert that had brought her here.

Experienced young woman required to catalogue extensive collection of rare books. Pleasant work in amenable surroundings. Applicant will be expected to do a small amount of secretarial work in addition to library duties, and should be prepared to live in.

The word 'experienced' seemed ambiguous, and the last stipulation about living in had been off-putting to the Rosie of a fortnight ago.

The Rosie of today still felt dubious about being experienced but she kind of liked its hint of naughtiness. She was also aware that her own small flat held too many memories of ecstatic nights with Geoff, so living elsewhere would be a blessing. Especially if it was in this house. The place was a palace and its elegant opulence was a pure, sensual thrill. To work in such a haven as this, she was beginning to think she'd do anything! Well, almost anything.

As if wishes could motivate action, the tall beautifully polished double doors to the hall suddenly opened, and in walked a quite different kind of beauty.

Oh no, not another God's gift! thought Rosie in the few seconds it took to assimilate the newcomer's appearance. She was infinitely glad now that she'd decided on her suit, her shoes, and her seductive new hairstyle. Because Mister Julian Hadey – if this was the same person who'd placed the advertisement – looked like a man who could probably only relate to women as sexually all-confident as he was. He wasn't the same blond god type as Geoff, but his dark, menacing, almost middle-eastern looks had an immediate and similar effect.

'Rosalind Howard?' he enquired, his voice like melting caramel. His brown-eyed gaze was already panning over her body as he strode forward and reached for her hand.

'Rosie, actually,' she replied, leaping to her feet and

21

letting him take her fingers in his, setting her inner parts shaking and shivering.

He answered with a narrow, assessing smile; a brief, telling twist of a mouth that was sinfully beautiful. 'Even better,' he murmured, squeezing the hand he still held and looking directly into her eyes. Directly and very, very probingly. 'And I'm Julian Hadey. Please,' he nodded to a long brocaded sofa some feet from the chair Rosie had previously chosen, 'take a seat and let's get to know each other.'

I can't cope! I can't cope! screamed the old, gauche version of Rosie, panicking silently in the face of such refined and unfiltered maleness.

Shut up! You can! the new look Rosie ordered from behind her armour of sleek suit, sleek make-up and a steel-clad determination to never again be bested by a glamorous, unprincipled man. A gut feeling already told her that this would be a job interview unlike any she'd ever had before; or dreamed of having. And even though she'd dazzled this Hadey with only two unimpressive words so far, she sensed an unaccountable rapport forming. A tension like fine wires stretched between them; as if she were face to face with a hot and sizzling new lover rather than a prospective employer.

Surprisingly, she felt quite poised. Matching his smile, she allowed herself to be led to the sofa, then sat down, wary of her slim, tight skirt. Hadey sank smoothly down next to her, his blue-jeaned knee just an inch or two from her gunmetal-stockinged one. He seemed to take note of her checking their proximity, and moved slightly closer on purpose.

'Please excuse me, Rosie, I don't usually dress so casually to interview.' The Arabian Nights grin widened, making his even teeth look white as ice in the olive-toned setting of his face. 'But at home I find a suit too restricting.'

There was a teasing note to his voice, something indefinably, yet appealingly suggestive – as if he'd just said he'd prefer to be naked and wouldn't she like to undress too?

22

You're going mad, Howard, Rosie told herself frantically. He'd said nothing of the sort! It was her own interpretation. Her own ridiculous idea. Her own desire
that instead of wearing those narrow jeans and that
fluidly-styled creamy-beige shirt, Julian Hadey should
be utterly and beautifully nude. For an instant she imagined him thus, and the picture almost threw her completely. Her well-planned résumé went flying out of the
tall Regency windows, and she could think of nothing
else but this handsome man and his elegant, unclothed
body. His beautiful shirt and jeans were there before
her, fitting snugly on his lean, muscular shape, but Rosie
could no longer see them.

He was smiling again, a wolfish, dark-eyed smirk; but
in Rosie's mind, the smile – and the man that went with
it – had shifted to a different location. He was lying on
a spacious bed somewhere, in a tangle of pale silk
sheets, his bare brown skin damp and gleaming. His
body was as swarthy and exotic as his dusky face and
hands had indicated, and he was peppered with dark
male hair: a thick, wiry mat at his chest, a soft fuzzy
forest at his groin. He was slim of waist, broad of chest,
and unequivocably solid of cock. And as the image of
that reared up like a club to torment her, Rosie prayed
that she hadn't started blushing.

Whether intentionally or not, this Julian Hadey
seemed hell-bent on stirring her libido. His every move
was both languid and graceful, and as he reached for a
manilla file that lay on a small table beside him, then
leaned back into the cushions of the sofa, his hard body
flexed and shifted explicitly as he crossed his jeans-clad
legs. It was almost as if he were aping the fantasy somehow, exhibiting himself, even though there was no way
he could know what she was seeing. Without speaking,
but still smiling, he settled the file on his lap and flipped
it open.

For what felt like a millenium, Rosie watched him pe-
ruse various papers; amongst them, presumably, her let-
ter of application and her photocopied diplomas. She

was mesmerised by the length of his coal black eyelashes as they flicked and fluttered in the course of his reading. She imagined them tickling the skin of her belly as his roving lips discovered her.

'Very impressive,' he murmured, looking up.

Blood surged ominously through Rosie's body, as all her most inappropriate responses fired up at once. She felt warmth surge through her belly, a tightness in her breasts, a hypersensitive readiness throughout all the surface of her skin. On the face of it, Hadey's words were an observation on her genuinely excellent qualifications, but his eyes said they were nothing whatsoever to do with certificates and references.

He was studying *her* now. Everything about her, and in blatant, indecent detail. This was the archetypal male 'undressing the female' look and this time, to her fascinated horror, Rosie basked in it.

She thought of how she'd seen this look so often recently, and how, when it had come from Geoff, she'd felt demeaned. But this time, here, she felt better for it, not worse. No matter how smoothly and suavely he projected himself, she sensed that Julian Hadey was a fundamentally straightforward man; an honest man who really was impressed with what he saw. With her, with her body, and even with her shaky façade of sexual *savoir-faire*.

'Tell me about yourself,' he said, facing her with the interviewee's perennial nightmare question.

'Well,' she began, wishing for just a second that the man was as ugly as sin, and that she wasn't so strongly attracted to him. At least that way she could have thought and answered coherently instead of sliding head over heels back into fantasy. 'Well, since I left University I've worked mainly in public libraries. Mostly doing reader enquiry work, but recently I've been doing more cat –'

'No, Rosie, tell me about *yourself*,' he interrupted. The emphasis on 'yourself' was silky and intimate, and she felt as if he'd asked her, straight out, what she liked to do best in bed. Insanely, she imagined telling him, but at the very last second, bit her tongue.

Not long ago, Rosie had attended a yoga course and learned the principles of bio-feedback. Now, under the intense, almost spot-lit scrutiny of Julian Hadey, she fought hard to remember those techniques, and to remain in control. Through sheer power of will, she suppressed the beetroot-red blushes she'd always been prone to, and managed to keep her breathing and her voice quite steady. There was nothing she could do about her arousal; it was running riot. She could only give in and enjoy it.

'Well, Mister Hadey,' she began, astonished by how together she suddenly sounded. 'I'm Rosie Howard, I'm twenty-eight, and I come from a small town in Yorkshire. I'm a chartered librarian. I love books and love being around books. But recently, something happened . . . and now I want a complete change. I want to work somewhere different. Somewhere quite unlike the sort of libraries I've always worked in . . . I . . .'

She faltered there, and felt her heart bound madly as Hadey's brown eyes thinned, and his attention visibly sharpened. This was a minefield, and she knew it. She braced herself for the inevitable questions, and when he didn't immediately ask them, she took a chance and plunged ever onwards.

'When I saw your advertisement, I decided I'd found just the change I wanted. I'm good at "cat & class", it's my speciality, but I'm fed up of dealing with romantic novels and books about knitting all day. Rare books in a private collection sound much more interesting. I also have no particular fondness for the flat I live in – and I'm a free agent in general – so living in wouldn't be a problem. Especially not here!' She waved in the vague direction of all the beauty and comfort around her.

She stopped for a moment then, wondering if she'd said too much. Hadey was still watching her closely, his dark eyes unwavering, his body motionless, his long brown fingers resting lightly on the papers before him.

25

To her increasing embarrassment, he said nothing, but just continued to look her straight in the eye.

He was challenging her to explain herself, to expand on her free agent notion. To admit she'd been ditched and sexually humiliated. Her heart speeding faster, she rushed on. 'I think I'd be perfect for your job, Mister Hadey. You'll have to go a long way to find someone with my qualifications who's available.'

The minute it was out, she realised she'd just blown all her personal PR clean out of the water. Available, indeed? What an air-head thing to say!

Julian Hadey smiled. Not the thin, judging smile of before, but a soft, mischievous grin that bordered closely on an out-and-out chuckle.

In that moment, he looked even sexier than ever, and if possible, both older and younger at the same time. His obvious amusement was as natural and unaffected as a boy's, but simultaneously, Rosie noticed the distinguished flashes of grey in his thick dark hair, the tiny crinkles of his laughter lines – and the almost palpable air of 'this man has lived' that seemed to overlay his entire persona. As she waited, breath on hold, he put her file aside and rose lithely to his feet.

'The name's Julian,' he said, reaching out for her hand to pull her to her feet. 'And I'm absolutely delighted you're "available". Because *I* think you're perfect for the job too.' His lips quirked slightly on the word 'job', as if that was a further source of entertainment, and somehow not quite what it seemed. But his brown eyes were so bright and compelling, and his smile such a welcome relief that Rosie dismissed her faint shiver of alarm.

'Come on, Rosie.' He drew her forward after him, 'I'll show you some of my books.'

As they made their way to the library, Rosie was struggling. Struggling to understand that suddenly, and without the interview really starting, she seemed to have acquired herself a job; struggling to cope with the presence of this Hadey – this Julian – and all the powerful effects he was having on her.

A lot of them seemed to stem from his penchant for touching. It wasn't offensive or gratuitous though; every time he laid hands on her, there was a relevance. He touched her to urge her to her feet. He touched her to guide her to the correct door amongst what seemed like a dozen in the huge spacious hall. He touched her very courteously to propel her into the library before him. All these small actions required that his fingertips rest somewhere on her body for a moment – and that he brand her skin with his heat through the finely woven cloth of her suit, and even, in some cases, through the fragile silk underwear beneath. When he touched her on the waist to lead her towards one of the tall, mahogany bookcases, she almost squealed aloud with unexpected pleasure. The intensity of the miniscule contact was so sensual that she felt it through the whole of her body: her flanks, her fingertips, her toes – and deep in the very centre of her sex.

As they stood before the serried ranks of books, ostensibly discussing their future disposal, it was all Rosie could do to stop herself from swaying towards him across the scant few inches that divided them.

The library around them was a wonder. A haven of words and paper; of rich, old carpeting; of angled light and the fragrance of leather upholstery. Under any other circumstances Rosie would soon have been lost in it, totally absorbed, but now, to concentrate, she had to fight the influence of its owner.

Julian Hadey possessed many thousands of books on dozens of topics, a great number of them rare first editions. Someone, at sometime, had begun to group them in a vague sort of sequence, but it was fairly haphazard. There was a lot of work to be done, but basically, Rosie didn't think anything more elaborate than the classic Dewey Decimal Classification would be called for.

That was until Julian touched her again, quite casually, and led her towards a set of four crammed book-cases which, unlike the others, were protected by leaded-glass fronts. As he turned towards her, his

27

expression had altered sightly, all the subtle sensuality rising up from within him and shining unchecked in his eyes.

'This is the most important part of my library, Rosie,' he said, his cultured voice infinitesimally thickened. Reaching into the pocket of his tight blue jeans, he drew out a key, and unlocked the first case. 'These are the books I want you to take special care of. The books I want you to cherish, and to read and understand.'

Running a finger along the bottom shelf, he pulled out a volume, a large leather-bound tome, then opened it, slowly and carefully.

Rosie was puzzled by the way he held the book at an angle so she couldn't see the contents. She was puzzled by the way his eyes seemed to widen and flare with heat as he flicked the precious pages; and by the way he unconsciously ran his tongue – his soft and very red tongue – across his lower lip, then smiled with an obvious enjoyment.

'This . . . and these,' he gestured elegantly from the open book to its companions still brooding on the shelves, 'are the very heart of my collection, Rosie. The books I've gathered for myself.' Staring at her from under strangely lowered lashes, he passed the open book to her.

'Oh my God!'

The priceless volume nearly fell, but Julian neatly supported it, his fingertips brushing Rosie's in the process, and lingering.

Mounted in the centre of a recto page was one of the earliest photographs Rosie had ever seen. Its sepia tones were a delicate, washed-out amber against the pure white backing sheet, but otherwise it was startlingly clear and beautifully composed.

It was also unrelievedly pornographic.

A moustached Victorian gentleman was reclining sideways across a tumbled bed, wearing a frilly dress shirt unfastened to show his open combinations beneath. His penis, photographed with astonishing clarity given the times, was being sucked by a buxom young woman who knelt between his legs, her own clothing in similar disarray to that of the gentleman she was pleasuring. Her pose was carefully arranged so that her ample breasts were shown to dangle between the gentleman's legs; and her bottom, which was artfully on display through a slit in her elaborate lacy bloomers, was being kissed by another girl – this one clad only in some sort of short, embroidered chemise and with her completely shaven sex on show for all to see. The faces of the man and the sucking woman were strangely mask-like and emotionless, but the bottom-kisser's bore the faintest ghost of an impish smile.

'Oh my God,' murmured Rosie again. Julian was supporting the book fully by now, and without thinking she touched her fingertip reverently to the photo. The title of the scene, hand-inscribed on the white paper beneath it, was 'The Pleasures of Mister Delaney.'

'So . . . What do you think of it?'

'I . . . I . . .'

Well, what did she think of it? The knee-jerk reaction, her old self's reaction, would be the metaphorical hands-thrown-up-in-horror. But after a deep breath, and a mental-shapeshifting into the new personality she was now supposed to be, Rosie discovered that she liked the photograph. That she more than liked it.

To her surprise, and in a way, with wonder, it suddenly dawned on her that the bawdy old picture excited her. Aroused her intensely. Aroused her physically. She wanted to be *in* the photograph. To be the girl in the middle; sucking that handsome man's penis and being sucked, obscenely, in return. The looks of that Victorian dandy were dark, and faintly exotic. He could easily have been Julian Hadey.

'It's wonderful,' she said finally, knowing in some deep and unfathomable way that she'd sealed her fate, passed a test, and confirmed that the job of cataloguing these outrageous books was truly hers. 'Are they all like this?' she enquired, looking up from the old-fashioned but incendiary image to the rows upon rows of similarly leather-bound books.

'I'm afraid so,' said Julian, grinning as he put the book he was holding aside and reaching into the case for another. He looked ever-so-slightly shamefaced for a second, but Rosie found this extraordinarily appealing. It made her wonder what he'd been like in his youth, when he'd been an innocent just discovering this breathtaking new world.

She shrugged. Julian Hadey could never be that way now; he was quite obviously steeped in worldliness, profoundly experienced and probably familiar with nearly every practice described in his sexual library. But the image of the untutored young man seemed to stick in her mind somehow, lingering in her thoughts to excite her as Julian laid a second open book before her.

This one was Japanese: a pillow book of outlandishly coloured woodcuts showing copulating couples entwined in bone-cracking positions. It was as much a curiosity as it was a work of erotica, but nevertheless there was much that was stimulating.

'I collect "mucky books", as they say where you come from,' Julian admitted frankly, in a fair approximation of a Yorkshire accent.

Without thinking, Rosie flashed him a sharp, disapproving look. It was nothing to do with his salacious choice in literature – she'd already admitted that she liked his erotic books. His gentle gibe at her origins however, had hit on her rawest raw nerve. She saw Geoff's laughing face in her mind, and heard him mocking her pronounced northern accent and her occasional provincial naïvety.

'I'm sorry. I didn't mean that to be in any way disparaging,' said Julian contritely, her fierce look obviously noted and logged for future reference. 'Your accent's charming, Rosie. Quite sexy in fact. And it'll be useful to have a Yorkshirewoman in the house just now. My wife's cousin is staying with us and he comes from Yorkshire. He's . . . Well, he's a bit of a shy young thing, and I'm sure he'll feel more at home with a familiar sounding voice around.'

Rosie was momentarily intrigued at the thought of a fellow 'Yorkie' to keep her company, but soon forgot the unknown house-guest as Julian pulled out more books.

The collection was a repository for what had to be some of the most exotic prose and images in the country. In addition to the illustrated volumes they'd started with, Julian's private case contained every imaginable classic of sexual writing available.

De Sade, Boccaccio, Restif de la Bretonne. The great and the notorious from all ages jostled with each other on shelves that were packed with books.

Nabokov, Anaïs Nin, Sacher-Masoch. The list of names was endless, and interspersed at regular intervals with that most prolific sexual scribe of all: 'Anonymous'. There were even, in the fourth case, a set of novels by contemporary writers; names that probably wouldn't go down in history, but who still seemed to be producing hot and blood-stirring fiction. Julian had no prejudice against these latter-day pornographers with modern names – the books were obviously mass-market in content, but even so, his copies were privately printed on superior paper and bound in leather just like their more literary counterparts.

'Here. Take these with you when you leave,' he said enthusiastically, taking three books down together from a high shelf. As he reached up, Rosie caught a subtle waft of fragrance from his armpit: a sophisticated perfume, his deodorant no doubt, and beneath it, just a tang of male sweat. For a second she felt dizzy, intoxicated by the images she'd seen and the snippets of raunchy prose she'd read, but even more so by the primal odour of Julian's lean, dark body. As he passed her the books she almost dropped them.

'Dip into them tonight.' His bitter-chocolate eyes twinkled wickedly. 'Get acclimatised.'

'Er, yes ... Thanks, I will,' muttered Rosie, still disorientated, as she stared down at the three slim books,

31

each embossed on the spine and front cover with the design of a domino. Acclimatised to what? she pondered, fingering the indented leather.

'Okay. That's enough porn for now, eh?' he went on pleasantly. 'Why don't we go back to the sitting room, have a glass of sherry and discuss all the strictly practical details?'

She's right. She *is* perfect for the job, he thought, and took a sip of the exquisite bone-dry sherry that Rosie had earlier refused in favour of a sweeter, more feminine variety.

The woman he'd just employed had left now, clutching her dark and educational books, and looking faintly bemused. Julian Hadey recalled her presence with some satisfaction, both applauding his own split second decision, and feeling a fresh wave of sexual excitement over the lovely young body he'd selected.

He smiled as he imagined her. A pretty, northern lass. Rosie. Well-named, because she did have a bloom about her. A sexy, innocent lushness that would be so useful for what lay ahead.

Good for me too, he reflected. Technically, he hadn't intended her for himself; but if she was willing – and he was perfectly certain she was – there was no reason why he shouldn't enjoy her as well.

He was back in his library now, and as he shifted his hips in the deep, leather armchair in an attempt to ease his erection, he pictured how she'd looked here earlier. The body that'd inspired his hardness. Specifically, he saw again the sight that had plagued him throughout the whole of the interview: that truly gorgeous cleavage between those long, charcoal pinstriped lapels. A deep and succulent cleft that was designed for the male mouth to forage in. And not just the mouth.

He wondered what she'd thought of his scrutiny. Julian had never hidden his abiding interest in women and their bodies; he felt it dishonest, somehow, to snatch furtive peeks and stolen leers. If he admired a woman, he told her with his eyes; and thus far his frankness had always been rewarded.

Putting aside his sherry, he laid his hand across his groin and considered Rosie Howard.

She was an intriguing and mouthwatering girl, and quite obviously not what she'd tried so hard to project herself as. Her performance had been good, granted, but he sensed that her smooth, sleek style had been a one-off act, or a persona that was still quite new to her. The idea that she'd been trying to deceive him – just as much as he had her – both aroused and amused him. There was much entertainment ahead, he decided, his smile widening. For both of them.

Beneath his fingers his cock was like iron. Had she noticed it? he pondered. Had she seen it pushing at the fly of his jeans? He'd felt her studying him as they'd talked – at least as intently as he'd studied her. What would she have done if he'd calmly unzipped and taken himself in hand, as he wanted to do now. He rather thought she'd be alarmed at first, her blue eyes wide with outrage. After a moment though, her look would soften and grow smoky, and she'd move forward and touch him. Stroke his silky stiffness, then fall down gracefully to her knees and take it deep in her scarlet-painted mouth.

'Oh yes,' he whispered aloud, aware that he'd pushed himself too far in his fantasy to back out now, in reality. Relief was essential. He saw no reason to suffer further. Sighing, he unbuckled his belt, drew down his zip, and pushing down his snug-fitting underpants, drew his penis out into the open.

After a moment of simply enjoying the air on his flesh, he began to adjust his position for further comfort. The people who worked for him were aware of his sensual nature, and never disturbed him unnecessarily. He had all the total privacy he needed to masturbate to orgasm, here in his own library; yet the fact that it was broad daylight, and others were moving efficiently about their duties not far away, only added to the piquancy of the act.

Pushing both jeans and briefs down to his knees, he pressed his naked bottom to the leather, and felt its cool surface kiss his inner cheeks. He wriggled slightly, enjoying the smooth hide rubbing against his balls and the slow majestic wave of his heavily rampant cock. He didn't touch himself directly just yet though. He was free for the rest of the day, so time had no meaning. He could extend his pleasure as much as he wanted. Or as long as his body would allow.

Leaning back, closing his eyes, he saw Rosie Howard spread before him on a bed. On her bed, the one that was prepared for her upstairs at his behest. The sheets were crisp cotton in the deepest pink – as if he'd known, uncannily, what her chosen name would be – and her white body looked paler than ever against them. Her delicious white body that seemed to cry out in silence for his dark one.

Because she was new to him, he'd made her nude. Tantalising clothing would come later, to add spice once the first fine madness was gone. Now he needed to see her rounded, bulging breasts, see their very fullness pull them sideways. He needed to see her lush limbs, her soft belly. She wasn't what he considered overweight, not by a long shot, yet there was a delicate ampleness about her that suddenly almost drove him to violence. His fingers tingled, dying to grab at his penis, but he refrained – tempering his need momentarily with a picture of a different, but equally desirable woman.

'Forgive me, Celeste,' he murmured to his absent wife. He knew that his lust for Rosie Howard was no threat to the happiness of his marriage, but he felt bound to acknowledge Celeste anyway. He always did as he took a new woman. Always afforded his spouse one moment of his attention, even as he enjoyed other flesh. It seemed particularly significant now, because this almost Amazonian Rosie was so different.

Celeste, bless her beautiful heart, had the body of a goddess. Every line, every toned and splendid curve, was aesthetically perfect. When he was with her, possessing her, inside her, she satisfied him utterly; and yet sometimes, he knew, it was just *because* she was such a paragon of perfection that he had a yen for someone who was flawed.

Like voluptuous Rosie, whose body was so delightfully more than svelte. In his increasingly vivid fantasy, he loomed above her now, on her bed. He'd made her naked, but he wore a robe. A favourite of his, a short happi-coat in a fine, but vivid turquoise cotton lawn that looked good against his deeply olive skin.

Returning his attention to his 'prize', he felt a moment of mischief, then saw her wrists fastened to the shining brass bed-rails by soft silken cords. He chided himself for such an easy, chauvinistic ploy, but accepted his predilection. Right now, he felt dominant. He felt the need to gently and kindly master her – and with her hands tied, she was perfectly displayed for his whims.

Behind his eyelids, her squirming body entranced him. Her breasts swayed and her long thighs scissored, giving him momentary glimpses of her soft, pink quim. She was glistening, already needing him madly. She wasn't struggling to get away from him, she was struggling to entice him to her sex.

'No, no, no! You pretty young thing!' he said aloud, regaining control of his own hot dream. He'd known what he wanted the instant he'd set eyes on Rosie Howard, and he'd have it now. Even if it was only in his mind.

Moving his dream-self over her, he straddled her belly, supporting his weight on his strong, lean thighs. He imagined the caress of her smooth skin against his testicles, the tickling sensation as she wriggled beneath him. Her blue eyes were like midnight now – the intense deep colour of the very edge of space – and she was imploring him for something. For anything. Begging that he continue his pleasures so that she might soon attain hers.

With a soft triumphant growl, he cupped her large, firm breasts in his hands and created the channel he'd been longing for. Settling lower, he laid his penis in its velvety containment, holding her flesh around him, careful not to hurt her, but quite set on the sensations he wanted.

Even as he moved and slid, and quietly groaned, he could still admire the physical composition before him. Rosie's pretty blushing face and her long wheat-coloured hair spread out across the pillow. Her white teeth snagging at her moist lower lip. Her pale, plump breasts distorted by his grip, his own long, darkly-livid cock, shining with pre-come, slipping and thrusting in its niche.

He'd wanted this to last, he'd planned for so much more; but suddenly, in the real world, his stimulated loins betrayed him. Barely aware of his actions, he'd been pumping his cock like a madman, and now, crying out, he felt the familiar tell-tale fire come roaring like a train through his guts. As his hips lifted high above the leather, he cupped his glans in his palm to contain his copious spurts.

But his semen escaped him, forcing its way through his fingers, oozing across his wrist, and dripping down onto his thighs, his jeans and the chair as he writhed in his self-induced ecstacy.

'Thank you, Rosie Howard, thank you,' he gasped as he fell back, his cock deflated, at peace, and temporarily eased from its aching. 'But next time, we do it for real.'

Chapter 3

The Wages of Success

'Oh God, I've really done it now!' said Rosie aloud as she settled the receiver in its cradle.

All through this odd, dreamy day, she'd had the comforting feeling that she could still change her mind, ring Julian Hadey and say 'thanks but no thanks'. But after hearing his suave, creamy voice just now on the phone, and realising how far things had progressed, it was obvious that a U-turn was impossible.

Strings had been pulled, wheels set in motion. There was no notice to work out because Julian had had a quiet word with someone on the library committee. He'd had a similar word with her landlord, it seemed, and she suspected that money had changed hands over that one; although Julian himself had refrained from mentioning anything so sordid.

All in all, her transition to his household would be both soon and trouble free. The only thing that remained for her to do was pack up her clothes and personal belongings. And even these would be collected by his chauffeur, when she herself was collected. Such luxury for a lowly librarian!

Hearing Julian's voice again had unnerved her. He sounded so close, so intimate; as if they'd known each other for ages, and been lovers for almost as long. How

37

on earth was she going to cope with that on a day to day basis? It sounded as if he took an active interest in his library, and spent time amongst his books. How the devil would she be able to concentrate on her cataloguing with his gorgeous dark body in the room? He'd played havoc with her judgement today, and they'd only been together an hour or so!

She'd walked down the steps of 17 Amberlake Gardens with a cushion of air beneath her feet, on a massive high from getting the job so easily and meeting a man, a truly sensual man who made no bones about finding her attractive.

His eyes, his voice, his occasional feather-light touches. All these had told her what he'd felt, and shown an admiration that was neither patronising nor glib. Unlike Geoff, Julian Hadey didn't make her feel he was doing her any favours by ever so gently and elegantly leering at her.

Yes, she'd really done it now.

The intoxication of the interview had spilled over into the rest of the day too. Rosie was usually quite a thrifty person, but half way along the Gardens, she'd hailed a cab and had herself transported to the West End – and the shops. For some reason best known to himself, Julian had assured her that a sum of money in advance of wages would be paid into her bank account. To cover her moving expenses, had been his explanation, but Rosie was dubious. It was as if he'd anticipated her qualms, and was trying to sweeten the pot even more to make sure she took his job.

She'd had precious few qualms in Bond Street though. And none in South Molton Street or the Burlington Arcade either. Buoyed up by success, and the lingering scent of her new employer's cologne, she'd spent and splurged in shops she'd never been in before, and flashed her plastic in fine style on the strength of his generous cheque.

It had started fairly innocently. She'd made her first purchase solely to get a carrier bag to put Julian's books in. They were so obviously treasured collector's items, and she didn't want to drop them or have them snatched. Treating herself had felt so satisfying though, and the prospect of using the scented body lotion she'd bought was so wicked and self-pampering that one thing had led to another. And another and another and another in a long, delicious orgy of unaccustomed and liberating spending.

Clothes, perfume, accessories. All sorts of notional knick-knacks. She was starting a new life, so she needed all the trappings of one. Julian had seen her in her one and only 'power' outfit, but she had no intention of disappointing him on Day One of the job by going back to her library mouse ways. He'd said she was perfectly at liberty to dress as casually as she liked while she was working; but there was casual, and there was casual. Whilst ever she was around Mister Hadey and his outrageous and indecent books, she decided she was going to look the part. Or at least as much the part as years of conditioning would allow.

But that didn't account for the lingerie, did it?

In a small, specialist shop she wouldn't have dreamed of entering a week ago, Rosie's groaning credit card had taken its hardest hammering of all. Pretty, curvy underwired bras had, naturally, to be worn with cobweb-fine matching panties. And that meant, automatically, a matching suspender belt for each set, and a few dozen pairs of sheer stockings. And with it being almost summer now, and the weather delightfully warm, some broderie anglaise camisoles with French knickers to match seemed like a good idea too. Thinking of such soft, unstructured fripperies, Rosie blessed all the toning exercises she'd always persevered with. Her bosom was big, admittedly, but it was also perfectly firm. She could easily get away without a bra.

And the nightwear had been out of this world. Touching the slinky, strappy creation she was wearing now, she thought of several other similar beauties that were still nestled in their tissue paper wrapping. Just waiting to be worn for her dark and dangerous Julian.

39

'Rosalind Howard! You bloody idiot!' she hissed at herself. It was·one thing daydreaming about going to bed with your employer, but buying lingerie on the strength of it? Good Grief, by all accounts the man was happily married anyway. If Julian Hadey had a wife as beautiful as the woman in the portrait in his drawing room, he was hardly likely to dally with his fat Yorkshire librarian, was he?

But as she looked at herself in the mirror now, she started to wonder. She wasn't fat. She wasn't even chubby really. It was only Geoff and his cruelly svelte friends that had made her *think* she was.

The woman who stood before her was attractive. Pretty even. She was most definitely sexy. Her body looked tempting and voluptuous in a deep rose-pink nightdress that clung lovingly to her firm, high breasts; and though her hips were generous, at least her waist was small, and her legs long and shapely. Drawing her fingers across her belly, then her midriff, then her bosom, Rosie started to smile.

'You look damn good, kid,' she told herself huskily, then reached for her celebration glass of wine and made a toast. 'To new beginnings, Rosie Howard! No surrender and no way back!'

The wine was sweet and cheerful: Asti Spumante, her rather unsophisticated favourite. Alcohol always made her randy, she acknowledged, drinking deeply; and tonight was no exception. For a moment, she felt a sad, masochistic yearning for Geoff. Then she remembered her toast, and her hopes, and banished him severely from her mind. The only way now was forward: towards a man named Julian Hadey.

A man who was truly the stuff of fantasy.

Topping up her glass, and giggling at how much of the wine she'd drunk, she sat down on the squashy old sofa in her flat and thought of the luxurious surroundings and superior furniture she'd soon be living with. She imagined the room that awaited her, and taking a few liberties, made it an exotic eastern boudoir – the

40

ideal setting in which to wait for an exotic eastern lover. For Julian, who'd revealed in the course of their conversation that he'd had a Sudanese grandmother; a princess no less, stolen away in her childhood and saved from arranged marriage and a life of domestic repression.

Closing her eyes, she imagined that she too had been stolen away. Rescued from tedious servitude at the Reader's Enquiry Desk, by Sheik Julian of Arabian Wonderland. She took another sip of her wine, put the glass aside, then dimmed the light, lay down and closed her eyes.

'I await you, my Lord,' she whispered, grinning at her own fancifulness as she arranged her arms and legs in what she imagined was an odalisque's pose. It was all very silly, she told herself, but suddenly, it was exhilarating too.

He'd look fabulous in a djellabah, she thought, trying to imagine the picture. Julian, in a long, snow white robe, with its neckline slashed to show his muscular brown chest and the curls of his crisp, dark body hair. It was a sublime image, and sinfully easy to embellish. Julian's romantic looks were clear and seductive in her mind, and his aura so powerful and male it seemed to sweep out across the city and engulf her.

It would be a thin robe too, she decided, mentally sketching in the silhouette of his hips and torso, and the hazy, but threatening shadow at the juncture of his long tawny thighs. He'd be erect already, his sex alive with his craving to possess her.

This is such tosh! said the cynic inside her; while the woman who was hungry for sex and magic and mystery said 'More! More! More!'

He was beside her now, his hand gently cruising her body. Sighing, she created the touch herself, placing her hands on her thighs and sliding the ruby coloured silk across her skin. It was a subtle caress, a gentle, courteous caress, but she knew it was correct. Julian would be a skilled lover, a considerate lover, building his mate's pleasure slowly, knowing in the final analysis that the better she felt, the better he'd feel himself.

41

The lighting in her dream was low and evocative, but even so she could clearly see his face above her; his eyes smouldering, his lips infinitesimally curved, his expression intense and thoughtful as if he were selecting exactly the move that would please her. She could smell his minty breath on her face, and both within and around that, a heady, dizzying perfume, the scent of his body, a body steeped in flowers and spices and musk. Her waking mind knew this was the expensive new fragrance she'd wallowed in, smoothed on – and generally gone over the top with – but her fantasy transferred it to him. He was a man who loved luxury and sensual refinement; when he came to a woman with love on his mind, he'd have perfumed his hair, his skin, his armpits, his every last hollow and niche.

In the fantasy, he kissed her, for the first time, his warm lips meltingly soft. It was exactly how she wanted it. A slow, gradually building experience; no hard-plunging tongue, no jaw-cracking force. Her dream-lips opened of their own accord, tempting him in, luring him, hinting at the parallel entering he'd enjoy in the heat between her legs.

But in this leisurely, fragrant dreamscape, there was still a long way to go. A whole night of simmering pleasure before the moment of ultimate joining.

Writhing involuntarily on her elderly and ordinary couch, Rosie sank deeper into a new and extraordinary dream. As she eased up the full skirt of her nightdress, Julian, miraculously, was nude in her mind. How easy it all was when you didn't have to struggle with clothing.

His body was strong and sturdy; lean, but almost buzzing with power. His penis was large, long and purple-tipped. She wondered for a second whether he'd be circumcised. In this dream he was supposed to be a sheik, so he was most likely Moslem. Did that mean he'd be cut? Not certain, and for purposes of now, not really worrying too much, she decided that he had been shorn of his foreskin, and that his glans was a neat round bulb, fat and shining and already running with liquid.

As she observed the sheen of his juices, she became keenly aware of her own, and the way her labia slid against each other as she moved uneasily on the couch. She felt swollen and puffed between her legs, all her intimate feminine flesh in a tingling state of readiness.

Unlike Geoff, her dreamy idealised Julian did not taunt her with his body. He didn't tease and make her wait and struggle and plead. Instead, he gently eased down the top of her gown and began kissing her breasts and licking them. His tongue was faintly rough, like a cat's, and its gossamer friction was heavenly. As he moistened her skin and caressed her, she felt a hot need stir in her sex. She moaned in her throat as long fingers stole between her labia: light as feathers yet deadly and accurate in their search. Within seconds the sweetest spot, her unsheathed clitoris, was being manipulated with fabulous delicacy.

He wasn't rough. He wasn't too fast. And neither was he too slow. His fingertip swirled on her flesh in a rhythm that was almost celestial, a clever little circular beat that synchronised sweetly with his tongue, as it slid round and round on her breast.

In the real world, Rosie was performing her own manipulations. Two fingers of one hand running rings around a nipple, while a singleton, from the other, palpated her aching clitoris.

She'd never been much of a one for masturbation until now, but suddenly she'd found a rare and special skill. It was as if Julian, or some powerful fantasy djinni, had taken control of her swiftly moving fingers and was guiding her surely to orgasm. She felt the loveliest of tensions building. A huge need to come, swelling in her quim like a crystal balloon that quivered on the edge of bursting.

Then it did burst, and she cried out hoarsely, her loins aflame, her heels drumming wildly on the sofa.

'Julian Hadey, you bastard! You bastard!' she

43

shouted, more in thanks than in insult as his dark presence slowly faded.

Was he really like that? she wondered, waiting for her heartbeat and breathing to steady. Was he really so courteous, so kind and so deliciously and erotically magnanimous? Somehow she didn't think so. A man as handsome, successful and confident as Julian was far more likely to be a patronising chauvinist like Geoff.

There was no harm in dreaming, though, was there? Dreaming of being wooed, not exploited. Pleasured to extremes, not used.

But the problem was, it had to *remain* a dream. Anything else and she could wave goodbye to her job. It was going to be difficult, very difficult. She couldn't avoid Julian while she lived in his house – and if she couldn't avoid him, what chance did she stand of resisting him?

On her first morning, however, resistance had been easy. There was nobody there to resist!

When she'd settled in and gotten over how luxurious her room was, she couldn't even find her employer, much less succumb to a seduction. The staff of the house were helpful, and thankfully, very friendly, but apart from them no-one else was home. Mrs Hadey – or Mrs Brent-Hadey, as Rosie discovered she preferred to be called – was in Paris for a few days with her cousin, and Julian himself was at a business conference and not expected home until late.

It was both a relief and a disappointment. A chance for Rosie to find her way round at her own speed, yet a huge anti-climax too.

Face it, Howard, she admonished herself, you actually wanted him to try something on. You wanted everything in one day. Mousy librarian to adorable, irresistible seductress with no stops on the way. You idiot, you're just dying to give in to him!

'You should write all this down, Rosie,' she murmured wryly as she entered the deserted library. The fantasies she'd been having for the last few nights were

44

as steamy as anything in the private case, she was sure. And some of them had even taken place right here, in this sunlit, leather-scented room. It was easy to believe she'd been taken on the opulent chesterfield, or been molested like a she-bitch on heat on the priceless Aubusson carpet.

And it wasn't only in the library. She was also starting to believe she'd had sex in a perfumed Arab tent, on a slatted wooden bench in a steam room, and in the back of a black limousine. She was going to have to disabuse herself of these rare notions soon though, she decided – or Mister Julian Hadey was going to get some awfully strange reactions from the newest member of his staff.

Looking around, she let the serenity of the books make her feel calm, like 'Rosie the Sensible Librarian' again.

It was such a beautiful room, and the contents of its shelves were priceless. It was hard to believe that this was only half of the collection, she reflected, studying the tall ranks of books. There was another hoard – at least the equal of this – stored at Julian's house in Norfolk. It was part of her job to catalogue that too. In situ.

Standing in the corner of the room, caught in a shaft of filtered sunlight, was an item Rosie hadn't noticed on her last visit: a black and gold lacquered chinoiserie screen. Curious, she walked across and looked behind it, only to smile and sigh with relief.

On a fine Regency library table was a device without which her labours would be decidedly tedious; a state of the art and obviously brand-new computer terminal, complete with printer and modem. She'd been wondering how she was going to create an integrated catalogue for the two libraries – and now she knew. Here was the modern technology she needed, masked by an antique object of beauty; just as the darkest realms of sleazy perversion were hidden amongst this treasured wealth of learning.

Reminded of perversion, she glanced down at the books she was returning, the three choice volumes that

45

Julian had already lent her. She'd expected them to be a spicy read, but what lay between these tooled leather covers was a domain of total eroticism. A world that was dark, bizarre and extreme. A realm of pain and its transformation into exquisite, unimaginable pleasures. A lifestyle that was entirely unlike Rosie's; yet which had some disturbingly familiar facets.

A disillusioned heroine who sought an escape from oppressive mediocrity. A woman in search of purpose, understanding and control. A woman going through changes. Like herself, after the débâcle of Geoff.

But in the novels those answers were only to be found in the world of fetishistic spanking. In exotic clothing; in whipping and beating. Stroking the strangely warm covers, Rosie wondered if their contents were a pure fabrication, conjured from the air; or some wild and deviant reality with which her old, dull life had never intersected. She couldn't see herself finding salvation in the rod – she found pain to be just that, pain – but even so the cleverly paced prose had stirred her. Her body had physically roused as she'd read: her sex had engorged and moistened, her nipples had swollen, and her pale throat had turned pink with the blood of excitement.

As she returned the books to their places – the private cases were unlocked now – she imagined the man who owned them enacting their principal scenarios. She imagined Julian spanking her, right here in the library.

He had that air about him of knowing everything, having done it all, and being adept. He'd take hold of her with strength, bend her bare-bottomed over his knee. He'd inflict pain with his hand, then soothe it, stroking her pale, shuddering body. For stimulation, there'd be nothing to choose between the two.

Rosie knew she shouldn't be thinking such thoughts. Fantasy was therapeutic and harmless, and the more she indulged in it, the better she liked it. But she was astounded that she dreamed of being dominated. It ran counter to her new internal politics, her vow not to be done down by men.

But no matter how incorrect they seemed to her, she still saw her wild, sexy visions. A spanking from Julian would demean her, yes, but in a sense it would also uplift her. Her new boss wasn't Geoff; he was a giver not a taker. He was a teacher and a tutor, not a person who mocked her and subtly sneered.

Oh my, this is all very heavy, thought Rosie, lining up the books with their neighbours and giving herself a strong mental shake. Julian Hadey was her employer. He'd flirted with her – extremely lightly – whilst interviewing her, and here she was now, considering kinky sex with him. It was absurd! Especially with his wife due home from France tomorrow.

And that was another thing, she thought, switching on the computer and finding, to her relief, a familiar operating system. Celeste was bringing this 'David' with her – the cousin that Julian had mentioned so pointedly. Rosie had a strong suspicion that being company for the lad was as good as on her job description. Julian had stressed repeatedly how helpful David would be. Apparently the boy was both an avid reader and an intellectual – albeit a more or less self-taught one – and he was also strong enough to hump books around when the library was assembled in its elegant new sequence.

Rosie was still dubious though. Goddamnit, the kid was supposed to have just had a nervous breakdown! He was hardly likely to be a scintillating conversationalist!

Almost immediately, she felt ashamed. She'd learnt hard lessons herself about being an outsider – most of them from Geoff – so she owed it to the boy to be nice to him. Keep him busy with interesting jobs; bring him out of himself; let him know she understood his problems.

She was still worried though. Julian had described his cousin-by-marriage as a shy young thing – and Rosie only hoped for both their sakes that this didn't equate with nerd, wimp or stuttering, anoracked oddball.

'Okay, Howard, let's get organised,' she told herself

sternly, opening a file, 'and we'll worry about David when we meet him, shall we?'

Day one in the library passed quickly. Rosie soon found her way around the computer, and in the notepad, found that her helpful-as-well-as-handsome employer had left the electronic address of a well-known software house, plus *carte blanche* to order whatever she needed. Such largesse was intoxicating after the privations of local government budgeting, and by the time Rosie logged off at five o'clock, she'd spent several hundred pounds of Julian's money!

Of the man himself, there was still no sign; just a message passed on by his housekeeper, Mrs Russell, when she brought in Rosie's afternoon tea. Mister Hadey had phoned, he'd be late, but he'd try and make it home for dinner. Rosie, however, was not to wait. He didn't want his librarian going hungry on her very first night in his house.

Hungry for what? mused Rosie as she made her way slowly to her room. Dinner wasn't until eight and she felt quite weary. She'd barely left the library all day, apart from a stroll in the garden at lunchtime, but she must have been up and down that step-ladder at least a hundred times. Her thighs and shoulders were aching, and her eyes were tired from poring over small print and the monitor. A short rest, to recharge her batteries, was what she needed; followed by a long, hot bath. But it was worth being tired, just to enjoy such a luxury.

Just over a week ago, she would have had an irritating stop-start bus journey after work, followed by a trudge round the local supermarket, and then more aggravation while she waited for an ancient immersion heater to heat up six inches of water.

Here, everything was done for her: laundry, meals, even the meticulous tidying of her room, which looked, incidentally, more like a courtesan's boudoir than staff quarters. Just to add icing to the cake, Mrs Russell had promised to pop up with a relaxing glass of sherry whilst Rosie was dressing for dinner.

48

This is the life! she thought dreamily as – having decided to bathe first, then rest – she sank into rose-scented water. She'd brought all her own cosmetics and toiletries with her, but the row of exotic looking potions in her private bathroom had been far too tempting to resist. Half-dizzy from sniffing most of them, she'd chosen Cosmetics to Go's 'Rose-tinted Spectacle'. 'Roses for a rose,' she'd whispered as she'd sloshed it in, aware of a certain irony, but too content at that moment to fret.

As she lay in the water, she let her hands move lightly on her body. She felt extraordinarily relaxed and sensual, and put it down to the sumptuous comfort of her setting. She considered indulging in her favourite new pleasure, masturbation, but couldn't seem to summon the energy. Just lying in the water was erotic enough for the moment. Her body was suffused with a delicate low-key excitement; a kind of soft, vague arousal that was so nice a state to be in that it simply didn't need changing.

The water cooled. She topped it up. It cooled again. Time seemed to melt and flow.

Finally, almost purring with self-indulgence, she hauled herself out of the bath, dried herself with leisurely thoroughness and moisturised both her face and her body. Letting her hair down from its knot, she wandered naked into her bedroom and noticed, by the small ormulu clock on her mantlepiece, that there was still a good hour to kill before dinner was served.

Outside, the edge of summer twilight was falling, but during the day, the sun had shone strongly into the room and warmed it. Cautiously ascertaining that she couldn't be seen, Rosie opened a window, drew the curtains, then lay down on the bed, still nude. It seemed distinctly decadent to be lolling around in the buff all of a sudden, but this was a new life, she reminded herself as a trance-like drowsiness overwhelmed her.

It's a new world, she thought, drifting. A new freedom. I can do anything now. Any damn thing I want.

* * *

49

She awoke with a furious start, aware of a presence in the room even before she'd opened her eyes. For a micro-second she reassured herself it was Mrs Russell with her sherry; then every nerve-end in her body started dancing and every instinct in her brain screamed danger.

'Sherry?' enquired a voice so silky and amused she seemed to feel it poured across her skin. With her eyes still tightly shut, she recognised a certain inevitability. This scenario had been in her mind from the very first moment she'd met her visitor; she just hadn't imagined it happening so soon. Intensely aware of her naked breasts and the soft patch of hair between her legs, she sat up and faced him.

'Yes, I'd love some!' It came out sounding almost blasé, but the heat in Julian's eyes made her quiver.

The way he was sitting on the edge of her bed, shirt-sleeved and tieless, seemed to suggest that the first thing he'd done on getting home was rush up here with *her* sherry. There were two glasses on a silver tray on her bedside table and as she answered, he took the one with darker, sweeter contents and handed it to her.

He was testing her; that was obvious. There was purpose in his look; a slow, assessing scrutiny, as well as just plain old desire. It was almost as if he were waiting for her to lose her cool and cover herself.

'You don't mind this, do you?' he enquired with a smile, leaving it to her to deduce that 'this' referred to her nakedness.

'Er ... No! Not really,' she answered cautiously, shifting her position on the bed then cringing within as her breasts swayed visibly. She took a deep sip from her glass and found the rich warm flavour revivifying. She'd been naked for a man before, but never so casually, or in a strange way, so comfortably. It was weird, but as she thought back to his question, it dawned on her that in her heart she *didn't* mind. At all. Julian was studying her bare body closely, but his luminous brown eyes weren't a threat.

50

There was no criticism in his look either. A fact which made Rosie's spirits soar giddily, and her confidence with them. Her lushness – her full, firm shape – seemed to please him not disgust him. There was none of the implied criticism she'd always sensed in Geoff: the unspoken but ever-present suggestion that she diet.

'Good!' he said crisply after a long long pause, 'because we tend to have a fairly relaxed attitude to nudity in this house.' He paused and sipped his own paler, clearly dryer sherry. 'A relaxed attitude to everything really.'

What was he telling her? That he expected sex? That his wife wouldn't mind?

'What's that supposed to mean?' she enquired, astounded at her own leading question. She took a last long hit of her sherry, then hurtled on. 'That sex is part of the job?'

Julian laughed and laughed, putting aside his sherry glass and reaching for her hand. 'No, Rosie, having sex with me isn't a part of your duties. Although if you want it, I'd be delighted to oblige.' He drew her fingers to his lips and kissed them lightly, his tongue flicking out at the very last second to tease her skin with its moisture. 'Just let me unwind. Have a shower . . . then we'll eat. And after that, who knows?'

'I didn't mean that,' she said quickly, snatching back her hand and fighting the urge to retreat, to drag the sheet over her body and cover herself. She'd just made the most enormous gaffe. She'd boldly gone and opened her mouth, and in a backwards about way, almost offered herself.

'Pity,' murmured Julian, reaching out again, and trailing the back of his hand against her breast. 'You're a beautiful woman, Rosie. I'd enjoy making love to you.' With a flip of his wrist, his fingers were pad-down against her skin, his hand curving slightly to cup her, his thumb settling neatly on her nipple.

To Rosie's horror, her nipple erected instantly, and seemed to burn. He was simply holding, not caressing

51

her, but the contact was electric. Clenching her own hands into fists, she fought an almost unbearable yearning to sway into his grip, and moan out aloud with desire.

Julian said nothing more, but just regarded her steadily, his hand warm and still on her breast. Rosie felt blood pulsing wildly through her body, making her skin turn pink and her sex start to quiver and engorge. It was terrible. In the space of a few seconds, she wanted him desperately. She imagined his lips on her skin, as well as his fingers, then his cock sliding slowly into her softness.

'Damn! This is unfair of me, isn't it?' he said suddenly, then before she could stop him, or protest, he leaned over and kissed her breast – exactly where his fingers had been.

This time, Rosie couldn't contain herself. She leaned towards him, almost presenting him with the curve. But Julian withdrew.

'I'm moving too fast.' He was on his feet now, smiling almost shamefacedly. 'There's something we've got to discuss first.'

'What something?' Rosie demanded. She was angry now, furious with her own arousal, furious that she'd revealed it and furious with Julian for rejecting what she'd offered.

'A proposition,' he said evasively, moving away from her. 'Something you could help with. But I won't go into it now. It'll wait 'til after dinner.'

Before she could dispute this, he was gone, and the room felt empty without him.

Rosie's thoughts whirled. Proposition? What proposition? He'd said he didn't expect sex, but he'd clearly wanted it. Was that what they had to discuss? The ground-rules for a clandestine affair?

The idea appalled but thrilled her, and she turned it over and over as she envisioned herself locked in Julian's arms. His after-image was strong in her mind, and it was easy to imagine his body. And how he'd use it. She could smell his cologne too, his insidious man-smell. And see that dark skin, those smouldering eyes, and that broad shouldered, slim-hipped male body.

She really didn't want to say no.

Dinner was delightful, but uncomfortable. Delightful in that the food was superb – a light meal, skilfully prepared from the finest ingredients. Uncomfortable in that the company was even more tempting.

Julian made no reference to the scene in her bedroom, although his look when she entered the dining room was patently admiring. She'd chosen a soft, cotton jersey dress in a deep shade of blue; a flattering thing that embraced her full breasts closely yet flared out from the waist into a full circular skirt. The neckline was low but not plunging, and to lengthen the line of her neck, she'd put up her hair in a cleverly coiled twist and left a few tendrils dangling alluringly so it wouldn't look too workaday. She'd considered dressing safely, but had abandoned the idea. Caution seemed pointless at this stage; she just prayed she could carry off the image.

It wasn't too difficult, though, because Julian's presence felt strangely unthreatening. He complimented her, but with no salacious overtones. He touched her as he guided her to her seat; and though Rosie trembled slightly, he didn't capitalise on it. Instead, he seemed intent on putting her at her ease: discussing his books and enquiring on her progress in the library. It was all territory she knew, and she guessed he'd chosen it deliberately. To put off the proposition.

But Rosie couldn't put it off, at least not in her mind. All through dressing and making-up, she'd mulled it over. She kept coming to the same conclusion. The proposition was sex – as a novelty for him, perhaps? A change from his beautiful wife.

And she was still battling with what her answer might be. Still fighting the urge to succumb.

When he'd left her room, Julian had left her unsatisfied. He'd touched her, with both his fingers and his glamorous male aura, then abandoned her. Her libido had been primed and made ready. Her juices had flowed shamingly, and were still flowing. Her breasts ached, her vulva felt heavy, and her whole body felt twitchy and restless. She was bathed and perfumed and deodorised, yet she still felt like a bitch on heat, surrounded by odours and pheromones.

Could Julian be aware of all this? Rosie took another sip of wine, and studied him covertly.

He looked gorgeous, but that was obviously normal for him. He was dressed elegantly yet casually, in chinos with a darker-coloured polo-neck sweater in just the same chocolate brown as his eyes.

Oh God, he's just edible! she thought, then blushed. She saw herself eating this edible man; kneeling between his legs, sucking obediently on his penis as he stroked her face, her hair and her throat.

'Are you alright?' Julian's soft voice brought Rosie rudely back to reality.

'Yes, I'm fine. Just a bit warm.' She fanned herself with her napkin in an attempt to distract him. She felt so visibly ready for sex that there was no way his sharp eyes could miss it.

'Yes, it's a lovely evening,' he answered easily. 'I'd offer to take you for a walk in the moonlight, but I'm afraid I've some paperwork to attend to.'

Rosie was flabbergasted. What about the proposition? What had happened to the man who was going too fast? Wasn't he interested any more?

'Oh,' she said, keeping her voice bland and trying to suppress her confusion.

'Don't worry, sweet Rosie. We'll get our chat.' A long, brown hand snaked out across the tablecloth and took hold of her pale, tensed fingers. 'And believe me . . . You won't be disappointed.'

Chapter 4

The Proposition

B east! thought Rosie later, as she lay on her bed still
waiting, and still fuming.

Sitting up, she looked across at the ormolu clock. It
was just after midnight and there was still no sign of
Julian. Rosie couldn't bear the edgy sensations that consumed her. She got out of bed and went to the window,
letting the moonlit calm soothe her soul.

The whole situation was mad. She'd applied for a job
to get over one man, and was now hung up about another. How stupid could you get?

And yet she knew that if Julian did disappoint her, it
wouldn't be quite in the way that Geoff had. In spite of
his arrogant, intimate touch, right here in this room,
there was still something detached about Julian, something that would always belong elsewhere. He loved his
wife, she presumed. His beautiful, sexy wife. Celeste's
portrait was breathtaking; she was one of the most genuinely lovely women Rosie had ever seen. And one of the
slimmest, she thought, gritting her teeth with envy.

Thoroughly unsettled, she returned to her bed, but as
she did so, she noticed that the drawer in the bedside
table was open very slightly. She'd put a box of tissues
in there earlier, and distinctly remembered pushing it
closed.

Flipping on the bedside light, she pulled open the drawer, then caught her breath. Someone had left her a present.

There, tucked innocuously in her tissue box, was a red plastic vibrator, and beside it a tiny glass pot containing a clear gel-like substance that looked suspiciously like lubricant. Rosie hardly dare reach in and touch either, but curiosity overcame her.

The vibrator was a surprisingly substantial little toy, and to her untutored eye, seemed well constructed. She'd seen pictures of such things in magazines, and though she'd never plucked up the nerve to send for one, she'd often wondered if she ought to – so she could think of herself as liberated.

So, Howard, you wanted to try a vibrator? Well, now's your chance. Courtesy of Mister Julian Hadey, one presumes, she observed wryly. Had he suspected his paperwork was going to over-run and left this rude approximation of his penis to keep her occupied? He could easily have secreted it here while she'd been drinking coffee in the library.

Hefting the slim plastic cylinder in her hand, she couldn't bring herself to turn it on.

'Come on, it won't bite!' she muttered, then twisted the bevelled end in her fingers until the small device started to purr. She wasn't quite sure what was normal for such things, but the vibrations were smooth and con-sistent, and instinct told her that this was a Rolls Royce amongst love toys. She twirled the control around a bit, experimenting with different speeds, while her con-scious mind avoided the issue.

Was she going to try it?

She imagined Julian lying in his bed right now – or maybe still sitting at his desk – and picturing her with this lewd red monster inside her.

To ignore it would be to resist him; but on the other hand, did she want to resist him? Even now, when he was so clearly playing games? Almost breathless with trepidation, she decided to try his gift.

But how did one go about it? Uncertain, she lay back

on the bed and spun the toy's bevelled end again. It buzzed cheerfully, and she pulled up the pink silk skirt of her nightdress, then slowly, very slowly lowered the finely trembling plastic to her sex.

The intensity of sensation made her squeal aloud. The vibrator's smooth, pristine tip seemed to shoot pure lightning through her innards as she pressed it unwarily to her clitoris.

'Oh God! Oh God!' she groaned, her frustrated body orgasming hugely under its first electronic kiss. She jerked her hips, she couldn't help it, then scrabbled frantically between her legs, desperate not to lose contact with her toy. Her vagina pulsed and squelched like a wet, marine mouth, and her juices were so copious she could actually hear the sound of her climax.

Instantly addicted, she soared again and again and again. She was just going for her fifth brilliant orgasm when a knock at the door broke the spell.

Julian! The bastard! He must have been planning to catch her all along.

This time, mercifully, he didn't walk straight in, and Rosie had time to stuff the vibrator back in its hiding place and shut the drawer on the evidence of her sins. She wondered, frantically, how thick the door was, and how long Julian had been just outside. The vibrator was far from silent; what if he'd been listening for it, purposefully?

Still panting slightly, she went to the door, glancing down at her body as she did so. A hot, rosy flush was making her chest almost the same colour as her gown, and when she looked in the mirror, she saw the same pink blotches across her throat and cheeks: lurid and impossible to hide.

'I didn't mean to be this late,' said Julian as she let him in and felt his eyes dart quickly over her. He was noting her pinkness, she just knew it. The blush felt so intense to her that she could almost imagine him feeling it too, before he'd even touched her. His gaze was molten in the dim, shaded light, cruising her breasts unashamedly through the thin, shiny satin of her gown.

Rosie herself had plenty to look at. Julian's short, cotton happi-coat was a brilliant, singing turquoise, and open to the waist showing chest-hair rampant, just as she'd imagined. Beneath its mid-thigh hem his muscular legs were bare. As were his feet.

Nervous, Rosie backed away from him, retreating to the bed and sitting down abruptly on its edge.

'Still warm, Rosie?' he enquired, settling himself elegantly beside her and reaching out to touch her glowing, reddened throat. She felt sweat beads start to form at her brow, beneath her arms, and in the creases of her groin. Why on earth did she feel so hot, when Julian – goddamn him – looked so cool?

'Yes, a little,' she answered, wanting to pull away, but pinned by the delicate caress of a fingertip that slid slowly down towards her breast. She hardly dare breathe, for fear it slide beneath her lacy bodice, touch her nipple, and sample its puckered hardness. Controlling her quivering, she looked him boldly in the eye. 'What is it you want from me, Julian? What's the proposition? An affair? Casual sex? My fair, fat body in return for that fabulous salary you're paying me?'

'Fair, but not fat,' he whispered, flipping down the thin silk ribbon of her shoulder strap, then exposing a single breast. Cupping the milky-pale orb, he held it for a moment, staring as if mesmerised at the arrangement of brown on white. As he squeezed slightly, and Rosie gasped, he looked up again, his eyes heavy-lidded, almost sleepy. 'It is sex I want you for, Rosie. But not casual. And not – primarily – for me.'

'What do you mean?' she asked, her voice wavering as a light clicked on in her mind. She didn't need an answer. She wasn't slow or stupid. The hints had been there almost since the beginning.

'It's your cousin, isn't it? You want me for this precious David of yours.'

'He's my wife's cousin,' he corrected, smiling. 'And yes, I do want you to have sex with David.'

'You're insane!' she cried, shuddering as his thumb

moved slowly on her nipple. 'That's outrageous! I'm a librarian, not a prostitute.'

'You're a gentle, beautiful girl, and David is an innocent young man who needs you.' The thumb flicked, then was joined, in a delicate pincer, by his forefinger. 'You'll be perfect for him. Sensual but not intimidating. Experienced but not jaded.'

'But I'm not experienced,' she blurted out, wriggling as he pulled, gently. 'At least, not very.'

From very close, Julian eyed her, his expression full of knowledge. 'It doesn't matter, Rosie,' he said kindly, touching her face with his free hand. 'In this case, the tutor doesn't have to be too learned. Too much technique would be frightening. The two of you can learn together.'

'But –'

'And you do have the experience that David needs.' He paused, slid his hand around the back of her head, and kissed her once on the mouth. 'You've been hurt recently . . . so you won't hurt him.'

How does he know? she thought as his lips returned to hers. She felt his strong, mobile tongue prise her open like a clam, then the kiss began in earnest. While he tasted and explored and sucked her, his fingers palpated her breast, squeezing gently and circling the flesh.

'Quite lovely,' he whispered, releasing both mouth and breast, only to tweak away her other strap and let her bodice slither down to her waist. With his prize uncovered, he shuffled a little way back from her, his smile narrow and triumphant.

Rosie felt even her breasts blushing now, especially the one he'd fondled. She remembered the portrait of Celeste, and how slim she was, how perfect and delicate her shape was.

'Not as lovely as your wife,' she said firmly, trying desperately to put him off-stride.

'Different, Rosie,' he replied, unfazed. 'Celeste has a magnificent body, but there're many different kinds of magnificent. And I suspect that David will like *your* kind.'

59

While Julian had been moving, his thin robe had been slipping, and as he reached towards her again – drawing her arms clear of the straps of her nightie – it seemed to slither like a wave and fall open, exposing his darkly-furred body.

Helpless, Rosie stared at his penis. It was risen and fully erect; a solid bar of ruby-toned flesh that reared up from his groin, its tip circumcised, just as she'd imagined.

When she lifted her eyes to his face, he was smiling again. Her fascination with his genitals seemed to amuse him and he made no attempt to hide either his feelings or his sex.

'See how you please me,' he said quietly, reaching for her hand and placing it on him. 'Think how you'll please David.'

'He mightn't like me,' she said shakily. His penis was hot and smooth and seemed to pulse in the palm of her hand. She felt a great urge to squeeze him as he'd squeezed her, to rub and caress him; to affect him as he'd affected her.

'He might think I'm too chubby!' she persisted, panicked into a simplistic objection.

'But you aren't,' he countered. He was really close now and their thighs were pressed together, his burning hers through the skirt of her gown. He put his arm around her shoulder and held her against him, his free hand settling on her belly, then beginning to snake beneath the bunched up silk at her waist.

'Your skin's so soft and your body's firm – a perfect combination.' His fingers continued to creep and search, creep and search, and she bit back a moan when he reached his ultimate target. 'And your sex is lush and wet. No man could resist you. I certainly can't.'

As if to validate his words, his cock leapt slightly in her hand, the tiny eye at its tip weeping slowly with a thin, clear moisture.

Julian's touch was gentle and clever. He nudged her clitoris to and fro in a delicate, measured rhythm that

60

obliterated all thought and reason. It seemed like a year since she'd parted from Geoff, and her frustration was enormous. She'd made her own pleasure, and it'd been good, very good, but she'd missed being touched by a man.

'But what if I'm no good?' she whispered, still doubting, while at the same time cursing herself. 'What if I don't know enough to teach him?'

'Let me be the judge of that.' There was a smile in Julian's voice, a kind smile that he pressed against her neck, just under her ear. 'And if I find anything you need to know more about, I'll tutor you in it myself.' He kissed her neck, his mouth wet and hungry, his tongue sliding and darting with a beat that matched his deft fingering. 'Now, hush! And let me make love to you!'

Rosie hushed. Words were becoming difficult anyway as she succumbed to Julian's sure hands. She sighed as he eased her back onto the bed, still stroking her clitoris, but with his thumb now because his fingers – one, two, oh God, three! – were inside her. Trapped by the satin of her gown, his wrist was pressed tight to her belly, and she could feel his pulse against her skin, its thud thud, thud thud, fast but perfectly even. Somewhere in their manoeuvre, she'd lost her grip on his cock and she searched around blindly to retrieve it.

'Don't worry about that. You're what matters now,' he breathed in her ear as he rotated his tormenting thumb. Her hips lifting crazily, she scrabbled still, desperate to touch any part of him; desperate to touch his smooth, fragrant skin, and convince herself this was real and not some disturbed dream brought on by an unfamiliar bed.

But Julian was not a man to be shaken off easily. Even as Rosie squirmed and wriggled, her body falling deep and hard into orgasm, he held her close, turning her in his arms until they lay on the bed spoon-style, her back nestled up against his front.

Rosie cried out hoarsely, her flailing legs hampered by her skirt, her heels beating Julian's shins. Around his fingers, her vagina pumped steadily, sucking and grabbing and contracting as her clitoris throbbed beneath his thumb.

'Oh God! Oh yes!' she howled, pressing back with her bottom to caress him in return. He was good. He was kind. Outrageous but, in his own way, caring. She wanted him to have pleasure now too. He made a low, throaty sound and pushed against her, his juicy tip wetting her nightie.

'Do you want me, Rosie,' he asked, his dark voice gruff and broken; and for an instant, she remembered Geoff asking the same sort of question, his attitude gloating and confident. Julian Hadey did not sound like that. His questions were genuine, as if he honestly wanted to be welcomed.

'Yes,' she gasped, coming again as his thumb dove and swirled.

'Good!'

As he spoke, Rosie felt him pull away and withdraw his caressing fingers with a last, affectionate pat on the tip of her clitoris. She started to turn towards him, reaching for her gown to get rid of it, but he placed a hand on her shoulder and said, 'Stay still, sweet Rosie.'

Lying motionless on her side, she watched their shadows shifting on the wall while Julian wiggled her nightdress down over her hips and thighs, and then tossed it away across the bed. After that, he shook off his own flimsy robe, and laid himself down behind her, his body pressed to her back and his hard cock poking at her buttocks.

Trembling and sweating, she felt him rubbing himself up and down the groove. Bizarre ideas flashed insanely through her mind, followed by an even weirder sense of acceptance. She'd never given anything other than her vagina and her mouth to a man – even though Geoff had hinted and wheedled – but with Julian things could be different. And he had promised to teach her what she didn't know already.

She felt his moisture pooling warmly at her anus, and felt the smooth acorn-shape of his glans. Flexing her inner muscles, she tried to catch him and tempt him, but as she did so, he adjusted her position.

'Not tonight, gentle Rosie,' he whispered, rubbing his face in the silken mass of her hair and reaching down with his fingers to guide his own stiff flesh to its goal. 'It'd be a beautiful thing to do, but we're not ready.' As the tip of his penis found her, he made a little shuffling movement and lodged it there – then took a firm, assured hold on her hips and tilted her body to receive him.

'Relax ... Relax ...' he purred in her ear, his grip unyielding but careful. She felt him pushing, pushing, pushing, and her own tightness yielding with a slow, delicious ease. Then in one smooth glide he was inside her – not deeply, because of the angle – but touching all her zones of pleasure completely.

Rosie sighed contentedly. The position was comfortable, and comforting. She felt cherished, treasured – something she'd never felt once with Geoff – and the sensation was so novel and longed for that it was almost a climax in itself.

Almost.

Her vagina rippled nervously around Julian as he shifted their bodies against each other, adjusting the fit of their flesh so she could get the best from him, and he from her. His cock slipped out as she moved too, but his fingers moved quickly to reinstate it. He laughed softly and Rosie found herself joining in. He was laughing with her, not at her, and somehow that seemed strangely erotic. Entranced, she wriggled her back against his front, feeling the tickle of his wiry male hair as it rubbed against the skin of her bottom.

She was almost lying on him now, cradled in the curve of his body, her hips angled so their sexes could mesh together snugly. His arms came around her: one hand cupping a breast, while the other slid down between her thighs, seeking what he'd sought out before. Burrowing in her fleece, he found her clitoris with ease, then made her groan as he unsheathed it and pressed it.

Without conscious thought, she put her fingers over his, guiding and encouraging them, as her other hand slid back, across his hip, and cupped his buttock.

'Lovely girl,' he whispered, his mouth seeking her ear through her thick, shiny hair as his fingers worked wonders down below. 'Your quim feels like heaven.'

Rosie had never heard that word spoken aloud, and it had a powerful effect on her. Her clitoris leapt and she had a small soft orgasm that made both of them gasp.

'God, you're wonderful,' he growled, bucking his hips and stabbing upwards into the white-burning heart of her. She was held tight against him, assaulted by splendid sensations from without and within, his cock pushing into her in short, hard thrusts, his fingertip dancing and rocking. She grunted, her voice uncontrolled and gutteral, wishing she could kiss him on the mouth to thank him.

As quickly as he'd started moving, Julian stopped, holding his penis quite still inside her, at the deepest point of his stroke. She sensed him containing a mighty force – checking himself for her sake – and even as this registered through her rapture, she resolved to remember it. It was a wisdom, and it could be passed on. Taught to one less experienced.

Filled already, she accepted more of his bounty. His kisses on her neck, her ear, her jaw. His swirling fingers, ceaselessly pleasuring her clitoris. His pure animal warmth like a blanket of tenderness around her. Never in her short sexual life had Rosie had a lover so giving. Geoff had been grasping, a chauvinistic taker, and the very few others had been fumbling incompetents when set beside Julian.

What will David be like? she wondered suddenly, then moaned and forgot the boy completely as Julian and his magic claimed her body.

'Will you do it then?' a creamy voice murmured in her ear.

'Do what?' Rosie queried, her faculties blurred by

sleep and sex. Bodyheat had been replaced by a thick, soft quilt that felt cool and fresh against skin that was sweaty and sticky. As she stirred, and bunched the covers around her ears, she sensed that the source of the voice was outside the bedclothes, that Julian was no longer lying beside her.

'Will you help him, Rosie?' he asked again, almost whispering. 'Will you teach David about sex?'

It seemed wild, peculiar, a request beyond her experience. Yet, she reasoned muzzily, isn't that just what I want? A wilder life, something different?

'Yeah, alright. I'll do it,' she mumbled into the pillow, her mind still drifting.

'Lovely girl, I knew you would.' Gentle lips kissed her exposed temple and she caught a waft of a now familiar cologne, then felt the brush of an ever so slightly stubbled chin against her cheek. 'He's damned lucky, you know.'

She wanted to roll onto her back, pull him down to her, reach again for his penis. But something told her their interlude was over: that he had to leave her now. Even as she realised it, she realised too that the idea didn't bother her. She'd had him, it'd been wonderful, but now she must sleep. Alone.

'Sweet dreams, Rosie,' Julian whispered, placing one last kiss on her passion-mussed hair. 'Sleep well. It all begins tomorrow.'

The last thing she heard was the pad pad pad of bare feet moving away across her carpet.

'Lovely girl,' Julian murmured again, to himself, back in his room.

He'd received precisely the answer he'd wanted. The one he'd known he'd get. What surprised him was that Rosie was so much more than he'd hoped for. He'd expected an average performance from a pretty girl; but what he'd received was an orgasm of dazzling clarity and intense pleasure from a full, fresh and deliciously responsive body. Rosie had come alive to him the instant he'd touched her, her moans and writhings luxurious and unstifled.

He smiled. She'd called herself inexperienced, and her history – as he'd discovered from various sources – seemed to confirm that.

Yet, when they'd coupled, her reactions had been wholly positive. And in a strange way, quite sophisticated. His penis twitched now as he thought of her hand closing over his, instinctively directing its movement. Once the dance of love had begun, Rosie Howard had chosen the steps. His and her own.

He knew he was right when he told her David was lucky. She herself was a jewel, a true rose; a hot, full-blooded flower who could reach into a young man's soul and bring his libido to life.

Suddenly Julian wanted to share his discovery, his elation. He wanted to tell Celeste that her worries for her cousin would soon be over; and as much as anything, he just wanted to hear her voice and let her share his delight in Rosie.

His bedside clock registered an unholy hour of the morning, but even so he picked up the phone and started dialling the number of a Paris hotel.

As he waited for the connection, he couldn't stop grinning. There was every likelihood that Celeste was occupied right now, indulging her voracious appetites just as he'd been satisfying his. He pictured her in their usual suite – her sleek thighs wide as some bell-boy or gigolo pounded and toiled between them. He saw a tight male bottom bouncing; heard Celeste's triumphant screams as her dark head tossed on the pillow, and her painted nails scratched and gouged at the back and buttocks of the convenient young man who was in her.

Or maybe it was a woman? His spouse had shown a marked interest in female lovers recently, mostly of the mild and submissive type. He imagined her riding some poor girl's head, mashing her sex against the tongue of a chit she'd enslaved with a single glance. When a familiar, smoky voice said 'hello' at the other end of the line, he almost couldn't speak. His mouth was swimming with saliva and the imaginary taste of his wife's sweet nectar.

'I've tested her,' he said without further ado, reaching down to take hold of his penis. It was semi-hard and blushingly warm, still glowing with the heat of recent activities, yet already anticipating more.

'And?' prompted Celeste huskily, as if she'd spent the few hours since their last phone-call just waiting for a bulletin on his progress.

'She's ideal, my love, just right.' He heard Celeste gasp and wondered whether it was a response to his words, or to some other, unknown stimulus. He half-hoped it was both.

'Yes,' he went on, working himself firmly. 'She's definitely the one for David. And I'm quite excited by the fact,' he enunciated carefully.

The key word was 'excited'– his signal to Celeste that he was masturbating and that he'd like her to do the same. If she was at liberty to do so, that was. If there was no finger, tongue or penis already on the move in her service.

'Yes, I find it exciting too.'

His wife's voice had deepened now, fallen almost to a modulated groan. 'Most stirring,' she continued, indicating that she was indeed stroking herself. He tried to picture her, imagine what she was wearing. Celeste was not one for nakedness in bed, and even when she was set on a long night of sex, she would always wear something. He thought of the nightgowns he'd seen her packing. One in black silk-gauze with panels of filligree lace; another in forest green, a mini-nightshirt that barely covered her bottom; a bias-cut forties-style tube in heavy flesh-coloured satin.

As he pictured her in each of these outfits, his cock ached furiously. She'd know he was speculating; she'd be waiting for him to ask. To tell him herself what she was wearing would be giving in, and beautiful Celeste had a habit of always, always making him the supplicant.

'So, what did you do to her?' she asked, panting slightly.

Before Julian had a chance to reply, there was a subtle click which indicated 'hands-free' operation at the Parisian end of the line. Reaching out – one-handed – he pressed a button on his own machine, then returned the receiver to its cradle. For an instant, he released his cock and stripped off his robe. Unlike Celeste, he *did* want to be naked, so he could submit his bare body to her whims.

'I went to her room after midnight. She looked very flushed and warm. I think she'd been touching herself. Or using the vibrator I left her.'

'Oh Ju! You wicked man! Was it one of mine?' Julian smiled and returned his fingers to his penis. Would he be punished for misuse of her toys?

'Yes, a red one. I found it in your secretaire . . .'

'A good choice,' gurgled Celeste, her sexy voice suddenly rough – as if she too was using a vibrator. 'And what was she wearing when you went to her?'

This was a prompt, a tease. She knew he was still dying to know what *she* was wearing.

'A nightdress. Low cut, satiny, the colour of cherries. It was very thin – I could see her nipples straight through it. And the hair between her legs.'

He could see it now – Rosie's soft, pale, fawnish fluff. Then the vision phased and the hair darkened to shiny ebon black – an elegant, heart shape – Celeste's precious, perfectly-clipped motte.

'Are you thinking of her now? Her body? How she felt when you took her?'

'Yes,' he murmured, squeezing the tip of his cock, his head full of lust, his loins full of fire and his heart full of love for his wife. He felt all these, and affection for a naïve yet strangely knowledgeable new bedmate. 'Yes!' he reiterated, squirming naked on his sheets, 'but I'm thinking of you too, my love. Imagining how you are now. Wanting you . . .'

Hard and quivering, and he rose, through pleasure, towards orgasm. And behind his closed eyelids, his beautiful spouse moved towards him, her divine, sexual mastery erasing all other fantasies. Even those about feisty girls from the north with big, blue eyes and large, curvaceous breasts.

'Celeste,' he groaned, his soul in another country: in Paris with a beautiful, masturbating woman in a night-dress as sheer as black vapour.

'Celeste!'

At the sound of her husband's tortured voice, Celeste Brent-Hadey groaned too – but contained the sound inside her by biting her left thumb, hard. The fingers of her right hand were moving firmly but delicately on her clitoris, sliding in her own heavy dew. Her fragile, misty-black nightgown was crumpled around her waist.

She loved her husband so much tonight. She felt so lucky to have him. He'd come through for her so wonderfully over this dilemma with David, and she was filled with gratitude and fondness. Emotions that turned easily to sexual desire.

As she listened to his broken voice, and his gasps and grunts, she imagined him at home in their bedroom, and wished him the greatest of pleasure in his own magnificent body.

Ju was such a handsome bastard! With his brown, sexy skin, and eyes that were even browner and so often sultry with passion. She loved *all* of her husband, relished every part of him. He was strong and muscular, graceful and light on his feet. She loved his sparkling white teeth, and his crisp black hair that was curly on his head, fuzzy on his chest, and thick and tickly round his cock. She adored the way that hair meshed with her own black curls when their bodies ground together in sex. She loved the way he was sometimes arrogant and sometimes so wryly self-mocking. She loved his boyish expression, his cheeky grin. It was hard to believe he was a 'forty something'. Her serious David, her quiet, bookish cousin, sometimes seemed older by far than her husband; and David was only nineteen.

And as she listened, and touched her own body, she began to consider David, and what a strange conundrum he was.

She'd almost wondered whether to educate the boy herself. The idea had a real appeal to it. A lover so unschooled would be quite a novelty, and in his own offbeat way, David was almost as handsome as Julian. It would be no hardship to go to bed with David, to sample that lean, creamy-skinned body and teach those long, flexible fingers what it meant to give pleasure to a woman. She'd been very tempted, but the simple truth of it was that they were cousins. Their relationship was several times removed, true, but even so, Celeste still felt a little uncomfortable with the idea of sex with her own kith and kin.

'Celeste!'

Ju's voice sounded frantic now, and Celeste imagined his lordly brown hand sliding and slipping on his cock. The skin on his member was fine and satiny, stretched tight, when he was erect, over a core as hard as bone. She pictured him spreading his own slickness as a lubricant; it was a sight she would never tire of, no matter how many times she saw it. She saw her beautiful, sensual husband, desperate to orgasm, rubbing himself like a callow young boy, yet afraid to come without leave.

'Are you naked, Ju my love?' she enquired archly, her own fingers working and moving. Her body was totally open now, her thighs rudely and lewdly spread. She had two hands pressed between them, caressing both without and within. She thought longingly of that stubby red vibrator, and how good it would feel in her channel as a surrogate for Ju's stiff flesh.

'Yes,' he said, perfecting her picture.

'I'm not,' she whispered, wondering if he'd hear. 'I'm wearing that black silk nightdress that you like so much. The one we bought together in Circe . . . Do you remember?'

'Oh God, yes!' His voice degraded into broken moaning, and Celeste wondered if the fight was lost already,

70

and he was coming. The memory she'd referred to was enough to stir a saint!

Slowly manipulating her clitoris, she slid off her heap of supporting pillows and lay splay-legged across the bed, her mind a maelstrom of images.

Not long after their marriage, when they'd been as silly and insatiable as teenagers, Julian had taken her to Circe, a fabulously exclusive lingerie boutique, and insisted on spending an obscene sum of money on lace and silk and satin. With a twinkle in his eye, and a huge and very visible hard-on, he'd insisted that she try on this particular gown – the wisp-like garment that so inadequately covered her now. And with the management of Circe so eager to pander to customers, no-one had turned a hair when Mister Hadey had followed his wife into the changing cubicle.

Inside, he'd made her stroke her own body as she disrobed, conveying his wishes by gesture alone because only a bolt of thinly-lined velvet divided them from the sales staff and fellow shoppers. When she was stripped to her high heels and hold-up stockings, he'd made her rest her foot on the seat of the velvet-padded reproduction chair, then finger her opened-out vulva until she reached silent and body-wracking orgasm.

The thought of that clandestine climax nearly made the same thing happen now. She felt her intimate tissues flutter as her juices flowed out across her buttocks, coating their glassy inner slopes. She pushed her finger in deeper, then gasped and writhed as her mind spooled quickly through her Circe memory.

Unable to stay on her feet, she'd let Julian grab her by the waist and drape her face down across the back of the chair. She'd lain there, mute and burning, while he'd mounded and fondled her bottom. She'd almost screamed with incredulous glee when she'd heard the distinctive whir of his zip.

She remembered muttering some muffled reply when the assistant had called out 'Is everything alright?', then almost biting the lush upholstery as Ju placed his cock

71

between her buttocks. She'd been prepared for him taking her – in fact she'd been aching for him – but when he'd started pushing his way into her bottom, she'd almost lost her nerve.

Just the thought of it triggered her now. She came violently, here in Paris, while she remembered what had happened in that high-class London knicker shop. With potential discovery just a heartbeat away, her husband had sodomised her vigorously, his virtually fully-clothed body jerking hard against her vulnerable near-nakedness. She touched her anus now and climaxed again, imagining that tiny sensitive portal stretched wide around his marvellous male girth. She'd had five distinct orgasms as she'd hung by her bottom from his shaft, and now she had at least as many more as she remembered her delicious humbling.

'Thank you, Ju,' she said at last, wondering if her breathy tones could be heard across the aether.

'Thank *you*, my love.' The words were filled with that beautiful smile of his, the most gorgeous of all his smiles – the relaxed, sated grin of a happy man who'd just climbed the highest peak of pleasure and was ever-so-slowly drifting downwards. For a moment, Celeste wished she was there to really see him; there, so she could kiss his mouth, his eyes, and his soft and satisfied cock.

She wondered if Rosie the librarian had sucked him, and found the vision intriguing. Julian had described his marvellous find in a previous phone call, and Celeste found herself looking forward to meeting her. Though slim herself, she had a penchant for curves in her female partners, and this lush northern girl sounded perfectly toothsome.

'So,' she purred, touching her breasts through sheer black lace and imagining them bigger, rounder and quite virgin to the hand of a woman. 'Will *I* like this Rosie of yours?'

Julian laughed richly. 'You'll love her, my dear,' he said softly. 'But I'd advise you to approach her with

72

caution. She's bright and sensual ... and very willing.'
He paused, obviously remembering just how willing.
'But our games might seem a little sophisticated as yet.'

'We'll see,' replied Celeste, easing down the bodice of
her nightgown and thinking longingly of a shy girl's
kisses.

Chapter 5

Enter the Lion Cub

*'L*ook, woman, this is a sophisticated household ...
Try and act sophisticated, will you?'

Rosie braced herself with yet another little homily as she put the final touches to her hairstyle. She'd heard the breakfast gong a while ago, but somehow it had been difficult to respond.

How should she behave this morning? As an employee? A lover? A woman employed to be a lover? She slicked on a little more lipstick and wondered if she looked like either.

Julian's proposition was so bizarre it was almost sensible. Almost. And she'd agreed to it, she seemed to remember. She was going to teach sex to a nineteen year old boy she'd never met. What's more she'd even taken a 'practical' for the post!

Ah, but did I pass? she pondered on the way to the dining room, her heart beating wildly.

Her throat tightened as she hovered in the hall, thinking of last night in her room. She seemed to feel a warm body pressed against her back again, and knew that beyond the dining room door was a man who'd promised he wouldn't disappoint her. A man who *hadn't* disappointed her.

Taking a huge breath, she smoothed at her soft, pink

74

angora sweater and touched the hairstyle she knew to be perfect. It was now or never. She reached for the door-handle, turned it and went in.

'Good morning, Rosie,' said Julian, his voice smoothly pleasant as he rose to his feet, the perfect gentleman. There were only two places set for breakfast – intimately close – and Rosie wanted to panic and run. Even in his dark business suit Julian looked poised for sex, and the combination of brown skin and white shirt made visions flare and bubble. She scarcely dare approach him. If she got one whiff of that cologne of his, she was finished. She was half dizzy with lust already.

'Good morning, Mister Hadey,' she said, flipping out her napkin as she sat, and wishing it was good form to tuck it into her neckline. Her nipples were hardening already and showed clearly through her thin, cuddly sweater. Even to her eyes, her cleavage appeared deeper somehow, far more of a plunge than it had looked in her bedroom mirror.

'Mister Hadey?' he queried, his eyes flashing sparks. 'Isn't that a little formal?'

'Er ... Yes, I suppose it is,' she said, reaching for the coffee he'd poured as she settled herself. What had he expected? she asked herself, sipping gratefully. An endearment? Some reference to last night? A kiss?

Studying Julian over her cup, Rosie realised her feelings were hard to quantify. He smiled at her, and as his mouth formed that beautiful curve; she *did* feel fond of him – not so much for the pleasure, which had been considerable, but for his kindness too. What she didn't feel was besotted. There was no shivery emotional mushiness, no fear of losing him, as there had been with Geoff. And surprisingly, as the coffee cleared her thoughts, she felt the welcome return of control. She desired Julian, even now, but to her relief, her heart was her own.

There was a bond between them, yes, but it was more like friendship than anything. A delicious sense of complicity. They were in a sexual conspiracy together.

75

Something risqué, but positive; and as Julian reached over and patted her hand, she knew she could do what he'd asked – always providing that David wasn't too much of a dork!

'I wouldn't worry about the library today, Rosie. I've something else I want you to do.'

Hot blood flared her cheeks as the night returned to her mind. She thought of things she would have liked to have done, that there hadn't been time or energy left for.

Julian laughed gently. 'No, no! Not this morning, alas.' He gave her hand a quick squeeze, then reached for his coffee.

As she watched this simple but elegant action, she saw Julian's plate was empty. He'd obviously finished his breakfast some time ago.

'I'd like to, Rosie, believe me.' He nipped at his lower lip with his teeth, and Rosie's loins warmed and wept. 'But I've some heavy meetings this morning and I can't put them off,' he continued, regretfully. 'What I want *you* to do is go to the airport in the limousine and meet Celeste and David. I'd go myself – she likes me to – but under the circumstances, I'm sure she'll be happy with you.' A slight lift of his head made Rosie meet his eyes – and she felt a fresh pang of lust as he winked. 'And the sooner you meet David the better, eh?'

In theory it was a good idea, but as she sat in the long, black car, Rosie had the jitters again. She'd hoped to meet these two separately, and ideally in the library where the aura of the books would empower her. But now she had to face them both at once, stone-cold, without even the questionable support of Julian. The wife she'd wronged and the boy she was going to have to teach – what a combination. She felt sweat break out under her arms, and prayed that her deodorant could cope.

The chauffeur, Stephen, wasn't helping matters either. He was a tall, black guy with an impressive, muscular physique, and a dazzling smile. Yesterday, when he'd

76

collected her from her flat, she'd enjoyed his frank male scrutiny; but now it just made her nervous. She'd sensed his eyes on her as he'd held open the car door, felt him studying her breasts in the thin, soft sweater, and the shape of her hips and thighs in her tailored linen trousers. There was nothing she could say to him really though, because his surveillance was too subtle to object to.

At the airport, Rosie tried bio-feedback: calming her nerves by sheer force of will, and suppressing the threat of blushes. Breathing deeply, she expanded her diaphragm and stood tall, projecting a sham of cool poise while her heart leapt wildly in her chest.

When the flight arrival was announced, she started counting silently and trained her eyes on the area where the passengers would emerge. At two hundred, the butterflies in her stomach turned to hummingbirds, flapping up a storm. Two figures – one male, one female – had appeared in the entrance, and every instinct she had said, 'They're here!'

The woman was unmistakably the one in the portrait at Amberlake Gardens: an exquisite sylph with a lovely face, a slender, perfect body, and thick, straight, shiny-black hair worn in an immaculate Cleopatra bob. She was clothed in scarlet lycra ski-pants and a matching form-fitting top that made everyone around her look drab. She wore boots and had a fringed, suede jacket draped around her shoulders. Her eyes were hidden by aviator shades and her lips were the reddest and glossiest Rosie had ever seen.

Beside her was David. The enigma.

Oh God, he's peculiar! thought Rosie, her spirits plunging. I can't do this, she wailed inside. I just can't!

But as the couple drew closer, something very weird happened. Rosie's perceptions did a sudden flip, and 'peculiar' and 'strange' seemed wrong. 'Different' took their place. And so did 'special', 'unique' and 'potentially wonderful'.

Celeste's companion was tall, lean and graceful, his

long body clad in black denim and a mustard coloured turtle-neck sweater. His skin appeared quite pale for a man's, and his features were sharply defined and startlingly symmetrical. His light pink mouth was firmly sculpted, and his nose noble, almost roman. His eyes were large, long-lashed, and a shade of brown so light and lustrous it was almost gold. As if to highlight this, he'd brushed his brown hair straight back from his brow in a style that was neat, yet vaguely leonine.

Rosie stood stock still for several long, countable seconds. The young man's gaze was intent and unwavering, and seemed to root her to the spot. She could almost believe that he already knew her, and her purpose; although common sense said that he was only staring at her because she was staring at him!

'Er . . . Hello,' she said finally, hating herself for being so dull in her choice of greeting. 'I'm –'

'Rosie, of course,' said a husky, feminine voice. Rosie jumped. Unlikely as it seemed, she'd almost forgotten about Celeste.

'I'm Celeste Brent-Hadey,' the dark-haired woman continued, her voice unexpectedly intimate, 'and this is my cousin, David Brent.' As she said this, the boy – man? young god? – stepped another pace forward and solemnly held out his hand.

'How do you do?' he said quietly, his soft voice surprisingly deep. It was only the shortest of speeches, but Rosie instantly warmed to his accent.

'A fellow Yorkie, eh?' she said, smiling to cover her shock. His hand was deliciously cool, the contact almost electrical. His long fingers seemed to fold around hers.

'Yes . . . Yes, I am.' His reply was hesitant, and his mouth quirked slightly as if he were afraid to smile outright. She sensed wariness, and if not suspicion, at least a certain confusion, yet he withdrew his hand slowly, as if he too relished their contact.

'Well, let's get to that car, shall we?' said Celeste briskly, diffusing the odd little moment. 'I'm about to die for a large gin and tonic in the comfort of my own home, and I'm sure you two must be keen to get into that library and start rummaging through all those books.' She turned to David with an innocuous smile, 'Rosie's the new librarian, David. I can't remember if I told you about her or not . . .'

Rosie felt grateful for Celeste. She was a natural hostess, and without overt manipulation, she filled in the spaces between them, her conversation soothing and fluid. Rosie found it easy to chat and answer questions, and while David didn't say much, he didn't seem unduly nervous either.

He was watchful though. Rosie sensed him observing her, and when she turned away from Celeste for a moment, she found his eyes on her, his look direct and fiery. He was sitting opposite her, in the jump seat, and in the car's tinted glass gloom, his great golden eyes were like beacons of scrutinising light. When he looked away it seemed more out of politeness than discomfitude, and Rosie felt both rattled and exhilarated. He wasn't at all what she'd expected.

While Celeste chatted idly of Paris, Rosie allowed her attention to wander. Towards David. Towards his differentness, and his possibilities.

He'd had a mild nervous breakdown, Julian had said, yet there seemed no outward sign of it. He was quiet, but it was the quietness of thought, not nerves. His body was still, his long legs stretched out in front of him, relaxed but somehow not casually so. There was a sense of feline readiness in him, but for what, Rosie couldn't discern. She could only be impressed.

More than ever now, she felt excited by the task ahead. Her pupil was quite beautiful in a silent, self-contained sort of way, and though she couldn't see much of his body, she sensed it would be as fascinating and fine as his face. She imagined hairlessness, quiet strength, wiry limbs, and a penis that was slender but long. Without thinking, she glanced towards his groin.

Her heart thudded. His black jeans were snug and well-cut, and there was marked fullness behind their neat double-stitched fly. Did he have an erection already? Because of her? Suddenly, she wanted to believe it.

Once again, she felt his focused attention, and when she looked up, something lurched in the pit of her belly. The pale boy was no longer quite so pale, she realised; there was a faint haze of a blush along the high, bright lines of his cheekbones, and as their eyes met, his skittered instantly away.

Good grief! Oh God! It *had* happened already. Before it was supposed to. He was aroused right in front of her, and she sensed it was against his will. She felt as if she'd drunk a dozen of Celeste's gin and tonics, and her body surged in response, its secret, female reaction concealed beneath the layers of her clothing.

It was all hidden, but it was as exciting as being thrown on a bed, stripped naked, then caressed until she moaned uncontrollably. She felt her breasts swell in the lace of her bra and the flesh between her legs start to tickle.

She imagined telling David what was happening to her, quietly describing the condition of her body and her sex. It would be his first instruction, and she'd place his hand between her legs and watch that faint veil of pink spread out across his face and throat. His fingers would move slowly in her moisture, examining it by touch. He'd make a sound of surprise, a soft, rough cry. She wished suddenly that they were alone in the car, so she could make her fancies real, take off her jumper and show him her hard crumpled nipples, thick and dark beneath her thin, silk bra. She pictured herself reaching out to him across this opulent, leather-scented space, then drawing his perfect young face to her bosom and stroking his sleek brown hair.

'It's alright,' she'd say when he trembled. 'It's alright, you're a man, it's your birthright. You can have me, David. Don't worry . . .'

How would it feel to lie there beside him? she wondered. To guide him on top of her, and into her? He'd be hasty, desperate. She'd have to steer his stiff, young penis to the right place, then steady his charge towards orgasm. Tempering her own need, she'd have to show him where to touch her. How much and how hard. Her vagina fluttered and she felt wetness in her panties, her body already smoothing his path. They were sitting several feet apart in a car, in the late morning London traffic, but in her mind, they were already making love.

'Are you okay? You look a bit dazed.'

Celeste's voice shattered Rosie's fantasies. Julian's wife was regarding her with mischievous interest, her violet eyes twinkling as if she'd seen the same visions herself.

'Yes. Thanks. I'm fine,' Rosie stammered, losing control now, blushing vividly pink and hot. 'I didn't sleep very well last night –' Her pulse pumped faster as she remembered part of the reason. 'A new bed and all . . . But don't worry, I'm sure I'll get used to it.'

'I'm sure you will.' Celeste's voice was strangely loaded, and for a moment Rosie was convinced the woman knew everything. 'But if there's anything I can do, just let me know, won't you?'

On any normal level it was a simple offer of help, but suddenly Rosie sensed more. As she turned to Celeste, she saw the same heat in those lavender eyes that she'd seen in David's golden ones; and the sight of it shocked her. She felt a deep, hard jolt of something that she wanted to ignore, but couldn't.

She's a lesbian! thought Rosie wildly. A bisexual. She wants me just as much as Julian did. As David does. Oh God, what have I got into?

Mercifully, the car soon slid to a halt before the front door at Amberlake Gardens. Patently delighted to be home, Celeste entered the house like a whirlwind, all sighs and melodramatic gestures, and smiles of greeting for her staff. David held back politely and let Rosie precede him, while somewhere behind them, Stephen dealt quietly with the luggage.

Rosie felt dazed and befuddled by Celeste and her

81

vibrancy, and by the strange feeling that on some deep, instinctive level, she'd already got through to David. They'd exchanged virtually no conversation, but it didn't matter. He'd looked. She'd looked. He'd seen her look. He wasn't yet conscious of her dual role in the household, she was sure, but he was certainly aware of her body. So aware that he was forced to escape, pleading tiredness, to his room.

'*He* hasn't been sleeping well either,' observed Celeste, looking at Rosie over her shoulder as she led the way into the sitting room. Rosie followed, then wondered whether she should.

Aren't I supposed to be working? she thought as she dithered on the threshold. Celeste seemed to be assuming her company, but when all was said and done, she – Rosie – was only paid help.

'Oh don't worry about the books!' Celeste twirled around, smiling, and her lovely hair fanned out like a glossy black bell. 'They'll keep a while. Have a drink with me. Let's get to know each other.' Without asking, she poured for both of them – and Rosie felt a frisson of alarm when she was handed a sweet sherry, the very one she'd told Julian she liked so much. As she sat down where Celeste indicated – next to her on the sofa – she wondered just how that knowledge had been imparted.

Up close, Julian's wife was extraordinary, her face as flawless as a jewel in the smooth, black frame of her distinctive Egyptian hairstyle. Her delicate features had a soft, sweet bloom that made Rosie wonder how old she was. Celeste looked young in years, but seemed old in confidence. And when she turned, Rosie almost flinched – those huge violet eyes were far too candid.

'So what do you think of David?' Celeste asked.

Rosie took a calming sip of sherry. What she said depended on what Celeste knew. 'He seems very nice,' she offered after a moment. 'A bit shy, but nowhere near as shy as I'd expected. Is his insomnia due to his . . . his illness?'

'No, not really,' replied Celeste with a slow, arch

82

smile. 'He's more or less over his breakdown now . . . It was fairly mild anyway.' There was an impish glint in her eyes now, a mischief that was almost dizzying. 'No,' she continued, 'I think his sleeplessness is the sort that afflicts most young men of his age. He's horny, Rosie. He's desperate for sex and lies awake half the night faking it with his own right hand!'

Without thinking Rosie drained her glass, and Celeste laughed.

'It's true!' she said blithely, taking Rosie's glass, then getting up to refill it. Her hips swayed sinuously as she walked across the room on her high, spike-shaped heels.

'He's ready, Rosie. It's as if he's just woken up from a sleep and his hormones are driving him crazy. He's had a sexually repressed upbringing so far and he needs to catch up. Soon!'

Celeste spoke quietly and sincerely now. She handed Rosie her drink and seemed to watch her intently as she sipped it.

She knows! thought Rosie, hardly tasting the sweetness in her mouth at all. She's in on it!

Rosie resisted the urge to drain her glass again. She'd have to think fast now, and clearly, because her job, at the least, might depend on it.

But Celeste began to talk about her cousin.

David had lost his parents at an early age, as had Celeste herself. But while she'd been wilful and headstrong, and come to live in London as soon as she was legally able, David had stayed put.

Being younger, he'd lived with his grandparents in the wilds of the Yorkshire Dales; and though the old couple had been kind to him, their smallholding home had been miles from anywhere, and the life isolated. After his grandmother's death, David had been left to care for his grandfather alone and his existence had become even more solitary. A natural genius, he'd more or less educated himself, devouring every scrap of knowledge he could find from books: both at home and in every library he could get to from his remote moorland locale.

83

'He's almost *lived* in our library since he came here,' Celeste said, nodding her gleaming head in the library's general direction. 'He's reading everything! Which was all very fine until he discovered Julian's special collection . . .' she let her voice fade delicately and looked Rosie straight in the eye. 'You can imagine the effect *that* had on him can't you? An impressionable boy just beginning to understand his own body . . .' She took a sip from her glass, and her slim throat rippled sensuously. 'It was like dynamite, Rosie. Pure dynamite. And now *we've* to do something about it.'

'We?' Rosie put down her sherry, carefully. She could see her fingers shaking.

'Oh come on, Rosie, you know why you're here.' Celeste's voice was silky and cajoling, a feminine echo of her husband's – as it had sounded last night.

'But I'm a librarian,' Rosie said firmly. 'What can *I* do?' Her innards were trembling and her heart pounding, and in her panic she clung to the safe, old Rosie.

'Yes, I know,' said Celeste with a laugh, 'and by all accounts a very accomplished one. But what about your other duties? The ones my husband outlined to you last night. When you were in bed with him.'

It was like being thrown into a river; a river of icewater. What could she do, or say? She opened her mouth and nothing came out. She couldn't look at Celeste at all.

After a moment, gentle fingers settled on her cheek and made her look up. At the same time, a surprisingly forceful arm slid around her shoulders and cradled her, just as a lover would. 'It's alright, Rosie, I know everything,' said Celeste like a zephyr of sweetness, her face all smiles. 'Last night was my suggestion. I thought you'd feel lonely in a strange house, and Julian agreed to help.'

Rosie gaped at her.

'It was a nice welcome though, wasn't it?'

Rosie nodded. She felt off balance, numb, shocked: by both Celeste's words and her scented closeness. The heat

84

in that red-clad shape was astounding, and Rosie could feel it warming her. She wanted to get closer, but she was frightened. She'd never responded to a woman before, never been held like this by one. She couldn't believe the way her own body felt.

'Julian and I have never had a conventional marriage.' Celeste's voice was even, clear, untroubled. Rosie was quivering, but her companion seemed to think nothing of stroking her and squeezing her with a touch that was far more than friendly. 'I love him and he loves me, but we've both always had other lovers ... Other men and women for sex.'

The emphasis was unmistakable, and it suddenly occurred to Rosie that men and women might apply to Julian also. Her fuddled mind boggled at the thought, but her body found it thrilling.

Celeste was speaking again, breathily, coaxingly. 'I would've ... I would've dealt with David myself, but he's my cousin. Third cousin, maybe more, but it bothers me.' She shrugged, her beautiful curves shuddering in their tight red shell. 'It's a shame because I think he's exquisite ...' She pulled away, her lilac eyes still asking the question.

'Yes, he is,' whispered Rosie. It was true, after that first sudden revelation at the airport, she couldn't deny it. He was as beautiful in his own way as his cousin: pure, erotic, and stunning.

Celeste seemed to pick up the thought.

'Imagine what you could do with him. A perfect, innocent boy with a fresh young body.' Her eyes sparkled. 'I've seen him naked, Rosie, and he's a gem! Don't let that pale face fool you, he's no wimp. His chest, his legs, his sex ... Everything about him is superb. Just think of it ...'

Think of it? She could hardly stop thinking of it. She saw David in her mind; his smooth body, his long, yearning penis. She saw his solemn face reddened with lust and contorted with pleasure. In her imagination, she gazed down at him from the heights of experience;

85

riding his impetuous flesh, bearing down as he thrust upwards. She was dimly aware that her eyes must be glazed, and that Celeste could see it. But there was nothing she could do about her fantasies, they were out of her hands. Uncontrolled. The coming task obsessed her, and made her body stir and prepare itself. She was wet in her silky panties, and she wished she was days or weeks advanced in it all, so she could go up to David's room now. And make love to him.

'Hey, wake up!'

Focusing slowly, Rosie saw knowledge in Celeste's brilliant eyes. Wicked knowledge. It was as if she really could see Rosie's thoughts.

'I'm sorry,' Rosie whispered. 'It's all so new. I want to help David. Really I do. But . . .' She hesitated, searching for the words. 'Until last week I had a tedious job in dull surroundings. A steady, monogomous relationship. We'd gone through all the normal stages. I was just . . . conventional. Then I came here –' She waved her hand in a small sweep. 'It's like being on another planet!' She paused again, thought, then smiled. 'It's a planet I like though. I think I could like it a lot. But it'll take some getting used to.'

'I'm glad,' said Celeste gently. 'I'm glad you like it here. I know it sounds corny, but I want you to feel like part of the family. I think it'll help with your . . . your objective. Make it easier for him to accept you.'

Rosie's head was spinning, but it wasn't from the sherry. Her mind was filled with strange pictures: images of a slim, pale boy with golden, almost cat-like eyes. A lion cub waiting to be blooded.

And she found Celeste befuddling too. Her beauty and her perfume, and the intimate nearness that should have seemed simply companionable, but which held the promise of more, much more.

'I . . . I . . .' she stuttered, at a loss to know what to think and feel, much less to say.

'I know, it's all a bit much, isn't it?' said Celeste kindly, compounding Rosie's confusion by closing the last gap between them and kissing her, just once, on the cheek. 'Why don't you take a lie down before lunch. Just relax, think things over. You'll see it all more clearly when you're rested.'

Rosie realised she must have looked alarmed, because Celeste kissed her again, then squeezed her hand reassuringly. 'Go on, off you go. I promise you there'll be no visitors.' She winked and urged Rosie to her feet. 'Well, not this afternoon!'

But as she ascended the stairs to her bedroom, then lay down, bemused, hot and bothered, Rosie realised she would have welcomed a visitor.

When a visitor did come, it was a dream.

In it, she was being led along a wide panelled corridor by a tall, black servant. He was silent and smiling and quite naked, but that seemed alright because she wasn't wearing much herself, just a beautiful slippy kind of underskirt made of pale pink silk, and high-heeled slippers in the rich red colour of roses. The tiny chemise was so short that her bottom was almost visible, and a warm, naughty breeze was tickling at her thighs and sex.

At the end of the corridor stood two tall doors that opened as they approached. The black servant entered first, then stood to one side to let her pass.

'The Dauphin's tutor!' he called out loudly, by way of announcement, and she walked past him into the magnificent chamber beyond.

Two high thrones stood at the far end of the room, and to one side was a cushioned and gilded stool. The thrones were occupied by the King and the Queen, smiling benignly, and on the stool sat the Dauphin, his oval face solemn and watchful.

'Approach,' said the King, augustly. He was a dark and beautiful man; exotic, a Moor from the Atlas mountains. His face was brown, his eyes were bright, and his fine strong body was clad in a turquoise robe. As he spoke he was fondling his penis, which was protruding boldly from the silken folds at his groin.

'Yes, please do approach,' echoed the Queen softly from beside him, her purple eyes darting from her husband's long, swarthy shaft to the shy girl standing before her.

The Queen was beautiful too, from the same continent as the King, but from a region more easterly, the vale of the fertile Nile river. Her hair was black as a raven's wing, and her face a vision of perfection. Her lips were brilliant crimson, the same bright colour as the long, shiny gown that clothed her fabulous body.

'And who are you, my dear?' the lovely monarch enquired.

'I am the English Rose, Ma'am, come to serve the Dauphin.' She could not help but look at him as she spoke his name. This boy, to whom she owed her body, was the most beautiful of the three, and his demeanor was calm and quiet. A torch burnt in a stanchion behind him, and its light seemed to glint like a diadem on his smooth, brown, brushed-back hair. His skin was the colour of cream and his lips were as pink as sugared almonds. A half grown lion cub was lolling on his lap, and its eyes, and his, had the selfsame yellow-gold gleam.

'Then serve him,' said the King, his voice heavy with lust and his bare legs shifting with pleasure. His dark eyes closed as the Queen replaced his grasping hand with her own.

The English Rose did as she was bidden, falling to her knees before the Dauphin's stool, her body stirred by the sight of him. As she crouched on the carpet, she felt her nipples ache and the nectar flow between her legs. Defying the wrath of the regal family, she lifted her slip and touched herself. Her core was hot and puffed and molten, and as she groaned, she saw the Dauphin's eyes flare with passion. Pressing a kiss to his pet's soft fur, he urged the cub gently up off his lap, then crushed his gloved fingers to his groin in a gesture of utmost torment.

'Hurry, girl! Give him your mouth,' cried the Queen,

her fingers on her husband's red penis, while her other hand caressed her own breast.

Her mouth? But where? On his soft pink lips? His long pale hand beneath its gauntlet? His naked chest, between the folds of his white silk shirt?

No, no, none of these! As she came up on her knees, the Dauphin reached forward and pulled her face against his loins. With trembling fingers, she unfastened his garment – a pair of black velvet breeches – and reached inside to seek out his treasure.

And when it sprang out, proud and free, it was a greater treasure than the English Rose had imagined – a stiff, rosy branch of flesh that wept silken juice from its rounded tip in anticipation of the delights to come. With a long sigh of content, the hungry, besotted Rose leant forward and absorbed him, sucking on his beautiful penis as daintily and cleverly as she could.

There were gasps from close by, small sounds of approval and of satisfaction. Even as they pleasured themselves, the Royal couple looked on, and the English Rose was glad of it. She licked rapidly at the fine warm staff in her mouth, and heard the Dauphin's voice join the others, groaning softly and brokenly in time to the swirls of her tongue.

In another chamber of the palace, a piano began to play, and as she reached between her thighs, to her damp and swollen-hot place, the beautiful music seemed to set the seal on the bliss of all of them. She heard the King and Queen sob out each other's names, and at that very moment the Dauphin whimpered loudly, caressed her hair, and graced her with his hot, sweet semen. And while her own sex throbbed hard beneath her fingertips, rippling like a wave in the sea, the piano played on and on and on . . .

Rosie woke up having an orgasm: her sweating face pressed into her pillow, her hips rocking, and her fingers jammed hard between her thighs. The cotton beneath her face was damp because she'd been crying with pleasure in her sleep; and in another part of the house, in a room somewhere below her, she could hear someone playing the piano.

Chapter 6

Early Learning

*F*or several minutes, Rosie just lay there. Listening to the music. Thinking about her dream. Touching her sex and riding her receding orgasm. She'd taken off her trousers to lie down and her silky knickers were soaked where she'd rubbed herself through them.

She recalled seeing the Steinway piano in the corner of the library, and wishing, not for the first time, that she could play – not as a virtuoso, she didn't really aspire to that, but it would have been nice to be able to play like the person who was playing now. The melodies had begun tentatively, with pauses for repetition of fluffed notes interspersed with outbreaks of keyboard doodling, but gradually the pianist seemed to grow in power and confidence, and the playing became more accomplished, the tunes more recognisable. Rosie's knowledge of the classics was slight, but all the same the muted sounds were soothing.

Was David the unseen musician? In his secluded life until now, there must have been plenty of time to practice, and the hesitancy of the early bars seemed to mesh with his shy, quiet reticence.

He hadn't seemed so reticent in her dream though. The Dauphin had been quite certain of what he wanted, and his eyes had been hot with lust.

It had been a vivid dream, textured and realistic, and needed little in the way of symbolic interpretation. It had just been Julian and Celeste, dominant and sexy, and their plans for David and herself. The lion cub? Well, that came from David's eyes, she supposed. And the way he wore his hair. And his light, cat-like grace. Nothing more sinister than that. Or was it?

As the piano finally fell silent, Rosie thought about getting up. The quality of the light that streamed in through her window looked strangely slanted, as if she'd slept longer than she'd planned.

The clock astounded her. It showed well past five. She'd spent the whole afternoon dreaming and playing with herself. She wrinkled her nose as she sniffed her fingers. They were pungent with her scent and the gusset of her panties felt sticky. As dinner was at eight, it hardly seemed worth changing twice, so she slipped into her thin silk robe.

When she looked around, Rosie found that some kind soul had brought her something to eat. There was a tray on the table at the end of her bed, with a plate of neatly cut sandwiches and a glass of milk. Her mouth watered, but just as she was about to wash her hands, an ominous thought occurred.

When, exactly, had the snack been delivered? Had someone watched her toss in her sleep with her hands rubbing hard between her legs? She reached out to the tray, then saw a small piece of paper tucked beneath the plate. It was a sheet from her own notepad, the one she used for jottings. The one that still lay on the table, along with a pencil.

Almost reluctantly, she picked up the note.

Dear Rosie, it said, *I didn't want to disturb you, your dream looked far more delicious than this sandwich! Please tell me about it later! Love, Celeste.* Below a long row of 'x's was a postscript. *Your bottom is beautiful. I nearly kissed it but I didn't want to wake you!*

Rosie's stomach felt tight and knotted, and she suddenly couldn't face her sandwich. Celeste had come into her room and seen her masturbating. Seen her bottom in only a thin pair of panties with the crotch ridden up in her groove. The idea was as hideous as it was exciting, and she wondered what would have happened if she'd woken. Would she have had her first taste of loving a woman? Or would she have resisted? Somehow she didn't think so.

With an age to go before dinner, Rosie took her time getting ready. First she washed and conditioned her hair, then she wound it in a towel while she took a leisurely bath, filling the tub as deep as was safe and slopping in nearly a cupful of scented bubbling essence from the vast selection on her shelf.

The room smelt like a herbalist's, and the perfume, as she sank into the water, made Rosie feel dizzy. The scents of frankincense and patchouli seemed to unlock something wild inside her, releasing a circuit between her loins and her brain that had been blocked until now. She'd had an orgasm in her sleep. Probably several. But she still wanted to play with herself, to touch her breasts, her belly and her clitoris beneath the veil of the heavy, silken water.

She brought lovers into her mind to share her sensuous stroking. Julian. Celeste. More than ever, David. She made herself focus on him, thinking about what she should tell him, and how to begin. What he might feel like when he used his lessons.

'There. Touch me just there,' she whispered, picturing him sitting on the side of the bath and reaching down into the water. She could almost feel his cool fingers. Feel them – guided by hers – slipping in through the grove of her pubis and finding her quivering core. Sliding deep into the water, she set her gaze inwards, and saw only a pair of hot, golden eyes with pupils darkened by pleasure.

Rubbing slowly, very slowly, she brought herself to a long, steamy orgasm, murmuring David's name as a mantra while she writhed, imprinting him on her brain and her senses. Making him what *she* wanted, so her task would be easier. Or not even a task at all.

The bathwater was much cooler when she got out, and the bubbles all gone. Her skin felt very smooth and slightly oily; sensitised and ready to be touched. As she dried off, it almost seemed to glow beneath the towel, and she began thinking about the evening ahead.

It was impossible to predict really. She'd spoken only a few sentences to David, so nothing much could happen just yet. Even so, she decided to dress optimistically. Standing naked before her wardrobe, she dithered over various outfits: both old ones, from her previous life, and new clothes she'd bought with Julian's moving in allowance.

Nothing too obvious, she decided. She had a few things that both plunged and clung, but she wanted to hold them back for now. Instead she chose a light, smoked-pastel chiffon two piece that achieved quite a lot by mere suggestion. The colours were blended and smeared – peaches, lemons, muted oranges and tans – all softly floating across a smock-like top and a full swirling handkerchief skirt. Beneath this she wore a camisole and french knickers in oyster satin, with matching suspender belt and sheer oatmeal coloured stockings. She felt almost like a bride in all her finery, and it was only when she stepped into her sandals – which were beige, strappy, and deliciously comfortable in spite of their height – that she felt a pang of disquiet. She remembered being with Geoff the last time she'd worn them, and suddenly realised it was the first time she'd thought of him all day.

Only a week or so ago he'd meant the world to her, and she'd have done anything to please him. Now, strangely, she could hardly bring his face into focus. He seemed blurred to her, indistinct. He was part of another world now, only significant as a negative experience. Someone who'd exploited her. The pain was still there, but it was dimmer now, like a nearly-healed sprain that only nagged occasionally. It would be gone soon, she realised. Would she then completely forget what he'd looked like?

Purging her mind of such unknowables, she turned her attention to her hair. It was almost dry, and combing it smoothly away from her face, she secured it with two mock-ivory slides in a simple, but sophisticated style. And she made up the same way. Smudged taupe eyes, lots of mascara, and a deep but lasting lipstain. Crushed cranberry that would endure and endure. If it needed to.

There was a knock on the door, and Rosie's heart leapt, but it was only Mrs Russell. Would she like an aperatif brought to her room? Or would she join the others in the library?

Downstairs, in the library, Rosie wondered if she'd strayed into a fairytale. Julian was in perfect, devastating evening dress, and Celeste wore a black, ankle-skimming tube-like dress covered entirely in sequins, with black silk gloves that sheathed her completely from fingertip to upper arm. Her black suede court shoes had heels that looked about four inches high, and her hair was sleeked back from her face and gelled, accentuating a flawless maquillage that was even more Cleo-like than ever.

'We've decided to go out,' she said as she undulated elegantly across the room towards Rosie, her deportment faultless despite her tricky shoes and her narrow dress, 'to an artshow. It'll give you and David a chance to get acquainted.'

'Er . . . Yes. Okay. Good idea,' replied Rosie, struggling to stay calm. She'd been banking on company tonight, with the Hadeys on hand to help her.

Julian's brown eyes flashed as he put down his glass and walked towards her, a girl's wet-dream in suave tailoring and a pure white shirt. Rosie felt a pang of pure lust at the sight of him. Her body remembered his, recreating the warmth of his skin against it. She glanced at Celeste, fearful of betraying herself, but the other woman's eyes were as vivid as her husband's, and aglow with expectation.

'Don't worry, Rosie,' said Julian softly as he pressed his lips against her cheek. 'He's a lucky boy. I almost wish *I* could start again.'

95

Rosie gasped as his hands settled knowledgeably on her body, exploring her breasts and her bottom through the malleable film of the chiffon. She felt her nipples respond immediately, and her cleft grow soft and moist, excited as much by Celeste's bright gaze as by Julian's long, roving fingers.

'You're beautiful,' he whispered, kissing her throat and moving his groin against her hip. His penis was semi-erect already, and hardening fast, and his kiss was wet and thorough. Rosie felt herself drowning, slipping deep beneath the high waves of need as his caress settled firmly on her mound, and he massaged her sex through her skirt.

'Julian, please,' she moaned. Celeste was grinning at her, over his shoulder, her violet eyes glittering like black-lined stars, and her slender silk-gloved hand at her own groin as if she found the sight of her husband groping another woman arousing.

The fondling seemed to go on forever, and Rosie's knees went weak. He was rubbing her insistently now, stroking her bottom through her paper-thin skirt. Without thinking she closed her eyes and put her arms around his shoulders, and as she did so, a pair of soft, feminine hands settled lightly on her shoulders.

'Relax, Rosie. Enjoy him,' whispered Celeste, her voice rough and compelling as her fingers slid and explored. Rosie felt them on her back, then sliding around her ribs to her breasts.

Rosie shook violently as they roused her, and made her respond to the touch of four hands. She locked her fingers around Julian's neck, swaying because her legs wouldn't hold her, and felt him rock her on her own hot vulva.

'Relax, Rosie. Give it up,' murmured Julian against her neck, swirling his hold, and making her come.

'Oh no! No! No!' she whimpered, her body betraying her. Her legs seemed to buckle and her strength leeched away. Only seconds later, she was being settled on the sleek leather sofa, still panting while her quim leapt and rippled.

'Why did you do that?' she gasped, as first one, then the other sat down beside her. Celeste produced a drink for her, the sherry that Rosie was oh-so ready for. As she drank most of it down, she felt a hand – Celeste's – settle gently, almost possessively on her thigh.

'To prime you, sweetheart,' the other woman said softly. 'To set you thinking of sex. So that David will too. With your eyes so sparkling, he'll know something's happened. And he'll want something to happen for him too.'

Rosie could feel heat in her cheeks and smell her own perfume swirling around her. She could well believe her eyes were glowing.

'You're very lovely, Rosie. Very sensual. He'll find you irresistible,' said Julian, giving her shoulders a squeeze as if what they'd just done was quite normal.

Maybe it is? thought Rosie suddenly, sipping her last drop of sherry, then letting Celeste take the glass and refill it. What had he said? *We're pretty relaxed about things here.* Maybe he and his wife shared women all the time? Lots of them? Men too? Maybe they had orgies a plenty, and needed to hurry up and get David eroticised so he could join in?

'We have to go now,' said Celeste, passing the glass back to Rosie. 'But don't worry. Nothing *has* to happen tonight. Although if it did . . .'

'David will be down in a minute, Rosie,' Julian interrupted, his voice ineffably kind. 'Just take a deep breath, be yourself, and I'm sure it'll all go well.'

Rosie watched, dumbstruck, as he rose, took his wife's arm and escorted her across the room. At the doorway, they turned – as one – blew Rosie a kiss, then left, their voices echoing softly in the passage.

Oh God, I don't know if I can do this! she thought, sipping quickly from her newly filled glass. The time of reckoning had come, and here she was still dizzy with pleasure from the weirdest, most unexpected kind of sex.

It wasn't a rape because she hadn't been penetrated,

or forced. Nevertheless, she *had* been railroaded. By a man, and his wife. Working as a team! Julian's fingers, and Celeste's eyes; it had taken both of these to make her come.

Pull yourself together, Howard! she told herself sternly, running her hands over her top and skirt, checking for any sign of what had happened. Everything seemed okay, but there wasn't time to make sure; even as she patted at her hair, then touched her fingers to her burning throat, the door handle turned, the door itself slowly opened, and David appeared on the threshold.

Oh dear Lord, he's amazing! thought Rosie, stunned anew by the boy's fresh, pure beauty. He'd clearly dressed-up tonight, whether in her honour or not, she'd no way of telling. She only knew he looked wonderful, and that his clothes were elegant and well-chosen: a pair of stylishly baggy black linen trousers and a rather Italian-looking maroon silk shirt.

'Hi!' he said in his softly accented voice. 'Have the others gone?' The bright, golden eyes looked wary, but to Rosie's relief, not unfriendly.

'Yes,' replied Rosie, sensing his nervousness, and feeling a strange surge of kinship. They were both in this: both strangers, both not quite sure of themselves. Apart from sexual experiences, they were more or less equals, and she felt instinctively that David could probably help her just as much as she could help him.

'They've gone to some exhibition or other,' she continued, finding it suddenly easier to smile. 'So it's just you and me ... Would you like a drink?'

As soon as she'd said that she wondered if she'd slipped up. What if he was on medication or something? 'Do you drink?' she added, cautiously.

'Yes. Yes, I do,' he answered, with a small tentative smile. 'Not a lot ... But I'm working on it.' The smile widened, and Rosie felt a slow, luscious softening of her innards. For a second, she wondered if she knew any jokes; because that tiny hint of what his smiling face might look like was more intoxicating than any amount of alcohol. And she was mad for more of it.

Trying desperately to pull herself together, she did her best nonchalant walk towards the silver tray, and its extensive cache of drinks. 'Sherry?' Her fingers hovered over the various decanters.

'Er . . . Yes, please.' He sounded hesitant again.

'Sweet or dry?'

'Oh, sweet, please. I know it isn't very sophisticated, but it's the only kind I like.' He shrugged his shoulders helplessly, and flashed just an instant of that smile again.

'Well, thank God for that!' Rosie said with feeling. 'I'm fed up with people who think I'm an uncivilised oik because I only like drinks that are sweet!' She had a split second vision of Geoff's disapproving face when she'd requested something that didn't suit his image. 'Try this!' she went on, pouring a glass of the same sherry she was drinking.

He took the glass very carefully from her, but still their fingers touched. She sensed that he was wanting to flinch, but controlling it.

Then he smiled.

Rosie had never seen a transformation like it. She could almost imagine the sun had come up, or the moon risen. The shy, edgy boy had gone and in his place stood a sexy young man with magic in his brilliant, golden eyes. It only lasted a second but the afterglow left Rosie dazzled.

After a moment or two, she realised he was holding out his glass towards her, offering a toast. Half-numbed, she topped up her own and chinked it to his.

'To being uncivilised,' offered David after slight hesitation.

'To being unsophisticated,' answered Rosie, fighting for self control as the smile appeared again, briefly but tellingly.

The ice was broken now, or at least dented, and as they sat down together, Rosie felt able to start a conversation. 'That's a beautiful shirt,' she ventured, with meaning. The rich, dark colour really suited him;

accentuating the distinct red tint in his smooth brown hair, and making his pale skin look paler than ever, and twice as dramatic and unusual. She wondered if the effect was intentional, and by extension, marvelled at how someone who'd lived in seclusion could manage to choose such good clothes.

'I got it in Paris,' he replied, smoothing his fingertips along his sleeves, the action measured and sensuous as if the texture of the cloth gave him pleasure.

Rosie felt a cool sharp frisson as she watched him. His fingers were long and narrow: very tapered and elegant. Without stopping to think, Rosie imagined them running slowly over female skin, caressing it thoroughly, comparing its consistency with that of the inanimate silk.

'Celeste took me around all the shops and boutiques.' He paused, then shrugged again. 'Or at least it *felt* like all of them!' His smile sent her composure sliding. 'I've never had so many new clothes in my life, and ... Well, it's weird, I actually enjoyed it once we got started. Choosing. Trying on. Buying. It's the last thing I'd ever have thought I'd be interested in, but there you are. There's always something round the corner to surprise you, isn't there?'

This was the longest speech Rosie had yet heard him make, and the most mature. His soft, even voice seemed to play across her nerve-ends; its richness, its slight northern lilt, affecting her strangely and powerfully. She wondered what it would sound like when he was whispering endearments, or gasping in ecstasy. She wondered how he'd react, and what he'd say, if she reached out and touched him right now.

'Too true,' she replied after a couple of seconds, belatedly responding to his philosophical observation. She'd had her own share of surprises in the last few days, and she was sure there were still many ahead. Probably from David himself.

As a speculative silence fell, the dinner gong rang out cheerfully.

'Shall we?' said David, rising. He held out his hand like a courtier, helping her up and onto her feet as if she were a visiting princess, rather than a member of his cousin's household staff.

'Love to,' she replied, taking the offered hand and trying not to tremble. David's fingertips were warm now, and his grip, for a moment, was surprisingly firm and confident. It seemed as if he was going to hold onto her hand, and keep holding it as they walked to the dining room. But, almost immediately, Rosie sensed he was unsure of her again. Unsure of how to act. Unsure, perhaps, of what he was feeling.

But what was he feeling? she thought as they sat down to their starter. She'd seen him react in the car, and instinct told her his disappearance afterward had been linked to it. So was the same chemistry at work now?

He seemed calm, and as they ate their beautifully prepared meal, he chatted quietly about books and about the time he'd spent in Paris. He even asked questions about Rosie's previous jobs, and where she'd lived and studied. But somehow, beneath the still exterior, she sensed an inner agitation. He was like a hurricane in reverse, she realised. More or less unruffled on the surface, but underneath, in a violent emotional turmoil.

Instinct – and wishful thinking – told her that this ferment was sexual. It could be due to his recent emotional upheavals, but something told her these had been transient, because basically his underlying persona was strong and stable. He was most likely reacting to her womanhood and her femininity because she was the first female he'd met since coming here who he could think of as a viable partner. His cousin – and presumably her female friends – were too experienced and sophisticated to approach, and there was no-one else around of quite the right age. He was too new to the City to go out seeking companionship – so that only left Rosie Howard. Rosie wasn't a member of the glitter set; she was older than he was, but only slightly; and she

101

was around in the house, and seemed perfectly placed to befriend him.

Good grief, it's no wonder he's nervy! she thought, trying not to watch him and make him feel worse.

But it was difficult not to watch him. It was almost impossible not to feel attracted to him, or to respond to his youth and his maleness – especially as his presence here tonight had been engineered for her just as much as hers had been contrived for him. The very artificiality of their pairing was a subtle but potent aphrodisiac.

Rosie couldn't each much, but she was glad that David's appetite seemed normal. He ate moderately, yet appeared to quietly appreciate his food and the single glass of wine he took with it. The movements of his slender hands as he handled the cutlery were strangely erotic. His fingers were long and flexible, and his actions neat and deft. She wondered what those hands would feel like on her, and now being almost certain that David was the phantom pianist, she began to speculate how long it might take him to transfer his artistry at the keyboard onto the flesh of a living woman; like herself.

Surely if he could play music so expressively, he could understand the beauty and delicacy of lovemaking. He clearly had a poetic soul, which meant he was halfway to being a lover already.

'Are you the one I've been hearing playing the piano?' she asked, taking a sip of wine.

'Yes. It's me. I play a bit.' He smiled modestly and shrugged his shoulders. 'I've never had any proper tuition, but I've had a lot of time to myself to practice. I hope there weren't too many duff notes!'

'You play beautifully,' said Rosie, knowing it was the truth. A feeling for the music meant so much more than sterile technical skill, especially for her purposes. 'Would you play again for me,' she asked, 'when we've finished our dinner?'

David looked doubtful, and bit his lip, snagging its full, pink softness with his strong, and very even white teeth.

'Please,' she pleaded, aware that the wine and the sherry she'd drunk were making her dangerously forward. She'd have to be careful not to push too hard. David was far more confident than she'd expected, but she sensed his self-worth was still fragile.

'Alright,' he agreed, smiling his amazing smile again. 'But don't say I didn't warn you.'

The rest of the meal passed smoothly, in spite of Rosie's growing excitement. David described how he'd more or less taught himself to play the piano by listening to recordings of the classical masters, and also learnt to read music from a book. It seemed a peculiar way to go about things, but Rosie was impressed. David was obviously determined and resourceful, and would work hard to get what he wanted, no matter how daunting the task. It filled her with a strange kind of awe.

When they returned to the library, someone had been there before them. A small fire had been lit to take the edge off the early summer evening chill, and a bottle of sparkling wine stood cooling on ice, with two tall crystal flutes beside it.

How clichéd, Julian, thought Rosie wryly, but she smiled when she saw that it wasn't champagne in the cooler, but the sweet Italian spumante she preferred.

'Would you like some of this?' she asked David, who was already perched on the piano stool, flexing his fingers and looking mildly apprehensive.

'I'll have some afterwards, if that's alright,' he said, then bit his lip again, the gesture small but innocently sexy. 'I'm bad enough when I'm sober!'

'Get away!' said Rosie, with a laugh, knowing she wasn't quite sober herself.

David didn't reply, but began a few hesitant practice phrases.

Half-entranced already, Rosie took a seat where she could discreetly watch him play without making him feel too nervous.

After a few minutes he launched into a fully fledged melody, although not one Rosie could name. It sounded vaguely familiar, as if she'd heard it in the background of a television programme or a film. Her knowledge of classical music and piano technique was negligible, but within moments she knew one thing. As she'd suspected this afternoon, David really could play. Play well – and entirely without music.

There was something exquisitely sensuous about the delicate flow of the notes. Rosie suppressed a sigh, her whole body alive and quivering as David unknowingly played magical tunes on it. The sweet wine helped, of course, but it wasn't only that. Rosie felt as if she could drift away, floating on a mist of relaxed and delicious languor. She forgot all her qualms about her task, and surrendered to fate itself. What would happen would happen; whether tonight or another night. All that mattered was a beautiful young man playing the piano for her.

Suddenly, Rosie recognised a piece she could put a name to: Beethoven's *Fur Elise*, a melody she'd always found disturbingly erotic. The rolling, rippling phrases seemed to synchronise perfectly in her mind with little forays of foreplay, rushes towards pleasure, then teasing moments of stillness and anticipation. The notes seemed to hover on the brink of being played, like a lover's fingers circling, approaching, but not quite touching a particularly sensitive zone.

Putting aside her glass, she sank back into the chair and closed her eyes, letting the music paint a picture of herself and David. Making love.

He'd undressed her cautiously and reverently, pausing as each garment was removed to admire what his hands had revealed. She could almost feel those elegant, pianist's fingers exploring the contours of a breast, a thigh, the slope of a hip. She could imagine those firm pink lips pressed gently to her belly, and the tantalising swipe of his inquisitive young tongue as it dipped into her navel, swirled around, then cruised downwards to areas more sacred.

She shifted her body on the shiny leather sofa, restless

as she wondered what David's naked body might look like.

He'd be pale certainly, but attractive. Lithe but strong, his limbs fresh and limber, his sex eager and untested. He'd be a natural gentleman, she sensed. Anxious to please her as much as himself. He'd push into her slowly, very slowly, the strain contorting his face. He'd cry out softly as he plumbed her waiting body, and she would too, enraptured by the stretching of her channel around the bulk of his warm, thick member.

With a start, she realised that she'd actually sighed aloud. And that the music had stopped, probably some time ago. She flicked open her eyes, and looked across at David.

He was watching her, intently, and almost fearfully; as if he'd seen her dreams and was screwing up his courage to ask if they could ever be real. She could almost taste his confusion and the way he was being torn by urges he didn't understand.

'That was wonderful, David,' she said, keeping her voice low as she would have done to an inquisitive but timid wild animal. He was so close, so close to being ready, but commonsense whispered 'beware'. A false move now and he'd be crushed.

'Shall I play something else?' he asked, his voice not quite steady.

'Yes, that'd be lovely.'

He still needed a breathing space, she realised, just as she needed a chance to cool off; to channel her desire, and regain control of the situation and herself.

With a slight nod, he began to play another tune she knew. Debussy's *Clair de Lune*, a piece so haunting and lovely that she recognised straight away that she'd made a mistake. Vivid images assailed her, more tempestuous and sexual than ever. In her mind, her young lover was playful, confident and virile. His timing was perfect and his hot, gleaming penis had a rhythm and purpose of movement that touched her right to the core.

Rosie felt a compelling urge to masturbate. To assuage

the unbearable hunger that the music, and the musician had triggered. She looked across at David again, and the sight was incredible. His beautiful face was a picture of concentration, and he was clearly as enraptured by his music as she was. He seemed so lost in the notes that flowed from his fingers that he barely seemed to have to look at the keyboard. His lips were parted, and his cheeks slightly flushed, and she could almost believe he was aroused. As he played a long, sparkling run, up and down the octaves, he sighed imperceptibly, and in that moment Rosie could have sprung to her feet, run across the room and kissed him.

Oh God, I wish I dare kiss her! thought David as he played almost without conscious control.

He'd always been able to do this; set half of his mind to a task, while the other ran free with something else. But tonight it wasn't just his mind running wild, it was his body too. His glands, his hormones, and the stiff wayward thing between his legs that was aching and as hard as a bone.

As his fingers danced smoothly on the keys, he could think of nothing but the beautiful woman who sat just a few feet away from him. Rosie Howard, the librarian, who perfectly embodied everything he longed for. Everything his confused libido had been craving for these past few terrifying weeks.

Sex. It had hit him all of a sudden, and rushed through his senses like a runaway train. No longer abstract as it had always been before – on television, and in books and films – sex had become real and irresistible and urgent.

It was right at the centre of things now, plaguing his every waking thought and his rampant, undisciplined body.

David had known the rudimentary technical details of sex for many years now. He'd read the entry on human reproduction in his encyclopaedia when he was ten, scanning the description with a strange sense of detachment, finding it hard to believe that his own genitalia could join with those of a woman. The word 'pleasure' had been just that, a word.

Things had begun to change in his teens. His body had responded occasionally to the prettier girls at school, and he'd blushed furiously, terrified that someone would notice his penis swelling in his trousers. He'd felt befuddled by what he knew was an erection – confused that it could feel so good and so bad at the same time. He'd started finding himself stirred by unexpected thoughts – and he'd been shocked at the sublime sensations that stroking his own flesh could produce. He'd dreamed luridly and often woken up clutching his penis, with his own sticky semen splattered all over the sheets and his body. For a while he'd felt guilty, then commonsense had prevailed. It didn't seem to do him any harm and afterwards he always felt glowing.

His interest in sex had waned when he'd left school at sixteen; swamped, he now realised, by his responsibilities to his grandparents. He'd sought solace in books, in the piano, and in solitary study; barely thinking of his body at all, except for the basic tasks of maintaining his health and hygiene.

He remembered little of the dark days after his grandfather's funeral, and it seemed now that he'd consciously blanked it out, living in a zombie-like state until he'd woken up one day, and suddenly felt alive again. Since then, he'd been constantly ravenous for knowledge and experience, his imagination going crazy, and his penis always ready to rise. Just the thought of a woman could do it, and the reality drove him to distraction.

Girls in the street. Girls in shops. His cousin's friends. Even Celeste herself, sometimes, although this troubled him. They were fairly distantly related; but even so, her kindness, and the way she'd taken him under her wing when there was nobody else seemed to exclude her from the list of women he could lust over. She was also married, and to a man she so obviously adored.

He'd been very attracted to Celeste's personal fitness

trainer – the quaintly nicknamed 'Ladybird' – a stunning red-haired sylph who came to the house almost daily to organise Celeste and Julian's exercises. She was a friendly and sociable woman, but despite this, David decided she was far too sleek and glamorous. And also probably far too sexually accomplished to have time for a nineteen year old virgin. Like all the other women he'd come into contact with in London, and more recently, in Paris, she simply seemed too experienced for him. He'd been forced to resort to masturbation again, using either vague images of women he'd met or seen, or the books that he'd clandestinely borrowed from Julian's library. Every night he'd pick something from the special case and take to his room to study.

But now, as he swept into the final romantic phrase of *Clair de Lune*, he knew he'd found a better inspiration: Rosie Howard, the custodian of both the chaste books and the rude ones.

Julian's new librarian was as good to look at, if not better, than any women he'd encountered so far – and also terrifyingly approachable. As his penis kicked hard inside his trousers, his fingers shook on the keys and the resulting discordant clatter made the object of his dreams look towards him.

'Are you okay?' she asked softly.

'Yes . . . I . . . I just lost my concentration for a second,' he answered, inwardly cursing the blush that was colouring his cheeks. When he looked too closely at her, her gorgeousness made him weak and unco-ordinated, and the lovely rounded curves of her body made *his* body throb and disobey him.

'Why don't you take a break? You've played so well you deserve a rest. Come and have a glass of wine.' She patted the settee beside her and nodded to the bottle in its cooler.

David felt a hot surge of nervousness. He'd managed pretty well so far, at a safe distance, with pianos and tables between them, but now she was inviting him closer. He'd have to sit next to that warm, soft body, and be near enough to touch it. Would he be able to control his erection? It felt as if it was standing out in front of him like a signpost, even though – after the way he'd reacted in the car – he'd chosen his underwear carefully, to try and keep his unruliness in check.

As calmly as he could, he sat down and accepted some wine. When he took his first sip, the sweet effervescence made him feel a bit more settled, so he drank half a glassful then put it back down on the tray.

'I love this room, don't you?' Rosie said, gesturing at the shiny polished woods, the thick carpet, and the great mass of books all around them.

'Yes, it's wonderful,' he whispered, agreeing but really more interested in the way her slight, graceful movement had made her top pull tight against her, the thin, gauzy stuff outlining the lushness of her shape.

She had the most beautiful breasts. He'd admitted to himself, and to his shame, that they were almost the first thing he'd noticed about her. This morning she'd been wearing a soft, tight sweater that had moulded to her curves and made his fingers tingle with the unbearable desire to touch her. He'd imagined how he might actually hold her breasts, cup them in his hands, and discover their weight and consistency. The floaty garment she wore tonight didn't cling in the way the sweater had done, but its slight almost ghostly consistency hid very little of her marvellous silhouette. The misty multi-coloured fabric lay closely against the long, firm lines of her thighs, and even hinted at the vee-shape between them, the greatest female mystery of all. David had seen topless women in newspapers, and even on television, but what lay between a woman's thighs was rarely so easily seen. He'd glimpsed the odd magazine, circulated secretly at school; but it wasn't until he'd had the run of this library that he'd finally seen the sight that so intrigued him.

Oh God, what a revelation! Unable to tear his eyes from the chiffon shrouded contours of Rosie's soft belly, he imagined what the body beneath the cloth must look like. The delicate creases of the groin. The deep, dark dent of the navel. The shadowy triangle of hair that he imagined would be the softest and prettiest on earth. He wondered what colour Rosie's pubic grove would be. The hair on her head was thick and glossy, a long heavy fall, perfectly straight, and a subtle ashy-blonde colour. He tried to transfer the same shade and texture to the hair that protected her sex, then decided it was probably curlier, like that of the women in the pictures.

When at last he managed to look up again, Rosie was looking intently at him, her blue eyes as vivid as corn-flowers and bright with a strange excitement. He shifted uncomfortably on the sofa, willing her not to repay the compliment and glance down at his crotch. *His* state would be no mystery at all!

'So what are your favourite books then?' she asked smoothly, her calm voice at odds with the brilliance of her eyes. He sensed that she was nervous too, and it comforted him.

'The Conan Doyle first editions,' he said after a mo-ment's thought. It was an acceptable lie; he had read most of them, before he'd discovered the erotic books and lost interest in everything else. 'I've always been a bit of a Sherlock Holmes fan, and those books are so rare it's a privilege to handle them.' And so it had been – until the sex books had become an obsession, and he'd spent hour after hour handling both the books them-selves, *and* the effect they had on him.

'And what about the other books?' she asked, sipping her wine, a faint sexy slyness on her face that both troubled and thrilled him. 'Have you looked at any of those?' She nodded in the direction of the glass-fronted cases that housed the erotica.

He was blushing again, he could feel it, and he was sure Rosie could see it. For an instant he considered de-nying all knowledge of Julian's spicy literature, but his pink face had already answered.

Rosie smiled, stood up, then walked across the room, her back view as entrancing as the front. She had a finely-shaped bottom that swayed and lifted as she walked, the firm lobes moving freely as if her underwear was as filmy as her skirt. David longed to be able to touch her, and hold that sweet, rounded rump as he made love to her. His penis twitched and ached, and he thought of how superior it must feel to be held by a woman's body, instead of his own sweating fist. What would it be like to kiss her while he was in her, and feel her soft breasts pressed against his chest?

The dream was almost but not quite agony, his desire exacerbated by the elegant, assured way she reached into the cabinet and took out books, one after another, stacking them in her arms and holding them to her bosom to carry them, just as he longed to be held there and cradled.

When she brought the books back with her, and placed them on the table, he saw they were all large format illustrated volumes, the sort that were filled with the very pictures that had inflamed him the most – and begun his sexual education.

'What an incredible treasury this is,' she murmured, running her fingers over first one shiny cover then another. There was something intensely sensuous in the action, as if it were a succession of lovers she was caressing, not inanimate sheaves of bound paper.

'Look at this, isn't it beautiful?' she opened the top book on the heap, a collection of photographs by a contemporary French luminary, all devoted to the joys of the kiss. *Les Baisers Erotiques* it was called, naturally enough, and from a previous investigation, David knew that some of the kisses were extremely hot indeed!

Nothing in his experience or reading had prepared him for such arrangements of mouths and skin. He'd trembled when he'd first seen them, and he trembled again as Rosie flipped quickly through the introduction.

The first kiss in itself was quite pure; a man and a woman with their lips delicately pressed together, the man's fingers cradling the chin of his partner with a tenderness that touched the heart. There was no other

111

contact between their bodies at all, but the photograph's piquancy arose from the fact that these considerate and courtly lovers were naked on a black silk bedsheet. The man's penis was erect and yearned towards his partner, its swollen tip resting just an inch from her gleaming white belly.

It was so easy to imagine himself in that picture. His own penis was yearning too. It felt tense and feverish, harder than ever now, and even though it was contained inside his underpants there was a sensation of it stretching and reaching. It felt as if it no longer really belonged to him and was gravitating towards Rosie of its own accord.

What would it feel like to touch her with his penis? Have her warm, flawless skin against the most sensitive part of his body? To press himself, stiff and burgeoning, into the hollow between her thighs, while he kissed her mouth and held her.

And he did want to kiss her. He wanted to taste her mouth and touch her face. He'd be happy, in a way, with just that; and would probably have an orgasm if that was *all* that happened. He'd had them recently from much much less. He'd come just from thoughts and fantasy images.

It almost happened now, from shock, when Rosie turned the page, her perfume drifting out from her body as she inclined herself forward in front of him.

He could see the shape of her breasts with perfect clarity now. They were large and rounded and looked seductively firm. He longed to cup them in his fingers, to gently squeeze her. He'd never seen a living woman naked in his presence, but the idea of her bare body was a sudden, burning talisman. He wanted to see her, see the texture of her skin, then feel it and put his mouth against it.

He imagined sampling her skin again and again, putting his lips here and there, licking at her throat, her bosom, and even – oh God! – her sex.

That in itself would be enough for him, he realised.

112

More than enough. His own body was so excited, so enraptured, that his crisis would come long before he ever made love to her; or tried to, he admitted realistically, aware of his paucity of experience. One disastrous, momentary fumble in the equipment store at his school didn't qualify a man as a lover. Especially as he had as little real idea of what to do now as he'd had back then.

Rosie turned the page.

The next image was the reverse of the first. The kiss it portrayed was savage, blatantly sexual, a reciprocal rape of the mouth. The participants were fully clothed, cumbersomely clad in the elaborate garments of the reign of Queen Elizabeth the First, yet somehow the man had his hand up the voluminous froth of the woman's layered petticoats, and from the splay of her legs, and the grimace on her face, it was clear he was caressing her vulva.

David moved uncomfortably on the settee. The pain in his penis and testicles was terrible now, but also marvellous beyond imagining. He felt like sobbing out loud, throwing himself on Rosie's mercy, forgetting his embarrassment and begging her to touch him. She was sitting quite still, yet obviously expecting something. It was as if she were waiting for a breakthrough. His breakthrough. She was staring down at the erotic kiss, but at the same time challenging him. Daring him. When she swayed slightly, then turned her head just the merest fraction, he gave in with a great sigh of relief.

Neither of them spoke, but Rosie's blue eyes told him volumes. Shaking violently, he leaned forward towards her, and tentatively put his lips against hers.

At first they just sat there with their mouths just touching. David was afraid to move a muscle. His penis was like a column of electricity, rigid and explosive, and even the slightest stimulation would trigger it. He felt as if it was wired to every single cell of his body, and he whimpered as Rosie's tongue stroked along his lips with a flicker and a dart, then pushed in a soft plea for entrance. He could feel the pressure of it, and its moist

113

burning heat, right on the tip of his cock. He wanted to scream and cry and rub himself wildly, but instead he just opened his mouth and let her tongue slide in and explore him.

'Hold me, David,' she said against his lips, the words breathing right into his soul. 'Put your arms around me. It's easy.'

It wasn't. It was the hardest, most dangerous thing he'd ever done. He knew it was crazy – because she had a full, strong, finely curved body – but she felt like egg-shells in his arms. Any false or crass move would break her, and destroy this incredible moment.

And yet when he dared to do it, she purred with pleasure and pushed herself against him. Those breasts that looked so beautiful, now *felt* beautiful; rubbing against his chest, their heat and firmness barely shielded by the thin, silk layers of their clothing. Her nipples were like pebbles, like the stones of some perfectly ripe fruit. His fingers itched to seek them out and squeeze them, but constrained by fear and emotion, he could only lay his hands cautiously on her back.

For a while Rosie kept her hands cradled around his head, holding his face to hers so she could taste the interior of his mouth. He felt her licking at his tongue, his teeth, his palate. He felt her challenge him again, and goad his tongue into a duel with hers. She lapped and sipped at him, opening her own mouth so wide that he could feel the tension in her throat and jaw just as clearly as he felt it in his.

It was sensory overload. Her scent, her taste, the pointy tips of her breasts against his chest. The line of her back, trembling finely beneath his hot searching fingers.

I'm going to come, he thought fatalistically. Any second now. It's going to burst out of me. It's going to spurt inside my underwear, and I'm going to shake and jerk, and she'll know exactly what's happening. With a jolt of delicious terror, he felt her right hand slide away from his head, dip down and tuck itself in between them, cruising his midriff and his belly.

114

'Oh God, please ...' he gasped into her mouth, not sure if he was begging her to touch him – or *not* to touch him. Whichever it was, she responded, her gentle hands closing on his groin, her fingers at the hub of his torment.

His trousers and briefs might as well not have existed. Her touch was infinitesimal, exquisitely light, yet he felt it as if he were naked. In some ways he was naked. He was raw and vulnerable and inexperienced, and she was holding him intimately, the first woman ever to handle his genitals with intent to arouse and excite him.

And how exciting it was. All-encompassing. As wild and thrilling as a wealth of complex, protracted lovemaking. Her careful, almost imperceptible hold was more stimulating than an hour of his own hand's rubbing. Tears filled his eyes, and he gurgled incoherently as his penis leapt and lurched, then turned to fire along the whole of its length. The same hot sweetness seemed to run like a flame up his spine, and he cried out harshly, his hips jerking uncontrollably as he came in the crucible of her fingers. He found himself falling against her, sobbing, his cock still twitching. Then he felt her sure, safe body take his weight.

It was like floating. His thoughts were hazy with pleasure, drifting free in a no-consequence place where only her warmth, and her sweet, fragrant flesh existed. His groin was awash with heat and stickiness, and he was astounded when he realised he was smiling to himself, still euphoric with the aftershocks of orgasm. Orgasm with a woman. With a lover for the very first time.

Slowly, the enormity of what had happened began to dawn. What a wimp she must think him. She'd hardly touched him and he'd ejaculated helplessly. He felt like an abject idiot. He was a callow untutored boy, but shouldn't he at least have tried to be a little more than that?

Suddenly he felt weak and utterly ashamed, and he tried to pull away. Rosie seemed to want to hold onto him, but he shook himself free, keeping his gaze fixed stubbornly on the table before them. He couldn't let her see the humiliation in his eyes, the failure. He thought of the other men she must know. Men who could make love to her for hours on end, attending to her pleasure. Suave, experienced men like Julian who had sexual skill, and who didn't come in their trousers after just one caress. He wanted to look down and see if there was a stain, but he couldn't bear to.

'What's wrong?' Rosie asked, her soft voice making him jump.

'I'm . . . I'm sorry,' he muttered. He felt disgusted by his body and by his soft penis, bathed in accusing wetness and still tingling inside his underwear.

'Sorry for what?' she persisted.

David wished for the proverbial opening of the earth. It was clear that this was not going to be ignored. Rosie knew what had happened to him, but she still seemed to want him to tell her about it. Every shameful detail.

'I . . . I . . . Oh God Almighty, you know what happened to me!'

He was surprised by the fieriness of his voice, and as he sprang to his feet, fighting the fact that his knees almost buckled beneath his weight, he was furious that he hadn't felt this energy a little earlier.

'You had an orgasm,' Rosie said calmly. Irritatingly calmly. She sounded too much like a teacher, too understanding. David suddenly felt irrationally angry at her, just for being older and wiser. And so beautiful that it made him want to come all over again.

'Yes! Yes, I did! When you'd hardly even touched me!' He strode away, shakily but keeping his body as straight and unyielding as he could, and sat down on the piano stool. Out of the danger zone, his subconscious told him slyly.

'And I'm sorry,' he went on, running a finger agitatedly along the edge of the keyboard and still trying to avoid looking at her. 'I'm hopeless. I've never had sex. I don't know what to do with a woman and I can't control myself. There, are you satisfied?'

The irony of that final statement hit him like a blow in the gut. 'No!' he cried almost immediately. 'Of course you're not! How could you be? It takes a real man to satisfy a woman, not a gormless, over-excitable idiot like me!' He pressed his face into his hands as fresh tears began to fill his eyes; tears of frustration and disappointment. He suddenly wanted more than anything on earth to be able to pleasure her, no matter how much her beauty laid him low.

Rosie was light on her feet, that was obvious. After a few moments, David felt her sit down beside him, even though he'd never heard her cross the room. He flinched when she put her arm around his shoulders, but almost instantly, he began to feel better.

'If you've never had sex, David, what do you expect?'

He couldn't reply, but her arm tightened reassuringly around him.

'Everyone has to start somewhere. It's not all that long since . . .' She paused as if about to reveal something that embarrassed *her*. 'Well, it's not all that long ago since I started myself.' Her pretty face pinkened slightly, and David felt a sudden rush of something quite divorced from sex, but in its own way, just as breathtaking. 'Would it help,' she asked, 'if I told you that I often feel gormless and over-excitable too?'

Chapter 7

A Room with a View

Now why on earth did I say that? thought Rosie a little while later, in her room.

Instinct. That was why. Her own impressions concurring automatically with Julian's. He'd said that David would never respond to her if she behaved like a worldly sexual superwoman, and he'd been right. Her honest 'I'm clueless too' approach had been the right one.

Even so, David had beaten another of his hasty retreats not long after they'd shared their kiss. Rosie supposed it was for the best, and that to rush now would be disastrous, but her hormones were completely at odds with her reason. David was beautiful and intriguing, a physical turn-on despite his naïveté, and he'd been quite right about her being unsatisfied. She *was* unsatisfied. Profoundly so.

She was so excited that her poor frustrated body was paining her. Her breasts were swollen and her vulva ached; her flesh had been primed to have an orgasm, and it hadn't happened. And she knew now that she'd have to bow to the inevitable.

The urge to masturbate was all-consuming, but she managed to resist while she undressed for bed. There seemed something so sordid about just lifting her skirt and rubbing herself. Something dirty and delicious. It was a huge temptation, but she had to control herself, if only to help David. Somebody had to be operating on a higher, more channelled level. Somebody had to rise above blind lust so they could guide, command and instruct. And that somebody had to be her.

Finally though, after completing her toilette with some difficulty, Rosie lay down on her bed, her tingling body clad lightly in a soft, white cotton nightshirt. It was a pretty thing, lace trimmed, and very short – reaching only to the middle of her thighs. She wore no panties with it, and the bedspread felt comfortingly cool against the uncovered backs of her legs.

Squirming slightly, she enjoyed the freedom and comfort of her surroundings: the temperate, well-ventilated room where she could do whatsoever she wanted in private. Julian Hadey's beautiful house suddenly felt more of a home to her than anywhere she'd ever lived, and its walls were solid and reassuring. Sound wouldn't travel far, she was sure; so she could scream out her delight in her own body and no-one would hear her. And even if they did, they wouldn't turn a hair. In this house the erotic was the norm.

Pushing her nightshirt up over her belly, she considered whether to reach for the vibrator. It was tempting, because its action was powerful and satisfying, but somehow she didn't think power was what she needed. Her sex felt puffy and expectant; almost in climax already. She was as excited and aroused as poor befuddled David had been, and she'd only need the barest of touches.

Closing her eyes, she brought his handsome image into focus, loving the fact he was so different, and so unconventionally attractive. She got the clearest picture of his pale, pale skin, and those eyes like two golden pennies. And yet in other ways he had all the standard male attributes. Beneath his elegant silk shirt, she'd felt shoulders that were strong and a chest that was hard and muscular. His legs were long and athletic, and between them she'd felt a mass so imposing it had shocked

119

her. Stroking her outer labia very lightly, she smiled at herself for being so predictable. Intellectually she knew size didn't matter – but even so, she couldn't help but be pleased that David had a big, thick penis.

What would it feel like, she wondered. In here. She put a fingertip to her vagina and felt the opening pulsate like a tiny, oceanic mouth. A hot, starry sensation began to build further in, spreading out rapidly to encompass the whole of her sex. Her clitoris was on fire, and she hardly dare touch it. She imagined David lying above her, pushing in, full and stiff and glowing with heat. No longer able to wait, she drew her finger up the length of her groove, then pressed hard on her clitoris, screaming at the intensity of a climax she'd been needing for what seemed like days. Her quim leapt and fluttered beneath her touch, and she came – deeply and powerfully – as if it were the first time in this house, and not something that had happened many times already.

And she couldn't believe it – just couldn't believe it! – that at the very same moment she started to throb, there was a sharp, insistent knock at her door.

Damn damn damn! Goddamn! she thought, clasping her whole crotch in her hand and rolling across the bed in aggravation.

Who the hell could it be? David, suddenly daring? Julian? Surely not, with his glorious wife at home. The Hadeys' sex-life seemed to have extraordinarily flexible boundaries, but surely Julian didn't hop from one bed to another on his wife's first night home? As she rose shakily from the counterpane, Rosie glanced at the clock. It was still only relatively early.

When she opened the door, her visitor was the last on her secret list of three.

Smiling like a goddess, Celeste swept gracefully into the room, filling it almost immediately with her heavy, exotic scent. As the door clicked shut, she paused, almost as if posing for a camera, and Rosie felt a rush of strange awareness.

This was the most beautiful woman she'd ever seen.

A woman whose attractions seemed to over-ride the strictures of gender, and make Rosie want something about which she understood very little. As little as David understood about heterosexual sex.

Celeste's nightdress made everything in Rosie's collection seem chaste. It was made of a satin so thin it looked like fluid. Peach-coloured, and suspended from the narrowest of shoulderstraps, it seemed to drip from the points of Celeste's dark nipples; it snagged on the wiry black tangle of her pubis; then trickled on down to her ankles. Rosie could see everything through it. Breasts. Pubic curls. Navel. All of it sexual and wantable. Her own body surged with feeling.

'Well, did it happen?' Celeste enquired, taking Rosie's hand and urging her to sit on the bed.

For a moment Rosie was confused. Had what happened? Her orgasm, just now? She glanced across quickly to the mirror and saw her own flushed face, and beside it Celeste's inquisitive expression. Julian's wife had removed her make-up now, but somehow her face looked equally vivid without it. Her hair hung down in thick glassy sheets, curving neatly around the line of her chin in its perfect Egyptian-style pageboy.

'Did you and David make love, Rosie?' she said softly, re-stating her enquiry.

'N . . . no,' Rosie stammered. To describe what had actually happened might make it sound like a failure. The success was too vague and non-definitive. To a woman like Celeste, it would just be an embarrassing fumble.

'I think – perhaps – you mean "yes",' said Celeste with a warm, gentle smile. Her long, scarlet-nailed fingers rested lightly on Rosie's blushing cheek. 'There are lots of ways to make love, Rosie . . .' Her thumb grazed Rosie's jawline as if framing her face for a kiss. 'And something tells me that you've made a good start.'

'Sort of,' Rosie admitted, imagining David's tortured groin and how it had leapt and pulsed beneath her fingers.

'Good,' Celeste replied crisply. 'I've got faith in you, Rosie. And now I'll show you something that'll help you.' Celeste's eyes flashed violet with mischief. 'The best way to find out what a man likes is to watch what he does for himself.'

'What do you mean?' whispered Rosie. She had a good idea what Celeste meant, but wondered how on earth they could achieve it.

'Come with me,' Celeste purred, reaching out to grip Rosie's hand. She raised it to her soft red lips and kissed. Kissed with all the seductive power and passion that Julian might have employed. The wife was as irresistible as the husband, she realised, and she was helpless to do anything but follow Celeste wherever she led.

In a moment, they were walking along a corridor, moving between walls full of collectable paintings in a part of the house she'd not yet explored. Rosie felt intensely conscious of her body; of the luxurious carpet beneath her unshod feet, and the cool air flowing up beneath her nightshirt, playing across her thighs and vulva. Every nerve-end alive, she watched as Celeste preceded her, studying the beautiful, easy roll of the other woman's buttocks as they swayed beneath pale filmy satin. Celeste's body was fine and slender; she should have made Rosie feel fat and lumpy but she didn't. The contrast between them only served to flatter them both.

'This is David's room.' Celeste indicated an anonymous, panelled door with a toss of her glossy black hair, but to Rosie's surprise, didn't stop. Instead she continued along a little way, then paused before a more concealed entrance – one painted to blend in with the wall.

'And this is the linen cupboard.' She pointed to the featureless door, and flashed Rosie a pantomime wink. 'Amongst other things.'

The room beyond the door was dark, larger than expected, and not just a storeplace for blankets – although there was a lot of fragrant, freshly laundered bedlinen stacked neatly on slatted wooden shelves.

On the other side of the room, however, opposite the shelves, was evidence of a pastime far less mundane than laundry. A long, lowish, plushly upholstered couch was set a few feet from the wall, parallel with the heavy velvet curtain that covered most of it. Rosie suddenly had a shrewd idea what was behind the thick draping, and her heart fluttered madly as Celeste led her in, switched on a tiny nightlight, then closed the door.

'Wha-' she began automatically, as Celeste pushed her down onto the couch.

A perfumed fingertip pressed lightly against her lips, and shushed her. Celeste's pale, silk-clad body was just a drifting blur, and Rosie could hear a subdued rustling as the other woman reached around in the darkness, and found the cord that opened the curtain.

Beyond the glass was a bedroom. Just as luxuriously decorated as her own, but in a cooler, more masculine style. It was a young man's room, done up in blues and light woods, and seen through what was obviously a floor-depth two-way mirror. An angular modern-looking lamp shed a glow across the centrally-placed futon-like bed, and more light shone from what was clearly a bathroom beyond.

Rosie felt a surge of horrified excitement. They were planning voyeurism. An invasion of privacy. They were going to slyly peep at David, and as much as the prospect appalled her, it also made her body stir with lust.

As if he'd heard her thoughts, their subject appeared in the bathroom doorway, switching off the light behind him, then walked forward into the bedroom. Rosie felt Celeste's fingers over her mouth again, stifling her cry before it started.

Wearing only a pair of pristinely white pyjama bottoms, David was even lovelier to look at than she'd imagined. His pale chest was as bare of hair as an angel's, but looked surprisingly strong and substantial, as did his shoulders and his arms. There was a faint gleam of moisture on his skin, and his hair was wet and slightly tousled as if he'd only just stepped out of the shower.

123

His feet were neat, slender and quite bare, and Rosie had a sudden sharp longing to kiss them and suck on his toes.

David frowned as he sank down onto his bed and stretched out; and regardless of the solid glass between them, Rosie could almost taste his tension. He looked uneasy, his limbs stiff and his body uncomfortable, and even as she studied him, there was an animal-like twitch beneath the white cotton fabric of his fly. He placed his hand on his crotch and squeezed himself, then Rosie heard him moan. The clarity of the sound was incredible, and told her that an even grosser intrusion was occurring; the room beyond was wired for sound as well as being two-way mirrored.

While David rubbed at his still-hidden penis, Rosie sensed movements much closer. The fingertips that had gently stopped her mouth now began to slide across the surface of her lips, stroking and exploring. At the same time other fingers settled on her nightshirt and eased it up over her belly.

She was caught between vision and sensation. Was Celeste going to touch her? Fondle her sex? The note left in Rosie's room had indicated that Julian Hadey's wife was blatantly and joyfully bi-sexual, and to stroke a fellow woman's vulva would be both natural and a titillating thrill to her.

But what about me? thought Rosie frantically. Will it thrill me?

The answer seemed to be 'yes'. With barely a moment's hesitation, she eased her legs apart, then felt the velvet of the seat tickle her bottom as Celeste tugged the nightshirt from under her. For a moment her view of David was blocked, and she felt a pair of firm, commanding lips press down onto hers. Husky words whispered against her mouth.

'Touch yourself, Rosie,' Celeste urged her. 'Share his pleasure. Masturbate your beautiful pussy while David plays with his cock. Rub yourself so you can both come together. It's the next best thing to making love.'

It was one of the most extraordinary speeches Rosie had ever heard, and for a fleeting instant she remembered how Geoff had liked to talk dirty, and how it had always sounded just that: dirty. Celeste's words were equally crude, but sounded sweet and caring too. Rosie obeyed her with a harsh little sob, sliding a fingertip down her belly to her groove, and there encountering a deep well of wetness.

David was moving on too. As if too hungry for sensation to stop, he was fumbling to unfasten his flies with one hand while with the other he carried on rubbing and squeezing. His actions seemed unco-ordinated, and slightly frenzied; but after a couple of moments, his pyjamas were unfastened and he'd ceased his rough pleasuring just long enough to expose his naked penis.

Rosie whimpered and pressed her fingers in hard between her legs. Squirming furiously, she squashed her clitoris against her pubic bone and came immediately, her eyes filled with David as he took his reddened sex in both his hands and worked it to a full, hard erection.

She'd been right about his size. His cock was large and sturdy, rising up from his groin like a tower, and crowned with a ruby-tinted glans. The whole length of it was already gleaming with fluid, and she could see him staring intently downwards, watching the tiny love-eye wink open as his fingers slid quickly on his shaft. He was both squeezing and pumping now, dragging his slick, penile skin to and fro on the rigid, stiffened core that it covered. The movements were ragged and violent, and Rosie almost sensed pain within his pleasure. She watched his bottom churn crazily, rucking up the bedclothes and making his pyjama fly gape and pull apart. She could see the thick, curly mat of his pubis, which was dark and wiry, less fine than the sleek red-brown hair on his head.

She was aching herself now, her sex-lips swollen, her clitoris engorged between them. Prising herself open with her fingers, she felt the whole zone shudder, and while half her mind prayed that Celeste would help her

125

and touch her, the other half still shrank from that final, sapphic strangeness.

When the contact didn't come, she slid two fingers of one hand inside herself, then took her tingling bud in a tight, pinching grip between the thumb and a finger of the other. She felt another hand cover her mouth, and like a baby, she nuzzled at Celeste's scented fingers, trying to focus and stay still as the pit of her belly went molten and her clitoris twittered and leapt.

David was arching himself clear of the bed now, rising on his heels and shoulders, his body a long stretched curve. His eyes were closed tight in his grimacing face, and Rosie felt splintered by the loss of them. She imagined their bright, golden beauty looking in at her, boring through the shadows, growing huge when they saw her fingers attacking her own sex.

In an instant, they were coming together; both spasming, both flowing, the liquids of their crisis rich and copious. Semen shot high in the air from the tip of David's prick, and Rosie felt her fingers, her quim and her thighs become trickly with her thick clear juices. Her belly shimmered wildly, then went taut, and when Celeste's hand pressed flat across her mouth, she was glad of it. If she'd screamed as loud as she needed to, it would certainly have been heard through the glass. As it was she let her own heart rise up with David's cry, soaring high and free on his long, orgasmic moan.

After many protractedly exquisite moments, she fell back into herself and away from their strange, sweet joining. She no longer needed to see David now. Their climax had been apart, yet mutual all the same, and though there was no way he could know she'd been with him, Rosie felt alive with his presence. What they'd shared had marked her; she could still see him coming, hear his sobs, almost smell and taste his semen. Yet as she opened her eyes in the darkness – hardly aware that she'd even closed them – she found the curtain had been drawn across the mirror and all she could see was deep, deep shadow.

'Remarkable, isn't he?' murmured Celeste from close by, her perfume assaulting Rosie's nostrils. In the darkness, she was just a silvery flicker in her pale nightdress, and yet Rosie felt a strong urge to touch her. She wanted to acknowledge Celeste and caress her, but she felt too weak and lethargic. Her limbs seemed to be weighted with sex, yet to her surprise she felt hunger stir anew between her legs. She put her hand out for Celeste, all her qualms dispelled by the cosiness and intimacy around them.

'Oh no, love. Not me,' laughed Celeste, her voice teasing. 'At least not yet.' As if in compensation, she crushed her mouth against Rosie's and kissed her, the contact as deep and lusciously punishing as genital sex itself.

Rosie felt completely at a loss. What was happening now? There had been a strange prophetic lilt in Celeste's husky tones, as if there was more yet to come. More than a strong, thrusting tongue; more than the delicacy of long, tapered fingers as they slid over Rosie's damp thighs.

'Wait here, Rosie,' said Celeste, in a voice that brooked no resistance. And Rosie didn't move because she couldn't. Pinned by inertia, her hands and arms limp at her sides, she let Celeste push her nightshirt up over her breasts and kiss each nipple in turn. Almost floating in the dim, ghostly light, Rosie felt the other woman licking her, laving her generous curves with spittle, mouthing and nipping. The feeling was shocking and wonderful, but just as she was rising to its sweetness, it disappeared. She sensed Celeste draw away from her, and as she did, even the night-light snapped off. There was a momentary slice of brilliance, and then Celeste was gone through the door, leaving Rosie alone, waiting.

Completely black now, the room had the womb-like quality of an isolation tank. Rosie had never been in such a structure, but this was just how she imagined it would feel. The featurelessness, the dense, yet comforting darkness, the blankness that let the mind range free;

127

especially a mind like hers with so much to range over. There was so much that was new and exotic that had happened in a few short days.

Backtracking just a little way, she considered the tableau she'd just witnessed: David in his solitary lust; his pure, private desire, untempered by company or censure. She wondered if she'd ever see it again, and then desperately wanted to. She longed to see it with his knowledge and his trust. She yearned to watch first and then, in tenderness, participate; caressing his firm young flesh just as he'd done.

Other faces swam into her mind's eye: two faces, that were disparate, yet strangely kindred; dark, exotic Julian and his beautiful wife beside him. Suddenly, Rosie had a yearning to see them together. Really together – their naked, contrasting bodies entwined in a sweating dance of love. She wondered fleetingly if there were any other cupboards around like this one. Oh God, what if there was a cupboard next to *her* room? What if Julian had watched her stroking herself, and seen the thrilling red vibrator at work between her tensing, jerking thighs? It was possible, in fact probable in this house. And how could she even feel outraged when she herself had so blissfully watched David?

The air in the room was warm and still, yet it seemed somehow to be stroking her, pressing down in waves on the soft, bare skin of her belly. Her sex was provoked by it, and the hair of her pubis felt sticky. More than ever, she wanted to touch herself, to play with her needy clitoris while her head filled with strange new visions.

She saw herself bent backwards, stretched across the leather arm of one of the library chairs while Julian stroked her vulva with a feather. Like an image from one of Julian's rare books, she saw Celeste in a bizarre leather harness, her sleek white body possessed by two bulbous vibrators. Beyond this, she saw Julian himself, hooded and gagged and being fondled by a faceless male lover. The last 'flick' was David, astride the end of his piano stool with his flies unzipped – while she, Rosie, sucked keenly on his thick, ruddy cock.

128

She was wriggling now, her bottom-cheeks split against the sofa to stimulate her dark, forbidden entrance. Between her thighs, she felt puffy and irritated, voracious for more pleasure; but when she reached down into her wetness to stroke it, a small warning sound stayed her fingers. The cupboard door opened slowly, then closed again. For a few seconds she saw the image of a figure, then nothing.

Not that she needed to see. Or ask. She knew who had come in. Celeste had said 'not me', and it was hardly likely to be David. Which left just one other person. One man, come to sample her body.

The footsteps were light, almost weightless, but the approach was swift. Someone confident was here, someone purposeful and skilled. She gasped as hands settled strongly on her thighs, drew them obscenely wide, then pulled her bodily forward on the couch until her tailbone lay on the front edge. A naked body moved between her legs, and an erection brushed the soft, inner slope of her rear. She sensed that the man had sunk gracefully to his knees so their sexes were precisely aligned.

The height, the angle and the moment were perfect, and Julian – wreathed in his telltale cologne – moved smoothly into the niche he'd created. Rosie tried to reach out and touch him, but he caught hold of her wrists before she could, and placed her hands on her own waiting body. One on her breast, one on her softly-curled pubis.

'Stroke yourself,' he said, echoing his wife's sultry order. 'I want you to be ready. I want you to be ravenous when I enter you. Starving. I want to coast straight into your flesh, ride in on a hot wave of hunger.' She heard him draw breath, moan almost, as if his own words excited him powerfully. 'Oh, Rosie . . . Oh God, yes, Rosie,' he hissed, grabbing her hard by the flanks as his velvet tip pushed at her entrance.

Mad for him, she pinched her tingling nipple and drummed on the bud of her clitoris – all the time shuffling and hitching herself forward in an effort to enclose and engulf him.

'Be still!' he commanded, his fingers closing on her body.

Rosie obeyed and let her muscles relax. At the same instant, and with total assurance, Julian began pulling as he pushed; dragging her hips towards him, as his penis drove in and took her. Rosie felt her sex-flesh give way and submit, her membranes deforming to take him.

The process was slow, deliciously slow. A lesser man couldn't have managed it, and would have come – in seconds – from the extenuated caress of her tightness. For an instant Rosie thought of David, and imagined him plunging in and losing it because the pleasure was too much and too soon. He'd cry out with agonised despair, slump across her, sob as the sensations overcame him.

But Julian wasn't David. They were both entrancing men, but Julian was – she realised happily – a lover of infinite experience. His mastery of his own body was unswerving, and the entry of his sex into hers was an event both extended and delightful which brought Rosie to a sudden sweet climax.

As her vagina throbbed and fluttered, she felt, sensed, and seemed to see in her mind that Julian lifted her up from the sofa; raising her hips and thighs so he could improve both his power and his leverage. He was handling her like a doll, a toy, a pretty, malleable indulgence to satisfy his whimsical desires – something she should hate with all her heart after Geoff. She'd come to this house fed up of being used – but now, in the blackness, she adored it, rippling around her possessor's fine stiffness, and crying out as her inner self massaged him.

'Ah!' was the only sound Julian uttered, but his fingers and his cock were more eloquent. His fierce grip hurt her unintentionally, and in her channel, his penis bucked and leapt – as if emitting a sharp burst of pleasure that made his climax become one with her own.

He held her until long after they were still, his cock

resting in her, their crotches joined in heat. His only physical action was to curve himself over her, kissing her upper body and nuzzling at her throat and shoulders.

Rosie felt as if she were still in that imaginary tank. Her thoughts were as loose and drifting as the water might have been; moving languidly between her recent, and most exotic memories. She made no comparisons or judgements, but just revisited the beauty and pleasure of each of them: the solemn shyness of David, and the challenge of his innocence; Celeste, and the lure of the utterly new; Julian, who was both exploitative and giving, and who used her body like an artist.

It seemed impossible to believe that only a week or so ago, she'd been barely more experienced than her 'pupil', and prone to blushing over her burgeoning libido. Sex had been private – between her and Geoff – and restricted to bedrooms at night.

Now, instead, she had erotic thoughts all over the place: any time, anywhere. And it was no longer just thoughts. She'd been made love to in the library by Julian and Celeste, and now, here in the linen cupboard, pleasured by them again.

And she had a feeling that this was just the beginning; that before long, lovemaking would be integral to *all* of her life, and as much her *raison d'être* as the study of fine literature was.

As she dreamily absorbed this fact, she felt Julian stirring. Very carefully, very considerately, he eased himself out of her and rose with noiseless grace to his feet, caressing her thighs gently as he did so. Rosie felt almost too sleepy to respond, too close to the edge of consciousness to reach out and touch him in return. She wanted to say 'thank you', to acknowledge what he'd done for her, but she was too tired to even lift up her arms. Somehow, though, she knew it didn't matter, and that Julian was aware of how she felt.

After the closeness of their joining, it was chilly to find oneself a separate body. Rosie shivered, then trembled in a different way as her legs were lifted and moved. She was being rearranged, she realised. Julian was shifting her into a new and more comfortable position, lengthways on the couch, and lying down. As she curled up foetally, smiling a smile he couldn't see, she felt her nightshirt being tugged down to keep her warm.

That was the most special thing about Julian, she thought contentedly. His most appealing quality. He was a Lothario, obviously, but he cared. He had respect for the women he slept with, and even though he made love powerfully, and drained you dry with his ravenous demands, there lay beyond an unexpected thoughtfulness. It was the very same tenderness that was making him drape fluffy blankets around her limp, drowsing form.

'Bless you, Rosie,' he murmured, easing her hair back off her face, purely by touch. 'You're a treasure.'

As his fingers slid over her cheek, she rolled and took the caress on her slightly parted lips, kissing his fingers and sighing with a voluptuous well-being. She'd have to come out of this cupboard eventually, she decided vaguely, but not just yet. She mumbled a muddled explanation, and Julian's mouth brushed her forehead, his breath like a soporific breeze.

'Go to sleep, sweetheart,' he whispered in her ear before he left her – and like a dutiful employee she obeyed him.

132

Chapter 8

What the Little Bird Said

O h God, I spent the night in a cupboard! thought Rosie as she showered the next morning.

Crazy as it seemed, she'd fallen deeply asleep when Julian had left her, and remained that way, perfectly dreamless, for several hours thereafter. Sometime in the early hours, she'd woken with a start, but remembered immediately where she was. The black velvet darkness hadn't frightened her.

Outside in the corridor, someone had thoughtfully left a light on, and in a couple of minutes Rosie had been safely and silently back in her room.

Now she had the same problem as yesterday – was it only yesterday? – which was how to face a lover over breakfast. There were three this time, but ironically, she felt less nervous instead of more so. She even found herself looking forward to it. She imagined herself swanning into the dining room, and meeting three sets of questioning eyes. Three intimate, remembering smiles.

This is so weird! she thought as she soaped herself. Her skin felt smooth and glowing to her fingers, as if it thrived and bloomed on excess. She looked down at her own body and found it improved somehow. She'd eaten well in Julian's house, but she didn't seem to have put on any weight. There was even a finesse about her shape

133

this morning that she'd never noticed before; a harmony to her curves that made her feel happy to have them. People in her old life – some people – had made it clear that they found her unfashionably podgy; but now, in this new and more sensual world, her lush form was prized and admired.

Breakfast, when she went down to it, was a peculiar meal. The events of last night weren't mentioned, but their echoes were real and perceptible; as tangible as the table they ate at, or the excellent coffee and food.

Julian had a full breakfast and looked disgustingly pleased with himself. As well he might, thought Rosie, sipping at her coffee and trying to stop her body wanting his. He'd taken – and given – great pleasure in that damned linen cupboard; it was no wonder his eyes were twinkling. Celeste seemed in good spirits too, although she ate very little, and Rosie wondered if the Hadeys had made love to each other after they'd finished their games with her. It seemed highly likely. She imagined them together in their marriage bed, writhing and shouting with passion, while she, Rosie, slept the sleep of the innocent in the linen cupboard.

And what of David? she thought, nibbling at a triangle of toast, and eyeing him over it, as discreetly as she could.

The boy seemed as quietly composed as ever, although he had blushed beautifully when she'd arrived at the table. He appeared to be quite calm now, but there was suppressed excitement about him. Her own heart started pounding as she realised he was waiting for something; expecting something from her. He was probably a little embarrassed about what had happened in the library, but he didn't seem crippled or upset by it. What Rosie sensed most was only his sweet and rather titillating shyness. His natural, almost juvenile modesty was as endearing as it was a huge turn-on.

It occurred to her, as she watched his neat, elegant way of eating, that he'd subconsciously accepted her role: her secret place in his life. His intellect might reject the true facts when they were presented, but his body wouldn't. More than ever she felt she was his tutor, and she liked both the word and what it signified. She was learning herself, at an astonishing rate, and whatever she discovered, she'd pass on.

After breakfast, everyone moved with purpose.

Julian was first on his feet, preparing to leave for his domain in the City. Rosie hadn't worked out what he actually did; but whatever it was, it earned him an obscene amount of money. Everything about the Hadey establishment was rare and opulent, and this was only one of their homes. Rosie had been intimidated at first, but it was funny how easy luxury was to get used to. She stared down at her Irish linen napkin, her bone china plate and her sterling silver knife, and realised she'd taken them all for granted.

Celeste didn't work, and certainly didn't need to, but this morning she was a demon of activity. She'd be shopping, meeting friends, keeping various appointments, and she'd be out all day. And she'd be taking David with her. He was to see his analyst, for the last time, and an educational advisor – to help him plan his future academic career. Tied to his grandparents he'd missed out on going to university, but that was now in the process of being rectified.

For a moment, as the others mapped out their days, Rosie felt slightly aggrieved, left out of things. But after thirty seconds further consideration, she almost laughed out loud.

Good grief! What the hell was she thinking of? Totally absorbed in her bizarre sexual duties, she'd lost sight of her genuine bona-fide job! She was as much on the Hadey payroll as Mrs Russell who'd served their breakfast. Remembering her place, and feeling strangely glad of it, she smiled, stood up and excused herself.

'I'd better get along to the library,' she said brightly. 'I've got a date with some books that need cataloguing.'

'I hate to think of you slaving away in there all day,' said Celeste, making Rosie smile again, but inwardly this time. It wasn't as if she was heading for the dark, satanic mills. She loved Julian's marvellous library, and even without all the esoteric perks, working in it was a dream come true in itself.

'Perhaps you could take the afternoon off and we could meet for tea or something?' the dark-haired woman persisted. 'I'm sure David would like that.'

It was tempting, oh-so-tempting, but Rosie felt a pang of guilt. She hadn't done much here yet on *either* of her projects, except enjoy herself, and the salary she was receiving was humungous. Shouldn't she at least *try* to earn it?

'That's really kind,' she said, wondering how to refuse without seeming ungracious, 'but the library is so huge and there really is a lot to do. It seems a bit much to bunk off when I've only just started. You don't mind, do you?'

'Of course not!' replied Celeste breezily. 'We'll do it another day.' She smiled then, a narrow, creamy smile, and something in her pansy-coloured eyes harked back to last night and their intimacy. 'We'll have a big shopping binge ... Harvey Nichols, Bond Street, the works ... Just us girls together, eh?' She walked forward until she was just inches away, then touched Rosie's arm, her aura overpowering. Rosie thought of those glossy red lips kissing hers, those delicate, manicured fingers in her mouth. Communication moved silently between them and she suddenly felt able to smile, and to promise.

'I'd love that. I'll look forward to it,' she said, imagining what David and Julian would think if she followed her instincts right now, and bestowed the kiss that Celeste so obviously wanted.

'You're a conscientious girl, Rosie. I'm impressed,' murmured Julian, moving to stand behind his wife, his expression intent and challenging. Those dark, middle-eastern eyes had been hidden last night, but had watched her all the same, she was sure; watched her as she'd bucked and heaved with pleasure, her body impaled and in orgasm.

He was teasing her, and for a moment it was infuriat-

136

ing. Men, with the notable exception of David, were such chauvinists. So sexually smug. Even the better class of men like Julian, the kinder ones. They all had that same irritating quality of believing they were God's gift to women – that because a woman had a climax with them, it made them Superman.

She had an urge to make a tart remark, then for the second time in a minute, felt like laughing.

Julian's faults were a good thing! They reminded her that the world outside was real and life was sometimes a bitch. One day she'd have to go back to an existence full of Geoffs and various other bastards. Living with the Hadeys was like living in a cocoon, a space capsule; it wouldn't do to forget the hard knocks.

'Thank you. I aim to please,' she said, flirting slightly, though she knew it was extremely foolhardy. Those scrutinising eyes were upon her. Pansy-purple ones; sharp, spice-brown ones; mind-bending, amber-gold ones.

'So I've noticed,' said Julian quietly. Rosie watched his hand drop lightly onto Celeste's shapely hip, and saw the other woman respond, swaying slightly, her lovely face softening for a second as if the touch granted instant, erotic pleasure.

'Me too,' Celeste mouthed, winking as she recovered her composure, then spinning away, her black hair swirling out around her in her eagerness to get started on her schedule. 'Come on, Davy, let's go,' she said, turning away towards David, who was on his feet already and pushing his chair beneath the table.

'I'll just get my jacket,' he said quietly, then made to follow his cousin from the room.

As he passed by Rosie, he seemed to hesitate, his eyes questioning. She could see a dozen strong emotions in their depths, but her heart hammered crazily when one of them came to the surface. He hunched his shoulders in a graceful shrug, then grinned at her. A real, beautiful, boyish gem of a grin that made her knees go genuinely weak.

137

'I'll see you later, maybe?' he said softly, his strange eyes as bright as sovereigns.

'Er, yes. Yes, of course,' she stammered, their roles all of a sudden reversed. She felt flustered, naïve, right back to square one; her experience cancelled and nullified by the beauty of the young man before her. 'I'll be in the library if you need me,' she finished lamely, watching the flip of his long pianist's fingers as he cheerfully bade her *'au revoir'*.

If you need me for *anything*, she added with silent emphasis, watching his precise, long-limbed walk as he followed his cousin from the room.

'Not long now,' murmured Julian, as he passed close by her, and Rosie trembled because she knew he was right.

In spite of her desire to work, Rosie found the library difficult that morning. The tasks there weren't beyond her, in fact under normal circumstances she would have relished them. It was just that she simply couldn't concentrate, couldn't focus her attention. A fact that didn't surprise her at all.

The books themselves didn't help her. The beautiful leatherbound volumes around her were as much works of art as the pictures on the walls, and the antique rugs beneath her feet. She couldn't just stick them in an arbitrary order, because most of them were bound as sets – even though their contents had little in common. She was going to have to create some sort of locational index as well as a classification sequence. The shelves themselves would have to be marked somehow, and in a way that didn't mar the elegance of the woodwork.

It was all a headache at the moment, no matter how good the computer, and how marvellous the books were to handle. And matters weren't helped by her inclination to open the private cases. She almost felt the books were calling her. She kept finding herself with one in her hands, scanning through it for particular words and images, for things she could teach David; things she could ask Celeste or Julian about.

At ten thirty, she gave up the ghost, knowing she could no longer function with a mind full of received eroticism, and a body that was yearning for release.

She decided to follow a suggestion of Celeste's, and take some physical exercise. One of the last things Julian's wife had said, before she'd left, was that Rosie should take a look downstairs if she wanted a change, and check out the gymnasium and the pool.

The more Rosie thought about this idea the more she liked it. In the shower, she'd been quite entranced by her positive new self-image, and exercise would only reinforce that. She'd always gone to Step classes when she'd lived at her flat, and she'd been wondering what to do instead. A gym on the premises was the perfect answer, and no doubt as de luxe as everything else in the house.

It was a simple matter to slip up to her room and change into a tee-shirt, some leggings and her Reebocks, then tie back her hair in a bunch. Grabbing a swimsuit and towel, and clean undies, she made her way down to the bowels of the house, in search of a hard, energetic, and hopefully distracting workout.

The gym wasn't as small as Celeste had led her to believe, and Rosie was impressed by the excellent array of equipment. There were benches, static weight machines, a couple of exercise cycles, and even the ubiquitous Step if she wanted it. There was also a mini-trampoline, and an elaborate looking rowing machine. The swimming pool wasn't huge, but it looked good for a decent length's lap. The whole complex was as beautifully appointed as the rest of the house, all done out in clean, aquatic blues, and complete with a spacious, towel-filled shower and changing area.

Static-cycling was the logical warm-up, and Rosie was pleased that there was a music centre in the room to offset the boredom. There were plenty of tapes and CDs to choose from, but it was a selection of what looked like home-recorded tapes that took her fancy. She smiled as she saw they were all clearly labelled, something she – a librarian – never did. She dithered over a collection of piano classics, presumably David's, then rejected them. A mental picture of *him* working out would defeat the whole object of her being here, so she picked out a rather cool-sounding dance tape instead. As the pounding beat filled the room, she climbed astride the nearest bike, set the resistance to moderate, and began to pedal at a fast but steady rate.

The rhythm of her cycling legs was hypnotic. Rosie felt her mind empty of all ethical debate about being a conventional woman in an unconventional situation, and her body found a deep relaxation. Endorphins rushed strongly through her bloodstream and she thought only of her rising metabolic rate and the burning off of excess calories. She'd never be a sylph, and it didn't seem to matter, but there was no harm in helping things along.

Grooving along smoothly with her eyes closed, it was a while before she realised she had company. There was a muted footstep on the rubberised floor, and in the split-second before her eyes flew open, Rosie imagined either Celeste, or Julian, or David standing there. Any one of them was likely to be grinning.

But the newcomer was a stranger, a young woman Rosie had never set eyes on before. She was tall, with thick, softly-curled titian hair and she wore a track suit. Her figure was one of the best Rosie had ever seen.

There was an awkward, music-filled moment, and Rosie stopped pedalling. The young woman walked over to the stereo and turned it down to a muted background pulse. 'Hello, you must be Rosie,' she said pleasantly as she moved towards the bikes, her tread very light and athletic. 'I'm Angela Byrd, Celeste and Julian's fitness trainer, but you can call me "Ladybird" if you like. Everyone else does.'

Rosie's 'how do you do' sounded stilted even to her ears, but 'Ladybird' smiled sunnily and began stripping off her tracksuit – a process that probably made everyone feel fat, not just chubby librarians.

'I expect you're wondering what I'm doing here,' she

said, kicking aside her tracksuit bottoms and revealing the longest and sleekest pair of legs: perfect pins in vivid pink lycra. 'Celeste offered me free run of the place when my usual gym's too crowded. You don't mind, do you?'

There was genuine concern in her eyes – eyes that were large and green with darkly mascara-ed lashes.

'No, it's fine. I'm glad of the company.'

It was hard to imagine anybody not wanting Ladybird around them. She seemed to radiate a natural good humour that was instantly attractive. To women as well as men, Rosie thought with a pang. The other woman's movements were neat and economical, and in seconds, she'd caught her pretty red hair into a ponytail and was slewing her lithe, shapely body across the bicycle next to Rosie's.

They pedalled without speaking for a while, although from time to time, Rosie found it hard not to turn and glance at her companion.

Ladybird was extraordinarily beautiful, though not in the classic sense, like Celeste. It sounded judgemental somehow, but the trainer's beauty had a commoner touch. Celeste had the look of a goddess descended to Earth, but Ladybird seemed more like someone who'd started with the same raw material as any woman, but just worked harder. To achieve a body like hers wasn't easy, and the grooming, the artful hair colour, and the carefully co-ordinated work-out gear that went with it, all spoke volumes about a determined desire to look wonderful.

And Rosie couldn't resent her. Especially when Ladybird breached the unrelenting whir of their cycling and began chatting, with a wry, pungent wit, about the Hadeys, their houses and their opulent, freewheeling lifestyle.

'So what do you think of Julian?' she enquired after a while, her voice warm and mischievous.

Rosie felt her emotional antennae start to quiver, and sneaked another sly look at the redhead.

141

Good God! Of course! The trainer and her boss had slept together! As the idea formed, she realised she should have known. Julian was a connoisseur of fine women and an unbridled sensualist. Ladybird was just the sort of choice female morsel he'd consume with the greatest of pleasure.

'I like him very much,' she answered cautiously. 'He's intelligent, kind, easy-going . . . The perfect boss really. I couldn't ask for better.'

'But don't you think he's sexy?' Ladybird's voice was intent and charged now, and even though so far the relentless pace of their cycling had had no visible effect on her, she suddenly started to blush.

'Yes, very much so,' said Rosie, deciding that here, perhaps, was a feminine friend she could truly confide in. 'Too much in fact . . .'

'Far too much,' echoed Ladybird, with feeling.

Their glances locked, and they both stopped pedalling. Rosie felt her instincts suddenly validated as a silent agreement flashed between them. A pact to be frank.

'I can't get into this today,' said the fitness trainer, leaping lightly from her saddle. 'Why don't we take a shower, then have a cuppa or something. Then we can really dish the dirt!'

Yes, the dirt, thought Rosie as she followed Ladybird's sleek shape into the showers. But whose dirt would be the dirtiest?

I like her. I really do like her, thought Ladybird as she emerged from the shower, and found a nervous looking Rosie trying to dry herself without dropping her towel or exposing her lush, exquisite curves.

Although it was partially her own doing that the librarian was here in the first place, Ladybird had – against her will – felt an initial inclination to resent her. This was irrational because she herself had declined the job anyway – the strange, sensual job that Rosie had so obviously accepted.

'So then, let's compare notes,' she said, dropping her

towel and hoping Rosie would do the same. Ladybird worked killingly hard to keep herself slender, but for some strange reason she didn't understand, she liked the sight of flesh on others. Especially on women she fancied.

'Come on, what do you think of Julian?'

In essence, it was the question she'd asked in the gym, but she sensed that Rosie understood its true meaning now.

'He's gorgeous,' replied Rosie softly, her eyes dreamy and her grip on the towel less vehement. 'One of the most handsome man I've ever met. And he's . . . he's . . . Well, he's what I'd call overpowering.' She paused, as if trying to say delicately what Ladybird confidently expected. 'I suppose it's a cliché to call a man irresistible, but . . . well . . . I didn't. I didn't resist him.'

'Me neither,' answered Ladybird, moving across to sit on the slatted wooden bench beside her new found friend. 'I had sex with him the very first time I met him. In the middle of a training session, would you believe?'

'I can believe it,' Rosie answered, grinning. With a curiously fatalistic shrug, she let her towel fall away from her bosom and started rubbing at her still-damp legs.

Ladybird tried to stay cool. 'Ah, but would you believe that after he'd had me, he went on and did the second half of his exercise programme?' she continued, trying not to ogle the glorious body beside her. Rosie was clearly fighting the giggles, which made her breasts shake softly and delightfully. 'And he'd hardly even broken sweat, the swine!'

'God, he is one, isn't he?' Rosie was laughing properly now, a sight that Ladybird found dangerously stirring. Her new friend was extraordinarily beautiful, and seemed prepared to confide, but that didn't mean she liked women in the way that Ladybird herself did.

'And how!' she answered, fighting her urge to touch Rosie's dark nipples. 'But he's nice with it, isn't he? You don't mind if he takes advantage, because basically, he makes you feel safe too.'

143

'That's exactly how I feel.' Rosie's voice was soft with wonder. Ladybird watched her closely, as ideas turned over in the other woman's mind. She found herself holding her breath, and hoping hard as Rosie spoke again. 'And I . . . I feel more or less the same way about Celeste too.' It came out in a rush, as if it had been an effort, and Ladybird felt her own body tingle as she sensed her hopes being answered.

'Yeah, she's quite something, isn't she?' she offered, trying to be non-commital. 'They're a very well-matched couple.'

It was an unbearably fragile moment. There were many possible futures in the balance, and Ladybird knew from bitter experience that to push now was foolish. What would happen would happen, and in the meantime, it was easier to concentrate on their mutual interest in men. And in Julian in particular.

'Shall I tell you about that first time with Julian?' she asked coaxingly, hoping that such a blatant offer would disguise her subtle change of subject. It seemed to work because Rosie's face became a picture of almost schoolgirl curiosity. She nodded, her blue eyes glinting as if she relished the thought of juicy revelations.

'Well, I'd spoken to him on the phone beforehand to make the arrangements, and believe me, that yummy voice had me creaming my knickers before I'd even see him!' As she launched into her account, Ladybird felt surprised at how the memories affected her. The tips of her breasts were throbbing already, and between her legs was a hot well of stickiness.

'It was a job I was really looking forward to, I can tell you, and when I saw him I wasn't disappointed.' She cast Rosie a conspiratorial look. 'Well, you've seen his body, haven't you? And a pair of satin shorts don't hide anything! To be honest, he hasn't the slightest need for a personal trainer, but who am I to argue? The salary is unbelievable, this place is a dream . . . I'd have to have been mad to refuse.'

Rosie's eyes were wide, and Ladybird wondered first

whether to edit her account or embellish it, then decided on the simple, delectable truth.

'He was in the gym early – on purpose, I presume – and just lying there on the pressing bench with his eyes closed. Rubbing his crotch!'

'You mean he was masturbating?' Her companion's voice was soft, but not shocked somehow, and Ladybird wondered if Rosie had seen something similar.

'You named that tune,' Ladybird replied. 'I often see men fiddling with themselves in my work, but it's not usually so deliberate. He wasn't just doing it without thinking. He was doing it on purpose. Putting on a show. For *me*.'

'And what did you do?' Rosie's voice was a breathy whisper.

'Well, I introduced myself and got on with the session . . . In the meantime trying to ignore the fact that he had a hard-on the size of a house!'

She could see the image now. Luscious, swarthy Julian in king-fisher blue shorts, his penis pushing like a ramrod against the satin that covered his groin. She could see his eyes too: dark and challenging; cheeky, if you could use such a word about a man in his forties.

It had been difficult for her to concentrate, although Julian had been totally unflustered. He'd listened intently to her instructions, and performed her carefully planned warm-up routine with just the right degree of concentration.

By the time both he and she were thoroughly loose and ready, his face and arms and legs were gleaming with the lightest of sweats – and his erection had barely diminished. It even looked as if it had stiffened slightly: aroused by the sensuality of the exercise, and by the sight of her lycra-clad body. Ladybird knew she looked good in her workout gear, and Julian wasn't the first man who'd got hard for her in the gym.

Then they began the weight training. Already armed with his health profile, Ladybird had a good idea of her client's capabilities, and had drawn up a general toning and hardening programme rather than intensive muscle-building for particular areas. For today, she'd set a target of two full circuits of the entire apparatus, but with only a few kilos on each.

At every station, she demonstrated the form she required for the exercise. It should have been child's play for her, doing routines she'd done hundreds of times, but instead it was extraordinarily gruelling. She could feel Julian's eyes following her every minute move, and even though that was what she *wanted*, professionally, she sensed that his scrutiny was twofold. He was studying the exercises, but he was also examining her body as he did so: staring at her breasts, her bottom, and the divided groove of her sex where it was visible through thin layers of nylon and cotton. As they approached the end of the first circuit, she could feel she was moist at her centre and suspected that it showed. She was certainly sweating far more than usual.

After a set of free weights, Julian suddenly placed the dumbells on the floor and rolled them away. Sitting up, he looked her squarely in the eye, but made no attempt to begin the next exercise.

A hot, familiar terror flared in Ladybird's belly. This was it. The way he'd been exhibiting himself when she'd arrived should've warned her he wanted more than a work-out, but somehow she'd expected a far subtler approach. His dark, sabelline eyes were inviting her to enjoy him – luring her sweating body to his, and her musky crotch to his penis. Like a mesmerised doll she moved towards him, and gasped when he took hold of her wrist and pulled her down roughly onto his lap.

No words were spoken, but none were needed. His fingers slid knowledgeably over her nylon-encased breasts, flicking at the already peaked nipples. She groaned when the hand moved on with purpose, and pushed rudely at the vee between her legs.

He cupped her, thumb pointing to her navel as his palm circled slowly on her mound, rubbing both the cotton of her panties and the lycra of her leotard deep

146

into the channel of her sex. Without conscious thought she wriggled, squirming her tautly honed bottom against his muscular, lightly haired thighs. She felt his lips settle on her neck, making the skin there quiver as he nibbled and sucked it. He was licking at her sweat in neat, delicate strokes, entirely unfazed by the sticky tangled strands of her hair, where it had come unbound from her ponytail. As his pressing hand dove further, and her clitoris leapt, she felt his white teeth close lightly on her throat.

The way he worked her was remorseless. His fingers pushed the layers of cloth right into her vulva, soaking them through and forming them moistly to her shape. She felt him rubbing at her clitoris, her labia, the fluttering mouth of her vagina, then pushing the juice-soaked fabric inside her, as another finger stabbed at her anus.

Ladybird screamed, her climax immense as her arms tightened around Julian in a death-grip. She felt herself almost falling, almost flying, her flailing body sliding on his knee. He was using his fingers on her bottom and sex like an infernal, prodding fork, while at the same time biting her neck – and it was the most erotic experience of her life. She screamed again, half choking as his supple wrist twisted and he thumbed her throbbing, pulsing clitoris and pressed it against her hard pubic bone.

But as she gasped and gobbled uncouthly, she felt his ruthless hands withdraw. Nearly tipping her off him, he made her stand for a moment, swaying on wobbly legs as he peeled away her sweaty sports clothes. First leotard, then leggings and pants, all in one bunch, although he ignored the snug white band of her bra. When he had everything as far as her knees, he took her and turned her; then laid her face down across the bench, her bare bottom high, and her upper body dangling down over the shiny black leather of the seat. She felt fingers prising at her thighs, opening her as far as the restriction around her legs would allow.

The same fingers tested her wetness, then teased her tiny pink bottom hole, making her eyes bulge with fear.

147

'And did he?'

Rosie's voice made Ladybird jump and her unfocused eyes see the real world. She'd been so entranced, so hypnotised by her own dream-filled voice, that she'd almost forgotten the woman beside her.

Almost forgotten? Completely forgotten, thought Ladybird, looking down. Her hand was wedged between her legs, pressing nearly as hard as Julian's had all those months ago, in the gym next door. She'd been masturbating, she realised, and for quite some time. She must have begun almost at once, unaware of her actions, although she was now keenly aware of their consequences.

Her flesh was heavy and aroused, and she could smell her own scent – fresh and thick and gamey in spite of her recent shower. She saw that Rosie's face was flushed, and that she'd been watching as well as listening; and yet she, Ladybird, didn't feel embarrassed. She'd often caressed herself to climax for a girlfriend; and often, in this house, for Celeste. She could even recall times when she'd done it for Celeste and Julian together.

But that was another matter. The Hadeys were freethinking libertines who had an open marriage. Rosie, she sensed, had only just begun to shed her inhibitions, and take the first, tentative steps.

And it was necessary to ask her permission, Ladybird decided. 'I need to come,' she said softly. 'Would it bother you?'

'No . . . Please . . . I . . .' Rosie's face was almost puce, but her eyes were twice as hot. 'Please, go ahead . . .'

'Thanks,' whispered Ladybird, her blood pounding, her heart elated. The woman at her side was cautious and still scared, but the sensual promise was there. And as Ladybird closed her eyes and leant back against the cool, tiled wall, it was Rosie who triggered her pleasure.

Last night David, and now Ladybird. Why oh why, pondered Rosie, do I keep on seeing people's closest secrets?

Nevertheless, she watched, enchanted.

Ladybird's body was as beautiful nude as it was clothed, and she seemed entirely without inhibition. Her long, sleekly-tanned legs were stretched out in front of her, and parted to display her precision-trimmed russet-brown pubis and the orchid pink lips it protected. A finger flickered in that pinkness, and as she rubbed furiously, her bottom wove and worked on the seat beneath her, and her small round breasts bounced and shook. Jerking towards a climax, she caressed one nipple too, pulling at the thick, roseate peak in time to her strokes down below.

Suddenly, the squirming girl stiffened, pointed her toes and whimpered very quietly. 'Oh! Oh! Oh!' she moaned, her fingers stilling and her knuckles turning white with pressure. For a moment, Rosie longed to do the same – to make herself climax. The urge was potent and compelling, but she couldn't quite obey it. The feelings were too sudden and too strange. She'd do it one day, but she couldn't now. Her body was left with frustration.

'Wow! That's better,' said Ladybird presently, her green gaze bright, yet still hazy. As she seemed to focus again, on Rosie, she frowned, her smooth brow crumpling with concern. 'I didn't embarrass you, did I?'

'No, it's alright ... It's just the first time ... with a woman,' she admitted, then smiled, thinking of David.

Ladybird's eyes narrowed. 'But not with a man?'

Rosie felt blood rush into her face and throat; she *was* embarrassed.

'It's okay. You don't have to tell everything,' the other woman said amiably, rising to her feet, all nimble, athletic grace. 'I'm going to take another shower. For some reason I'm all hot and sweaty again. See you in a bit.' With a grin and a flip of her fingers she walked through into the shower area – closing the connecting door firmly behind her.

Rosie blessed Ladybird's tact. She needed solitude now, and her new friend the trainer understood that.

Without wasting a second she slid a hand between her thighs, and sighed with relief at her own hungry touch. Just a few long, slicking strokes and she burst through the barrier, biting her lips as her quim throbbed deeply and gratefully. Sighing with relief, she slumped back against the wall, turning her head first to one side then the other to cool her glowing cheeks against the tiles.

By the time Ladybird returned, Rosie was composed again, and pristinely clad in her clean bra and panties as she combed her hair at the mirror.

'So, who's this man you've seen tossing off?' Ladybird enquired salaciously as she slid into her own undies – a pretty lace-trimmed bodysuit, Rosie noticed, that made a perfect shape look even better. 'Is it the sumptuous Julian?'

Rosie could quite imagine that, and thought Ladybird's adjective well chosen. The vision of Julian touching himself was intoxicating; but somehow it couldn't match what she'd seen from the linen cupboard. Julian's self-pleasure lacked the perfect jewel-like innocence of David's. With him there was no delicious aura of guilt, no atavistic, juvenile dread of indulging in a vice. Masturbation would be an everyday experience for Julian, with no sinful overtones. A de luxe way of scratching an itch.

'Well, is it?' persisted Ladybird, grinning.

Rosie shook her head.

'Stephen?'

'Stephen?' Rosie couldn't say she hadn't noticed the handsome chauffeur, but she hadn't really considered him sexually.

There was no denying that Stephen was a gorgeous piece of work. He had a strong, muscular body beneath his uniform, and an exceptional smile: strong and white in his smooth-skinned, oak-brown face. There was something in Ladybird's glittering eyes, Rosie observed, that said she'd noticed these assets too. More than noticed them.

'Yes, why not?' the trainer said questioningly.

'I've never been near enough,' replied Rosie, 'except in the car.'

'I have,' Ladybird said, quirking her pretty pink mouth, 'and much good it did me!' She adjusted the fit of her bodysuit as if it were suddenly too tight. 'I know he fancies me, because he's started coming to my gym occasionally instead of working out here . . . But can I get him to fuck me? No! He's playing hard to get, the bastard! Either that or he's completely gay and he's getting what he needs elsewhere and only teasing me out of spite.'

Rosie analysed this astonishing statement carefully, and realised how tame her life had been until these last few hectically erotic days. She'd thought herself quite daring trying new things with Geoff, but now lesbianism, bisexuality, voyeurism, and Lord alone knew what else, all seemed to be almost common practice!

'He looks so macho,' she said in a small voice.

'Oh, I'm sure he is,' replied Ladybird evenly. 'But he's certainly into men some of the time, because . . . Well . . . I've seen him with one!'

The beautiful redhead hesitated, her inner debate obvious. There was another revelation imminent, and with her appetite now thoroughly whetted, Rosie couldn't resist the question.

'Who?'

Ladybird still dithered. She bit her lip, looked troubled, then made a small gruff sound of resignation. 'Well, considering why you're here, I suppose I'd better tell you everything. I once came in here quite early one morning and found Stephen making love to Julian. Right there on that bench . . . He had him doubled up, nearly folded in two. Neither of them noticed me. Julian was sobbing and moaning, in seventh heaven, and Stephen was pounding away like a steamhammer.'

It was an appalling picture, yet unthinkably arousing. Rosie tried to imagine her all male Lothario boss being taken and used like a woman, and the thought made her ache with desire. She wanted to see it for herself; see the strong, assertive Julian made weak by the act of sodomy.

151

'It seems unbelievable,' she breathed, wishing she had the courage to touch herself again.

'Believe it,' said Ladybird firmly, reaching for her tracksuit.

The two of them stayed silent for a while, and continued getting dressed. Ladybird put on her tracksuit and began to pack her various belongings, but Rosie just pulled on her white tee-shirt. It was voluminous, and covered half her thighs, so she didn't need her tight sweaty leggings.

'What did you mean by "considering why I'm here"?' she asked, as the significance of the phrase suddenly dawned.

'Uh huh . . .' Ladybird looked evasive.

'Just how much do you know about me, Ladybird? About my job, I mean?'

'Well, I know there's some pretty strange things in your job description . . .'

Rosie felt confused and angry. It seemed that all and sundry knew about the tutoring. She wondered how many more members of the staff were in on it. Stephen? Mrs Russell?

Sounding worried, Ladybird rushed on: 'Don't take this the wrong way, but they asked me first. They asked me if I'd take David under my wing –' She grinned nervously. 'Joke! Ladybird? Wing? Get it? No? Oh well . . . They asked if I'd teach him about sex, and help him get rid of his virginity.'

'So I'm just the second choice?' Rosie said tightly. 'The substitute.'

'No, it's not like that at all!' Ladybird seemed cross with herself now, her ruddy hair tossing and her eyes as sharp as green glass. 'I fancy the lad . . . He's beautiful. But I couldn't take the job 'cos I'm too thick!' She thinned her mouth, as if admitting to shortcomings wasn't pleasant. 'He's too clever for me. Too intellectual. Always reading and playing the piano and stuff. I'm a body person, not a mind person.' She touched her breast lightly to illustrate the obvious. 'He needs someone a bit

152

brighter to relate to . . . Someone to talk about sex with, not just screw. And someone who isn't *too* experienced, so he won't feel put off and fail . . .'

'Enter the naïve librarian,' commented Rosie dryly, although her initial irritation was fading.

'No. Honestly. You were the first *real* choice. They only asked me because I was handy. I don't think either Julian or Celeste really thought I was suitable.'

The irritation was gone now. Ladybird was too open, too honest – and far too attractive! – to resent. She was also doing herself down, Rosie decided. The other girl was perceptive, considerate, and physically beautiful; David couldn't have been put in better or more tender care.

'Will you help me?' Rosie asked on the spur of the moment, reaching for Ladybird's hand in a purely instinctive gesture. When she squeezed it, she felt her shaking. 'I'm not as green as David, but there's a lot I don't know either. I could use some guidance. A list or something. An A–Z guide to sex!'

Ladybird laughed full-bloodedly. 'On index cards, maybe?'

'I don't think so,' replied Rosie, grinning. 'Although when I want to find out how to do a thing, I do usually try and find a book on it.'

'What a logical girl.' Ladybird reached into her sports bag and took out a shorthand notebook and a pencil. Rosie could see what looked like lists of exercises on the top sheet, but Ladybird flipped this over, and wrote the figure 'one' at the top of the next sheet. 'Okay then, here we go.' She chewed the pencil, then her lip, then made a quick note.

'Well first you've got to teach him anatomy. Sexual anatomy, that is. What makes *his* body feel good and what makes *your* body feel good.'

'He knows what makes *his* body feel good. He's the one I saw masturbating.'

'I might've known in this bloody house! Was it one of Julian's trick mirrors?'

'Yes, it was,' Rosie admitted. 'Celeste thought it would be helpful.'

'And was it?'

'Oh yes ...' The memory was dreamlike, almost unworldly. The sight of a beautiful innocent exploring his pale, almost saint-like body.

'Ooh, I bet he's lovely,' purred Ladybird, licking her lips. 'I've seen him in his swimming trunks ... and I was impressed! He isn't a little boy, is he?'

'No, he isn't,' whispered Rosie, seeing nothing at that moment but David. David with his hands on his sex, and his eyes tightly closed in ecstasy.

'Does Julian have many little hidey-holes?' she asked, after a pause – still wondering if she'd been watched too.

'Oh yes. Lots,' replied Ladybird. 'Both here and at Stonehaven ... They're behaving themselves at the moment, I think. Because of David ... But some very strange things go on at Chez Hadey, I can tell you. I've seen things you could hardly credit. Honestly.'

Rosie could imagine the concept if not the acts, and felt intensely curious. Would she get her chance? she wondered. Would she be allowed to sample these barely credible pleasures? It all still felt vaguely sinful, but she couldn't help hoping just the same.

The two women got on with their list; stopping from time to time for wild fits of giggles and heavy, arousal-charged silences. The compilation was a work of erotica in itself, given all the extravagant acts they'd itemised.

'Now most men turn to putty in your hand for oral ... Or maybe not putty.' Ladybird chuckled knowledgeably. 'So I think you'd better do lots of sucking and licking and nibbling. He'll love it, and then, when you've made him your absolute slave, you can get him to go down on you!'

Rosie mentioned some of the books she'd perused. 'There's just about everything in Julian's collection. If I can't find a way to talk about something, I can always give David a book!'

'I should read more,' Ladybird said pensively. 'I bet there's still plenty I could learn.'

'You want to experiment with a few simple positions, Rosie,' she said later, scribbling more notes. 'Nothing too fancy. No performance tricks. And then you could try a little gentle kinkiness. Show him how to use a vibrator on you, perhaps? Or tie him up with silk scarves. Keep it light though. Just fun.'

'You should be a sex therapist,' said Rosie, feeling a great rush of fondness for this raunchy but sensitive woman. 'You'd be wonderful at it!'

'I'm wonderful at screwing!' replied Ladybird smugly. 'But I'm a doer not a talker . . . I can teach people how to make themselves fit, but when it comes to sex, I'd rather just get on with it!'

'Maybe so,' said Rosie cautiously, 'but I'm still grateful for your help . . . Are you here often?'

'Two or three times a week,' replied Ladybird, suddenly frowning. 'God, what a dummy I am! I should've given you a massage . . . Shown you how to do one . . . It's a perfect way of getting into sex!' Her frown changed to a deep, glowing blush. 'For David, I mean . . .'

Rosie knew what she meant, and either way, she liked the idea. She liked it very much. To either give or receive a massage was a delectable prospect. 'I'd love that. Maybe we could do that next time you're here? They don't seem to be too bothered about me doing much in the library.'

'Well, it's only one of your jobs, isn't it?' Ladybird winked, then got back to her point. 'Yes, I'll give you an aromatherapy massage.' Her lively voice became softer, deeper, and more intimate. 'And then you can practice giving me one.' She moistened her petal-pink lips. 'You'll enjoy it both ways, I promise you . . .'

'I'm sure I will,' answered Rosie, part certain, part fearful, and wholly excited. 'Believe me, I'm sure I will.'

Chapter 9

On and Off the Road

'Change of plan indeed!' muttered Rosie as she threw clothing willy nilly into a holdall. 'It's alright for her. She's used to all this! I'm not. I haven't even settled in here yet, never mind slogging all the way out to the wilds of Norfolk!'

Rosie knew she wasn't really all that cross, but letting off steam reassured her. It was normal and manageable and ordinary, while almost everything else around was extraordinary.

The 'she' and 'her' in question was Celeste. She'd come home unexpectedly – with David – just as Rosie and Ladybird were coming upstairs from the gym.

'Change of plan, Rosie,' she'd said with a smile as winning as it was imperious. 'We're all going to Stonehaven for a few days. Ju and I can't drive down until tonight, but you and David can go this afternoon. David knows the way, and he's good with maps. Can you drive?'

'Yes, I can,' Rosie had replied, then added with some smugness, 'And I'm pretty good with maps too!'

It was true, she did have a knack for routes, but she wished now that she hadn't been so pert with her employer.

Fortunately, Celeste had seemed oblivious.

'Marvellous! That's wonderful!' she'd continued cheerfully. 'I'll run you off some directions on Julian's routeplanner, just in case, but in the meantime pack a few holiday type clothes, and I'll have Stephen bring the small car round.' She'd paused for breath then, as if sensing Rosie's irritation. 'I'm sorry, I didn't think . . . Have you had lunch? Perhaps Mrs Russell can whip up a picnic for you? Would you like that?'

'I've not much option,' observed Rosie wryly as she stuffed the last item in her bag and zipped it up. Picking up a fresh white tee-shirt from the small pile of clothing on the bed, she began to dress – all over again – for the journey.

Twenty minutes later, after a detour to the library, she stood on the pavement outside the house juggling with her bag, her holdall, and a dozen or so carefully chosen books – feeling nonplussed by what Celeste had considered a small car.

Although no expert on the matter, Rosie could still recognise a Mercedes when she saw one. And this one was a sleek, black two door number that crouched by the kerb like a panther. It would be by far the most luxurious vehicle she'd ever ridden in – apart from the Hadey limousine – and the first, and probably only supercar she'd ever actually drive.

'Beautiful, isn't it?' said a soft voice behind her, and when Rosie turned around, David was with her, changed into a black cotton tee-shirt and jeans, and carrying a soft, squashy hold-all of his own. In his other hand were the keys to their technological chariot, and he was holding them out towards her.

'Can you take these?' she asked, gesturing with the books she was precariously balancing. Exchanging their various belongings, and getting organised in the car was quite a performance; something Rosie suspected had been contrived on purpose. The two of them were being thrown together as innocent travellers on a voyage into the great unknown. This was a perfect parallel with their bigger adventure, and she tipped a silent salute to the

157

clever, but absent Celeste for her highly effective strategy.

'Where's everyone else?' she asked, surveying the dashboard layout while David fastened his seatbelt, the routeplan dutifully on his lap.

'Celeste's gone to lunch with someone. Stephen's driving her. And Ladybird's gone back to the gym she works at . . .' He paused, faintly frowning, 'Celeste's invited *her* down for the weekend too. She's coming tomorrow.'

Good, thought Rosie. Ladybird was beautiful and kind, and to have her on hand would be invaluable.

'Let me have a look at that,' she said, nodding towards the sheet of directions.

David passed it to her and she perused it quickly, recognising place names and road numbers, and seeing the way quite easily in her head. The distance was 136 miles and the programme said it would take them three and a half hours. She checked the dashboard clock, and it read just before one. They could get there for teatime, no problem. If there were no interruptions.

'Here, thanks. I shan't need this.' She passed the sheet back to David. 'Are you hungry? Celeste said something about a picnic . . .'

'Yes, there's a basket in the boot,' answered David. His voice was soft, slightly husky, and she wondered how nervous he was, and whether he was still thinking of last night, and what had happened in the library. He was all hers now, with no outside influences; and the idea of having him cocooned inside this close, luxurious space with her, strapped in and with nowhere to go, was sharply and viscerally thrilling. She only hoped it wouldn't affect her driving.

'Shall we get a few miles under our belt first, and then eat?' she suggested. 'I'm not really hungry myself.' For food, that is, she amended silently.

'I'm not either,' he replied, his voice still muted. 'Do you want me to shout out when we're getting towards junctions and things?'

'No thanks . . . It's alright. Trust me,' she said, hiding a grin. 'Why don't you put some music on, then take a look through those books.' She'd slid a few of the choicest volumes into the well beside his seat; ones she'd selected after her talk with Ladybird.

While David sorted through the CDs in the glovebox, Rosie snapped her seatbelt in place, flipped the ignition and set the car in gear. There was no traffic in the quietly exclusive Gardens, and as she pulled away from the kerb on the very first stage of their journey, she revelled in the effortless response of the Mercedes. By the time they got to Norfolk, she decided, she'd be too spoiled for anything less.

It took them forty minutes to clear the northern periphery of London, and while Rosie's attention was mainly on the roads they were travelling, she was still intensely aware of David. She sensed he was uncomfortable, but trying not to show it. There was a Mozart sonata playing, but even so she could hear every nuance of his breathing, and the delicate rustle of paper as he turned the pages of his book. He'd chosen Anaïs Nin's *Delta of Venus*, and that pleased her. Her hopes soared as she realised he was becoming absorbed in it. Would its gallic eroticism arouse him? And what about the fact that it was written by a woman?

'Good book?' she enquired, as the car slid out onto the M11 and she could relax on a long straight road.

She felt him look at her sharply, and sensed him wondering whether *she'd* read the book too. And if so, could she still remember it.

'Yes, it's very good.'

His voice was contained but slightly unsteady, and his attempt to seem unconcerned made her smile. She decided to let him stew for a few minutes, and just listened to more pages being turned. When finally she did steal a glance at him, she felt a powerful surge of excitement. He was blushing.

'Do you find it arousing?' she asked, and though she couldn't look at him just then because she was

159

overtaking, she could almost feel the intensity of his colour. She heard the rustle of cloth as he moved again, adjusting his body in his seat. Was he hard? she mused. Was he trying to ease the pressure on his penis?

The answer to her question was a long time coming.

'Yes,' he whispered, the word barely audible, but heavy with embarrassment. The effort it took him to speak told her that he *was* erect. That he was aching and swollen in his jeans, and plagued by a sensation not dissimilar to the sensations she was feeling herself: heat, fullness, engorgement; the delicious hunger for sex.

Her own jeans were uncomfortable too. The seam between her legs had ridden up into the cleft of her sex and was caressing her clitoris like a lover. She longed to be able to close her eyes and surrender, but she was trapped by the road and the car. The motorway ahead seemed to mock her; all she wanted to do was screech the car to a halt, embrace the boy beside her, and bring relief to their mutual torment.

Across the screen of the dull grey road, she saw the sight she'd seen last night – a penis that quivered and was beautiful – and she wanted it so desperately it stunned her. If she could stop the car now, there would be no doubt, no hesitation. She'd engulf him. Possess him. Feel his nervous majesty within her, filling her warm female body with reality instead of just fantasy yearnings.

'Read to me,' she said suddenly, wanting his voice if she couldn't have his flesh. 'Please. Read me a story from your book.'

She felt him glance at her like a startled fawn, his golden eyes wide with astonishment.

'I . . . I'm not sure if I can,' he stammered, but even so, she felt his psyche rising to the challenge, and trying to shake off fear and inhibition.

'You can,' she said, making her voice confident, so his would be too. 'You've got a nice voice, David. You'll be a wonderful reader.'

As she overtook another car, she heard pages flicking

quickly, as if he were looking back, searching for something he'd already read.

'It's called "The Veiled Woman",' he began without preamble, then launched straight into a story that Rosie knew quite well. It had recently been reprinted in a magazine.

In spite of everything, David's voice was strong, and his familiar accent evenly modulated. He spoke every word with a strange, telling clarity, and caught the natural rhythm of the sentences with an aptness that was almost uncanny.

Rosie found herself entranced, and aroused all over again by the story of a mysterious woman who'd enslaved a complete stranger in a bar – purely because he *was* a stranger. She drove the car as if on auto-pilot, listening to the erotic tale of 'George', and his dealings with a nymphomaniac temptress who seduced him in a bedroom of baroque and mirror-filled splendour.

The mention of mirrors made Rosie quiver and grip the wheel tightly. David had made love before a mirror last night, and his natural, solitary pleasure had been as sensual as anything by Nin. For a second Rosie wondered if David had been aware of his watchers, then commonsense told her he hadn't. He was too honest and guileless to dissemble.

Should she ever tell him what she'd seen? At the end of the story George had felt betrayed because the veiled woman had only really wanted him as a performer. For a paying audience.

What would such a situation feel like? she wondered. Could she 'perform', sexually? Staring at the road ahead she saw a different vista – herself on a bed, entwined with David, while Celeste, Julian and even Ladybird looked on. The shock of the thought was so immense that she had to concentrate hard on holding the wheel while her centre throbbed and vibrated. She was having a secret, hidden orgasm and it was a battle to keep the car steady.

As David finished the story, it was Rosie who had to

161

lick dry lips. She heard the book slide away onto the floor of the car, and when she dared look quickly across, she saw that David was slumped in his seat with his eyes closed. His face was tense, he was biting his lip, and his hand was resting squarely on his crotch.

'I'm sorry,' he muttered, his fingers squeezing involuntarily.

'What for?' she enquired, keeping her voice light. She had the sensation again that she was dealing with a wild, young animal – a creature whose nascent trust would be shattered by the slightest false move.

'For this,' he gasped, his fingers tightening. 'For last night . . . For getting all worked up and being too young and too stupid to control myself!' Rosie didn't even have to look to know that his face was agonised.

'But you'll learn . . . It'll happen naturally when you get used to sex,' she said reasonably, even though her heart was pounding fit to burst. She sensed the approach of some indefinable, irrevocable watershed and she wanted to reach out and touch him, to help him cross it. Words teemed in her mind, but she realised – in a moment of astonishingly cool rationality – that they were almost at their motorway exit. Praying that a great chance hadn't just been lost, she negotiated the traffic stream, slid neatly into her lane and indicated.

'But how can I get used to it if I don't do it!' he almost sobbed as they cruised along the slipway.

Braking at the junction, Rosie had to concentrate for a few more eternal-seeming seconds, but mercifully they were soon moving smoothly forwards, along the road that would take them to Newmarket.

'That can be changed,' she said quietly.

'Wha . . . What do you mean?' He knew, she could tell, but she could also tell he was having a hard time making himself believe it.

'You can "do it". You can have sex. Make love. Whatever you like to call it.'

'When?'

'Whenever you're ready.' He hadn't asked 'who with',

162

she realised, as if he knew he didn't need to. An idea formed in her mind, and she glanced at the passing scenery.

Soon, she told herself. There was a magic place somewhere, but she knew they hadn't yet reached it. She pressed her foot to the accelerator as her wild idea became a plan.

'Read some more,' she commanded quietly, feeling her loins thrill at the sound of her own controlled voice. Did she really know what she was doing?

David started reading again, this time a longer story, about a woman called Elena who discovered certain inner hungers whilst reading D. H. Lawrence on a train. It seemed an ironical choice, and prophetic; it was the written word that had brought David to the brink too.

They drove for nearly an hour before Rosie saw what she needed. David had already finished the story by then. He seemed distracted, lost in a deep sexual fugue, and she wondered what on earth he was thinking. He wasn't touching himself any more, but his erection was still clearly visible, pushing against the fabric of his jeans.

Turning from their route, Rosie followed signs for a forested picnic area, and when she found it, she parked the car. The place was beautiful, but deserted, and she thanked whatever kind spirit was protecting them for making conditions so ideal for her scheme.

You're crazy, Howard, she told herself as she swung her legs out of the car. This is all mad, self indulgent and ill thought out – and if it goes wrong it'll be David that suffers.

Even so, she felt confident. It was the most foolhardy decision she'd ever made in her life, but the simple act of making it was exciting. As was the sensation of being in control, instead of controlled.

'Let's see what's in this boot,' she said crisply to David who'd followed her example, and got out of the car. She could see his nervousness in every gesture, in every facet of his expression, but in a strange way that made her admire him more. He was scared to death, yet he still stood tall and straight, and made no effort to hide his tumescence.

Rosie decided not to insult him with euphemistic talk about picnics. Instead she just pulled out a thick, luxurious car rug and passed it to David; and then took out a half bottle of wine and two glasses from the picnic hamper. It came as a surprise that it was actually champagne this time, not her usually 'sweet and fruity', but somehow the fine vintage wine seemed totally appropriate. Hopefully, they'd soon be celebrating.

'Come on,' she said, nodding to a path that led further into the woods. 'Let's find somewhere a little more secluded.'

After a few minutes of silent walking, they broke away from the established trail, and passed through a thick shady copse. Further on, they found themselves in a sort of half clearing where the sunlight was broken and dappled. To one side was a softly mossed hollow which could almost have been designed for their purpose.

Thanks again, whoever you are, thought Rosie, feeling amazed and grateful that sometimes in life, things just went right without you even trying. Almost as if he'd read her mind, David flicked open the rug and spread it out across the moss.

As he stared intently at the soft, tartan fabric, Rosie wondered if he was having second thoughts. Sitting down as elegantly as she could in her tight jeans, she patted a space on the rug beside her.

'It's time, David.'

The serenity of her own voice amazed her. Now the moment had come, she felt calm and assured. Somewhere along the road from London, she'd left behind the last remnants of her girlish gaucherie, and become completely and powerfully a woman; and everything that David needed.

As if protected by the same magic spell, even the champagne opened perfectly, and Rosie poured them both a brimming fluteful.

'Here's to knowledge,' she toasted, clinking their glasses together. David said nothing, but just looked back at her, solemn and unblinking. When he finally put his wine to his lips, he drank it all down in one swallow.

Rosie watched his pale throat undulate, then followed suit, swallowing the crisp golden wine, and for the first time in her life, truly enjoying it. The dry, mellow taste had an effervescent radiance that warmed and enlivened her, titillating not only her mouth and palate, but the whole of the rest of her too. Her limbs, her belly, her sex.

Together they put their glasses aside, and then Rosie reached out, slid a hand behind David's head, and pulled his mouth on to hers for a kiss. She felt him shake as she touched him, but his lips opened eagerly and his champagne-drenched tongue found hers, stabbing forward with an unexpected boldness. His arms came around her too, holding her in close to his body, his fingers massaging her back as her breasts met the heat of his chest. He made a low, anguished sound as she shimmied against him, caressing his body with her own and revelling in his muscular, young torso as it pressed against her aching nipples.

Every part of her felt sensitised, every nerve end sang with rich feelings. She cooed with approval as she felt him tugging at the edge of her tee-shirt, then smiled into his kiss as his warm hand touched her bare back. Her shy-boy had taken the initiative.

She didn't want to rush him, or damage his fragile confidence, but her breasts felt so tender and needful she could almost have described it as pain. Crushed against him, they were tense and swollen. She wanted him to squeeze her, explore her, be a little rough, perhaps – anything to distract her from the greater ache lower down; the wet, burning need to be filled by him, and to possess his rampant young beauty in the very act of him possessing her.

Novice or no novice, David seemed to read her effortlessly. He fumbled, but within moments he had her tee-shirt pushed up to her armpits and was working on the

165

single front catch of her bra. The small hook yielded easily, and as the pretty silk cups slid away, her full breasts swung free towards his hands.

'Oh God,' he groaned, sitting back a little so he could study what he'd revealed. Rosie guessed it was the first time he'd ever seen such a sight in the flesh, and she cupped her own lush shape in her hands and held her breasts up towards him like an offering.

David's great golden eyes were enormous now, with discs of pure black at their centres, his pupils dilated with arousal. He reached forward with a trembling hand, and brushed his fingers to first one nipple then the other, exploring their absolute hardness. Rosie gasped, shocked by the delicate, ghostlike contact that shot directly to her quim and her clitoris. She hadn't expected an orgasm from this encounter – it was David's time, not hers – but suddenly she was balanced on the edge of one. As his fingertips flexed, then squeezed her, she started rocking convulsively on the blanket, working her furrow against the seam of her jeans until a great wave of pleasure engulfed her.

As she throbbed and swayed, David let go of her, an alarmed expression on his face. Through her haze, she realised he was frightened he'd hurt her, and quickly, she took his hand, pressed it to her breast, and curled it round the firm white flesh.

'Squeeze hard! I like it!' she hissed, one hand still folded around his, the other rubbing furiously at her crotch.

David frowned for a moment, then smiled and obeyed. Rosie couldn't help herself now, she was writhing and panting, and it was obvious what was happening to her. With the hand he had free he reached for her, pulled their faces together, and in a move that was exactly what she wanted, needed and craved, he kissed her through the tumult of her climax.

When she was finally calm again, or as calm as was possible, Rosie reclaimed the kiss. Abandoning her own needs, she let her hands run freely over David, examining his body through his clothes.

The process made him gasp, his breathing coming hoarse and heavy as her fingers flowed indulgently over him. And just like her, he seemed to be unable to keep still, shifting this way and that on the rug, and shivering as she discovered first his nipples, then the bulge at his groin.

'Let's get these clothes out of the way, shall we?' she murmured, pushing him gently backwards until he was lying before her on the blanket. Working quickly and deftly, she eased his tee-shirt out of his waistband and pushed it upwards. His chest was white as milk against the dense black cotton, and his nipples were as sweet and dark as berries. Running her tongue across her lips, she leaned forward and nibbled him, mouthing at his tiny male teats. As she sucked one, then licked it, she pinched its twin with her fingers and made David groan softly in response. Surrendered beneath her, he rolled his slim body on the rug, his hips weaving this way and that. Out of the corner of her eye Rosie saw him reaching downwards, rubbing at his groin in desperation.

'Oh, please,' he gasped, his voice so sharp and clear and young that she could deny him no longer. Now it really was time, and with a last swirling lick at his nipple, she straightened up, then started unfastening his jeans.

Underneath his black denims, he wore plain white jockey shorts, and as his fly slid open, his erection forced them out through the gap. She could see the shape of his cock quite clearly, pressing up against the thin white fabric and deforming it with the power of his lust.

Rosie considered simply easing him out, letting his flesh spring up, then sliding down on it straight away. It would be a perfect poem of rudeness. Instant gratification. A gallop in jet black, silky russet, and vital quivering red. She imagined his penis rising up like a tower, questing towards her, reaching out for a new world of sex.

Sunlight glinted on the teeth of his zipper, and those sharp little points changed her mind. 'Hup,' she said softly. 'Lift your bottom.' When he obeyed, she pulled his jeans and underpants down to his knees, and made him bare from armpit to thigh. His chest and belly were a pale, naked band with his burgeoning cock at its focus.

She watched his flesh sway, as if played on by a breeze, and felt her own sex ripple in answer. She wanted him, she desired him, she needed him and hungered for him as much, if not more than he was hungering for her. It would be cruel now, to wait or delay, and in a flurry, she pulled off her trainers, then her jeans and panties. Moving as gracefully as she could, she stood astride his body, nude below her tee shirt, and showed him the treasure he longed for.

The sensation of displaying herself was intoxicating. She saw David swallow, take huge breaths, then try to struggle upwards, reaching for her. But with a slow smile, she brushed aside his hands, then steadied herself, placing her feet squarely and strongly. Very very gradually she began to sink down towards him, revelling in the way her thighs opened and stretched. Reaching down, she parted her labia, showing him her bright, swollen pinkness as she descended. His golden eyes grew wider than ever at the beauty of her folds and her clitoris.

Her thighs were taut and aching, yet the discomfort barely touched her. She held herself, hovering, her jewel just an inch from his glans. She could almost feel the heat of him, the tip of his burning hot penis, and as her muscles screamed in protest, she sank down a minute degree further. Her body tried to waver and unbalance, but she fought it, stabilising her pose with her weight and the elegant outstretching of her arms.

Seconds ticked, and somewhere a bird sang, then Rosie forgot the awkwardness, forgot the tension, forgot everything but the thick, hard pressure of David as his stiff flesh made contact with her entrance. It was suddenly the easiest thing she'd ever done – the easiest thing in the world – just to let gravity carry her downwards and onto him.

* * *

It's the easiest thing in the world! shouted David in the silence of his mind.

He felt relieved. Triumphant. He hadn't had to struggle. He hadn't had to fumble. He'd just lain there almost serenely and let her beautiful body slide over him, then watched in gratitude and wonder as she'd neatly rearranged herself into a kneeling pose, tucking in her sleek legs beside his hips. The only thing David found difficult was stopping himself thinking he was dreaming!

A strange laden stillness seemed to engulf both the glade and their bodies, a crystalline quiet that astonished him. In every sex-dream he'd ever had, in every masturbation fantasy, he'd always pictured thrusting and wild, violent action. A headlong dash towards the peak. But in reality, everything was calm. He felt steady. Almost composed. He didn't have to rush or thrash, just lying still brought the sweetest sensations. Even his eyelids – closed now – were motionless, and perhaps in a way that was best. If he opened his eyes, he might discover he was imagining things. Rosie might be just a warm, perfumed illusion; and the delicious containment of his penis might only be his own gripping hand.

But his hand had never been like this; never felt like both satin and velvet at once; never been so exquisitely warm and snug; never pulsated; never fondled every inch of him so lingeringly.

Was this marvellous phenomenon natural? he wondered – aware that he was grinning like an idiot, but unable to prevent it or worry. Did all women ripple like this, or was it something special and skilled she was doing? His captured body didn't care which, but there was a part of his brain still thinking. Thinking – and hoping – that this particular and magical effort was contrived to increase *his* pleasure.

As she began, very slowly, to move up and down, he took the huge risk of opening his eyes.

He needn't have worried. Rosie was real. And her own eyes were closed in an expression of rapt, almost trancelike intent. She was concentrating utterly on the even rise and fall of her body. Her face was a flushed pink mask, finely shining with a light trace of sweat, and David had never seen anything so lovely. She exceeded every fantasy, every fevered, passionate dream, and he was too excited and enraptured to breathe. When he did remember to do so, he gasped in air like a bellows, his head as light with happiness as his loins were heavy with desire.

Not knowing what to do with his hands, he started stroking the slopes of her thighs. Running his fingertips up and down them, he travelled closer to their apex with each pass, yet felt afraid to take the last step. He wanted to reach up and hold her breasts too, but he held back, not wanting to still their delicate, syncopated jiggling.

Framed by her pushed-up clothing, Rosie's bosom was a glory to his eyes, each individual breast a harmonious, delicately pointed round that was capped by a dark, puckered nipple. As he watched, she lifted her hands and cupped herself again, her delight in her own beautiful body just as obvious as his would have been. He longed to copy her action, and hold the full, veined weight of her – a breast in each hand – but awe kept his fingers on her thighs.

'Touch me, David,' she said suddenly, her voice an urgent purr, like a cat requesting attention. For a moment he was puzzled. She was gripping her own breasts tightly now, squeezing in an arcane, complex pattern that forbade interruption. She didn't seem to need *his* hands.

After a couple of seconds, though, he understood the significance of her words. She didn't want him to touch her breasts. She wanted his fingers between her legs, touching the place, almost, where he was inside her. The tiny, tender spot that even he knew was a woman's greatest pleasure. Her bud. Her berry. Her clitoris.

Tentatively he reached forward, letting his fingertips comb her silky hair and travel in search of her centre. The lips of her quim were slick and puffy, and seemed to stand away from her body, stretched, engorged and pouting. Using both hands, he parted the tangling curls so he could see what he was doing, see the gem he sought to plunder, the tiny pink droplet he could almost hear begging to be rubbed. He could actually see it moving, twitching in its niche like the beat of a miniaturised heart.

'David! Please!' she groaned, rocking on his body to push her clitoris towards him. 'Rub me . . . Please! Just do it! It doesn't matter how!'

Her tone was both urgent and commanding. She'd said – gasped, groaned – 'please', but she wasn't pleading at all. She was telling him, ordering him to pleasure her with his fingers while his cock remained lodged in her body.

Remembering books and pictures, and drawing on his deepest internal instincts, David let his fingertip settle on its target, then pressed, lightly. Rosie cried out, her voice incensed, her head tossing, and her long hair swirling around her like a cape. Her body was in heaving, thumping motion, riding him; yet he knew that the contact between them must stay constant. Concentrating when it should have been impossible, he swirled her clitoris with his finger, delighting in its subtle mobility and the way it leapt and throbbed beneath his touch.

Rosie howled, and suddenly her whole body went rigid. Her neck, back, and thighs all tensed before David's astonished eyes – while her inner muscles spasmed around him.

She was coming, he realised, but even as the knowledge hit his brain, his own senses blanked out the thought. Long, gut-wrenching waves of feeling slammed up through his belly and loins, eclipsing everything he'd ever felt before. It was like being hit by a cattle prod or a massive electric shock, yet it filled his whole world with raw bliss.

There had never been sensations like these, not even in his most successful dreams. His penis felt indescribably

171

wonderful, pulsing and jumping in her silkiness, his ecstasy blending with hers as he too shouted and groaned.

At the very pinnacle of his pleasure, David suddenly had to be closer. Closer than having her. Closer than in her. Curving himself up from the ground and the rug, he slung his free arm around Rosie's body, caressing her back, her spine and her rib-cage while his fingers still moved at her core.

'Oh David,' she whispered, bending down to hug him to her in return, then pressing her lips to his mouth.

'Oh David,' she seemed to say right inside him – lighting up his yearning soul with her spirit as their joined flesh danced in the sun.

Chapter 10

Stonehaven

S o this is the famous Stonehaven, thought Rosie, lying
in – or more properly on – her very first four poster
bed.

The canopy above her head was made of elaborately
tented canary yellow silk, and if the librarian's bedroom
was as beautiful as this, she decided, then the master
bedroom must be beyond all imagining. The whole
place was like a film set, and twice as opulent as the
London house – and that was certainly no hovel.

She supposed she was musing about interior design
to distract herself. The 'event' that had occurred on the
road was so special, so marvellous that it was difficult
to believe it had even happened. It was as if one of Anaïs
Nin's stories had come to life; the little-known one about
the boy virgin and the woman who looked after books.
Even the setting had been too perfect to be real.

David, she reflected, was a revelation. As simple as
that. He'd been shy, understandably, but he'd taken to
sex like a natural. An adept. She'd sensed him wanting
to please her, felt him trying to please her, and then
instinctively getting things right. She was physically
tired now, from the drive, and from their time in the
glade, but at her innermost core she was awestruck.

And David felt the same, she could tell. It was obvious

he'd surprised himself. She thought of his face, and how it had looked as he'd lain beneath her after his orgasm. His expression had been a blend of pure shock, and grinning, almost imbecilic happiness – the classic ear-to-ear grin of contentment. She'd been on the point of kissing her way from one end of that grin to the other, when a faint sound from the direction of the picnic ground had set both of them struggling with their clothes, each helping the other with garments that were tangled or bunched.

By the time they were decent, and free of bits of stray grass, a family of four and their dog had been visible, approaching through the trees. Rosie had been most impressed by the cool way David had gathered up the blanket and their other belongings, then nodded politely to the newcomers as they'd passed.

'So?' she'd said when they were in the car, noticing that David's dazed smile had returned.

'I never realised,' he whispered. 'I thought it'd be like . . .' He paused, and Rosie saw a blush flow up his pale throat. 'I thought it'd feel how it does when I do it myself. But it doesn't. It's not a bit like . . . like that.'

'Is it better or worse?' she asked, teasing.

'Better! Different . . . Oh God, I don't know!' He was really quite pink-faced now, but curiously, he looked all the more handsome for it.

They both fell silent then, and the car seemed to hum with deep thoughts. A little while later, as Rosie saw a rather pretty looking roadside pub ahead, she glanced at the dashboard and realised it was just about opening time. There were rustic tables and chairs in an adjacent beer garden, and without hesitating, she pulled the Mercedes into the car park just beyond.

'Let's stop here, shall we?' she said, not giving David a chance to object. 'I need the ladies, and I could do with . . . with a breather or something.'

Within ten minutes, they were sitting one on each side of a roughly-planed wooden table top. Rosie, mindful of the champagne she'd drunk, had a tall glass of Perrier before her, but David had a pint of best bitter.

174

Another rite of passage, thought Rosie, smiling inside as he eyed the drink suspiciously. Real men drank pints, so people said, but although David was now most certainly a real man, he didn't seem too sure about the beer.

'Cheers!' she said, then took a sip of her icy cool water.

'Cheers,' answered David, drinking cautiously from his pint. Rosie felt a fresh spasm of lust when he licked his lips slowly, as if deciding whether he liked the taste or not. His tongue was very red and looked uncannily long and flexible; just right for exploring her body.

'So?' she enquired, nodding at his beer, unable to resist the parallel.

David laughed out loud, his golden eyes sparkling with merriment. 'It's good actually. Great.' His face coloured even more, but he was already instinctively flirtacious. 'But I think I like what I had earlier better.'

'I'm pleased to hear it,' she said softly, reaching out to touch his hand, her flesh thrilling at the thought of him: his delicious young body, his innocent *savant* lovemaking; the gentle playful wit that was emerging now the first shock was over.

It was an erotic moment, though only their hands were in contact. Messages passed between their eyes, feelings were compared and marvelled at. Rosie felt her sex rouse and her pulse race madly, then had her attention suddenly distracted by something black and shiny flashing by in the corner of her vision.

She turned quickly and saw a familiar shape speeding away along the road. 'That's the limousine!' she cried, turning back towards David. 'Julian's limousine. They're going to get to Stonehaven before us!'

David made a panicked face. 'What shall we do? Try and go another way and get past them?'

'No. I don't think so . . .' It seemed pointless. Celeste had engineered the situation anyway, and there were bound to be questions. It seemed logical to just face the inevitable.

They sat and finished their drinks, the atmosphere

between them a strange mix of ease and slight nervousness. Several times, she caught David taking sneaky looks at her breasts over the rim of his glass; but they didn't discuss sex, and they didn't compare notes. It didn't seem necessary. They'd been perfectly attuned when it mattered, and Rosie had a bone-deep feeling that the same thing would happen next time. Whether in an hour or two, or several days hence.

When their drinks were done, they moved on, motoring steadily but not slowly and arriving at their august destination just as the first shades of evening were falling.

Stonehaven was a huge, gothic looking house, made of beigey-grey softly-weathered stone, just as its name suggested. As Rosie had suspected, the Hadey limousine had been sitting accusingly in the carriage yard, but when she and David had entered the lofty, pillar-lined hall there had been no sign of either Celeste or Julian. Instead, a tall, very thin woman with grey streaked black hair had greeted them.

Rosie's immediate thoughts had been of Daphne Du Maurier's 'Rebecca' and the fiendish housekeeper Mrs Danvers, but when the lean one had smiled and introduced herself as Mrs Bright, her manner had been as sunny as her name, and her welcome as warm and friendly as that of her London counterpart, Mrs Russell.

Rosie had felt a glow of old-fashioned femininity when David had insisted on carrying her bag upstairs, and an entirely different kind of jolt when his hand had touched hers as they'd paused outside her room.

'See you later,' he'd said, his voice husky, his eyes intent. And as she lay now, in this elegant room, with its gilt, its space, and its smell of spiced pot-pourri, Rosie wondered how *much* he expected to see.

She was surprised that Celeste hadn't allotted her and David a shared room. But then again that was perhaps a bit too blatant. Even for Celeste.

It was disappointing though.

Rosie had never actually slept with a man. Not even

with Geoff, who'd always made a point of either going home afterwards, or chivvying her to do the same. She'd tried to tell herself this was okay, and that she preferred her space; but now she wasn't so sure. What would it be like to wake up in a man's arms? To shake out the kinks of sleep with each other? To smell another person's sweat on her body?

She imagined waking up with her lover's cock already inside her, and him moving gently and smoothly to rouse her in the nicest of ways. If all went well in her endeavour, she'd try it, she vowed. She'd spend the whole night with David, and feel his warm young body against her as she slipped into the sweetest of dreams.

This room she was occupying was more of a suite than a simple room, and when she got up to look around, she discovered that not only did she have a private bathroom, but there was also a dressing area too.

It was very pretty and very feminine-looking, and full of mirrors. Thinking of London, she wondered if anyone was watching her. Waiting behind her own reflection for the moment when she peeled off her clothes. She was tempted to strip immediately, and make a proper show of it, but her attention was distracted before she'd even begun; by a stack of boxes and parcels piled one on top of another on one of the brocade covered dressing chairs.

Rosie's stomach fluttered when she saw a note lying on the top of the topmost box. That reminded her of London too.

Dear Rosie, it said, *I just couldn't resist getting you a few things to wear for David! Just a few naughties to tickle a young man's fancy. I took the liberty of checking your sizes yesterday, while you were sleeping. I hope you don't mind. Love Celeste.*

Do I mind? pondered Rosie. Gifts of clothing were fine for an intimate friend of the family, but she still wasn't quite sure she was one. Her position was delicate, nebulous, but even so, she prised open the first box, feeling full of both guilt and greed as she plunged in,

177

then shredded away the soft pink tissue that was printed with a world famous logo.

'Good grief!' she whispered, lifting out what seemed to be a collection of black silk cobwebs elaborately trimmed with lace. It was the product of an elitist lingerie house, an abbreviated camiknicker and suspender belt set, as insubstantial as it was exquisite. Its beautiful satin-bound edges seemed to invite the hand – the male hand – to slide beneath them and explore. Rosie could well imagine what such a whimsy would do to an excitable boy like David! Instant orgasm, just from looking. For her part, it made her think of something more lingering. Long, sumptuous bouts of tender, yet decadent pleasure.

She held the camiknicker against her, and imagined what she'd look like inside it. She'd be clothed, yet more than naked; her pale, lush breasts barely masked by the smoky black fabric. She put David's hands into the image then too, holding her through the sheerest of barriers, pressing the texture of the lace into her skin.

The rest of the clothes were just as erotic. Some more so. From a set of boxes marked 'Circe', she took a basque made of plum-coloured satin; a white voile g-string; a black net bra with holes cut in it for her nipples, and panties that were similarly punctured. Rosie's fingers shook as she pushed them through the lace-edged gap.

Some of the smaller boxes had other things in them. A slim, chartreuse-coloured vibrator to replace her red friend from London. One or two small contraptions of narrow leather straps, whose purpose she had only the vaguest idea of. A velvet *commedia dell'arte* mask. And even a fully functional pair of stainless steel handcuffs!

'Good grief,' she said again, surveying her esoteric cache. Ladybird had suggested a few mild 'kinks', but straps and buckles and handcuffs? That all seemed a little advanced just yet.

The camiknickers were okay though, and she put them aside to wear straight away.

Remembering how much David had seemed to admire last night's outfit, she picked out another 'something floaty' for the evening ahead. This time it was a long, black muslin, handkerchief-pointed skirt, with a matching tee-shaped top; and when she slipped the ensemble on over her expensive new lingerie, she smiled a slow, catlike smile. The clothes she'd chosen last night had made David want to masturbate – would this lot have the same effect?

After brushing her hair to glossy smoothness, she let it hang dead straight down her back, then made-up carefully but vividly. She added some big silvery costume jewellery to create a chic, slightly off beat effect, then finished with a rich, flowery perfume.

'How beautiful you look tonight, Rosie,' murmured Julian, ever the flatterer, as she walked into the large salon that joined onto the entrance hall at the foot of the main staircase. It was an airy, spacious sort of room, crammed with superb antiques, but because of its sheer size, not cluttered. Julian welcomed her into it as if she were a visiting monarch, not his own employee.

When he took her hand and kissed it, Rosie trembled, thinking first – and rather strangely – of David. After a second though, her thoughts went winging back to the linen cupboard, and the man who'd enjoyed her in the darkness.

'Thanks. One tries,' she murmured, wishing she could accept compliments without feeling embarrassed. She felt a brief pang of fury at Geoff. Because he'd put her down so much, she now found it difficult to believe that sophisticated men like Julian could find her extremely seductive.

Covering her nervousness, she accepted a drink. It was the same sweet sherry she'd had in London, and its delicious warmth made her innards feel delightfully peculiar: sort of warm and sparkly and randy. She realised she'd had virtually nothing to eat since breakfast, and resolved not to drink anything else before dinner.

Under the guise of letting Julian show her some of his artistic treasures, she admired him too, thinking how

179

handsome he looked in a simple white silk shirt, and loosely tailored trousers. It seemed outrageous that after having one man this afternoon, she could now be desiring another – but either the sherry, or the situation, was making it happen. She felt her body responding to Julian's, her sex reacting to his wine-dark voice and his aura of unfiltered maleness.

'Good evening, Rosie,' said another velvety voice from the direction of the open double doors.

Celeste looked stunning too; her long, draped, off-white gown a perfect foil for her shiny black hair.

'So you got here eventually,' she continued, walking slinkily across to the drinks table and mixing a large gin and tonic. 'When I discovered we'd beaten you here I couldn't help but speculate.' She took a sip of her drink as she walked towards Rosie, then bestowed the same greeting that her husband had. A kiss on the hand, but on Rosie's palm this time, with lips cooled by the well-iced gin.

'We ... We stopped to stretch our legs,' stammered Rosie, knowing that Celeste certainly didn't believe her. The other woman did a thing with her perfectly plucked eyebrows that said 'who are you kidding?', and Rosie felt her face start to redden.

'So you stretched your legs, did you?' Celeste's grin was perfect, beautiful wickedness. 'And what did David stretch?'

At this, Rosie went pinker than ever. She'd tried to prepare a nonchalant explanation whilst in the shower, but now the crunch was here, she'd been rendered quite speechless.

'I see,' said Celeste triumphantly. 'Well done, my dear ... I'm tempted to say "I knew you had it in you", but that's probably just a little too crude.'

Rosie took another long sip at her sherry, then allowed an amused, but solicitous Julian to refill her glass. His brown eyes were as bright as his wife's amazing lavender ones, but they also held a spark of respect. Rosie suddenly realised that in spite of her obvious embarrassment, the Hadeys were genuinely impressed by her.

Then, as if she'd unconsciously summoned him to support her, David appeared in the doorway. He looked shy, eager, nervous, happy – a whole array of emotions seemed to shine out of his huge golden eyes. He looked as if he'd had a hundred thousand volts put through him, but in the most joyous and enriching of ways. Rosie felt herself melting all over again.

She sensed, too, the almost hawk-like scrutiny of Celeste and Julian. It was as if the couple were imagining her and David making love, picturing them entwined together on the richly patterned carpet, their sexes meshed, their sweating limbs tangled in passion.

Their stares didn't surprise her really. If she could see such a difference in David, the Hadeys must surely be able to. There was an indefinable lustre to him now, a brilliance. His pale skin seemed to glow, highlighted by a shirt of sombre midnight blue, and trousers in the same dark shade. His sleek, nut-brown hair was as neatly combed as ever, straight back from his face, but something about its very tidiness seemed to suggest a previous dishevellment.

Expecting either Celeste or Julian to make some kind of fuss over David, Rosie was relieved when they behaved quite normally. There was a very slight atmosphere while they all sipped their aperatifs, but as the evening wore on, and dinner was served and eaten in the elegant oak-panelled dinning room, even this disappeared. It seemed as if nothing unusual had happened at all.

Perhaps nothing unusual *had* happened? thought Rosie, as she set off with Julian and David for a tour of the house, and Celeste settled down to watch a play on TV.

Two people who were strongly attracted to each other had made love. What could be more natural and normal than that? Or more beautiful? It had been straight sex in a sunny, woodland hollow. Orgasms for two. An open air idyll.

Stonehaven was as astounding inside as it was out –

181

a moody, magnificent mansion house, straight out of a Victorian pulp novel. To Rosie it seemed more like 'Manderley' with every room they passed through. The furniture and pictures were perfectly chosen, the carpets rare, and the whole ambience a curious amalgam of the intimidating and the homely. Modernisations – to pander to conventional standards of comfort – had been made throughout, but so subtly done that the eye did not immediately perceive them. Even the heated indoor swimming pool looked 'right'.

The rooms that appealed to Rosie most were the library, of course – which was in far more of a jumble than the London one, but which mercifully contained a computer and a modem – and the conservatory, a lovely glassed-in area full of fragrant plants and shrubs. Its intense green eroticism reminded her strongly of being with David in the woods, and the whole place seemed to ring with echoes of pleasure. It was easy to imagine people making love amongst the ferns, to see Celeste riding Julian on the long, buttoned chaise, and hear their combined climactic cries bouncing back off the bright panes of glass.

From time to time, as they walked, she'd catch David watching her closely – and if their eyes met, he'd smile shyly. He was staking no claims on her, she sensed, as if he was still very wary of his own sexuality, but curiously she liked that. A cocky, boastful David would not be 'her' David and she enjoyed having a kind of control over him. The power of 'yeah or nay'. When he was an experienced lover, she knew he'd be amazing in a different kind of way, but for now his demi-innocence bewitched her. And she didn't want to rush him into changing.

When she saw him yawning, she suspected he'd had enough for one day. Probably of everything.

'I think I'll turn in now,' he said as Julian turned back towards the drawing room, where Celeste was still viewing. 'I'm really tired . . .' He turned towards Rosie, his golden eyes questioning. Was he letting her down?

182

they seemed to say. 'You don't mind, do you?' The question was asked of both herself and Julian, but she sensed it was really aimed solely at her.

Julian nodded amiably, said 'goodnight', and strolled away; and Rosie felt a warm rush of gratitude. He was such a chauvinist in a lot of ways, but in others, his discretion and sensitivity were quite faultless.

'I feel a bit weary too,' she told David quietly. 'It must be all that fresh air.'

A complicit smile passed between them, the carrier wave for a dozen silent messages. It was okay *not* to have sex too. There was no hurry. There would be more soon, and better. No pressure.

Without thinking, Rosie leaned over and touched her lips to David's, stroking his pale face as she did so. His skin was very soft, and she wondered how often he had to shave. He was nineteen, but seemed so much, much younger. His mouth moved a little under hers, sighing slightly, and she felt a sharp, sweet stirring that ran counter to their wordless pledge. As she savoured the warm, luring velvet of his lips, she reprimanded her greedy inner self.

'Goodnight, David. Sleep well.' Drawing away, she let her fingers trail across his jaw, then turned and walked briskly down the hall.

'Goodnight,' she heard, spoken softly in reply, but didn't dare turn or halt in her stride, for fear that temptation would sway her.

When she entered the drawing room, two pairs of eyes seemed to pin her like a moth to a board.

'Have you put him to bed?' enquired Celeste, rising from the sofa like Aphrodite from the waves.

'With a goodnight kiss, perhaps?' suggested her husband, his tone light and inquisitive.

Perplexed, Rosie thought of London and the library. Separately, each of these people could easily seduce her; but together they were omnipotent. She felt boneless, without will, completely at their mercy.

'Well, did you kiss him?' Celeste was in front of her

now, and deep in her personal space. Rosie quivered as the other woman's fingers curved lightly around her neck and drew their faces together.

'Did you?' Celeste persisted, her wine-scented breath fanning Rosie's face.

'Yes.'

'Like this?' Her mouth plunged down onto Rosie's, quick and hard, her tongue demanding instant entrance, then retreating to leave need in its wake.

'No, not quite,' Rosie whispered, so stunned that she let Celeste guide her helplessly to the sofa, with just the lightest of pressures on the curve between her neck and her shoulder. As she sat down, the Hadeys did too, one on either side of her, like brackets.

'But you kissed him like that earlier, didn't you?' said Julian, picking up the thread. Caught between the two of them, Rosie wondered if they were telepathic. For all their mutual, sexual freedom, she sensed that Celeste and Julian were intensely in love with each other, on a level she could barely understand. They were like two aspects of the same person, and she was trapped at the focus of their power.

She tried to remember, but her mind was numb. Yes, she and David had kissed, hadn't they? She'd kissed him, but he'd kissed her back. And with far more skill than she'd expected.

'Yes,' she said quietly, 'We kissed. It was nice. David seemed to know what to do . . .'

'Did he kiss you anywhere else? Other than the mouth?' asked Celeste, her thumb stroking Rosie's lip, then sliding down her face, her jaw and her throat. At the edge of her tee-shirt, it dipped inside, hooking in under her camisole top and resting on the curve of her breast. Acutely aware of its movements, Rosie also felt another hand at work. Julian's hand. Sliding between her lower back and the seat, flattening and going lower, cupping and squeezing her buttock through the cotton and silk of her clothing.

'Did he kiss your breasts, Rosie?' he whispered,

184

kneading her. 'Did he put his face between your legs and kiss your wet little pussy?'

'No!' she squeaked as his finger probed her crease, and at the same moment, Celeste pushed aside the loose neck of her top and held her breast through her flimsy camisole. 'No, just my lips,' she groaned, then felt the pressure of Celeste's supple lips against hers, tasting her and making her yield.

And then there were two tongues working: Julian licking her neck as his wife probed the cavern of her mouth. Fingers also palpated her wickedly: Celeste's moulding her breast, Julian's teasing her bottom and prodding at her anus through her clothes. She was their victim, and she despised herself for her weakness, but at the same time she acknowledged their artistry. Her head, her heart and her loins all told her that they'd done this before; taken a willing, defenceless lover and quartered his or her body between them.

'Did he touch you?' The words were moist against Rosie's lips, and the fingers were cruel on her nipple. 'Did you let him fondle your breasts?' Celeste asked, pinching. 'And squeeze your nipples? Like this?'

Rosie struggled, her body alive in every pore. Celeste had asked questions, but given her no chance to answer. She was being kissed again, aggressively, the tongue in her mouth stabbing deep as the fingers tweaked rudely at her breast.

'And did he touch you here?' asked Julian slyly, letting his free hand settle on her belly. He had her loins in a sandwich now, his hands warm and intimate behind and before, but not quite doing what she craved. She felt his fingers in the channel between her buttocks and playing at the edge of her pubis. They seemed to dance there – hovering tantalisingly, but not pressing down to bring ease to her sex.

'Yes!' Her answer was garbled by Celeste's thrusting tongue, and her hips jerked crudely in Julian's unwavering hold. To her horror, Rosie realised she was unconsciously trying to entice him. She could feel herself

185

soiling her lingerie, her juices running out like a stream across the fragile silk strip between her legs.

'And did you let him touch your quim?' asked Celeste, switching her attack from Rosie's mouth to her ear, nibbling at the lobe beside her ear-ring and sucking it like a fold of her sex.

Had he or hadn't he? She could barely remember. 'I don't know,' she whimpered, feeling Celeste on the move again. She felt her breast freed for a moment, her tee-shirt adjusted, then Celeste's hands were beneath the garment, tugging down the lace beneath and wedging it under her breasts. The thin straps slid down off her shoulders, trapping her arms and seeming to pin them at her sides. Her hands lay useless by her thighs, and her breasts were loose and free with only a thin layer of cotton to cover them. Rosie had never felt so vulnerable.

'Surely you let him finger you?' asked Julian as his wife now tucked Rosie's tee-shirt out of the way, and exposed her bosom – like two white, cherry tipped globes suspended between twin bands of black. One glance at the lewdness of her own body made Rosie try and turn her head away, but Celeste wouldn't let her. She gently urged Rosie to look downwards, then stroked each of her nipples with a fingertip, to make them harder and darker than ever.

'You did let him touch you, didn't you?' she cajoled, flicking ceaselessly, one nipple then the other, again and again and again.

Remembering, Rosie nodded, then whimpered as Julian's hands were suddenly at her crotch, working on the set of miniature press studs that held the gusset of her camiknickers in place. When he had them unfastened, he eased the sopping fabric aside, then raised her skirt and rolled it up to her waist.

Rosie closed her eyes again, aware that her face was red with shame. She felt fingers working neatly between her legs: combing open her wet pubic hair then dividing her thickened outer labia to expose the very softest parts within. Cool air flowed over her moistness and the distended bud of her clitoris, making it ache and almost cry for contact. She wiggled her hips, trying to invite either one or the other of her tormentors to touch her, but they didn't. She felt hands on her inner thighs, fingertips tracing the lines of her suspenders, someone tugging very gently on her curls.

The same someone – or maybe not – then turned their attention to her breasts, and began torturing them with little tickles, touches and licks. The very featheriest of caresses designed solely to arouse, not satisfy.

It was the same at her crotch.

'Did he touch your clittie,' murmured Celeste, while someone traced the creases of Rosie's groin, and blew on her pubic mound. 'Well, did he?' the beautiful voice persisted, while the tormenting fingertips went right inside Rosie's outer labia and performed a series of tiny fluttering strokes on either side of her clitoris. Madly engorged, the little bud seemed to pound like a drum, the beats so heavy and profound she could almost hear them. She tried to rock her body so the sliding fingers would accidently nudge into climax, but the one who wasn't stroking her – probably Julian – held her tight by the thighs and kept her still, her clitoris burning with an intense, but exquisite agony.

'Yes!' she shouted, sobbing in desperation. Just a few short minutes, and a few expert moves, had brought her to this. The very pinnacle of frustration, a state of desire so huge it was terrifying. If she didn't come soon, she was afraid of the consequences.

'And did you need him then, as you need him now?'

It was Celeste again, breaking the pattern of him, then her, then him again. Rosie groaned and struggled. She needed something now, needed orgasm by any hand, including her own or even David's.

'Yes,' she croaked, trying to jerk herself free and touch herself, because the stroking fingers would not. 'Oh God, please, I need to come!'

'Then go and find David,' purred Celeste, biting her neck just beneath the ear. 'Seek him out, Rosie. Enjoy him. He's beautiful . . . He's young and ripe. He's yours . . .'

'But he was tired,' said Rosie, confused. Her brain felt addled, her memory twisted. The fingers kept slicking and slicking, less than a quarter of an inch from her clitoris.

'Nonsense!' Celeste was laughing, pressing tiny kisses to Rosie's face and neck, licking her hot skin as the fingers squeezed gently then withdrew, and another tongue pressed delicately to each of her naked nipples in turn, wetting them, then pulling away completely.

'That's nonsense,' repeated Celeste, sweeping the damp hair back from Rosie's brow. 'Young men his age are sex machines. He's just unsure of himself. *You* have to be the prime mover, Rosie. You've got to go to him now. He's in the room at the end of the corridor on the right ... Two doors down from you.'

All hands, all mouths, all presences slid away, and Rosie was left alone on the sofa, slumped and sleazy, her breasts and sex exposed and damp. For a few moments she just lay there – numbed and half naked – and then a small sound roused her from her stupor. Weighed down with sexual discomfort, she heaved herself upright and opened her eyes.

Celeste and Julian were lying on the rug, entwined and kissing. Celeste had one thigh jammed between her husband's legs and was rubbing it rhythmically against his crotch; while Julian had his hand up his wife's white dress, making short, stiff, stabbing movements with his arm. Their mouths were fused, their tongues working. They were already oblivious to her presence, or at least making it seem that way.

Clumsily, Rosie straightened her clothes. Her legs shook as she got to her feet. Avoiding the writhing couple on the carpet, she made her way to the door in a daze. When she reached it she turned, unable to resist another look.

Celeste's body was writhing furiously against the carpet now, and every so often her white-gowned body would lift from the floor and arch. Her partially bared thighs scissored wildly as she rose, and as her bottom seemed to float in mid-air, she wriggled like an eel on the pivot of Julian's rubbing hand. She was orgasming violently but in silence, her husband devouring her screams at the source as his own body pounded against hers. It was obvious that he was coming too.

Rosie almost ran from the room, groaning as her swollen breasts bounced. Her sex felt wide and bloated, and every movement seemed to goad her more and more. Her body was riven with longing, with a desperate need to climax. She pressed her hand to her crotch as she raced up the stairs, then almost fell as a spasm assailed her.

It was as if her sex was crying out for release, begging her for it, and on the landing she stopped, crouched gracelessly and rubbed herself roughly through her clothes.

Almost instantly a long, hard wave raced through her; the orgasm she'd yearned for, but too sudden and too soon. It felt more akin to pain than pleasure, and she grunted like an animal as she came, her pelvis pumping and weaving as she wallowed in the black depths of shame.

Chapter 11

Stealth

'What's happening to me?' whispered Rosie as she slid down against a wall and collapsed in a heap on the floor.

To put it in its crudest terms she'd just rubbed herself off in an open, accessible part of the house, here on the upper landing. And she couldn't have stopped, even if someone had come by and caught her. One of the staff, on their way to turn down the beds, or perhaps Celeste and Julian, refreshed by their own swift pleasure and ready for further mischief.

And the worst of it was, she wasn't even satisfied. She'd had an orgasm, granted, but not one as powerful as she needed. She'd simply partially defused some tension; not made love – as she'd wanted to – either with herself or with any other person.

But her other person was close by now, and available, and struggling to her feet again, Rosie forced herself not to dither. Striding along the landing, she twisted the large glass doorknob, then pushed gently on the door. To her relief it swung open soundlessly, revealing the dimly lit room beyond.

Closing the door as quietly as she'd opened it, Rosie found herself in a suite not unlike her own. The same wonderful antiques, the same abundant space, and even

190

a similar four poster bed – although this one had draperies of forest green instead of yellow.

On the bedside table, a nightlight burned, shedding its soft, muted glow on the bed and its single occupant. A figure that was sprawled face downwards; calm and still, yet at the same time subliminally restless.

David had changed.

It dawned on her again, here, just as it had in the dining room. He was a different boy altogether, sensualised somehow. Lit from within. He still looked the same, though, but with just one quantifiable difference – he wore no pyjamas tonight. He was quite clearly sleeping in the nude, with only a twist of sheet across his hips and buttocks to preserve his masculine modesty. His back, his arms and his shoulders, and his smooth, muscular legs were all naked and gleaming in the half-light.

Rosie drew stealthily closer.

Although David's face was pressed into the pillow, she could see his features in a pure, perfect profile. His bold, slightly roman nose; his crisply defined mouth; his closed eyes with their sooty black lashes so unfairly long for a man. While she watched, those lashes fluttered just once, like fans, and she took a nervous step backwards. She saw him frown in his sleep and wriggle slightly, and she wondered if he was dreaming. About sex; and maybe about her.

Suddenly her own desire seemed to ravish her. David looked so vulnerable, so available. He was something sweet and tempting she could feast on. She could have him and touch him, taste him and fondle him. Any part of him. He was an independent young man, whose trials, she suspected, had only made him stronger. But right now, she – as his tutor – still had the controlling upper hand.

Drawing close again, she carefully lifted the thin, light draping of the sheet.

His bottom was superb – neat, hard, and male – and his smooth, slender thighs were parted. Between them his balls nestled shyly, and shielded his penis from her

191

eyes with their fuzzy, reddish bulk. In the deep, shady vale between his bottom cheeks, his anus seemed to wink like an eye; tiny, tight and alluring.

Not sure of what she wanted, but sure she wanted something, Rosie started stripping; tearing off her tee-shirt and skirt, then flinging them on the floor with her shoes. Her camiknickers had twisted during her writhings downstairs, and her nipples were peeking out the bodice. Between her thighs, the slender, fragile gusset was only half fastened in place, and her curls were poking out, on show. She could smell her own odour rising up: perfume, sweat, and the distinctive, pungent musk of a vulva that had seeped with pleasure. As she studied David closely, she saw his nostrils flare, and wondered if he'd smelt her too. She yearned for his scent in return.

Very carefully, Rosie tested the springs of the bed. It dented slightly, but the mattress seemed resiliant. She took a chance, and climbed up onto it beside David – holding her breath in case he woke. His only response, however, was to stir slightly, then still again almost immediately, muttering and nuzzling his pillow.

So far, so good.

Sweeping her hair back over her shoulder, Rosie leant over him, holding her face just an inch from his body and breathing in deeply.

She smelt the faintest hint of sex-musk, plus some kind of green-scented shower gel and the unmistakeable freshness of baby talc. It was really the weirdest of aphrodisiacs, but Rosie felt a giant surge of lust; a rushing need to explore his body, that was focused in the strangest of ways. Pressing her lips to the centre of his back, just between his shoulder-blades, she began kissing her way down his spine.

She felt his skin quiver finely beneath her progress, and when she reached the watershed between his back and his bottom, she sensed strongly that her pupil was aware of her; completely conscious, but not moving or speaking for fear that she'd stop her exploration. It seemed to signal both trust and trepidation, and Rosie

192

vowed silently neither to betray the first, nor completely banish the second.

When he still showed no outward sign of wakefulness, she began an attack on his perfect young bottom. Covering it in kisses, she rubbed her cheeks and her nose against it, then licked at his firmly muscled lobes. Attending to every last millimetre of skin, she played around and caressed with her tongue, and at the moment when she sensed relaxation, she switched her efforts to the area of his cleft, and used her fingers for the first time too.

Prising apart his cheeks, she exposed the seductive little hole, amazed at its delicate prettiness. It looked like a small, mauve flower, the tight, crisp bud of a cultivated rose. Flexing her fingers, she opened him further and watched the miniature orifice dilate.

Alarming thoughts passed through her, odd feelings that defied her gender. It was as if she were a man suddenly: a possessor, a taker, a penetrator. She was going to have this gentle creature below her, have him and enter him. She was to use the small and sweetly puckered hole that he so innocently and openly offered her.

Using her thumbs, she stretched him even more, then moved her face in closer. She'd never indulged in play like this before, not even with Geoff. Whenever she'd touched *his* bottom, he'd complained, and she realised now that it was because he feared for his masculinity. Liking having your bottom stroked was for 'poofs' and 'queers' in his opinion, which only confirmed to Rosie that her ex wasn't quite the sexy guy he thought he was. You were wrong about a lot of things, Geoff, she thought, almost laughing against the cheeks of her lusciously surrendered young lover.

And clearly David himself wasn't hampered by such negative pre-conceptions. He was a blank slate, an open book, and she could write whatever she wanted on him. Phrases that were full and rich and strange. She could make him receptive to anything and everything, and as she pressed her lips to his exquisite, immaculate bottom, she relished his cry of delight.

As she kissed him, he started moving wildly beneath her: his feet kicking and scraping, his hands gouging at the sheets. His hips rose up, pressing his anus hard against her mouth, then plunged down again and circled, so he could massage the mattress with his groin.

Mastering him effortlessly, and encouraged by the sweetness and freshness of his body, Rosie opened her mouth and began to use her tongue on his flesh; licking at the forbidden little opening and teasing it with short, sharp dabs.

David was moaning continuously now, babbling gibberish, his face still pressed into the pillow as his body writhed and trembled. 'Oh God,' Rosie heard him whimper as she furled up her tongue and pushed it determinedly into him. She felt like a raider, pillaging him anew for a deeper and more telling virginity. For the second time in as many minutes she wished she was male. Or at least had a cock. She wanted desperately to penetrate him; to go in further than her tongue could reach; to feel what it was like to be inside him, and possess him in complete dominion.

As his body went rigid, she sensed him teetering on the edge of orgasm and made a split-second decision. She'd prolong the game, make more of it. She pulled back a little way, and watched his bottom and his whole back shake. He was tense as a wire, every nerve and muscle keyed up for climax. She could almost hear him screaming for release.

Half expecting him to break his silence and beg, she was pleased when he made not a sound. He had guts, and an instinctive sense of adventure, and she was proud of him. Keeping her touch ineffably light, she ran her fingers over the incurves of his cheeks and up and down his hot, tense thighs. Unbidden, his legs opened wider to expose the rich, dark bounty of his balls. She slid her hand up and delicately enclosed him.

When she squeezed, infinitesimally, she saw his toes

clench and a pulse start to leap behind his knee. He made a rough sound in his throat, but otherwise stayed silent. When she leant over him, she saw that his lips were compressed in a thin, tight line, and his fine brow was crumpled with effort.

It was time. She couldn't torture him any more. Moving as smoothly and as quietly as she could, she unfastened the crotch of her camiknickers, threw her leg half across him and let her quim kiss the back of his thigh – just at the point where it merged with his buttock. Letting her weight take her down, she pressed the furrow of her sex against him, wetting his skin with her juice as she massaged her swollen membranes against the smooth, hard line of his haunch. His heat made her clitoris quiver, and as she rocked her body against him, she worked his flesh too; fondling his balls with her fingers while her momentum ground his cock against the sheet. It was as close as she'd ever get to being a man; the nearest she'd ever come to fucking him.

As her orgasm came, she inclined across his back like a willow, pressing her open mouth against the nape of his neck as her free hand searched blindly for one of his. In an instant, their fingers laced, and when David's grip grew vicelike, and he groaned, she felt his hip jerk up against her vulva.

'Oh! Oh!' she heard him gasp, as his pelvis rode the bed beneath him, and his balls leapt and pulsed in her fingers. 'Oh God,' he whimpered again, his voice just a thread in her splintering mind as pleasure sent it spinning from her body.

The next morning, as she jogged away from the house, Rosie turned and looked backwards for a second. There was a window open on the first floor, and its lace curtains fluttered cheerfully in the breeze.

It was David's room. And as she ran on the spot a few steps, then launched herself off towards the woods, she couldn't help thinking of what had happened beyond those curtains last night.

195

It'd been the strangest event of her sexual life so far. A union, but without intercourse, or even mutual touching. She hadn't seen David's penis, and she certainly hadn't handled it. And yet it had been under her control. She'd governed his responses completely, and possessed him in a way she'd never expected. It had been sublimely and quite beautifully peculiar, and though they hadn't exchanged a single word, she'd felt closer to David than to anyone ever in her life.

But how do I feel now? she pondered.

Taking pleasure in her own smooth stride, she decided that the word for her condition was 'great'! She'd slept well, and felt full of vitality and pep. And she could only ascribe it all to David.

After their mutual, but separate climax, she'd lain beside him for a while, listening to the rhythm of his breathing and trying to sense the current of his thoughts. He'd refrained from conversation, she deduced, because – like her – he was still mulling over what had happened. It was a pretty kinky thing they'd done between them, especially for a sexual novice. Did he have a few of Geoff's fears after all, she'd wondered. The perennial atavistic dread. The macho man's 'am I gay?' nightmare.

'Don't worry,' she told him remotely, as she pounded lightly away across the grass. 'You're a real man, my sweet. And even if you are bi-sexual, it'll probably make me like you even more!'

And that was another can of worms. One of several it seemed silly to open right now when the morning was so lovely and the sun so bright and uncomplicated.

When she'd woken up at dawn, and back in her own bed, the first thing she'd wanted to do was get out for a jog and explore. Last night, when she'd arrived, she'd been too pre-occupied to look around properly; but this morning, out on the long veranda that ran along the side of the house, she'd been thrilled by the breath-taking view.

Stonehaven stood in the centre of its own vast park.

196

The flat Norfolk panorama had been landscaped slightly to make it interesting, moulded into gentle rolls and hillocks that were dotted here and there with shrubs and bushes. The house itself was ringed by an elegant, formal flower garden that seemed to melt into the wilder zone around it.

Heading in the direction of the wooded perimeter, she kept her pace steady, and felt surprised by her own strength and liveliness. It was amazing. She should have felt like death warmed up after all that debauchery and creeping around the house in the small hours.

Rosie's relationship with jogging was a hit and miss affair; sometimes love, sometimes hate. This morning it was love, especially when a cooling breeze caressed her deliciously as she ran. Her clothes – a thin jersey sweat top and shorts – hardly kept her skin from the air at all, and her trainers almost flew across the turf. She felt healthier than she'd ever felt, and could only conclude that a life rich in sex was good for you. For a moment, she wished David was running beside her, but then accepted she couldn't have everything. Maybe they could swim together later? And afterwards discuss what they felt.

She also supposed she ought to get herself into the library – and do some of the work she was paid for!

When she reached the tree-line, she skirted its edge, looking for a clearing or a gap – then found a faint but quite definite path. Confident that her inbuilt sense of direction would eventually get her home, she set off boldly down the track, walking briskly but not running, so she wouldn't trip up or stumble.

Being in woods reminded her poignantly of the previous afternoon; and she smiled. It had been a cliché, but a good one. An unforgettable memory. She imagined David recounting it to some future lover, a wife or fiancée perhaps? They'd be lying in bed, in that glorious euphoria when sharing minds is as sweet as sharing bodies.

'Tell me about your first time,' the unknown woman

197

would say. And David would smile that slow, solemn smile of his and describe a sunny afternoon on the road to Norfolk, when he'd lost his virginity to his cousin's librarian.

Why aren't I jealous? thought Rosie, pausing to peer through the trees. She'd been thinking of David with someone else and it hadn't hurt – even after yesterday's intimacy. She did want him for herself, yes; in fact she wanted him a very great deal. But she couldn't find envy in the feeling. She tried picturing him with Ladybird – and had to stop dead because the image was so vividly arousing.

Ladybird was limber and beautiful, an exotic, superbly fit animal. Her gilded body would look amazing against David's creamy pallor – once she got over her curious notions of intellectual inferiority – and Rosie longed to be there at their blending. Or even be a part of it.

Is it all that stuff with Celeste and Julian that's changed me? she wondered, enjoying the way the branches above made the sunlight dapple and flicker. She'd never even considered making love to more than one person at once until she'd arrived at Amberlake Gardens, but now the idea seemed quite natural.

As she turned the concept over in her mind, she noticed that up ahead the trees seemed thinner. Between them there was the sparkle of water, some slowly flowing river or stream. She broke into a trot again as the path became wider and more definite.

The woodland track disgorged onto a tow-path, and where they met was a large and solidly built boathouse. Made of stone and timber, it reminded Rosie of a similar structure she'd recently seen in a film. Something arty by Merchant Ivory, she seemed to recall; and in it, two homosexual lovers had embraced in a boathouse at night while all the 'straights' snoozed on unaware in the 'big' house.

I bet this place has seen some action, she thought, pushing open the side door and stepping cautiously inside. It was an ideal trysting spot. She imagined Julian and Celeste bringing their various paramours here; either separately or in some complicated menage. There were a couple of moored rowing boats bobbing in the water, and nearby a sturdy joiner's trestle. In a flash of shocking clarity, she imagined a sleek, writhing body stretched face down across the bar, while another figure laid intimate hands on it. The picture crossed her mind so quickly that she couldn't even register their genders.

Shaken, she backed away from the sawhorse and the slowly lapping water. It was foolhardy to stand so close to the edge when she was hallucinating, so she made her way carefully to the back of the building – stepping over spare oars, coils of rope and half empty pots of varnish – and ascended the narrow staircase that led to an area up above.

Upstairs, she found a curiously cosy little set up. The storeroom, loft, or whatever it was, had been divided by a partition and made into a kind of apartment. There were a couple of easy chairs, a coffee table, a TV and even a surprisingly large bed. At the back of the room was a sink, some cupboards and a worktop, complete with a small microwave and fridge. Beyond the division was a tiny but squeaky clean bathroom – with a sink, shower and lavatory.

A love-nest, she thought with a smile, its ambience made all the more charming by the fact that from the upper level one could look down through a large, open trap-door and see the whole of the boathouse below.

Rosie looked down at the gently rocking boats for a few minutes, and tried to picture what these walls might have seen. Celeste, on the bed, entwined with lovers of either sex. Julian, ditto, if Ladybird's wild story was true.

It'd be a lovely place to bring David, she decided, her smile widening. It was comfortable, romantic, secluded, and provided she knew the whereabouts of *both* her employers at the time, well away from the Hadeys' watchful eyes. She and David could relax better here. Celeste and Julian were basically well-meaning, but their obsession with David's 'education' might embarrass him more than it helped.

Resolving to get him here as soon as possible, Rosie made her way to what seemed to be an exit. She opened a door right at the back of the room, and beyond it found a set of stone steps – on the outside of the building – that descended down to the tow-path.

She was just about to use them when she suddenly heard the sound of running. Two people running. Not really knowing why, she ducked back into the boathouse flat, and pushed the outer door quietly shut. On the lightest of feet, she crossed to the trap-door, and peered down into the area below; knowing she was trapped by her own nosey subterfuge if the newcomers chose to come upstairs.

But they didn't.

The runners were Julian and Stephen the chauffeur. They moved into the centre of the boathouse, and just stood facing each other, by the trestle. Both wore sweaty sports gear, and both were panting with exertion, but their faces bore a matching, narrow-eyed expression. The look of pure, naked lust. Without either of them speaking, they moved forward as one and began to kiss. Their mouths were ravenous and passionate, and their hands were the same; exploring each others bodies, squeezing and groping quite freely.

Oh God, it's true! thought Rosie, stunned and breathless. She'd half suspected that Ladybird had been storytelling, but obviously she hadn't. The two men down in the boathouse were clearly lovers. Why else would Stephen be palming his employer's genitals and bending him back across his arm with the force and fury of his kiss?

The chauffeur's dominance was a shock, in spite of her being forewarned of it. She was so used to Julian being suave and confident, so used to him being the boss, and a heterosexual. It seemed out of character for him to yield. Nevertheless, Stephen was handling him in a way so crude it could only be intended to demean him.

'You want it, don't you?' Rosie heard Stephen growl. Then she watched, open-mouthed, as his big, dark hand slid down into Julian's thin shorts, and resumed the rough stimulation.

It was total role reversal. Julian looked soft-faced, enraptured, malleable. Rosie heard him whimper in his throat as Stephen caressed him, and saw him clutch at his lover's thick arms, every inch the pathetic, quivering submissive.

Rosie felt her blood stir dangerously, and her own flesh grow tense and excited. She remembered what Ladybird had described to her, and compared it with scraps of her own fantasies – the wild outrageous ones that came from nowhere. The ones that set her stroking her body compulsively and feeling guilty at the resulting orgasms. She'd always found the theory of man-to-man loving a turn on, but down below was a practical demonstration. Her hand stole slyly to her mound.

The men looked dynamic together. A poem in contrasts. Stephen was like a column of ebony, sparsely clothed in a grey vest and shorts; while Julian wore pale blue, a delicate eggshell pastel that gave his honeyed middle eastern skin the subtle bloom of velvet.

'Slut,' murmured Stephen huskily, biting at Julian's bared neck. 'Little pansy. You want me don't you? I saw you waggling your bottom . . .'

'Oh please, yes!' groaned Julian, arching even more.

Rosie had never heard a more unlikely conversation. Julian was completely in Stephen's control, completely domineered, yet she sensed there was a deep bond between them. Stephen's face was stern, but there was a strange respect there too – even though Julian was clearly quite happy to be used.

'Please,' she heard him croak, his usual extensive and sophisticated vocabulary torn away by the rawness of his need.

In a jerky, shaming movement, Stephen pulled down

201

his victim's shorts. Julian's erection bounced up hungrily, its red tip straining and pointing towards the man who was currently its master. Rosie bit her lip, her own crotch aching, when Julian's hips began to weave.

'What's this then?' enquired Stephen, as he almost dropped Julian at his feet, then reached out to flick at his stiffness. 'What do you think you're up to? Did I say you could get like this?'

'No,' said Julian in a small voice.

'It's disgusting,' Stephen scorned. 'You need punishing . . . For being a dirty little pervert.'

The chauffeur's tone was pure theatre, grim and harsh. The men below were acting out a drama, an entertainment for their mutual pleasure, and Rosie found herself smiling as, quite suddenly, Julian started flirting.

Giving his companion a creamy, almost coquettish look, he insolently stroked his own prick and wiggled his hips like a hussy. He was playing the effeminate to the hilt this morning, and to Rosie, it was a wonder to behold. Especially when he closed his eyes, bent his knees and flirted his pelvis to and fro with an expression of pure sleaze on his face. His shorts were still pushed down to his knees, which only increased the impression of lewdness.

With the speed of a striking snake, Stephen slapped his employer's face.

'Whore!' snarled the chauffeur, his voice soft and steely as real tears formed in Julian's eyes, and Rosie could have sworn she saw his lip tremble. There was a clear, pink handprint adorning his smooth, tawny cheek.

'I'll stop you,' Stephen went on, eyes narrowed. Looking around, he snatched up a short length of cord from the assortment of nautical detritus that lay scattered across the stone floor. With unnecessary force, he grabbed Julian's wrists and tied them together behind his back; leaving Rosie wondering how there just happened to be such a convenient length of rope to hand. Did they play these games here often?

Utterly fascinated, Rosie thought of all the sights

she'd seen in the past few days and tried to pick a high-light from amongst them. In her mind's eye she saw David again, masturbating; then pictured him as he'd appeared last night, stretched naked on his sleep-tossed bed, his long pale back and his firm young bottom exposed to her like an offering.

But even as she focused her attention on Julian again, and the expanse of his rudely bared loins, she sensed a movement at the edge of her vision. Something close by, in the loft itself.

She turned her head very slowly, then almost toppled head first through the trap-door when she saw David just a few feet away from her. He'd obviously come up via the outdoor steps, and the fact that he wore a tee-shirt, tracksuit bottoms and trainers indicated that he too had been out for an early morning jog. His smooth brow was creased in puzzlement, and as he opened his mouth to speak, Rosie pressed a finger to her lips to shush him, then nodded towards the trap-door. As he moved forward with a silent, almost feline grace, she wondered if she was doing the right thing. Watching was a good way to learn, but was David really ready for such strangeness?

But as he crouched noiselessly over the opening, his face showed only fascination. Rosie was torn between the urge to watch the action down below, and the desire to see David's reaction. She settled for observing the lovers. She might never get the chance again.

Stephen's hands were back on the move. With slow luxurious strokes he was examining Julian's helpless body, pushing his hand up his victim's vest and tweaking his nipples, then swooping down over his ribcage and flanks to settle his naked hips. He didn't touch Julian's penis, but instead, slid both hands around his back, then dropped them to his trim, masculine buttocks. Julian's cock seemed to yearn towards the dark man before him, but Stephen stepped teasingly away, denying the comfort of contact.

'Oh no you don't,' he purred to his employer, and

even from several yards away, Rosie saw Stephen's arms flex. He was squeezing Julian's bottom-cheeks as hard as he could, treating the taut, smooth flesh like raw clay.

Julian was panting heavily, and had sweat standing out on his brow. He whimpered like a girl when Stephen brought one hand forward, and his eyes widened and bulged. Rosie couldn't quite see what was happening: she could only deduce that Stephen was attacking his employer from both back and front now. Playing with his penis or his balls, whilst caressing the crease of his bottom. After a couple of seconds Julian's hips lurched forward, and his mouth fell slackly open.

On impulse, she glanced towards David. His face was a picture of conflict. He looked excited and intensely turned on, yet there was an edge of worry there too. Was he alarmed by the implications of what he was seeing? The connotations of having enjoyed something similar – his bottom being fondled and kissed?

It was impossible to reassure him without revealing their presence, but even so Rosie tried. 'It's alright,' she mimed. 'Just enjoy . . .' It didn't make a lot of sense, she realised, but even so he seemed to relax. He gave her a confused grin, then shrugged and looked down his own body. There was a bulge in the front of his trackpants.

'It's alright,' Rosie repeated in silence, then on impulse, slid her hand into the waistband of her shorts – seeking out her warm, moist centre. The pressure of her own fingertips was exquisite, and she rolled her hips to increase the sensation, and hoped that David would copy her.

For a moment, his eyes went as round and bright as two gold coins, and he just gaped in amazement. Then with a soundless sigh of acceptance, he laid a long pale hand across his crotch.

Down below matters were progressing. The men had shifted around slightly, and made their contortions easier to see. Stephen had a rhythmic, pumping finger at work in Julian's tight anus and he was complimenting

204

this by holding the tip of his employer's penis in a tight, pinching grip, just below the glans. 'Sexy little queen,' he murmured huskily, then swooped down and bit Julian's neck again. Hard.

Julian was sobbing now, his face beatific. It was clear that in this quasi-feminine role he took a genuine pleasure in weeping and mewling like a damsel in direst distress. His slim hips were waving and swaying, and it seemed that no matter how firmly Stephen held on his cock, he was still about to come any minute.

Then, with a sudden, wrenching cruelty, the chauffeur withdrew both his hands, and Julian was left high and dry. His gleaming body seemed to hum with tension, and his cock stood out like a tortured, crimson prong. His eyes turned beseechingly towards his tormentor. 'Please ... Bring me off,' he pleaded, pushing forward with his hips.

'No way,' snarled Stephen, and Rosie felt her own flesh quiver beneath her fingers – as if the chauffeur had proscribed her pleasure too. She hardly dare look at David, but minute almost subliminal rustlings told her he'd either slid his hands down inside his tracksuit, or eased his stiff sex out into the air.

'Please,' repeated Julian below them. 'Please, I need to come. It hurts ...' His voice was pathetic and wheedling, quite unlike his usual confident drawl. Bizarrely, Rosie found this peculiar new persona a turn-on, and without thinking, began to rock against her fingers.

A strong hand settled on her shoulder, and made her still before the sound became incriminating. She looked up into David's lambent eyes, and realised that he'd edged ever so slightly closer. He was lying with his body almost touching hers and his erect penis pointing at her belly. He smiled, and she felt her quim shake again, excited by the sweet blend of shyness, arousal and conspiracy she saw on his handsome young face. Like the wonderfully quick study he was, he'd plunged into voyeurism like a pro and was as turned on by the strange sights as she was.

Stephen's voice refocused their attentions.

'Hurts, does it?' he taunted, taking Julian by the shoulders and virtually throwing him face down across the trestle. 'Well, we'll see about that!'

First gay love. Then bondage and humiliation. Was it spanking next? Julian was draped over the hard wooden cross-piece, with his naked bottom perfectly positioned. Stephen had said – hours ago it now seemed – that Julian needed to be punished. Rosie stole another peek at David.

His golden eyes were still hugely wide, and as she watched him he bit his lip in a sort of semi-worried eagerness. He was lying in a position that precisely mirrored her own; stretched out, half sideways on, one hand supporting his chin while the other worked steadily at his groin. Rosie realised he must have read about people beating each other – Julian's library was stuffed with such literature! – but the difference between reading about and seeing for real was astronomical. She was terrified herself in a way. Her sex was already throbbing and the tableau had barely begun.

Down below, Stephen was opening up a weathered oak store cupboard and reaching inside. From where Rosie was lying, its contents were hidden, but she wasn't at all surprised when he returned to the trestle with a thick leather strap in his hand. She saw Julian's back shake, and his bound hands curl into fists when the cruel thing was drawn slowly, oh so slowly, between his buttocks. His prick was partially hidden from view by his body, but as the leather slid idly up his channel, a string of clear fluid began to snake down towards the floor from his visible and very swollen glans.

'Kiss it,' ordered Stephen, holding the strap to Julian's lips. Julian craned his head forwards and rubbed his mouth lovingly over the sturdy chunk of leather; as if it were the body of someone he worshipped and not an instrument of punishment and pain.

The chauffeur turned away, hefting the strap in his right hand, while with his left he made some small, tugging movements. Rosie couldn't actually see what he was doing, but she could imagine. And when he turned back round again, she swallowed, then blinked, then swallowed again.

Stephen had pulled down the front of his shorts and exposed his penis and testicles. They were resting on the bunched up cloth like treasures exhibited on a cushion. And they were enormous.

Astounded, Rosie looked away quickly towards David; who in turn glanced briefly down towards his own genitals, then shrugged, shook his head, and cracked a grin so droll that Rosie had a hard time not bursting out laughing.

As her hysteria began to bubble, she had to take her hand out of her pants and bite her knuckle. She was dying to giggle, almost wetting herself with the need to roll about and howl, and David wasn't helping matters either, because he seemed to be having the same problem. He was pressing his face into the rug they were lying on, his cotton-clad shoulders shaking with the effort of containing his mirth.

Eventually though, they were able to resume their surveillance, and down in the bowels of the boathouse all was dark and deviantly erotic.

Stephen stood before Julian's upturned face, his penis almost touching his employer's trembling lips.

'Kiss it,' he said, repeating his earlier command, but in a voice that was soft and cajoling as he gently stroked Julian's black curls.

Edging himself forward, Julian complied meekly, pressing his lips and tongue to his lover's imposing sex. He went at the long, purplish bar as if he were starving, his stubble-darkened cheeks going hollow as he sucked and slurped with gusto. The noise was even audible in the loft.

Rosie wondered what David was thinking. Having his penis caressed by someone's lips and tongue must be high on any young man's agenda. It was something she hadn't done for him yet, but after this she knew he'd soon want it.

207

'Enough,' said Stephen, his strong voice suddenly shaky as he pushed Julian away from his prick. The pleasures of fellatio were clearly undermining his role, and Rosie admired the way he could forego them for another man's benefit. It was all a psychodrama, she realised, because in spite of his mock subjugation, Julian was still, and always, the master. All this was his fantasy, his pantomine; a piquant and highly seasoned side-dish in the life of a sexual gourmet.

She felt David move a little closer as Stephen strode around and stood behind Julian. She and her pupil were lying face to face now, and she felt a shuddering thrill when the tip of his cock touched her leg. He made as if to pull away, but she put her hand on his hip and stilled him. Being hidden away like this was as intimate in its own way as yesterday afternoon had been – in the open, the woods and the sunshine.

Below them, Stephen swished the strap experimentally and Julian wriggled on the bar, his bare rump glistening and gleaming in a thin shaft of slanted yellow light. Rosie found the sight of it delectable, and more so for having David beside her. She shifted her position slightly, feeling the urge to touch herself again, then supressed a wild gasp of happiness when her wish was suddenly anticipated. With a bit of a tussle, David slid his free hand up the loose jersey leg of her shorts, and then in under the elastic in the leg of her panties. He hesitated for a second, as if unsure, then seemed to get his bearings and start burrowing inwards.

Rosie moved again, to make things easier, and David responded instinctively, wiggling his finger in her secret, humid softness and making contact with the point that he sought.

Overcome, forgetting where she was, Rosie moaned when David tickled her clitoris. The urge to thrash and groan was agonising, but as awareness returned, she controlled it. Looking down, her sex still on fire, she saw Stephen pause and seem to scent the air like a puma. As unobtrusively as she could, she drew back, taking David with her, but the chauffeur didn't even raise his eyes. If he knew they were there, he was ignoring them. He had things more immediate on his mind – like Julian's naked bottom.

As Stephen lifted the strap, David's finger found her sweet spot again and she rocked infinitesimally against it. In the still claustrophobia of their hideaway, her sensitivity and her pleasure were compressed. Her vulva convulsed into orgasm, the first spasm breaking and cresting as below them the leather whistled down, hit Julian's tense flesh, and made a sound that echoed like a gunshot. She moaned again, but in perfect safety this time because down below the agonised yowls were louder.

Somewhere at the back of Rosie's mind, a cool, calm observer was surprised. Not because of the sweetness of her sudden climax – although it was very sweet and very sudden – but because she'd expected her boss to be braver. He was sobbing and gulping, juddering his hips about, and when he turned his head sideways for a moment, she saw he was actually weeping. Great, fat tears were streaming down his face, and shockingly their presence aroused her. As another blow fell, and Julian shrieked like a baby, David resumed his gentle stroking.

Already roused, Rosie's flesh leapt immediately; and as a new climax came, she rolled in tightly against her caresser, and caught his cock between her slowly working thighs. He gasped, but again the sound was lost in the cacophany from below: Julian's desperate high-pitched yells and the increasingly fierce cracks of the strap.

It was impossible to watch now, but the sounds of Julian's punishment lingered on like a strange, spicy soundtrack, and David's rubbing became suddenly less accurate.

Rosie was too sensitised to worry. Her quim was in a continuous, fluttering state of orgasm, and somewhere in the heart of their tangle, she could feel David's prick oozing warm fluid. As she sighed, it seemed to answer.

It shuddered against her, leapt once, then spat semen in long, pulsing bursts. Curling her arms around him, she cradled David to her breast, and felt the force of his rapture like a wave. His mouth was moving and muttering against her shoulder, his sobs of joy muffled by her sweatshirt.

For a long while they lay just glowing and listening. The blows rained on and on, and Julian yelled harder with each one – his voice high and shrill, yet laced with a strange edge of triumph. He was enjoying himself, crazy as it seemed, even though Stephen was showing him no mercy.

Then, quite suddenly, the quality of the sounds changed. The strokes of the strap stopped for one thing, and Julian's cries metamorphosed into moans. Long, voluptuous moans. Stirring from David's hold, Rosie wriggled forward a little way and looked down, then pursed her lips to stop herself gasping.

Stephen was kissing the very flesh he'd just punished, his mouth moving slowly and wetly over Julian's reddened bottom while his big hands sensuously explored him. Julian was writhing like a snake against the trestle, but he stiffened and bucked upwards when Stephen reached around for his prick. What followed was hidden by their bodies, but Rosie could tell what was happening. Julian was being masturbated, energetically, by the man who'd just beaten and abused him.

Rosie felt David slide forward beside her, and she reached up to place her hand across his lips. The ultimate act was almost upon them – upon *all* of them – and she sensed that even after what he'd already seen, the reality of sodomy might shock him. She wasn't even sure if she could watch it herself.

But as Stephen kissed his way up Julian's spine, she experienced it as an echo – in reverse – of what she'd done to David last night. And the process looked equally as beautiful as it had felt. She caught her breath as the chauffeur nuzzled the nape of his master's neck, then held the same breath as he moistened his fingers

210

with saliva and transfered the slick fluid to his cock. That done, and still using his hand he pressed his glans against Julian's anus.

Julian was still moaning, but the low throaty sounds spoke only of passion and need. Rosie saw him straining backwards against the man who was mounting him, then heard his long, bleating cry of acceptance as Stephen gave a last telling push.

'Oh God, my darling, yes!' Julian gasped, and Rosie was struck by the clear sound of pleasure in his voice. He was responding to being sodomised as if it were something tender and loving; when in fact he was being ruthlessly used and crushed against a rigid wooden bar. More than this, his hands were still tied behind his back, and trapped between their two heaving bodies.

With her gaze locked on the twin, tensing rounds of Stephen's black buttocks, Rosie felt David react yet again. Nervously, but with growing confidence, he drew her hand to his newly stiffened penis, then slid his own hand back into her shorts.

And then, as Stephen pounded and thrust, and Julian shouted and wailed, it seemed quite natural that all movement should synchronise – and four people's bliss be as one.

Chapter 12

De-briefing

'It's not all ...' David paused, and seemed to debate what to say. 'It's not all fucking, is it?'

Rosie smiled as she picked her way along the woodland path beside him. It was the first time either of them had spoken since they'd crept down the outside steps of the boathouse, and she was glad he'd broken the ice. And broken it so frankly!

'No, sweetheart, it isn't,' she observed, turning the smile his way. They were walking separately, because the going under foot was uneven, but she still felt wonderfully close to him.

He was absolutely right too. Entwined together in the loft, they hadn't made love in any conventional, penetrative sense, but they had given each other great pleasure. It reminded her a bit of a time not all that long ago when she herself had been back at David's stage. A time when nervous forays in awkward places had sometimes yielded up magic. It hadn't happened to her much, admittedly, and certainly not as much as she would have liked, but in her heart she'd always been waiting.

And it all seemed a long, long way from her present situation, she reflected. For the past few days, she seemed to have been surrounded by people who wanted her. Men *and* women. And it was as fabulous as it was unexpected.

As they moved along in companionable silence, David seemed to be mulling over her latest pronouncement, so Rosie took her first proper chance to observe him. In the gloom of the boathouse loft, all she'd really got was just an impression. His eyes, his mouth and his prick – and a warm body clad in sports gear.

Her charge appeared even younger than ever this morning. He had his hands stuffed in his trackpant's pockets, and he was scuffing the toes of his trainers in the dirt with all the gusto of Dennis the Menace. His usually smooth hair was sticking up endearingly, and there was a long smudge of dust down the side of his arm. In the tree-filtered light, he looked nearer to pubescence than adulthood – apart from his height – and far too young for their antics by the trap-door!

For reasons she didn't want to analyse, this made Rosie want him more. He wasn't quite the innocent he'd been when she'd first set eyes on him, but there was still something untouched about him; a lingering layer of virginity that she wanted to gently peel away.

'So . . .' About to blurt out a question, she hesitated. Was he really ready for all this? Julian's pecadilloes were, after all, complex stuff for a novice. He's seen it now though, she thought resignedly, so what the hell!

'What do you think about Julian and Stephen then?'

He turned to her as they walked, and she saw an unexpected humour in his face. 'To be honest, I don't know. My mind's still in overload. Not to mention my body.'

'Me too,' echoed Rosie softly, aware of a flow of secret moisture. Ten minutes ago, she'd been satisfied, but seeing David lithe and beautiful in the morning sunshine had changed all that. She wondered if she dare stop and lead him into the trees, to finish what they'd started in the loft. It was a very tempting idea, but maybe they needed to talk a bit first? Have a de-briefing, she thought, grinning at the double entendre.

'I knew that sort of thing happened,' David went on pensively. 'I'd read about it. But Julian's the last man I'd

213

have imagined being ... being like that. He seems so *male*. Don't you think so?'

Rosie quivered at David's penetrating sideways glance. Did he know something? she wondered. Did he suspect about *her* and Julian?

'Yes. He's very strong and sure of himself,' she said non-commitally. 'It was a surprise to see him so submissive. Although I had been warned ... Ladybird said she'd seen them together in the gym. I didn't believe her ... and I certainly never expected a demonstration!'

'Wow,' murmured David.

They strode on, each deep in thought. Rosie was debating whether to tell David more, and at the same time, wondering whether David was screwing up the courage to ask *her* questions. As they reached the edge of the park, and saw Stonehaven standing majestically at the centre of its gardens, his hand shot out and grabbed hers.

'Have you been to bed with him?' he demanded, his eyes like golden fire.

'With who?' Prevarication.

'With Julian.' David's pale young face was intent, and at first Rosie thought he was angry. Then she looked more closely and saw something more like passionate curiosity than ire. 'I bet you have,' he went on, letting slip the faintest of smiles. 'He's handsome, he's accomplished and clever. Obviously he's a poof on the side, but he's sort of macho with it. I think if I were a woman I'd fancy him ...' He paused there, and Rosie realised he'd said more than he'd meant to. His smooth brow crumpled as he continued. 'And any man with breath in his body would have to be blind, deaf *and* stupid not to want you!'

Rosie was amused and flattered. 'Thanks,' she said, starting to blush and feeling the nag of desire. David's naïve yet knowing persona was an alluring sexual cocktail, and the sight and scent of his body didn't help matters. It was too late to drag him into the bushes now, but in the distance the tall house beckoned. She thought of

214

comfortable bedrooms and secluded, out of the way corners whose darkness welcomed lovers.

But were they secluded? What was it Ladybird had said about two-way mirrors and suchlike? Stonehaven was just as riddled with peeping opportunities as the house in Amberlake Gardens was, it seemed; and she wondered suddenly if she'd been watched already. Either alone or with David.

'You haven't answered my question,' David said slowly.

There was no point in lying. David might be unschooled in some ways, but he was no fool. 'Yes, I've had sex with Julian. Does it bother you?'

When he didn't answer, and she daren't look at him, Rosie found the urge to confess irresistible. 'I've sort of had sex with Celeste too. And I think I wanted it with Ladybird as well. I don't quite know what's happening to me, David. I've changed since I took this job. I used to be a bit of a prude, and unimaginative. And now I feel like a nymphomaniac. I mean . . . Well . . . Even after what just happened, I still feel sexy. Crazy, isn't it?'

'Join the club!' said David with feeling. He was staring at the grass around his feet, but suddenly he kicked aimlessly at a pebble, then looked with a smile so mischievous, and so wickedly yet innocently sensual that her vulva quivered wildly in response.

'I feel the same,' he said, pushing his fingers through his disordered hair. 'I seem to have travelled from nothing to everything in the space of days. I want to do it again now,' he finished, shrugging, then looking down towards his crotch, where his cock was clearly stirring in his trackpants and pushing out the thin black fabric.

'Well, aren't we a pair,' said Rosie, moving close and putting her arms affectionately round him. In that moment she just felt so fond of him, and so kindred. It was an intimate feeling, yet pure too. She suddenly felt she could tell him anything and he'd understand. Even the true reason for her employment. She was just on the point of speaking the words when he leaned forward

215

and put his mouth over hers, pulling her body against his as he did so.

It was a long kiss, and unexpectedly assured. David's lips were soft yet forceful, prising hers open so his tongue could taste and explore. She marvelled that he could have learnt so much so soon, and know how she melted when her tongue was played with and sucked. He drew on it in a way that set up other resonances: the suckling of a nipple or a clitoris. The tips of her breasts grew hard, became delicate yet sensitive points that he caressed with the wall of his chest. And between her legs, her sex seemed to swell into a fat ball of heat that she lewdly massaged against his thigh.

As she rubbed herself, David made a sound of profoundly male satisfaction, and for a moment, Rosie's mettle was stung. So he *was* an embryo chauvinist after all, she thought, then mellowed as her sex-flesh rippled against him and he gripped the firm lobes of her bottom. She could feel his penis butting against her, iron-hard again because he was young and strong and had so much catching up to do. She swayed, her whole body boneless as she wished she was flat on her back and being taken in one long stroke.

I'm going to come again, she thought in a panic, feeling David nip her tongue with his teeth. His fingers flexed around her bottom, sliding craftily into the cleft. He'd learnt a hundred lessons in no time at all, she realised, and his ability to use initiative was devastating.

She was jerking now, dancing like a puppet and grinding her sex on his leg. She felt her juices flowing freely, seeping out onto the cloth of his trackpants and soaking it, while David's sly fingertips plagued her. He was touching her anus through her shorts and panties, pressing and prodding and rubbing as her mind filled with flash-frame images. She saw herself being taken from behind by Julian, and being tickled by his wiry pubic hair. She saw David himself, sprawled on his bed, his perfect young rump accessible to her fingers and her tongue. Then Julian again, martyred on the trestle, his eyes and his penis weeping as Stephen possessed him completely.

As each picture appeared her sex convulsed. She tried to moan, but David sucked harder on her tongue, his fingers flicking and tormenting. She felt her legs buckle, but he held her tight, her open vulva balanced on his thigh. He was controlling her pleasure with all the skill of years of experience, and the poise of an accomplished sexual roué. It was hard to believe that less than twenty four hours ago he'd been a virgin.

Rosie was awed. She hugged him hard, crushing him to her breasts, and felt her climax bloom anew as they kissed. She wanted more and more of him, and as he began to lower her to the grass beneath their feet, and their bodies momentarily lost contact, she whimpered.

Seconds later she was cooing with delight again, and wriggling in her efforts to help him strip off their lower garments. Her shorts and knickers went flying across the turf, closely followed by his trackpants and briefs – which got tangled round his trainers in their haste.

A de-briefing! she thought hysterically, then stopped thinking altogether when he entered her with a swift, vital thrust.

'Oh David, David, David,' she groaned as his lips touched her face, her neck and her ears. He was kissing her hair too, where it had come free of her ponytail, mouthing the thick silky strands and rubbing his cheeks playfully against it. She could feel him biting and nipping and nuzzling as his penis moved strongly inside her.

Rosie cried out again, wordlessly, when her flesh seemed to flutter and vibrate around him in a delicious high frequency wave. She could feel him jerking inside her, and held him tight as his whole body bucked and leapt. He was taking his pleasure in her arms, but instead of shouting or screaming, he just let out a long, falling sigh that flowed like a breeze across her throat.

It was the heat of the sun on her legs that roused Rosie. She sensed that they'd both nodded off for a moment, still joined. Suddenly, she felt concern for David's bottom. It was bare, pale, and had probably never been exposed like this before. Trying her best not to shatter the moment, she urged him to get up and get covered.

But for several seconds, he wouldn't budge. He just raised the upper part of his body and looked down into her face, his eyes huge and golden.

'See,' he said softly. 'You're not the only one . . . I can teach *you* a thing or two!' There was something so knowing in his voice, so triumphant, that she struggled like an eel to shake him off.

Goddamn the young bugger, he knew! He knew what she was here for! What her *real* job was!

'What do you mean?' she enquired warily as at last he climbed to his feet, then reached for her panties and shorts.

'You're here to teach me, aren't you?' he said, passing them to her, his manner smug and jaunty. 'You're my tutor. For sex. Aren't you?'

Rosie studied the lace inset on her panties as if she'd never seen it before, then concentrated intently upon sliding the garment on, while David put on his things too.

How could she answer, she wondered. She couldn't deny what was true. There was nothing on paper, but she had said 'yes'. And she was certainly being grossly overpaid for her library work.

'I'm a librarian, David,' she averred stubbornly as she wiggled her shorts up over her hips.

'Bullshit!' he said with relish, as if he'd just discovered the word and been dying to use it. 'I've hardly ever seen you in the library in the daytime!'

'Cheeky tyke!' she said, lunging at him. 'I've only worked for Julian a few days, and it takes time to set up all the systems and stuff!'

David was ticklish, Rosie realised as she grabbed him round the waist. Very ticklish indeed. Within seconds, he was giggling uncontrollably and squirming on the

218

grass beneath her as she sat astride him. If they hadn't only just made love the position would have been dynamite; and even so, Rosie felt temptation stir again. His body was so strong and fit and solid as he thrashed and bounced between her legs.

'Look, you,' she said leaning over him, breathing in the fresh tang of his sweat. 'I *am* here to catalogue Julian's library, both this one and the one in London –' She hesitated, unable to resist touching his fine pale brow and his shiny fox-brown hair. 'But I admit there *is* another dimension to the job. And it *is* what you said . . .' She shrugged, thinking back and trying to remember just how she'd agreed. 'It just seemed liked a good idea at the time!'

'So you really are my teacher,' he whispered, gazing up at her, his eyes a brighter gold than ever. Between the cheeks of her bottom, Rosie felt his penis try to rise; then felt her own sex grow sticky in response. In a panic, she sprang to her feet, almost frightened that she could want him again so soon. She also had a powerful sixth sense that someone was watching them from the house, even though they were still a fair distance away.

'Yes, I am,' she said lightly, reaching out to urge David to his feet, 'but I think we'd better postpone the next lesson. I've a sneaking feeling that someone's spying on us.'

As she spoke, there was a bright flash of reflected sunlight from the direction of Stonehaven.

That's Celeste's window! thought Rosie, with absolute certainty. Oh God, what if she's got a pair of binoculars?

'Come on, let's jog,' she said crisply, starting to run on the spot. She carefully kept her distance from David, not quite sure if she could resist him if he grabbed her.

'You're kidding,' he gasped. 'I've just –' He stopped and blushed furiously.

Rosie smiled to herself, glad that he still had at least some of his shyness left.

'Look, young man,' she remonstrated, in an affected schoolma'am tone. 'If you want to learn, you're going to have to build up your stamina. So look lively!' Then, without waiting for further protest, she turned in the direction of the house and set off at a fairly fast run.

Almost immediately, she heard the thud-thud of his feet behind her, then within seconds he was jogging at her side.

'Race you, miss!' he cried cheekily, then launched himself forward with a breathtaking energy and speed. Several yards ahead, he turned around and stuck out his tongue, then was running again in an instant, his muscular thighs pumping and working in a stride that was as long as an athlete's and as graceful as a big hunting cat's.

'You're on, lion cub,' said Rosie softly to his retreating back, then set off more slowly in pursuit.

As he ran, David relaxed and let images flood his brain. Pictures, impressions, sensations; some strange and many-faceted; others familiar, but seen with eyes that were brand new and knowing.

In less than a day, everything had changed. The thing he'd beem dreaming of since his arrival in London had happened. He'd made love with a woman. Had sex. Fucked. That last word seemed hard but had its own earthy splendour; a rawness that perfectly expressed what had happened just now on the grass.

David could feel his sex bouncing as he jogged. It felt warm and lingeringly sensitive, as if his flesh were imprinted with the memory of Rosie. He imagined himself still inside her, sheathed and embraced by that living sleeve that had a mind and movement of its own. Please no, he thought in confusion, as his penis began to stiffen again, and ache from the motion of his run. It was as if he could still feel those concentric, rippling waves. Still feel the heat of her body, and still hear her shrill cries of pleasure.

To carry on running took a supreme effort of will. Desire brought a soft, giving sensation to his belly and a precarious weakness to his joints. If he stopped con-

centrating for a second, his legs would buckle and he'd
fall down onto the sun-warmed turf; clutching at his
painful erection and rubbing it to a frenzied relief.

But do I love her? he thought, deliberately choosing
the thorniest question to try and rise above his tortured
body.

Love for David had always been a warm, gentle feeling that he equated with safety and security. The patient
kindliness of his grandparents, that inspired love. So did
the wayward, contrary affection of the cat he'd had as a
child.

But now these sentiments seemed meek and mild
compared to the crazy things he felt about Rosie. He felt
like a savage, in both mind and body, whenever he even
looked at her. She was warm and gentle towards him,
and he would have liked to be more that way towards
her. He'd managed it in the boathouse loft, but it was
difficult. And getting even more so. One hint of the
shape of her body, and he was gone. The curve of a
large, luscious breast, or the sweet little dink of her navel, or the long, smooth sweep of a thigh; and he was
like a poker inside his briefs. The more he got, the more
he seemed to need. And seeing such sights as he'd seen
in the boathouse didn't help either.

From his readings and responses so far, David had
deduced that he was a perfectly normal heterosexual.
He liked looking at women and fantasising about them,
and he certainly knew now that he adored making love
to them. He'd never thought about men sexually at all.
Or at least not until this morning.

Seeing Julian and Stephen had excited him intensely;
both the sex act they'd shared, and the bizarre ritual
drama that had gone with it. Easing at last into a
smooth, but automatic stride, he let his mind run unfet-
tered and free. He wondered what it would be like to be
smacked with a strap, or to take, or be taken, by Julian.
His bowels felt hot as he imagined the pressure within
and the pain without. After last night, he knew that his
bottom and anus were especially sensitive, and though

221

he couldn't quite summon the texture of the strap across his buttocks, he could certainly understand penetration. A penis couldn't feel all that much different to a finger or a tongue; it was only a question of size. He imagined something very stiff, yet velvet-skinned pushing into him, and almost stumbled because the sensation was so vivid. Breathing heavily, he banished all thoughts of men from his mind, and returned his attention to Rosie.

Specifically to the concept of having her spread out and subjugated before him. He pictured her tied across that bar in a really beautiful dress, something silky and blue that made her skin and hair gleam and her eyes look like sapphire stars. Her bottom was ignominiously bare and her panties were dangling around her knees. This exposure seemed totally rude to him, and far more exciting than full nakedness. Between swathes of clothing, her skin looked whiter and more nude. He liked the thought of seeing the purse of her sex from behind. Seeing it moisten and swell as he stroked her, the pink flesh glistening, and the soft leaves puffing out towards him. As he charged on towards the house, he imagined putting his hands on her buttocks, and squeezing them and mashing them until she groaned. Then he'd take a stick or a whip, and beat her bottom to fuchsia pinkness, and thrash it until her throat was raw with her screams.

What's wrong with me? he thought wildly as he reached the edge of the formal garden and suddenly hit an oxygen deficit. He'd been racing like an olympian, running from what he wanted most, and as he turned round and leant forward – hands on knees, gulping in air – he saw Rosie had fallen behind, and was running at a steady prudent pace, her limbs moving smoothly and easily.

God, she's lovely! he thought as he got back his breath and felt his heartbeat settle. His tutor was no sylph-like supermodel by any means, but her overall shape was superb. She was a modern classic; voluptuous, yet sleek. She went in and out exactly where she should do, in a series of lush, harmonious sweeps.

And it wasn't just her body. She had a pretty face too, with big, stormy-blue eyes, an impish, slightly turned-up nose, and a mouth that was as pink as raspberries. Her long hair shone, and always seemed to fall into a stylish shape; even now when it danced and lifted as she ran, or some minutes ago, when it had fanned across the grass like a halo while he'd taken his pleasure in her body. She was everything that was beautiful, David realised, and he could only thank fate for having met her. With his parochial background, and his sexually constrained upbringing, it was a miracle things had worked out so well. He could just as easily have lost his virginity to some nervous girl back in Yorkshire; some-one from school, perhaps, who would have meant no-thing to him. Both he and this hypothetical partner would have been too young to know what they were doing, and both would have ended up disappointed.

Instead, though, through destiny and the good offices of his unconventional cousin, life had worked out very differently. He'd been shielded from sex until he was ready. He'd been preserved until there was a warm, grown-up, incredibly fine-looking woman who was spe-cifically around to teach him. It was the most bizarre and unlikely of arrangements, but he was desperately, desperately glad of it.

Especially when Rosie padded to a halt in front of him, and stood catching her breath as he had. Her round breasts heaved and shook in a way that made his belly twist with lust. He almost wanted to fall down on his knees and weep with gratitude. Gratitude towards Rosie for simply existing, and towards Celeste and Julian for helping him find her.

'Good grief! I must be really out of shape,' panted Rosie, hands on hips and head tilted back as she drew in deep breaths of air. The run had been exhilarating and sur-prisingly easy considering what had immediately pre-ceded it. She could hardly believe she'd made violent love on the grass, then jumped up and run half a mile afterwards. She hadn't raced with David, but her pace had been good. In spite of what she'd just said, she was impressed by her own fitness. Lots of sex must be good for your stamina, she observed wryly, resolving to test out the theory some more.

David regarded her steadily. 'Your shape is wonderful, Rosie,' he murmured, as he stepped towards her, his eyes bright and golden. Rosie sensed that he wanted to kiss her again – and not leave it at a kiss for that matter – and her insides quivered at his touch.

'Somebody might be watching,' she whispered when his arms folded all the way around her, and his lips settled gently on her neck. She could feel him hard as stone against her belly, and marvelled at how quickly a young man could recover and be ready for another round of sex.

'I don't care!' he hissed, moving his hips suggestively.

'Well, I do!' she answered, fighting him, yet failing to get free. His strength was unexpected, and his arms were like tempered steel binding. Rosie felt a lovely melting, yielding sensation start to pour through her loins like honey, and was profoundly tempted to encourage him. She imagined making love right here on the stone-flagged path in full view of the house; with Celeste and God alone knew who else watching from behind the curtains. It would be outrageous, but she longed to try it.

With obvious reluctance, David finally let her loose. 'I'm sorry,' he said quietly. 'I don't know what's got into me. I . . . I feel aroused all the time.' He looked down at his tell-tale bulge.

'Come on. Let's have a swim,' said Rosie with sudden inspiration. She'd seen the pool briefly on her first look around, and right now its cool, blue water seemed the perfect solution to their heat. They could dowse their unruly fires a bit, gain respite and have time to think. 'And after that, I really must show my face in the library.' She stuck out her tongue at David and his sceptical 'you're kidding!' look. 'Because no matter what you want to believe, I *was* taken on to look after Julian's books!' David was grinning now, trying not to laugh. 'As well as one or two other little matters . . .'

The poolhouse, when they reached it, was a veritable tropical paradise, part of a big, open plan conservatory that abutted onto the side of the house. At one end of the pool was a lounging area, complete with a selection of thoughtfully cushioned wrought iron garden furniture; and at the other was a tiled deck and changing complex – complete with showers, cubicles and lockers. Tubs of flowers and flowering shrubs were dotted around this area too, and the whole of the poolhouse was like some kind of 'green' environmental bubble, filled with the fresh scent of foliage and alive with the gentle, pervasive lapping of the water. A door at the far end of the complex led – unsurprisingly, given Julian's obsession with fitness – to a small but well equipped gym. There was also, Rosie noticed as they entered, a full size leather-covered massage table in the changing area. A fixture that reminded her of Ladybird, and the promise of aromatherapy.

'What a gorgeous place,' whispered Rosie, then jumped when her voice echoed off the high glass roof over the pool. 'It's like a Caribbean holiday without the hassle of flying . . .' Her voice petered out as a discouraging fact dawned on her. The water was sparkling and deliciously tempting; but she had no swimsuit. She could swim in her underwear she supposed, but it was all sweaty and sticky. Not a particularly inviting prospect.

'Celeste and Julian swim in the nude, apparently,' said David from behind her, having obviously read her mind, 'although I've never actually seen them myself.'

'But what about the staff?' Rosie queried, turning the idea over and finding it dangerously appealing. All her body and her clothing felt grubby, and there were shreds of grass sticking to her bottom, she was sure of it. The thought of plunging into all that crystalline clarity was so alluring it almost made her ache. She wanted

225

to dive in and be renewed; made ready to do everything again.

'They tend to stay out of the way most of the time.' David quirked his fine dark brows. 'Well, you know what Julian and Celeste are like . . . They're always doing *something*!'

'Too true,' murmured Rosie, deciding that the tendency towards exhibitionism must be catching. It wasn't more than half an hour ago that she and David had been putting on a performance – rolling around on the turf half-naked, making love in plain sight of the house.

'Shall we, then?' asked David, a touch of trepidation in his voice, in spite of his previous assurances.

'What . . . Swim naked?' The water shimmered and danced and Rosie could no longer resist it. Without answering, except for a wink, she began pulling off her small amount of clothing. Trainers and socks, sweat top and shorts, pants and bra; she let them fall to the tiled floor around her. She caught her reflection in the glass of the opposite wall and saw a curvaceous wood-nymph about to descend into the water. As she half-twirled she realised she'd been right about her bottom. She was indeed festooned with stalks and grass, not to mention dark, earthy smears where she'd been slid along by David's strong thrusts.

Mindful of the purity of the water, she decided to shower before she went into the pool. She needed to urinate too, and slid discreetly into one of the several closed cubicles, set modestly out of the way around a corner. As she sighed with relief, she heard an adjacent door close quietly. Wild, plunging sex had obviously had the same bladder-stimulating effect on David, and the picture of him holding his penis and peeing had a powerful sexual resonance. Rosie had a sudden wish to be standing beside him, cradling him tenderly, kissing his neck as she directed his stream.

Banishing the bizarre thought, she finished, flushed, then made her way into the changing area. Beneath one of the open, Japanese style showers, she began to sluice off the grime and greenery. The water heat was adjust-able but she kept it cool; anything to zap herself to wakefulness and shake off her strange erotic cravings. She closed her eyes, and let the water cascade over her face, her hair and her body, vaguely aware that David had stripped off too, and had stepped into the shower beside her to wash off the grass on his body.

Wet and naked, they walked together to the water's edge, then slid in. Rosie was intensely aware of the beauty of David's body, but somehow the feeling was more tender now than lustful. She knew she'd soon want him again, but for the moment it was nice to just swim together as friends, as companions, and to laugh and splash and frolic for the sheer, high-spirited fun of it.

The sensation of swimming naked was unusual, but extremely pleasant. It was the first time Rosie had ever swum in the buff, but she decided that from now on she would take every opportunity to do so. There was a delicious but subtle excitement in the flow of water where it didn't usually flow; the silken rush as it slid over her breasts and buttocks, and the delicate tantalis-ing drag as it filtered through her soft, pubic bush. Sur-reptitiously, she took a sideways glance towards David, and wondered what effect nude swimming was having on his penis.

David was a strong swimmer, and he cut through the water very smoothly, his thick hair plastered dark against his scalp like the pelt of an otter or a seal. He appeared completely unperturbed by his naked state – at least until the tap tap tap of footsteps sounded on the tiles of the conservatory, and Rosie saw his face start to colour with embarrassment.

She hardly dare look up herself, but when she did, she saw Ladybird. The fitness trainer was standing on the poolside, smiling and staring into the water, her green eyes bright with pure mischief.

Chapter 13

A Scentsational Experience

*L*adybird looked wonderful; sleek and beautiful in form-fitting blue lycra leggings and matching skimpy top. Her red hair was loose on her shoulders, and her whole expression was one of devilment. It was obvious that she knew they were naked, and thoroughly approved of the state.

'Hi, you guys!' she called out cheerily. 'Mind if I join you?'

'No . . . Of course not,' said Rosie, treading water in the deep end. David closed his mouth where it had fallen open in surprise, and this caused him to splutter and cough.

Ladybird seemed to take that as a yes and began peeling off her clothes. In a trice, she was magnificently stripped and walking to the edge of the deep end, where she dived in neatly and cleanly. She was no paddler either, and didn't stop to chatter when she surfaced. Using a long, easy crawl, she powered cleanly from one end of the pool to the other at a speed that made Rosie feel distinctly hippopotamus-like.

Even so, Rosie couldn't find it in herself to resent Ladybird; and as she swam along at her own slower, but not unrespectable pace, her mind was filled with the striking but all too fleeting vision of the fitness trainer's perfect golden body.

David was obviously thinking of it too; from time to time he stared across the pool intently as if his unusual eyes could see clean through the light-distorting water to the superb female shape beneath. Rosie's thoughts drifted back to his penis, and its state as he swam. Was he hard again? Turned on by this streamlined, super-fit woman?

Taking the idea further, she wondered how David would react to being with *both* of them. Given this opportune gathering, it was the next logical step. She'd been shackled by conventions of one-on-oneness herself for far too long, but now she could see new ways to love. Could he? Or was it still too soon? Too early? Considering his progress so far, she thought not. He was quite a free-thinker in the making; an untrammelled, generous soul who could give himself joyously to many.

As if reading her mind, Ladybird suddenly broke out of her series of disciplined lengths and swam across to tread water at Rosie's side.

'Are you up for that massage then?' she asked, wiping the water from her face, and grinning challengingly.

'Yes, I'd love it,' Rosie answered, feeling her heart skip wildly in her chest. 'And I think David would too.' She nodded over to where their companion was floating in a corner and watching them closely. 'Do you do men as well?'

'Try and stop me,' crowed Ladybird, striking out strongly for the side of the pool, then climbing from the water in all her glory, clearly proud of her fabulous shape.

Rosie was slightly less proud of *her* shape, but felt a hundred per cent better about it than she had a couple of weeks ago. And what doubts she had were quashed when both Ladybird's and David's eyes widened appreciatively at the sight of her.

Their scrutiny was like wine surging straight to her belly. She felt intoxicated and aroused, consumed by a rich sensuality that made her slow her steps and almost flaunt her nudity as she walked across to the leather covered table.

229

'Ladybird's going to give me a massage,' she called across to David, who lingered in the water. 'Do you want to watch?'

His pale face looked flushed, and she saw him swallow. It made her smile. He was erect in the water, she guessed, and too embarrassed to emerge while they watched him.

'You can probably see from where you are,' she suggested, tacitly acknowledging his condition and making him blush even harder.

'Yes, I can,' he said quietly, then agitated the water around him as if to make sure they couldn't see his stiffness. 'I think I'll stay here a while . . .'

'No sweat,' she answered, feeling a lazy thrill of power. 'Just remember you've to come out eventually.'

David's face showed non-commitment, and he ducked under the water to avoid the issue.

'Don't worry,' whispered Ladybird, setting out an assortment of bottles and other nick-nacks on the tiled counter near the table. 'By the time I've finished with you, he'll be in such a state that he'll kill to get on this table!'

Rosie shivered. She'd never had a massage before, and the thought of Ladybird's long flexible hands working her over made her body feel hot and weak. What she'd said earlier to David was now more true than ever. She was suddenly ravenous for pleasure, and her sex felt a mile wide and yearning. Even the smallest movement was uncomfortable, and the urge to touch her clitoris made her dizzy.

'Just lie on the couch and relax,' urged Ladybird, as if sensing her arousal. 'That's it. On your front first.' The trainer had covered the leather surface of the couch with a thick fluffy towel, and when Rosie settled gingerly down, the soft nubbly fabric seemed to caress every part of her it touched. Moaning under her breath, she flexed her hips and thighs luxuriantly, then pressed her sex down hard against the couch.

She'd closed her eyes as she'd lain down, but after a

230

second she opened them again and turned her face towards the pool. David had come to the water's edge and was staring back at her, his own eyes huge with wonder, as if he'd heard her tiny, hungering cry and correctly interpreted its cause. His gaze was so intense it was an embrace in itself, triggering heat in her vulva and her breasts. She was simmering, sizzling, at boiling point – and Ladybird hadn't even touched her. Unable to help herself, she wriggled again, holding David's almost agonised look as she rode her own surging desire.

As she began to gasp, her nostrils were suddenly assaulted by fragrance. A strong floral scent was drifting across from where Ladybird was concocting her magic – the sweet blend of aromatherapy oils that were intended for Rosie's bare body.

'Oh God, what's that? It smells beautiful,' Rosie murmured, drawing in the sumptuous vapours.

'Well, basically it's sweet almond oil, blended with a few stronger essential oils in a combination that both stimulates and soothes the senses,' said Ladybird authoritatively, drawing close. 'It's an aphrodisiac,' she whispered in Rosie's ear, moving her long hair carefully out of the way and tying it with a soft towelling cord. 'When I massage you, you'll come and come and come.' Her breathy voice sounded just as much threatening as it did promising. 'And I'll hardly even have to touch your pussy.'

'What . . . what is it I can smell though?' gasped Rosie, knowing she barely needed touch now.

'Let's see,' said Ladybird, making slick, slurpy squishing sounds as she charged her fingers with oil, 'There's a mixture of jasmine, rose maroc, sandalwood and cumin . . . It's my own favourite blend. I use it when I want particularly strong orgasms.'

This time she didn't lower her voice at all, and as Rosie looked again towards David, she saw him almost salivating with lust, his young face a taut, aroused mask. She couldn't see his hands, but she had no doubt at all that one of them was folded round his penis.

'Brace yourself,' purred Ladybird softly, then placed her slender hands on Rosie's shoulders and drew them slowly down the full length of her torso in one fluid, extenuated sweep.

The sensation of being oiled was so exquisite that Rosie trembled all over. The epicentre of the shivers was in her groin, but as Ladybird coated her scrupulously, the warm, slippery substance made every part of her tingle with pleasure.

Closing her eyes again, Rosie groaned without shame. Her yearning for genital contact seemed to double and treble as the oil sank into her skin, yet perversely, she wanted the wait to be drawn out and prolonged. Ladybird began the real massage on the back of her neck for starters, humming a tune as her fingers skimmed and circled. As she went lower, along the shoulders and down the back, Rosie was possessed again by a massive need to touch herself, to slide her hand between the couch and her belly and drive her fingers into the core of her sex. Just the thought created tension in her arm, which Ladybird was instantly aware of.

'Bad girl! Mustn't touch!' she hissed, as if Rosie's craving had been written on her flesh.

'Please . . . Oh God, I'm dying,' whimpered Rosie as her masseuse moved on and began to concentrate on a small patch of skin just an inch above the crease of her buttocks.

Rosie cried out, louder this time. It was as if that minute area was a button – a switch – connected by a fine hot wire directly to the tip of her clitoris. She whined and wriggled, unable to stop herself, electrified by the giant wave of feeling. Her hands clenched automatically at her sides, shaking as she fought to control them.

'Very well then,' said Ladybird, her husky voice revealing that she too was affected by the odours. 'Here, David, make yourself useful!' she called out, and almost immediately there was a commotion in the water.

Half delirious, Rosie opened her eyes, and saw David moving towards her from the pool. His penis was sticking out before him, superbly erect, with a stream of

232

water flowing lewdly from its tip. Rosie remembered her peculiar fancies in the lavatory, and moaned again at this new rush of yearning.

As he reached the side of the table, Rosie felt two sets of hands touch her body; Ladybird's guiding David's. She lifted her belly to give them access, then screamed out in an instantaneous climax when a wedge of laced fingers rubbed her clitoris. Dimly, she felt Ladybird withdraw and resume her uniquely skilled massage, while David's hand remained, and worked diligently in the chink of her sex. His narrow fingertips seemed to have absorbed Ladybird's talent somehow, and the masturbation he gave was slow and delicate, yet still sufficiently forceful to bring Rosie to peak after peak.

Amazed, she heard her own shouts and yells echoing off the glass roof of the poolhouse. Her crotch was a well of burning pleasure, and her whole body alive with juddering swells of blissfulness that swept out from her vulva in circles and were stirred by Ladybird's kneading. She felt as if she were going to expire, orgasm herself into oblivion, and when she knew she could take no more, she begged her tormentors to cease.

Whimpering and snuffling into the couch, she was aware of them gently complying, then kissing her – one after the other – on the heavily oiled lobes of her bottom. In a brief lucid instant, she wondered where David had got the idea to do something so ritualistic, then surmised that he'd merely copied Ladybird. Whatever, the tender little gesture was beautiful.

For many minutes, Rosie floated in a spaced out, slack bodied haze. It was as if she'd been a bomb of sensation that had gone off with a bang, then left perfect inner silence in its wake. She could hear the ripple of the water, and small sounds of movement nearby, indistinct and unattributable. She could feel the diffuse heat of the sun on her back, filtered by the creeping vines that grew up the inside of the glass, and also by the glass itself, that seemed to offset the fiercest of the rays and admit only beneficent light.

233

Pleasure such as she'd experienced wasn't easily gotten over, but at length, she pushed strongly with her hands and sat up as gracefully as she could.

A charming sight met her eyes. David and Ladybird were kneeling on a pile of towels – and she was slowly massaging his back. They were both still naked, and David still erect; yet there seemed nothing overtly sexual about their actions. David was stretching his shoulders from time to time, and making small sounds of contentment – but clearly only from the easing of knotted muscles.

'Ha! It lives!' said Ladybird pertly, pausing in her slow digital glide across David's scapulae.

Rosie managed a lopsided grin. Her body was fully satisfied now, but there was still a heart-tugging attractiveness about the couple before her. If she'd had the energy, she would have wanted one, or more probably both of them, but instead, she accepted a temporary hiatus. There would be other days, and all just as delicious.

'Do you want this table now?' she asked, her voice coming out in a soft, almost mouselike squeak.

'Yes,' answered Ladybird, rising lithely. 'But only if you can stand, sweetheart.'

'I'll try,' Rosie said, then slid her feet cautiously to the floor. When she straightened her legs and tried to stand, her knees felt like water and she swayed. In a flash both David and Ladybird were beside her. David pulled up a nearby stool and helped her to sit down on it; while Ladybird draped her around the shoulders with another of the freshly laundered towels.

'Are you alright now,' the beautiful trainer asked, crouching down to touch Rosie's cheek. David just stood to one side, an expression of concern on his fine young face, while his erection was as solid as ever. It jutted out imposingly in front of him, pointing towards them, although David himself seemed barely aware of it as he looked worriedly in Rosie's direction.

'Believe me, I feel fabulous. Never better,' she replied, feeling her strength and vitality flood back. She fixed

David with a long, steady look. 'And I seem to think it's your turn now, if I remember rightly.'

'Right, my boy, up onto that couch,' said Ladybird with a fair degree of authority. Whatever doubts she'd had about relating to David were now obviously gone. She looked strikingly confident and physically stunning. In the realm of the senses, she was queen, supreme and empowered by her skills.

With a sure, natural elegance, David did as he was told, but then hesitated, kneeling on the couch. Rosie covered a smile with her hand, although really it wasn't funny. To squash a hard-on like that beneath him would be painful. Poor devil, she thought, watching him stare bemusedly at his own stiff manhood.

'On your back, Sunny Jim!' said Ladybird, reaching out to touch the offending member. 'We'll need full access to this . . .' She tapped his penis playfully and he gasped. Rosie saw his face contort, and his flanks quiver with effort. Slowly, and with extreme care, he lay down on his back, his splendid but unruly young cock pointing proudly at the distant glass roof. As he closed his eyes and settled back into stillness, Rosie could sit no longer, but rose to her feet and moved in closer to the table, knotting her towel around her waist as she walked.

Ladybird said nothing, but winked broadly, reaching into the sports holdall she'd placed on the counter earlier. From its depths she pulled out a bunch of the same soft towelling ties that she'd used for Rosie's hair. Her green eyes glittered like shards of emerald, and Rosie sensed a game beginning.

She bit down on her lip and held in a gasp, when Ladybird began arranging David's body on the couch – with his arms bent back above his head, and his legs widely parted. Rosie had noticed that there were metal rings bolted to the four corners of the couch, but she'd not really thought about their purpose. She'd supposed they were something to do with shifting the weighty contraption around, but realised now that they weren't.

They were for bondage. To secure some unwilling –
or willing – subject to the table for the purposes of erotic
stimulation. Even as the idea dawned, Ladybird nodded
pointedly in the direction of David's feet, and handed
Rosie two pieces of towelling, while taking two more for
herself.

David had been strangely passive on the table, but as
he felt their efforts to secure him, he began to struggle.
'What's happening?' he demanded, his right leg kicking
and snaking in Rosie's grip.

'Keep still, David,' commanded Ladybird, her voice
steely and strange.

Rosie was impressed, then suddenly realised that this
role wasn't new to her friend. Ladybird had done this
before, obviously, and her tangible aura of dominance –
and the way she'd co-ordinated the restraints – suggested that she was intimately familiar with the more esoteric uses of this particular table.

I wonder who it was last time? thought Rosie as she
fastened the ties around the ankles of a chastened and
motionless David.

Julian? Very likely. He obviously liked that sort of
thing. Or perhaps Celeste, who seemed quite catholic in
her sexual tastes and probably loved anything slightly
decadent.

Rosie's fingers faltered and she fumbled with a knot.
What if Ladybird had chosen to tie *her* up? Then done
exactly the same exquisitely arousing things that she'd
done earlier? As she finally managed to make the tie
safe, Rosie imagined it was her own body stretched helplessly on the couch. She could almost feel David's finger on her clitoris, rubbing it gently as she bucked and
heaved in her bonds, torn apart by overpowering sensation.

And more shocking than even the fantasy of being
tied, was the realisation that she actually wanted it.
Watching Ladybird scrupulously wash her hands, then
begin mixing her oils again, Rosie made a silent vow to
sample these strange delights as soon as she was able –

which in *this* household could be a matter of hours rather than days, she concluded wryly.

'Can you dry him off for me, please,' asked Ladybird as a new and equally delectable aroma-blend seemed to fill their immediate environment. This mix seemed more robust somehow, sharper in its top notes, and decidedly male. Combining oils and their perfumes was clearly an art form, and one that Ladybird excelled in. Picking up a fresh towel from the heap, Rosie made a second mental note. She'd like to learn this skill too, just as soon as she could think straight again.

David shuddered as she pressed the soft fabric to his skin. Instinct made her avoid his genitals though; mainly because his prick was so stiff and inflamed that the slightest of touches might trigger him. She'd come quickly herself under Ladybird's scented ministrations, and been glad of it, but she wanted David's experience to last longer. She wanted his pleasure to endure and be extended to its utmost limit. This was yet another whole new world for him, and she didn't want it rushed or hurried.

Smoothing the towel over David's body, she dried his face, his torso and his limbs. He kept his eyes tightly shut throughout the process, but his strong-featured face was revealing. His mouth narrowed with strain as she neared his groin, and he stirred restlessly, tugging at his bonds. On a whim, she leant over his prick and blew on it, and immediately he cried out, his hips bucking up towards her.

'Naughty!' said Ladybird chidingly, but to which of them, Rosie couldn't tell. The scent of the oil was overwhelming – it made her feel giddy and daring. It filled her head with smells that were hot and animal and spicy. She caught a citrus note somewhere in the blend, and found its bite both exciting and euphoric.

'Stand by . . . He'll need you,' said Ladybird calmly as she poured the potion onto her hands, then moved closer to David's quaking body. With the lightest of strokes she began annointing his arms and shoulders, then worked smoothly across his chest and his ribcage.

The massage was brisk and businesslike, and it was hard to tell which element affected David most: the kneading or the pungent aromas. He began shifting around on the couch and moaning in a long, sub-vocal chunter. As Ladybird reached some particularly sensitive spot, he'd squirm like a wild thing and gasp; then relax again when she moved on to somewhere less critical.

Quite soon though, most parts of his anatomy seemed critical. Feet and forearms, shoulders and kneejoints – wherever Ladybird patted and circled and rubbed. His hips were in constant lifting motion and his penis swayed and jumped, and ran freely with a clear, shiny fluid. Rosie felt her own resolve weakening too. She wanted to reach over, glove him gently in her fingers and bring ease to his rampant stiffness. She longed to hear him wail with rapture and gratitude, and see his grimacing face grow soft and calm. So focused was she on David, that Ladybird's sudden, faint cry, and the stilling of her deftly moving fingers came as a complete and rather piquant surprise.

'Oh God, Rosie, you're going to have to help me,' she whispered, leaning weakly against the table. David's eyes flew open as he absorbed the slight jolt, his face a picture of puzzlement and lust.

At a loss, Rosie glanced towards the bottles and the bowl with the oil in. Not quite sure what to do, she made a start towards it.

'Not that, *me*!' gasped Ladybird, swivelling around against the table, parting her long, sleek thighs and bracing her feet on the floor. 'Help me come, Rosie,' she begged. 'I know you're not sure about this, but please . . . just put your hand here and let me do the work.' On the word 'here' she flaunted her slim pelvis forward and made her moist sex open and pout between the delicate red curls of her motte.

Remembering how she'd felt in the gym back in London, Rosie didn't hesitate. She moved close and slid her hand between Ladybird's legs, gasping at her friend's

238

heat and wetness. Instinctively, she waggled her fingers
and rubbed them from side to side across Ladybird's
large bud-like clitoris. The other woman groaned heavily, and true to her word began to work herself roughly
and rhythmically on Rosie's rigid fingertips. Her slim
hips rocked and swayed, then after only a few seconds,
she let out an uncouth gurgling grunt and jammed her
hand in hard over Rosie's, almost hurting her.

'Yes! Yes! Yes!' chanted Ladybird, in the age old cliché
of orgasm, her hot flesh rippling and her juices trickling
and flowing. The spasms were deep and distinct to the
touch, but as they faded, she slumped forwards, her
slender body finding momentary support against
Rosie's. Then, just as quickly as she'd demanded her
pleasure, it was over, and the trainer stood straight
again, bouncing lightly on her toes and clearly ready to
proceed.

'Let's get on then, shall we?' she said, pouring fresh
oil into the palm of her hand as if nothing unusual had
happened.

Returning her attention to David again, Rosie saw a
man tormented by need. His handsome face was a mask,
his skin white and stretched, and there were great jag-
ged spots of high colour daubed across his elegant
cheekbones. His penis was vivid too, harder and more
angry-looking than ever. Ladybird's casual climax had
only exacerbated his lust, and he seemed only a couple
of breaths away from coming.

'Please,' he entreated softly as Rosie leant across to
stroke his sweaty brown hair off his face. As her fingers
strayed, tempted by the beauty of his features, he craned
up towards her and sucked her thumb into his mouth,
pulling on it urgently, like a comforter. It was the first
time a grown man had ever done such a thing to Rosie,
and she felt a thin twist of pleasure between her legs,
that seemed to flutter in time to his suction.

'I think he's ready,' said Ladybird suddenly, her fingers lying flat on David's belly. Rosie realised she was
meant to do something. She drew her thumb out of

David's mouth, moved behind his head, and pressed her hands against his tied-down wrists. Her hold on him was ineffectual really, but the gesture was primarily symbolic. She felt the muscles in his forearms tighten as Ladybird slowed her oily stroking, very delicately took hold of his cock, and at the same time – with her free hand – reached down between his legs to hold his balls.

'Dear God,' gasped David as Ladybird began handling him with the measured precision of a surgeon. Her grip – and her syncopated motions – remained constant even though he struggled; and within seconds he was shouting and groaning and jerking his body on the couch. Without his bonds, Rosie couldn't have held him, and she expected them to snap any moment. Oil, and his own thick fluids were squelching and squeaking through Ladybird's fingers; the noise revealing and graphic as she worked on his hard, red member. Rosie was utterly captivated, and felt her own sex drip and swell too. Especially when Ladybird's fingers slid down to the cleft of David's bottom.

'Kiss him,' she ordered curtly, nodding to Rosie and rotating her grip on David's prick. As she did so he screamed, his dark flesh leaping visibly and his rich creamy seed jetting out. Rosie wanted to watch, and to taste it, but obediently she dove around to his side and pressed her mouth down onto his.

As she pushed with her tongue, his lips yielded, even though he still tried to shout out and rave. Moulding his mouth with her lips, she drew his joyous cries inside her, absorbing the sound as if it were his very life itself. She felt like a vampire goddess, devouring his rapture and feeding on the essence of his orgasm. She wondered casually if Ladybird was sucking his penis, but found she didn't really care. His sweet young voice was born of his brain, his heart and his soul, while his semen came merely from his baser parts: his cock and his blind, aching balls.

As he finally grew still, she let her mouth rove over his face, kissing his chin, his cheeks and his eyes. With

240

him quiet at last, she straightened up and watched Ladybird finish her ministrations. There were strings of silky whiteness on David's thighs and belly, and these she massaged into his skin like an unction. It was as if the product of his magical loins was the final ingredient in her spell.

Rosie moved to stand beside Ladybird, and stared downwards. Still bound to the couch, David looked angelic, his face and body both divine and wasted. His skin was slick and gleaming, and his hair – usually so neatly combed – was all tousled into spikes and points where he'd tossed and strained in his ecstasy. He seemed only semi-conscious, but he was smiling – a perfect, innocent, beautiful grin that turned Rosie's innards to fire all over again. His cock was flaccid now, but still held a marvellous promise – as if at any second it might stretch into the long, magnificent baton she'd felt move and swoop inside her as they'd squirmed and bucked on the grass. It seemed like a lifetime ago now, but as she glanced up towards the glass, and the sky beyond, she realised it was only an hour or two. If that.

As she remembered their sunlit frolic, she wanted it again. Wanted to be back there, kissing him, tasting his tongue, breathing his joy into her mouth as he came and she came too. She looked down at his soft, sticky cock and wished it a hard hot pole that she could mount and ride to glory. She thought of their first time, on the way to Stonehaven, and of how she'd taken exactly what she wanted back then.

But if David was too tired to perform now, wasn't there always Ladybird, whose sexual power was prodigious? The beautiful trainer had said Rosie wasn't ready, but maybe she'd been wrong? Maybe now was the right time to experiment?

Then, suddenly, Rosie's anticipatory musings were shattered. She heard a high, clear voice calling her name. Someone was approaching, and looking for her. They weren't here yet, but they weren't far away either – probably in the passage that led to the main hall.

'Rosie? Are you there?' Celeste's bell-like tones rang out, much closer now. 'There's somebody here to see you!'

Rosie glanced desperately towards Ladybird, and then saw a truly extraordinary phenomenon.

It was like watching Wonderwoman, or Supergirl – naked. Rosie had simply never seen anyone move so fast or in such a highly co-ordinated fashion. In a flash, Ladybird had the ties off David's wrists and was handing him a terry-cloth robe from the selection piled nearby. To Rosie she just nodded significantly, and made folding and tucking motions.

Her heart beating wildly, Rosie picked up the cue and lashed her towel somewhat higher around her body in a makeshift but decent sarong.

By the time the double doors to the passage swung open, both she and David were clothed – although he still looked blank-eyed and dazed. Smiling broadly, Celeste swept into the room, preceding whoever the visitor was, and as she did so, Ladybird walked naked to the side of the pool and executed a smooth, almost world class dive straight into the water of the deep end.

Rosie would have liked to have congratulated her friend for her incredibly quick thinking. She would also have liked to have given David a little shake, to help him wake up. She would even have liked to have taken a closer look at Celeste, who appeared to have only just risen from her bed, and was wearing a sheer silk kimono that revealed far more than it hid.

Rosie would have liked to do all these things and more, but the sight of a familiar figure – stepping out from behind Celeste – stopped her dead and froze up her limbs.

The 'somebody to see her' was Geoff.

Chapter 14

Metamorphoses

*H*e's still as handsome as ever, thought Rosie, studying her ex over the rim of her glass. So why does it seem as if he's changed?

They were sitting in the library, at right angles to each other on matching buttoned-leather couches which were duplicates of the ones in London. Celeste had suggested that they retreat amongst the books for a private and undisturbed chat.

The introductions had been brief and disjointed. Rosie had been shocked mute for a few seconds by Geoff's unexpected arrival; but to her surprise, the impact had faded quickly. She'd even felt a bubble of excitement; a frisson of power as she'd stepped forward, smiled easily, and said 'hello'. With a poise that seemed to come from nowhere, she'd found herself playing the hostess, with the usually all-dominating Celeste mysteriously demurring to her.

And that wasn't the only change. For the first time ever, she'd looked at Geoff and seen him completely out of his depth. He had, and still did seem completely at a loss, and it amused Rosie no end. She suddenly realised that she was now quite at home in the bizarre Hadey menage; that it was perfectly natural to be amongst people in various stages of undress, some with their faces still flushed with sex. She almost giggled when Ladybird popped up out of the water to say 'hi' and displayed her beautiful breasts. Geoff nearly choked, however, and then was overcome by a fit of furious coughing when Celeste's kimono started sliding sideways and showed a flash of her black pubic hair.

The only person Rosie had been mildly worried about was David – but even he non-plussed her ex boyfriend. He held out his hand and offered a courteous 'how do you do', his expression as grave as that of an alien prince inspecting his guard of honour. Rosie felt the giggles surge through her again, then an instant later, felt a wild flash of anger. David's composure had been so exquisite she could have kissed him, yet she'd also noticed Geoff's swift but familiarly dismissive expression at the sound of a second northern accent.

Bastard! she'd thought silently, making an inner vow to get him for that. Although even now, some quarter of an hour later, she hadn't quite worked out how.

Geoff was still in a state of semi-shock.

A few minutes ago, Celeste had tottered in, swaying theatrically on her flimsy high-heeled mules, and carrying a bottle of wine and two glasses. 'I thought you'd like this,' she said, her voice soft and suggestive, then sashayed out again, her robe drifting clear of her bare white bottom as she wiggled and simpered outrageously. Rosie had had to cover her grin with her hand, and was still smiling now, thinking of the other woman's complicity. She'd seen Celeste glide like a mannequin in far higher heels, and in even trickier dresses. The whole performance had been an attempt to deliberately unsettle Geoff.

And it's bloody well worked! thought Rosie, taking another sip of wine and appreciating its sparkling fruitiness. She suspected that the wine itself was another ploy. Although it probably wasn't something she'd drink herself, Celeste had brought them Rosie's favourite sweet Italian spumante – as if tacitly stating that in this house, *her* preference was the correct one, and not the dryer, more sophisticated product that Geoff might have expected. Draining her glass, she reached discreetly for the bottle. Her stomach was empty, and she'd been giddy with sex to start with, but she didn't care. Against all the odds, and when the mood should have been high trauma, she was thoroughly enjoying herself.

'Who is that woman?' demanded Geoff peevishly, running his fingers through his thick blond hair.

Rosie had to admit he looked particularly attractive this morning. He was wearing a soft fawn shirt, and chinos; the sort of colours that had always suited him. Designer casuals were perfect for his upwardly mobile image, and his sleek golden boy style. For a moment, Rosie thought of being in bed with him, and despite all the unkindness of his betrayal, she still found the idea appealing. She considered seducing him to assuage the desire that had been building again – just before his arrival – then stopped dead in the middle of her thought-stream.

Oh God, the changes were more profound than she'd realised. It's *me*, not him, she thought wildly, smirking into her wine, then sipping again. *I've* changed. *I've* got the advantage now, and the snivelling weasel's scared of me. She put down her glass, realising that alcohol was now superfluous, and regarded Geoff steadily and silently.

'Who is she?' he repeated, clearly rattled because she hadn't answered promptly, as she'd always done.

'Celeste?' She paused, drawing out his wait like toffee. 'She's Mrs Brent-Hadey ... My boss's wife. Isn't she beautiful?' She imbued the short description with as much sensuality as she could muster: echoes of Celeste's touch, her lips, her voice and her perfect, available body. She could feel her own sex responding to all the inferences, and hoped that Geoff would be as affected as she was. When she looked down at his linen clad groin and saw the beginnings of a bulge, she wanted to leap up and down and shout 'gotcha!' – but instead she just looked him in the eye, and studied him as intently as she could.

245

This was so much fun.

'And those others?' he persisted, his voice slightly higher than usual. Shriller. 'Who the hell are they? What's going on here, Rosie? I thought you were here to work?'

Rosie stayed quiet and calm, turning her attention inward, and as she did so, somewhere in the house, someone started playing the piano.

Oh, David, she thought, I hope I'm not hurting you. She imagined him puzzled and confused by her sudden disappearance with Geoff, then seeking solace in his artistic gift. She remembered passing through a small music room last night, and saw David in it now – at the piano, in just his trackpants, venting his frustration on the keys. The music was violent and passionate; she didn't know what it was – maybe Beethoven or Tchaikovsky perhaps? – but there was fire and lust and longing in it. She wished she was there beside him on the piano stool, ready to embrace him and offer him her body the instant the last note died away.

Meanwhile, back here in the library, she seemed to be winning a game of sorts. She had an upper hand she'd never had before, and the thrill of it, combined with the diffuse, background presence of David, made her more lustful than she could ever have imagined.

'I am here to work,' she answered, with a slight smile. 'But you know what they say about "all work and no play" . . .'

'What do you mean by "play"?' Geoff was flushed beneath his tan now, and he took a long, deep gulp at his wine – no longer bothered, it seemed, by its unfashionable fizzy sweetness.

Rosie crossed her legs before she answered, remembering an actress in a film doing something similar, to unbalance *her* inquisitor. Given the angle she was sitting at, she doubted if Geoff could actually see her pubis, but the possibility alone made him swallow.

'Well, David and I had been for a long run together, and then we had a swim.' She leaned back, and saw

Geoff's eyes lock onto the upper edge of her towel now, where it almost hung from the points of her breasts. 'After that, Ladybird arrived, and as she's an aromatherapist, we all spent some time giving each other massages ... With perfumed essential oils.'

Again, the erotic potentials weren't lost on Geoff. 'But you were all naked!' he spluttered.

'You can't do massage with clothes on,' she pointed out blandly.

'What, even with the boy?'

'The man,' said Rosie softly, touching her tongue delicately to her lower lip. The old tricks were always the best. 'David is a dear friend of mine. We've become very close over the last few days.' She paused again to let the significance sink in. 'And anyway, Geoff, what does it matter to you? You were the one that said we should split up.'

'I –' he began, but changing pace rapidly, Rosie cut him off.

'What are you doing here, Geoff? How did you find me?'

Two questions at once seemed to throw him, and he put his glass down clumsily on the table, almost spilling his wine. 'I rang the library and they told me where you were working in London. And when I went there, they told me you were in the country with the Hadeys. It's not all that hard to find!'

'But why?' she persisted silkily, then adjusted her towel.

'Because I knew I'd made a mistake. We were good together ... we shouldn't have split up.' As he spoke, he shifted uncomfortably in his seat, his eyes darting from her breasts to her legs and back again. At his own crotch, the bulge had visibly grown.

'Split up? Eeh lad, I thought you'd chucked me,' Rosie replied, making her voice a blunt, northern caricature. 'What about your new girl? Mizz "Happening" in PR?'

Geoff had the grace to look shamefaced. 'It fizzled out. She was too pushy. She was after my job, not me. The PR department was just a stepping stone. And so was I.'

247

Rosie said nothing. 'Serves you right' would have been too childish, and inappropriate for the mood she was trying to build. As she considered her best response, she realised that the piano had just fallen silent, and in her mind she followed David to his room. She imagined him stripping naked; imagined herself naked too, falling to her knees before him, kissing his body, mouthing his cock to ease his –

'Rosie, please, listen to me! Can we give it another chance?'

The interruption made her angry. Would Geoff never realise he wasn't the centre of the universe? That other men could interest her?

'We could be good together, I promise you,' he went on, oblivious to the fact that she'd barely even been listening to him. 'You could be the best possible thing for me right now. The new managing director comes from Leeds. I thought we could invite him and his wife to dinner. You know, impress him? Show him how settled we are?'

Rosie felt another huge swathe of anger. You pig! She yelled silently, wanting to rage and fume, but channelling the force of it inside her. Making it steel her resolve, and stoke the fires that burnt for others. Geoff was still a handsome brute, and if things had been different, she might have found a way to forgive him. But now he'd revealed himself to be just the same user he'd always been. And it was time to make him pay for using *her*!

'So it's not my voluptuous body you're after?' she enquired, keeping her voice smooth and pleasant as she slid across and sat beside him, then let the towel fall artfully from her breasts. It was a move worthy of Celeste herself, and the shock on Geoff's face – the instant naked lust – cried out for a polaroid camera.

'Rosie!' he hissed, glancing nervously towards the door, then looking back hungrily at her breasts.

'Ah . . . Maybe it *is* my body after all?' she said quietly, reaching for the bottle again, and making the towel fall completely apart as she poured herself another glass

248

of wine. 'Not just the fact that I could make you look good with your boss?'

'No! Yes! I don't know . . .' Geoff seemed mesmerised by her lush, pale curves. He was licking his lips, making fists with his hands. His stylish, creamy chinos were pushed out grossly at the crotch, as if her flesh was new and exotic, and he hadn't already made love to her dozens of times in the past.

'God, I can't think straight!' he stormed. 'You're so beautiful, Rosie. I'd forgotten . . . I want you so much it hurts!'

'So you want me, do you?' she said, a delicious idea forming. A scheme Celeste would have adored, 'Why don't you show me how much?'

'Oh yes, Rosie,' he murmured, launching himself towards her, his movements unco-ordinated and desperate.

Rosie held him off – even though she was tempted. He *was* a good lover. Selfish sometimes, granted, but he did have a certain brute flair.

'No, that's not what I mean,' she said, smiling obliquely, then letting her gaze drift down to his crotch. 'I said *show* me . . .'

Geoff frowned and looked downwards too, as if not wanting to believe what he suspected.

'Rosie?'

She nodded slightly, lifting her eyes to meet his.

It was a pivotal moment. Her true metamorphosis. Rosie was reminded of the heroine of the erotic novel she'd been reading. That contemporary classic she'd dipped into in London and brought with her here to Stonehaven. There had been such a moment for Josephine – the character in the book – when she stopped being a woman who let fate jostle her, and became one who took life in her own two hands and made it do what she wanted. Josephine hadn't faltered when the time had come, and she, Rosie, wouldn't either. She looked at Geoff unblinkingly, her expression controlled yet amused.

And then he shuddered. A long hard shake from head to foot as *his* change became irrevocable too. Rosie watched impassively as he fumbled with his belt, unbuttoned his stylish trousers, then reached into the folds of his boxer shorts.

His cock was rigid as he eased it out, the skin red and stretched and gleaming. A picture of need. Of abject male hunger. Of surrender – at last – to her supremacy.

'Very nice,' she said quietly, turned on but not tempted any more. His penis was just a toy to her now; something to play with. Or for *him* to play with because she wanted him to. 'Why don't you stroke it a bit? It looks as if it needs it.'

'Rosie! What's the matter with you?' he demanded, his voice unsteady.

Rosie didn't answer. Instead she leaned over and kissed him slowly on the mouth, slightly off centre. She pushed her tongue inside, then flicked it like a snake's, goading his but giving him no chance to push back. His lips were still parted as she drew back. They were moist and slack, and his eyes looked stunned. Rosie nodded briefly towards his cock and like an automaton, he took it in his hand and started squeezing.

It looked so incongruous. A crude, earthy act performed by a man so smooth and self-aware. He almost seemed not to know how to masturbate, and curiously that added a certain charm. Rosie felt arousal building but kept her expression mask-like and unrevealing. Her body was simmering, but she reserved the knowledge for herself; to make use of it later with one who better deserved it. She kept her legs neatly closed, although it cost her real discomfort. Rather that than show her flesh all shiny-wet and swollen.

Geoff was wriggling his bottom now, and his face was flushed and sweaty. 'Please,' he gasped, his teeth gritted as he pushed his pelvis towards her.

'Please what?' she murmured, reaching for her glass and taking a small sip. She barely tasted the wine; the action was only for effect.

'Please, Rosie, I need you,' he groaned. 'I really want you. You're so gorgeous. Please, give me a blow job.' He jiggled his penis winningly in her direction, trying out his old sexy smile and failing miserably.

Rosie winced inside at the crudity of his language, but on the outside remained quite still. She studied his erection sardonically, narrowing her eyes as if it were some particularly tedious cataloguing chore, and pursing her lips to increase the disapproving image. Finally, she put her glass down with a soft, decisive clump and steepled her fingers before her naked and still oily breasts.

'But I don't want that, Geoff,' she said simply, nodding downwards at his cock and the fist that enclosed it. 'And I don't especially want *you*. At least not at the moment.'

It was only a partial lie. She didn't want Geoff, the man who'd treated her so shabbily; but she did want a man. And there was no denying Geoff was a virile and good-looking one. Even with his face full of horror and incredulity.

Steeling herself magnificently, she rose gracefully to her feet. 'Goodbye, Geoff,' she said softly. 'Maybe I'll see you when I get back to town? You could introduce me to that new boss of yours. I've always thought Yorkshiremen were sexy . . .'

'But, Rosie,' stammered Geoff. To his credit, his erection remained solid, despite his obvious frustration. 'You can't do this! You're kidding . . . You're not going to leave me like this, are you?' He looked down at his body.

'I can and I will,' she replied with a blithe heart. She'd been worried about a moment such as this, but it, and Geoff had been almost childishly easy to cope with. 'Any problems, use this,' she suggested, picking up the towel and tossing it neatly across his hand and his penis.

She turned, then, and walked away from him; secure in her beauty and confidence. She could hear him protesting vehemently behind her – berating her, the house, and all its other inhabitants – but she couldn't

251

be bothered to listen. Geoff and his voice were the past, and the future was far more alluring.

As she showered and dressed in her room, there was just one picture in Rosie's mind: David, when she'd turned to look at him as she and Geoff had left the pool-house. While the water was running, she suddenly imagined she could hear music again, then saw that pure, pale face of his, and how it looked when he played the piano. She saw his solemnity and the concentration in his sovereign-coloured eyes, but when she turned off the shower, the music was gone, and she saw only his confusion once more, and the hard lines of pain and disappointment.

And yet, despite this, David had been the epitome of grace under pressure. He'd clearly suppressed what he'd felt, and been completely amenable and polite. There was no question of him not knowing who or what Geoff was but he'd shown no animosity. Rosie didn't quite understand how such gentlemanly behaviour could be erotic; but it was. She thought of his quietness, his preternatural stillness, and felt her body grow hot and needy in spite of her cool clothes, her soft, fresh perfume, and the fact that her just-washed hair was still damp where it hung on her shoulders.

She'd made a special effort to look good. Her delicate lavender skirt and camisole were light as air, almost transparent, and she wore virtually nothing beneath them. She'd rifled through her makeup box, then studied her face in the mirror and decided that in this case, less was more. Her complexion had a glow of its own, even though it was nearly as pale as David's. She'd caught a little sun this morning, but that only accounted for *some* of her radiance. The sheen on her skin and the twinkle in her smile were down to sex. To highlight the colour of her eyes, she'd applied a soft grey blue line around them, and darkened her lashes, then finished off with a soft cherry tint on her lips. She'd done nothing with her hair, except run a comb through it, once. Its

252

natural gloss and thickness were all the ornament it needed.

'You look nice,' said Ladybird as Rosie reached the bottom of the stairs.

The fitness trainer was in clothes now too, but only minimal ones, noted Rosie with a grin. A red lycra halter top and cycling shorts looked surprisingly good with Ladybird's vivid hair, and they clung to her body like paint.

'You don't look so bad yourself,' Rosie offered, feeling momentarily shy. What had passed between them by the pool had been sweet and intimate, but the fact that she'd begun making love with women as well as men was going to take some getting used to. But it would be well worth the effort, she thought, looking sideways at Ladybird's long thighs.

'Where is everybody?' she asked, suddenly realising it must be lunchtime. She wasn't hungry, but she did wonder what it would be like to sit around the table with the residents of Stonehaven after what she'd seen – and done – this morning. Then another thought occurred. Oh God, what if Geoff hadn't gone yet? What if he was still hanging around somewhere, determined to get his own way?

'Well, your blond friend went tearing off about half an hour ago.' Ladybird waggled her beautifully groomed eyebrows. 'He was burning rubber like crazy and there was gravel flying everywhere . . . What on earth did you say to him?'

'I think he was a bit annoyed,' said Rosie calmly. 'He showed me his willy, and I said I didn't fancy it. What can you do when a man can't take "no" for an answer?' She tried for deadpan, but a snigger still broke through.

'You turned down good manflesh? Shame on you!' Ladybird waved an admonishing finger.

'I'd seen something I liked better,' Rosie countered, thinking of David, and how he'd looked on the massage bench, aroused and writhing. She wished he was still there right now, waiting for her.

253

Ladybird smiled knowingly but said nothing.

'What about the others?' asked Rosie, pleating a fold of her skirt between her fingers, then noticing the other woman eyeing its sheerness.

'David was playing the piano, but he seemed to be making a bit of a meal of it, so now he's gone for a walk, I think. I saw him heading in the direction of the river,' Ladybird said very pointedly. 'And if you want to know where Celeste and Julian are, just follow me.' Her green eyes glittered, and she took Rosie by the arm and led her towards the conservatory.

When they reached the open door, Ladybird touched a silencing finger to Rosie's lips, then crept forward like a cat burglar, utterly noiseless in her high-tech trainers. Rosie followed her. Very carefully.

As they approached the pool, under cover of a thick bed of shrubs, they heard a medley of two familiar noises. The rhythmic slapping of water against tiles, and the breathy, disjointed moans of a woman being sound-ly pleasured.

Julian and his wife were in a corner of the shallow end. Celeste was lying in the water, clinging onto two handholds, while Julian was standing between her out-spread thighs, thrusting hard, with an expression of de-termined passion on his face. With one hand he was gripping his wife's hip tightly, and with the other he was bracing himself against the pool's edge. Rosie had never seen him look more male.

It was a stunning contrast to his performance earlier, when he'd cried and cringed before Stephen, but as Rosie was rapidly coming to understand, there was a sexual shapeshifter in everybody. She'd been stuck in one role herself for far too long, but now she wanted adventure. Be flexible and daring, try the strange, the outre, and the new.

Lucky David, she thought suddenly, who could be free and adventurous from the beginning, and not have to go through all the conventional mindgames she'd gone through with Geoff and his ilk.

But as she was about to draw away, and go looking for her fortunate pupil, a noise from the pool made her stay. It was Julian, crying out fiercely.

He was half-groaning, half-shouting, his slim hips a mad pumping blur as the water flew and danced in his wake. Rosie saw his hand slip on the side of the pool and just as it did, Celeste responded with an age old female gesture. She tried to enfold her climaxing husband in her arms, but with nothing at all left to anchor them, the couple went down beneath the surface in a wild, thrashing tangle of limbs.

The commotion was enormous. For a moment, it looked as if someone had thrown David's piano into the water, but eventually two bodies surfaced, still embracing and kissing and fondling, despite a lot of spluttering laughter. They were no longer joined at the groin, but they were pressed together so closely they seemed glued to one another. As they rocked and swayed, their hands ran affectionately over each other's bottoms, and they kissed and nibbled and nuzzled like a pair of sex-crazed animals.

It was an affecting sight. Rosie felt both aroused, and touched in another, deeper way. Julian and Celeste were both unprincipled libertines, yet clearly they were profoundly in love. They would both happily share their bodies with others, but at the heart of things they were devotedly married. Rosie imagined them old and grey together yet still behaving outrageously. Behind her, Ladybird sighed, as if she'd seen the same picture too.

What happened next was even more like a romanticised movie. Julian suddenly lifted his wife up in his arms and placed her gently on the side of the pool. Then, while she gazed at him lovingly, he climbed out of the water, picked her up again and carried her to one of the thickly upholstered mattresses that were set out nearby. As he lowered her onto it, Celeste locked her arms around his neck and drew him down on top of her, kissing his face with great fervour as he arranged his body over hers.

Julian's penis had been softened by his orgasm and his chaotic dowsing, but as they watched, Rosie and Ladybird saw it stiffen again and butt against Celeste's rubbing thigh. It changed, before their eyes, from tender quiescence to a rampant, demanding shaft that shone dark and red against his consort's smooth pale skin. As Rosie touched Ladybird's arm and led her away and out of the conservatory, he was just entering Celeste yet again.

'Beautiful, eh?' said the fitness trainer when they were out of earshot, and Rosie noticed her eyes were misty. She felt a bit that way herself. Sentimental. That, and incredibly aroused and hungry to enact such a scene of her own. With David.

'Yes,' she agreed quietly. 'It's the best of both worlds. Sexual freedom, but with trust and love as well. I envy them.'

'Me too,' murmured Ladybird, then shrugged and smiled, her expression good-natured. 'But I'm going to make the most of what I've got,' she said philosophically, smoothing her hands over her sleek red-covered hips. 'Seeing as David's out walking, Julian and Celeste are busy, and you're here, that means Stephen's on his own somewhere. I think I'll see if he needs a little company.'

'Go for it, girl,' said Rosie, and on impulse, leant over and kissed her friend's soft mouth, feeling an instant of piquant temptation. 'Good luck,' she whispered as they drew apart. 'Not that you'll need it. You're far too gorgeous for anyone to resist . . .' She let her voice trail away, but knew that Ladybird had understood the subtext. Their own particular time would soon come – on a day when a man wasn't quite what either of them wanted.

Rosie's heart felt light as she set off out across the grass towards the distant tree-line, and beyond it, the river and the boathouse. Every instinct she had told her David had already gone there, and in her delicate, filmy clothes and with her body fresh and perfumed, she felt like a bride going expectantly to her groom. Wrapped in

256

that sense of romanticism again, she thought how neatly the lovers in the household had divided themselves into couples. Such conventional arrangements wouldn't last long, she was sure, but for now it was a happy situation.

And the sight of Julian and Celeste had primed her perfectly. She'd been vaguely aroused to start with, having denied herself Geoff, and now she was hungry – ravenous for David's almost, but not quite virgin beauty; for his strength and his gentleness; his eagerness to learn, and his startling ability to absorb sexual wisdom at a speed that left her gasping. When he came into his prime, he was going to be quite a phenomenon; and even if she wasn't around to enjoy him then, Rosie felt privileged to be the one who had him now.

As she approached the boathouse, her nerves began to dance and tingle. She halted for a moment on the track, and ran her hands over her breasts, her belly and her loins. Sliding them up the inner slopes of her thighs, she caressed herself slowly through the fabric of her skirt. Her body felt warm and alive. Totally ready. Her sex was open and moist, her nipples hard and puckered; the moment couldn't have been more right to offer herself. Walking forward, still stroking herself, she made her way to the foot of the outside steps.

The boathouse loft was receiving more sun now. The light was filtering in through the windows that looked out onto the river and the room had a soft, golden ambience instead of its earlier gloom. When Rosie entered, she was struck for an instant by a sense of peace and stillness, and almost thought the place was empty.

But it wasn't, because like a vision from her fantasies, David was lying motionless in the centre of the large low bed. His eyes were closed and his face was as pale and smooth as a graven image. He had one hand pressed lightly to his groin, and around him lay a dozen or so books. They were strewn on the bed and on the floor, and all open at blatantly erotic illustrations. Rosie recognised *Les Baisers d'Amour* and several others she'd brought from London.

257

She'd half expected him to be naked – undressed and ready for her – but instead he lay on the quilt still clothed, the only bare part of him his feet. His trainers were on the floor, among the books, and presumably he'd not bothered with socks. Without the rest of his nude body to distract her, she couldn't help but notice the slenderness and elegance of his toes, and the vulnerability of his insteps and ankles. She was tempted to drift forward and kiss him there, but as if he'd tuned into her thoughts and intentions, he opened his eyes and regarded her steadily. His hand flexed slightly at his crotch.

Now he was looking at her, Rosie hardly dare approach him. He looked perfect and almost unattainable, even though she could now see his erection quite clearly. It was a promising bulge in his stone-faded jeans; and he'd no doubt been stroking it as he waited for her. His shirt, a soft cloud-white thing made of cheesecloth, was unbuttoned half way to his waist. She could easily imagine that just a moment ago, he'd reached inside and caressed his own nipples.

'I was thinking of you,' he said without preamble. His voice was quiet, but very calm and strong, without any hint of uncertainty. As she watched he clasped himself slowly and deliberately, announcing a readiness that balanced her own.

Shaking now, Rosie walked up to the bed, and stared down at him. 'I'm flattered,' she said, nodding down at his tumescence. She felt far more nervous now than David apparently did, and her fingers trembled as she edged a book out of the way and sat down on the bed beside him. She nodded questioningly at the volume she'd just moved. It was open at an antique, colour-washed drawing of a man and a woman entwined in the *soixante-neuf* position, licking each other's genitals with tongues that were long and flexible.

'Just doing my homework,' he muttered, sitting up. A bit of colour had come into his face now, as if her nearness had affected his confidence. 'I didn't quite know if

I'd see you again ...' he added after a moment. 'I thought you might be gone by now. I heard a car ... and I wasn't sure if you were in it or not.'

'A fortnight ago, I might have been,' she said, letting her fingers cruise his denim-clad thigh. 'But not now.'

David shifted slightly, rucking the quilt beneath him, but he managed to meet her eyes. 'I thought he was your boyfriend. He seemed very possessive. He didn't seem to like us all being together.'

'He *was* my boyfriend. But he was only possesive when it suited him,' Rosie observed, thinking how true the statement was. 'But I'm not into that any more. All that "I'm your one and only" stuff ... I've seen a better way. I want to be free to care for anyone I choose. Any man. Any woman. No limits ... and no lies.' She grinned at David, hoping he'd understand, then felt a plume of almost physical elation when he smiled back shyly and reached down to cover her hand with his, just an inch or so from his groin.

'That sounds very sensible,' he answered, squeezing her fingers and slyly edging them upwards.

As her hand closed over his manhood, Rosie sighed with pleasure. This was an instance of masculine pride she *could* accept – and enjoy without capitulation. He was beautiful and he knew it; as strong and virile as the young male lion she'd likened him to from the very beginning. And yet in spite of this, she sensed that David would never try to manipulate her, as others had done, or make her do things for his benefit at the expense of her own wants and needs.

Beneath her fingertips, his sex seemed to radiate life and heat. She could feel the clear shape of him through the denim of his jeans, the thick, hard line of his yearning. He moaned as she traced his trapped erection; then suddenly he sat up and wrapped his arms around her, kissing her and pressing softly for entrance with his tongue as she rubbed and fondled at his crotch.

The kiss was a revelation, a summation of how far he'd progressed in his studies. His mouth bore the taste of his growing power; licking, nipping and sucking at her as he eased her backwards and down onto the pillows, then rolled on top of her. Still kissing, he reached between them and drew her hand away from his penis. Pressing his loins against hers, he circled his hips where he lay, massaging her body with his weight and with the solid mass of his flesh. He was imposing himself on her at every point of contact, yet Rosie did not feel oppressed. She welcomed the dominance of this man, encouraged it, crying out around his firm intruding tongue as he slid his hands between her and the bed, and cupped her bottom through her tissue-thin skirt.

They kissed for several minutes, rocking their pelvises against each other in a dry imitation of sex. Their tongues swirled and stroked around in each others mouths, exchanging moisture and faint murmurs of passion.

'You're beautiful,' gasped David, lifting his face from hers and looking down into her eyes. Rosie felt a soft, weakening sensation in her belly as if his hot golden eyes were melting her right down to her vulva. The flesh of her sex felt as warm and yielding as gellified honey, and against the division of her labia, his penis was a long, rigid bar, probing blindly in search of her niche. Her clitoris was swollen and inflamed, and it throbbed insanely beneath the down-bearing pressure of his sex.

As her legs began to shake, and her breath caught in her throat, David lifted himself away from her, his expression intense, almost possessed. Rosie groaned. She was almost coming. She *needed* to come. Yet David plainly had an inner agenda.

With exquisite grace, he rose to his feet and slowly began to strip off his clothes. His shirt he unbuttoned meticulously, exposing his smooth skin inch by inch, then letting the white cloth swish sensuously down his arms and catching it behind his back as a model would. Rosie smiled inside, wondering how he could instinctively perform so well. She doubted if he'd ever even seen a female stripper, never mind one of the newer breed of male ones.

260

Beneath his faded jeans, his underpants were black and very brief. His stiffness was altering the shape of them and jutting out boldly before him as he shimmied his way free of his denims.

Rosie wanted to leap up and grab him, run her hands luxuriantly over his body and enjoy its strength and vitality. She wanted to pull off his neat black underpants and caress the beautiful organ beneath them. She wanted to kiss him, revel in him, devour him; yet instinct held her back. This was David's show, his moment, and it would be selfish to undermine him. Instead she just held out her arms.

With a small, composed smile, David slipped off his briefs and lay down beside her again. He seemed unembarrassed by his nakedness, and untroubled by his swaying erection. Still smiling, still calm, he began unbuttoning the front of her camisole, popping the tiny pearl spheres from their buttonholes with all the care he'd used on his own buttons. His movements were measured and tantalising, and it was all Rosie could do to hold back, and not rip open her clothing herself and offer her naked body to him.

When he flipped open the two wings of soft fabric, David sighed. She was bare beneath the camisole, and she saw his eyes grow heavy with lust as her breasts gleamed whitely in the sunlight. Bowing his head like a penitent, he started kissing her nipples – first one, then the other – wetting them with long, moist swipes of his tongue and nipping with his hard, straight teeth.

Rosie could hold back no longer. With a cry of relief, she clasped at his head, rumpling the smooth, sleek line of his hair and fondling his ears and his neck. The sensation of being bitten was delicious, and it shot towards her groin like a dart. She moaned and pushed her hips towards him, tugging at her skirt as she did so. The floating lavender garment had a loose elasticated waistband, and in seconds they were sliding it down her legs as a team. When it reached her feet, David sat up and flipped the skirt away with a flourish; while Rosie kicked off her shoes and sent then tumbling over the edge of the bed.

All she had on below the waist was a minute white silk g-string – an almost transparent triangle of fabric that seemed to enhance far more than it covered. Her soft, bushy pubes peeked out from satin bound edges, and the silk itself was damp with her dew. She reached down, about to strip it away completely, but surprisingly, David stayed her hand.

'Leave it,' he murmured, touching a finger to the small white scrap. 'It looks pretty.' The exploratory fingertip pressed, and then wiggled; working the gossamer-light cloth through the tangle of her hair until it lay against her hot, liquid core.

Rosie dug her heels into the bedspread as a huge wave of pleasure overcame her. She was climaxing and she could not contain her hunger any more. She pulled David against her as she came, crushing his caressing hand between them and grabbing at his back, his buttocks and his flanks – any part of his warm body she could reach. His penis was jammed against her leg, hard and fiery, burning like a thick, living brand.

Rosie's eyes were shut but she could still sense David's golden gaze; it felt like a shimmer of heat on her cheeks where his face hovered just above hers. His breath was tickling her chin, his gasps faint and light as he buried a hand in her hair, then swept his mouth down forcefully on hers, sealing her lips with a kiss, his timing instinctive and perfect.

'I don't know how much I can teach you, David,' Rosie said presently, when her mind and her voice were her own again. She was lying on her side, facing David as he lay facing her. She was relaxed and replete, her body loose and satisfied, and she was holding his penis in her fingers, stroking its still-enduring hardness with slow and teasing swirls.

'It's like I said in London,' she continued, letting her hand loosen as he shuddered. 'I'm not all that experienced myself. I only really started to learn when I came to work for Julian.'

'Well, we'll just have to work it out together then, won't we?' he said faintly, his hips rocking back and forth as he struggled to control his reactions. 'Have intensive tutorials ... Read books ... Ask the experts ... There are enough of them around,' he observed, grinning wickedly, then gasping with pleasure as her fingers closed round him again.

He was truly a wonder, this pupil of hers, decided Rosie, as the devil in her own belly stirred. 'Where shall we start?' she asked, leaning forward and kissing his cheek. As she did so, she stroked the groove under his glans with her fingernail, and smiled in slow, female triumph as he hissed her name through his tightly gritted teeth.

'There's a book on the floor,' he gasped, his head lashing from side to side on the pillow as she squeezed with one hand and stroked with the other. 'It was open at a picture ... Teach me *that*! Now! Please!'

Rosie glanced down at the picture of the top-to-tail lovers, kissing each other's sexes in an entanglement as old as yin and yang. Then she looked back to the resplendent young maleness in her hands, and felt her mouth water and her vulva slicken in readiness.

Oh yes, my gorgeous boy, I'll try anything! she told him silently, curling down towards his crotch to lick his penis, while his strong hands pulled her hips across his face, then dragged aside the thin silk that covered her.

He tasted salty and delicious as she sucked him, and his penis seemed to swell and fill her mouth. Yet as thought began to blur, a single question assailed her, popping in her mind like a lightbulb the very instant she surrendered to his tongue.

This is glorious, my sweet, beautiful David. But is it you who's being taught here ... or me?

The Gift of Shame
Sarah
Hope-Walker

Chapter One

*H*elen lay her head on this stranger's belly and contemplated the source of her pleasure.

His cock, in repose, she decided, was quite beautiful. Much more complicated and intricately worked than she had ever before noticed. Thick veins ran their complicated patterns under its fleshy surface. The skin shone with the buffing of its recent exertions. Exertions which still burned deep in her belly. Taking it delicately between the tips of her fingers she lifted it to feel its dead weight and then, moving her head, probed it with her tongue. It moved like the live thing it was, and she could feel it tensing in expectation. An answering response came from deep inside herself and reaching just an inch or two more she took him, limp still but already stirring, between her lips where she savoured him for a moment before taking him wholly into her mouth.

His body flinched and he moaned, but all she cared for was the stirring in her mouth. With rising excitement she felt him growing, hardening, and she raised herself slightly so that the downward thrusts of her lips could become whole-hearted engulfments. As she felt him reaching down to caress her head she knew she wanted to swallow him whole. She pounded him against the back of her throat and only wished she could reach further and deeper to take him in completely.

He called out and broke the mood but the Devil rose in her. She resented his intrusion on her private pleasure. She didn't want him involved in this. Didn't want his voice, his needs, to interfere with her own pleasure. For hours she had submitted to his demands, but this, she was determined, would be hers alone. She wanted this pleasure for herself – he was a necessary accomplice but she didn't want him interfering.

Taking her mouth from him she whispered urgently. 'Be still!' She saw that his own pleasure had caused him to thrash his head from side to side. Raising herself up, she swung her thighs across his fully roused sex. 'I'm going to have *you*,' she told him. 'This has nothing to do with you. Be still.'

Tucking his huge arousal inside herself, she looked down on his closed eyes, clenched teeth, and knew that this was difficult for him. It was his initial assertiveness that had brought them to this pass in less than twenty-four hours from meeting. She was as astonished as he that she was taking the initiative – asserting herself in a way she had never done before.

Her hands pressing down on his hips allowed her to more precisely control her own body's movement. As she did so she tried to, objectively, study her body's pleasure. Outside of this room, beyond this bed, she knew there was a world resounding with sophistication, constructed to man's own arrogant pleasures but here, at the junction of her loins with his, was the oldest, most exquisite pleasure known to human-kind. Needing no artifice or machines, it was a lust unchanged from beyond the birth of civilisation and one she intended to have in full measure.

Her head flung back as she ground slowly down onto him, the fire licking deep into her belly, she felt his hands on her breasts. 'No!' she admonished him. 'Don't touch me! This is mine!'

Still moving with a smooth, slow, rhythm, refusing to respond to her body's increasing urgency, she swayed herself into a circular motion and reflected on how this exquisite moment had come about.

This man had found her out. Less than twenty-four hours previously she would have been offended if anyone had thought of her as anything other than a virtuous widow.

Kenneth had died ninety feet under the Caribbean. His air tanks, they told her, had become entangled with the loose hawsers of the wreck he had been diving on. She should have been with him. Regulations insisted that divers go down in pairs. Kenneth had been the expert, she his novice diving 'buddy' but, suddenly appalled at the weight of water surrounding them, she had panicked and surfaced.

The Diving Master had told her not to worry. It happened to novice divers. She would do better next time. Reassured, and quite proud of how she had managed the surfacing drill alone, she lay down on the deck to work on her tan. She had forgotten to report that Kenneth was now alone. Had she done so she would have saved his life because Kenneth, his air tanks holed and running out, was at that moment fighting for his life. His diving 'buddy', who should have been there to seek assistance, was instead contemplating that night's renewal of their sexual revels.

No one but herself had blamed her for Kenneth's death and she had told no one of the guilt she felt so no one understood why she had gone into such social seclusion.

'You'll have to start going out sometime, Helen, darling,' Millie had insisted. 'Either that or join a religious order. Besides there's someone I want you to meet.'

So, after six months of grieving she had forced herself

269

to accept the relentless invitations and gone to the pre-Christmas party.

The moment she arrived she knew it had been a mistake. Too many sidelong glances at the woman who had returned from her honeymoon alone.

Jeffrey had come out of the mix of faces and she knew at once that this was the one Millie had meant her to meet. Guiltily, she realised that Millie had been right. As she spoke to this tall, quietly spoken man she found herself thinking the unthinkable. By sitting and talking with this stranger she felt as obvious as a whore sitting in an Amsterdam window.

'Are you all right?' he had asked.

His tender enquiry broke her. She knew if she didn't leave now she was lost. Rushing away she went to find her coat, intending to leave.

Millie caught up with her as she searched among the piled coats. 'Helen! Whatever's the matter?'

'I'm sorry Millie. It's just – I just can't do this. I have to go.'

'What happened?'

'Nothing happened. I shouldn't have come. It's too soon.'

It was then that Jeffrey caught her arm. 'I'll drive you home,' he'd said. 'St John's Wood, isn't it?'

Looking into his eyes, so full of real concern, she knew she was defeated.

She waited with embarrassing docility as he found his own coat and then, taking her firmly by the arm, had led her out to his car.

It was a long-slung Continental sports coupé of a kind she had never seen before. The seat into which she sank was so low that her legs were forced flat out along a luxurious carpet. This was a car totally out of tune with her mood.

As he drove she looked across at his profile. Somewhere deep inside her there had been a gear-shift of emotions. The empty guilt she had felt at the party fell

270

away to leave, in its place, an emotion so powerful and direct that she felt instant shame.

With a feeling of growing unreality, an internal denial that this was really happening, she had let him escort her to her door.

As she fitted her key she had meant to say. 'Please *don't* come in,' but somewhere between her brain and her tongue the negative had got lost and came out sounding like a brazen invitation.

For a long, agonising moment he had looked directly into her eyes. 'I don't think you mean it,' he said. 'I'll call you and we'll meet when you're less upset.'

Then he had gone, leaving her with a perverse feeling of rejection.

Miserably, she went to bed feeling shame tighten round her like an instrument of torture. She felt hollow inside while her outer shell became rigid with the horror she had been about to perpetrate. She told herself she might as well have gone to the cemetery and squatted over Kenneth's grave.

Helen woke from a fitful sleep to the sound of the telephone. It was an anxious Millie.

'What happened?'

Wearily she tried to read the face of the bedside clock which always eluded her. 'Millie! What time is it?'

'Good God, girl, it's nearly noon.' Millie took in a long, pretend shocked breath. 'Don't tell me he's still there?'

'Who? What are you talking about?'

'When I saw the way he whisked you off last night I was certain – well, that there would be *developments . . . ?*'

She knew precisely what Millie meant and she was ashamed that, but for Jeffrey's understanding, it would have been true. She hated being that transparent before her friends and so, perversely, continued to play at confused virtue.

'Millie? Are you talking in riddles or what? I haven't the faintest idea of what you're talking about.'

'Jeffrey . . . !' prompted Millie. 'Don't pretend you don't remember!'

'Oh. Him. Yes, well he just drove me home. That's all.'

'Not even a late night coffee?'

'Nothing. I told you.'

Millie drew in a long, exasperated breath. 'I really don't know what we're going to do with you.'

'Nothing. You don't have to do anything with me. I'm quite happy as I am. But, Millie, could we talk about this later? I've just woken up and have to run to the bathroom.'

'All right, but be sure and call me back for a long gossip.'

'About what, Millie? I told you nothing happened.'

'So *you* say!' said Millie, and hung up.

Almost immediately the telephone rang again. It was her mother. She felt trapped. It had been accepted and, she had agreed as always, to spend Christmas with her parents. She was meant to be travelling down to the coast that very afternoon. She was being reminded of her promise to bring liqueurs as her contribution to the festivities.

What once had seemed the commonplace of family courtesies was, suddenly, an intolerable burden.

'So you won't forget them, darling?'

'No, mother. I promise.'

Her mother took one of her long pregnant pauses before repeating what was, these days, a constant theme.

'Perhaps you'll find the idea of living at home again a little more appealing after you've spent some time with us. It'd be for the best, you know.'

'Mother – we've been through this so many times . . .'

'I know,' said her mother in that familiar dismissive

272

tone, 'but I'm your mother and I worry about you. Kenneth's gone and there's nothing we can do to bring him back. I worry about you, alone in that flat with all those memories. I really believe you would do better to come home.'

She wanted to tell her mother that, in her mind, she *was* home but where could she find the words to soften the ultimate rejection? Her mother had thought of her leaving home – even for marriage – as a temporary condition which, by a twist of fate, was now capable of remedy.

Mother loses daughter to husband, daughter loses husband, ergo, mother regains daughter. The logic of it, seen from her mother's perspective, was flawless.

How could she explain that she didn't see it quite so simply? How to explain the agony of the guilt she felt about Kenneth's death? A guilt as yet unexpiated, since no one but herself had ever laid it at her door? Far less could she hope to explain the crushing burden of having contemplated adding sexual betrayal to her list of crimes.

She took her nagging guilt with her to the shower. There – never having learned the trick – she couldn't avoid getting her hair soaked and so had to hunt the drier out from where it had, inevitably, hidden itself.

She sat on the base of the bed and watched herself drying her hair in the mirrored closet doors.

She remembered going with Kenneth to buy them, both feeling wicked because they reflected the full length of the bed and the erotic possibilities that they offered. She remembered those images and, bitterly, the images they would never show.

Switching off the drier she had the feeling that the telephone had been ringing for some time. Thinking it would surely be her mother with some more last minute instructions she lay across the bed to reach for it and spoke her 'hello' a little wearily.

'I didn't wake you did I?' Jeffrey asked.

273

Startled, she sat up, reaching for a bath-robe to cover her otherwise naked body. 'No. I just didn't hear the telephone, that's all. My hair got wet and I was just drying it. I've got a very noisy drier.'

She cursed herself, even as she spoke, for this over-long explanation. Why hadn't she told him she was naked? She'd mentioned everything else!

'I was wondering, somewhat forlornly perhaps – it being Christmas Eve – if you would be free for dinner tonight?'

'No. I'm sorry. No. I'm going down to Eastbourne tonight.'

'Tonight? What time?'

'Well. Usually I like to drive down and get there before dark but I overslept so that isn't possible.' Why was she going on at such length like this?

'Suppose we met for an early dinner?'

'No. I really would like to get away as early as possible. I hate driving at night.'

'I could drive you down there.'

Suddenly she was vulnerable. He was pushing too hard and she felt she ought to mind but found she didn't.

'To Eastbourne? No. That would be ridiculous. Besides I need my car down there.'

'I could drive your car.'

'And what would you do then?'

'Take a train back.'

'They stop running early on Christmas Eve. There aren't any on Christmas Day.'

'Then I could take a cab.'

'From Eastbourne to London? You must be mad.'

He paused and she found herself hoping he could think of something more acceptable.

'Look,' he finally said, 'I'm only about ten minutes from your place. Why don't I come round. I really would like to see you before you go away.'

274

Aware of the unmade bed, her own nakedness and wrecked hair she tried to put him off.

'I'll only be gone three days. We could meet when I come back.'

'No,' he said decisively. 'I'll give you half an hour.'

She laid down the phone and stared at it. Was she really going to allow this? What was the point? What time would they have? None. An hour at the most and then she would have to leave. This was insanity. This time yesterday she didn't know of his existence and now he was making assumptions and invading her life.

Hurrying back to the bathroom she stared at herself in the mirror. What would she wear? How could she get her hair into some semblance of order? Should she try and rush to make-up her face?

Settling for a vigorous brushing, a smear of foundation and a sweater and jeans, she was still feeling harassed when he rang the bell.

'I really don't have time for this,' she told him as she opened the apartment door to him.

'I've been up most of the night thinking about you,' he told her.

'Me?'

He came to stand intimidatingly within her space. 'You needed me last night and I walked out on you.'

' "Needed" you . . . ?'

'I'm sorry,' he said and, reaching, made his arms into an embracing arc and brought her tight against himself. The move had been so sudden, even if half anticipated, that she made no protest.

That first real kiss had unnerved her. Swept along, without thought or protest, she had come to be naked under him, feverishly rising to meet his every harsh, cruel, thrust.

Her brain, protesting her libidinous body's betrayal, had sought to transmute pleasure into punishment. His powerful shafting flesh had caused her to thrash helplessly from side to side, blocking protest, preventing contrition, denying resistance. That first time her eyes had been tight shut to block out the contempt she was sure he must feel for the abandoned person under him. A woman now so crazed and out of control that she heard her own voice begging for pain, then sobbing and screaming as his fingers responded, digging deeply, painfully, into her frenetic buttocks. It had hurt and it had been punishing, but it had also thrilled and intensified her pleasure.

Then came the moment of her body's final betrayal as she felt the clenching throb of her own internal orgasm against his. It was a mutuality she had never achieved with Kenneth in a thousand tries, but which had ceded to this man on his first assault.

When he had exhausted himself she had not resisted the downward pressure on her head but had gone to greet the fallen, sullied, warrior with an enthused mouth that sought only to bring him back to full erection so that he might plunge into her again.

And he had.

And she wanted to die of shame.

Now, barely minutes later, she lay listening to him in the shower and wondered how she could face him. He must have known, Millie would have gossiped about her, that he had made her from resolutely virtuous widow to voracious wanton in less than a day. Could any man respect such a creature? How was she going to bear the lash of his contempt? She lay in wretchedness, a hollowed, empty victim awaiting the inevitable humiliation.

When he finally emerged, smiling, naked and even half erected she wanted to hide. Certain of his scorn, she was even more shamed when he took a firm hold on the pillow with which she had covered her face, and looking down into her wide, defensive eyes, had gently kissed her full on the lips.

'That was marvellous.'

She braced against his contempt, lay still and frozen.

276

She had heard only the words she had expected and not those he had spoken.

Looking down at her widened eyes, and still lips, he was puzzled. 'Something wrong?' he asked.

'Please go.'

His brow furrowed even deeper. 'Go? I thought we'd agreed I'd drive you to Bournemouth?'

'Eastbourne,' she corrected him.

'Wherever. Didn't we?'

'It's not a good idea.'

'I think it's an excellent idea,' he said, and his hand sought out her traitorous loins that both burned and flinched at his touch. 'I have lots of excellent ideas.'

Summoning the will to move she thrust aside his hand, swung her feet to the floor and raced to the bathroom. She would have closed and barred it to him but he was already there gently preventing its closure.

'You don't regret what just happened, do you?'

'No. But please leave the door . . .'

He pushed against it even more firmly. 'No. I want to watch you shower. I haven't seen you properly naked yet, you know.'

Now close to tears she turned to begging him to leave her alone, and he, looking wounded and puzzled, finally relented and let her close the door on him.

Feeling safe for the moment she turned to confront herself in the full-length mirror which Kenneth had installed so he could watch her face while he took her, fresh from the bath, from behind. Now she could only beg its forgiveness.

Standing in the shower she felt her legs weaken and had to hold onto the pipes to allow the water to do its best to wash away the dirt and the guilt. Guilt that rose not so much from what she had done but from recognising just how thoroughly it had excited her.

She was still there when she became aware of the hammering on the door. Turning off the water, she called out angrily.

'It's the telephone,' he called through the door. 'It just keeps on ringing and I thought I'd better not answer it.'

Illogically angry at him, Helen wrapped herself in a towel and opened the door to hear the phone still ringing. He stood back to make a respectful space as she crossed the room to answer it.

'Darling!' cried Millie. 'I was sure you'd gone off without thinking to call me back!'

'Not now, Millie. I'm all in a rush. I'll call you from my mother's.'

She hung up, careless that Millie would be offended. The call had brought her out of hiding and now she was face to face with him, with nowhere to hide.

'What are you so guilty about?' he asked.

'It shouldn't have happened. I shouldn't have let it happen.'

'I'm sorry.'

Had he said any more she might have been able to summon up anger, but he hadn't. She cursed silently as she felt herself weakening towards tears. Without warning they engulfed her and she found herself wrapped tight against him begging for comfort.

She cried herself out for some minutes pleased to be within his warm embrace but hating herself for seeking this unsafe and dangerous sanctuary.

'Do you want me to punish you?' he asked in a soft, gentle tone that belied the enormity of his words.

Thrusting herself away from his body, made suddenly chill, she stared at him.

'What did you say?'

'I asked if you wanted me to punish you,' he said again in patient, even tones.

The words were plain but their meaning, to her at that moment, obscure.

'What for?' she finally asked.

'Whatever is haunting you.'

'Are you mad?' she asked, throwing out one last desperate lifeline towards sanity.

'Not at all. You seem upset about something. Guilty, even. Guilt left unpunished can fester.'

She stared at him, not wanting to believe what she had heard. There was only one possibility – of the many which raced through her mind – he was insane!

'I think you'd better go now,' she said as evenly as she could manage.

'No,' he said. 'I'm driving you to Eastbourne.'

Aware that the towel was the only thing between them she felt suddenly vulnerable and went to walk round him to the relative safety of the bathroom. She didn't make it. He caught her arm, reached for the towel, stripped it from her and threw it aside. In an attempt to minimise the feeling of vulnerability that now engulfed her, she sat down on the bed, staring up at him through tear-stained eyes.

He reached for her, turned her naked body onto its stomach and holding her down firmly, slapped her repeatedly on the soft flesh of her buttocks.

Wriggling for freedom from his firm grasp, yelling to be let up she felt the heat from the blows suffusing her entire body.

Still angry, she was flipped onto her back as easily as if she were a pancake on a hotplate, and looked up at him in fear as he loosed the belt from the loops of his trousers.

'What do you think you're doing?'

'Something you need badly,' he told her.

She watched mesmerised as the belt was flipped up into the air and then brought down across the bed within millimetres of her tender flesh. Yelping with sudden fear she dived from the bed and made for the bathroom. He caught her wrist and lashed at her calves and buttocks – anything that was presented to him.

Now she was yelling, sobbing and protesting all at the same time. Next she felt her burning, outraged body thrown to the bed where she could do nothing to prevent his further invasion of her spreadeagled self.

The fire that had played about her buttocks and loins was now being pressed deep inside her. He felt huge against her inner flesh, as, desperately hating herself, she found her nails digging into his back which he answered with sharp digs into her buttocks. Effortlessly he held her hips high as he drove even deeper into her again and again.

She felt flames licking her every nerve as she abandoned herself to the inevitable orgasmic climax.

He knew. Oh, how humiliatingly well, he knew how abandoned and lost she was. How easily her wanton body dismissed her protesting reason, how readily her thighs rose to answer his every sortie with greedy, clenching attack. She had surrendered everything of herself and now only regretted she could find nothing more to give.

They lay exhausted on the bed for a long moment before she could bring herself to articulate the one word that had resounded in her head since her climax.

'Bastard!' she breathed with an intensity born of real hatred.

He had smiled, she had lain her head down on his belly and, with the heat of the beating still burning on her flesh, felt the need to assert herself.

'Now I'm going to screw you,' Helen had said and then, as she rode astride this man, almost still a stranger, she knew she was venting months of guilt and frustration on his body but, also, that it was directed mainly into her own soul.

Assertive and positive he might have been but now he was passively submitting to the slow tortuous pleasure she wrought out of him. He had even, at her urging, placed his hands behind his head while she used him.

Then something snapped inside and she realised she

280

was losing control. Her body was taking over, insisting she increase the pace and its pleasure. Violently now, she started to move on him, beating her pelvis into him with punishing force, finding she could no longer protest when his hands reached for her, dragged her down and forced her to receive his gushing tribute, spread helplessly on her back. 'Yes!' they screamed in unison and knew that this was right.

There was an appalled silence during which it seemed even the walls of her bedroom held their breath, until, raising himself on one elbow to look deeply into her vulnerable eyes, he spoke. 'I have no intention of letting you go,' he said. 'You're mine. I've claimed you.'

'I have to go to my mother's,' she said, hating the intrusion of a little girl's tone into her voice.

He nodded. 'But afterwards . . .' he said.

'Afterwards,' she agreed, and felt inside her the first real happiness she had known since that soporific afternoon in the Caribbean.

They were half way to Eastbourne before she noticed the car following them.

'Isn't that *your* car?' she asked.

He nodded.

'Luckily I managed to get Turner at home and he agreed to follow us so that I'll have my car for the return journey.'

'Who's Turner?'

'My chauffeur.'

'You have a chauffeur? I'm impressed.'

'Strictly speaking he's employed by my company. He usually drives the company car but he's been dying to have a go in the Maserati. It was that that lured him out tonight.'

It was another reminder of how little she knew of the man who had so comprehensively invaded her life and her body.

'What do you do?'

'I've got some property.'

She lapsed into silence. Kenneth had hated people who created paper profits and produced nothing. 'Economic leeches,' he had called them. She had, with Kenneth, developed some radical attitudes of her own. Now she was consorting with one of 'them'. Yet another betrayal – the third or fourth – she was rapidly losing track.

Helen spoke defensively as if he had been listening in on her silent thoughts. 'You must have a very low opinion of me.'

'What brought that on? Have I offended you in some way?'

'Not you. Me.' She looked across at him behind the wheel and saw him smiling. 'I'm not usually like "that",' she added quietly.

'Of course not. I think you're a very special lady and I intend to cherish you.'

'Is that why you thrashed me?'

'I thought that was what you needed.'

'It won't happen again.'

'Didn't it excite you? At one point you asked me to hurt you some more.'

'It's very bad taste to repeat things said in the throes of orgasm.'

'Did you?'

'What?'

'Orgasm.'

'You know I did.'

'I'm one of those men that is never sure. I'm glad.'

She fought down an impulse to say 'So am I' and reached out a hand to lay on his forearm.

He acknowledged it by looking down and smiling. Feeling that his smile meant he was patronising her, she withdrew her arm. Arrogant bastard, she thought, he thinks he's got me precisely where he wants me.

'I have an unfulfilled fantasy,' he said so suddenly

that, at first, she wildly thought he must be speaking to someone else.

'Haven't we all?' she asked.

'You have unfulfilled fantasies?' he asked sounding genuinely interested. 'I'd love to help you fulfil them.'

She laughed. 'You'd need a limitless resource.'

'I have a limitless resource,' he said, very soberly.

Looking across she could see no trace of a self deprecating smile or laugh. 'So what is this unfulfilled fantasy?' she asked.

'I want a girl to go down on me while I'm driving. It's never happened to me.'

'I've news for you,' she said. 'Nothing's changed.'

'You won't do it?'

She looked directly at him but his eyes never left the road. 'Do you seriously think I would? We've barely known each other for twenty-four hours.'

'You did it in the bedroom. What's the difference?'

She stared out the side window. Resentment, she neither wanted nor could cope with, was rising rapidly in her.

This man was supposing too much, too readily assuming that she was his creature, willing to devote herself to his pleasure.

There rose a need to assert herself. To establish that she was an independent being, not some appendage he'd taken from a dusty shelf. She might have done so then and there but for her crippling guilt.

Her mistake, she thought, had been to allow him to drive her down to the coast. She wanted him to stop the car and let her out, before reminding herself that this was her car and that his was following behind.

So there was the solution! He could simply step into his own car, turn round and return to London. She need never see him again.

He broke in on her thoughts. 'Do it for me and I promise I'll fulfil any fantasy of yours. Absolute promise.'

283

'Now you're treating me like a casual pick-up.'

'I love whorish women,' he murmured, almost to himself.

'Then I've an idea,' she told him. 'Why don't you stop the car, get into your own and drive back to London? You might even be in time to catch some tired prostitute on her way home. I'm sure, given the right incentive, she would happily oblige.'

He laughed out loud for nearly a minute. 'Not the same thing,' he said when he finally finished. 'I want a whorish woman – not a whore. There is a very big difference. Of course it would be perfect with someone who loves me.'

Helen reached deep down inside for all the scorn she could muster. 'You don't imagine I'm in love with you, do you?'

'I'm determined that you will be.'

Now it was her turn to laugh.

'Too late now,' he was saying. 'We're nearly there.'

In the context she thought, at first, the remark had been directed at their relationship but, looking up, she was surprised to see the first of the town's signs. The time had flown, the mileage dissolved. It was the most painless drive from London to Eastbourne she could ever remember

She directed him to her parents' home, conscious that it was much later than they would have been expecting her. A further problem was that she could see no way of avoiding inviting him in to meet them.

Perhaps his generosity would ease the inevitable tension this would cause. As they were driving through the London suburbs she had remembered her promise to provide the cursed liqueurs without which her Mother didn't consider it to be Christmas. She had asked him to stop at a store and, when he understood why, he had insisted on buying a bottle of every kind they had.

Now, in the trunk of the car were bottles of liqueurs

284

she had never even heard of, supplemented by a huge mixed box of every conceivable kind of liqueur chocolate ever created. Her mother was going to love this man!

In the event, her optimism proved false. Her mother's smile of greeting froze the moment she saw Jeffrey following Helen into the house burdened by the bottles of liqueurs.

The display of abundance did nothing to diminish the chill edged reception. She could see that her mother's intuition had sight read the situation. Her only consolation was that her mother couldn't possibly guess at the depth of her daughter's debauch.

Jeffrey stayed just long enough to drink a cup of begrudgingly offered coffee before departing.

The only positive response to his visit came from her father who was impressed by the expensive sports car parked outside the house. Her mother had dismissed it as a ridiculous extravagance.

That night Helen thought about the past twenty-four hours. She remembered the guilt, but also the thrill in her total surrender of self and inhibition. Before sleeping she had recalled his every word and conjured up his every gesture; probing them, turning them this way and that, in a search for hidden meanings.

She decided that there were none, or room for very few. He had a directness about him which was disconcerting but, in its honesty, attractive.

Most particularly, she recalled his fantasy in the car and knew for a certainty that, one day, she was going to do that – and much else – for this uniquely demanding man.

Christmas Day was, as always, disappointing. Some distant relatives turned up. Her mother fussed over the strewn wrapping papers, lunch was late and the turkey burnt. Her parents got irritable with each other and, when all the 'outsiders' had departed, rounded off the festive day with a row.

In need of some time alone she walked alone through

285

the early night streets and she found herself thinking about Jeffrey, tempered only by the memory of the previous Christmas when she and Kenneth had been here together.

She remembered Kenneth's tentative experiments with her body. Last Christmas, slightly drunk, he had wanted to sodomise her. She had refused when his clumsiness had caused her too much pain.

She wasn't sure about Jeffrey. Somehow she suspected she would feel no pain.

It wasn't until she was almost on the point of leaving that her mother mentioned Jeffrey.

'Who is he?' she had asked suspiciously. 'I don't like him. Not one little bit.'

'He's someone I hardly know. He offered to drive me down, that's all. You know how I hate to drive after dark.'

'Long way for someone to come who hardly knows you.'

'I think he was going to his own parents' house. They live along the coast somewhere.'

The lie hadn't convinced her mother. Mothers know their daughters too well, she concluded, because they were once daughters themselves.

Chapter Two

*T*he return to London was an unexpected anticlimax. What she had expected, she couldn't imagine. Jeffrey on the doorstep, perhaps? How could he be when he could have no idea when she was coming back?

Wandering around the empty apartment she felt unutterably lonely. With the holiday season still in full swing to call Millie or anyone would seem to be begging for an invitation. Instead, she consoled herself with a bottle of whisky and the endless stream of movies which seemed to be pouring out on every TV channel.

At some point she must have dozed off and was quite shocked on waking to find her first memories were of Jeffrey. She had, in those first unwary wakening moments, for the first time, found it difficult to summon up Kenneth's smiling face.

She dragged herself to bed – to sleep and hope for better things from the following day.

It was close to three in the morning when she woke to the frightening sound of voices in the other room. Fear paralysed her until her more rational mind told her it was the sound of her own voice on the answering machine. Someone was calling her at this unbelievable hour.

Cursing herself for having forgotten to switch off the call monitor she got out of bed, eased open the door and listened, uneasily feeling that she was intruding on herself.

Her own announcement ended, she waited with bated breath to see if the caller would dare leave a message.

'Hello. This is Jeffrey. It's just past midnight . . .'

Liar! . . .

'. . . and I wanted you to know I was thinking of you. Please call me the moment you get back. Speak to you soon!'

Listening to the machine re-set itself she heard the micro-chip date and time monitor record the truth and wondered why he had bothered to lie about so apparently insignificant a detail.

Puzzled, she rewound the tape to hear the message through again. Was it possible that a man of his experience and resources didn't know that the new generation of answering machines recorded the time and date of the call?

Even supposing he didn't know, was he so unworldly that he had not even allowed for there to have been an intervening call which would have also exposed his lie?

She found herself having her first real doubts about the true nature of the man who had assumed so much over her.

It was then she realised that she had overlooked the most illuminating facet of the call. Had Jeffrey been lying awake at three a.m. thinking about her? Thinking so deeply that he had been moved to call her with no expectation that she would be there? Then, having done so, been too coy to admit that he had called at such an ungodly hour?

Of course, he might simply have been returning from a night out and had thought to impress her with his devotion. But for what reason?

She replayed the tape, listening carefully for any signs

of slurred speech which might have indicated a drink inspired call. There was none. He sounded endearingly sincere and, but for his lie about the time, she might have, there and then, called him right back.

Instead, she turned off the call monitor and went back to bed.

Some hours later she woke in a state of confusion. This had happened to her several times in her life and more especially since Kenneth's death, but this morning was something different, something more intense and frightening.

Nothing seemed to make sense and nothing was as it should be. Rationally she knew where she was but the images that haunted her dreams remained hovering, undefined, on the edge of her waking mind. Something was bothering her. A problem that her dreams had left unresolved.

The feeling grew and no amount of coffee could drive the apprehension away. Something out there in the mists of the future was lurking, waiting in ambush. She would have liked to call somebody but there was no one.

Millie was her closest friend but she already knew that talking to her would be met with a furrowed brow and the admonishment to 'pull yourself together'.

Something more stopped her calling Millie. It was the knowledge that, no matter how great her resolve, she would, in minutes, have confessed everything that had passed between her and Jeffrey. That was a shame she wasn't yet ready to share. Not even with Millie, whose own answer to depression was a romp in bed with someone new.

Millie was without doubt the most outrageous woman she knew. Flagrantly unfaithful to her adoring husband. Drooling to know the details of everyone else's sex life, and scornful of anyone that espoused the slightest regret no matter how outrageous their behaviour. Millie had once said: 'In life you should only regret the things you *didn't* do.' No. On this precipitous edge Millie was not the person to confide in.

Trying to distract herself by tidying up the apartment she came face to face with an echo of her own debauch. Lying half concealed under the bedcover was the belt he had used to beat her. Seeing it, she had involuntarily reached out to pick it up but then hesitated as if it had become a venomous snake. All her unsettling images suddenly resolved themselves into one. Jeffrey. He was the serpent gnawing at her mind. A cancer that needed immediate surgery. Going to the telephone she dialled rapidly, anxious to put her impulse into effect.

'Hello? Jeffrey?'

He sounded excited. 'Where are you? Are you in London?'

'Yes. At the apartment . . .'

'I'll be right there!'

'No!' she yelled into the phone, but her voice bounced back off the already dead microphone.

Infuriated, needing to stop him at all costs, she dialled his number again. His answering machine came on. He couldn't possibly have left immediately, so when the tone came she spoke urgently hoping that he had also left his monitor switched on.

'Jeffrey, please pick up the phone. I have to speak to you. I can't possibly see you. Not today.' She waited a moment more before the answering machine clicked off and returned her to the baleful dialling tone.

Putting the telephone down she found herself in confusion. What did he want of her? Why this instant response to her call? Why had she told him she was home? Why hadn't she told him she was still in Eastbourne?

It was then that she discovered the leather belt was still in her hand. She stared at it. When had she picked that up?

His imminent arrival left little time to tidy herself or the apartment. Refusing to listen to the inner voice which plaintively reminded her that she had intended telling him she didn't want to see him, she flew about the flat and made some semblance of presentability.

The street door buzzed and, picking up the security videophone, she saw his monotone image, making him look like something from an old newsreel. If she were going to turn him away this was the moment to do it. All she had to do was tell him he wasn't coming in and then not open the door. She was about to do just that when he spotted the monitor lens and, sticking out his tongue, smiled broadly into it.

Unable to resist this childish behaviour she pressed the door-lock release and watched as he disappeared from the video screen.

Opening the apartment door to him she was still intending to make a token protest, but was greeted with a doorway filled with flowers through which poked a magnum of champagne. From behind the floral screen came his voice.

'Don't say a word!'

She stepped back as the flowers advanced on her. His face appeared grinning impishly over them.

'You are forbidden to speak!' he told her. 'I'm here to look.'

'Look?' she gasped.

The champagne was thrust into her hands – it was chilled – and an admonishing finger laid lightly on her parted, protesting, lips.

'Not a word! Not one! Nothing. You are sentenced to be silent.'

Having freed one hand, he reached back into the hallway and dragged in a huge white box tied all over with golden ribbon. Saying nothing about the box he swept by her into the kitchen leaving her to hold the champagne. He was back in a moment carrying a huge vase – he'd found an unwanted wedding present she couldn't have found if her life had depended on it.

He arranged the flowers – which only now did she

register as predominantly, unseasonal, roses – while humming a joyous tune to himself.

'But—' she started to say before the finger again admonished her to silence.

She sighed and turned away wondering exactly how drunk he might be. On the other hand it was refreshing to find a grown man – who, she thought, did know how to behave – prepared to play games at the nursery level.

The flowers placed precisely where she would have put them herself, he turned his attention to the champagne. Keeping to the rules she stayed silent as he flushed out yet another wedding present – fluted champagne glasses.

Beginning to warm to the kindergarten atmosphere she held the glasses as he opened the bottle – without any explosive overflow – and poured repeatedly until, the bubbles subsiding, they were filled.

In the manner of a Head Waiter she was conducted to her own couch where she was sat down, the glasses touched and they drank.

He settled on the matching couch opposite and smiled at her.

'You are the most lovely lady I know,' he told her, and then, as she opened her mouth to deflect the outrageous compliment, he again held up his finger. 'Please!' he said. 'The things I have to say will be much more easily said if you say nothing.'

Intrigued, she saluted him with her glass, sipped, smiled and looked expectantly at him for him to begin his promised monologue.

She was disappointed. He simply sat opposite her, smiling, and looking at her. Twice during the long minutes he spent at this, she opened her mouth to speak and twice he raised his admonishing finger to stop her.

Deciding the only dignified way to support his game

was to pretend to ignore him, she sat back and did her best imitation of a silent movie vamp.

He clapped his hands in delight. 'Perfect!' he cried. 'Listen, I could just sit here all day drinking with you but – I wonder – would you do something else for me?'

Staying in character, she swept a hand through the air in a regally dismissive arc.

He leapt to his feet and going to the door, picked up the huge white box in one hand and came back to hand it to her across the couch table.

'Wear this for me,' he said.

Taking the box she saw the famous designer name discreetly engraved in gold in one corner and instinctively, although only half-heartedly, opened her mouth to protest, but again that finger was there, readied and threatening.

This created a dilemma. Should she open it here or take it into the bedroom? What if it were something she wouldn't be seen dead in? Could the contents, given the name on the box, possibly be construed as a Christmas gift between friends or was there something inside that would create an obligation or, at least, an expectation.

He settled her internal argument by reaching down to pull at the gold ribbon bows himself.

Under layers of silky white tissue she found a gown of very fine black silk that looked, in the hand, to be practically shapeless. She looked across at him and wondered why he had brought this to her and puzzled over whom it could have been bought for. Certainly not her – couturiers didn't work over Christmas and they would not, anyway, sell such an item without fittings.

'Put it on,' he enthused. 'If there's anything to be done to it we can fly to Paris and have them fit it properly.'

Feeling slightly light headed and thinking she might have, like Alice, fallen down some mythical rabbit hole, she stood and held the dress against her – it still had little form or even shape. 'Please,' he was saying. 'Try it on. If you don't like it we can change it.'

Allowing herself a deep sigh, she turned past him and went into the bedroom where she, firmly, closed the door.

Hurrying to the mirror she again held the gown in front of her and was undecided what to do. Was she going to join in this 'game'? What if the dress looked as awful on as in the hand? Could this be some kind of fetish of his? Distantly, she heard his voice calling out asking her not to be too long.

Consciously thinking that this was ridiculous, her hands were already unbuttoning the denim shirt she had worn to greet him and pulling off cotton leggings, she shed the brassiere, unwearable since the top of the gown consisted only of two panels held by buttons at the shoulders and then not caught again until the waist. It took some few attempts before she got the dress on and when she turned into the full-length mirror she got a tremendous shock. The fine silk had immediately clung to the warmth of her body. What had seemed shapeless now had taken form – her form! The material, clinging to every nook and cranny of her body, delineated the thrust of her nipples, which she observed had gone into instant erection. The effect was breathtaking. She saw herself as transformed and, although she had never thought of herself as any more narcissistic than the next girl, exciting. To wear a dress like this was not only to proclaim the naked body beneath but to advertise to the world that the woman inside was ready for sex.

Responding to his further admonishment not to take too long she searched out a pair of high-heeled shoes – Kenneth had called them her 'tarty' shoes – and slipped into them. She would have liked to do something more with her hair, but settled for a spray of perfume before taking a careful, assessing, look at herself.

There was only one flaw in the reflected image and

that was the way in which the silk, now thoroughly warmed to her body, and clinging ever closer, outlined her panties.

With a tingling sense of daring she raised the flowing skirt and, hooking her thumbs into her briefs, pulled them down and stepped out of them.

Looking at herself she became shocked and aware that her breasts were thrusting hard against the silk and her nipples ached – a sure sign of arousal. 'Cocktails are ready!' he called through the door.

With one last regret at not having more time to do anything with her hair, she moved to the door, took a long breath, and stepped out.

He was clear across the room holding two tall, stemmed, glasses which he had filled with some kind of champagne cocktail.

'Stunning!' he said.

She got as far as saying 'I—' before he again intervened.

'Rule still applies!' he told her coming forwards to hand her a glass with one hand and, catching her other hand, raised it to his lips.

'You can only wear it for me,' he said. 'I mean you look gorgeous and all but I think something a little more subtle, more understated would ensure you didn't get ravished the instant men saw you. Model it for me. Let me see the full effect!'

Tingling from head to toe, she did her best impression of all the catwalk models she had ever seen.

'Superb!' he called along with other compliments. 'Again!'

Turning, she swished and sashayed as best she could on the high heels that had suddenly started to pinch, before coming back to accept the drink he had been holding out all this time.

'Who was the gown made for?' she asked.

'For you,' he said.

Her laugh was short and scornful. 'And how did you get a dress made over Christmas?'

He looked bashful. 'The truth is I saw the dress on a model many years ago and loved it so I bought it. I didn't have anyone to wear it for me, then or since – until I met you. I knew immediately that this dress had been made for a body like yours. I was right.'

'True?'

'I promise you. We might have only just met but I've been searching for you a long time.'

Enormously aroused, she found her apprehension growing. This man was different. He had mistaken her for someone she was not but as she stood there she knew that she wanted, desperately, to become that woman.

'There's something else about this dress,' he told her. 'But before I show you what it is you have to promise something.'

'What?' Now she was fully aroused. Secrets and promises were like aphrodisiacs to her. She only wondered how he knew.

'You have to promise me that whatever happens to that dress in the next five seconds you will not interfere.'

She was puzzled. Did the dress dissolve or what? 'I don't understand,' she said.

'But do I have your promise?'

She nodded and he reached out to the top fastening buttons, tweaked them and the dress slid, like a caress, to the floor leaving her completely naked before him.

Four days – or was it a century? – ago, before she knew him, she might have instinctively grabbed at the dress to stop its downward slide but something about this man made her trust him and his judgement completely. She was proud to be naked for him and willed herself to be as still as a statue as he looked at her.

'Breathtaking,' he said. 'I knew I was right. You're perfect in or out of that dress. We'll have more of them made. It'll be exciting to know I can have you naked in seconds.'

Trembling before him she realised that he was as aroused as she was and as she fought for breath she brought her uncertain eyes to his and read in them that he knew. In that moment there was nothing more important to her than that this man should be sexually satisfied and then found she had fallen to her knees.

He was standing over her.

'Incredible. Beautiful!' he was saying as he tried to reach down and lift her to her feet, but she didn't want that. In close proximity lay his cock, veiled only by the thin material of his trousers. It was that fleshly pleasure god she wanted and eagerly she reached for it. He had to help her trembling hands seek him out, but the moment his arousal was free she sank her mouth down on to it like an eager calf at the teat.

Greedy now, insatiable even, choked by his growing erection, she tried to cry out and let him know what she was feeling, but his member gagged her. Her mouth clung to him, worked him, fearing that if she let go, took her mouth from him, she would fall backwards into an abyss of oblivion. This cock and its coming gift were, in that moment, her entire life. She was greedy for the taste of him, wanting him to fill her, choke her, punish her. Then, as she felt him start to throb, she found her own release as she redoubled her efforts to suckle from him. Suddenly, without seeming transition, she was on her own bed and he was burying himself deep inside her. She felt another wave starting as he moved against her. It came and she knew another was close behind. This was impossible. Sensation was crowding in on her brain, confusing her, leaving no room for thoughts beyond satiating her body's needs. There came only one other sensation – a sudden pain on her nipples.

'Yes!' she screamed. 'More of that! Hurt me! Punish me!'

His words started then in an excited stream. Words that assured her she would feel his pain, feel his come, feel his cock and at each teeth-clenched imprecation she yelled back him 'Yes!'

When did it stop, she wondered? She was lying flat on her stomach, streaked with sweat from his and her own overheated bodies, knowing only that somehow it must have stopped since she now lay in a velvety haze that held her swaying in the most comfortable position she had ever known.

She moved gently so as not to dislodge him only to find that he was lying turned away from her. What she had thought was his risen flesh inside her was only the bruised, happy memory.

Turning her head she could see the tendons raised on his strained neck where it pulsed with life. Fascinated, she watched the flesh vibrating. Somehow she wanted to match the rhythm of it, feel his pulsating life inside herself.

Reaching down she cupped herself in both hands, not caring that this spread her naked thighs obscenely. There was only him to see and she already knew that nothing she did would ever be obscene to him. Watching his neck pulse she imagined that it beat deep inside her. Matching her self caress to his pulse she could fantasise a situation where the throb would be constant, never detumescent, just a constant never-ending drip of infinite sexual arousal.

Never had she felt like this. Now she knew the meaning of insatiability. As her own libido sang she had to resist her bodily demand to increase the tempo of her searching, teasing finger. Instead she forced herself to endure this self-inflicted arousal as a regiment of men looked down on her spread thighs and waited their turn with her. Yes! Now she was a cheap whore – the brothel girl who would do anything, satisfy any man's craving. She was the dirty bitch that would crawl to them, beg them for their cocks and cry with gratitude when one deigned to put his shaft in her . . .

She came gently enough but lay gasping for breath as she fought for control of her own thumping heart. As her more rational mind took over from the wanton that lived inside her, she marvelled at what this man had done to her. He must have known at a glance what she was – what she craved. He had even known she wanted to be beaten when she would have been appalled if anyone had suggested it instead of, like him, just done it. She was startled to realise that, since meeting him, she had been in a constant state of arousal. Even in Eastbourne she had known that, deep inside, it had been still simmering, unacknowledged, within her.

Just seeing him brought that simmer into a searing life. If any man could take her by the hand and lead her to paradise then it was this man. A man she must cherish and satisfy, no matter what the cost, for fear of losing him.

Her secret fantasies had always been extreme. Here was a man that would drag those fantasies from her subconscious and uncritically watch her play them out in life.

The thought liberated her. She had beside her a man who had taken her beyond anything she had ever before imagined and, she knew, would take her even further. She only needed the determination, and the courage, to go with him.

She imagined herself standing beside him on some formal occasion wearing the gown as she had today and knowing that at any moment he could reach out, tweak those buttons, and leave her naked. She trembled at the thought of so delivering herself into his hands knowing she would never be able to refuse him anything.

Nothing was impossible – no fantasy beyond his imagination or their mutual exploration. She was free of constraint, of the need to pretend that she was anything other than a newly liberated, decadent, totally filthy-minded wanton – something which, until now, she had only ever admitted to herself in fantasy.

He was a fantasy made real and the thought frightened her a little.

Finally, she reached up and drew the top light cover gently over them both and immediately felt secure.

If she felt herself precariously on the edge of an abyss she also knew that, should she fall, she could be confident he would be there to catch her before she hit the rocks.

Smiling with contentment, she finally slept.

Chapter Three

S he had woken early and stood at the foot of the bed looking down on his sleeping face filled with a sense of wonder.

He looked so vulnerable in repose. No sign of that energy that could prompt searing orgasm in her. She had never imagined such intensity of feeling existed. With Kenneth their love-making had been tender, only pretend daring and adventurous but always neatly compartmentalised, tagged as something the mind turned to at bedtime. Never had she imagined that there could be a passion so all consuming that she wouldn't be able to rid herself of it even when asleep.

Acknowledging that her abstinence since Kenneth's traumatic death had created an almost unbearable pressure, she knew that this was more than the sudden, and finite, release of a bursting dam. Jeffrey had, she suspected, tapped a deep resource and opened her to a continuing, renewable flow.

As she watched him sleep she was afraid that he might wake and find her wanting. What he had to give was so precious it should be given as a tribute to perfection and that, she knew, she was not. What she needed was artifice and the good luck not be found out too soon.

It was as if all that had gone before had been simple preparation. In his presence she had found a fierce pride in her body. Until now it had been appreciated, tenderly kissed and caressed, but never before had she felt it so openly worshipped. With this man she could go confidently naked. With this man she could be openly wanton.

Then, aware that his eyes were open and watching her, she straightened her back, put back her shoulders, and made the best of her pose.

'Come,' he said throwing back the covers to show his risen flesh.

Like a supplicant approaching a holy relic she crawled onto the bed and gratefully did as he wanted.

First she licked, nuzzled and kissed him, and then, carefully, alert to any contrary instruction he might give her, raised her loins to straddle him, and reaching down, guided him into herself.

His intake of breath was all the goad she needed. Now he must be ridden like the thoroughbred he was. First, the trot, then the canter and finally the gallop.

It wasn't until he cried out and grasped her that she realised that the flame that had been heating her had come as much from his hands, rhythmically, slapping her buttocks, as from the reliquary buried deep between her thighs.

Feeling him gone from the field she lay beside him and wished away the time that would pass before his next arousal.

'What am I to do with you?'

'Anything you want,' she told him.

'You know that I can't let you go?'

'I've nowhere I want to go.'

They lay silently exchanging caresses for a moment before she found the agony of him not being inside her more than she could bear. 'Shall I make some coffee?' she asked.

'I insist,' he said softly, and added a kiss to the breast closest to his mouth.

She reached for his head as tiny darts of flame came from his lips through her nipples to the pleasure places in her brain.

'Coffee,' he said bringing her from her tantalising fantasies.

Reluctantly, she rose from the bed and, in a reflex born of custom, reached for her robe.

'No,' he told her. 'I want you naked.'

She felt inclined to tease him. 'I was always told a woman's body looked better if she was wearing a little something.'

'A man would have to be mad to acquire a perfect Ming vase and then want to cover it with a cloth wouldn't he?'

'Am I your "Ming"?'

'You are exquisite and very precious and beside you Ming is a commonplace.'

She felt liquid with the release from months of remorse and self denial. She wanted to rush at him and re-pledge herself but instead, feeling that she was exercising super-human control, she turned away from the extravagance of his compliment and went into the kitchen.

As she went through the mindless ritual of coffee making she wished she had something more exotic, something undreamed of, to offer him. But, she wistfully understood, there was only herself – and that, too, was soon to be found out. She had an uneasy feeling that they had started too quickly and, too soon, gone too far. She feared that anything travelling at this velocity must surely come off the rails at the first curve.

Towards noon he was to surprise her yet again.

Ordering her to stay as she was, he produced a pencil and a pad of notepaper and started sketching her. At first she was happy enough to have a reason to stay still for a moment and expected his sketches to be no more

303

than amateur crudities. So she was pleasantly surprised, when he handed them to her, to see a vibrant, naked young woman – one who just happened to have her face – drawn with great economy and directness.

'You're an artist?'

'An early ambition, quickly squashed.'

'What happened?'

'My father. I wanted to go to art school but he insisted that I should study something more vocational. The closest to art he would allow was architecture.'

He placed her in another pose and as he worked she thought she had found the first weak spot in his, until now, apparently impregnable armour.

'Isn't it a little unusual to give up art to become a property tycoon?'

'In the first place I haven't given up art. Secondly I became – what you are pleased to call – a "property tycoon" by accident. The same father that denied me my earlier ambitions left me a seedy, run down, rambling apartment block whose only asset was a good address. I used my newly acquired architectural skills to refurbish it. Everyone told me I was crazy and that it didn't make economic sense, but I couldn't stand owning anything that was that shabby and that ugly. Then the controlled rent laws were changed. I had moved it up market and it became the collateral asset from which I spread upward and outward.'

'And what happened to the art?'

He shrugged off the question and only the sound of his pencil spoilt the absolute silence until he heaved a huge sigh.

'It's time you knew about me,' he said.

Allowing her only a raincoat and a pair of shoes, she found herself being hustled out of her apartment to feel the chilly December wind invading parts she would never have normally exposed to the winter chill.

'Where are we going?'

'To my place.'

They got to a street corner and he hesitated. She didn't notice his concern at first. She was too busy eagerly scanning the faces of passers-by trying to judge whether or not they could sense she was naked under the coat. She found it particularly thriiling when she understood that no one was noticing. Either that or they just didn't give a damn!

His cursing brought her back to the present reality.

'The bloody car's gone!' he exploded. 'I wasn't sure at first but now I distinctly remember parking it there outside that shop.'

'Stolen?' she asked.

'What else? Come on, we'll have to get a cab.'

He was one of those people for whom taxies miraculously appeared on cue. It was in the cab that she was reminded that he loved to play erotic games.

He urged her to move from the rear seat to the jump seat directly in front of him. Aware of the taxi driver just a foot away from her back, she understood the point of the game and moved her thighs apart allowing the coat to fall away from her legs, fully exposing herself to him.

He mouthed to her that she should play with herself and for the first time in his presence she hesitated. The cab driver couldn't see but she feared other passing drivers – especially those sitting high in trucks or buses – might.

'Do it!' he said in a loud authoritative voice that made the cab driver think his words had been intended for him.

'Not you, driver!' he yelled back. 'I was talking to my whore!'

The cab driver chuckled but she was mortally offended. Snapping her legs together she carefully drew the coat back over her thighs to cover herself. She found she couldn't look at him.

'That . . .' he said in a soft even voice, '. . . was very naughty of you.'

Still refusing to look at him, she stared instead out of the side window.

Minutes later the cab drew up in front of the prestigious address that was his flagship property and she sat tight, undecided whether by going home directly she would be punishing herself more than him. It was then she realised her predicament. If she took the cab home she would have nothing to pay the man with and, then again, wouldn't it be silly to take the one cab driver in London who might guess at her condition and lead him to her home so he would know where she lived?

When Jeffrey turned to offer a hand out from the rear of the cab, she took it, telling herself she had no choice.

She still didn't feel like talking to him but was, despite herself, impressed as they crossed the refurbished, somewhat kitschy, lobby towards the elevators.

The receptionist called out a greeting, as did the man in a porter's uniform who hurried from some back room as if anxious to look alert in his employer's eyes.

Once inside the elevator she couldn't help noticing the Yale key he used to unlock the mechanism before it would respond to the PENTHOUSE button. She noted she was with a man who valued his security.

The elevator moved swiftly up but she kept a hurt distance. She felt pained that he made no attempt to break the silence and ask her what was wrong. She knew he didn't have to – that he already knew precisely at which moment the deep freeze had set in and why.

The doors opened into a small lobby and he had to use a magnetic key on a second set of heavy double doors before they would open.

When they did she was treated to an apartment of, literally, breath-taking proportions. It had the dimensions of a hotel lobby but there was little evidence of the over-zealous symmetry which some interior designers imposed. Instead, the main living room was split into groupings of furniture with a profusion of potted, semi-tropical plants that reduced the vast expanse to human proportions.

There were several messages on his answerphone so, in response to his invitation to have a look round, she started on a self-conducted tour.

Everywhere she looked was evidence of abundant affluence. Its corollary – bad taste – was totally absent. Jeffrey had managed to make a display that avoided vulgarity and ostentation. Although it was demonstrably impossible she got the feeling that this apartment had been here for some long time. There was no questioning its modernity but he had gifted it permanence.

She remembered being told how an aristocrat had made a 'put down' remark about someone he considered a parvenu. 'He's the sort of chap that buys his own furniture.'

Jeffrey had done that but avoided being too precise, too matching. She couldn't help noticing that the bed would accommodate four people with comfort. She wondered how many times it had.

When she returned to the living area she heard him telling a girl, his secretary, surely, about the stolen car and asking her to make the necessary steps, including informing the police. Did this man do nothing for himself?

When he laid the phone down he turned to her.

'It's a beautiful apartment,' she said.

'So! You've found your voice again!'

'You shouldn't have called me a whore!'

'I didn't,' he said, 'call you "a" whore. I called you "my" whore. There's a difference.'

'Well I'm not.'

He shrugged. 'You're free to leave,' he said.

She was standing in front of him, separated from the desk by two metres of velvety carpet. His words had stunned her. She even felt tears beginning to threaten her composure.

307

'Are you tired of me, then?' she said.

'No, but if you want to play then you play my rules.'

'Don't I get any choice?'

'Only when to stay and when to go. Do you want to go?'

'You know I don't.'

He nodded, stood up and closed the space between them to stand directly in front of her.

'Get rid of that coat and bend over the desk.'

Angry at him and herself for knowing that she would accept this humiliation, she tried to protest, but he cut her short by grabbing her, turning her and almost literally ripping the coat from her body. As she yelled desperately at him he propelled her forward to the desk and forced her face down to crush her nose into the smell of polished leather.

She opened her mouth to protest again at this treatment, but the word became a cry; then she felt him firmly entering her. Suddenly all protest seemed superfluous. Anger turned to joy as his words battered her ears.

'You disobeyed me in the cab, didn't you?'

'Yes!' she yelled.

'Are you sorry?'

'Yes!'

'Are you going to be my whore?'

'Yes!'

'What happens to disobedient whores?'

'They get fucked over desks!'

'Wrong!' his words seething into her ears like liquid lava. 'They get punished!'

'Yes! Punish me, screw me! Do anything you like to me!'

And then, in unison, they came.

Later that evening she stood tied loosely between two posts. Her feet firmly on the ground and though not strained she was, nevertheless, tethered, as immobile and fearful as any creature awaiting an unknown fate.

He had come to her and, without explanation, tied her wrists together with a silken cord. Then leading her to stand between the posts, had first tied her and then gently fed a knotted bandana into her mouth to silence her.

Without a word of explanation, not a look, nor a backward glance, he had left her among the ornamental plants that crowded for space in his heated solarium as if she was just another passive ornament among the many. The worst moment came when he turned off the lights in the solarium leaving her with only the incidental light escaping from the living area.

She had been there for what seemed to her an eternity. Her thoughts were confused by the dull ache that had started in her raised arms but one message repeated and repeated until she was sure it would become engraved on her throat. She hated him. Hated this. The moment she was released, it was over. How dare he do this to her? How dare he assume that there could possibly be any pleasure for her in such humiliation?

If he had stayed, if he had watched her, it might have become marginally supportable, interesting even, but she could hear him somewhere in the apartment making phone calls – arranging to go to a New Year's Eve party – and then, worst of all she could hear the drone of the TV.

Deep in her discomfort she tortured herself with the thought that she knew very little of this man . . . that wealth did not prevent someone being mad – only from being locked up. Suppose he was a maniac and intended to kill her? There was nothing she could do about it!

Hate him! Hate this! It's over between us!

She saw him coming and watched, her face muscles tensing, her vocal cords rehearsing the invective she intended showering on him. Punishment? He didn't know the meaning of the word.

'So, are you suitably chastened?'

His finger tips reached out and gently touched her nipples. It was as if he had touched her with heated needles.

The hands moved outward and encircled her breasts. His lips nestled to her throat, from which she couldn't escape. His hands circled her belly and then gently, with the subtlety of a soldering iron, touched her most vulnerable bud of flesh.

Then a switch was thrown and a gear moved in her body. She found herself moaning, pressing herself against his caresses, and desperately wanting him. But please God, she thought, first, please, set me free!

'I love you like this.'

God. No. Not like this! Please don't let me come!

His fingers returned to her nipples, now extended and sensitive. Gently at first he tweaked them then, increasing the pressure, he bit his nails into her tender flesh.

Using one hand he reached up and loosened the silk gag, and threw it from them.

'I want to see you smile,' he said, increasing the nail given pain.

She was breathing too hard, her throat too constricted to say anything.

'If you smile for me and tell me you love me then I'll set you free.'

Her uncertain eyes managed to still his swimming image and she saw his eyes – those eyes! Then, straining every muscle in her face, she managed to smile. 'I love you,' she said.

It was late evening before they spoke of anything other than their pleasure.

'Why did you do that to me?'

'You deserved it.'

'Why did you just leave me there and walk away?'

'I had things to do.'

'I hated you. You know that, don't you?'

He smiled to himself and by doing so rekindled the anger he had washed away with a gesture.

'I think I still hate you.'

'That's healthy. Hate is closer to love than any other emotion.'

Earlier he had shown her the tanning lamps built into the solarium to bring a touch of summer to even the dreariest winter's day.

They now lay side by side enjoying the counterfeit sun.

'Are you frightened?' he asked her.

'I'm not sure. I think I am but it's like a recurring nightmare. You know it will come at you in the night but it doesn't stop you wanting to go to sleep.'

'I have a technique for destroying nightmares. What you do is turn and face them. Stops the pursuing horror dead in its tracks. When you know your fear you can face it.'

'That's how I feel about you. Unknown. And yes, that frightens me.'

'Sure it isn't yourself that frightens you? Haven't you found out things about yourself you never knew?'

'Also.'

Even as she spoke she discovered something new about herself. She could lie here next to him and calmly, objectively, discuss things which would have, previously, shamed her in any context other than the throes of passion. Of course the protective eye shields they were wearing helped. The past few days had taught her that direct eye contact can be the most excoriating experience between two people.

Warmed by the lamps, confident to be naked yet masked from the world, she felt totally relaxed.

'What do you want of me?' she asked him out of a lengthening silence.

'To be allowed to worship.'

'Worship what?'

'You.'

'Is that what you think you were doing when you tied me up in the solarium?'

In truth she still harboured a hate of what he had done to her but also recognised that there was emerging a perverse recognition that the price was worth it for the joyous aftermath. When he had finally released her, the pain, if anything, had increased. The blood rushing back into her veins had seemed loaded with liquid fire rendering her totally helpless – and therefore without responsibility – for what had followed – an unfathomable depth of pleasure.

He had stayed silent for a long moment. 'Do you know how incredibly beautiful you looked?'

'How could I?' she asked with a degree of asperity.

'You're right,' he said. 'There should have been a mirror. Selfish of me. Next time. Promise.'

'What makes you think there'll be a next time?'

'There won't,' he said. 'Unless you want it.'

This struck her as a bizarre remark and left her feeling curiously bereft. Must she be forced to ask him to torture her? Did he imagine she ever would?

At that moment the timer that controlled the ultraviolet dosage clicked off and broke the mood.

Lifting the shields from their eyes they looked at each other as if for the very first time. Curiously, she even felt a little shy.

'Say it,' he said. 'Say the words you have often thought but have never dared say to a lover.'

The challenge struck her to the core. The words were there instantly, known to her since puberty and although never spoken they were now brazenly echoing in her mind and insisting she give them life. Words that, if she spoke them, would be the most terrible of all her betrayals of Kenneth. Fight as she might she couldn't stop them as they leapt into life from her lips.

'Fuck me in the arse,' she said and, unable to take breath until he answered, she listened, horrified, to the dying echo of the words.

Had he laughed. Had he leapt on her and taken her cruelly in that place where she knew she would suffer, she might have been able to plead a moment of madness, but he didn't. Instead he held her eyes for a whole heart-stopping minute then, standing, he reached down a hand to help her to her feet. 'Come with me,' he said softly.

Now quite frightened by what she might have started she padded beside him across the wide carpet and into his bedroom.

Throwing open his closets he indicated the rank upon rank of suits, shirts, ties and underwear.

'If you are to be taken like a man you will dress like one. You have one hour before I greet your identical twin brother.'

Turning, he left her alone with a heart-pounding dread at what she had done. Damn him, she thought. Why couldn't he have just taken her? Why force her into this humiliating ritual and make her responsible for her own madness?

If she did as he asked there was no escape, no turning back, no excuses she could make to herself in some future sleepless night. She was alone with her own wantonness.

Finding a full-length mirror she questioned her reflection. 'Shall you be his whore?'

After a moment's pause the image in the mirror, eyes wild with light, smiled and nodded.

313

Chapter Four

Confusion.

Her mind was racing and outstripping her brain's capacity to process the bombarding stream of thought.

His clothes. Where did she start? Choosing her own clothes for any occasion was stressful enough but deciding what to wear for her imminent sodomisation, with her immolator impatiently waiting, was the very stuff of which panic attacks are made.

Very few useful ideas were getting through to her oppressed brain.

Her body was not much help either. Her heart was pumping blood at a rapid rate. Her hands shook as they fluttered over the serried ranks of shirts and sweaters, while her breathing was audibly hoarse.

She was in no shape to go shopping!

Feeling the task had overwhelmed her, she turned away from the closets to sit down heavily on the huge bed, almost ready to let the threatening sobs break through and, head in hands, simply give up.

Either that or run away and hide.

What a good idea! Where would she go? Home? What would she use for clothes or money? Her decision had been made – forced on her – when she got out of the taxi. What would she do now? Put time on re-wind and delete that decision?

Damn him!

Why couldn't he have just done it?

Why put her through this hell?

Because he liked it, that's why!

In retrospect she saw her predicament as the result of a carefully engineered plan.

Bringing her to his apartment wearing only a coat and shoes he had ensured that she was his captive as surely as if he had bound and chained her. What initially seemed a spontaneous, mad caprice, she now realised, was the first move in a diabolical plot!

Testing her, that's what he was doing. Even now he was probably gleefully chortling at the prospect of her tear-stained appearance before him to admit defeat.

It then came to her that he might be expecting her not to go through with it. That would explain why he hadn't just done it. He was counting on her cowardice! It was entirely possible, she thought, that his plot had extended that far!

Well, to hell with him!

Picturing him, confidently waiting for her capitulation, angered her. Out of anger was born resolution. She'd damn well show him she was not going to play his 'little woman'. Now she was determined to call his bluff!

Returning to the closets she found her anger had calmed her. This was, after all, a simple, if unfamiliar task. Take it a step at a time and anything was possible.

First, imagine what her identical twin brother would have looked like. No problem. Exactly like her. Except, of course, for the hair.

Solution? Obvious. Find a hat!

She looked but there were no hats. A cap then? Sports clothes. Not this closet. Try the next. No. Maybe he kept his sports gear, supposing he had any, in a different closet.

Looking round she could see none that weren't already open.

Intending to look in the bathroom, she had started towards it when she noticed a closet standing between the bedroom and bathroom doors. In there she hit pay dirt.

Rackets for squash, tennis and a curious basket-like glove. Caps? Top shelf. Bingo! Baseball style caps in profusion, a multi-coloured curiosity with a gold tassel on it, cricket caps and then she saw it – a wide brimmed panama. Perfect!

Going to one of the many mirrors, she piled up her hair and placed the panama on top. Untidy wisps showed through. She needed to wind her hair onto the top of her head and then find something to keep it there. Dismissing the possibility of finding any hair pins or grips, she spotted a pair of his shoes. The lace from one of them would have to do.

Her hair bound into a bun, secured by the lace, wasn't the perfect solution but it served. Slamming the hat down over the piled up mess, she smiled. Great! Next a shirt.

She didn't waste time on it. She took down the first silk shirt she could find. There was a momentary confusion with the left to right buttoning, but she finally got her clumsy fingers to work that out. Oversize and looking ridiculous but, with the sleeves folded back and a jacket on top, she thought it would be acceptable.

Underpants? Why not. In a bottom drawer she found some pretty exotic ones. Not a whole lot unlike panties. An unworthy thought came into her head but, considering the determined stamina he'd shown in administering to her, it was immediately dismissed. However, some of his underpants were little more than posing pouches. It was possible they were unwanted Christmas presents, but whatever they were they fitted snugly round her waist and hips. God knows what they did to him!

Now trousers. This was an immediate problem. All his seemed to have been made to accommodate two of her, and there was no way her waist and hips could keep them up. She didn't want her own brother to look like a baggy-pants comic.

Skis! She remembered seeing skis stacked in his 'sporting' closet, where there were skis there would be ski-pants. Tight, clinging ski-pants! Perfect!

After a moment's search she found them folded neatly in a drawer. Pulling a pair over his suspect posing pouch she saw that they fitted well enough except for the inordinate length of the legs. Sitting down she found that by pulling and stretching she could fold the excess length up and into the bottom of the pants.

They were loose under the crotch but she took up that surplus by rolling the waistband in on itself.

How did she check out so far? Not too bad. She needed a sweater, loose but not too much, a wind-cheater, also loose, on top of that and things were taking shape. Socks obscured the bulge where she had rolled in the leg length of the pants. Shoes? Despair gripped her. There was no chance she could find shoes to fit.

Her own shoes! They were only medium heeled. They would do but the trouble was she had lost them while being taken over the desk. How could she retrieve them without risking him seeing her before she was ready?

Simple. Let him do something for once.

Crossing to the bedroom door she opened it a few inches and called, 'Hello!?'

No answer. She opened it a few inches more and put her head out. She could hear his voice murmuring somewhere off in the distance. Cautiously, she slipped into the living room, darting from potted plant to potted plant, peering round them to make sure she wasn't spotted.

As she got closer to his voice she could hear that he

was on the telephone, but fortunately for her, at the far end of the apartment and not at his desk.

She found one shoe lying where she would have expected it, but no sign of the other. Thinking it couldn't be far she started anxiously looking round. She had just spotted it partially obscured by the valance of one of the couches when his end of the telephone conversation impinged on her.

'Yes, he's quite young and inexperienced. I want the young lady to, you know, give him something to remember when he goes back to school.'

She listened, mouth open, and horrified. What was he plotting now? She had no doubt that the 'he' of the 'inexperienced' was meant to be her. She couldn't believe he was hiring some kind of call girl.

She heard him winding up the call. 'You can? Oh, excellent. Straight away? Fine. Yes, here's the address.'

She listened, her mouth so wide open that it became dry, and as he gave his address she wondered what he was playing at.

Realising the conversation was coming to an end she scuttled back to the bedroom wondering why *she* felt guilty.

That he had some further complication to add to her already overburdened worry banks, there was no doubt. Just what it was she couldn't imagine. Well, she *could* . . . but surely not 'that'? If so the 'young lady' with her 'memorable experience' was due for a surprise of her own!

She pulled on the shoes and stood to look into the mirror. What she saw was a completely outmoded, expensively dressed, idiot. She looked like a boy who had got hurriedly dressed in a bomb distressed ballet chorus dressing room. The panama didn't go with the jacket. The jacket might have gone with the ski-pants – but nowhere she would have wanted to go. The shoes were the only familiar thing about herself.

What was she going to do? She looked a disaster and felt worse.

She was about to give up when she heard a brief tap on the bedroom door and, as she whirled round, ready to explode if he so much as smiled, saw him hesitate only briefly before breaking into an overly hearty greeting.

'George!' he beamed, 'I was wondering where you'd got to! Come, I've got us both a drink. You *do* drink don't you?'

Feeling that he must be either blind or more easily pleased than she thought, she followed him out of the room.

With a comradely arm about her shoulder he walked her across the expanse of the living area. 'I've been looking forward to having a talk with you, George.'

Leading her to a bar which seemed to have been born out of a bookcase – the first hint of crassness she had found in his furnishings – he handed her a tumbler of whisky.

'As you know,' he was saying, 'I've been seeing a great deal of your sister and quite frankly there are some things about her that puzzle me. I thought you might be able to help me with a pointer or two.' Jeffrey paused and smiled with patronising indulgence. 'Drink all right?'

She had gratefully taken a sizeable draught of the smooth malt but, still unsure of her voice, simply nodded in reply.

'Good!' he cried, leading her to sit on a couch opposite to his own. Sitting himself down he beamed across at her. 'I mean, frankly, she's a bit of a tart, isn't she?'

She frowned and conveyed her dissension as best she could without, yet, daring to try out her voice.

He seemed to pick up on her dilemma and sorted it out. 'Now, George, I know your voice is about to break

319

and you're embarrassed about it, but you can talk if you want to, you know.'

'She's not a tart!' she said positively.

'Well, you would say that wouldn't you? Being a loyal brother and all, and, of course, I respect that, but tell me, George, have you ever had a woman yourself?'

She reverted to a resentful shake of the head while waiting to see if this was going to lead to an explanation of the phone call.

'No, I suppose not. The Old School keeps to its regime of cold showers and avoiding "evil" thoughts, eh?' He paused and drew in a long breath as if contemplating the 'good old days', before going on. 'Matter of fact I was reading the other day that cold showers actually *stimulate* the libido. Did you know that?'

She shook her head.

'So you see, the Old School idea can lead to a lot of mischief in the showers.' Idly picking an imaginary thread from his jacket sleeve, he went on. 'Much of that going on still?'

Again she shook her head aware that her 'twin brother' wasn't being very good at this. Despite the sanctioning of her unmasculine voice, she still couldn't speak because, having been reminded of where all this was supposed to be leading, she was scared to death. He *hadn't* been bluffing!

Seeing Jeffrey in the role of an 'old queen' intent on seducing a 'young boy' was unnerving to say the least. He was just a little too smooth and convincing for her taste. An added concern was the knowledge that there was a 'surprise' on its way.

Perversely, she also resented him thinking that any brother of hers, imaginary or not, would fall for such a line!

Jeffrey, who had been watching her/him for some silent moments, now gave the most sickly smile she could imagine before patting the couch beside him.

'You look so distant sitting over there. Why don't you come and sit by me?'

Feeling sickened and revolted – Jeffrey was that good at 'it' – she warily moved to sit next to him as he had asked.

Jeffrey, laying a careless arm along the couch behind her, smiled again. 'Got a little treat on its way for you, George.'

A very real shudder of revulsion went through her body. 'Really?' she squeaked.

'Yes. Possibly, something a young lad like you has never seen before.'

Quite suddenly she felt she wasn't there. It was as if her body had been invaded by another creature. Everything was suddenly unreal, even surreal. She really was starting to respond like a nervous schoolboy in the company of a disreputable uncle.

This was ridiculous. A waking nightmare. Could it be that she had been subtly hypnotised or even drugged?

When the arm, which had been 'carelessly' laid along the back of the couch, became a hug, she actually felt quite sick.

Abruptly, not quite sure where the impulse had come from, she found herself on her feet blurting out that she wanted to go.

Jeffrey was staring up at her, obviously taken aback. As they looked at each other in confusion the apartment door bell cut through the tension like a knife.

'Not now,' he said, getting to his feet. 'Surely,' he added, before turning away to answer the door.

She looked around for succour but none was apparent. She began to think she might be going mad when she strained to hear the subdued murmur of voices coming from the apartment's lobby.

Now, in total confusion, she felt as if she was suffocating. Her brain had simply ceased functioning and the earlier 'disassociated' feeling grew even stronger.

The voices drew nearer and she turned to see Jeffrey

321

returning accompanied by a tall slender girl wearing a full-length 'gowny' dress and, of all things, a feather boa over her shoulders.

'This is my young nephew, George,' he was saying to the girl. 'George, this is Lesley.'

Lesley came forward with a graciously extended hand. 'George' found 'himself' awkwardly shaking her hand and not knowing where to look.

Lesley, fortunately, seemed oblivious to anything about her but her own appearance. 'Darling,' she said, addressing Jeffrey. 'Put my music into a suitable slot, would you?'

Jeffrey, who seemed to be enjoying himself enormously, took a cassette from her and went off to place it in its 'suitable slot'.

Meanwhile Lesley was casting an assessing eye around the apartment which gave Helen a chance for a good look at her.

The hair looked as if it was fighting for its life under layers of lacquer. The face had been made up by an undertaker and the word 'glitz' had been invented to describe the dress. All in all, Lesley was what her mother would have called 'extravagant' and she would have called, enamelled.

Jeffrey rejoined them to be received by an anxious enquiry from Lesley. 'My music, darling! Aren't you going to play it?'

Showing her a black box he was carrying, he smiled. 'Remote control,' he told her. 'Any time you're ready.'

Casting another, despairing, eye about the apartment Lesley spoke again. 'Yes, darling, but we'll have to do something about the lighting . . .' Lesley moved off around the apartment, turning off this lamp, turning that one on, until she came back murmuring, 'I suppose that'll have to do,' and struck a startling, dramatic pose; standing in profile to them with one hand raised in the air and the other knuckled to her forehead.

Turning to 'George', Jeffrey indicated that she should

come to sit next to him on the couch, as Lesley hissed: 'My music, darling!'

Jeffrey hit the play button on the remote and, as the brassy show music filled the apartment, Lesley started making swooping, leg dragging movements about the space before the couches, only occasionally tripping on the hem of her gown in the deep rug piling.

Feeling that things were moving from the surreal to the preposterous Helen realised that Lesley was about to launch into a strip-tease of the most excruciatingly embarrassing kind. She couldn't bring herself to look at Jeffrey – on the other hand, she could barely tear her eyes away from the ludicrous Lesley – but she did begin to wonder when he had decided to turn their 'affair', if their relationship could aspire to so grand a status, into farce.

Mouth involuntarily open in stupefaction she watched as Lesley slipped out of the gown to reveal black stockings on a garter belt framing surprisingly good legs, then used the feather boa to play peek-a-boo with her undersized breasts.

Having thought that things couldn't get worse she was appalled when Lesley started waltzing towards her, flicking the boa into her face. 'Have you been a *really* good boy? Lesley *loves* really good boys!'

Fortunately, Lesley waltzed off into a series of crotch-probing poses, enabling Helen to stop herself throwing up on the glass couch table before her.

When was this nightmare to end? She had never felt more shamefully distressed in her life. Distress for the totally untalented Lesley who, somewhere, waited like a taxi to be summoned out to embarrass people.

The music was building to what had once been a show-stopping climax and she could pray that it signalled the end of this torture – a prospect which focused her mind on the horrendous potential the aftermath presented. Suicide would be the only rational response if Lesley were to be included.

Now their 'dancer' was dramatically sticking one long leg before the other as she advanced on 'George' with fixed gaze and malice aforethought. Then, throwing her arms and boa wide in the air, she exposed her almost non-existent breasts as, looming menacingly closer, Lesley placed one leg on the glass table, threw her thighs wide to expose the diamante G-string, which 'George' realised, with horror, was about to come off!

It did! To reveal an even greater horror. There before her eyes was an unmistakably male penis! She felt unable to take her eyes from it as the music died away and total silence reigned.

'Want to feel it, darling?' asked the voice of 'Lesley'. 'It's a real one.'

Mesmerised, she heard Jeffrey speak. 'You have my permission . . .'

Slowly, she raised her eyes to the now grotesque face of 'Lesley' to see that he had whipped off the lacquered wig. As their eyes met Lesley spoke. 'I don't do penetration, darling, but if you want me to go down on you, that's cool!'

She heard a silly, squeaky voice protest, 'But I'm a girl!'

Lesley chuckled. 'That's all right, love. I don't discriminate.'

Feeling as if she had been transmuted into a waxworks tableau, she could find no thought, no words, other than a silent prayer that somehow the floor would open up and get her out of this.

Her prayer was answered by Jeffrey. With a sonorous clap of his hands he stood up and spoke the first sensible words she had heard all evening. 'Wonderful! Absolutely marvellous. Thank you Lesley, but, sorry, that's as far as we can take it tonight.'

Afraid to meet anyone's gaze Helen sensed Lesley immediately dropping out of character to fussily gather up 'her' discarded props as Jeffrey shepherded 'her' away.

Meanwhile 'George' sat feeling as if a dentist had sneaked up and injected her entire body with novacaine.

There was more murmuring at the door but, this time, thankfully, it was the sound of 'Lesley' departing. It was then she realised she was still wearing the hat. How long ago her preparation all seemed now! The hat lay in her hands like the reminder of another life.

When he came back into the room, thankfully alone, she found her voice. 'Why did you do that?' she asked him.

'It's what "us chaps" do.'

Silently, she looked at him. Were men an alien species? Had he imagined that what they had seen could, on any level, be construed as titillating, arousing or anything but humiliating to the onlookers?

'Sad, isn't it?' he asked, voicing her thoughts exactly.

When he came and reached down for her she went into his arms with a sob of relief. The nightmare was over and the world could resume its axis.

But not quite.

'Look,' he said, and she watched as he reached under the glass table and, pulling away a furry rug, revealed a mirror laid to reflect upward.

'What's that for?' she asked.

'For you,' he said. 'You told me you liked to watch yourself suffering.'

She felt herself jellifying. The protest her brain was making was choked off by the excitement in her throat.

His voice softly insistent, he said, 'Kneel on the table.' When she hesitated, he added, 'It won't break.'

Suddenly, the role intended for Lesley was clear. 'She' had been hired to witness her humiliation. As she tentatively did as he said, she reflected that, comparatively, it made what was to come an act of love.

'Stay quite still,' he murmured as she knelt on the table and looked through its transparent surface to her 'twin brother' looking back up at her.

325

She watched as Jeffrey reached round and loosened the rolled up trousers tops and then eased the elasticised top over her hips. Fascinated, she felt distanced, like an audience watching a play, as he ran his hands over her rump. Then she flinched and gasped as she felt the lubricant jelly being worked into her.

Now she knew he really meant to go through with it she felt her body preparing itself – except it had gone into action in the wrong place!

'You're going to get a thorough screwing,' he told her, moving her raised buttocks towards the end of the table. 'You can scream and shout all you want. It won't make the slightest difference.' He was standing behind her now, as she stared down at the frightened face of her 'brother's' reflection as he waited with her.

Standing behind her, she felt him hard and probing. She gasped in anticipation of pain as he found her and tried to force entry.

With a tight grip on her hips he thrust again and she found herself falling forward to rest her arms, to the elbows, on the glass top.

Then he withdrew, but the respite was fleeting, since he had withdrawn only to better prepare the ground. His jelly laden fingers searched her out and acted as warning precursors for the giant that would follow in their path.

Again he addressed himself and this time the resisting sphincter muscle surrendered to him and she screamed as he surged into the breach.

The mirror relentlessly recorded every flicker of expression, each and every one of her protests against the strange sensation, but there was no escape now. He was lodged firmly and moving smoothly while she stared, in horror, at the maddened face in the mirror.

Now the rushing sensations were close to unbearable. Layers of pain and pleasure so intermingled they seemed inseparable. Now she saw her reflection screaming and she cried out for the lash of him.

'Yes,' screamed the demented creature in the mirror. 'Yes!' and he responded, bucking and rearing into her with even greater vigour, ever greater cruelty. Now, having transmuted pain into pleasure, she rejoiced, she no longer cared about what he was doing to her. Happy only that he could harvest such pleasure from her body, she felt herself threshing in the grip of an orgasmic wave.

Insensate to anything, overburdened with delight, she felt him throbbing and pumping, and filling her with his pleasure.

When his exhausted weight bore down on her she slid forward to lay on the glass, her head now turned sideways away from the indelicate, mirrored, vision and thanked any interested god that she had lived long enough to know this moment.

They lay for long minutes, he still inside her but now of more accommodating size, in silent communion until she got an uncontrollable fit of the giggles.

'What's so funny?' he asked, defensively acerbic.

'I was just thinking of poor Lesley,' she said. '"No penetration"! She doesn't know what "she's" missing!'

Chapter Five

They woke like lovers.

Lying side by side in his huge bed beneath a single sheet, they held hands in silent communion, feeling no need to question or explain.

She was the one to break the potent silence. 'Yesterday, when I saw you on my door monitor you looked exactly like someone in an old newsreel.'

'God news or bad news?' he asked in a slightly puzzled tone.

'At the time I didn't know, but now I do.'

'Really?'

'Yes. Because now I feel exactly the same.'

'As what?'

'As if I was in an old newsreel.'

Raising himself on one elbow he looked down into her smugly smiling face and was puzzled. 'Have I missed the point of this conversation – or what?'

She shook her head. 'I haven't come to the "point" yet.'

'Would you mind hurrying up? I have this uncontrollable urge to fuck you.'

She smiled, cat-like, into his face. 'You must have seen those old newsreels of the Allied troops liberating France.'

'Of course.'

'Well, right this minute, I feel like one of those French women, beside themselves with joy, clambering onto the tanks.'

Looking down, his expression was still puzzled.

'Liberated,' she told him. 'That's what you've done to me. Liberated me after months of oppression.'

His eyes flickered during a momentary stunned silence. 'I think that's about the best compliment I have ever received.'

'My hero!' she said, but couldn't contain the giggle.

His mouth nuzzling into her throat, he murmured, 'And how, exactly, did those newly liberated women reward their conquering heroes?'

Purring with pleasure at his caresses she could barely contain her mounting excitement. 'Well, first they would permit their "hero" to bring them chocolates and then, perhaps, allow a kiss. All most proper, of course. Then, another day, perhaps he would call with flowers and get two kisses. Some days later she might receive chocolates *and* flowers . . .' His lips on her breasts were creating tidal waves, making it difficult for her to maintain her little girl, bantering tone so she broke off to indulge herself in moaning restlessness.

'And, after all this long drawn out courtship – what did he get?'

'Movietone never showed that,' she managed – the words barely escaping her throat.

'Shall we try an educated guess?' he asked as his lips moved to cover her urgent mouth.

Suddenly the bed was a battlefield. No more a place for bantering philosophers or, even, thought. Here only the animal responders could survive. Joyously, her body greeted his penetrating surge while her brain became fixed in a loop of joy.

This was right! This act between these two people at this time and place, she thought, was the true definition of consummation; the saturation and the wholesome, natural completion of self.

She welcomed his unstoppable climactic surge with genuine joy, screaming out with an intensity more appropriate to fear than pleasure and then as suddenly they fell apart like broken dolls to lay appalled at the pleasure they had known at each other's loins.

She was the first to find words. '*Ah, mon Colonel! Où sont les autres?*'

He was still gasping for breath. 'For God's sake don't talk French to me. I can barely think in English!'

Filled with the joy of a confident temptress she rolled to press her breasts against his heaving chest. 'I wanted to know where the rest were?'

'Rest of what?' he gasped.

'Your Regiment! We liberated women do not stint to reward our liberators and we show no discrimination!'

'Or mercy!' he gasped.

Kissing her way down the centre seam of his chest and belly she came upon his fearful pride.

'*Pauvre petit!*' she murmured. '*Je crois trouver un héros tombé!*' With sinuous tongue she reached out to tease the 'fallen hero' now limply lying in repose, bringing a moan of delighted protest from him.

'I see it all now,' he said. 'The entire Machiavellian plot!' Reaching down he seized her head and turned her grinning face towards his own. 'You've insured me for a million pounds and now you're set on fucking me to death!'

Her laugh rang out in delight. 'The way I see it, is that it's got to be worth a damn good try!'

Dragging her up the length of his body he brought her nose to nose. ''Tis a far, far better thing I do now than I have ever done.'

Laughing with delight she joined in to mangle his quote. 'That a man should give his life for a woman's pleasure?'

Closing his eyes against the intensity of his sigh he

pushed her head to rest on his chest. 'This is a moment of such exquisite pleasure I feel there ought to be a way of preserving it forever in amber.'

Each pleasurably confident that their thoughts were identical, they lay in silent communion for some minutes before he spoke.

'Tell me something,' he said.

She smiled upward. 'Like yesterday?'

'No. Yesterday I asked you to say something you have never before dared say to a lover. This is different.'

She waited, confident that there was nothing she couldn't tell him.

'Tell me something about yourself that you've never told anyone. Not even your best friend.'

A twinge of pain, discomfort, shuddered through her. This man had plundered her body in the most absolute manner possible, and she had rejoiced in the surrender but now, it seemed he wanted to assault that most intimate part of her body – her mind.

She knew exactly what he wanted to know. Just as yesterday the five words that had hovered on the edge of her lips, unspoken for years, had struggled free, now her greatest secret was there, fully formed, and impatiently waiting its turn but it was too painful to share, even with him.

When she was very young and still experimenting with her own sexuality she had discovered that the man who lived opposite her in Eastbourne had been spying into her bedroom with a telescope. Night after night she had tormented the man, sometimes giving him full view of what he sought and on others coming to the brink and then closing her blinds before he got what he wanted. She had been knowingly cruel in her exhibitionism and thought herself a monster while consoling herself with the thought that he was only getting what he deserved.

Night after night she had revelled in knowing his eyes were on her, and goaded into even more daring

331

acts she had felt like a latter-day Scheherazade and found fuel for her own fantasies. One night her mother, looking out from another room, had discovered the man spying from a tree to which her exhibitions had lured him, and called the police. The man had been dragged into court and lost his highly placed position with the local authority. He had, to his honour, never mentioned what must have been obvious to him – that she had known and conspired with him – while shame had prevented her saying a word about her own repeated complicity, and he had been hounded out of town, his reputation in ruins. This incident was known to no one but themselves and remained her most shameful secret. From time to time she would calculate how old the man must be by now, and by what standard he must judge her own behaviour. While that man lived, the only other guardian of her guilt, she knew she could never be truly free. Not even now, not even with this man who had brought her to the edge of paradise, could she share it. Instead she sought to divert him.

'I used to run an airline,' she said and then waited as he absorbed her meaning before reacting precisely as she had hoped he would.

Raising himself on one elbow he stared down at her. 'You what!?'

She laughed, delighted by his reaction. 'I did!' she insisted.

'An airline?' he asked.

She nodded, almost unable to contain her happiness that she had managed to surprise him.

'A real airline? I mean, one with aeroplanes that flew?'

She nodded again.

'Which one?' he demanded.

'Well, all right,' she confessed, 'it wasn't exactly an *airline*, but we did have planes and they did fly.'

'What was it then?'

'A club. There was this small airfield near where I

332

used to live. The owners would sometimes rent their planes to other people and sometimes, if they were qualified, they would fly them as air taxis. I used to run the office.'

Sinking back onto the pillows he sighed with relief. 'For a moment I thought I was in bed with the Chairman of British Airways!'

Her laughter rang round the bedroom.

'I always wanted to learn to fly,' he said, and when she stayed silent, went on. 'Never had the time.'

Her silence had become palpable and, curious, he looked across to see that tears were flowing from her eyes.

'What's the matter?' he asked with immediate concern.

'That's where I met Kenneth.'

'Kenneth?' he asked and then immediately felt stricken as he remembered. 'Your husband?'

Her chin trembling now, she nodded.

'Christ!' he said feeling an idiot. 'I'm sorry. Look, I blundered into that! Millie had told me what happened, of course. The last thing I wanted was to upset you.'

Her shoulders were shaking now, and she turned away murmuring into the pillows.

He reached for her but she, now openly weeping, shrugged him off.

'Look there's nothing that's happened between us for you to be ashamed about.' He felt helpless seeing her pain and feeling he had nothing to offer. 'You're a young woman. No one could blame you. Please don't . . .'

She spoke savagely into the pillow. 'You don't understand! I killed him!'

Her words jolted him for a moment until he understood they couldn't have literal meaning. Now he reached for her more positively and forced her anguished face to look at him. 'That's crazy!' he told her. 'How could you have "killed" him?'

Throwing off his hand which sought to placate her, she fled to the bathroom. He would have followed and caught her but, as he moved, he found his foot tangled in the sheet and was held long enough for her to have shut and bolted the door.

'Open the door,' he pleaded. 'Please. I want us to talk.'

Her only reply was a muffled: 'Go away!'

Reluctantly, he forced himself to give her the time and space she so obviously needed.

Using a guest bathroom, he found himself making a mental inventory of his own bathroom for anything with which she might harm herself. With relief he concluded there was nothing. Not even aspirin, for which he had a lifelong aversion. The windows were fixed against the air-conditioning so it was impossible for her to hurl herself down the eight floors of the building. Even so he was concerned enough to come silently to the door and press his ear against it, listening for any sound inside.

His worst fear was that he would hear nothing so he felt almost pleased to hear the shower noisily gushing.

Dismissing his fears as melodramatic, he turned to dressing. She was, he assured himself, far too sensible a person to do anything like that.

Finally, remembering that this was a business day, he went out to the office section of the apartment, still cursing himself for having brought Kenneth into their bed.

'Idiot!' he yelled at himself, before picking up the telephone to tell Annabel that he was ready to start his working day.

She sat huddled in the corner of the shower cabinet and let the water pound down on her naked body. Not all the waters in all the world would be enough to wash away the self-disgust that gripped her. How could she have so piled treachery on betrayal? Even, back then, when Kenneth was dying, choking, drowning, she had lain, pleasuring herself on the deck, sensuously aware that the Diving Master was looking at the breasts she had bared to the sun.

When they had brought up Kenneth's body and she saw the agony of his dying in his face she had felt cursed by all the gods that ever were. Had she not panicked and left him she would have been, as she was meant to be, there to summon the help that would have saved him. Instead, she had been lying in the sun dreaming of what they would do to each other that night in the hotel bedroom.

She had been sickened then as she was sickened now.

Emerging from the bathroom, wrapped in an over-sized robe – a reminder that she had come to this flat practically naked – she hesitated as she heard voices. His, and then the answering voice of a girl or woman. For a moment she shuddered at the memory of Lesley, and, then, as she came closer, she heard they were talking about the claim on the stolen Maserati.

The girl was tall. Her black hair was cut so dramatically close to her head it looked almost like a cap. She was strikingly attractive, perhaps a year or two older than herself and when she looked up she revealed the most beautiful eyes Helen could ever remember.

'Ah,' Jeffrey cried, following Annabel's eyeline. 'This is Annabel,' my personal assistant.'

The two women smiled and then warily waited for some sign that the other intended to shake hands. Neither did.

'Let's all have some breakfast. Annabel, would you?'

Annabel picked up the telephone and spoke quietly in the background as he came to her. 'You all right now?' he asked, and when she nodded, went on, 'I feel a complete idiot. I'm sorry.'

Looking at him she managed a smile. 'It's hardly any of your fault.'

'It was my fault for blundering in like that. Especially then, at that moment.'

'What "moment"?' she asked.

He looked at her awkwardly. 'Well . . . just then I felt we were so close. You know,' he finished artlessly.

Looking at him she suddenly realised that this assertive, dominating man could also be vulnerable. 'It wasn't your fault,' she told him. 'It was a passing idiocy on my part.'

He was holding her now but not so close that they couldn't look into each other's eyes. 'I know that's not true. I know the memory of him is still an agony. I just want you to know that I will do anything to make it easier for you to bear.'

Laying her head against his chest she let the tears flow again, now a blending of gratitude and a feeling that his solicitude was welcomed but misplaced.

Annabel, coming to announce that breakfast was on its way up, was stilled by the intimacy embodied in their embrace. Silently, and a little in awe, she turned away unable to disturb them.

Later that day as she lay in the solarium, listening to the distant voices of Jeffrey and Annabel as they worked, she found that she had regained some of her confidence. Having worked through the self-hatred of the early morning, she had concluded that if she was of no worth to herself she could, still, be of use to others. A category which was hastily reduced to an exclusive one. Jeffrey. He had shown concern. Consideration. Appreciation. She was capable of lighting his eyes with delight. If that were not a worthy function then she couldn't imagine what else might be.

Naked, she went to where he worked at his desk. Annabel was at a distance feeding paper into a fax machine, as Helen willed him to look up.

When he did, she saw with pride how his eyes flickered from her face to her breasts, to her naked pubis and back again.

'You don't demand enough of me,' she told him. 'If you want a whore then you have me.'

336

Jeffrey's mouth quivered, his lips tried to form words but none came.

Peripherally aware that Annabel was openly watching her, she turned and walked away across the deep-piled space to the bedroom.

It had been almost an hour since her declaration to Jeffrey. An hour she had spent staring into a mirror and asking, over and over again, the same question: 'Who are you?'

The real question she was asking of herself was 'Why did you do that?' Why had she made such a determined attempt to close down all her previous life and throw herself so totally into Jeffrey's hands? Chillingly, she realised it was not the first time she had made such a gesture.

When Kenneth had asked her to marry him she had been excited less by the culmination of a romantic dream but rather as a means of escape from her mother. For as long as she could remember, her mother had terrified her just as she had dominated her father.

'Extravagance!' was her mother's verdict on every birthday present, every Christmas gift her doting father had ever bought her. From an early age she had been aware that her mother thought of her as a rival and that never once, during all those years of her growing, had she ever managed to gain her approval. Kenneth's proposal had given her ammunition against her mother. An act of defiance to counter the many years of helplessness as she watched her beloved father sink further and further under the yoke of domination. How many times had she seen that smiling acceptance of his subservience and wanted to shake him, force life into him, because his acceptance of her mother's domination robbed her of any chance of successful rebellion. That was why she now sought out strong willed men. Men behind whom she could find shelter from her mother's wrath.

Guiltily, she now saw that Kenneth had not been that man. He had simply been the means of escape and she doubted that she had ever truly loved him. Whether or not he would have developed the strength to provide the protection she so desperately craved, had never been put to the test. The accident had ended any such hopes and instead returned her to her mother's unrelenting pressure. The question now was could Jeffrey be that man? In going to him as she had, speaking as she had done, she now realised it had been an act not of submission to Jeffrey but another attempt to distance herself, to shut out forever, her mother.

When the door to the bedroom opened she saw Jeffrey coming into the room and, standing, she turned to face him.

'You are not my "whore",' he told her. 'When you are free I will love you.'

'"Free" – of what?' she asked.

'Of your guilt.'

'You mean Kenneth?'

'There's a great deal more troubling you than simply Kenneth,' he said with finality.

His words struck so directly into her own thoughts that she felt almost elated that he could be so understanding. For confirmation she sought to challenge him. 'What makes you think you know so much about me?'

'I've been there,' he told her in the flat tones of confession. 'I know what it is to have guilt tearing into your guts. My father . . .' His words trailed away like water spilled in a thirsty desert. 'Let's just say: "I know".'

'So what do you propose doing about it?' she asked.

'I told you yesterday that the best way to beat a nightmare is not to run away but to turn and face it. I propose that we test that theory together.'

'How?'

'By means and times of my choosing. If you put

yourself in my hands I think we could work it out. Are you willing to try?'

It was another demand for commitment. Once more he was asking for her submission. She had now, in this time and place to make a decision which she knew would be irrevocable. As she stood there facing him across a room, which seemed suddenly a continent wide, her mind raced through the alternatives. If she refused this man she might be turning her back on her one salvation. If she submitted she had no idea of where it might lead. Remembering his earlier, milder, challenges and his talent for bringing her to previously unimagined heights of pleasure, she knew what her answer was going to be.

He may be offering her a voyage on an uncharted sea but beyond the fear lay the possibility of undreamed of discovery. Excitement gripping her like ice, she slowly, deliberately, nodded.

'You have to say it,' he urged.

Looking him directly in the eye for the first time in many minutes, eyes flaring, she said: 'Yes. Do what you will.'

339

Chapter Six

Standing before the mirror and staring at her gilded nipples, Helen was appalled by the commitment she had made. Five short words had condemned her to whatever dark fantasy might lie in the darkest recesses of Jeffrey's mind. Fear and excitement had always been close allies in her fantasy subconscious but she had declared herself to a man in open acknowledgement of what she was doing and left herself no escape clauses, no excuses she could make, and no means of dignified retreat.

Along with these fragile certainties came doubt. What had he thought of her? After hearing her declaration he had said nothing but had stared at her for what seemed an agonisingly long time. His lips had moved but the thought had withered before being spoken until, still wordless, he had turned away and out of the room.

The dull echo of her unanswered words, intended to be a challenging submission, now echoed in her mind like mere bravado. The garishly decorated breasts no more than a clown's make-up. Had he seen it as such? Had she assumed, too soon, that she had some hold on this man she, even now, barely knew? Was he now trying to grapple with the dilemma of what to do with a woman who had offered up a commitment he didn't want?

Her thoughts lashing her, she realised that what she dreaded most was total rejection. The thought terrified her. She knew that, should he do so, her confidence would be crippled and her soul seared for life. Once more she trembled on the edge of a precipice knowing there was only one person in the entire world who could save her.

When the door opened again she turned fearfully towards it, to see Jeffrey standing there smiling.

'We have a visitor,' his voice light with confidence. 'Someone I know you will want to meet.'

The words had no real meaning – it was the melody with which he spoke them that warmed her. Had he said 'we' have a visitor? Had he said 'I know you will want'? Somewhere in her relieved mind the other words 'visitor' and 'meet' only signified that she had not been rejected and that there was something he wanted to share with her. At that moment she might have run to him, thrown her arms about him, and sobbed with relief, but, instead, she simply smiled and murmured: 'Thank you.'

'For what?' he asked.

His puzzled face warmed her. The ice slid from her, melting before the beat of a renewed heart that reminded her she lived. Confidence surging back, she sought to challenge him. 'Shall I come naked?'

'Why not?' he asked.

Excitement triumphing over doubt she came, eyes fixed on his, slowly towards him, hoping, perhaps, that he would back down, decide, she might, after all, cover herself. When she realised he was not going to back down before her challenge she felt a liberating thrill – as if passing through the bedroom door, licensed by Jeffrey to go naked to greet a stranger, was the threshold to a new dimension in her life. One thing was

341

certain – her commitment could now be nothing but total.

The visitor was short in stature but huge in presence. A man, completely bald but vibrant with the simmer of a fulfilled life, he stood burned dark brown by endless summers whose aura of warmth he seemed to carry with him. Disdainful of the season, he was dressed for the sun in a light cotton short-sleeved shirt and white linen trousers, while on his feet he wore open espadrilles. His eyes, looking large in so small a face, widened as he saw her and she knew immediately who he was even before Jeffrey spoke the introduction.

'Qito, I'd like you to meet Helen Lloyd.'

'Magnificent!' cried Qito holding up both his hands as if to prevent her coming any further forward. 'How wonderful to meet a beautiful woman naked! Like a goddess! Such beauty *should* be brazen! The goddesses knew that but it is rare in mortal woman.'

Coming forward, Qito took her hand and, with a courtly bow, kissed it. Helen unconsciously squared her shoulders while his kiss travelled the length of her arm creating ripples of pleasure in her. His touch seemed to infuse her with some part of this extraordinary man's energy and, when he looked up at her with his sparkling eyes, she felt disconcerted – as if she had shamelessly initiated some form of intimacy with him – while his open admiration filled her with a fierce pride.

It was then that her eyes fell on the glass-topped table on which she had been sodomised the night before. There lay scattered the sketches Jeffrey had made of her before bringing her here. How distant that time seemed now. It was the time before commitment. Was this to be Jeffrey's first 'test' of her?

Her thoughts were brought from reverie by words which resonated with future promise. 'I shall paint her!' Qito cried, then, coming even closer, his perfect teeth gleaming unnaturally white against his walnut skin, he smiled into her eyes. 'You are deserving of immortality.'

She felt, uneasily, as if his piercing gaze could see deep into the wanton soul that now lived behind them. 'Come, child,' he said, and taking her by the hand led her to stand before him as he sat on the couch and brought her hips square to his eyes. 'Open yourself to me,' he murmured.

Helen knew exactly what he meant but hesitated. Glancing to Jeffrey she saw he had seated himself at some distance and now regarded her with an expression of aroused amusement before he gave an almost imperceptible nod. Even as her incredulous brain questioned its instructions, her hands reached down to the lips of her labia and, with a curious feeling of innocence, opened them.

'You see!' cried Qito. 'We look into the gateway of all life and the portal to Paradise!' Qito's fingers had joined hers to probe deeper into her. 'There are so many petals to this rose, and as each unfolds it reveals yet more mystery.' Addressing himself to Jeffrey, who discreetly stayed behind Helen, he cried: 'So why did Nature hide it away? Disguise it, entangle it with brambles through which every man must find his way back to his source? To hide such beauty while the male equivalent is flaunted, exposed, and displayed is ludicrous!' Qito's fingers left her warmed and now throbbing 'source'. 'Nature made a grotesque mistake!' Qito's scorn softened as he spoke directly to her. 'Come, child,' he said. 'Look!' Glancing down she saw that Qito had opened his trousers and was fully exposing himself. 'Compare this pathetic male answer to your woman's mystery.'

Drawn, either by his hand or her own volition – she was never able to say which – she found herself kneeling before the couch and taking his limp and wrinkled penis in her hands.

'It is a blunt instrument. No?' he was asking her. 'Without the tender hand of a woman it has the significance of wet string. Tell me what you see,' he urged.

Her mind raced. She held in her hand the penis of a

343

man who might be a world acclaimed genius, but was also a man she had only just met while her lover stood silently aside and watched.

While she struggled for coherence she could only wonder why this act of intimacy with a stranger felt so natural and normal – as if she had previously greeted a hundred men this way.

Oppressively aware that Qito still waited for her answer she wondered what words she could use? *Were* there words for such a moment? At the same time she felt filled with a sense of discovery – as if this was the first penis she had ever seen or held – and, with Qito's eyes, she saw it as something strangely closed, hooded, vulnerable – timid even, and she felt moved to bow her head and tenderly kiss it as she might have to comfort a suffering child.

'A mother's response!' Qito's voice sounded filled with delight as she reached forward just an inch further to take him softly and tenderly between her lips. When the penis flexed like a living thing in her mouth she felt triumph flooding her body, soaking her with confidence. Filled with a sense of giving life, she now eagerly reached for him, suckled him, and was gratified by the fleshy swelling response. On her knees, naked before a stranger, she was consumed by a zeal to bring the helpless infant between her lips to threatening, punishing adulthood, yet curiously she also felt detached – as if what she was doing was not real but being done merely to prove Qito's point.

The act had no context unless it was that Jeffrey watched and, hopefully, approved – but did he? Beyond his initial nod she had heard no word of encouragement – no sign that he was even aware of what she was doing. She sucked on Qito but wanted the pleasure to be Jeffrey's. Her mouth fully enthused, she could not beg his judgement. With her eyes bent close into Qito's surprisingly firm belly she could not see him and so, her nostrils filled with the slightly pungent perfume of

344

the man, she could only strain her ears for some sign
that Jeffrey was near and knew that this was for him,
not for Qito and far less for herself.

When she felt the first sting of leather on her buttocks, excitement flooded through her entire body and
she almost cried out with relief. Suddenly what she was
doing made sense, was parenthesised and made a part
of her relationship with Jeffrey. The leather stroked fire
from her loins, and, like a whipped horse, she
redoubled her efforts, sinking the fully erected and
engorged shaft deep into her throat.

Now she knew that Jeffrey was not only near but
taking a part, punishment became reward. Hearing Qito
begin giving out muted sounds of pleasure increased
her excitement and she knew that victory was hers,
even as Jeffrey raised her crouched haunches to make
more prominent a target of her all too willing flesh.

As she felt the first awakening seed, low in the now
fully hardened shaft, she impulsively broke off for a
moment to call to Jeffrey for harder, faster strokes and,
as they came, her spirit soared, exulted beyond anything she had ever before known and, predatory now,
sank the flesh deeper into her mouth while her buttocks
sang with the pleasure of Jeffrey's whipping. It was the
first time she had known pleasure and absolving punishment to be served on the same dish – and it tasted
sweet!

Qito came with the stinging heat of a volcanic erup-
tion, and she was determined that not one drop of him
should escape her voracious mouth. Feeling Qito
softening in her mouth she wanted to cry out and voice
her frustration. She wasn't finished, but so close she
thought it would be a crime if she should be left
distracted but unsatisfied. Then, even as she drew
breath to protest she knew she should have trusted in
Jeffrey.

His hands reached around her to lift her, bodily, still
curled up in the kneeling position, from the carpet to

the glass-topped scene of last night's immolation, and was thrilled to see that the mirror still lay there. Kneeling again, she looked down into the sweat-streaked face of a totally distracted, almost demented woman, who moaned in anticipation as she felt Jeffrey addressing himself.

'Fuck me!' that demented creature cried and then let the words become a long moan of pleasure as she climaxed the moment Jeffrey thrust himself deep inside her. 'Yes!' she screamed, and, when Qito came to stand before her raised, kneeling figure, she grabbed for his hands and brought them to her lips. Jeffrey was so roused and hard that his thrusting, savage and punishing, was exactly what she wanted. 'Punish me!' she screamed into Qito's caressing hands. 'Punish me! Fuck me!' and then felt Jeffrey surging, erupting, embalming the pleasure forever in her mind.

Exhausted, Jeffrey withdrew and let her sink to lie, in a curled foetal position, on the glass table, where Qito looked down in glee. 'See!' he cried. 'Her whole body lies in the shape of a smile!'

Qito looked from the satiated, but defensive posture to Jeffrey, where after a momentary exchange of locked glances they turned away, avoiding each other's eyes with the shy awareness that they had both been savagely aroused over the body of the same woman – an act that both united and separated men at one and the same time. It was to that same woman that Jeffrey leant, to kiss her, gently, on the neck.

Helen, roused by the kiss, moaned and reached out a blind embracing arm and drew him into a kiss while turning over on the glass to offer up her whole body. Holding him close, so that she could look directly into his eyes, she smiled. 'Is your wanton forgiven?' she asked.

Jeffrey shook his head. 'She is cherished,' he murmured.

Confidence soaring, she looked for Qito and bending

her head backwards found him stuffing his penis out of sight but still standing over her. Her arm now reached for his blessing and Qito – his eyes bright against the walnut colour of his tan – looked almost aflame as he leaned forward and, awkwardly, upside down, confirmed on her the benediction she sought. 'Where did you find such a glorious creature?' he asked of Jeffrey.

Jeffrey, sitting tentatively on the glass-topped table, put an arm about her shoulders and drew her to him as he answered. 'Well, you know, Christmas and all, you get the most surprising gifts!'

Qito's laugh resounded. 'Every man should have such a gift!'

'Well, now, you've had her, too!'

'To "have" is not to "possess"!' Qito said.

Listening to the two men, Helen could hardly believe they were talking about her. Turning to Jeffrey for comfort she asked: 'Am I "possessed"?'

'Totally,' he assured her.

His words gave her comfort. 'Thank you,' she murmured.

Turning her face to him and begging a kiss, she marvelled that she had done something that a week before would have been unthinkable and then heard it discussed as if it had been no more than a social courtesy.

Qito was turning away, his voice fading as he spoke. 'An old man has no place between lovers,' he declared. 'I am going to leave you . . .' He was coming back to them, shrugging a bulky fur-collared coat over his summery clothes. '. . . but I shall never forgive you if you do not bring this wild woman to my show tonight!'

'I've no intention of going *anywhere* without this woman!' Jeffrey retorted, and then, standing, hugged the diminutive teddy bear the top coat had made of Qito. Springing upward from the table Helen felt filled with enough love to spare a little for Qito. She had to dip her head to kiss his cheek as he pulled her into a strong, wiry, embrace.

'Together we shall make a masterpiece,' he told her. Then, waving a hand to Jeffrey, turned for the door. 'Until tonight,' he called.

It was only as she saw Annabel hurrying to see Qito out that Helen remembered her existence. Suddenly shocked with herself she turned to Jeffrey. 'Annabel was here?' she asked. 'Did she hear everything . . . ?' The look on Jeffrey's face told her that she had, and Helen stood, aghast – hand over her mouth – as she heard the door close and the soft sounds of Annabel's return.

'Would anyone like a drink?' Annabel asked with such insouciance that Helen almost burst out laughing.

'We'd love one,' answered Jeffrey.

The moment Annabel had gone, Helen turned to Jeffrey. 'Whatever must she think?' she asked in hollowed, self-horrified, tones.

'She probably thinks, as will everyone else, how lucky I am.'

She looked into his eyes and noticed for the first time that they were grey with exquisitely placed segments of black. They were beautiful eyes she decided, and she felt herself melting before them. 'Don't ever let it stop,' she whispered then, feeling her body starting to tremble, and hastily added, 'I rather like the idea of being "possessed".'

'And *I* meant it – I want to "possess" you rather than just "have".'

'You already do. I just need you to keep reminding me.'

They stood apart, like duellists looking for an opening, with distinctively differing thoughts. Jeffrey felt blessed while she felt an irresistible, masochistic mist enshroud her.

'Do something to me,' she breathed. 'Now – this minute!'

Jeffrey's smile was lazy. 'Don't you think you ought to think about getting ready?'

'For what?'

'Didn't you hear Qito invite us to his showing this evening? It's a huge affair. A gala in fact. I want you to look devastating.'

'In *what*?' she seethed. 'You brought me here naked.'

'That would be "devastating",' he agreed. 'But hardly suitable for presentation to the French President.'

'The President of France is going to be in London?' she demanded in a voice filled with sudden alarm.

'No,' said Jeffrey patiently. 'We are going to be in Paris.'

'Tonight?' she squealed.

'Well that's where Qito's gala preview is being held.'

Helen's mind was running wildly beyond coherence. 'But . . . Paris? Tonight?' Exasperated, she turned to Jeffrey. 'It's impossible!'

The infuriating smile still on his lips he spoke. 'No it isn't. Paris is a thirty-five minute plane ride – little more than a cab ride when you think about it.'

'But I'm not ready! I've nothing packed! Nothing *to* pack! Jeffrey – this is impossible!'

'Nothing's impossible,' he said, coming towards her and seeking an embrace. 'You have the gown I brought you.'

'That's still in my apartment!' Bustling with sudden urgency she turned back to Jeffrey. 'I'll have to go back to my place. What time are we expected?'

'A President of a Republic doesn't "expect" – he commands. We must be there by eight.'

'Oh Lord! How will I . . . how can I . . .?'

Jeffrey smiled. 'You will,' he told her. 'I'll have Turner drive you home and I'll pick you up from your place at six, but you'd better put something on in the meanwhile.'

Panicked, she started a fervent hunt for her long discarded raincoat only to find that a smiling Annabel was already holding it out for her to slip into. 'I take it you've no time for the drink?' she asked.

'I've no time for *anything*!' Helen protested, then, as the coat settled about her shoulders, she was reminded that she had rarely been other than totally naked for the past twenty-four hours. The close proximity to Annabel also brought about another crushing memory. 'Did you . . . ?' she asked, then, as Annabel smiled non-committally, went on, 'I'm sorry if you were embarrassed.'

Shaking her head Annabel's smile not only continued but brightened. 'Envious, perhaps,' she said. 'But certainly not embarrassed.'

Flashing the girl a grateful smile, she turned as she heard Turner arrive. 'Jeffrey?' she called. 'I'm going.'

Jeffrey appeared from the depths of the apartment and reaching out his arms gave her a gentle kiss on one cheek and then as he leant into the other whispered, under the eyes of the patiently waiting Turner, 'I'm tempted to fuck you again before you go.'

'No!' she laughed, her protest forcefully loud. 'I've got far too much to do before six!'

Smiling, Jeffrey handed her to the care of Turner before turning back to the attentive Annabel.

'Think you can handle her?' Annabel asked.

His answer was a spirited: 'It's got to be worth a try, don't you think?'

'I'll say!' she agreed.

350

Chapter Seven

Standing under the teeming shower Helen felt like a tired child on Christmas night trying to remember her new presents. So much had happened since she was last in her own apartment that she could barely believe it had been only two days. She knew she was not the same woman who had stepped out from this shower two days before. Not only was there Jeffrey and his exquisite talent for erotic surprise but the change that had been wrought in herself. She could now confidently cope with something like the sad Lesley; been made aware that her body was something in which she could take fierce pride; had, under the eyes of one lover, orally taken another, and then, under the eyes of the other, given herself fully to her true lover. With pride she considered she had carried all before her with creditable aplomb. The excitement was not knowing where else this path, on which she had taken only the first few, faltering, steps, might lead.

Drying herself and hurrying to offer her hair to the salvage of heated rollers, she realised that tonight she was going to an event she had not even heard of hours before and there, in the company of an enviable escort, would meet again the legend for whom even the

President of France turned out, and whom she had sexually satisfied. It was then that the echo of his promise to have her pose for him returned. It was enough to still her hands as they curled up her hair. Was it possible that the face staring back out of the mirror was really worthy of, as Qito had claimed, immortality? Would, centuries from now, some man from an, as yet, undreamed of generation, look on her body and feel lust for her? Had, she wondered, Mona Lisa harboured similar doubts before going to Da Vinci's studio when her immortal image was but an idea in the artist's mind?

One thing was certain, she thought, as she started on her base foundation, no woman had ever been so filled with certainty as was she at that moment.

When Jeffrey arrived she had yet to pack and still to dress and barely opened the door to him before fleeing back into the bedroom aware of how little time there was before they had to leave.

'I'll only be a minute!' she called out to him as she sat before her mirror to apply an antique golden lip-gloss to her already made-up lips. Then she searched out a pair of silk stockings she'd bought the previous year and never, until now, found occasion to wear. Slipping into the fine silk gown she remembered how it had looked on her the first time she had worn it. How quickly it had responded to her body's warmth and clung so closely as to even outline her navel. Again she was reminded that to wear anything, even stockings, under the dress was impossible. The thought of going to this event near naked both bothered and thrilled her. Slipping into a pair of elegant evening mules she gave herself one last head to toe scrutiny before bracing herself for the presentation to Jeffrey.

'Well?' she asked him coyly. 'How do I look?'
'Unique!'
'"Unique"?'
Jeffrey nodded. 'There are very few women in this

world who can look equally beautiful dressed or naked. You are among them.'

Pleased by the compliment she felt ready to be pedantically teasing. 'To be "among" a number is not to be "unique",' she said with as much false petulance as she could muster.

'Exquisite, then?' he offered. 'Is that better?'

Pretending deep consideration she loftily replied: '"Exquisitely beautiful" would be no more than acceptable . . .'

Jeffrey laughed and, his eyes alight with pleasure, started towards her, meaning to embrace her, but she turned away. 'No! I've spent ages on my hair and make-up and I'm not having you ruin it!'

'I was just going to remind you that you're pledged to me!' he said. 'What if I want you naked? Now, this minute!'

'Absolutely no way!' she cried, and as he reached for her again, she remembered that the gown would be gone in seconds if he got his hands to the shoulder catches, and ran from him in a move which soon became a halting chase.

The chase was ended before it really got started when the telephone rang. She knew immediately, as if sensing it from the sternness of the ring, that it would be her, almost completely forgotten, mother.

Seeing Jeffrey stilled by the interruption she went to the telephone and lifted it.

Her mother's excited voice poured into her ears. 'Where on earth have you been? I've been calling and talking to that stupid machine of yours for days. Why haven't you called me back?'

'Mother, I've been busy . . .' she looked back over her shoulder and shrugged an apology in Jeffrey's direction.

'Too "busy" to return the messages I left on your machine?'

'I'm sorry, Mother, I haven't had time to play them

back and I'm in a tremendous rush just at the moment – can I call you later?'

'No!' cried her mother. 'We've been worried sick about you . . .' with the stream of non-stop complaints ringing in her ears, Helen had dropped her guard against Jeffrey only to be forcefully reminded of that oversight when she felt his hands at the fastenings of the gown. The telephone in her hand prevented anything but the weakest attempt to still the downward slide of the clinging silk. Covering the mouthpiece she turned, genuinely angry, towards Jeffrey. 'No, Jeffrey . . . we have to . . . this is my mother . . . I—'

Determined and unsmiling Jeffrey gently took away the one hand that stopped the gown from uncovering her entirely and she stared helplessly, and pled speechlessly, as the gown slid to the floor leaving her facing him, naked. 'Please . . .' she begged, but Jeffrey was implacable.

She was turned and he thrust hard into her from behind. Her gasp at his penetration carried all the way to Eastbourne.

'Are you listening to a word I've said?' her mother was demanding. 'It's that man, isn't it? The one you brought down here? I suppose you've been with him all this time with never a thought that we might be worrying about you? I think I have a right to know . . .'

Her mother's words were now only background as the convulsions Jeffrey was creating in her took command and extinguished all will to do anything but respond.

'Helen?' her mother's voice was calling down the line. 'What on earth is going on . . .'

'Mother, please . . .' she managed. 'Not now. There's someone here . . .' she broke off, trying to silence her rising climax.

'*Who* is there? *Him?*' asked her mother and then, after a steely silence in which Helen could almost sense the keening ears, added in horrified tones, 'Oh, my God!

You're doing "it" with him right this minute aren't you? What on earth . . . ? How *dare* you?' Helen heard the phone being slammed down in her desperate ear.

'You bastard!' she seethed even as her body begged release.

Jeffrey pulled her hips tight to him as she, still holding the telephone in one paralysed hand, bent forward and gave him even greater access. 'You're my whore!' he breathed throatily as he bent over her to sink his teeth into her shoulder.

'Yes!' she yelled into his face. 'Fuck me! Fuck me, fuck me!' then gave vent to a scream as the onrush of orgasm vibrated inwards before bursting out to encompass her entire body. Within a second she felt him straighten and then, as his grip dug painfully into her flesh, surge into her.

'God I must look a mess!' she said the moment she managed to disentangle herself from him. 'My hair! What am I going to do?' she wailed.

'You'll go as you are. The "just screwed" look is all the rage this year!'

Turning from the mirror where she was surveying the damage she was enraged. 'You pig!' she yelled at him. 'How could you do that to me?'

'Because you looked so beautiful,' he smiled. 'I had to put my mark on you.'

'My hair!' she wailed. 'My face! I spent hours getting ready and then you have to do that to me! I haven't packed anything yet, and . . .' her voice trailed into silence as she remembered with horror what her mother had said as she slammed down the phone. 'And my mother heard us!' she cried.

'You mean, until now, your mother imagined you were a virgin?' His tone was so close to a bantering sarcasm that she felt a sudden urge to hit him.

'You know perfectly well what I mean!' she said defiantly. 'Well, we'll just have to be late. I'm going to repair the damage.'

Jeffrey physically blocked her progress to the bedroom. 'There isn't time,' he said. 'You'll just have to do what you can in the car!'

Filled with a sudden need to show anger, she remembered she had once been told how grimly her face set when she needed to express rage. Fully aware that she now wore that expression she decided to let it out. 'Jeffrey, I'm warning you – I really mean this – get out of my way.'

Jeffrey stayed where he was. 'Shall I go?' he asked quietly.

The rush of blood that was carrying an affirmative response to her lips stopped dead in its tracks as with sudden, chilling clarity she saw the space where Jeffrey now stood would, if vacated, be nothing but a yawning void which, she knew, would haunt her for the rest of her life. All anger was suddenly frozen. Icicles, she would later swear, formed in her gut at that moment. 'No,' she murmured so quietly that he made her repeat the words more loudly.

'No, you bastard!' she yelled at him.

Seemingly much relieved, Jeffrey smiled. 'Lucky thing for you I changed my mind.'

'About what?'

'When I saw how gorgeous you looked I wanted to put my mark on you in another way.'

It took a moment to realise his meaning. 'You were thinking of spanking me – just before going out . . .'

'We aren't "out", yet.'

'*Don't* think about it!' Her voice was pitched half way between plea and resolve.

'All right, but you should bear in mind that you will have to be punished later.'

Annoyed that the threat both warmed and thrilled her she agreed that there would be time in the car to repair her face and hair, and after throwing some things into an overnight bag, happily went down to the waiting Turner feeling that she had narrowly escaped disaster.

The limousine whisked them to a part of Heathrow she didn't know existed. This was the terminal, far from the commercial terminals, from which private planes departed. Jeffrey, she discovered, had rented an air taxi and so, with the minimum of formalities they were in the air and *en route* to Le Bourget airport which, she was informed, was even closer to Paris than the sprawl of the Charles de Gaulle.

Waiting there was another chauffered limousine which took them directly to the reception hall. It had all been so effortless and quick that she understood what Jeffrey meant by Paris being only a cab ride away. All it took was money and a willingness to spend it.

Feeling pampered and flattered she took wicked pleasure in thinking of how horrified her mother would be by all this 'extravagance'!

They were barely inside the exhibition hall and had no time to pick out one face from another when an authoritative voice started calling out that the arrival of the President was imminent and the person behind it fussily started lining up those who were to be presented.

Falling back among the lesser guests Helen and Jeffrey could now see Qito, who had deferred to the admonitory 'formal' dress only so far as donning a black T-shirt under a darkish jacket, and, towering over him, was the unmistakable figure of Carla Colardi. It was only then that Helen was reminded that Carla, still overwhelmingly beautiful, was Qito's wife of almost twenty years. Dressed in a glittering silver gown, cut aggressively low to display her famous bosom, the 'glitter' theme continued with her jewellery which, all platinum and white gold, flashed in the lighting as if powered from Carla's own formidable personality which seemed further emphasised by her 'big hair'.

Two legends in the same household should have been fertile ground for the gossipmongers yet nothing had ever been found to besmirch their union.

Looking at Carla, Helen could not help relishing the thought that she had, if only momentarily, shared Qito with her. The *frisson* of excitement this engendered was rapidly followed by the daunting thought of what the formidable Carla's reaction might be if she ever found out.

It was then that Qito spotted her. 'Helen!' he called out with such excitement that she felt all eyes, tensed ready for the arrival of the President, turning to her. Qito was gesturing wildly for Helen to come to him. Aware of Carla's huge black lustrous eyes searching her out from top to toe, Helen turned to Jeffrey. 'What?' she asked.

'He wants you in the line up,' Jeffrey smiled. 'Go!'

Aware that everyone in the crowded room was now looking at her and wondering who the hell she might be, she felt Jeffrey's hand on the small of her back urging her forward. With a growing sense of unreality that this was really happening Helen found the crowd opening up before her and the fussy organiser, looming before her to demand her name. Having hastily added her name to the official list he ushered her forward to where she found Qito insisting that she stand to his right, between him and Carla.

'*Cara mio* . . .' Qito spoke across the highly embarrassed Helen to the highly interested Carla. 'This is the English girl I told you about. Isn't she incredible?'

Carla's look to Helen was, to say the least, smouldering but, whatever verbal response she might have made was lost in the sudden stirring of interest as the President's party arrived.

Standing next to Qito, Helen had the unsettling feeling that she was caught up in a fantasy made real. She watched with blurred vision and bated breath as the President's party paused in the doorway, as they

358

were welcomed by the Gallery officials staging the exhibition. Then her vision was filled with the sight of the President making directly towards Qito. It was only then Helen realised she had absolutely no idea how one greeted a President and since it seemed she would be the first female to be introduced she would have little chance to learn by observation. Grimly, as the President all but embraced Qito, she thought it would have been simpler if the man had been royalty. Then it would only have been a matter of a quick curtsey. Desperately, her mind raced over the possibilities only to find her brain otherwise engaged when the thought of her recent violation at Jeffrey's hands chose that moment to leap into her head creating a stirring in her groin, and the resulting fervent juices to start trickling down her thighs.

Her heart thumping out a drum beat of impending disaster, she heard her name, as if at a great distance, being spoken and a Presidential hand being extended to her.

'My new inspiration,' Qito was saying by way of further introduction, and Helen, totally lost, settled for an ingratiatingly embarrassed smile.

'How charming . . .' mused the President in a tone that managed to convey its uncertainty at why such a nonentity should be being introduced, and she felt enormous relief when the hand shaking personage moved on to greet Carla with more obvious enthusiasm and genuine warmth.

It was then that her swimming vision brought Jeffrey's face, grinning at her from across the channel left in the crowd and, for a passing moment, she hated him for exposing her to such an occasion with barely an hour's notice. Carla's voice broke into her seething mind. 'Qito tells me you have inspired him.'

Looking into the familiar famous face, Helen felt even more lost. What is there to say to a wife when her husband has declared that he has been 'inspired'?

Fortunately, Carla didn't wait for any cogent reply but instead murmured, 'So no doubt we will be meeting again,' before being caught up in a surging crowd of admirers which somehow managed to elbow Helen to one side. Jeffrey caught her arm. 'Hungry?' he asked.

'Aren't we going to look at Qito's work?' a bewildered Helen asked.

Jeffrey indicated the great crowds. 'We'd see nothing in this scrum. We can come back tomorrow if you want. Meantime, I don't know about you but I'm starving.'

Not sure if she was hungry, she was certainly ready to flee from the confusion of this sudden exposure to so many famous faces, so she readily agreed to his suggestion that they go and eat.

It wasn't until they were seated in the small but exclusive restaurant that she realised this was the first time they had formally eaten together.

Jeffrey's choice of conversational topic was, initially, surprising. 'When I was ten,' she heard him saying, 'my father caught me smoking one of his cigars. I thought he would be furious with me but instead he fooled me into thinking he was delighted. He sat me down and lectured me on the proper way to prepare and really appreciate a cigar. In fact he watched me smoke my way through that first one and then insisted I had another. I got about half way through it before I turned green and spent the rest of the evening in the bathroom. I have never smoked a cigar since.'

Smiling politely, and wondering why she was being exposed to such a mundane tale, she was startled when he came to the point. 'That's how I intend to deal with your masochism.'

Gripped with apprehension she managed, '"Deal" with it? Is it a sickness then?'

'Not *the* sickness – a symptom. To get at the root we have to cut away the undergrowth.'

Stilled with fear of what he might be about to propose

360

she nevertheless found herself anxious to be told. 'To face my nightmares?' she asked.

'To find out whether or not the nightmares really exist.'

'I see,' she said filling in time as her mind raced. 'And how do you propose to do that?'

'I don't,' he said. 'You have to do it yourself, but what I can do is show you the way. It will be up to you whether you go down that road or not.'

Again the challenge! Again, he was forcing her to commit herself. Once more she found herself excitedly willing to do just that!

'I'm in your hands,' she told him.

Jeffrey smiled and reaching out laid an admonishing finger on her lips. 'Now I sentence you to silence,' he murmured as she, with mounting excitement, reached her lips forward to nibble at his lingering finger. 'I've dismissed the limousine and rented a self-drive car instead,' he said as her lit eyes fixed alertly on him, 'so I will be driving. You do remember our drive to East-bourne, don't you? I asked you to do something that night and you refused. You will not refuse me tonight.' For answer she drew his fingers deep into her mouth and, uncaring what other diners or waiters might think, kept her eyes firmly fixed on his and suckled on them.

'It is quite a short drive so you will have to be particularly expert since you will be performing that small service totally naked.' As she stopped sucking on him and stared instead, he added, 'However, you may remain clothed until we are in the car. Shall we go?'

The formalities of paying the bill, him signing his charge slip and their finding the car seemed to take forever. Her body was totally encased in the excitement of the moment and the trivial interests of others were merely obstacles in the way of opportunity.

Still trembling she was seated in the car as he turned the heater to full and waited for it to warm up.

When he drove away she, with a sense of assertiveness, reached to her shoulders for the catches that held the dress and let it slither down into her lap leaving her breasts bare to the flash of passing lights and the eyes of passing pedestrians. It was then only a matter of shifting her weight, first this way then that, before she was completely free of the gown. Laying her head across his lap, her fingers sought out his already risen flesh.

The steering wheel rubbed hard against her head as she plunged him deep into her throat, there was only one thought in her mind – he must come before they ended the short drive. At that moment it became her only aim in life beyond which there was nothing. Feeling an exquisite moment of total self-abandonment she worked her lips and tongue feverishly around his stiffened cock trying as she did so to remember everything she had ever learned or read about this particular pleasure. She felt almost total despair as she realised that the car had stopped and she had yet to feel his first convulsion. Desperately, she ignored the possibility of passing strangers looking in on her and increased the tempo and intensity of her lips and mouth.

Eerily aware that Jeffrey had remained silent, she continued working on him while dreading that he might intercede and stop her and tell her she had failed. Sensing his first flesh quickening throb she sucked deeper and harder forcing herself to concentrate on what she now knew was inevitable. Feeling his hand resting lightly on the back of her head she waited eagerly for his gush but, even as it started, she heard him add yet another condition. 'Do not swallow it!' he gasped as he started to issue. 'I want you to take it and guard it in your mouth. You understand me?'

All she could do was nod as he filled her mouth. When he nudged her to indicate that she could now sit up, she found his imperative that she must not swallow his tribute almost impossible to obey. Having to fight against instinct she was aware that her puffed cheeks and strained throat must be making her look ridiculous. As he got out of the car she sat, still naked, and only vaguely aware that they were stopped in a wide, tree lined avenue.

When Jeffrey opened the car's door a blast of the winter's night air flooded in to remind her that she was still naked. 'Come,' said Jeffrey.

Stepping out of the car she found herself keeping her eyes strictly to the front, not wanting to know if there was anyone there to see her. Instead she kept her eyes firmly fixed on his until he, smiling, turned away and led her, still naked, up the steps to a substantial villa. There he rang the bell and she had to wait interminably, the cold now piercing her body in places she was only vaguely aware existed, and wondered where it was she had been brought and what might lay behind the glossy shine of this green door.

Chapter Eight

*H*elen caught barely a glimpse of the girl who had opened the door before Jeffrey, taking her elbow, urged her into the long, high ceilinged hallway. At the far end a woman appeared wearing the kind of long floral evening gown that overweight ladies use to disguise their widened hips. She was directing a broad smile at Jeffrey. 'I had almost given up hope,' she was saying, before directing her gaze to Helen.

'Helen, this is Madame Victoria. She runs the most famous House of Pain in Paris.'

Madame Victoria smiled. 'And all completely English. We English are renowned for our expertise in this field just as the French, in England, are sought out for their cooking. Each to its own, as it were.' Madame Victoria, whose eyes suggested she had seen everything, looked a little puzzled as Helen stayed silent. 'Doesn't she speak?' she asked Jeffrey sharply.

'Not at the moment. Her mouth is full.'

'Of what?'

'Of me.'

Victoria's mouth wrinkled into a smile. 'Excellent!' she cried and immediately took Helen's arm and walked her the length of the hallway and into a large room which seemed furnished entirely with a variety of couches. Here Helen registered two girls, one naked and one in an abbreviated rubbery looking dress that constricted rather than fitted her, while a man sat crosslegged on the floor before the naked girl's feet. Conscious that all eyes were on her, she was led to stand in the open centre of the room. 'Kate!' Victoria waved to the naked girl, 'come here.'

Kate came forward looking directly into Helen's eyes as if expecting a challenge of some kind. 'You kneel,' Victoria said and it took a moment for Helen to understand that the order had been directed at her. Thankfully the carpet was thick and quite comfortable to her knees. Helen felt her hair taken and grasped firmly, though not cruelly.

'Be very careful, now,' warned Madame Victoria. 'You are going to open your mouth but when you do so you must not swallow. Do you understand me?'

Desperate now that she could no longer see Jeffrey, Helen nodded, aware that she didn't know how she could avoid swallowing. The moment she had agreed she felt a slight tug on her hair and bent her head backwards until she looked directly up at the worked plaster ceiling. The movement had caused her eyes to close, shutting out the sight of Victoria, but leaving her aware that the woman was peering deep into her mouth and must surely see the liquid which she could feel thickly coating her tongue.

'Ah, yes,' murmured Victoria. 'Do you see it, Kate?'

Helen felt a pang of excruciating humiliation as she sensed movement in the room and knew the others were coming to peer into her mouth. Kneeling there, mouth open like a hungry chick in a nest, she wondered how Jeffrey could have known how excruciating this would be for her. She had always dreaded visiting the dentist. Not because, in these days of sophisticated painkillers, she would feel any discomfort beyond the initial needle, but because the man would be peering into her mouth which she thought of as more intimate than a gynaecological examination. Gynaecologists didn't loom over her mouth like a threatening lover!

'Kate will clean your mouth,' said Victoria in such quiet conversational tones that Helen didn't understand the significance until, opening her eyes, she saw the bright eyed Kate leaning closer to her, her mouth closed on hers and a seemingly huge tongue probed into her mouth, leaving her desperately breathless, while scooping and seaching out every last drop of Jeffrey's deposit. Helen wanted to scream protest at being so intimately invaded by another girl. Her hands moved as to fend off Kate but were taken, even as they moved, and lightly but firmly clamped behind her back. Her vision filled with Kate, she was uncertain who had taken her hands until she heard, close to her ear, Jeffrey's voice. 'You are being tested.'

These simple words flushed away the protest of her rational mind. What was being done to her was now sanctioned – gifted to her – licensing her to dismiss any consideration but that Jeffrey wanted this to be done to her. An overwhelming sense of relief flooded through her. What she was doing was being done for Jeffrey which gave it sense and meaning.

Eyes closed, she now gave her mouth to Kate's searching tongue, opening to it as if she opened to Jeffrey. It no longer mattered if four people – or four hundred – watched her as, giving way to a gentle pressure on her shoulders she felt herself being laid back to stretch full length onto the carpet.

Kate had shadowed her movements and now Helen felt the full length of another girl's naked body on her own for the first time in her life as the tongue pressed deep into her mouth. Consciously or otherwise she had opened her thighs and Kate lay between them – one pubic bone pressing hard against the other – and to her astonishment Helen's loins began to flow as if in answer to a lover. Confident that nobody but her could tell of this shaming response she became alarmed when Kate suddenly lifted herself and knelt to straddle Helen's belly but, instead of covering her, she felt an unseen hand searching out the damning evidence of her arousal. Distracted now she sought to wriggle free of the unknown fingers that probed her outer lips before entering her, but Kate's firm pressure restricted any such protest, which soon turned to writhing as she felt the hand replaced by the gentler pressure of a tongue. Doubly invaded she wanted to scream to them to stop before she betrayed herself totally but then she heard the benediction of Jeffrey's voice: 'Relax! Go with it!'

Tearing herself free of Kate's relentless kiss she let go a long repressed orgasmic scream as her entire body convulsed under tidal waves of release. Now, with Kate's head tucked in against the side of her own, her eyes were freed to roam wildly and search out Jeffrey.

In response to her silent appeal he came to lie beside her, his hands gently caressing her breasts. As she reached to embrace him he closed on her and gifted her a deeply searching kiss. The wave came again as the unknown tongue at her loins probed even more deeply and she was forced to break off from Jeffrey's kiss as yet another wave engulfed her.

Looking manically down to see who it was inducing such pleasure from her abandoned loins she saw the thinning hair of the other man which unnerved her only momentarily until Jeffrey renewed his kiss.

'Screw me!' she gasped into his open mouth but was then shattered to hear Victoria's voice cut through her consciousness. 'Enough!'

Suddenly, all activity had ended. Kate had gone, the man with thinning hair had gone and Jeffrey was standing at a distance, leaving her spread and totally exposed on the carpet, the centre of all eyes and feeling like a beached whale. Wildly she looked from one face to the other trying to divine the meaning of this sudden abandonment. It was then she realised that everyone was waiting for Victoria to speak. 'Come with me,' she said, and it was Jeffrey who reached down to offer a hand to help Helen to her feet.

Looking at Jeffrey she saw him suddenly unwilling to look back at her, which filled her with foreboding. 'I'm waiting,' said Victoria from the door, and so Helen followed her flowing gown out of the room, along the hallway and into another room in which stood a shower in what might have once been simply a bathroom, but was now swamped with closets and shelves.

'Take a shower and then I will dress you,' Madame Victoria told her, and then had her stand in the disconcertingly pliable plastic shower tray before turning on the water.

As the hand withdrew from the cascading water Helen experienced a crystal clear image of another time and another place.

Just short of her eighteenth birthday she had left home, for the first time in her life, to start a course of business studies. It was a confusing environment for someone so used to being completely cared for especially as she sensed that none of the other girls were suffering the same maternal withdrawal symptoms as herself. It had been only after long and prolonged campaigning by her mother that she had been found a room in the scarce Halls of Residence accommodation without which her mother would have forbidden her to leave home at all.

On the second night in the room which she shared with another girl they had been invaded by a group of girls from the more senior, second year, who had told them they were about to be 'initiated'. She and her room-mate, Caroline, had been frog marched out of the Halls of Residence and into the nearby gymnasium. There they had been forced to strip naked and had their hands tied behind their backs.

After a great deal of pummelling and squeezing of their breasts they had, now quite distressed, been taken to the showers where their hands were tied to the shower spigot pipes and the water repeatedly turned on, first cold then hot, until both girls were tearfully pleading for the torment to end.

It was the vision of the girl's hand that had turned off the water before leaving them there in the dark that had now returned so forcibly. Helen had hung there, helplessly listening to Caroline's sobs until they were found in the early hours of the morning by a Security Guard who, having released them, made a report which, somehow, got lost in the bureaucracy and never came to anything.

She and Caroline, although becoming firm friends, never talked about the incident which Helen felt had shamed them both, until the celebration held to mark the successful end to their first year. More than a little influenced by the amount of wine she had drunk Caroline had remarked how much she was looking forward to getting her hands on the new intake of first-year girls. Helen had been shocked. 'You wouldn't really do that to the new girls, would you?' she had asked.

'Damn right I would!' Caroline had laughed. 'And I will! Come on, be honest – that night – didn't it turn you on?'

Helen stared at the girl with whom she had shared a room for almost a year and who she never once suspected shared her own shameful secret. The incident, only in retrospect, had seemed exciting. In fantasy she had even extended the experience and made the middle-aged Security Guard into a handsome young buck who had taken advantage of her helplessness and ravaged her. It had never occurred to her that her emotions of that time could possibly be shared by another living being and for the first time in her life she began to think of her own fantasies as something other than a private sickness lodging in her head alone.

Jeffrey had brought a great deal of her secret thoughts

into the glare of reality and tonight she had taken yet another step forward. The memory reinforced in her the resolve to rise to his challenge no matter how daunting it might become.

Madame Victoria's voice brought her back to the present. 'You haven't dozed off in there, have you?'

Turning off the water she stepped out of the shower and, taking one of many warmed towels, started drying herself as she watched the indomitable Victoria returning, holding in her hands an intricately worked basque in layers of appliquéd green and black leather. 'I'm going to put this on you,' she was told before being peremptorily turned as Madame Victoria's expert hands wound the leather about her waist.

Submitting to what she considered to be the inevitable she stood passively as the corset was tightened about her torso to just under her breasts which the leather left exposed, and then gasped as with firm hands Madame Victoria started drawing on the strings causing the leather to groan as it compressed about her rib cage. She made gasping protests as the process continued until she was afraid she might faint.

'Please . . .' she pleaded. 'It's too tight. I can't breathe!'

'Nonsense . . .' replied Victoria and gave another breath-taking pull on the strings.

Helen's body felt gripped as if in a vice as she desperately gasped for air. 'I can't . . .' she managed.

'Relax,' Madame Victoria told her. 'Enjoy the constriction, you'll find yourself forgetting about it. Here . . .'

Desperately Helen looked round to see impossibly high-heeled boots being laid at her feet. 'Put these on,' she was told. Knowing that she couldn't possibly bend, Helen had to put one hand out to balance herself as she forced her feet into the tight-fitting boots. She was relieved to find them a little too large for her feet so there was no crippling pain from her toes.

Still trying to orientate herself to the new high elevation to which the heels had raised her, she felt her hair being brushed back from her face before being wound into a tight pony-tail. 'Hold on to that,' she was told as Victoria turned aside only to return with a fearsome looking head-dress, combined with a mask made in leathers to match the corset, which, after threading her pony-tailed hair through a hole in the back of the head-dress, was lowered and fitted snugly about her face to outline her eyes but exposing her mouth and nostrils.

'Now you may look at yourself,' smiled Madame Victoria, turning her to face a mirror set into one wall.

There stood a fearsomely beautiful creature who might have stepped from a fantasy science fiction novel labelled as a bare-breasted Amazon queen. The heels gave her enormous height and, while the corset still felt oppressive and the boots constricting, she felt a surge of excitement as she registered that the creation in the mirror was a reflection of herself.

'There,' said Madame Victoria. 'Don't you think that image is worth a little discomfort?'

Continuing to stare at herself she thought she had never imagined how her breasts could be so engorged by contrast with her tiny waist, how firm and rounded her thighs could be made. In the mirror she saw not herself but a woman, so distanced and of such imperious sexuality it excited her incredibly. 'Yes,' she breathed.

'You look wonderful,' cried Madame Victoria. 'Think what effect it will have on him!'

Suddenly her mind was filled with Jeffrey and the excitement of showing herself to him like this. Guiltily, she became aware that her hands had gone, seemingly of their accord, to cup and caress her own breasts. 'Can we go to him now?' she asked.

'Of course, my dear. But you will need this.'

Looking down Helen saw that she was being offered the haft of a shiny lacquer-handled whip. Looking up, eyes wide with surprise, into Madame Victoria's clear, unblinking gaze, her question was transparent to the other woman's greater experience before she had asked it. 'You'll see,' smiled Madame Victoria and, still confused, Helen found herself being turned and urged out into the hallway.

She had expected to be returned to the sitting room so was surprised when she was turned instead in the opposite direction and led into a room where another shock awaited her. Strapped naked to a wooden frame which dominated the room was a man – his back facing her. At first she thought this might be Jeffrey but was soon able to see this man was both heavier and older. Led round the man to face him she saw Kate kneeling naked before him, looking expectantly for her instructions.

'How are you this evening?' asked Madame Victoria in casual conversational tones.

'Very well, thank you,' replied the man who Helen now saw was somewhere in his florid-faced middle fifties.

'This lady is the Mistress Helen,' said Victoria. 'She is to assist me this evening.'

The man's eyes glowed as they lighted on the masked, tall, leather-encased figure. 'Thank you, Mistress Victoria,' he murmured.

'I intend we play a little game,' Victoria was saying. 'Kate here, will arouse you – make you naughty – while the Mistress Helen will punish you for the naughty, filthy little tyke we all know you to be. You understand me?' asked Victoria, reinforcing her words with a resounding slap about the helpless man's face.

'I do, Mistress,' gasped the man.

Turning to Kate, Victoria nodded. Still haunched, Kate sat up slightly and, reaching forward, took the man's flaccid penis between two fingers and delicately addressed it to her lips.

The man gasped. 'No, please Mistress,' he pleaded.

372

'Don't make me "naughty". I promised Mummy I'd be good today.'

'Silence!' roared Victoria. 'We already know what a liar you can be! Kate will prove it.' Victoria turned to Kate. 'Well?' she demanded.

For answer Kate withdrew her ravaging mouth and exposed the man as already half aroused. 'Time for firm measures!' said Victoria who, taking the whip from Helen's nerveless hands, took a measure before delivering three quick blows across the man's buttocks.

'Well?' demanded Victoria of Kate, but she got only a muffled reply since Kate's mouth was already back and hard at work.

Helen felt absent – as if none of this was really happening. She felt that if she stayed silent they might forget she was there and so neither involve her nor dismiss her. These thoughts forced her to acknowledge that she would hate to be sent from the room. She felt hypnotised by the man in bondage, and the livid patterns Victoria's whip had created. Having no doubt that this was what the man wanted – indeed had come to Victoria for – she found herself more than intrigued to find out just how such matters could be managed.

'How old is your daughter?' asked Madame Victoria of the man.

'Please . . .' the man sounded more pained by the question than the whip that had been laid across his quivering flesh.

Madame Victoria's hand made only the tiniest of flicks but the whip seared into the man's flesh again. 'I asked you a question.'

'Twelve!' gasped the man.

The whip snaked out again. 'Liar! How could she be twelve when you told me she was about to make you a grandfather. The truth now!'

'Twenty-four!'

Helen watched Madame Victoria nod. 'Twenty-four.

That's more believable. Now let me see – that would make four groups of six strokes, would it not?'

'Yes, Mistress!'

'Good. You will keep the accounts and ensure no mistake is made. You understand me?'

'Yes, Mistress.'

When Victoria rapped out 'Mistress Helen!' she waited until the startled Helen looked at her. 'You will go to his front and report on his condition. You understand me?'

Nodding, feeling even less real, Helen moved to the front of the man and saw how Kate's kneeling efforts had raised the man yet again to full erection. 'He is ready, Madame,' called Kate.

'I said that Mistress Helen would report to me!'

Fascinated, Helen moved forward and reached out a hand to touch the rigid flesh, made slick and shiny by Kate, and then looked up into the man's eyes. They looked desperate as he met her gaze and for a moment she felt sorry for him, but then as her hand, seemingly of itself, began to stroke and caress the man's phallus she saw a smile play about his lips and all sympathy vanished from her to be replaced by a sudden lurch in her loins.

Madame Victoria's voice cut into her reverie. 'Well?'

'He is ready, Madame,' Helen murmured, her eyes once more peering into the man's face.

'Very well, then,' said Victoria and Helen held her eyes on the man's face and continued to caress him as Kate sat back to cede her place.

The sound of the whip cutting through the air and then biting deep into the man caused him to yell out as a convulsive wave swept through his body and into Helen's arm, shooting through her upper body before sinking like an electric surge to clench at her loins.

'One, Mistress,' cried the man.

Helen's eyes never left the man's face nor did her

hand stray from his softening penis. Again the whistle then the impact as the whip cut into him.

'Two, Mistress.' His voice now rising against the cumulative gathering of pain.

Helen turned to see that Kate was watching her closely. With a quick gesture Helen brought her forward to fall hungrily on the detumescent cock.

'Three, Mistress.'

The strokes became more rapid and the man's voice more forced as he kept what Victoria had called the 'accounts'. Helen watched the man's face, contorted when the blows landed, breathing deeply between each one, with a growing sense of excitement. She had never seen anyone else beaten before and found the experience uniquely powerful.

'Mistress Helen!' Victoria's voice brought her once again to understand that this was all really happening before her eyes. Looking up she saw Victoria looking directly at her with a curious smile on her face. 'Take it!' she said and looking down to Victoria's extended hand saw the whip being offered to her.

Feeling an emotion that might have been fear or excitement, or both, she took the ebony handled whip in her hand and found her breathing shortening as her hand tightened around its sculpted haft.

'You will deliver the next six,' Victoria told her and brought her to stand in precisely the right place.

Helen looked at the already heavily marked buttocks and felt, curiously, that she was the one about to be tested. 'I want to see each of them leave its mark,' Victoria warned her before moving out of her swing's reach.

Her entire body started to quiver as she measured out the first stroke on the vulnerable flesh before her. She swung back and then brought the stroke feebly across his outraged buttocks.

The man didn't even flinch. 'We shall have to do better than that!' scoffed Victoria. 'Strike harder.'

Suddenly, seized with a desire to make this one count, Helen found her arm swinging back further and her wrist snaking in faster to deliver the next blow. The cry of the bound man shot through her, electrifying every nerve in her body.

'Thank you Mistress,' gasped the man.

'Keep the count!' Victoria reminded him.

'Thirteen, Mistress!'

The words meant nothing to Helen's brain which was seized in a paralysing madness. Almost completely detached from what the man might be feeling she was aware only of the tremendous sense of power that was charging her entire body. Now she struck out barely waiting for the man's count, until his voice rose to almost total incoherence as the blows followed close on one another.

She had become totally unaware of the man or the pain. She knew only of herself and the alien excitement which had laid siege to her senses and only when Victoria stepped forward to grab her already raised hand did she realise that she had been, literally, flogging the man until his 'count' had become a continuous wail.

'That's enough,' said Victoria sharply. 'Go to your Master.'

Helen felt her brain empty. 'Master?' she asked.

Victoria turned her to the door and all but pushed her through it. 'He's waiting for you in the sitting room. Go to him. Leave this to us.'

Resentful at being so peremptorily dismissed she went, feeling she had failed the 'test', to find Jeffrey rising from one of the deep couches, his eyes wide at the sight of her in the leather costume. 'You look magnificent,' he told her. 'Tomorrow we must have something like this made for you.'

This sudden transition from the unbelievable events taking place just a wall away, to Jeffrey's presence, confused her.

'Here,' Jeffrey was saying, as he held out a drink to her. 'You look as if you need this.'

Taking the glass Helen was only vaguely aware of the other girl, to whom she had not been introduced, sitting legs curled under herself on the couch opposite Jeffrey. Noting that the girl, who when last seen had been wearing a dress, now wore only a dressing gown gaping open to show most of her naked breasts, and wondering if, in her absence, anything had happened between the girl and Jeffrey, she heard herself asking: 'Did you fuck her?'

Jeffrey smiled. 'No. I was saving that for you.'

'Here,' her voice continued.

'No. I thought we'd go back to the hotel.'

'That wasn't a question,' she said with an assertiveness that surprised even her.

His face quivering with surprise, Jeffrey looked at her. 'Here?' he asked.

She nodded and turned to the girl. 'Is there another room – like that one?' Helen indicated the room she had just left.

The girl nodded cautiously. 'Show it to me,' she murmured.

Rising, the girl glanced at Jeffrey for confirmation that she should do as Helen asked, before leading the still masked Helen into the hallway. She was led past the room from which she had so recently been sent and into another, slightly smaller but equally well equipped. As she looked around she was aware of the girl watching her.

'Help me out of this,' she said indicating the basque.

The girl came forward immediately but made a mild protest. 'But you look so good in it. Didn't your man just admire it . . . ?'

Impatiently she started tugging at the front hooks herself but knew the strings at the back would need help. 'Do it!' she rapped, surprised at how like Victoria her tone sounded.

The girl's fingers moved nimbly over the restraining strings and soon Helen felt her abdominal muscles relax with relief as cooler air touched her heated skin.

Freed of the basque, but still masked, she went forward for a closer look at the chains that dangled from a ceiling frame. Extending one wrist she closed the leather band round it and motioned for the girl to come forward and secure it.

In seconds the girl's obviously well practised fingers had closed the clasps, and she looked to Helen to have it confirmed that the other was to be treated in like manner.

When she was fully secured, feeling deliciously open and vulnerable she sent the girl to summon Jeffrey. Balanced on the high pointed heels of the boots, only the mask gave her any confidence that she would not disappoint him when he came to her.

On coming into the room Jeffrey was stunned by what he saw. Every sinew in her upper arms and shoulders seemed defined by the restraint in which she had been secured. Her stomach had all but disappeared into her rib cage while her breasts appeared firmer with their nipples, aroused and engorged, pointing almost ceilingwards.

'The whips,' she gasped to him. 'Use them . . .'

When Jeffrey nodded as if to dismiss the girl from the room, Helen called out again. 'No! I want her to stay!'

Jeffrey, smiling quietly, came to stand directly in front of her. 'Since the girl is to stay I suggest we make use of her. Shall I have her whip you?'

Feeling something akin to anger at his delay she spat her words out through gritted teeth. 'I don't care who whips me just as long as it hurts!'

'What a greedy little slave you've become!' said Jeffrey quietly, reaching out to tease both nipples with his fingers. 'Every time you tell me you love me she will strike five times,' he added.

Taking a deep breath Helen braced herself before uttering the fatal words.

When, some thirty minutes later, she saw, through hooded eyes, Victoria come into the room she felt immense pride as that jaded lady winced at the sight of Helen's lividly marked buttocks and thighs.

The man that was with Victoria looked unfamiliar to her until she realised that his strangeness was due to the fact that he was now dressed. The man's eyes bulged at seeing her whip marks but he came forward, and reached both hands to encompass her head before kissing her lightly on both cheeks. 'Thank you, Mistress Helen,' he murmured.

Victoria looked significantly to Jeffrey before turning to usher the man out of the room leaving her once more alone with Jeffrey and the girl. Defiantly, she held Jeffrey's eyes as he looked back at her. 'Now you can have me,' she told him.

Chapter Nine

*H*elen woke, thick headed, and feeling as if she might be coming down with something, only to find an enthused Jeffrey at her side.

'Helen!' he was excitedly calling before she was even fully awake. 'Marvellous news. They've found my car!'

Her head still heavy with sleep, Helen tried to concentrate. 'Your car?'

'Yes. At, of all places, the German/Polish border! Annabel called me from London. Apparently the border police got suspicious because the thieves – who can't be very bright – had put false French plates on a right hand drive car! They checked it out and found it was listed as stolen.'

'What on earth were they doing trying to take it into Poland?'

'Apparently there's a big market in Russia for that kind of car at the "right" price. Isn't it marvellous? I thought I'd go and collect it and drive it back. You could come with me if you want but I don't think the German/ Polish border is the most appealing of places. What do you say?'

Helen felt confusion closing in rapidly. 'I'm sorry, Jeffrey, I'm not awake yet. As a matter of fact I feel exhausted still.' She paused trying to absorb this sudden change of plan – an effort made worse by Jeffrey's obvious excitement at the prospect of getting his car returned. 'What do you suggest I do?'

'I'll only be gone a couple of days at the most. Why not just stay here?'

'Alone?' she asked.

'No! Annabel's coming over. I need the registration documents, the insurance – all that kerfuffle – to prove the damn thing's mine. She can stay with you – you two could go round the shops together.'

'I'd rather wait until you get back.'

Jeffrey nodded and then looked as if there was something else on his mind. Watching him she was filled with a sudden dread.

'Is something wrong?' she asked tentatively.

The question seemed to surprise Jeffrey and he looked, for a moment, as if he'd been caught out in thinking something shameful.

'No!' His denial was too effusive to be convincing. 'It's just that – well, there is something I wanted to discuss – later – but my having to go off like this . . .' He let his voice trail off. 'No,' he said as if his mind was made up. 'This isn't the time to get into that.'

'What?' she asked sharply.

His eyes, avoiding hers, focused randomly about the room for a moment before, taking a deep breath, he turned back to look directly at her. 'I'm a fraud,' he finally sighed.

Stricken with the thought that she was about to hear something she'd rather not she spoke with quiet insistence. 'What sort of "fraud"?'

'You came to me with your guilt-stricken vulnerability, looking for strength and the means to forget – obliterate, if you like – the agony you've been put through. The trouble is I'm not as strong as you might imagine,' he hesitated as she watched him. Filled with a sudden feeling that everything was about to go wrong

381

she, nevertheless, felt obliged to give him the space he so obviously needed. 'This may sound crazy but, you see, I've never felt entitled to anything I have,' Jeffrey said flatly. 'Not even you.'

His last words startled Helen. They had come so suddenly and sounded like the crack of doom to her apprehensive ears. 'What do you mean?' she asked. 'You have me. I'm here. My God, Jeffrey, we might not have known each other long but the things we've shared . . . don't start doubting "us".'

'I don't doubt *you*!' he protested. 'You're a fantastic girl. You're beautiful, sexual, intelligent and . . . maybe that's the trouble. I've begun to think I'm exploiting your vulnerability.'

'That's total nonsense! I haven't done anything I didn't want to do – and there's things we've done I want to do again. Please don't feel guilty about me. I meant it when I told you you'd liberated me. Jeffrey, I need your strength – don't start doubting yourself now.'

His smile was wry as he looked away, staring blankly and without interest, at anywhere but her. 'My "strength"?' he asked with heavy sarcasm. 'Don't you realise that my only "strength" is in your submission?'

It took her a moment to absorb this surprising concept but when she did she found herself encouraged. 'Fine!' she said. 'That's fine with me. I'm totally yours.'

His smile remained glacial but at least, she thought, he's looking at me again. 'My father once told me that the only time you ever know what you possess is when you give it away, sell it, dispose of it. Only in losing it could you be sure you ever had it.'

The ice rushed back into her soul making her next words brittle. 'Are you saying you want to be rid of me?'

'That's not what I'm saying at all. My greatest fear is that, having found you, I might lose you. I couldn't bear that.'

382

'So that makes us even,' she told him. 'I don't want to lose you either.'

As he looked steadily at her she read agony in his eyes. The source of this worried her. He had been in a confessional mood but had said nothing to explain this sudden despair. At the same time there was, gnawing at the back of her mind, the certainty that he hadn't told her everything. She couldn't imagine ever again being as intimate and open with anyone other than Jeffrey and she found the thought of being without him terrifying. More terrifying than knowing the worst. 'What is it you're *not* telling me?' she asked.

'You might hate me,' he finally said.

'I doubt it,' she answered, her voice edgy with preparedness.

'I started some enquiries . . .' he said hesitantly.

'"Enquiries"? About me?'

He shook his head as if dismissing that suggestion as ridiculous. 'About Kenneth.' Seeing her go into a shocked and puzzled silence, he rushed on. 'Millie told me about the accident and everything before I even met you. It didn't sound right to me then but it was none of my business so . . .' he shrugged before going on. '. . . But after we'd met – when I realised how affected you were by what you thought had happened I started some enquiries . . .'

Helen stayed silent. Her first reaction was much as if she had found him rifling her diary, reading her letters or checking her bank account, but then she remembered that she had felt precisely the same during the police enquiries and the inquest and when the facts – as the world saw them – had become public property. There was no reason Jeffrey shouldn't know as much as total strangers but his phrase 'by what you *thought* had happened' rang discordantly in her ears. 'And what did you find out?' she asked.

'Nothing. Not yet, anyway. I mean it's only been a few days – the real investigation hasn't even begun yet.'

'And what do you expect to discover?'

Jeffrey looked painfully awkward. 'I honestly don't know. I've done some scuba diving myself but I'm not expert, so I checked with a friend of mine who is. He confirmed my first reaction.'

'Which is?'

'That it is extremely unlikely that in a properly supervised dive, a member of the team could go missing for over an hour and not be missed. You told me Kenneth was an experienced diver and yet he got entangled with some wreck's hawsers and just stayed there waiting to die? That doesn't ring true. There had to be something they didn't tell you.'

'What?'

'That's what I hope we'll find out.' He looked at her with eyes pleading their sincerity. 'Whatever it is, or might be, it can't be worse than your imaginings – or the guilt you're carrying around.'

Feeling increasingly that the situation was becoming weird she attempted to inject a note of realism. 'Jeffrey, there was an investigation, then an inquest. If there was anything to find out it would have come out.'

'Inquest verdicts are not always what they seem,' he murmured.

'Are you saying that the verdict on Kenneth was fixed?'

'Of course not. All I'm saying is that, sometimes, a verdict isn't what's true but what's best.'

'For who, or what?'

'Who knows? It could be politics – it could be a negative effect on tourism . . . It could be – right now – almost anything. All I'm saying is that what you were told doesn't sound right – an experienced diver could have done a dozen things to alert people to what was going on. The last thing he'd do is just hang there and wait for his air to run out.'

Helen felt totally numb. She almost wished she could feel anger but recognised that Jeffrey thought he had acted in her best interests. What concerned her was that he had thrust himself so deeply into her business without consulting her feelings. Suddenly the wonderful lover sitting opposite her was not the man she had imagined him to be. 'Jeffrey,' she murmured out of her confusion, 'I think I'd like some time alone to think.'

'This is what I was afraid of,' he muttered. 'Please don't go cold on me now. I did this because I was worried about you.'

'Apparently not "worried" enough to discuss it with me first.'

'I thought you'd try and stop me!'

'Maybe I would have,' she said. 'It's something I've been trying to put behind me. Something I don't want to think about any more than I have to!'

'That's where you're wrong!' cried Jeffrey. 'What you've been really trying to do is run away. Do you imagine that by ignoring what happened you'll be able to forget it? You never will – all you'll succeed in doing is putting up barriers – barriers which, sooner or later, will come tumbling down and crush you. I knew that. I knew that's why you came to me. I didn't flatter myself that it was my magnetic personality that drew you. You wanted just to stop *thinking* – and not only about Kenneth, but everything. In me you imagined you'd found someone strong enough to distract you. You won't ever be able to put this thing to rest and I can't do it for you, unless you turn around and face it – for better or worse.'

'Like nightmares?' she asked with a wry smile.

'*Exactly* like nightmares!'

While recognising that there was truth in Jeffrey's words she also recognised a greater truth – she now needed nothing so much as time and space to sift through the many confusing thoughts that were saturating her mind. She was experiencing her first doubts about Jeffrey but wasn't quite sure where they were coming from. Finally, she spoke quietly. 'Maybe it's not the best time to be talking like this. I'm too tired. I'm afraid I might be going down with flu, and I would like to get some more sleep if I can.'

Nodding, Jeffrey rose from the bed. 'Sorry, I was so excited at the news I didn't stop to think. Is there anything you want? For the flu, I mean?'

Helen, amused at his sudden concern, shook her head. Jeffrey nodded. 'OK. Get some sleep and maybe later you'll feel well enough to have dinner with us.'

'"Us"?'

'Annabel. I told you, she's on her way over. Should be here any minute.'

Jeffrey left her with many sudden doubts. Cursing the dead feeling in her head, she remembered her chilling naked walk to Madame Victoria's and, mentally, upgraded her symptoms from flu to pneumonia.

Helen's next memory was of being gently woken by the sound of Jeffrey's concerned voice. 'Helen, I'm leaving now. There's an early plane to Berlin – the sooner I get started the sooner I'll be back.'

Still asleep, a befuddled Helen tried to rouse herself to understand what he was saying. 'Tonight?' she asked.

'It isn't "tonight". It's morning. You've slept round the clock.'

Startled, Helen stared at Jeffrey. 'Morning? How long have I been asleep?'

'On and off – something like eighteen hours but you obviously needed it. I'll be gone at least two days, I suppose, it's a chance for you to get rested.'

With a vague feeling that everything was coming unravelled, Helen tried to put her arms around Jeffrey, feeling it was important to hold on to him at that moment. Gently Jeffrey unwound her embrace. 'I have to go or I'll miss the flight and that'll make the trip that much longer.' Leaning in he gave her what, in her present mood, seemed no more than a patronising kiss and left her gazing after him as he hurried off to the door. 'I'll call you this evening and let you know how things are going.'

Muddled and cursing herself for being barely awake at the moment of his leaving, she lay back on the bed engulfed in a growing sense of unease. The bedside clock told her it was barely seven a.m. – six a.m. London time she told herself for no logical reason she could think of.

Turning on her side she ruminated that she had a great deal to consider but the problems grew more indistinct the more she thought about them. Gratefully she felt sleep once more overtaking her and decided to slide into its comforting embrace and worry about her indeterminate troubles later.

At first she thought she was dreaming of being attacked and became panicked when she realised it was real and that she was awake. A man was holding her in his arms and laying fervent kisses on her forehead and cheeks. Anger pumping adrenalin, she started fighting the man off furiously until she, amazed, saw that her 'attacker' was Qito!

'You are a very strong woman,' he was saying, ruefully nursing a bruised cheek before a broad, tooth sparkling smile broke out of his deeply tanned face. 'You looked so beautiful lying there – I couldn't resist you!'

Dragging the covers defensively about her she stared at Qito. 'What are you doing here?' she demanded.

'We came to invite you and Jeffrey! Carla and I are leaving at noon for Basse Terre. We wanted you both to come with us. I want to paint you.'

'Jeffrey's not here,' she told him, aware that he must already know that. 'How did you get in?'

'Annabel kindly let us in. She and Carla are having breakfast right now. Will you come?'

'To breakfast?'

'To Basse Terre!'

'I don't even know where that is.'

'It's the capital of Guadeloupe – a *département* of France – a domestic flight from Paris.'

Helen felt herself being buried under an avalanche of confusion. Jeffrey had wanted to take her to Germany. Now Qito was proposing she go, immediately, to a place she had never heard of. If she had been tied between two horses and about to be torn to pieces she couldn't have felt more perplexed. She just wished her head, seemingly filled with concrete, would clear.

'You'll have to talk to Jeffrey about that, and he's not here.'

'I don't need Jeffrey. It's you I want to paint.'

'Well, I'm sorry, I can't go anywhere – I . . .' Helen broke off and then, feeling distinctly uncomfortable, made a more direct appeal. 'Look, I can't think like this. Let me get up and then we can talk.'

Spreading his hands expansively Qito rose from the bed. 'Of course, but we haven't much time. We have to be at the airport in an hour. Don't take too long!' he cried breezily before going out.

Left alone Helen lay in the bed and considered that her world, already disordered, was now in chaos. The one thing she knew for certain was that she wasn't going anywhere before she spoke to Jeffrey but that thought only served to remind her that she, presently, had no way of contacting him.

Emerging into the suite's sitting room she was surprised to see Annabel rising from the breakfast table still wearing a dressing-gown. This item brought a rush of even more confusing thoughts about just where Annabel and, more especially, Jeffrey had spent the night. Carla was agitatedly mobile, filled with, to Helen, crushing energy and busily inspecting the hotel suite as if she might be considering buying it.

'They've re-decorated since I was last in this hotel,' Carla was saying as she looked disapprovingly at a silk lamp shade. 'Pity they didn't take the opportunity to *improve* it.' Then, finally acknowledging Helen's presence, she swooped towards her. 'It seems we are fated to meet constantly!' she cooed as she grabbed a startled Helen and delivered a swift kiss on each cheek. 'Qito is positively enraptured by you, darling!' Carla's words managed to convey that she did not entirely go along with that assessment.

Annabel came to Helen's startled assistance. 'How are you feeling?' Annabel asked. 'Jeffrey said he thought you might be coming down with flu or something. In any case you look as if you could use a hot drink. Come.'

With a growing feeling that she had, during her sleep, become something of an outsider – even an intruder – it took an effort of will to remind herself that she was here with Jeffrey and it was they, if anyone, that were intruding on her. Burying herself in the fine porcelain teacup, Helen felt some of her vital life signs slowly returning.

Carla, meanwhile, was continuing her peripatetic inspection of the premises. 'If you are having influenza stay away from me. I catch everything!'

Qito joined in. 'The best thing for the grippe is warm sea air! Guadeloupe is just the place for that! Take my advice – pack a bag and jump on the plane with us!'

'Qito!' Carla's voice contained a threatening note of caution. 'Give the girl a chance. There's always another time!'

Qito's response was explosive. '"Another time"! You don't know what you're talking about. You never understand! I have my muse – ' Helen was startled to find that role assigned to her. 'I have the place – the island we found last year – and I have the inspiration! You imagine I can switch such things on and off like a tap?' Turning to Annabel he demanded, 'Where is Jeffrey? I must speak to him immediately!'

Annabel shrugged. 'Not possible, I'm afraid. He's probably somewhere in the air between here and Berlin.

After that he has to find his way to the Polish border but I'm sure we'll hear from him tonight.'

'Ridiculous!' cried Qito. 'We will be on our way to Guadeloupe by then. There's only one solution. Helen comes with us and you tell Jeffrey to join us later in Guadeloupe.'

'Wait a moment!' cried an exasperated Helen. 'Don't I count for anything in this conversation? In the first place, I'm not going anywhere – certainly not to some place I've never heard of – without, at least, speaking to Jeffrey and, in the second place, I don't even want to.'

Qito stared at her in horror. 'You don't know what you're saying!' he cried. 'Don't you understand? I *need* you!'

Suddenly angry, Helen found herself on her feet and shouting at Qito. 'What an arrogant little man you are!' she cried. 'You *"need"* so the whole world has to fall into line? Well *I* don't!'

Having left herself with no other place to go Helen fled the breakfast room, taking with her the image of Qito's astonished face and leaving behind a solid stunned silence broken only by Carla's cry of approval and solitary applause.

In her bedroom Helen was still seething. Everything, this wakening, was off kilter. Immediately realising that her anger was due to an uncomfortable feeling that she had been 'dumped' in Paris in favour of Jeffrey's almost frenetic enthusiasm to recover his 'precious' car. There was also the unsettling discovery that Jeffrey had spent the night in the suite where the only alternative to Helen's bed had been Annabel's. Added to which this ludicrous assumption that she would be thrilled to go off to some unknown destination with a virtual stranger, made her feel as if she had stumbled into a Parisian version of the Mad Hatter's Tea Party.

Agitated wasn't the word for it!

When Qito came cautiously after her she felt ready to

vent herself more fully but his soulful eyes dissuaded her until he'd spoken. '*Caro* . . .' he murmured, coming forward and reaching out for an embrace which she, with conscious petulance, avoided. 'I didn't mean to upset you,' he was saying in his softest tones. 'Truly, Jeffrey is one my oldest and truest friends. Had he been here, I know he would have agreed at once – maybe not to come with us immediately – but, maybe, to follow on in a day or two. I meant no insult by my suggestion.'

Despite herself Helen found his obvious sincerity beguiling, but she still had no coherent answer to make.

'I have a suggestion,' Qito was saying. 'I will leave first class tickets at the airport desk for both you and Jeffrey. That way you can join us as my guests, whenever you wish. Is that fair?' he asked before adding in the face of her continuing confusion, 'Am I forgiven?'

Finding his tone conciliatory, and the pressure of the need to make a decision lifting, she managed a smile. 'I'm sorry. I just feel a little irritable this morning. I don't know what's wrong with me. Maybe I am coming down with something but I shouldn't have spoken to you as I did. I'm sorry.'

Qito's face positively beamed with relief. 'Then everyone forgives everyone else!' This time as he came forward she allowed him to take her into a light embrace. 'When you've spoken to Jeffrey, and you feel better, come. It's a beautiful place. The sun shines, the water is warm and, there, they don't know what a grey day is. It would do you good!' Holding her at arm's length he beamed. 'And I need you to inspire me!'

The cosy warmth that had been established between them was peremptorily interrupted by the cutting edge of Carla's voice. 'Qito!' she said sharply. 'We have to go if we are to catch that flight.'

Stepping back with an alacrity that suggested guilt, Qito turned to his wife. 'Of course. *Subito!*' he said.

Helen found herself quite pleased – even flattered –

to be the subject of a withering look from Carla before the lady turned abruptly from the bedroom.

'So, I may hope to see you in Guadeloupe!' Qito was insisting.

Smiling, Helen told him she would have to speak to Jeffrey and see what he said. This answer seemed to satisfy Qito as he turned, chastened, to join the impatiently waiting Carla.

'Don't forget!' Qito cautioned her on leaving. 'Tickets will be waiting!'

With the barest of polite goodbyes Carla all but dragged Qito from the suite leaving Helen to face Annabel whose dressing-gown reminded her again of unresolved doubts, best left, she decided, until another time.

'Aren't you excited?' Annabel asked.

'About what?'

'That Qito, of all people, wants you to pose for him. He would immortalise you!'

At any other time Helen might have found Annabel's enthusiasm faintly comic but, in her present mood, she could find nothing even remotely funny. 'Maybe!' she said as she made her way into her room and, settling on the bed, felt in need of a damn good cry.

That evening, feeling that Annabel had dragged her across half of Paris, Helen returned to the hotel anxious not to miss Jeffrey's promised telephone call. She was frustrated to find a message from him that he was sorry to have missed her and would call again later.

Beginning to find Annabel's presence oppressive, she bluntly asked her how long she meant to stay. Annabel shrugged. 'Jeffrey did ask me to look after you while he was gone.'

'I don't need "looking after",' she said, not bothering to disguise her acid tone.

Annabel seemed quite at ease and Helen got the distinct impression the girl was enjoying the discomfort of her presence. 'It's a little late to go back to London tonight.' Annabel smiled. 'Perhaps in the morning – that is, if Jeffrey doesn't want me to stay on.'

Aware that she had been subtly reminded that Jeffrey had the last word in the arrangements, Helen felt a surge of bitterness. 'Well, at least,' she said with deliberate sarcasm, 'you'll have the bed to yourself tonight, won't you?'

Annabel opened her mouth as if to say something but settled for a dulcet smile which infuriated Helen even more. Turning on her heel Helen went to her own room and closed the door with noisy emphasis.

When, later, Annabel called through the door to ask if she should order a room-service dinner, Helen told her she wasn't hungry and settled in for a grumpy night not caring that she was behaving badly.

Jeffrey's promised call didn't materialise and so it was an even more unsettled Helen that faced Annabel the following morning.

In answer to Helen's somewhat forlorn enquiry, Annabel told her that the only call had come from the airline to confirm that they were holding tickets in the names of Helen Lloyd and Jeffrey Hacking.

Not wanting to leave the hotel in case she again missed Jeffrey's call, Helen waited impatiently throughout the morning until close to two in the afternoon she finally heard Jeffrey's voice.

'Hi! I'm sorry about this. There's more red tape than you can imagine. I've had to hire a local lawyer to try and fight my way through it but he hardly speaks English and my German is atrocious. I'm afraid this could take longer than I thought. There's talk that they will have to hold the car as evidence until the smugglers come up for trial.'

'But that could take weeks!' Helen protested. 'Surely you don't intend staying there that long?'

Her heart sank as she heard Jeffrey's sigh. 'Well, no, but I think I should stay at least another couple of days and see what can be done to speed things up.' As if trying to cheer her up, he added, 'By the way, I've seen the car and it's totally undamaged. That's something, don't you think?'

Helen didn't think it was much and let that into her tone as she answered. 'I feel pretty silly sitting in Paris on my own. The best thing I can do is go back to London – but I'm not sure how to settle the bill.'

'Don't worry about that. Let me talk to Annabel . . .'

Handing over the telephone to her Helen felt even more out of place than before Jeffrey's call.

She heard the efficient Annabel assuring Jeffrey that she would take care of everything, and then, without offering Helen the chance for a last word with Jeffrey, hung up.

'Nothing's easy,' smiled Annabel. 'I even told him not to expect too much before he left. He's crazy about that car.'

'To the exclusion of all else it seems,' murmured Helen.

'What a shame you didn't accept Qito's invitation,' said Annabel brightly.

Reminded that she hadn't even thought to mention the invitation to Jeffrey she asked, 'You don't imagine I had any serious intention of going, did you?'

Annabel looked bemused. 'How many chances at immortality are you going to get?' she asked. 'I know what I'd do,' Annabel added.

Looking up, Helen saw a strangely thoughtful looking Annabel handing her a drink. As she gratefully reached for it she had little idea that her, already shaky, confidence was about to be totally shattered.

'You do know he's married, don't you?' asked Annabel.

Helen smiled. 'Qito? Of course. Carla was right here.'

'I meant Jeffrey,' said Annabel.

Chapter Ten

*T*o be confused was one thing. To be confused about why she was confused was demeaning. She had run away. That fact was clear in her mind even as she had blundered out of the hotel and taken a cab to the airport. They had the ticket and, since nothing could be too much trouble for anyone connected with Qito, she found herself caught up in a highly efficient process which demanded nothing of her but her presence. She had given no thought to where she was going but only to what she was leaving behind.

She felt emotionally violated. She had opened herself more totally to Jeffrey than any other living being and he had betrayed her. She remembered him telling her that there were things he had yet to tell her, but thought the basic fact of his being married left unsaid was unforgivable, and it was this that was the source of her confusion. The issue of marriage had never been mentioned and, indeed, given the short time they had known each other, it would have been ludicrous. However, given that, in little more than a week, they had explored each other's sexuality with such complete abandon, she did consider that it entitled her to believe that a bond of trust had been formed, which Annabel's news had totally shattered.

Now, riding in this plane to an unknown future, she could not wipe away the image of Jeffrey as she had seen him in arousal, and the knowledge that behind that face, during all those excursions, had been this other man who had kept a secret.

It was this that confused her confusion. She had been made foolish in his eyes, which was demeaning enough, but there was also the knowledge that, somewhere in this world, was a woman with a greater claim to him than she had.

Stupid! Stupid! Stupid! These two syllables repeated endlessly in her mind, blocking out any attempt to rationalise what she was really doing by flying in this aircraft to an unknown and, until yesterday, unheard of destination.

When the dinner had been cleared away and the choice of movies announced she realised the flight was going on for what seemed an inordinate length of time for an internal French domestic flight. It was only then that it occurred to her to check her ticket. The 24-hour clock system always confused her but she was still able to work out that the scheduled flying time was four hours and, she thought, that must include some time-zone reduction – maybe an hour or so – so, having been already in flight for two or more hours they must, surely, be almost there. Could it be that it was possible to fly by fast jet for three hours and still be in France? It was then she realised she hadn't the least idea where Guadeloupe was. She had imagined it might be some off-shore possession in the Mediterranean like Corsica, but even with her limited knowledge of geography she didn't imagine Corsica to be more than two hours flying time from Paris, yet they had announced that they were about to show a movie!

She cornered a passing attendant and asked her for an explanation.

'But, madame, the explanation is in the time zones. The flight only appears to be four hours because those

396

are local times. To that you must add the five-hour time difference.'

'*Add* the time difference?' a bewildered Helen asked. 'But surely if we are flying east the time difference is deducted?'

'But we are flying west, madame,' the girl explained in patient tones.

'"West"? You mean across the Atlantic? But I thought this was a domestic flight.'

'It is. Guadeloupe is a *département* of France, but it is in the Caribbean. Our flying time will be a little over eight hours.'

The smiling girl moved off, little realising that her words had left a corpse in the shell of Helen's body. She who had, but moments ago, felt herself betrayed was now herself a betrayer. She was flying into the ocean that had killed Kenneth. Before her eyes lay his pain-wracked death mask which now stared at her to ask what she thought she was doing.

Why was it she had never once in her life ever asked the obvious questions? Sometime, in the few quiet moments she had known with Jeffrey, there had been room to ask why a man of his age and affluence had not married. Surely, before so precipitously fleeing that man, she might have taken a moment to ask where Guadeloupe was? Had she known it lay in the same ocean that had taken Kenneth she would never have come. She felt totally lost in a nightmare of her own making and, but for the almost sepulchral dignity and quiet of her fellow passengers, she might have broken out into a primal scream. Instead, she sat in her seat numbed with the thought that she had already died.

She felt trapped. Once more committed to an insanity because she had failed to ask the right question. Catching the arm of the passing attendant she asked for more champagne. If there was no physical way out of this sealed cigar in the sky she would seek escape from herself and the self-loathing that was suddenly welling inside her, and champagne seemed as good an anaesthetic as any other.

Two or three glasses of their excellent champagne later, the movie seemed to be getting duller and more out of focus. It was a welcome relief when the flight attendant came back to lean in on her confidentially.

'Madame, the Captain asked if you would like to visit the flight deck?'

Thinking that one of the best ideas she had heard in a long time Helen got to her feet and was surprised to find the plane's floor seeming so unstable. The attendant even took her arm as she led her forward and through a door into the capacious cockpit.

This was a totally different world to the passenger sections. Here was a confusing array of different coloured lights, dials and switches most of which seemed to be displayed on television monitors. It looked like a video-game player's heaven.

From out of the left-hand seat a shirt-sleeved man in his middle forties was smiling at her as if from a toothpaste ad.

'Welcome to our workbench,' he called in a warmly accented voice. A younger man rose and came to lead her even further into the alchemist's kitchen of confusing technology. With the champagne singing in her blood, Helen was gently edged towards the right-hand seat.

'Would you like to sit there?' the younger man asked.

He helped her into the extremely comfortable control seat and she was thrilled by the thought of sitting before the controls of a powerful machine, but terrified of touching anything in case she caused a sudden disaster. The younger man was meanwhile fitting a headset over her hair and arranging it about her ears. Suddenly the Captain's voice was a whisper in her ear.

'Have you ever been taken up front in a plane before?' he asked. The question struck her as extremely funny and she went off into peals of laughter. 'What's funny?' the captain asked as she fought to control her giggles.

'No,' she said. 'But I'm willing to try anything once.'

It took a moment for the Captain to translate his own double entendre but when he did his voice became a great deal warmer.

'Well, in that case, we must see what we can do for such a lovely lady.'

Helen looked across at the man's face, lit as it was by the green glow of the electronic instrument panel, and decided he was extremely attractive. 'My name is Lucas,' he told her. 'My First Officer is Hubert.'

Helen turned awkwardly in the seat to shake the hand of the younger man. Hubert was even more attractive she decided.

'Are you going to Guadeloupe on vacation?' asked the Captain's voice close in her headset.

The question, confused as she was about her own motivations, stilled her for a moment. Rather than launch into a long explanation she decided it would be simpler to agree.

'Alone?' was the next question.

'As you see,' she told him.

Aware that a meaningful glance had passed between the Captain and the First Officer, Helen felt a surge of returning confidence. The questions, and the revelation that the Captain already knew she was travelling alone, made it clear to her that she had been 'targeted'. Obviously the Captain had sent his cabin staff to scout for an attractive woman travelling alone, and she had been selected. Helen found she didn't mind one bit!

'We have a two-day stop over in Guadeloupe,' the Captain was saying. 'Maybe I would be lucky enough to have dinner with you one evening?'

While looking across at his chiselled profile Helen realised that ten days ago she would have fled, embarrassed, from such an open pass but Jeffrey had taught her differently. That and the generous amount of champagne she had drunk seemed suddenly to have fired up her blood and she found nothing wrong in answering the Captain boldly. 'It might be that you could get *very* lucky,' she told him. His answer came as a confident chuckle into the intimacy of her ear.

It was then, keenly aware of a glow in her loins, that she noticed something missing from the area immediately in front of her. There seemed to be no control stick. 'Excuse me,' she asked. 'But shouldn't there be something here to steer the plane by? What do you call it . . . a joy stick?'

'Not any more,' the captain told her and pressing himself back into the leather of his seat, indicated a tiny lever by his left hand. 'These days we have only this.'

'It seems very small,' Helen murmured, then hurriedly added, 'I mean to control such a huge machine.'

'Size is not everything,' smiled the Captain. 'Mind you,' he added in his warm French voice which was, by now, insinuating through her like warm treacle, 'we still carry joy sticks in case of emergency.'

'You do?' asked Helen innocently.

'Of course,' smiled the Captain and turning round called to his First Officer. 'Hubert will be happy to show you his . . .' The Captain broke off and Helen, turning to see what had caused his hesitation, saw that they had been joined by one of the flight attendants – a somewhat subdued looking, pretty young woman.

The Captain greeted her. 'Ah! Of course – our *nouvelle*.'

Helen, realising that the Captain had spoken in English for her benefit, turned to study the newcomer with some interest.

The girl had fine blonde hair, fine china-blue eyes which flashed uncertainly from one to the other of the three but finally centred on the Captain whose voice continued to whisper into Helen's headset.

'Michelle is newly graduated from our training school. This is her first operational flight. We have a tradition of initiating our new girls in a particularly interesting little ritual. Would you be interested in witnessing it?'

Her interest even more aroused, Helen turned fully in the seat to study the stewardess even more closely. She saw the young woman's lips parted in an uncertain smile with the lower lip visibly trembling. Helen clearly read aroused sexual excitement, barely repressed, in Michelle's expression. She not only saw it but began to feel it herself!

'I'd love to,' breathed Helen.

The Captain nodded as if this confirmed his own judgement. Looking across at his maturely handsome face Helen felt a stab of insight. This man, in charge of a highly sophisticated aeroplane, was all that stood between her – along with approximately two or three hundred others – plunging to her death. It was his skill that kept her safe and, quite suddenly, she thought of him as no longer a man but, given his power of life or death, some kind of latter-day deity. That thought combined with his obvious good looks – not to mention the uniform – caused her loins to heat up as an air of highly charged eroticism blanketed the flight deck.

Meanwhile the Captain was addressing the apprehensive Michelle. 'Are your passengers settled down?'

'Yes, Captain,' murmured the girl.

'And so you have some time to devote to us?'

The girl flashed a side-long glance at the attentive Helen before nodding.

The Captain's voice whispered into Helen's headset. 'There is a strict dress code for the new recruits,' he said, his voice light and amused. 'It is my duty to now check that Michelle has conformed to that code.'

'What "code"?' asked an avidly interested Helen.

'You will see,' said the Captain before turning to address Michelle directly. 'Are you properly dressed?' he asked.

She nodded, her hands already anticipating his next order as she reached for the buttons of her blouse.

'You understand it is necessary for me to confirm your report?'

Michelle, anxiously nodding, whispered, 'Yes.'

'Very well. Continue.'

Helen's eyes grew rounded with excitement as she saw the woman's trembling fingers complete the opening of her blouse to reveal her pleasantly rounded, pink tipped breasts.

In her ear the Captain continued his commentary. 'New girls are not permitted underwear on their inaugural flights,' he told Helen.

Helen found herself, enormously aroused, unable to take her eyes from the woman now unzipping her uniform skirt and handing it to the First Officer who was hovering behind her ready to take it. Michelle then turned to face the Captain wearing only a pair of high-heeled shoes, self supporting stockings and an apprehensive expression.

'At this point . . .' the Captain whispered through the headset, 'it is necessary to check if the initiate is truly enjoying herself. Would you care to assess her condition?'

Barely believing she was doing this, Helen agreed enthusiastically and with no doubt of what was being asked of her, removed the headset and stood to look directly into the face of the startled flight attendant.

Feeling that the past few days had primed her for this unconventional moment, Helen spoke words which, even to her ears, sounded alien. 'Hands on your head.' The girl nervously obeyed but visibly shuddered at Helen's next order. 'Spread your legs.'

Michelle almost stumbled and fell as she shuffled her uncertain feet apart and the First Officer had to extend a steadying hand.

Filled with a surging sense of power Helen held her gaze as she reached down and, with her fingers, felt the woman's spread inner thighs which were seemingly melting with excitement. Helen's voice came out burdened with an unfamiliar huskiness as she reported Michelle's condition. 'She ready for anything.'

'So what do you suggest we do with her?' he asked.

Helen looked to him. 'You need me to tell you that?'

The Captain shook his head. 'But what about me?' he asked. 'Do you not wish to check on my "readiness"?'

Helen hesitated a moment as her impulse to go immediately to the man was tempered by an even greater impulse to survive. 'Who's going to fly the plane?' she asked.

'Madame!' protested the Captain. 'Computers have been flying the plane since we left the Charles de Gaulle air-traffic control. You have nothing to fear but my penis.'

Fearlessly, Helen went forward and kneeling at his side felt a surge of unutterable daring as she reached for his trouser zip. He was standing tall and aroused as she searched him out and leaned forward to tease him before plunging him deep into her throat.

As she hungrily sucked she fantasised about the context. The Captain had her life in his hands since he controlled the sophisticated machine that contained them all and it thrilled her to imagine that her safety depended on this man's pleasure. It was, therefore, with some affront that she felt Michelle's breasts brush past her bobbing head and realised that the attendant was being bent over her own kneeling figure to plunge her tongue into the Captain's mouth. She was even more distracted to feel Michelle's knees pressing against her and breaking off for a moment she turned to see that the First Officer was vigorously taking Michelle from behind!

A slight pressure on her head brought her attention back to her 'duties' and she plunged the Captain once more into her mouth as Michelle started screaming in orgasmic ecstasy. Then, pressing forward, Michelle all but thrust Helen to one side in her anxiety to reach and straddle the Captain in his seat, where, having torn his cock from Helen's grasp, thrust it deep into her own spread thighs.

Helen had little time for resentment when she, at the First Officer's urging, turned to be confronted with an enormous, risen penis standing out from his uniform trousers. The distant roar of the engines sang in her ears. This was a moment out of time and she felt like a woman truly privileged to be breaking every one of polite society's conventions. Thinking only of the hurt Jeffrey had delivered to her, and revelling in this opportunity for instant revenge, she took the risen flesh deep into her throat where her taste buds were immediately assailed by the taste of strawberries. It was the first flavoured condom she had ever tasted and for some reason it struck her as hilariously funny.

Chapter Eleven

*H*elen stepped from the plane feeling more an alien than a visitor. Even the pristine blue sky and the all embracing heat seemed to mock her – and ask her what she imagined she was doing. Having left Paris in precipitate haste, feeling feverish and confused, she now found herself filled with the doubts and bewilderment of a refugee and the suspicion that she might have made a momentous mistake. Since the flight from Paris to Guadeloupe was classified as domestic there were few formalities on arrival other than to reclaim the baggage.

It was in the baggage hall that Carla, accompanied by a stick-like young man, found her. 'There you are!' she cried closing to embrace Helen as she might have her oldest and dearest friend.

Surprised as much by the warmth of the greeting as anything else Helen relaxed, aware that everyone in the baggage hall was excited to find a famous face – Carla's – in their midst.

'Qito is beside himself with excitement,' Carla told her as she supervised the young man retrieving her one, sad looking, bag. 'Did I introduce Jimmy?' she asked as they started from the baggage claim hall.

'Jimmy travels with me everywhere. He claims to be my hairdresser but actually he simply cannot live without me.' Only Carla's self-deprecating shout of laughter took the edge off her remark. 'We are only two minutes from the harbour,' Carla added.

'Harbour?' asked Helen.

Carla nodded. 'We are guests on my friend's yacht.'

Coming out of the airport was, for Helen, fresh from the wintry north, like stepping into an oven. On the short walk to the waiting car, Helen was struck by the fetid balmy air, perfumed by the scent of uncountable flowers striking at her nostrils like a cheap perfume. There was a spiciness to it that caught at the back of her throat like the very essence of excitement.

It seemed impossible to believe that this place, drenched in sunshine and filled with the colour of flowers, could be on the same planet as the wintry grey streets of Paris or London.

'I'm surprised Jeffrey hasn't come with you,' murmured Carla as they sped through the alien streets of this other world.

Distracted from gazing in awe at the colours of the overwhelming green of the flora and the equally colourful dress of the people, Helen turned to her. 'He doesn't know I've come yet,' she said adding, in the face of Carla's incredulous stare, 'he was still in Germany when I made up my mind.'

This seemed to give Carla pause for some thought until, her brow clearing, she smiled. 'Qito will be flattered,' she said.

As the car started drawing into what appeared to be a mixed mooring for expensive boats and workaday fishing boats she was reminded of the yacht. 'Whose yacht is it?' she asked.

'It belongs to a man called Martinez. He has loved me for twenty-two years and will do anything for me – or, of course, Qito.'

Beginning to wonder just how many devoted

406

admirers, like Jimmy, Carla might have, she heard herself blurting out: 'He's your lover?'

The scorn seared through Carla's reply. 'No! He loves me but that doesn't mean we are lovers. Impossible!' Carla's tone suggested she thought the question was ridiculous.

A chastened Helen was further distracted when the car drew to a halt at the gangway of a boat which seemed to her to have the proportions of a minor warship.

A white uniformed crewman leapt forward to open the doors of the car and Helen stepped out to better see the sleek lines of the beautiful craft. Two other crewmen, both oriental, appeared as if by magic to seize on her one piece of luggage while she and Carla, with the weedy hairdresser, Jimmy, coming a poor third, walked up the gangway to where a smiling man in his mid-fifties was waiting to greet them.

'Martinez!' cried Carla on greeting the man. 'This is the English girl that Qito is so madly in love with!'

Martinez wore a moustache and his fiftyish, handsome face was sparkling with two rows of teeth which seemed to be crowding out of his tanned face. Murmuring in Spanish he bent low over Helen's hand before straightening to add, in a pleasantly accented English, 'Qito will be beside himself that you've come.'

Never having seen a yacht like this before, far less ever been on one, Helen found it hard to believe that anything like this could be private property. On board the boat seemed even bigger than it had from the outside. Martinez waved forward a petite, slim Chinese girl who wore a very tight-fitting cheongsam and what appeared to be a permanent smile.

'Tsai, would you show our guest to the Golden stateroom.'

'Of course,' said the brightly smiling girl.

Helen was led from the aft deck through a huge sunlit deck cabin furnished with an extravagance of white leather couches set about beautifully carved oriental tables. Beyond that was a carpeted hallway leading to a short flight of winding stairs which gave, in turn, into a lower hallway which was bounded on one side by wide windows and on the other by several doors, each of which seemed to have a panel of different colour. The door which was opened for her revealed a room walled with gold panelling and soft velvets, while the gold bordered white carpet was so silkily smooth she felt guilty to even tread on it.

'This will be yours,' Tsai told her and started a conducted tour of the facilities during which she noted that her baggage had not only arrived but been unpacked and her clothes hung in closets. She marvelled at the speed with which this must have been done.

Gazing in at the glittering gold bathroom, the dressing room and the king-sized bed, Helen could only reflect that her own apartment would comfortably fit in here and leave room to spare.

'It's incredible,' she murmured when, at the end of the tour, Tsai stood smilingly awaiting her verdict. 'I never imagined there could be cabins like this on a yacht.'

Looking around Helen felt uneasy with her lack of experience with anything as grandiose as this before and, since there was no one to ask but Tsai, turned to her. 'What do I do?'

Tsai seemed puzzled by the question. 'Do? You do as you wish.' Helen nodded and let the girl go before turning to survey her meagre wardrobe. This totally unexpected journey to a warm climate left her with very little choice. She was still pondering on the best compromise when her legs felt suddenly weary and in need of rest. Not wishing to further crease her dress she slipped out of it and lay down on the top of the bed intending to close her eyes for a few moments. Helen drifted into a dream in which she imagined she was flying in an aircraft so big it had a dance floor on which naked couples were either upright and dancing, or horizontal and copulating.

Ghostly hands seized her and lifted her to be impaled on a huge pink phallus that dominated the interior of the aeroplane. Jeffrey was there encouraging the two uniformed pilots to bear down with all their weight on her legs while her mother sat on a high stool knitting and shaking her head in disapproval.

She was startled awake as she consciously felt a hand laid gently on her forehead. Opening her eyes she saw Tsai standing over her. 'Madame is not well?' the girl asked.

Helen, in truth, was not sure how she was and, for a moment, even felt unsure of *where* she was. It was only when she heard the slap of water against the yacht's sides that she remembered where she was. Seeing Tsai was still patiently waiting for an answer she shook her head. 'No, thank you. I'm fine.'

Swinging her legs to the side of the bed she realised that she had lain down naked. Someone had, while she slept, covered her with a white linen sheet.

'Madame Carla sent me to enquire if you would wish to join the company for dinner tonight,' Tsai said. 'If so it will be in one hour.'

'Is it night already?' asked Helen looking to the long narrow windows that lined the seaward wall of her stateroom.

'It is seven o'clock in the evening,' Tsai said. 'Come, let me help you. It is difficult if you are not used to the sea.'

Beginning to suspect that life had become unnecessarily complicated Helen allowed herself to be led into the bathroom which, she saw, was now dominated by a massage table which must have been put there since she last saw the room.

'I make you feel better,' Tsai said with enthusiastic confidence. 'Just lay on the table and I massage you. You'll feel better.'

Feeling that she could cope only with the least line of resistance Helen obediently stretched herself face down on the towel covered bench, and, feeling that her body was a mass of knotted tensions, was grateful to feel Tsai's hands soothing away the aches with oils. 'That's marvellous, thank you,' she sighed, giving herself over entirely to the girl's expertise.

Helen lay moaning with pleasure at the girl's ministrations until she realised with a start that she could easily be lulled back to sleep if she allowed her to continue. 'I think that's enough,' she said, turning to sit up on the couch and looking into the Chinese girl's worried face. 'It's not that I don't appreciate it. It's simply that you're relaxing me so much I might doze off again.'

The worried frown on the girl's face cleared to be replaced by a sunny understanding smile. 'Ah, no!' the girl cried, 'I know it. Do not worry.' The girl reached forward to push firmly on Helen's shoulders until she lay on her back. 'I fix that,' the girl told her and produced a bunch of twigs. 'This stimulates the blood,' said the girl.

Worried that the girl might be about to beat her with the twigs, in Finnish sauna style, Helen moved to protest but then groaned with pleasure as she felt the twigs drawn firmly along the length of her legs to leave in their wake a tingling, scratchy feeling that aroused her flesh to the most delicious sensations. 'That's nice . . .' she murmured lying back and closing her eyes to better concentrate the sensation as the twigs progressed across her belly and then made a tingling Devil's dance on her breasts. Embarrassed to feel her nipples rousing and hardening she moved her hands to protect them from further stimulation only to find Tsai's own hands intercepting them and pressing them back – this time above her head. 'You wish?' asked the girl. Not understanding what she was being asked Helen opened her startled eyes as she felt Tsai's fingers seeking out her

410

clitoris and the Chinese girl's lips hovering only centi-metres above her interested nipples.

'No!' she cried, sitting up and aware that the middle-class girl from Eastbourne was reverberating with shock at the oriental girl's suggestion.

The beautiful girl from Taiwan was now standing back with the expression of a whipped puppy. 'I am most deeply sorry,' the girl was saying. 'Others like me to do that for them. Please forgive me.'

Helen still felt ruffled as she wrapped herself in a towel but seeing the hang-dog expression on the girl's face felt Eastbourne rapidly draining from her. 'I'm sorry,' she said. 'I would enjoy it too, I'm sure but, for the moment, I'm so tired it might exhaust me.'

Looking up Tsai's face looked much brighter. 'Now I give you shower and after you feel much better.'

'I can do that for myself,' smiled Helen and tried to shake off the girl by ducking into the shower stall and turning on the water. She was still trying to keep it out of her hair when she was startled to see a, now naked, Tsai joining her.

'Look, this isn't necessary . . .' she started to protest.

Tsai's face furrowed as if worried that her expertise was being challenged. 'I do this all the time,' she assured Helen, 'please.'

Deciding that further protest would only lead to greater misunderstandings Helen relaxed and let the girl's, admittedly expert, hands go to work. Tsai's promise to make her feel better was more than fulfilled until the point where Helen found herself again becoming embarrassingly aroused. 'That's enough for now,' she told the girl as she, brusquely, moved to snatch up a towel before Tsai could offer it to her.

'You are angry with me?' Tsai asked.

'Of course not,' smiled Helen. 'Tell me, have you any idea how the ladies dress for dinner?'

'Very formally,' said Tsai Lo, her expression still anxious. 'All the ladies look most beautiful for dinner.'

411

This was bad news for Helen. She had packed only the gown Jeffrey had given her and both Carla and Qito had already seen that. She was still trying to decide what might best serve in its place when she noticed a long pale pink dress with intricate gold thread embroidery hanging from the closet door. 'Where did this come from?' she asked.

'It's Madame Carla's suggestion that you might like to wear this for dinner.'

'How did "Madame Carla" know I hadn't brought anything suitable?'

Tsai stared at the carpet as she murmured, 'She asked me after I unpacked for you. Are you angry with me, madame?'

Somewhere deep inside Helen did indeed feel that she was being treated as something akin to a charity case but, after a moment's reflection, saw that the gesture did solve a difficult problem. 'It's beautiful,' she said finally and was amused to hear Tsai's held breath audibly exhausted.

'I shall help you with your hair and make-up,' the Chinese girl enthused. 'I have training in such things.'

Giving herself once more over to Tsai she found the multi-talented girl able to work minor miracles with both her hair and make-up with amazing facility. After dressing in Carla's gown, she surveyed herself in the mirror and only then noticed the distinctly oriental lift that Tsai had given to her eyes. It was different but not at all unflattering. Giving herself a final check over she announced herself ready and as Tsai bowed her out of the stateroom Helen thought she could, so easily, accustom herself to this life.

Tsai led her to the door of the aft deck saloon where the company were assembled for aperitifs. Carla, seeing her, hurried forward. 'My dear, how lovely you look!' Linking arms, Carla brought her the considerable distance across the salon to where the others were gathered. Martinez rose politely as she would have

412

expected, but Qito's reaction was startling to say the least. Hurrying forward he brushed aside the bowing Martinez to pull Helen into an embarrassingly close embrace accompanied by multiple kisses on both cheeks.

'I thought you'd never get here!' he was enthusing. 'I know exactly where I will paint you. I have the island all picked out and ready for us. Together we shall make it immortal!'

Overwhelmed by this unexpected deluge of affection Helen looked up to see Carla's steely eyes fixed on her – a look which silently spoke warning volumes.

'Well,' said Carla with an undisguised sarcasm. 'Now that our revered guest of honour has joined us, I suggest we go into dinner.'

Qito and Carla took the heads of the long, gold laden, dinner table while Helen was seated to Qito's right. Martinez, who as Host, might have been expected to head the table, was seated to Carla's right hand, while Jimmy was placed on her left. Qito seemed determined to dominate Helen's entire attention to the exclusion of all others. He enthused, almost with pause, over 'his' island where, she learned to her consternation, he intended to isolate both himself and her, for several days. 'I am filled with fire,' he told her, eyes shining. 'I have never before been so certain that I shall create a masterpiece.'

Carla's voice was the only one to which Qito attended. 'Qito, *caro*, please let our guest have some peace.'

'Peace?' cried an indignant Qito. 'For what does she want "peace"? She is to be the instrument of immortality!'

Carla's voice was carefully even tempered but cutting in tone. 'Qito . . . If you want to fuck the girl go ahead but don't bore us with hyperbole.'

The stunned silence which greeted this remark only increased Helen's embarrassment which became intense

413

when Qito threw down his napkin and leapt to his feet to let go a stream of Italian which Helen was grateful not to understand.

Carla too was on her feet answering in equally angry tones and the two were soon standing almost toe to toe exchanging what were obviously gutter insults. Helen dared a glance towards the others at the table. Jimmy, the hairdresser, sat with eyes closed and visibly shook, as if the insults being hurled at Carla were digging out pieces of his heart. Martinez had risen to his feet and gone to stand at Carla's shoulder as if willing to intervene if the shouting match came to blows. Helen, who felt the cause of all this, just wished there was some way to slide invisibly out of her seat and to the calm of her own stateroom.

The raised voices had attracted a worried gathering of the stewards who were standing, staring in from the service door.

It ended with Qito raising a hand as if to strike Carla but, as she challengingly stuck out her head as if defying him to strike, he turned to stalk from the dining room with Carla in hot pursuit and still shouting.

In the nervous silence that followed the warring pair's exit, Martinez turned to the remainder of his guests. 'Shall we take coffee and brandy in the library?' he asked.

Grateful to be distracted Helen and Jimmy dutifully trooped after Martinez to an upper saloon whose walls were lined with books – all trapped behind panelled wire and glass doors to prevent them being dislodged during rough weather.

There, already in place was a large screen, high definition, projection television whose presence Martinez explained as the silent stewards distributed after-dinner brandies. 'I have my favourite movie of all time to show you,' he told the guests. '*Messalina* which, of course, stars our honoured guest Carla.'

The opening music and titles were played out over a

scene of Carla wearing little more than a superior expression and a sprinkling of diamante, as she was carried through the streets of ancient Rome. Helen was just marvelling at how fantastically beautifully Carla photographed when the original herself came storming into the darkened library and, pausing only to pick out Helen in the reflected light from the screen, marched to her, grabbed her hand and dragged her to her feet. 'You!' she all but screamed in Helen's face. 'Come with me!'

Dragged off balance by Carla's determined tow, Helen feared for the hem of the gown she was wearing as her uncertain feet sought to keep up with her body. Feeling that an angry protest was in order she tugged her hand free of Carla's. 'What do you think you're doing?' Helen demanded.

It was when Carla turned back to face her, here in the fuller light of the passageway, that Helen was shocked to see Carla's eyes brimming with tears. Suddenly all the aggressiveness was gone from her stance. 'I love him!' she cried, and Helen found herself moving forward to take her in her arms. They stood, frozen in mutual surprise, for some minutes before Carla made an effort to control herself. 'Come,' she said.

In Carla's stateroom, even grander than the one assigned to Helen, Carla appeared to have regained her self-control.

Without asking she poured them both whiskies from a side table, lifted her glass in salute before sitting down to stare directly at Helen from a couch. 'How could you understand?' Carla asked a bewildered Helen. 'Look at you! Comfortable bourgeois upbringing. Nice school, where they taught nice manners and how to be polite. My school was different,' Carla said sourly.

Not having the least idea of how to respond, Helen sat silent.

'I had no childhood,' Carla was saying, so quietly it seemed she might be speaking only to herself. 'At nine

I found out that begging bread was not enough. Men were the answer. Dear God – the men! When I was twelve I met this skinny little guy who said he was a painter. He took me to his studio where I found out he was eating even less than me. So now, genius that I was, I had two mouths to feed instead of just my own.' Carla looked up at Helen with eyes that could coruscate a soul, let alone a camera. 'But now I had a purpose other than just surviving. You see? I became a much better whore, and we ate well. I fed my genius when he would have starved. I kept him alive to be the Qito who now has the world kneeling before him.' Carla fell silent and stared into her glass for a long moment. 'Never once has he ever touched me.' Those terrifying eyes flared upwards to fix on Helen. 'Not once!' she added.

By some means other than her own volition Helen found she had moved from her chair to sit next to Carla on the couch. Reaching out a hand that was meant to be comforting, she murmured, 'Carla, I'm sorry. Look, if it will make things any better, I'll leave.'

Carla's street-loud laugh filled the room. 'Stupid girl,' she murmured. 'We're in the middle of the Caribbean – at sea! Where do you suppose you can go?' adding scornfully, 'Don't you understand anything?'

Startled at the sudden mood shift, Helen took back her hand and stared at Carla. 'What do you want me to do?' she asked.

Carla indicated a bedside panel of buttons. 'Press that second button down,' she said, a curious smile now playing about her mouth.

Helen did as she was asked before turning back to Carla.

Carla's voice when she spoke was deeper and more controlled. 'It's time for a lesson your polite school never taught. You want Qito? Then you'll damn well pay your dues!'

Helen protested. 'But I don't want Qito. Not in that sense! He wants to paint me – nothing more!'

Carla's smile was like that of a contented serpent who knew the kill was certain. 'Get naked,' she said.

The blood thundering in her ears, Helen stared, stunned, for one moment as she decided whether to stay or run.

Reminding herself that it was, after all, Carla's gown and that she was at sea with nowhere to run and, since even the owner deferred to Carla, there was no one on board to whom she could run. With those huge, famously beautiful eyes, scrutinising her she felt something undefinable.

Fear certainly, but also a mixture of pride and resentment which amounted, so her liquid loins proclaimed, to excitement. Coyly turning away from the blaze of Carla's gaze, Helen reached for the fastenings and, as gracefully as she could manage, stepped naked from the gown. Taking a deep breath, she turned to face Carla.

Carla rose from the couch and came forward to stand immediately in front of her. 'You have a beautiful body, but let's make it more so. Put your hands on your head . . . and brace your arms back . . . You see what that does for your breasts?'

Helen found her voice lost in her throat and could only nod.

'Now open your legs a little,' she said as she reached out a gentle hand to cup the side of Helen's face. This touch caused Helen to flinch as if struck, and when the hand travelled down her face to her neck and the firm flesh of her shoulders she shuddered and, involuntarily, turned towards the hand as if to beg that it move to her breasts. 'Look at me,' murmured Carla. 'Look only into my eyes.'

Bringing her own eyes to meet those dazzling, devastating eyes, Helen felt lost.

'Do you know what I am doing to you?' Carla asked, and reading the answer in Helen's desperate eyes, she smiled. 'And is that what you want me to do to you?'

417

Finding a hoarse voice and nodding, Helen said: 'Yes!'

Carla lifted her head and, reminding Helen to keep her eyes open and on hers, moved her hand with agonising slowness to caress her breasts, first with her fingertips and then with nerve tingling trails of her long nails, brushing against Helen's urgently roused nipples. 'Ah!' sighed Carla. 'You like that, do you? Do you like pain?'

Her throat once more numbed, Helen could only nod.

'A flicker of pain to spice the moment or the crescendo of feeling that comes with the whip?'

Helen shook her head. 'Not the whip,' she managed.

Carla nodded as if that answer was pleasing to her. 'But my caress? You find that pleasant?' Helen's nod was answered with a sudden nip of Carla's nails on her aroused flesh. 'Answer me properly.'

'Yes.'

'Look nowhere but into my eyes,' Carla said as her hands sought out the swell of Helen's belly and the fingers of one hand traced the contours of her pubis while the other gently played with Helen's half-opened lips.

Despite everything Helen raised up onto tip-toe to thrust her pubis towards Carla's hand. Carla's smile showed she understood the plea in Helen's eyes, which now stung with the effort of holding Carla's gaze. 'Do I judge that I may do with you as I will?' asked Carla.

'Yes. Please!' Helen all but screamed as Carla's roving fingers plunged deeply, causing her body to crease almost double, an action which brought her mouth into contact with Carla's throat where her lips, as if of their own volition, kissed greedily. A tug at her hair brought Helen's head suddenly back to stare into Carla's now wild eyes. 'I will tell you when you may kiss me,' she seethed through angry lips as the hand left Helen's belly to streak across her cheek. 'Now apologise.'

'I'm sorry,' Helen murmured.

Carla, still holding Helen's hair in a tight grip,

nodded. 'Good.' There was a pause while Carla seemed to be considering what she might do next. Helen was startled to hear her address a third party.

'Tsai, my lovely, come here.'

Into Helen's peripheral gaze came the beautiful Chinese girl who had come into the stateroom so silently that this was the first Helen knew of her presence.

Tsai Lo, wearing a green silken cheongsam, came to stand at Carla's shoulder. Her flawless face reflected no emotion as her clear eyes looked into Helen's. 'Earlier,' Carla was saying to Helen, 'you had the temerity to refuse Tsai's caresses. You will apologise to Tsai. Get onto your knees.'

Feeling that her entire body had been eviscerated and replaced with ice, Helen knelt.

'Look at us,' Carla ordered.

Raising her eyes, Helen was immediately struck with the resemblance between the two beautiful women – born ten thousand miles apart – but as similar as sisters with their black hair, almond-shaped eyes and flawless skins. The only real difference between them was the structure of their facial bones and that the slim and dainty Tsai looked like a two-thirds scale model of the exquisite Carla. Helen was now forced to watch as Carla's hands caressed the shoulders of the impassive oriental girl until one hand sought out the fastenings of the cheongsam and, flicking them open, let the material fall away to reveal her perfectly formed small breasts. It was Tsai who stepped from the cheongsam and cast it aside before resuming her docile stance in Carla's half embrace. 'You may kiss Tsai's feet and tell her you are sorry for your impudence,' Carla murmured.

Kneeling further forward Helen felt that she had somehow been caught up in an oriental ritual. Tsai's feet were shod with green silk sandal-like shoes of such exquisite beauty that it added to the electric thrill of humiliation she felt. Kissing first one then the other of

419

the tiny feet that seemed sculpted from ivory, she murmured her plea to be forgiven to Tsai.

'Good,' said Carla in a more positive tone. 'Now you will move yourself to lie on the bed.'

Rising to her feet, unable to look at either woman, Helen obediently padded to the bed where her uncertainty about how she was to lie was ended by Carla. 'On your back,' she told her.

As Helen lay back she had a rush of understanding of how well she had been prepared by Jeffrey for this moment. It was as if he were there in this cabin continuing her sensual education. The memory of Madame Victoria's brought her a sudden rush of confidence. 'May I be tied?' she asked as Carla came to loom over her.

Carla nodded and presented two thick ribbons of padded silk. 'I was about to do just that,' she answered. Making a loop at one end of the silk ribbon Carla snapped it closed about Helen's wrist before turning it several times about the bed-head as if tethering a horse. Moving round the bed she stretched Helen's other wrist to the fullest before securing that. Helen lay there revelling in her now total helplessness.

Her excitedly lit eyes came once more to Carla to see that she held yet another band of silk in her hand. 'Yes!' she purred in agreement as the silk was tied about her eyes to make a blindfold.

There followed a period of almost total silence in which the only sounds were of rustling material which, Helen's heightened senses judged, must mean that Tsai was undressing Carla. When she heard murmured whispers passing between the other two women, the waiting Helen, her loins now totally liquid, felt a stab of jealousy as she imagined caresses passing between them while her own body was crying out for their touch.

'Please!' she called out of her voided sight and, as if in answer, she felt a slight sway of the bed as someone's

420

weight was lowered to it. The next sensation was that of fingernails being drawn the full length of her leg to score inside her thighs, making earthquakes under her skin. The hand that came to press down on her pubic bone was answered with Helen's own upthrust and thrash of her legs as she sought to wrap them about her tormentor. The girl, now identifiable as Tsai, lay her weight to still those searching legs, and Helen felt Tsai's soft breasts pressing against the answering muscle of her inner thighs. Slim fingers sought to open her vulvic lips and peel back the inner layers before the searing contact of a firm tongue sought Helen out causing her to cry out her pleasure in a fully vented scream. Her legs, now freed, went out to wrap themselves about the slim Chinese girl as Tsai's tongue went deep inside to expertly ravage her.

A gentle finger, laid to her lips, stilled her cries and she quietly reached to take the finger into her mouth, sucking on it and the two others that followed, with a rising need to have everything.

Next she felt Carla's generous naked body stretching out alongside the length of her own and the suckled fingers withdrawn to be replaced by soft lips closing on hers, and a clash of tongues as her own sought to duel with Carla's. Devastated by the twin attack on her senses she felt her body convulsing as the sheer pleasure of total surrender overwhelmed her.

Tsai's lips had, meanwhile, found her aroused clitoris where they alternately sucked and then nipped the tender bud. The sensation redoubled as Carla's teeth closed on her soaring, marble hard, nipples.

Then the sheer joy of Carla's, now liquidly aroused voice murmuring into her ear. 'Shall I ravage you?'

Without waiting to question the feasibility of the suggestion, Helen heard her own voice calling out in affirmation. She waited, breathless, as she felt Tsai's, slight weight leaving her to be replaced with the more substantial Carla. Keening to feel everything that might be done to her she felt a nudge between her soaked loins and then the entry of a solid phallus. Her pleasure echoed at the top of her voice, it mattered nothing that this might be counterfeit. It mattered only that Carla's arms were round her, Carla's mouth on hers and that the upward thrusts of her own body were met with the generous press of Carla's breasts.

Her legs wrapped about the other woman's body, bliss searing deep inside her, the thought that she was giving pleasure to this wondrous creature only served to heighten the pleasure that was being returned.

Orgasmic waves rolled thunderously throughout her delighted body and she would have cried out but for the deep penetrating tongue that ravaged her throat.

It was only when Carla broke off to voice her own mounting climax that Helen could join in the relieved chorus. Pounding into her with welcomed savagery, Carla finally fell exhausted, her heated body sliding to one side and dragging the counterfeit phallus from Helen as she did so.

Now Helen regretted her tied hands since she wanted nothing more desperately than to reach out and embrace Carla as she lay beside her with her head heavily on one of Helen's arms. 'Thank you,' Helen murmured into the stillness that ensued then, almost immediately, was once more convulsed as she felt Tsai's hands, now oiled with the scents of jasmine and rose petals, soothing her sweated skin.

From the pleasured murmurs coming from Carla, Helen judged that Tsai must be anointing them both simultaneously and, delighted, she opened her mouth and reached with her tongue to test the air and savour the taste of the oils that now filled the room.

The massaging ended, Tsai stretched herself out on the bed and Helen heard the sounds of tiny kisses being exchanged between the other two women before Tsai's body moved across Helen's to lay on the other side of her as Carla's fingers came again to tease her painful nipples.

Carla leaned in so that her words breathed across Helen's open mouth. 'You imagine that Qito could do anything like that for you?'

Startled to be reminded of their differing status, Helen could only shake her head. Carla laid a finger on her lips.

'I promise you he cannot,' she was murmuring with a throatiness that was excitingly threatening. 'So, our little beauty is to spend five days alone on an island with my husband, is she?' Carla broke off for a tiny chuckle. 'And what do you suppose is going to happen to that "little beauty" when she is delivered back to me?'

'I'll probably be screwed senseless,' Helen groaned.

Carla chuckled ominously. 'You imagine an anxious wife would *reward* you?' she asked, indicating that she would answer the question herself with a tut-tutting sound. 'Oh, no! That is not the way of the Italian wife. You will scream for me again – but not with pleasure.'

Helen's racing excitement at these words was quenched in a deluge of kisses. Opening herself wide to Carla she gasped as she was re-entered.

'Yes!' called Helen as the phallus once more battered at pleasure's gate. It mattered little when she realised that it was now Tsai that was entering her. The slim girl's weight pressed down on her, her smaller, but firmer breasts clashing with her own as she rose to meet the Chinese girl's thrusting pressure, even as her body protested that there was now soreness and discomfort amounting to pain in this new assault, since in her ear was the balm of Carla's threatening voice.

'I shall enjoy myself with you,' Carla was saying. 'Every gram of pleasure you have ever known will be paid for with a kilo of pain.' Carla's voice was becoming strained and excited as her hands thrust between the slight body of Tsai and Helen's to dig her nails viciously into Helen's nipples. 'Will you scream for me?' Carla was asking.

'Yes! Yes! Yes!' cried Helen as pain gave way to a totally consuming pleasure. Tsai, who had not uttered a sound, much less a word, during her assault, now withdrew leaving Helen spread and gasping with no inclination to close herself.

Swaying gently on the couch from her own gratification, Helen heard some whispering and then the opening and closing of a door.

Carla took the blindfold from her eyes and Helen looked up into her huge eyes, now bright with tenderness. 'I dismissed Tsai to spare your blushes,' the fabled beauty told her.

Hearing the door open once more Helen looked in astonishment as she saw Martinez come into the room, totally naked except for black leather straps which crisscrossed his body. Rising from the bed Carla went to greet the newcomer who stood trembling – whether with fear or excitement, or a mixture of both, Helen could not judge. 'Do you love me?' Carla asked of the man.

'You are my mistress and entitled to do with me as you wish,' he answered in careful English.

Beaming with delight Carla brought Martinez to stand over the wide eyed Helen. 'And what do you think of my friend?'

'She is beautiful, mistress,' murmured Martinez.

Nodding, as if acknowledging this to be the correct answer, Carla moved away, admonishing Martinez to stay as he was, only to return a few moments later carrying a short handled, many-tailed whip.

Helen's eyes blinked rapidly from Martinez to the whip in Carla's hands and wondered who it was intended for. The answer was not long in coming.

Carla's hand snaked out to bring the whip lightly across Martinez' buttocks. 'You have my permission to become erect,' she told him.

Helen could only watch in amazement as the sanctioned member started immediately to stir and grow. More light taps of the whip followed as Martinez' tumescence rose under Helen's eyes until it stood, frighteningly big, straight out from his firm belly.

Her loins beginning to drool in expectation, Helen was disappointed to hear that Martinez' erection was not for her.

'You have my permission to bring yourself off on her body!' Carla drawled.

Immediately Martinez' shaking hands went to his phallus and started stroking it as the slaps from Carla's whip became both harder and faster. As if anxious to keep pace Martinez' hands flew up and down on his burgeoning penis.

'It's going to be wasted!' Helen cried out.

Carla stared at Helen, as, smiling, she moved to the other side of the bed. 'Did you say something?' she asked.

Helen, looking at Carla and knowing she was about to feel the sting of the whip, felt her body convulsing. 'Let him take me!' she spat.

For answer the leather strips were brought down on Helen's thighs, the ends seeking out and stinging her pubic lips. Defiantly, Helen raised her body to meet the blows but before Carla could take advantage Martinez cried out, and, shouting, begged permission from Carla to come.

Carla's attention turned to him as she, in furious tones, ordered Martinez to kneel up on the bed.

As he did so the whip snaked out and rapped him sharply about the chest as, with a great cry, he spouted a copious stream of sperm which landed, hot and wet, on Helen's heaving belly and breasts.

Feeling cheated, Helen gasped out a protest which Carla ignored as she spoke to Martinez. 'You have my permission to clean her with your tongue,' she told him.

The tongue touched off a totally unexpected wave deep inside Helen and she, under Carla's approving eye, twisted and turned her body to bring Martinez' cleansing tongue to her loins, but it wasn't until Carla gave her express permission that Martinez dared to do as Helen wanted.

Being far less expert than either Tsai or Carla he managed, nevertheless, after much effort to bring her to a quiet, but perfectly satisfactory orgasm.

Chapter Twelve

It was the strong tang of freshly brewed coffee, irritating her nostrils, which woke Helen to a new day. Opening her eyes she saw Tsai moving about the stateroom in her usual wraith-like manner. For a moment she lay as if still asleep while she worked on the problem of precisely how to greet the girl after the previous night's intimacies and it was quite a surprise to herself to realise that this was her only problem. She felt no shame and certainly no regrets about what had happened. As she allowed herself to stir she felt only a strange release, feeling as if she had been admitted to a sorority of freedom in which guilt and regret had no place. Deciding that the simplest approach was the best, she sat up in the bed and sang out a 'Good morning'.

Tsai turned towards her smiling. 'Good morning, madame,' she said, hurrying to pick up a breakfast tray, appetisingly laden with a mixture of croissant-like rolls and fruit. 'I was uncertain whether madame would prefer to bathe or to shower.'

'Shower,' decided Helen sitting up feeling wickedly indulged to be fussed over so thoroughly. Gratefully starting with the tiny glass of orange juice she went quickly to drink greedily on the delicious coffee while watching Tsai move about the room as if determined to find something to tidy. It was then that it dawned on Helen that the almost imperceptible vibration caused by the boat's engines had ceased.

'Are we moored somewhere?' she asked.

Tsai turned to her, face beaming. 'Yes, madame. At an island which, I was told, is called Far Lee Island.'

Throwing back the covers Helen hurried to one of the long narrow windows and drew up the slatted blind that covered it. She could see nothing but the endless ocean. 'Where is it?' she asked.

'On the port side, madame. We are looking to starboard from here.'

'Well, what sort of place is it?'

'Nothing, madame. No one lives there. Mr Qito has chosen this place for you and he to work on.'

'And there's nobody else on it?'

'No, madame.'

Helen turned away with a great deal to ponder. When Carla had said she would be alone with Qito she had taken that as a figure of speech. Had it really meant they were to be little more than castaways? Finding her appetite for breakfast gone Helen went directly to the bathroom where she turned on the shower full blast.

Tsai was waiting for her with warmed towels as she stepped from the shower, seemingly willing to dry her back and legs as Helen caressed her front. Her breasts seemed rowdily aroused by this double assault and Helen's mind took her to the massage bench which still stood erected in the bathroom.

Without a further word she lay down on it, face down. With equally tacit silence Tsai Lo's hands started to stroke oils into her skin.

Lying there Helen contemplated what the next five days might bring. She felt that she had most certainly paid the admission price but wondered precisely how the performance might play. She vaguely remembered seeing a film about a girl stranded on an island with a man she came to hate and the memory of it brought her little comfort. These thoughts, combined with Tsai's expert hands, led her to dreamily remember the last occasion she had lay on this bench. Times had since changed!

Languorously, she turned her awakened body onto its back and looked up into Tsai's beautiful face. She awaited the girl's reaction with a feeling of voluptuous abandonment. Tsai allowed herself only the tiniest smile of satisfaction at this overt gesture as her hands began spreading their fiery message across Helen's stomach and breasts. Tsai said nothing until her hands were gently massaging Helen's throat. 'Madame would like?' she asked.

'"Madame would like" very much,' said Helen and, closing her eyes, passively gave herself over to the now openly arousing caress.

Using only her soft hands Tsai gently stroked Helen's most sensitive flesh, her oiled fingers stimulating and stinging her openness to a convulsing clitoral climax.

Opening her eyes she saw that Tsai, duty done, had turned away and was once more the purposeful maid, picking up the dampened bath towels and turning back with them in her arms. 'Has madame decided what she wishes to wear today?' asked the girl as if nothing untoward had occurred between them.

Picking up on the workaday mood, Helen shook her head. 'What is the usual dress for morning?' she asked.

Tsai smiled. 'Perhaps a simple sarong, madame?'

'Sounds perfect except I haven't got one.'

'Oh no!' cried Tsai. 'We have plenty!'

Curious, Helen followed Tsai out into the stateroom where she watched as drawer after drawer was opened to reveal neatly folded ranks of the soft silken garments. Called upon to choose, Helen arbitrarily pointed out one decorated with oversized red flowers which seemed to please Tsai who insisted on showing her how to wind it under her arms to tuck in above the left breast which, Tsai insisted, was the way it was worn in the Polynesian islands. From the breakfast tray Tsai took a fresh flower which was almost the twin of those on the material and hesitated over which side of the head Helen would prefer to wear it.

'What difference does it make?' Helen asked.

'Is very important,' cautioned Tsai Lo. 'For the unmarried woman it is worn on the right, but a married woman wears it on the left side.'

'What do you mean by "unmarried"?'

Tsai glanced coyly away. 'Virgin,' she whispered.

Helen laughed. 'Let's not push our luck,' she said taking the flower and carefully pushing it into her hair above her left ear.

Coming up onto the main deck gave Helen the first sight of the island on which Qito apparently intended they should spend some days alone. The yacht was moored in a pristine bay, some hundred yards offshore.

At first sight it seemed as if a careless deity had dropped a handful of greenery in the middle of the ocean. From behind the edge of the white sand beach, dotted with clumps of elegant palms, rose the steep sides of a volcanic shaped hill, covered in a verdant carpet of shrubs and trees.

Looking at it Helen thought that it, at least, was not the desert island of legend. On the contrary it looked quite cool and inviting.

An approaching steward interrupted her reverie and offered her breakfast which she refused. Since there seemed to be no other guests about, Helen took the opportunity to have her first real look at this amazingly huge boat. From the dining salon there was a view forward over an immaculately clean deck of polished mahogany to the elegantly shaped bows.

Stepping out of the salon Helen was overwhelmed by the scents being wafted seawards from the island. Looking to the source of Nature's perfume she caught a flash of reflected light and, guarding her eyes against the gleaming sea, saw that one of the yacht's motored tenders was dragged up on the beach and manned by two of the white uniformed crew.

'Good morning, madame,' said a quietly accented voice beside her. Turning, she saw an officer in a white duck shirt and shorts. He was shorter than herself and looked vaguely Latin. 'I am the Captain,' the man was saying. 'Captain Miguel de Soledad. Most of the guests have gone ashore. May I show you the ship?'

Accepting, Helen was led up a flight of steep chrome-railed stairs to a quarter-deck which spread the full width of the ship and seemed filled with a confusing array of instruments and many television monitors.

'The boat is equipped with most of the very latest navigating and guidance systems.' Fearing that her technological blindness would afflict her she tried to look intelligent as it was explained to her that satellite positioning made it possible for the crew to know the yacht's position to within a metre or two, anywhere in the world. Of more interest was the array of communications equipment by which they could send or receive fax or telephone communications. It occurred to Helen that she might try calling her mother to tell her where she was, but then decided against it as her mother would surely consider it 'extravagant'.

Although she had no knowledge of such things it was still impressive to learn that the yacht had a displacement of 750 tons, was nearly four hundred feet in length, and carried a crew of twenty-nine.

'It must cost of fortune to run a boat like this,' she said.

'More money in a year than most people would expect to see in a lifetime,' the Captain smiled.

One of the crew came into the wheelhouse to report something to the Captain in what sounded like Portuguese.

The Captain turned to her. 'The others have started back from the island,' he told her.

Looking down from the wing of the bridge Helen saw that the launch was fast coming back towards the boat. On board she could see Martinez and Jimmy but no sign of Carla or Qito. Leaving the bridge she moved down the steps to the main deck, ready to greet them as they came aboard.

Martinez was the first to come on board. From the warmth of his smile and his bear hug of a greeting, Helen judged that he must have enjoyed the previous night's events. 'It's going to be fantastic!' he told her. 'Qito is like a crazy man waiting for you.'

'He's already ashore?'

'Ashore and raring to get to work. The tender will take you to him.'

'Now? But I haven't prepared anything . . . I've no idea what I'll need.'

Martinez smiled expansively. 'Nothing,' he said. 'You'll want for nothing. It's like a paradise on there.'

'But what about food and . . . ? I presume we *are* going to eat?'

'My crew have been working since daylight,' said Martinez. 'What you have on there is a mini Hilton,' adding, with an encouraging shoo-ing motion, 'Go. The tender is waiting just for you.'

Still confused by the pace of events, Helen suddenly saw Carla on an upper deck looking at her with an expression that threatened thunder.

'Go!' said Martinez urging her forward to the gangway with a gentle nudge.

One more glance in Carla's direction made the possibility of getting away onto the island more appealing. Still feeling that this was completely unreal she stepped onto the gangway and into the assisting hands of the two crewmen.

The launch started away from the yacht the moment she was on board and looking back Helen suddenly realised a sense of just how isolated she was going to be.

Turning away from the impressive lines of the yacht and looking to the island, she couldn't shake off the feeling that she was being transported as some form of ritual sacrifice. Rapidly she tried to remember what she knew of Qito. That first meeting with Jeffrey . . . the reception in Paris and then his visit to the hotel. Their encounters on the yacht added very little, and she might, for all she knew, be about to be delivered to an ogre to do with as he wished. One thought, above all others, seethed in her disordered mind – that whatever he might do to her, Qito, secure within his international prestige, would not be held to account. Throughout her sexually aware life she had always sought to pass the responsibility for her actions to others, secure in the knowledge that the man would behave to a set of principles. Now she was being offered, almost literally naked, to the mercies of a man who would not likely be held accountable, in a place from which she had no escape.

She tried desperately, as the launch nudged up into the soft sand of the beach, to take refuge in her masochism and be thrilled by her jeopardy, but somehow the call went unanswered and, as she stepped from the boat onto the beach, she felt only a cold dread of what might be to come mingled with the feel of warm water and soft sand.

Seeing no sign of Qito and so having no idea of what she might be expected to do next, she hesitated. One of the crewmen called out to her. 'Lady?' Turning back to the man she saw him pointing into the palms which fringed the beach area. 'You go there,' the man added as she still hesitated.

Seeing little alternative, Helen started blindly up the gently shelving beach to the line of sighing palms. As she began to peer into the shadowed gloom under the trees she heard the murmuring of the launch's motor and, turning, saw that it was already backing away from the beach.

433

Fighting off an impulse to run after it, she heard a sound in the shrubs to her front and, turning, saw a smiling Qito, his compact but powerful body completely naked, coming towards her. 'It's perfect!' he cried. 'At least we won't have those cretins . . .' he waved a hand at the yacht, '. . . disturbing us. Come.'

When Qito turned, Helen followed him across some grass which bit coarsely at her bare feet. Within a few yards the colourful undergrowth opened up to a sandy based clearing in which stood a very substantial looking tent around which were piled crates and boxes, while a little way off from the tent stood a propane fuelled cooking range that would have looked well in her kitchen. At least they weren't going to starve to death.

Qito had momentarily disappeared into the tent only to emerge carrying a large plastic bottle. 'Get that off,' he said indicating the sarong she had wound about her that morning.

Defensively she asked, 'What for?'

'So I can spread this on you,' he told her indicating the plastic bottle. 'Sun shield. You're going to need it on your white skin. It's factor fifteen so you should come to no harm.'

Somewhat reassured, she reached for the bottle. 'I can do it for myself,' she told him warily.

'Nonsense!' cried Qito, 'besides, I want to feel the contours of your body. If I'm to paint you I must feel the plasticity of you.'

Not at all sure that his statement had any validity, Helen felt curiously shy as she unwound the sarong and, not for the first time, stood naked before him. Qito came forward and humming an unfamiliar tune through closed teeth, set about coating her body with the sun-screen. As he worked, he talked. 'After we get you protected we can walk up to the spring. Fantastic! You'll love it as I do. God is a wonderful set decorator.'

Helen stood submissively as Qito, the infuriatingly repetitive tune endlessly repeated, liberally coated her

434

body, actually going on his knees before her to stroke the oil into her legs. 'You'll have to do this every morning and, again, after you swim,' he told her.

Filled with a sudden sense of the absurdity of the situation, Helen felt brave enough to quip, 'Aren't you going to do it for me, then?'

'No time,' said Qito as he stood up and looked critically at her to seek out any spots he might have missed. 'You trimmed your pubic hair and shaved your armpits,' he told her as if noticing for the first time.

'I usually do,' she told him.

'Ridiculous habit,' muttered Qito. 'Hair is grown for a purpose and you're supposed to be my wild creature of the forest.' With a deep sigh he turned away to return the sunscreen to the tent.

'Now,' he said, 'I'll take you up to the spring and afterwards I'll make us some lunch. After lunch I like to sleep a little and then this afternoon we'll start work. That suit you?'

Helen shrugged. 'I could cook if you like,' she offered.

Qito let out an exasperated gasp. 'Women can't cook!' he told her and then turned away, obviously expecting her to follow.

Helen picked up the discarded sarong and was about to wind it about herself when Qito, already some yards off, called back, 'You don't need that. There's nobody here but us. Come on.'

Unwilling to so immediately assume the status of naked savage, but neither wishing to dispute with Qito – already out of sight in the trackless bush – she compromised, and, bunching the strip of material in her hand, started after him.

Qito may have been thirty years older than her but his legs seemed to carry him up the hillside with the facility of a mountain goat. Helen found her heart and lungs protesting as she ground up after him, so it was

435

with som e relief that she saw him halt at the top of a rise.

Puffing up to stand beside him, Helen looked down into a rocky depression. From half way up a sheer rock face came a shimmering, but sparse, column of water which, sparkling in the sunlight, looked like so many diamonds. The sun's heat seemed focused on the water and before it struck the smooth, saucer-like depression in the rock beneath, it almost completely petered out so that what fell was no more than a mist which drifted airily away on the breeze. It was magical. A fairy-tale place where legends could be played out.

'Isn't it wondrous?' asked Qito.

'Fabulous,' breathed Helen.

'Imagine how long that water must have been falling. It must have taken millions of years for that drizzle to have worn away the rocks. It's inspiring,' he told her. 'Civilisations, worlds even, have been created and lost while that steady drip waited for our eyes to find it.'

Looking to Qito's absorbed profile, his eyes fired with delight, she felt a surge of privilege. This *was* a truly magical place – the kind she might have wanted to share with a lover, and for one passing moment she all but promoted Qito into that role.

'Is this where you mean to paint me?' she asked.

'Down there!' cried Qito. 'Exactly where the water strikes the ground. I mean that you should look as if the water had carved you out of the rocks.'

His enthused tone fired her so that she could see what the finished picture might be. Suddenly everything – the flight to Guadeloupe, the yacht and being stranded on the island with Qito – made sense. The chain of events which had brought her here, ragged and unplanned, now seemed like an intricately stitched tapestry. In that moment there was no other world and, it was almost possible to imagine, no other people. In such a place, she decided, anything was possible.

It was Qito who broke the mood. 'Let's go and eat,'

he said, and started back down the path they had so recently created through the coarse undergrowth. Helen hesitated and gave one more lingering look into the magical dell. No matter what was to come, she decided, it was going to be worth it.

While Qito monopolised the cooking range Helen wandered through the thin screen of shrubbery to the gently lapping water's edge. Tiny fish were being driven up onto the beach with every eddy. Looking further out into the translucent waters of the lagoon she saw the flash of other bodies as they teemed, seemingly fighting for sea room, in their crowded world. Impulsively she waded knee deep into the water and laughed out loud when she saw how her legs appeared to bend in the mirrored clarity of the water. Fish eagerly approached her intrusive legs and she yelped with delight as they fearlessly nudged against her in the hope she might present them with a meal.

Lifting her eyes to look beyond the white water breaking on the reef she saw an endless placidity and imagined this to be a friendly place that had opened its arms in welcome and granted her peace.

A half-heard yell from Qito brought her wading back from the busy ocean to find him already greedily scooping up forkfuls of a creamy pasta and drinking deep into a glass of blood-red wine, she felt an intense sadness for the workers who, she imagined, sweated in the dark noisy factories to produce durable goods which had been brought to a paradise they would never see.

Qito indicated her plate set down on a table. The sauce was delicious – tangy enough to soften her conscience at enjoying the rich creamy indulgence. Qito, who seemed to wolf his food, was almost finished. She had barely had time to savour hers, and compliment him on it, before he was on his feet, stretching, belching delicately, and turning into the tent. 'I'll sleep for an hour then we'll make a start,' he told her.

Grateful not to have been invited to join his siesta

Helen, after eating, walked down to the water's edge to sluice the plates and watch the fish excitedly nudge at the dregs of the meal. She idly wondered how they might react to this new taste sensation before having a pang of conscience about how it might also damage their digestive systems.

'The hell with it!' she called to them. 'A short happy life is better than a long miserable one! That's my motto!' Consoling herself with the thought that these creatures had never known a wet, grey city landscape she paused for a moment and looked towards the shrubs that screened the campsite and was overwhelmed with a sudden stabbing need for a lover to magically appear beside her and throw her to the sand. With a guilty start she realised that this lover had no face. At that moment she would have allowed herself to be taken by anyone – including Qito who, anyway, would give her no choice.

For some reason this thought inflamed her. Going to the folding table, so immaculate with its clipped on, pristine white linen cover, she poured more of the heavy red wine and drank it down in one huge gulp. With her head buzzing with alcohol she turned away and found a sensuously curved palm tree. She lay there, her back against the sharply ridged trunk, while letting the fingers of one hand seek out her loins.

Opening her thighs slightly, so not to disturb her evenly balanced body, she sought out her hardened and aroused bud. Moistened and ready, her fingers gently stroked the apex of her pleasure, dispatching waves of toe-curling energy to the furthest ends of her body.

Giving way totally, she felt the warm tropical air blanketing her as she rocked herself harder and faster into an unconscious riot of emotion leading to her heavily breathed, choked words. 'Hurt me!' she gasped. 'Hurt me, take me! Hurt me!' she told the palm as she

438

ground her naked back into the tearing ridges of the tree bark.

At the moment of orgasm there was only one thought in her head. 'Jeffrey!' she called into the still warm air, and then collapsed as all the energy flooded out of her.

Levering herself from the tree, aware that she had all but rubbed her back raw, she lay on the mattress-like texture of the sand and felt totally miserable.

'Why did you have to be married?' she asked the gritty sand.

Chapter Thirteen

Standing beneath the drifting mist of water Helen had time and space to think. Posing, she decided, was a mindless task, but the thoughts that crowded in to fill the unengaged space in her head were unsettling.

Mentally, she marvelled at the pandemonium of events which had brought her to be standing naked on an uninhabited island in the company of a man whose name had, less than a week ago, been but a legend.

With only the occasional screech of an outraged bird to break the all pervading silence, her mind was free to retrace the steps that had brought her here.

Carla. Astonishing that she had shared intimacy with yet another legend and done so without remorse or shame. The yacht, although a magnificent experience in itself, had become no more than, as her mother would have said, an 'extravagant' means of transportation peopled by beings from another world in which she remained an alien.

In boarding the jet which had brought her from Paris she had been taking flight in more senses than one. She had been fleeing from Jeffrey. A man with whom, in the intimacy of a bed, she had exposed her body, and, even more intimately, her inner fears, more totally than to any other living being. That he had harboured significant secrets while presuming to delve even deeper into her own life, had shattered her. It wasn't the fact of his being married that bothered her so much. After all she had no such expectations of him, but that he, in the face of her confessions, should not have found time to mention it, appalled her, and told her that he was not the man she had thought him to be.

The incident with the flight crew had been sheer vengeance. As that thought entered her head she wondered why she didn't think of the intimacy with Carla in the same light, before realising that there was a very great difference. What she had done with the pilots had been of her choice, while Carla, while not coercive, had *imposed* intimacy on her.

The same was true of Jeffrey. He had come into her life like a whirlwind and, gathering her up like a latter day Dorothy, had taken her down the yellow brick road which had led, not to Oz, but to disappointment. She had wanted Jeffrey to be the all-knowing Wizard, able to grant her every wish, but instead she found him to be the Tin Man who had no heart. Of even less comfort to her was the suspicion that she had cast herself in the role of the Scarecrow – all outward appearance and no substance – a victim but now resolved to be a victim no more.

'The light's going. Let's call it a day!' Qito's voice echoed dully about the glade and was heard by Helen with enormous relief. Her arms, which she had been holding, spiralled, above her head throbbed with relief when she lowered them and for a moment she was back in Jeffrey's penthouse recovering from his bondage of her in the conservatory.

Hoping for a glimpse at his progress Helen was disappointed to see him hastily lower a canvas flap to cover the painting. Anticipating her protest he told her she could only see it when it was complete.

Her offer to help him carry the canvas back to the

441

camp was dismissed. 'No need,' he told her. 'There's no one else on the island.'

'It might rain.'

'Not likely and, in any case, the cover is waterproof. Moving a wet oil is likely to do more damage than leaving it where it is.' Helen saw that Qito looked drawn and tired as he turned and started leading the way through the flowering shrubs to the beach.

'Shall I help with the evening meal?' she asked.

'No. I can't stand people watching me work – whether it's painting or cooking. You go have a swim or something. I'll call you when it's ready.'

Standing on the beach watching the sun redden and start its seemingly headlong plunge over the horizon, Helen felt a sense of acute isolation as she realised the immensity of the ocean at her feet and her own insignificant occupancy of this tiny speck of earth. Had it not been for Qito she would, at that moment, have thought herself totally forgotten by the teeming outside world. She sought refuge from her thoughts by wading hip deep into the warm tropical water and then, plunging head first, sought to swim herself into a state of exhaustion.

Tiring quickly from her initial exertions, she turned on her back and gazed upward into the even greater immensity of a sky which was already starting to light up its stars. Lazily, she swam and floated until, feeling more relaxed, she was overjoyed to hear Qito's voice calling her to come to the table.

Qito had lit and strung three or four oil lamps from a rope suspended between the trees, while on the table lay dishes of food which stingingly reminded her she was famished.

Qito had magicked a dish of an exotic fish under a thick piquant sauce with pasta and a salad which, as she ate, filled her with a reassuring sense of well-being. 'This is delicious,' she told him. 'Where did you learn to cook like this?'

442

'Only when you've known real hunger,' he told her, 'do you learn to appreciate food.'

Looking at the famed face in the light of the lamps Helen remembered Carla talking about finding someone even hungrier than she had been and, with a pang of envy, she saw that the bond that had been forged between the two was close to unbreakable. Idly, she played with the idea of scouring the attics of London to find herself a similar cause deserving of devotion but then decided, with her luck, she would devote twenty or thirty years to a no-hoper and, in any case, thirty years was a long time to wait for posterity to catch up.

Helen ate silently for some moments, aware that Qito, having wolfed down his food, was now enjoying his third or fourth glass of wine, and was watching her closely. She hoped his mind wasn't speculating on anything sexual and she was startled when he seemed to have tuned into the thought.

'Is it too boring?' he asked her.

'Posing?' she asked. 'Not boring, but I had no idea how tiring it could be.'

'I meant being here with me,' he insisted. 'With a lover this place could be paradise for a young woman. Unfortunately, when I work, I am impotent with everything but my paints, so I cannot fill that role for you even had you wanted me to.'

Uncomfortable with the thought that he might be reading her mind, she sought to divert him. 'Carla did warn me.'

Qito nodded. 'Carla is extremely possessive of me, but she earned that right.'

'Aren't you jealous of her?'

This question was greeted with a scornful laugh. 'Any man who marries a beautiful woman and imagines she cannot be tempted by other admirers is a fool. Jealousy is a total waste of energies which can be better employed in seeking redemption.'

Helen found the word 'redemption' laying heavily on

the table. Big philosophical concepts had always made her uneasy since she suspected she would never understand them. 'Are you a religious man?' she asked.

Shaking his head Qito reached out to refill her glass. 'I believe in the soul. That is my perception of what life is – a striving to find a soul. When we have that, we have redemption. Not in the eyes of some prescient, all-seeing deity, but for ourselves. A simple self-justification for having lived.'

'You've found it then,' smiled Helen. 'In your art, I mean.'

'In the eyes of others, perhaps. I have yet to find it in myself. Redemption calls for discipline; gratification is much more accessible so we take the easier path and, in the struggle, lose purity, without which, all is lost.'

'Your philosophy sounds almost monasterial.'

Roaring with laughter Qito rose from the table. 'The monks wouldn't have me!' he cried and reaching for a bottle of brandy poured himself a generous draught. 'Which of them was it prayed: "God grant me chastity – but not yet!"? That is my downfall, you see?'

Helen shrugged off the question as Qito came round the table, cupped his hands about her face and lifted her bodily to her feet. 'You are a very beautiful woman,' he told her, 'but I am a tired old man and must now go to my rest. We shall meet again at dawn.' Planting a chaste kiss to each of her cheeks, he wished her goodnight and disappeared into the tent.

Helen watched the tent flap drop back into place behind him and couldn't escape a feeling of rejection. Perversely, she felt he might at least have tried something with her if only to give her the virtue of rejecting him. Now, instead, she found herself, revitalised by food, facing a long empty evening.

A stir of the palm fronds reminded her that a night breeze had sprung up, so, finding a blanket, she wrapped it around herself and was drawn towards the brilliantly moonlit beach.

There, watching the liquid silver ocean rippling under the full moon, she thought of herself as standing on the edge of eternity. Qito had said life was a quest for the soul and here, she decided, was as good a place to look for it as any other.

Spreading the blanket, she lay down on the still warm sands and looked into the immense sky above her aware that the combination of wine and sun and Qito's philosophising – not to mention his working 'impotence' – had induced in her a warm glow of relaxation which, for Helen, always brought about a sensual awareness. Qito had been right in one thing. This was a place to be shared with a lover but where was he to come from? With one hand trailing over her groin and another cupping her breasts she was reminded of Qito's words: 'Gratification is much more accessible,' and that, her questing fingers reminded her, was certainly true but she lacked the fantasy to stimulate herself. Carla? The pilots? Both conjured up a background of sophisticated technology which was far from her mood.

Closing her eyes she sought out her old favourite. The regiment of sex-starved men, but even they were out of ear-shot, and she was left with nothing but the physical stimulation of herself.

It was then that some sixth sense, or, perhaps, some tiny sound caused her to open her eyes. There, rearing above her, the whites of his eyes bright in the moonlight, stood a man. Curiously Helen felt no fear and was, only afterwards, to understand why. In the moment of opening her eyes and registering the man's presence she had imagined him a manifestation of her own longings.

After a moment of stilled surprise Helen found herself smiling a welcome. The man said nothing. His body, bare to the rope that supported his baggy sailcloth trousers, was athletically dark and polished, with the moonlight bright enough to shadow the deep contours of a powerful chest. Feeling that to speak would break the magical moment, she instead spread her thighs and arms in invitation. The man's expression barely flickered and she saw that more was demanded of her.

Reaching up she laid a hand on the man's groin and, feeling him already hardening, reached for the knotted rope that supported his trousers. The man brushed aside her feebly questing fingers to quickly dispose of the knot himself. The baggy trousers slid from his taut, muscular stomach and Helen, now more fervent, took him fully into her fist, thrilled to find that her fingers could barely meet about the thickness of the still-growing phallus. She drew him down to kneel beside her in the sand. Unwilling to lose her daring initiative she guided the intimidating size of him down over her belly to where her readied sheath awaited his sword.

It was then, inevitably, that she ceded all control. Now the man, his body tangy with salt, lay above her, staring directly into her widened expectant eyes, seeming to ask if she had enough courage to take him. Gathering both her wrists in one huge, roughly textured, hand he effortlessly pulled them rigidly above her head, pinning her helplessly under his body which now bore down on her with threatening weight and slab-like solidity. Searching the man's eyes she could see no sign of curiosity about who she might be and, more worryingly, no sign of mercy. Helen wanted to speak – to give consent, reassure him that her reaction was that he paid her homage rather than rape, but his intense, set, expression muted her, and made her know that what was about to happen would be devoid of tenderness and that pain and pleasure would be mixed in equal parts.

When he moved to gently probe at the outermost sides of her pubis she could not suppress the gasp of welcome that escaped her tight lips. Urgently she rose to meet him, swallow him, but he paused, teasing her to the point of torture. Shuddering with expectation, she tried tearing her hands from his indomitable grasp to wind them round him and use her nails to goad him into her, but still he waited, his face expressionless. As her body begged, he ended the agony of expectation and so it was with relief and apprehension that she felt him pressing gently forward, opening her nether-lips, to penetrate, with deliberate slowness, deep into the centre of her soul, until she writhed, her body pleading, even as her fear mounted that she could never accommodate him. Just when she was certain she would be split in two he began to withdraw – so slowly and with such deliberation that she feared he meant to drive her to distraction.

Shamelessly, fearing that he meant to abandon her, she pressed herself against him, her legs around his broad hips, until she was all but lifted from the blanket. It was then, when she was at her most vulnerable, that he plunged with surprising accuracy deep into her to rub against the tender flesh inside her and bringing forth a gasp which ripped through the silence of the night as, having shown her the worst, he once more withdrew with tantalising slowness to hover at her loin's gate.

There his solid cock rested, teasing and threatening before, when she least expected it, it again plunged deep into her, ravaging her senses to be immediately followed by another, even more hearty thrust, causing her to voice yet another scream of triumphant pleasure.

His movements became a mix of slow withdrawals and inward thrusts. There was no tender smile, no brush of his lips to reassure a vulnerable Helen. Instead, he held himself away from her upwardly arching body, creating a space of intense heat between them, making her skin as liquid as the fire that he stoked in her loins. Not one word had passed between them as he plunged himself, huge and vibrating, inside her. The sheer strength of this assault excited her as she conspired to her own pain by squeezing her stretched, outer lips, vainly attempting to trap his huge, pulsating cock.

The only sounds between them had been her alternating cries and sighs lending an almost ritual air to her exquisite torment. When she felt the helpless embrace of her own orgasm rushing through her it seemed almost impertinent. He, this man, this stranger, this totally unknown lover, gave no sign that he felt anything other than a delight in assailing the willing flesh laid open to his mercy.

Consciously aware that this was animal savagery she cried out in the certainty that this was right. To couple without preliminary, without even a word, was totally in tune with the primaeval setting and her own mood. Waves of orgasm swept through her, as she abandoned every doubt and restraint imposed by hundreds and thousands of years of social pretensions. Qito had spoken of redemption and now, naked and savage, she felt she was close to knowing it – red in tooth and claw!

His expression didn't alter one iota as he continued orchestrating one unstoppable wave after another – his heavy sac banging into her until, without warning, he pulled completely out of her. His grip still firm on her wrists, he raised himself until she could feel the dead weight of him between her breasts. With his free hand he took both her breasts to squeeze them tight about his huge erection so that she felt his throbbing climax long before the first gouts of his heated offering spurted forth to lay a sticky trail across her throat and lips. With this came the first sign of humanity in the man as his body relaxed and his weight came down, threatening to crush her as her freed hands forced themselves between their sweat-streaked bodies, to seek out the precious fluid that lay there.

Smearing her breasts and belly, as if anxious to coat herself in the memory of him, she reached up and tried, with the other arm, to draw him down to her, shamelessly seeking some moderating tenderness in which

448

she could express her thanks in the only language her fevered mind could recall.

The man seemed puzzled by this gesture and, despite her protest, levered himself out of her attempted embrace to stand over her. Muted by the immensity of him, she continued to work the rapidly cooling semen in a vain attempt to soothe her aching breasts. Unable to summon the will to move, she lay, her eyes filled with the still half-erected hugeness of him, and passively watched him reach for his discarded trousers and, with eyes that never left her, put them on, tie the rope and, still expressionless, turn away.

Only then did she find the strength to move. Scrambling to her feet she saw that he was walking down the beach to where – she saw for the first time – a small dinghy-like boat, a bright lamp hung over its stern, was drawn up onto the beach.

She stood silently watching as he pushed the boat out into the water before athletically leaping aboard. The rasp of rope on the pulley signalled the raising of the one triangular sail which, filling immediately, with the light night breeze, brought throbbing but silent life to the boat as it arced its way seawards leaving a phosphorescent trail in its wake.

As the boat gathered pace, Helen felt filled with something akin to awe. This stranger had appeared, full fledged as if from a fantasy, and now was, it seemed to her inflamed imagination, returning to the mythical Valhalla from which he had sprung.

Breathless, she watched the bobbing bright light which marked his boat's passage and began, even then, to wonder if it had really happened. The tingling ache in her loins reassured her that it had, but it was still difficult to believe that anything that fierce and animalistic could be so satisfying. Drawn to the water's edge, she scooped up water to wash herself down in its warm saltiness while her eyes remained fixed on the lighted boat until it was lost in the vastness of the ocean beyond the reef.

When she did turn away she was filled, not with sadness at something lost, but a certainty that she had lived a day which would be fixed forever in her memory. Had she perhaps, she wondered, found the first strand of what Qito had called her quest for a soul?

While certain that such a momentous experience must have more significance than mere gratification, the stranger had left no room for her to take refuge in any delusion of romance.

He had come out of the night and delivered precisely what she had craved. More than enough, and certainly nothing less. If he had been a messenger from the prescient deity that Qito denied, he had left in her a soaring confidence which filled her with joy.

As she came into the tent and saw that Qito slept on undisturbed by the activities, the sounds of which must surely have carried to the campsite, she felt even greater pleasure in knowing that the experience was hers alone with no need to explain or account to anyone.

Hugging the memory of the night close to her breasts, as she might have done with a favourite teddy bear, she summoned up the image that had lodged most firmly in her mind – the moment when, satiated, he had stood over her, his still half-hardened cock standing proudly out from his muscular stomach. Her groin went into spasm as she regretted that he had not allowed her the pleasure of re-arousal – nor the wanton abandoning of self that taking him into her mouth would have given.

Had the stranger even understood how completely he had been welcomed? Demanding only her submission, he had not even allowed her the pleasure of acquiescence, but, once more safe, she acknowledged that he had been right.

They had coupled as two animals meeting in the night. No words had been used and, what words were

450

needed, she wondered, to communicate the most basic of needs?

In the dark stillness of her desert island tent, with only Qito's nasal snorts for company, she felt herself in communion with thousands of past generations of women. Tonight she had known what it was to be truly, consentingly, *taken*. Not romanced, not seduced, with no pretence at anything other than an urgent response to a mutual need.

She knew with certainty that nothing was ever going to be the same again.

Content that she now knew something granted to few women, she slipped into the sleep of the innocent.

Chapter Fourteen

Waking the next morning Helen was pleased to find she was alone. It gave her the space to appreciate the sensation of peace and a freedom from guilt that warmed her entire body. To be able, as she was, to rise naked from the light covering of her camp-cot and step out of the tent into an unthreatened peace and bathe in warm sunshine, was, to her, the definition of what it is to be alive.

Finding coffee, still warm, in a pot she poured herself a cup and stepped through the margin of brush that separated the campsite from the beach to feel the comforting ooze of warm sand pressing between her toes. Looking out over the sparkling lagoon towards the white water of the reef she imagined that anyone looking at her would see a body carved, as Qito had once remarked, in the shape of a smile. To be happy was one thing but to *know* it – to feel it settled about her shoulders like a comforting blanket – was sheer bliss.

Suddenly, it was important to her to establish the reality of last night's 'fantasy' encounter. Walking around a slight bend in the immaculate shoreline she came upon an area of disturbed sand. Was this the place? She wasn't sure. The tide had lapped away at where the boat might have been beached while the sun beat down, bleaching out signs of where she might have lain and received the man. Deciding it would take the skill of a forensic scientist to find traces of the night's debauch, she smiled happily in the knowledge that it didn't matter. Nothing mattered. This morning, as no other she could ever remember, she felt in love with a world which had, it seemed, suddenly chosen to focus all the blessings it could offer on herself.

Wading into the bounteous sea she washed herself down with the warm water, and felt her stimulated body sing with happiness. A distant voice, calling her name, carried to her. Looking round she could see nothing but the extravagant greenery of the island's vegetation soaring steeply up the hill towards the glade in which Qito had posed her.

Making her way up the scarcely discernible path, her body being rapidly sun dried, she came upon Qito sketching a detail of the rock formations with such concentration that he hadn't noticed Helen's arrival.

She stood a moment and watched him at work, filled with a throbbing awareness of being in the company of genius. Bathed in the glowing awareness of privilege, she moved forward to let him know of her presence.

'There you are,' he said, straightening from his crouch. 'I was beginning to wonder if you were ever going to wake.'

'Sorry if I'm late.'

Qito shook his head. 'The light won't be right until the afternoon anyway. Have you noticed how the rocks soften in the evening light?'

Shaking her head she happily felt she would never again be able to rid her expression of the smile which seemed to start somewhere deep in her body.

'You look different this morning,' Qito murmured.

Nodding happily and, prompted by her overwhelming feeling of invulnerability, she went towards him and gently wrapped her arms about his diminutive

453

body. 'I feel different,' she told him. 'This is a magical place. It makes me happy.' Aware that Qito was standing very still and making not the slightest attempt to return her loose embrace, she drew back her head and looked down into his widened brown eyes. 'Today anything is possible,' she told him. 'Today I love you.'

Qito's eyes softened before suddenly flaring with decision. Reaching for her hands, now resting lightly on his shoulders he drew them aside. 'My God,' he said. 'I must have those eyes.' Turning her so that she was half faced into the sunlight filtering through the overhang of foliage, he took up his sketch pad. 'Your eyes are incredible this morning. If Carla saw them she would know.'

'"Know" what?'

'That you were in love.'

'With you?'

'Since I'm the only other being here she might be justified in thinking so, don't you think?'

Helen felt her inward smile turn to a satisfied grin. How little this intense man knew! Content that her fantasy was lodged safely and secretly, she found she could look back at him innocent and unblinking as he stared into her eyes, the silence broken only by the scratch of his pencil on the coarsely textured pad.

Throughout that morning Qito seemed quietly intent on capturing every tiny detail of her face and its unvarying expression of happiness, until hunger drove him to thoughts of lunch.

Dismissed from witnessing the mysteries of his preparations she went again to swim in the lagoon, exquisitely conscious that the same water in which she bathed was, somewhere, lapping at the keel of the fisherman's boat which would, that night, bring him to her.

Called back to the campsite she found chilled melon, Parma ham, an odoriferous but delicious cheese and bread so flakily crisp that it forced its way between her teeth to edge sharply against her gums.

454

'Do we have a refrigerator on the island?' she asked.

Qito nodded enthusiastically. 'And a freezer.'

'That's incredible. How is it powered?'

Qito waved a hand vaguely in the direction of a panel of glass. 'Solar panels,' he said. 'Just because we have left civilisation it doesn't mean we have to reject it.'

As she ate Helen found herself filled with unworthy suspicions about the source of Qito's gastronomic feats and decided that she would have to investigate the contents of their amazing freezer.

Immediately after eating, Qito took himself off for his hour's siesta while Helen decided to force all thoughts of skin melanoma, and Qito's insistence that she coat herself in sun blocker, from her mind while she lay on the sand and worked on getting some colour into her skin.

It was Qito's angry voice that roused her from an intense but immediately forgotten dream. 'Are you crazy?' he was shouting at her while dragging her to her feet and back to the shaded campsite. 'Look at you! You're on fire! You'll be lucky not to have sun-stroke. My God, you could get ill and we wouldn't be able to work. You Anglos go crazy in the sun!'

'I'll be all right,' she murmured, feeling her earlier felicitous mood rapidly diminishing.

Later that afternoon, posing in the sylvan glade, she needed all her will-power to disguise from Qito just how light-headed and dizzy she felt. Daunted by the belief that Qito knew just how much she was suffering, but determined not to acknowledge it, it was with great relief that she heard him finally call 'enough'.

Back at the campsite Qito insisted she lay in the cool of the tent where he carefully smoothed more cream to her outraged skin. Feeling quite sick Helen was happy to agree to his suggestion that she rest while he prepared the evening meal.

She had gone to bed with no intention of sleeping for any length of time but when she woke she found the evening had slipped into the deep silence of night. Qito was asleep and it was with the excitement of a daring teenager eluding the vigilance of a parent that she started towards the beach. She had been staring out to sea, eagerly watching for the dancing light on the stern of his boat for some minutes before she found the night breeze, striking chill on her still outraged breasts, intolerable and turned back to sneak out a blanket.

The moment she came out of the tent she saw, through the shrubs, the gleam of a light out at sea and rushed, breathless, to watch with rising excitement as the boat found the break in the reef and turned towards the shore.

Unable to contain her patience, discarding the blanket she waded into the still warm water for some yards before plunging headlong into it and swimming out to meet the oncoming boat. There was a moment when she feared her headlong dash would end in disaster as he, not seeing her in the dark water, might have run her down. Seeing her only at the last moment he turned the boat so that she was swept along its side. With one immensely strong arm he reached down to lift her bodily from the water and cast her, breathless and spread, across the wooden slats at the bottom of the boat which were still slimy from the entrails of past catches.

There was no pretence possible between them. Both knew why she had come so eagerly to greet him, but he had other things to do. Turning aside from her brazen, open invitation he knocked away a piece of wood which brought the single sail crashing down the mast.

Flinging out a sea anchor he turned to her as if she were but one more chore to be taken care of before work could begin. Pulling away the rope that held up his trousers he came to stand magnificently naked and fully aroused over her liquid body.

Scrambling up she would have paid homage to his risen flesh with her mouth but this man had no patience

456

for such subtleties and instead caught her up, turned her around and penetrated her conventionally from behind – all in one swift movement which knocked the breath from her body.

Ravaging her, she felt his hands tight about her shoulders as if to prevent her escape, he brought her gasping to a rapid climax and while she hoped for more, he pulled out of her and let her feel the shower of him pulsing onto her arching back. With a murmur of protest she tried to turn to take some part of him into her mouth but instead found herself lifted into his arms and carried over the side of the boat. Fearing that he simply meant to dump her she rejoiced when he stepped into the now shallow water and waded ashore while she felt a featherweight in his arms.

Dumping her unceremoniously on the sand he came down heavily on her, her legs pressed wide and high, and she was astonished to feel his already fully re-aroused flesh probing deep into her.

Anxious to hear him speak she tried to provoke him with urgent murmurings, but received only grunts as his hugeness delved deeper and more painfully into her. Reaching a climax, she wound her legs about him, gripping him tightly, determined that, this time, he would deliver himself into her and not on her belly, but this man had some deeply imprinted objection to coming inside her and, with great force, wrenched himself from her loins and levered himself upward. Not to be cheated, letting out a cry of frustration, Helen grabbed at his already erupting penis and sunk its convulsive size deep into her mouth. He made a move as if to protest but his orgasm had weakened him so that she had little difficulty in easing him onto his back where she triumphantly sucked on him until the last convulsive spurt. Straddling, she looked down into his closed face and felt that she had conquered. The beast, now moaning with pleasure, lay vanquished between her thighs as she felt a soaring sense of fulfilment.

'Say something!' she told him harshly.

The man's eyes opened and she was shocked to see in them a flicker of shame.

Suddenly, it occurred to her that it was possible that no woman had ever taken him in her mouth before. Their few encounters had been animal – wild, even. Could it be that he thought of women as simple victims who could only be taken by brute force?

As the man continued to stare silently up at her, as if at some strange alien species, she was overwhelmed with the feeling that she had made him vulnerable – frightened of her, even – and moved to reassure him. Moving her body down over his she laid her head on the firm muscles of his tensed stomach and reached for his now saddened looking penis. Taking it gently between two fingers she reached out with her tongue and touched its most sensitive point.

His reaction was instantaneous. Two huge hands reached about her ribs and lifted her bodily, as if she were no more substantial than a china doll, while turning her so that she was held at arm's length above his body with only her legs drooping to contact the ground. The breath driven from her, she felt totally vulnerable as fear rushed in to replace her earlier feeling of superiority.

His lips parted to reveal a shining row of perfect teeth and she felt herself being lowered onto his waiting loins. There she felt his flesh re-erected and waiting for her. Gasping at his entry, still dangling helpless above his head, she was effortlessly raised and lowered as he teased her by plunging her deep down onto him and then lifting her so that only the point of him nudged at her flowing gate.

He was reasserting himself, reminding her that he was master here and that her attempts to take the initiative were not to be held of any account. The ache of her ribs, where he held her, lessened in direct ratio to the reawakened fire in her loins. Gasping, breathless, she felt deliciously helpless and used. As her body burned, her mind lashed her with the thought that she was, literally, no more than a toy in his hands to be used and tossed aside like any other masturbatory aid.

In the fear and humiliation she found an intense and worrying excitement. The power of the man that could so easily dispose of her as he wished, brought her quickly to climax and, as she gasped out her appreciation, she heard him murmuring the first word she had ever heard him speak. *'Puta!'* he growled.

Two things then happened so synchronously that they appeared for a moment to be cause and effect.

The man beneath her rammed her rigid body down onto his throbbing flesh, surging fully and cruelly deep into her, while a blinding white light shone into her face.

Concentrating on the one, and, for the moment, ignoring the other, she yelled out in climactic orgasm which became protest as the man under her unceremoniously dropped her, and scrambled to his feet.

Lying abandoned and helpless in the soft, warm sand she heard Qito's voice murmuring something that sounded like an Italian apology. Abstractedly she realised that her cries must have drawn Qito to the scene but she, still light-headed, found she didn't care.

The torch was switched off and allowed her to see Qito turning away down the beach. The man had disappeared by the time she looked for him and, resenting the abrupt end to their encounter, she got to her feet and hurried towards where the boat had been beached.

Frustrated to see the bright lamp at the boat's stern already some metres from the beach, her first impulse was to call out and reassure him that there was nothing to fear, but the hand she had raised to wave him to come back, went instead to smother the cry that had come to her lips as she stood and watched helplessly as the beacon that signalled her pleasure sailed away.

Coming back to the campsite she found Qito, his back resolutely turned to her, making coffee. Feeling curiously assertive she spoke to challenge his silence. 'Did we wake you?' she asked.

Qito turned and looked at her. 'Do you know what *"puta"* means?' he asked her and, when she shook her head, went on. 'It means whore,' he said before walking round her and into the tent.

Had there been a solid door on the tent frame Helen felt certain he would have slammed it. Instead, she savoured the word and its meaning in her head to combine it with the, almost certain, feeling that Qito had been jealous. Self-embracing her own tingling body she was, even, tempted to offer herself to Qito as he lay on his tent cot, but instead she turned away to the beach where, registering that the light of the dinghy was now far out to sea, she waded into the water and washed herself.

The following morning she woke to find Qito fussily working the camping oven and producing hot crispy croissants while keeping his back turned, firmly, towards her.

Amused at his petulance she sang out a 'Good morning' with all the genuine happiness that she felt.

Putting the coffee pot heavily in front of her he stood over her with just enough silence to let his annoyance show. 'Who is he?' he demanded.

'None of your business,' she told him, happily ladling butter and delicious apricot jam on her already over-rich pastry.

'It is my business when you are too tired to stand still!'

'Yesterday wasn't anything to do with that. I'd had too much sun that's all. Besides I'm not your employee. I do as I want.'

For a moment she thought Qito was going to explode with anger but, to her relief, the fight went out of him

460

as he sank down to sit at the table and look steadily at her. 'Jeffrey is my friend,' he said flatly.

'It has nothing to do with him either.' She let Qito wait while she sank her teeth greedily into the flaky croissant. 'He's married.'

Qito looked genuinely surprised. 'Married?' he asked. 'Jeffrey? No. It's not possible!' Qito paused a moment as if searching his memory to see if he could be mistaken before going on. 'I have known Jeffrey since he appeared on my doorstep fifteen years ago. A tall, skinny student who could talk sensibly about my work. We have been friends ever since. I have never known him to be married.' Qito paused a moment. 'Who told you of this marriage?'

'His assistant.'

Enlightenment, along with a knowing smile that bordered on the amused, crossed Qito's face. 'You mean that pretty girl – what's her name . . . ?'

About to supply Annabel's name, Helen was crushed with the sudden realisation of just how precipitately she had accepted Annabel's word. It was obvious that Qito didn't believe Jeffrey capable of such a deception and, in the colder perspective of time and distance, she found it hard to believe herself. What if it were not true – or a misunderstanding? The thought that her every revenge might have had no basis appalled her.

Looking into Qito's waiting sceptical eyes, she found the only response was defensive. 'Why would Annabel have lied about something like that?'

Raising his hands as if to ward off an intruder, Qito smiled. 'You are asking me, a *man*, to divine the motives of a *woman*? Impossible! All I can say is that, until you have spoken to Jeffrey, I would caution you to withhold judgement.' As he was speaking Qito gathered up his sketching pad and bundle of pencils. 'I'm off to do some work on my own,' he told her. 'We'll work on the canvas this afternoon.'

Alone with her thoughts Helen considered what she

might do if Annabel had been lying or misleading her. Would Jeffrey ever forgive her for her 'revenge'? The likelihood of keeping it from him after last night's 'discovery' by Qito seemed distant. The more she thought, the more her newly discovered paradise became fragmented and fragile.

Not for the first time, she felt bits falling off her life. Suddenly the glorious colours of the flora, the fine white sand of the beach and the pristine sparkle of the ocean, became a mocking reminder of her isolation.

Jeffrey had reimposed himself into her consciousness and his presence made her feel guilt.

Wandering aimlessly in search of something to distract her thoughts she came upon the chest freezer under its canopy of solar panels and, remembering Qito's boasted skill at preparing meals, lifted the lid to look inside.

There, arranged in neatly labelled plastic boxes, were all the meals they had so far enjoyed and several that were, as yet, untouched. So Qito, for all his worldly pre-eminence, had been prepared to let her believe he was a master chef when all the meals had been prepared on the yacht and delivered to them frozen, needing only to be de-frosted.

Closing the lid, Helen felt the discovery somehow more profound, and less amusing, than it might have been in any other context.

Was deceit endemic to the male species, she wondered?

Chapter Fifteen

That afternoon Qito worked with greater intensity than ever before. He had, previously, broken off to comment on the cries of the birds and identified them for her – his knowledge of the flora and fauna of the island was impressive – but this afternoon he worked in total silence which, she felt, was creating a distance between them.

As she posed she painfully considered just how she might face Jeffrey if Qito's confidence in him proved to be justified while, at the same time, resenting the confusion that the previously unconsidered possibility had brought. She had behaved mindlessly, she decided, and felt that retribution, should he take the trouble, would be quite painful.

Her lurking masochism, driven by guilt, roared into her head on a flight of fantasy. Standing under Qito's penetrating gaze she wished she could close down time and space so that she could immediately – this instant – confront Jeffrey with her suspicions so that he would have to either confirm or disprove them. Quite suddenly the prospective confrontation had taken on a quite exciting connotation – whichever way it went. The only immediate question her loins presented was what was she to do when, as she confidently expected he would, her mysterious fisherman lover reappeared?

Her mind told her one thing while her body urged quite another. The dilemma was still unresolved when, after a silent dinner – which reminded her of Qito's posturing as a resourceful chef – Qito took himself off to his bed.

Tonight she decided to take a bottle of the delicious, heady, wine down to the beach and there sat on her blanket and gazed out into the lagoon, her eyes keening for first sight of the lantern which marked the dinghy's progress. Uncertain of the passage of time – she wore no watch – she waited in vain for what seemed several hours before, wrapping herself in the blanket, she lay back on the sand and drifted off into the welcoming arms of a wine induced drowse.

It was the birds' dawn chorus that woke her in time to witness a spectacular sunrise. She woke irritated and chilled and, spurning an early morning bathe, turned through the shrubs to the campsite. For once she had risen before Qito and, feeling an urgent desire for coffee, found matches and started the propane gas cooker. She hesitated to fetch croissants from the freezer since this would indicate to Qito that she had discovered his 'secret' but then did it anyway, popping them into the oven to crisp.

'What are you doing?'

Looking round she saw Qito had come out from the tent and was standing watching her. She was almost embarrassed to notice that his naked belly was adorned with a soaring erection. 'Making breakfast,' she told him, then, brimming with devilment, turned to fully face him and fixed her eyes on the exclamation mark at his groin. 'On the other hand would you like me to do something about that?'

Qito frowned darkly at her and turning away moved some way into the bushes where she heard the splash

464

of his early morning urination. 'There goes your hard-on!' she sang gaily after him. 'It's too late now!'

When a still disapproving, but now detumescent, Qito returned, he found her already at the table eating a hot croissant and coffee. When he reached for the coffee pot she reproved him. 'First wash your hands,' she said as primly as she could manage.

'You're in a funny mood this morning,' he said acidly. 'What happened? Didn't your mysterious lover show up?'

'None of your business.'

Qito laughed and sat at the table and, ignoring her injunction, helped himself to the coffee. 'So he didn't! I probably frightened him off. Maybe he thought I was an angry husband or lover!'

She felt the urge to puncture the pleasure he was having at her expense so said: 'More likely *grandfather!*' but immediately regretted it when Qito, provoked, got up and walked away from her. Rising, she went after him to find him looking out across the lagoon. 'I'm sorry,' she said, putting a hand to his broad shoulder. 'You're right. He didn't come and I am irritable.'

Turning to her, his face wreathed in a smile as warm as the morning sun, he put out his strong arms, and she, feeling curiously self-conscious, went into his embrace. 'And I'm a silly old man,' he told her. 'You know just how silly? Seeing you with that man, I was jealous.'

Enveloped in a rush of warm affection she looked into his soulful eyes. 'And not only that,' she smiled, 'you're an old fraud!' In the face of Qito's offended expression she went on, 'You've not been cooking – you've been defrosting!'

'When did you find me out?' he asked with heavy mock contrition.

'Yesterday.'

Nodding, Qito pulled her back into the embrace.

465

'What we old men lack in virility we have to make up for with guile. Forgive me?' he asked.

Nodding into his shoulder, she murmured. 'We have to make allowances for a genius.'

Qito laughed and thrust her away. 'What was it you said: "Too late"? You were quite right! Twenty years too late. My God that Jeffrey is a lucky man! Not only is she beautiful, a perfect model and knows what she wants but is also charitable to old men. Get thee from me, Satan's child!' he cried before grabbing up her hand and kissing it.

Together, hand in hand, she aware of a feeling of great privilege, they walked into the lagoon's water and indulgently washed each other down.

Later that afternoon, as she posed, she was consumed by the intensity which Qito brought to his work, and regretted that while he looked at her, he saw only a shape worth putting to canvas. Having said he had been jealous of her fisherman and complimented her outrageously, she discovered a great longing to seduce the great man. She imagined herself, some distant day, opening a newspaper to read of his passing and regretting not having taken the opportunity which currently presented itself. The incident in Jeffrey's penthouse she discounted, since that had been for Jeffrey's pleasure more than anyone else's. Standing there she determined that before this idyll ended she would make a memory of a shared moment with Qito.

It seemed that moment had come when, as the light began to fade, Qito called a halt and, coming to her, took one of her wrists firmly in hand to lead her to a glade of bamboo.

'What are you doing?' she asked as he took a vine, previously tied to one of the bamboos, and bending it down, tied her wrist to it.

'Taming a wild banshee,' he told her.

She protested further, but to no avail, when he tied her other wrist and, letting go of the springy bamboos, had her stretched helplessly between the two of them. About to protest that she had daydreamed something gentler and more intimate between them, she watched, silently aghast, as he started to move away. 'You can't leave me here like this!' she shouted after him. Unmoved, Qito sauntered away into the gathering night and didn't look back.

Her mind in tumult, it took her several moments to find the breath to scream further protest. Aware that the spaces between the trees were already darkening she had begun to feel real fear when, without warning, she felt herself grabbed from behind. The man, there was no doubt it was a man, put one arm about her breasts while the other sought out and penetrated her groin. Outraged and screaming, she tried to twist herself out of the unknown man's grasping arms.

'Be quiet,' said Jeffrey's voice in her ear.

Her body instantly stilled, her mind went into confused orbit. 'Where did you come from?' she gasped.

'Never mind that now. There are urgent things to be done to you.'

Even as she twisted in her bonds, trying to catch a glimpse of his face, she felt him probing, then penetrating her to unleash in her an outrush of frustration. Still she protested. 'No!' she cried. 'We have to talk!'

'Don't talk!' he murmured, his voice now harsh. 'Screw!'

Her writhing had dragged one of her loosely tied wrists free and she swung on the other still tied wrist, to stumble and almost fall as Jeffrey continued to hold her, now bent almost double, and mercilessly impaling her, took all the breath from her body and smothered the protests of her brain.

'Bastard!' she screamed.

'Filthy slut!' he answered her.

'I *hate* you!'

'You disgust me!'

Just then, at the expense of rope burns, she managed

to free her second wrist and, with a violent thrashing movement, pulled herself away from the urgent liquid fire he had stoked deep inside her and turned to face him with fists bunched and anger flaring.

Her small victory was short-lived as, his face fired like some wild forest creature, he caught her up and, his weight bearing her to the ground, again penetrated between her defiant thighs. Pinned firmly now, she was consumed by the moment. All thoughts of betrayal and guilt fled from a mind overwhelmed by the sensations he was creating in her. Nothing mattered now other than to answer her bodily urge to surrender. Her legs wound around his heaving loins, she dug her nails deep into his back the better to urge him even deeper and more firmly into her body.

'Yes!' she cried as naked lust forced her body to rise to meet his every thrust. As he savaged deep into her their cries rose into the night canopy stilling those of the other night creatures who, it seemed, had paused to lend an indulgent ear to the human intruders so noisily locked together on the floor of their domain.

'Yes!' she screamed again as the now familiar surge laid siege to her breathless body as he led her to all-consuming completion.

After the mutuality of climax they lay in each other's arms, he still lodged deep in her, and the rasping of their desperate lungs fighting for breath was now the only sound in the quieted night, until she spoke. 'Annabel told me you were married.'

'Annabel lied,' he told her.

Immediately assailed by two conflicting reactions – relief and a flood of guilt at her precipitate 'revenge' – she groaned. 'Oh no!'

Jeffrey raised his head to look at her. 'You're disappointed?' he asked.

Everything she had done since fleeing from him, flashed before her with lightning speed and explicit detail. 'Not with you. With me,' she murmured. 'Why would she lie about something like that?'

'Jealousy.'

'You had an affair with her?'

'No. It seems that for years she's been having an "affair" with me. Purely mental, I hasten to add. I sensed it but ignored it. I have a strict rule never to mix business with pleasure.'

'She just invented it?'

'Not entirely. I *was* married. We were students – I was in a state of depression. The whole thing was madness. The marriage barely outlasted the honeymoon before we both agreed it had all been a terrible mistake. We waited the statutory two years and got a no-fault divorce by mutual agreement.'

'And that's all?'

'That's all,' he answered flatly.

Feeling that 'madness' was the word to describe her own state of mind since running away from Paris, she fell into a morose silence.

'What's the matter?' he asked.

Pushing him from her she rose, only now aware that her back had been pressed into a patch of prickly thorns, and shook her head. 'There's things I have to tell you,' she murmured.

'Confessions?' he asked.

Only able to muster a nod in reply she turned away desolate in the knowledge that she had behaved badly – at the very least, foolishly – and terrified in case he would not forgive her. As they stumbled through the night towards the campsite she sought to divert her fear filled mind. 'You still haven't told me how you got here.'

'Annabel confessed what she'd done and showed me the fax. I called Carla on the yacht, heard where you were, and took the next plane.'

Mention of Carla and the yacht made her realise that her idyll on the island was at an end. Attempting to make light of it she murmured: 'I suppose that means I'll have to put some clothes on,' but inwardly she felt she was losing a great deal more than that. It was wildly impossible but she had a longing for things to stay just as they were – she left to wander primitively naked, visited at night by an undemanding lover, and leaving the complications of civilised relationships to others less enlightened.

Coming to the campsite she saw the yacht's crew had all but dismantled it, leaving little of the tranquil sanctuary she had known.

Tsai Lo, appearing out of the shadows, came forward with a broad smile, holding out a sarong for her to wind about her body. Looking into the girl's porcelain beauty she was reminded to add the Chinese girl's name to the list of confessions she would have to make. Suddenly the thought of returning to the sophistication of the yacht overwhelmed her. Turning to Jeffrey, aware that her voice was tinged with desperation, she asked, 'Couldn't we stay on the island tonight? There's so much to talk about.'

'But they've taken everything away,' Jeffrey protested.

'It doesn't get cold at night. We could sleep on the beach.'

'You're nuts!' he told her, smiling. 'Besides the Captain's anxious about a hurricane warning and wants to sail immediately. We can talk on the yacht *and* sleep in a bed.'

Defeated, she allowed herself to be handed into the waiting launch and silently, morosely, even, watched the boat's growing wake stretching back to the island like some umbilical cord that must inevitably snap. The sense of impending loss caused a shiver to run through her.

Thinking her chilled, Jeffrey put his arm round her shoulders. 'I have a confession to make as well,' he said.

470

'You do?'

Jeffrey nodded. 'I find your interest in my marital status highly flattering.'

'Oh? Why?'

'Could it be that your thoughts have wandered in the same direction as mine?'

Feeling that he had broken into her mind and was rifling through her innermost thoughts, Helen reacted defensively. 'I don't know what you're talking about,' she told him, adding hastily, 'and I don't think I want to.' When his response was merely to chuckle she felt infuriated. 'Anyway – we have yet to talk.'

The launch was coming alongside the anchored yacht and she took the opportunity to distance herself from further discussion by standing up as if preparing to disembark.

Jeffrey didn't let her go that easily.

'What will we talk about? Carla and Tsai? Qito? Your fisherman?'

Shocked that he knew about even that, she was pleased to note he had left out the two pilots from the roll call. 'Among others,' she said tartly and got perverse pleasure at seeing the surprise on his face.

At that moment the launch crew turned to hand her to the lowered gangway and she stepped out of the small boat and climbed to the deck. Not waiting for Jeffrey she made her way aft to the stairway that led down to the stateroom deck.

Coming into the stateroom she felt overwhelmed with a sense of claustrophobia. The walls seemed to be closing on her. She felt an almost panic stricken impulse to turn and run before it was too late. 'Too late' for what, she had no idea. Could it be that after only three days without walls she had grown unaccustomed to being in an enclosed space?

When Jeffrey followed her into the stateroom she felt a spasm of resentment at his presumption. Staring at him as if at an intruder, she felt confused. 'Who told you about the fisherman?' she asked, even though it was blatantly obvious.

'Qito saw you.'

Perversely aware that she had him at a disadvantage, but not sure why, she insisted, 'Saw us doing what?'

'According to Qito you were enjoying yourself.'

'True!' The word exploded from her. 'And I hope you realise that it's all your fault!'

'*My* fault?'

'Certainly. If it wasn't for you I would still be a virtuous widow.' Seeing his stunned silence as an opportunity for a good exit, Helen turned on her heels and went into the bathroom where she firmly locked the door.

Unwinding the sarong, which though light seemed suddenly constricting, she was about to turn on the shower when she caught sight of herself in the mirror and came to an astonished halt. She barely recognised the honey coloured creature reflected there. Hair wild, eyes savage, breasts more prominent than ever above slimmed down ribs and belly, even she could find herself exciting.

'You've changed!' she told herself.

When there came a knock on the door she assumed it must be Jeffrey and called a caustic 'Go away!' only to hear Tsai's voice.

'Miss Helen?' asked the melodious voice. 'Do you need anything?'

Crossing to the door Helen looked beyond the smiling girl to see no sign of Jeffrey. 'Come in,' she told the girl. 'I feel like being indulged. You can wash my back.'

Tsai's eyes rounded with pleasure. 'You have such a beautiful colour,' the girl smiled, stripping herself of her cheongsam. 'Afterwards I will give you a beautiful massage. Yes?'

Standing under the shower with Tsai's expert hands soaping her back she found it titillating to imagine Jeffrey's face should he come upon them both just as they were now. So titillating that she found herself turning, without inhibition, to present her naked breasts to the soothing caress of Tsai's hands.

Very titillating, she decided.

When Jeffrey returned it was to find Helen stretched naked on the massage table and the subject of Tsai's expertise. Watching him reflected in a mirror above her head she was amused to see him hesitate, and thinking himself unobserved, take a moment to admire the sleek lines of Tsai's body. Thinking she had given him more than enough time, she turned on to her back and pretended to see him for the first time. 'Jeffrey, you're just in time! There's a phrase running through my head and I can't remember where it came from – perhaps you'd know?'

Looking puzzled Jeffrey came a pace nearer the table and looked down on her. 'What "phrase"?'

'I don't know if I remember it exactly but it goes something like: "Brave are they that dare to do what others scarcely dare to dream". Do you know it?'

'No. I don't think I've heard it before.'

Sitting up, and for no good reason feeling extravagantly pleased with herself, she put out her arms to Jeffrey who, awkwardly, came to the side of the table and returned the embrace. 'It's true though, isn't it? We "dared to do", didn't we?'

'You make it sound as if it is over.'

'Not "over". Perhaps a little different.'

'In what way?'

Lying back on the massage bench Helen allowed herself a long, deep reflective smile. 'Who knows?' she asked as she reached, taking Tsai's hands, leading her to stand at her head and laying her hands on her breasts. 'Did you have something to tell me?' she asked a startled, completely engrossed Jeffrey.

'Yes,' he said, then seemed to hesitate as if his mind, centred on the sight of Tsai's hands moving over Helen's breasts, had wandered from the subject.

473

'What?'

'What?' he echoed as if looking at the two naked girls had completely distracted his thoughts.

'What is it you have to tell me?'

'Oh!' cried Jeffrey flushing guiltily. 'Yes. The Captain's decided not to sail. Apparently, the hurricane is skirting the area just out to sea and he thinks it might be dangerous.' Jeffrey's voice was trailing away as his highly eroticised thoughts centred on Helen's openly naked body.

'So we could have spent the night on the island?'

'Sorry?' asked Jeffrey as if he hadn't heard a word she had been saying.

Delighting in the distraction she and Tsai were providing, Helen laughed. 'Come here,' she said, waving to a place at the side of the bench where she could reach him. Jeffrey obediently moved to one side of the bench where, reaching out, Helen's hand felt him standing erect under his linen trousers. 'Darling!' she cried, as if delighted by the discovery. 'Is that for me or for Tsai?'

Jeffrey flushed with embarrassment as Tsai failed to totally smother the giggle that had come to her throat. Jeffrey, totally distracted, looked from Tsai to Helen in confusion as she sought to unzip his trousers and bring his risen flesh into view. 'Helen!' he protested. 'We're expected for dinner!'

Her fist firmly encompassing him she murmured, 'You didn't answer my question . . .'

'What question?' Jeffrey asked, embarrassment giving edge to his voice.

'Is your cock hard in tribute to me or Tsai?'

'That's a ridiculous question!' Jeffrey protested.

'To us both, then?' she insisted.

Forcibly removing her hand, Jeffrey turned away, attempting to stuff himself back into his trousers, until Helen's ringing voice caused him to hesitate. 'I wouldn't do that if I were you, darling!'

474

Turning, Jeffrey looked startled. 'What are you talking about?'

'You have to be punished,' she said with a bright smile.

'Punished?' he asked. 'What for?'

Noting that he had asked only the reason for his impending 'sentence' without questioning the principle, Helen, much emboldened, went on: 'For spreading false information that deprived me of another night on the island.'

Jeffrey's expression froze as he stared at her while, apparently, searching for a suitable response. 'We'll discuss this later!' he said firmly and made a dash for the bedroom door. Delighted to see him retreating in confusion, Helen let her laugh follow him as he called from the bedroom. 'You'd better hurry up. Dinner will be waiting.'

Feeling that she had won an, as yet, unquantifiable victory she lay back and looked up into Tsai's serious, slightly puzzled, face.

'I've definitely changed,' she told the puzzled girl.

Chapter Sixteen

That night dinner was a noticeably subdued affair. Helen, sensing that Jeffrey was wary of her, felt filled with a wholly new self-confidence, while Carla's unusually subdued mood and constant assessing glances at her made Helen feel that she had, somehow, moved to centre stage in this glittering company. Martinez, the yacht's owner, paid particular attention to her every request and Qito was positively beaming every time he looked her way. Further confirmation that Carla saw her as a threat came from the total silence of Carla's 'creature', Jimmy, who reflected his 'mistress's' mood by sullenly avoiding eye contact with anybody.

'Qito tells me he has created a masterpiece,' Carla's voice, laced with ice, rang down the length of the stateroom table to Helen. 'You must have offered a great deal of "inspiration",' Carla added with barely disguised sarcasm.

Helen smiled sweetly. 'I don't know about that. I just did what I was told.'

Carla's response was heavy with threat. 'What a good little girl you must be,' she said.

'I do do my best whenever possible.'

'And so generous, too,' smiled Carla with all the warmth and affection of a cobra about to strike.

Jeffrey's voice, unusually hesitant, broke the silence that followed. 'Are we going to be permitted a sneak preview?' he asked.

'There is still work to do,' said Qito. 'Perhaps tomorrow night – after dinner.'

'How lovely!' cried Carla. 'We must make it an occasion.' Then, surprisingly turning to Martinez she added: 'Musn't we, Carlos?'

Martinez looked a little uncomfortable before murmuring, 'If you insist, Carla.'

Carla nodded. 'I do,' she murmured before sipping on her wine and challenging Helen with a direct stare. 'I've already seen the result of Qito's devotional labour and come to *my* conclusion. You will all have the chance to play at critics for the evening – and, afterwards, come to your own verdicts,' before adding with a gay laugh, 'Along with plaudits and punishment, of course.'

Since everyone at the table had immediately looked at her, Helen had no doubt to whom the last word had been intended. Under the flare of Carla's steady gaze she found herself confused by feelings of resentment which immediately rose only to be instantly swamped in a contrary emotion of excitement. Inwardly aware that her shiny new armour of confidence was being exposed as only paper thin, she looked to Jeffrey for comfort only to see that he seemed to be, not only aware of, but amused by the conflict that Carla's words had created in her.

Quelled by Carla's display of petulance, Helen took the first opportunity she could of escaping onto the deck where the multitude of seductive perfumes wafting to sea on the evening breeze reminded her of the short idyll that now seemed to have been irretrievably lost. She could barely summon the will to turn to greet Jeffrey as he joined her at the ship's rail.

'What's wrong with you tonight?' he asked.

'With me?' she asked. 'What about Carla? Why is she being so bitchy to me?'

Putting a warming arm about her shoulders, Jeffrey laughed. 'That's obvious. She's eaten up with jealousy about your days alone with Qito. You should be flattered.'

'Well, I'm not and she's got no reason. Nothing happened between me and Qito on the island.'

Jeffrey smiled. 'I believe you. But you don't know what Qito's been saying. He takes a great deal of adolescent pleasure in seeing Carla provoked.'

'Then I'll put the record straight the first chance I get.'

'And spoil Qito's pleasure? Surely not?'

Helen turned to Jeffrey angrily. 'You saw and heard her in there! I was starting to worry in case she came at me with a knife!'

Jeffrey's scornful laugh made Helen turn away with an unsettling feeling of anger. Still bristling, she was suddenly alert.

Out to sea, obviously approaching the island, she saw the lonely bobbing light that marked the stern of her mysterious lover's dinghy.

Overwhelmed with a rush of warmth to the man's loyalty – he must surely have seen the moored yacht – she, unawares, spoke her unbidden thought out loud. 'He's come back!'

'Who has?' asked Jeffrey before going on to answer his own question. 'Your fisherman?'

Nodding, Helen pointed out the light on the moonlit sea. 'That's his boat.' She hadn't realised how silent and thoughtful Jeffrey had become until, turning to him, she asked. 'Why does he have that bright light hanging over the water like that?'

It seemed Jeffrey had to wrench his mind to her question before answering. 'To attract fish. The light excites them and brings them in close – like moths to a flame.'

478

Involuntarily, Helen found herself shuddering. 'Weird!' she murmured.

'What's weird?'

'To be standing on the deck of this sophisticated pleasure machine in sight of a primaeval game of life and death.'

Jeffrey was silent for a moment as both watched the light getting ever closer to the island. 'It seems fish aren't the only creatures he draws to his lamp.'

'What does that mean?'

'You want to go to him, don't you?'

Meaning to make a pretence at protest she turned to look directly at Jeffrey's serious face and suddenly read there a complete understanding of the other, darker, impulse which had risen in her loins. 'Yes,' she said, flatly. 'As a matter of fact, I do!'

'Then go,' said Jeffrey. 'I won't stop you.'

They were still making silent challenge and answer when Carla's voice cut through the night. 'But I will!' she said, coming to stand close to the startled Helen. 'One man – two men – aren't enough for you, huh? You want to play the slut for some seaborne peasant!'

Bridling, Helen demanded, 'What business is it of yours?'

Carla answered with an equally brittle tone. 'Jeffrey is my friend and Qito is my husband! I'll not allow you to insult either one.'

Startled to find herself angered but able to stand up to the formidable Carla, Helen flared back: 'If you're bothered by what might have happened between me and Qito on the island, you can relax. Nothing happened! But, in the second place, it's downright patronising of you to appoint yourself defender of either Qito or Jeffrey. They're both old enough to speak for themselves! In the third place, I don't give a damn what you think!'

The resonating silence that followed Helen's outburst was broken by a curiously disarming Carla. 'Our little

479

mouse has grown fangs!' she cried in tones suggesting a delightful discovery. 'It's obvious that something must have happened on the island.' Reaching out a hand she laid it gently to Helen's face. 'However shall we tame this wildcat?' she asked of Jeffrey.

'I don't think I want her "tamed",' he murmured.

'Are you going to let her go ashore then?'

'That's her decision.'

'And will you take her back without conditions?'

'Yes.'

Smiling beneficently at Helen, Carla went on: 'How wonderful young love can be,' she murmured. 'And you, lovely child, how did you mean to get ashore?'

Looking out to the seductively moonlit island, lying less than a hundred metres from the yacht's anchorage, she turned back to Carla to speak defiantly, 'Swim, if I have to!'

Carla laughed with delight. 'I think you should. Life should never be too simple. And what of your return – what then?'

Puzzled, Helen asked, 'What do you mean?'

'All indulgence has a price. We shall have to punish you on your return, don't you agree?'

Looking into Jeffrey's face Helen could see the equivocation in his expression. Challenged and feeling that to retreat now would forever condemn her in his eyes to weakness, she braced herself to once more face Carla and, realising that Carla's threat merely added spice to the excitement coursing through her veins, said, 'All right. I agree.'

'Lovely!' cried Carla and then reaching forward opened the single catch that held Helen's dress, leaving her naked. Helen kicked off her shoes and turned to the yacht's rail. 'Did you think I wouldn't dare?' she asked Jeffrey.

'Just remember to come back,' he called as Helen, waving, turned to face the ocean and made as perfect an arc as she could in diving into the sea.

Jeffrey watched her strike for the shore, leaving a glowing phosphorescence in her wake, and tried not to think of this as rejection.

'What a wonderful girl!' breathed Carla in genuine admiration as they both stood watching Helen, clearly visible in the silver moonlight.

Jeffrey was about to reply when the First Officer appeared at their side and, leaning forward, peered into the water. 'Did someone just dive over the side?'

'Yes. Helen did. Why?' asked Jeffrey.

'Because this afternoon we spotted a bull-nose shark in the lagoon!'

'Oh dear,' murmured Carla. 'Are they one of the dangerous kinds?'

'Vicious,' said the excited First Officer. 'More dangerous than the Great White. Can you see her?'

It was then, scanning the beach, that they saw Helen rise from the surf and trot gently along on the dry sand.'

'She made it!' breathed Jeffrey.

'She still has to get back,' Carla reminded him as the First Officer moved off.

Seeing a teasing light in Carla's eye, Jeffrey had a sudden insight, 'You knew, didn't you?'

Carla affected a casual air, 'I do believe that someone did mention that we shouldn't swim.' Not even bothering to disguise her total insincerity, she went on, 'It completely slipped my mind until that charming officer reminded me.'

'She might have been killed!' Jeffrey protested.

'What is life without, at least, a little excitement?' Carla asked. 'However, nothing was lost.'

'Yes, but what do I do now? I can't let her swim back in the morning, but suppose she decides to come back before then?'

Carla shrugged. 'It sounds to me as if you will have to maintain a whole night vigil.' Leaning in, Carla

481

kissed Jeffrey firmly on the cheek. 'Pleasant thoughts,' she said before turning away to the boat's interior.

Stooping to pick up Helen's shoes and dress from the deck, he turned with them in his hands to look out across the glistening waters of the lagoon and tried not to imagine what was happening behind the screening shrubbery. His mind in conflict, he tried to rationalise what he had done and imagine what might have happened had he objected to Helen going ashore. Her words, spoken just hours ago, resonated in his mind: 'Those that do . . .' fought for pre-eminence with another, half remembered, maxim: 'A man will never know what he truly owns until he gives it away.' The question remaining was – would he ever regain her?

Standing at the rail on this warm sub-tropical night Jeffrey recognised that it was the most important question he would ever ask himself.

Rounding the promontory of rocks and shrubs that separated her from the beached boat, Helen hesitated. She could see the man in the light spilling from his stern lamp, looking one way and then the other along the beach, looking for her and wondering if she were still on the island or on the yacht. What, she wondered, had brought him back to the island when he must know it was, given the presence of the yacht in the lagoon, more than likely she would be on board. How could he have sensed that she might do exactly what she had done – thrown caution to the winds and come, eagerly, to his side?

In considering his motives she was also forced to question her own. If she were to believe Jeffrey's forthright denial of his being married then she, Helen, could no longer excuse herself on the grounds of inflicting punishment on him. The anger and frustration she had felt alone on the island with Qito was also no longer any kind of justification.

So she was left with pure lust. Lust for a totally

unknown, silent, man who came and went with the tides. In her dilemma she felt she was two separate persona. Her hungry body urged her forward but her mind whispered caution. The choices were there in stark contrast. The bright glare of the primitive gas lamp on his fishing boat was in front of her while, by turning her head, she could look back to the riding lights of the anchored yacht. She had also to ask herself why she had hesitated. How simple it would all have been, had the impulse that had caused her to dive from the deck's yacht been enough to carry her forward to the man's waiting arms. Rationality, she considered, was the ultimate passion killer. Either that or the comparative chill of the waters had sobered her up somewhat. She had come to prolong the 'wild child' freedom of her days on the island but knew that it would be only for this one last night and as ephemeral as making a grab for a ghost.

Her indecision mounting to be almost physically painful, she had started to turn sadly away when there was a movement in the bushes to her immediate right. Looking there she saw the man's face gazing, expressionless, directly at her. For a moment they stood facing each other before Helen felt forced to speak.

Unsure, even, of which language the man spoke or understood, she tried communicating with the universal shake of the head. 'No,' she said, her voice shaky with indecision. 'I only came to say goodbye.'

If the man understood he showed no sign of it and came forward to face her directly. Looking at the fine definition of his muscular body, the quietly confident and totally impassive face, she wanted to turn and run from her own bodily urges.

'He knows about you. They all know about you,' she offered, and then as confusion engulfed her, pleaded, 'They're going to punish me if I stay.' Mentally she added: 'And even if I don't', and suddenly everything was excitingly clear to her. She had licence. All was possible – everything permissible. This magnificent man before her was to be had at a price and she had only to decide if the price was worth it.

The man, though so close she could feel the heat of his body, made no move to reach out for her and was making it clear that if there was to be a first move then it was going to have to come from her.

Perversely angered, as she always was by being made responsible for her own actions, and even while wishing he had resolved her dilemma by simply taking her, she reached out to take his ever readied magnificence first into her hands, and then as it flickered and convulsed like a live creature, gently lowered her lips to him in supplication.

The man towering over her groaned his protest and reached to lift her to her feet and again she was forced to fight him off. 'No!' she told him as sternly as she could muster but when he knelt, wrenching himself from her, and bore down on her shoulders there was no protest that could be of any avail. Furiously she tried to roll clear of his grasp but it was hopeless. His sheer animal strength pinned her down, spread her and soared deep into her. Now able to tell herself that she had no other choice Helen was able to surrender with dignity.

The man, suffering no such inhibition, went about seeking his own satisfaction and played her like the accessory to his own pleasure that she revelled in knowing she was. Her protests gave way to pleasured gasps and cries as he created turmoil in her, thankfully deadening all thought of right and wrong, as the sand played mattress to their heaving bodies.

Her body, writhing with satisfaction at finally getting its own way, hushed her mind but her mind fought back with vivid images of Jeffrey – and Carla – as if they loomed over the writhing wanton bodies and smiled in satisfaction of the dreadful price they would demand as the price of re-entry into rationality.

'I'm to be punished for this!' she gasped into the

uncomprehending face of the man who ravaged her. 'Beg forgiveness! Humiliate myself!' but even as the thoughts lashed her she knew they were only adding to the pace of her rising climax. Soon she was screaming in orgasm as the relentless man thrashed on inside her. On and on. No longer caring whether she was willing or not, he brought wave after wave of exquisite torment, until she felt she could stand it no more and started beating her closed fists against his stone-like chest. She had never felt more helpless as he effortlessly picked her up and standing, still locked deep inside her, carried her into the lapping waters where her extreme vulnerability to the man was apparent as, to quiet her highly vocal protests he simply bent her backwards until her head went underwater.

Panicked, she felt herself swallowing water even as the fire between her loins intensified. When he lifted her, gasping, from the water and allowed her to breathe she used much of the breath to beg mercy, but he held her transfixed and pounded even deeper into her.

Sobbing, even as the fire within her grew more intense, she had one massive orgasm after another as she imagined herself fighting for her life where only his pleasure could save her. When he relented and waded them both back to shore she was once more borne down onto the beach where the sand welcomed her by forming a perfectly shaped base to their final debauch. Still lodged deep inside her she felt him surge, felt him throb and begin to move and, desperate to contain him this time, wound her legs about him, but to no avail. Once more he was pumping his warm seed onto her belly, leaving her feeling distraught and cheated.

Exhausted, she lay for a moment, eyes closed, and awaited his comforting embrace, but when, not feeling him close, she opened her eyes, he was already walking away towards his boat. 'Damn you!' she screamed after him. 'Go to hell!'

The man didn't bother to look back to her until,

standing in his boat, his hand already on the rope that would raise the sail, he waved her to come forward. Not knowing where he might take her she came forward and climbed into the boat, looking up at him wide-eyed and feeling entirely bereft of free will.

The sail, once raised, immediately filled with the off-shore night breeze and the tiny dinghy moved smoothly forward into the night waters of the lagoon.

Looking round she saw, not without a pang of disappointment, that he was returning her to the yacht. Looking back she saw him pointing into the moon silvered waters. 'Shark!' he said. 'Dangerous to swim.'

Suddenly terrified Helen gazed down into the clear waters which she now saw as filled with menace. 'Sharks?' she asked the man, hollow voiced, and then swallowed hard as she saw him nod. Aware that only thin wooden planks separated her from a nightmare, she wished away the distance between the frail craft and the safety of the yacht.

As that extravagant craft loomed larger she saw this return as almost a metaphor for her own state of mind. Out here, distanced from civilisation, was a primitive and savage world while the yacht now took on the aspect of sanctuary and safety. Only her stomach quelled at the price she might be expected to pay for re-admission.

When the boat nudged gently against the lowered gangway of the yacht she scrambled for it half expecting the manacing shark to leap up in the tiny gap between the bobbing dinghy and the gangway. So intent was she to put distance between her and the monsters of the deep that by the time she turned to wish her mystery man farewell she saw his dinghy had already slid away and was headed for the gap in the reef.

She was startled to hear Jeffrey quietly calling to her and turning, saw him leaning anxiously over the rail just above her head. 'I was watching for you,' he said as he handed her up onto the decking. 'I meant to bring

486

a boat for you when you were ready to come back. Did you know a shark was spotted in the lagoon this afternoon?'

Staring at him her mind was doing loops. Was this to be the only question he was going to ask? 'You knew?' she countered. 'You knew and didn't tell me?'

'I didn't know until after you'd reached the beach. I was worried as hell that you might try to swim back.'

Knowing that Jeffrey must have seen the fisherman, she felt embarrassed. 'I'm sorry,' she murmured. 'What I did was an act of madness.'

'The swim in shark infested waters?' he asked.

She shook her head. 'Going at all. I'm sorry.'

Relieved to see the smile that lit his face, she went on. 'It's over now,' she murmured as she went gratefully into his welcoming arms.

'Not quite,' he murmured. 'There's still your forfeit to pay.'

487

Chapter Seventeen

*T*he discreet vibration of the ship in motion woke Helen. It was close to midday as she rose from the bed and drew back the blind that masked the long windows to look out onto the startling close passage of the water. Seeing the ocean at almost window level, and understanding that where she stood was actually below the sea level, reminded her of the shark in the lagoon, which changed her perception of the ocean from a thing of amorphous beauty into a viscous mass, masking the frightening savagery within its depths.

Pressing her head hard against the thick glass of the screening window she craned her head to look backwards, hoping to catch one last glimpse of the island but there was nothing to be seen but the swell of the ocean as the yacht carved its disdainful way forward. Just for a moment she felt uneasily undecided which of John Milton's titles might best express her feelings – was it 'Paradise Lost' or 'Paradise Regained'? Only the day would tell.

As she showered and dressed the intangible uneasiness she had felt on waking grew in her. There was a feeling of absence. Tsai had not come to attend her, she had seen nothing of Jeffrey and as she emerged onto the main deck she could almost imagine she was alone on the yacht. It was only the ever-attentive Korean stewards who welcomed her into the dining room that reassured her that the yacht had not become another *Marie Celeste.*

Having brought her a chilled, delicious melon, satayed prawns and a green salad she was still savouring the chilled, heavy white wine and craving coffee when a totally naked Tsai came padding silently to her side. 'You must come with me now,' the girl had spoken in a voice so soft it had been almost a sigh.

'Where?' she asked.

'I must prepare you for this evening.'

Tsai's use of the word 'prepare' left little doubt about what she was to be prepared for. With the promise of excitement came also the darker shadows of doubt. 'Where's Jeffrey?' she asked of the girl.

Tsai shook her head in a gesture that might have been meant to convey that she didn't know or had been instructed not to say. Suddenly the earlier expectation of coffee had become a craving along with an alien urge to smoke a cigarette – a habit she had only experimented with in her early teens and then, she imagined, dismissed from her life. Now it was back, searing her tongue and coating her throat, unsummoned from wherever childish impulses are consigned. The reason became apparent when she reached for the table bell that would summon the stewards, she saw her hand shaking. Excitement, like warmed molasses, had seeped into her blood and was causing her heart to race along with her mind. 'I want some coffee,' she told the waiting girl.

Tsai again shook her head. 'All the men crew have been sent below and must not come out again until tomorrow.'

This news caused a convulsive shudder to pass from head to toe and, standing, Helen looked around the ship even more aware of the 'absence' she had sensed earlier. While the yacht clipped smartly through the ocean there was no sign of the ever-attentive deck crews. Pausing, uneasily aware of the unique isolation surrounding her, she felt the welcome onrush of helplessness. Knowing she could do little to protest at whatever might be about to be done to her, rendered her guiltless. Standing there, Tsai anxiously awaiting her reaction, she realised the care with which she had been prepared for this moment. It was as if Jeffrey had known from the outset that she was going to be presented with this test and had gently accustomed her to accept it when the time came. She turned to look into Tsai's porcelain face and finally smiled her acceptance of that which she was now convinced was inevitable. 'Let's go,' she said.

Beaming with relief Tsai led the way from the dining room and down the stairway that led to the main stateroom deck. Confident that she was to be taken to her own cabin she was a little surprised when, at the base of the stairs, Tsai turned left instead of going straight on.

Tucked away, almost under the stairs, was another stateroom.

Opening the door Tsai stood aside to allow a now curious Helen to precede her.

Stepping into the darkened cabin the first word that came to Helen's mind was incongruity. The room was furnished more like a medieval chamber than a space on the modern hedonistic machine that was the yacht. Chains and leather lined every wall, while the whole was lit with what, at first, seemed guttering candles but turned out to be cleverly disguised flickering lamps. None of these accoutrements to bizarre pleasure took her eye like the more human element in the room. Strapped naked to a wooden cross was the yacht's owner – Martinez. His eyes, hugely rounded, were fixed on Helen as she stood staring at him but, she saw, his silence was explained by the leather thong that gagged his mouth.

Propelled forward by an instinct she recognised as having been instilled in her during her visit to Madame Victoria's, Helen came to stand immediately before the man with his deliciously desperate eyes. Between her and this man, with whom she had barely previously spoken, sprang an immediate affinity. The light sarong that was all she wore became constricting so, tugging at the knot that held the sarong, she loosened it and let it slip to the floor where Tsai immediately moved to pick it up. The widening of Martinez' eyes as he looked on her honey coloured body was all the goad she needed to go further.

Looking directly into his eyes her hands sought out his hardening flesh. 'Have you been whipped?' she heard her huskily toned voice ask and, when she saw his nodded reply, felt enveloped in an intensity of excitement that scorched her body and threatened her soul. Reaching forward she kissed his gagged mouth, then his throat. An explosive grunt escaped Martinez' constrained mouth as her lips sought out the matted hair on his chest and nipped affectionately at his nipples.

All consciousness of another world – even of her surroundings, and the excited, cautionary, protests of Tsai – fled from her mind as her hands gave him pleasure, so paying tribute to their companionship of pain. Even as she worked and teased she understood that once, before finding total freedom on the island, she would never have dared do this without Jeffrey's prior sanction and she was engulfed in a soaring sense of triumph.

Standing before this helpless man she was her own arbiter, with no need of excuse or alibi to explain her self-indulgence. This too, she appreciated, had been gifted her by Jeffrey, but what followed, as Martinez erupted convulsively into her manipulating hands, came, unheralded, from some dark resource of her own mind.

Carefully conserving and guarding every drop of him in her hands Helen rose and looking Martinez, squarely and without shame, directly into his eyes, offered up his cock's harvest to his lips. 'Clean them,' she told him. The act seemed to pleasure Martinez enormously. His eyes closed in sublime acceptance while his grunts were far from protests.

A kind of madness gripped Helen as shock-waves of arousal sought out every last nerve in her body. She trembled with excitement as she reminded herself that a man stood helpless, his eyes pleading for savagery. It was as if she could read his mind. How well she had been taught the joy of submission – of surrendering free-will to the whim of another. She knew that Martinez' mind would be racing with expectation, be willing the surprise and shock of her pain. His silent demands begged not to be disappointed. Still looking directly into his eyes she found herself wondering what avenue Martinez had come to this knowledge. She knew only too well her own guilt and her own needs and was, conversely, angered.

'Bring me a whip,' she murmured to the attendant Tsai.

For a moment Tsai hesitated and Helen knew the Chinese girl was about to protest but seeing Martinez' eyes lit with expectation she spoke again. 'Do it!' she insisted.

Tsai moved to the display of instruments pinned to the walls and, after a momentary pause, returned with a long pliable stick of many tails. The moment Helen's hands closed about the leather stem a surge of live power raced upwards from her closed fist to lay siege to her quaking body. At the same moment she was assailed by the knowledge that having come this far, having raised expectations, she must not disappoint and her confidence wavered. Needing sanction she spoke to Tsai. 'Loosen the gag,' she told the girl and was momentarily relieved of the oppression of his eyes, so full of pleading.

Gasping with the relief of his mouth's bondage Martinez smiled on Helen. 'You are so beautiful, mistress.'

The title, spoken so fervently, shocked Helen. Was that how he saw her? A dominant woman able to deal with him as she chose? Standing there she knew her eyes were filled with fire but her mind was full of doubts. She felt she was to be tested by this man far more than she had ever been with Jeffrey. For a moment she yearned for the simplicity of submission just as Martinez' eyes begged her now. She was to find the hesitation fatal as the doubts flooded in to quench the fires that had so recently been lit.

'I'm sorry,' she told Martinez. 'I cannot be your mistress.'

His eyes clouded with disappointment. Martinez pleaded, 'Please, mistress, I am helpless before you – you give me your pain.'

Turning away from the oppressive eyes, Helen shook her head. 'I cannot hurt you. I do not love you.'

A warm laugh startled Helen and, turning, she was in time to see Carla stepping through a door which had previously seemed merely a panel of mirror set into the wall. 'Well said!' Carla was smiling as she came forward to embrace the surprised Helen. 'Isn't it fortunate that I *do* love you?'

'Were you watching me?' Helen asked.

'Of course I was. Why else should I arrange your temptation?' Carla smiled. 'You fulfilled my every expectation. I have always maintained that the submissive will, given time, makes the best master. Jeffrey disagreed but you have proved me right and him wrong. Congratulations.'

'Jeffrey saw?'

'Everything!' cried Carla then, leaving Helen to absorb this, Carla's eye lighted on Tsai. 'You, however, have disappointed me. Why were my orders not carried out?'

As Tsai stood trembling and incoherent, Helen stepped forward. 'What "orders"?'

Carla turned to Helen, her eyes lit with delight. 'But your punishment, darling. Tonight I shall prove to you just how highly I regard you. We shall, all of us, hear your confessions and then pass judgement. Even Carlos,' Carla smiled, moving to stroke the helpless man's face. 'Won't you darling?' she asked before bringing a resounding slap to his cheek. 'Say you love me.'

'I love you,' murmured Martinez.

'Good!' Carla turned to Tsai. 'You will bring Helen before my tribunal at precisely seven tonight. She will be prepared as I ordered and you will also be required to present yourself as a penitent. I trust I am understood?'

Tsai dipped her head and let out a sigh of acknowledgement as Carla, bestowing a dazzling smile on them all, swept from the room.

Looking to Tsai, Helen found herself shaking. Whether it was fear or excitement was impossible to know. Within her were two quite separate emotions which were equally difficult to recognise. There was only one thing of which she could be sure: Tonight, whatever was to happen, would resolve her emotional conflict one way or the other. Shivering, she felt the breath of change settling about her like the first of winter's chill.

Looking at the result of Tsai's skilful labours in the mirror Helen felt a little bewildered. After Carla's departure from the peculiarly exotic stateroom Tsai had indicated that they should complete Helen's preparation for the coming evening's events in her own stateroom, which was where they now stood.

Helen had imagined that her 'preparation' for Carla's

494

punishment would result in her being dressed in something fetishistic and submissive – leather and, possibly, chains. The exotic make-up Tsai had applied to her face had done nothing to diminish this expectation and so it was with some surprise that she now looked into the mirror and saw herself dressed in a crisp, white peasant blouse and a knee-length skirt which flounced out from the waist. Barefoot and bare-legged she looked like nothing so much as an Italian peasant girl about to attend a village dance.

'This is it?' she asked of Tsai.

Tsai nodded. 'It is Madame Carla's instructions precisely.'

It was unexpected but also, subtly exciting. She wore nothing but the blouse and the skirt and so, although presentable, she also felt deliciously vulnerable. Adjusting the top she saw how its cotton laced neckline could be loosened and simply pulled down to reveal her breasts while the skirt needed only to be lifted to leave her, essentially, naked.

Tsai, by contrast, looked severely formal in her white and gold oriental dress. Feeling her heart fluttering in her breast like an agitated live bird, Helen smiled. 'So . . .' she said, '. . . what happens next?'

'Mister Jeffrey will come to fetch you and escort you to the party,' Tsai hissed urgently. 'All the stewards are confined below so I must serve the evening meal.'

Remembering the veritable squad of stewards that normally attended the yacht's guests, Helen was surprised. 'All by yourself?'

With a secretive smile Tsai beamed, 'Not by myself alone. I shall have a French maid to assist me.'

Judging from the delighted light in Tsai's eye Helen was able to judge that the 'French maid' was also to be something of a surprise. Turning to look at the healthy 'peasant' girl in the mirror she could also see that, thankfully, it was not to be her. 'Do we have a 'French maid' on board?' she asked.

'Oh yes!' hissed an excited Tsai.

Sensing there were other intriguing elements yet to be revealed about the forthcoming night, Helen was about to insist on being told more about them when the stateroom door opened and a Caribbean pirate entered!

It took a moment for Helen to absorb that the tall figure dressed in an elaborately ruffled shirt, a thick black leather belt securing his wide-bottomed black trousers tucked into knee-high, wide topped black boots, was Jeffrey, his face half disguised by the eye patch he wore over his left eye.

He looked magnificently threatening and Helen felt a comprehensive rush of excitement in looking at him.

Jeffrey dismissed Tsai from the room with a gesture and then turned to the trembling Helen who, nervously excited, attempted to cover her rising excitement with an essayed humour. 'I might have guessed it was to be fancy dress,' she said on a nervous laugh.

Still silent, Jeffrey stood, hands on hips, in theatrical parody of a pantomime pirate but his voice bore no trace of humour as he spoke. 'Bare your breasts,' he told her.

Trembling with excitement at this peremptory order Helen challengingly held Jeffrey's gaze as she reached first one hand and then the other to slowly draw the crisp cotton top down to her waist. As she did so she realised that the half sleeves restricted her arm movement, so imposing a subtle bondage to the action. Her breasts naked, she squared her shoulders to present herself more flatteringly to his eyes, all the while looking challengingly to Jeffrey. The memory of everything this man had taught her to enjoy – things no other man had ever dared hint at – flooded in on her. All the dominant conflicts she had experienced standing before the helpless, submissive, Martinez fled before her overwhelming excitement at recovering the experience of surrender to Jeffrey.

His next words confirmed her most delightful fantasy. 'On your knees,' he said, his voice sure and certain.

Careful to flounce out the skirt to its fullest, Helen sank gracefully to her knees before the figure of the man her racing mind told her was, truly, a pirate confronting a captive princess. Raising her eyes to his as he came forward to stand over her kneeling, bare-breasted figure, she, unasked, raised her hands to place them on her head – a gesture which indicated her total submission while, at the same time, she was consciously aware that it presented her breasts even more prominently.

'I had almost forgotten how beautiful you are,' he told her, his words flushing away any last residual restraint she might have nurtured.

'I am what you want me to be,' she murmured, feeling the anguish of their locked eyes.

Jeffrey smiled and came forward to take her head in his hand and press it against the groin of his trousers where her cheek felt his excitement already stirring. 'You couldn't possibly know what I want of you,' he said through an excitement slurred throat.

'Anything,' she pledged urgently.

'Remember that,' he said, 'because tonight may be difficult for you.'

Moving her head so that she could look up at him towering over her, she whispered, 'If you're there, nothing is going to be "difficult" and nothing . . .' she added, '. . . impossible.'

His face wreathed in a delighted smile, Jeffrey reached down to gently raise her from her kneeling position to stand expectantly before him. 'It's almost a shame to share you while I'm feeling like this. It seems ages since we last made love.' As he spoke he carefully rearranged the peasant blouse to cover her breasts.

Emboldened by this implicit declaration of love, she smiled. 'Is that what's to be done with me tonight? Am I to be "made love" to?' The flicker of doubt crossing

497

his face only increased her excitement. 'I was led to believe I was to be punished.'

'Do you deserve to be punished?' Jeffrey asked.

Helen felt a lava-like rush of heat which emerged from her throat in one word. 'Terribly,' she murmured.

His voice throbbing, he asked, 'And you're mine?'

With a curious feeling that she, though dedicating herself to his will, had the initiative, she nodded before challenging him directly. 'I ask only that you don't disappoint me,' she murmured.

Helen watched him struggle between an obvious desire to take her where they stood and the promise of the unknown night ahead, before reluctantly and resignedly deciding to honour their hosts. 'They're waiting for us,' he said, ushering her to the door.

Together they moved silently through the curiously quiet, but vibrantly alive ship, mounted the stairs until they stood together for a moment on the threshold of the dining salon. From inside came the sound of sonorous music as Jeffrey took her by the shoulders and turned her wide eyes towards him.

'Whatever happens tonight,' he said, 'remember I love you.'

His words encompassed her soul with the warm glow of security and the certain knowledge that tonight they would be making memories that would last them a lifetime. As they came into the dining salon she felt invulnerable. Nothing could harm her now.

Chapter Eighteen

*H*elen stepped into the heady atmosphere of the candle-lit salon to be immediately confronted by the turned back of a towering French maid. Standing over six foot in seven-inch high heels, it wasn't until the startling apparition turned towards her in greeting that she discerned, somewhere under layers of make-up and sweeping fake eyelashes and moustache, the more familiar shape of Martinez. With the shade of Lesley rearing before her it was some moments before she understood she was being offered a glass of champagne from the silver tray in the 'maid's' hand. Taking the offered glass and almost laughing out loud at the 'maid's' wobbly attempt at a curtsey, Martinez' bulk moved aside to reveal the much more sobering figure of Carla.

Her rounded figure was emphasised by a red and green leather basque drawn about an incredibly small waist from which stemmed rounded hips and thighs, making her legs incredibly long. A high leather collar about her throat was ablaze with an encrustation of diamonds and emeralds which seemed to dazzle in the candlelight as the devastating figure swayed forward to greet them. She was almost on them before Helen quailed at the sight of the riding crop which Carla was playfully slapping into the open palm of one hand.

'Jeffrey!' she mewed. 'You look so authentic! Absolutely terrifying!'

Helen might have used the same adjective to describe Carla as the famous eyes centred on her. 'And Helen! You look ravishing, my dear. Almost good enough to eat!'

As they exchanged cheek kisses Helen saw over Carla's shoulder the grinning figure of Qito, dressed in a vaguely Middle Eastern robe and turban that might have been meant to present him as a simulated sultan or as if he had been caught on his way to take a bath. Qito was there to take her hand to his lips the moment she was freed of Carla's embrace. 'Tonight is to be the first viewing of our collaboration,' Qito told her.

Having all but forgotten the real point of their isolation on the island, Helen's interest immediately quickened. 'I hope you're not disappointed?' she asked as he led her towards an easel which was still covered with a shroud of canvas. 'Can I take a peek?'

Qito shook his head. 'Later,' he said. 'For the moment we must not detract from Carla.'

Looking round, Helen saw that Carla had assumed proprietorial rights over Jeffrey and was standing, arm in arm with him, talking to a flamboyant parody of Carmen Miranda, complete with fruit bowl head-dress!

Momentarily unable to discern who might be under this extravagant disguise she turned to ask Qito.

'Jimmy!' he cried with delight. 'Don't tell me you've forgotten Carla's ever-present little hairdresser.'

'He makes a very authentic woman,' said Helen, adding, without thinking, 'Is he gay?'

Qito laughed. 'He's whatever Carla wants him to be.' Qito pulled her into a confidential whisper. 'I'm planning to throw him overboard later tonight and I'm counting on your assistance.'

At that moment they were distracted by the raised

voice of Tsai. Helen turned to see the diminutive Tsai shrilly berating the 'French maid' who had, it seemed, tottered once too often on his high heels and spilled a tray of drinks. 'Stupid!' Tsai was yelling at the trembling man who stood at least a foot higher than Tsai. 'You are a very stupid maid and, if that happens again, I shall have to beat you most severely!'

Martinez had dropped to his knees before the seemingly furious Tsai and was begging her forgiveness as Helen turned to Qito. 'Can Tsai talk to him like that?'

'Tsai occupies a very special place on this boat. Tonight she speaks for Carla.'

There was a sudden explosion of energy from the direction of 'Carmen Miranda'. Jimmy was suddenly on his feet, waving his hips in an impersonation of the forties Latin singer/dancer, and, noisily rattling maracas, danced around the still kneeling Martinez singing one of Carmen Miranda's best known songs. 'Aye-aye-aye I like you very much . . .' while Carla, joining in, added an incredible sexuality to the scene.

It was just then that Helen caught sight of Jeffrey's eyes. He had taken a chair, his long leather boots crossed one over the other while his stare was fixed, eyes soft and unsmiling, on Carla in her fetishistic costume. The message in his eyes struck home to Helen with a clarity she found startling. Jeffrey, unguarded, wore the expression of a puppy being teased with a chocolate biscuit! That the 'biscuit' was Carla and not herself sent a stab of jealousy racing through her. Propelled forward by a determination to claim those eyes for herself, she came to stand directly before Jeffrey. As he looked on her, smiling, she spoke. 'Do you want her?' she asked.

'Carla?' he mused, as if he thought she might have meant 'Carmen Miranda'.

Nodding, Helen could only wonder why she was provoking a situation she wasn't sure she could handle. Was it possible she could extend her masochism to

501

encompass watching Jeffrey with Carla? She wasn't sure. All she knew was that it was important that his eyes were on her and not Carla. Aware that she had placed herself in a ridiculous position she was grateful when, still sitting, he gestured her forward.

'Come here,' murmured Jeffrey.

Standing over him, acutely conscious that he could no longer see the display behind her, she thrilled to feel his hands running up under her skirt to caress her thighs. 'There are many beautiful, highly desirable, women in the world and Carla is one of them. A man would have to be dead not to respond to her but he would have to be a fool not to know what is truly important – and *you* are important to me.'

Helen was still trying to frame a response while cursing herself for the weakness his caressing hands were inducing in her, when she heard Carla's voice ringing out above the music. 'The painting, everybody, is about to be unveiled!'

'We'll talk later,' Jeffrey murmured as, standing, he put his arm about her waist and led her to the veiled canvas.

Carla's flaring eyes fixed on Helen in a way that caused her stomach to quell. 'We are privileged to be the first to see Qito's latest *oeuvre* – a work he has told me he considers among his best to date and, of course, inspired by the lovely Helen.'

The words, while sounding like compliments, carried, to Helen, a sub-text of threat in which she found a curious satisfaction.

'And here it is,' said Carla, dramatically throwing back the cover to reveal the canvas.

For a moment there was a stunned silence. Glowing out of the canvas was a riot of colour which momentarily stunned the senses and obscured the central figure of a woman, eyes wild and threatening as if proclaiming herself to be a creature of this world but somehow above it, challenging onlookers to gaze any-

502

where but at her eyes. The power Qito had created from colours and canvas was astonishing. This feral woman was both beautiful and terrifying.

'Great God!' cried Jeffrey into the silence. 'She is beautiful!'

Startled that Jeffrey should have spoken of her as if in the third person, Helen looked to see that he was transfixed by her image in precisely the same manner she had resented when he had, earlier, looked on Carla. There was a message in this but, for the moment, she found it difficult to decode from her own internal tumult.

As cries of congratulation and applause broke out Helen turned back to see that Carla had come to stand directly before her. 'Congratulations,' Carla smiled as she leaned forward and cupped Helen's chin in her hand to place an open-mouthed kiss on her lips. Leaning back Carla looked directly into Helen's startled eyes. 'Any woman that can inspire Qito as you did deserves our thanks, but should also remember that those that play with the gods play a dangerous game. The world may see a creative work of genius wrought from paints and canvas but I see a tribute of love from my man to another woman. Such aspiration has a terrible price.' So saying, Carla released her hold on Helen's chin and turned away to join the small group, Jeffrey among them, about the easel.

Qito came to Helen's side. 'Did I do you justice?' he asked.

Astonished to find tears welling, Helen turned to him and put her arms about his neck. 'Carla hates me,' she blurted into his ear.

'Nonsense! That is simply a measure of how much she loves you,' Qito murmured back into her ear.

'I don't understand that,' Helen told him as she straightened from him.

'You will,' promised Qito.

Carla's voice rang out. 'Let's now enjoy our buffet supper!' she was saying.

As Qito, caught up in a flurry of congratulations, was carried towards the buffet table, Helen was left standing alone floundering in a quandary of confusion, to which Qito's image of her only added. Jeffrey had unequivocally declared his love yet Carla's kiss still burned on her lips reviving memories of how totally she had surrendered to her in the 'scene' with Tsai. She had earlier that day been tempted to dominate the willing Martinez and yet had melted into submission before Jeffrey. This flood of confusing signals left her feeling uncertain as to who or what she really was. When she told Qito she didn't understand she had, she now realised, been voicing an uncertainty which went far beyond a simple response to her present dilemma. Remembering Qito's last words: 'You will,' she fervently hoped she might.

Jeffrey's voice, close in her ear, startled her from her own internal debate. 'Let's talk,' he said and taking her arm led her from the dining room onto the deck.

The warm, balmy air, stirring only lethargically in the night's breeze, calmed her as they paced the deck to come to look out over the swell of the ocean, silvered in the moonlight.

'The canvas is extraordinary,' Jeffrey was saying. 'Incredibly lyrical – totally unlike anything Qito has done before.'

With Jeffrey's words fluttering about her ears with the irrelevance of a moth about a flame, Helen found far more urgent topics to discuss. 'Do you really love me?' she asked. 'After all that I've done can you forgive me?'

'What *did* you do?' asked Jeffrey lightly. 'React impetuously to what Annabel told you? I can forgive that. I even find it a little flattering.'

'Flattering?'

504

'Yes. After all it does show your feelings for me run deeper than just a passing affair.'

Surprised to hear that he hadn't yet appreciated that, Helen mused: 'I thought I'd already adequately demonstrated that . . .'

As he turned to her she rejoiced to see his eyes lit with pleasure. 'I had hoped so,' he murmured as he reached out to embrace her.

Nestling against his chest Helen had never felt more safe in her life. Out of grief she had stumbled a rocky, sometimes shocking road but now felt she had come safe home to harbour. Raising her head she invited a kiss which Jeffrey greedily accepted. Afterwards, they stayed close in each other's arms and allowed their mutual pleasure the silence it deserved until Jeffrey spoke – his voice so soft and quiet that she had to strain to hear him above the soughing sea sounds around them.

'When I was very small . . .' he murmured '. . . my parents took me on holiday with them to the Lake District. I can't remember a single thing about it except, on the drive back to London, they stopped off at a pub. I stayed in the back of the car half asleep until my mother came out to bring me a drink – probably orange juice or Coke, I don't remember – but the one thing I do remember is the sandwich she gave me. It was delicious. Cheese – no pickle – but that taste stayed on my palate for years. Even after college, even when my father died, I still remembered that sandwich.'

When Jeffrey broke off Helen looked at him and saw that he was deeply moved. She waited, sure he was about to confess something extremely important.

'It was the cheese, you see? Strong and tangy. It was the most delicious thing I'd ever tasted and I spent years trying to rediscover it. I must have tried almost every cheese there was in the world but the closest I ever came to it was a mature Cheddar. I searched every cheesemonger in London and everywhere I went trying

505

to find that elusive something. I got close, but never quite found "it". There was something missing, you see? Something about that sandwich I had yet to identify.'

Jeffrey paused again while Helen listened, willing him to come to the point and desperately hoping that when he did she would understand why the telling of this anecdote was so important to him.

'Then one day – quite by accident – I found it! There, singing on my palate was the taste I had remembered since I was four years old. Do you know what it was that I had been missing all those years?'

Helen remained silent as Jeffrey went on. 'A slice of onion!' Jeffrey cried triumphantly. 'For years I had tried all those variations of cheese and eaten onions but it had never occurred to me to put them together into the same sandwich! You see? Two very ordinary elements, under my nose for years yet only when they came together did I realise they constituted something I had searched high and low to find. It was magical. I was four years old again, half asleep in the back of my father's car. Do you understand what I'm saying?'

Bewildered, Helen shook her head.

'I'm saying that you can spend your life looking for something – a smile, a light in someone's eyes, a voice or accent, and, somehow, although it may be close to what you are searching for, it isn't exactly what you want. Then, one day, someone comes along who just happens to mix two ordinary enough elements to make a dream come true. Now do you understand what I'm trying to say?'

'I think you're saying that I'm the onion in your cheese sandwich . . . ?'

'Exactly!' cried Jeffrey triumphantly. 'You are beautiful, intelligent and charming – but I've known all those qualities in other women. You bring something else – something elusive but not frightening or dauntingly other-worldly. Something unique that I can cherish. I

506

saw it tonight, defined for me by Qito's canvas. Seeing you through his eyes I have no doubts. I love you,' he added simply. 'Is that enough?'

Renewing their kiss, Helen felt suddenly appalled at ever having mistrusted him, but equally there arose in her a furious need to be purged of this new guilt. 'Jeffrey, there are things I have to tell you . . .'

Smiling, Jeffrey nuzzled her face. 'And you are going to,' he murmured. 'But I haven't forgotten you asked me not to "disappoint" you.'

Her loins suddenly in convulsion, Helen wondered at the shift Jeffrey could effect in her emotions. With barely a change of tone or even inflection he had wrenched her from the warm glow of affectionate embrace into quivering submission. Involuntarily, her arms had dropped from his, her back straightened and, as she looked into his still warm eyes, she felt her loins heating. She cursed her quavering voice as she spoke. 'You don't know every stupid thing I did.'

'Do I need to know?' he asked with quiet firmness.

'*I* need you to know,' she answered.

Nodding, Jeffrey moved away a pace before turning back to her. 'Do you love me?' he asked.

Helen nodded.

'Do you believe I love you?' he insisted.

Her throat, constricted with rising excitement, would only permit her to nod in reply.

'Bare your breasts,' he said in a voice so low that it was almost lost in the quiet sigh of the sea breeze.

Excitedly mute, she reached one quivering hand to her right shoulder to pull down the laced top while raising an elbow and awkwardly freeing it. Her eyes, blurred but firm, remained on his while she repeated the movement to her left side, then, her arms freed, she drew the blouse down, flinching at this tight bodice top flicked against her engorged nipples. Drawing back her shoulders to make better display of herself she stood in silent challenge.

507

There was a tiny dull clink of metal as Jeffrey came forward and caught up her wrists. Glancing down she saw a handcuff clicking about one wrist and only then raised her eyes to his, half expecting that he would now turn her and so pinion her wrists behind her. As always Jeffrey was to surprise her. Instead, she found herself facing the ship's rail and looking out at the silvered sea glistening under a huge tropical moon.

With one swift movement Jeffrey had hooked the other cuff about her wrists with the ship's rail in between. Tethered to the rail, she could not fully straighten, and as if following some natural law, found herself most comfortable by leaning slightly forward and resting her fore-arms on the varnished wooden rail, a posture which a distant observer might think of as simply relaxed but, to her just then, was the most exquisite form of bondage she could imagine.

When Jeffrey moved behind her she found she could no longer comfortably turn her head to watch him. When he came to embrace her, pressing himself hard against her, she gasped with urgent need of him to take her there and then. When his hands closed round her to cup her breasts and tease her raging nipples she gasped out her demands in the coarsest words she could summon.

'Not quite yet!' Jeffrey muttered through teeth clenched tight with excitement. 'You don't get off that lightly!'

Her heart racing, her breathing so deep it caused her bared torso to convulse, she cried out in frustration as his hands sought out the hem of the full skirt and drew it with agonising slowness up her thighs to be finally tucked into the waistband of the skirt, leaving her naked from the waist down. 'Please!' she begged as her libido threatened to go into overload. 'For pity's sake take me!'

Jeffrey's voice was close and insistent in her ear. 'Have no fear,' he murmured, 'you are going to be ravished, and much more besides – but at a time, and by persons, of my choosing.'

'No!' she screamed. 'I want *you! Now!*'

His chuckle all but sent her into instant spasm. 'Do you really think you're in any position to make demands?' he asked, his hands caressing her as, her questing loins finding him pressing hard against her, she again sobbed out her need.

'All pleasure must be paid for. Pleasure past and pleasure to come, both carry incredibly high price tags – and I would hate to *disappoint* you.'

Abruptly, Jeffrey stepped back from his tight embrace and her heated loins struck chill even against the sultry night air. Her mouth was already open – readying yet another plea – when his bare hand struck firmly against her exposed buttocks. The sting of the blow stayed in the one small area for only a moment before its heat flooded through her hungry body and all but consumed her. 'Yes!' she cried out across the empty ocean.

In answer his hand came down again – three more times in rapid succession – before he spoke. 'Tell me about your lover on the beach. Was he beautiful?'

Helen tried to force her mind to think – to concentrate – on what she might say, how best to say it, but she was in such confusion that only the truth seemed to have any validity. 'Yes!' she yelled defiantly.

Three sharp stinging slaps of his hand followed in quick succession and she rejoiced that the currency of her guilt was now established.

'Tell me everything,' Jeffrey insisted into her ear.

'Yes!' she cried. 'He would appear – just be there – at night . . .' She broke off as she received three more rapid slaps. Her breath now difficult to control, she went on. 'He was brutal, we never made love – we just screwed!'

The slaps this time stung as her already roused flesh became more sensitive with each successive blow.

'He was huge – his cock was enormous . . .'

509

Slap – slap – slap.

'He would tease me with it. Hold back and then plunge so deep he would hurt me!'

Jeffrey's hand rose and fell and he was forced to put his free hand out to grip her tightly as her body sought to escape the implacable rise and fall of his hand.

Recovering, grateful when he left his hand resting on her inflamed flesh and drew away the heated pain, she gasped: 'Then he would make me wait. Make me beg. I loved it! I loved his savage pain!'

This outburst earned her six blows and it took her a moment to recover before inviting more of his punishment. 'But when he came he would pull out. He would never come in me – never let me feel everything!'

Three more, the more intense yet, seared into her convulsing flesh.

'His hot sperm would shoot on my belly, on my breasts and into my mouth . . .'

Wildly out of control Helen could feel only the heat of the blows which now rained down in quick succession. As each landed she heard herself greeting it exultantly and demanding more – and harder.

'And you . . . ?' asked Jeffrey. 'Did you come?'

'Yes! Gloriously! Wonderfully!'

'Like this?' he demanded as his probing fingers first spread her and then plunged deeply into her, all but lifting her off her feet.

'Yes!' she screamed in defiance.

Jeffrey's probing became more violent, more vicious and for one distracted moment she thought he might be about to plunge his entire bunched fist into her.

Instead, as she writhed on the fleshy spike he had made of his fingers, he reached with one finger of his other hand and expertly sought out her risen fleshy rosebud. His touch was like that of a trigger to a detonator. Totally out of control, uncaring who heard, she proclaimed her orgasm in a scream that went forth like sheet lightning into the calm blackness of the night.

Her knees buckling to come into painful contact with the lower rung of the deck rail, she recovered in time to realise that Jeffrey was moving away and leaving her there. 'No!' she called out desperately. 'Don't leave me here! Not like this!' Twisting herself awkwardly against the rail she could see him stepping from the deck into the saloon. 'There's more!' she called vainly into the night.

By turning herself to stand, still firmly pinioned by the wrists, the other way, she found she could follow Jeffrey's progress as he made his way through to the library where she saw Carla rising from a couch to greet him. She could hear nothing of what was said through the thick armoured glass of the deck windows and could only guess that they were discussing her. Seeing Carla's laugh and quick embrace of Jeffrey only increased her feeling of isolation and vulnerability. His chastisement had excited her beyond measure and the fire of it, though dampened by his absence, still worried away at her hungry loins. When she saw Carla, magnificent still in her fetishistic leathers, move to leave the library she knew immediately where she would next appear.

She was not to be disappointed. Carla stepped out onto the deck and came towards the quelling Helen, smiling and making deliberate display of the riding crop laid across one open palm. 'Well now . . .' mused Carla '. . . it seems this is my turn.'

Biting back an urge to plead, Helen stared fixedly into Carla's dancing eyes. 'Face front!' Carla suddenly snapped, adding as Helen turned to obey by staring out into the moonlit sea, 'Spread your legs!'

Immediately, helplessly, liquid, Helen did as she was ordered and mentally braced herself for a sterner test than any Jeffrey had inflicted.

'Four days, was it?' Carla asked so quietly that she might almost have been speaking only to herself. 'Four days and three nights? Is that the sum of the time you spent alone with my husband?'

Helen, unable to do more, nodded then flinched as she felt the first of Carla's contacts. Expecting a cut from the whip it took her a moment to realise that what she felt was merely Carla's hand reaching out to caress her inflamed flesh.

'And, in that time, how many times did you screw him?'

'None! We never did anything on the island.'

'Too busy with your fisherman, then?' asked Carla.

'Yes! He exhausted me.'

'And you never gave a thought to what Qito might be feeling?'

'I did. Yes, I did, but he was too intent on his work. He's a serious man. He took me there to paint and that's all he did.'

Ignoring the last of her answer Carla insisted she concentrate on what, to her, was the most important business at hand. 'So he never thought about you as a woman – what about you? Did you not want him between your greedy legs?'

For a moment Helen, remembering the one moment when she had invited Qito to respond to her, hesitated. To answer truthfully she knew would invite pain against which she had no defence. When Carla, impatient for an answer, cut a stinging blow aimed with expert evenness across both buttocks, she cried out. 'Yes! I wanted him. I wanted him to fuck me!'

Carla's voice sounded almost affectionate. 'The truth at last!' she murmured triumphantly. 'Tell me, could you love him?'

'I admire him. I could worship him. I don't know if I could love him.'

'And me?' asked Carla.

The inference of the question escaped Helen for one startled moment and even more when Carla reached out and, cupping her face in one strong hand, turned her head to face directly into her own. 'Could you love me?' she breathed so close that Helen felt the sting of her breath against her opened mouth.

'Yes,' she murmured, astonished at her own realisation.

Carla's lips opened to reveal strong white teeth set into a beatific smile. 'And what more do you have to tell me about you and Qito?'

Trembling in the face of Carla's relentless pressure Helen reached for the truth as if it were a lifeline. 'I sucked his cock,' she murmured quietly. 'I had to. Jeffrey was there and told me to.'

Still close, Carla's smile became even more serpentine. 'What a good little girl you are,' she hissed. 'So young and beautiful – and *so* obedient!'

Breaking from the intimate closeness Carla stepped back a pace and Helen, bracing herself, faced forward once more to look on the placid swelling of the passing sea.

'What do you suppose happens to "good little girls" who indulge themselves at another woman's expense?' Carla asked.

'I don't know,' breathed Helen.

'Yes you do,' Carla insisted. 'They get punished, don't they?'

Eyes closed, Helen waited unable to bring herself to beg for what she knew was inevitable. 'Answer me,' snapped Carla.

'Yes!' screamed Helen.

Carla's tone was immediately conciliatory. 'Of course they do,' she said with satisfaction. 'Now you will have to help me . . .' She paused as Helen urged her outraged brain to ignore the searing heat at her buttocks and prepare to make answer to Carla. 'I was always so terrible at arithmetic,' Carla was saying. 'Let me see . . . you did say it was *four* days to which must be added three nights – which, of course, count double. How many does that make? Four, three and three?'

513

'Ten,' managed Helen through gritted teeth.

'Ten?' asked Carla as if savouring the number on her palate. 'Plus an allowance of, shall we say, *five* for your unfortunate lapse into enforced fellatio? Would you think that fair?'

With a flare of spirited defiance Helen snapped back, 'You're going to do it anyway so why don't you just get on with it?'

Delighted, and after a carefully judged intimidatory pause, Carla asked, 'How many does that make in total?'

The tension on Helen's expectant body caused a shuddering rebellion to sweep through her and setting her teeth she gave no reply. 'Well,' Carla sighed. 'If you're not prepared to help me with the calculations I shall just have to guess when to stop.' Pausing again as if waiting for an answer which, defiantly, never came, Carla went on. 'I intend that you shall have your punishment in groups of five. After each group there will be a pause during which you may recover and then, after thanking me for my indulgence, ask me to proceed. Do you understand?'

With Carla's hand lovingly caressing her buttocks and her entire body visibly shaking, Helen could not force any reply from between her tight-set teeth.

'I'm waiting,' murmured Carla.

With flaring anger at this tormenting wait, Helen spat out, 'For what?'

'Your permission to begin, of course!'

Her voice wild, Helen snarled: 'Bitch!' only to hear the cry becoming a wailing scream as, without pause or pity, the lash descended. The first five strokes were so swiftly given that they overwhelmed her brain, taking away Helen's power to voice her indignation. As the heat spread across her buttocks Carla's cooling hand, placed caressingly on her, felt like a benevolence.

Head bent, each sobbing breath drawn noisily through flaring nostrils, Helen fought for control as her

514

brain raced to rationalise what was being done to her. Yes, she had behaved foolishly towards Jeffrey and welcomed his punishment as a purging of sin. But what of Carla? What hurt had she inflicted on her? So why then should she submit to this punishment? The only possible answer was in Carla's pleasure. For some reason this sent Helen's daunted spirits flying. She had wanted Qito's pleasure for his fame and to make a memory. She was astonished to find she wanted Carla's pain for the same reason.

'Well?' insisted Carla.

Raising her fallen head from her chest Helen took a deep breath and knew the response expected of her. 'I thank you for your indulgence and am ready to receive more.'

'Well said!' called a delighted Carla and into the grim and painful interval that followed she allowed only Helen's anguished voice to be heard.

Once more bowed into recovery Helen was startled to hear Carla speak. 'Ah! I see we have attracted an audience!'

Raising her head, Helen turned to see that Jeffrey, surrounded by the ludicrous 'Carmen Miranda' figure and Martinez, had, drinks in hand, come to see the 'show'. Only Qito was absent.

Deluged with humiliation, Helen sought out Jeffrey's eyes. Smiling, he came forward and, taking her chin delicately in his hand, placed a light kiss on her lips. 'Be brave, my darling,' he told her before turning away from the plea in her eyes.

From behind the assembled group came Tsai, eyes on Helen before turning to Carla. 'Let me take her punishment,' said the girl.

'How delightful!' cried Carla. 'That you should, on so short an acquaintance, be willing to sacrifice yourself.' Carla paused. 'I leave the decision to you all,' she said. 'Shall Tsai be whipped in Helen's place!'

The first to answer was Helen. 'No!' she screamed.

515

Carla's surprised eyes rounded on her. 'What do we have here? Can this truly be love at first sight? What more has a woman to give than that she should be whipped in another's place? Such nobility deserves reward.' Carla paused as if searching her mind for the one touch that would exquisitely fit the moment. Her eyes falling on the 'French maid' she beckoned Martinez forward. 'You may serve our noble friend with the sweetness of your tongue. On your knees before her!'

Martinez scrambled down onto his knees and worked his way through Helen's legs to kneel up, and like an excited puppy, reach with his fingers to spread Helen's labia and wait on Carla's orders.

'My pain combining with his pleasure – sweet and sour!' cried a delighted Carla, addressing herself to the anxious Tsai. 'Fitting, don't you think?'

Helen once more facing forward heard what sounded suspiciously like a sob from Tsai and, in confusion, wondered what was in the Chinese girl's mind. There was little time for further thought as Carla's voice rapped an order to Martinez. 'You may begin!' she told the kneeling man.

Helen flinched as his searching tongue probed deeply into her but even as the pleasure began she felt the barrage of five swift strokes scorch into her. Her knees giving way under her she, simultaneously, found a steadying grip about her loins from Martinez who still fervently delved for pleasure between her thighs, while she felt hands softer than Carla's, caress and soothe the fiery pain that marked her flesh. Realising the soothing hands must belong to Tsai she leaned forward and, giving herself up to the pleasure-sparks being struck at her loins, decided to get the remaining five strokes done with as soon as possible.

'Thank you, Carla, for your indulgences and I am now ready for more,' but even as she braced herself against the coming pain she heard Jeffrey intervene.

'How much has she had already?' he asked.

516

'Ten of fifteen.' Carla's voice was challenging.

Helen heard a slight shuffle of feet as people re-positioned themselves and wondered what was going on as she felt Jeffrey's hand on her as he examined the site of the thrashing. If Helen had hoped Jeffrey might be about to intervene his next words dashed all such hopes. 'You haven't cut her skin,' he said as if sur-prised. 'Truly an expert.'

'I aim to give satisfaction.' Carla's voice was filled with amusement. 'May I continue?'

Helen, straining for the sound of Jeffrey's voice as, remembering she had already recited her designated chantra, braced herself and cursed the pain that was her due until her eye caught something that, in that moment of trauma, seemed magical. Far out in the silvered night she saw a bright light bobbing on the water! For a moment she fantasised her beach lover sailing to her rescue but, as she strained to make out the boat marked by the light, she saw others appear, bobbing like so many fireflies on the swelling ocean. An armada coming to her rescue? Realising her mind was racing towards the fanciful she was brought abruptly back to the present by the smarting of the riding stick. Her voice raised in vain protest she found her eyes were staying open despite the pain, and fixed on those bobbing lights which seemed to be speeding closer. So intense was her concentration that she absorbed this final beating with ease.

Feeling the heat was soothed from her by Tsai's soft hands she became aware once more of the compensa-tory pleasures being fired by Martinez's tongue as he continued to work doggedly, even frenziedly, between her thighs.

Carla's voice jolted her back to the present. 'Well?' she demanded.

Ignoring her, Helen kept her eyes on the fishing boats which, for a moment, seemed to be speeding towards them side on, until she rationalised the distance

517

between them was being closed not by their motion but the speed of the yacht. Would they pass between them, she wondered. Would fishermen have binoculars or telescopes which, even now, might be fixed on her? Memories of her adolescent Peeping Tom flooded in on her as she pulled her torso upright and prepared herself for the combination of whatever was to come next and the fishermen's eyes.

Jimmy's voice screeched out in sudden surprise. 'Hey, look! There's a fishing fleet out there! We're going right through them!'

Helen smiled to herself as she imagined her own recent thoughts now flooding through Jeffrey's mind. 'Well?' she demanded over her shoulder. 'What are you waiting for?'

Her defiance received quick answer as she heard Jeffrey demand that he be given the riding crop. 'Turn her!' he snapped and it was Jimmy, having discarded his ludicrous fruit bowl head-dress, that came forward with the key to the handcuffs and, leaning over the rail, unlocked them.

Turned, Helen found herself looking directly into Jeffrey's livid face and had no doubt about his intention as he murmured an angry: 'Bitch!' into her boldly challenging face. 'Hands on your head,' he told her.

With as much dignity as she could muster Helen slowly raised her hands and with infinite care, placed them on her head while at the same time impudently thrusting her breasts forward from the waist so that they reached to the tip of the stick. Her eyes alight she made plain that she was daring him to do his worst.

Jeffrey seemed to hesitate. 'Those boats are very close now,' he murmured. 'So you suppose "he" is out there and can see you?'

'I hope so,' Helen replied, her defiant spirit soaring.

'Hold her upright!' Jeffrey ordered, and Helen felt Martinez rising from his kneeling position to take her about the waist and pull her hard against his own

518

body. She had barely time to register that Martinez was pressing his own full arousal against her before all such thoughts were driven away by the resulting four stripes of the crop. Summoning every last ounce of will that could be scavenged from her outraged body, she raised her head and as Martinez' hold on her relaxed, smiled directly into Jeffrey's dumbfounded face. 'Thank you,' she said keeping her voice firm and managed.

Jeffrey hesitated a moment, seemingly disconcerted by her response before reaching forward to catch her, lifting her into his arms and carrying her like a bride swiftly from the scene.

Down through the boat and directly into the state-room Helen found herself being unceremoniously dumped on the bed. Resentfully she tried getting up into a sitting position, her bottom still on fire. 'Bastard!' she screamed at him.

Jeffrey, his 'pirate' costume thrown to the four corners of the cabin, advanced on her, furiously aroused. 'Slut!' he seethed as he caught her up, spread her and penetrated her as she continued to scream protest while pummelling the solidity of his heaving body with her closed fists.

Silencing her with a hand across her mouth, Jeffrey spat his words into her face. 'I've "marked" you! You're mine! Understand? Nobody else's!'

Despite her rising orgasm Helen managed to keep her anger going even when it was obvious to them both that it had been reduced to pretence. Rising to meet his every cruel thrust, she greeted his aggression just as she had welcomed the expiation of Carla's whip. Nothing mattered but the combustion at their thighs. When Jeffrey explosively exhausted himself she moaned in protest. The fires dampened, they lay in each other's arms, recovering their breath and knowing that they had in each other a relationship fired in the kiln of forgiveness.

They lay in astonished silence for some moments,

listening to each other's breathing, until, driven by an urgent need for full confession Helen thought of the in-flight episode of which she had yet to tell Jeffrey.

'There's something more you have to know before you forgive me . . .'

Jeffrey raised himself slightly on the bed and looked tenderly down into her widened, apprehensive eyes. 'There's nothing more I need to know,' he murmured. 'Nothing! Except . . .'

'What?'

'Do you want to be with me?'

'Yes,' she said.

'Permanently?' he insisted.

'Yes.'

Chapter Nineteen

A blast from a car horn half roused Helen from a deep velvety sleep and, annoyed at the intrusion of traffic, she had turned over to return to it when realisation dawned. A car horn? In the middle of the ocean?

Instantly alert she sat up, noted Jeffrey's absence, and going to the long side window opened the slatted blinds to find herself looking at the feet of people passing along a quayside. They were in harbour!

Excited to know just where they might have fetched up she would have hurried on deck to find out, but first there were urgent preliminaries to be taken care of in the bathroom.

It was there she caught a vision of herself in the mirror.

The sight of her battle 'honours' brought about an ineffable surge of energy. Filled with the need to share her excitement with Jeffrey she positively raced into the shower then dried herself, wincing as the towel passed over her bruised buttocks, brushed out her hair, grabbed up a sarong and was in the act of reaching for the stateroom door when it startled her by opening, seemingly, of its own will.

Looking up she saw a beaming Jeffrey standing. 'Great news,' he told her.

Feeling her entire body alive and open to experience she reacted sourly to his obvious excitement. 'Don't I get a good morning kiss?' she asked.

Smiling broadly he caught her up and their kiss added further fuel to the smoulder in her loins. Overwhelmed with an urgent need she took his hand intending to lead him to the bed, but he, infuriating her, pulled himself free. 'Don't you want to hear my "news"?'

'Can't I hear it later?'

'No. Now. We have to pack.'

'Where are we going?'

'Los Angeles,' he said, his excitement bursting forth. 'One of the investigators I hired has turned up a witness there.'

Helen became almost angry to have this reminder of her guilt thrust at her. Since meeting Jeffrey, especially since Paris, she had concentrated her anger and then guilt on him and their relationship. To be reminded of her previous, greater, guilt in the context of her lustful mood was enervating. 'Must you bring that up now?' she wailed sitting heavily on the bed and mourning the loss of her earlier mood.

'Absolutely!' cried Jeffrey. 'If half what my man reported is true it will change everything.'

Helen looked up at Jeffrey and felt a great gulf opening between them, just as she had over dinner that night in Paris. 'Do you want everything to change?' she asked.

'Not between us – of course not. What I want is to lift this burden of guilt from you.'

'And how will you do that?'

'By going to Los Angeles and talking to this man. He's a student at UCLA.'

'And what does he know about anything?'

'That's what I want you to hear. First hand. From him.' Taking her by the arm Jeffrey insisted she stand

522

up. 'We haven't much time. I've chartered a private jet that'll have us there in six hours. We're three hours ahead of them in time zone terms so, if you hurry, we'll be there in time to talk to him tonight.'

Looking at him Helen felt a sense of foreboding. Life had already cruelly demonstrated how one cruel trick of Nature could destroy an apparently seamless happiness and she feared any new intrusive element coming between her and Jeffrey. 'Do you think this really is a good idea?' she asked plaintively.

Normally excited by surprise, Helen, instead, felt sulkily depressed by this abrupt change of pace. Their goodbyes to those left behind on the yacht had been warm enough but Helen felt a deep sense of loss at leaving Qito and Carla and also the tearful Tsai. The luxuriously appointed interior of the aircraft had eight armchairs – they were far too grand to be described as 'seats' – grouped in two facing sets of four which the stewardess, not without a sly smile, indicated could be converted into two huge king-sized beds, then turned to demonstrate the video and music as if they were to be grouped, along with the beds, as further potentials for in-flight entertainment. After telling them they were cleared for immediate take-off she made a discreet withdrawal.

'Pretty girl,' commented Jeffrey as the twin engines rose to screaming pitch and the extravagant machine began to move.

Helen's tone was more acid than she had intended as she answered, 'No doubt she would happily demonstrate the beds for you.'

'Something wrong?' asked Jeffrey with much injured innocence in his voice.

'Nothing,' said Helen shortly and turned to stare out of the window as the jet raced along the tarmac and lifted into the skies.

Shutting Jeffrey out by feigning sleep she cursed her

523

present mood. She was in flight with a man who had declared his love for her and wanted nothing more than to bring her peace of mind and she couldn't understand why she resented him as if he were an intrusive stranger. Finally, just before genuine sleep overtook her, she understood. He was wrenching her from the refuge of forgetfulness that had made these past weeks possible and was now forcing her to face the root of her guilt.

Fearful of what might come from such a confrontation she knew for certain that, whatever the outcome, nothing would ever be the same again.

True to Jeffrey's prediction the plane made it to Los Angeles by four p.m. local time, landing not in the sprawl of L.A. International but at Burbank in the San Fernando valley. As they transferred, with very little formality, from the jet to the long black limousine waiting for them, Jeffrey explained that, after the recent earthquake damage the traffic in Los Angeles was chaotic and made Burbank handier to the UCLA campus at Westwood, than the downtown LAX.

Wesley Pike was a tall rangy young man, standing six feet four and blinking at Helen through pebble glasses that made his eyes look as if they were in a permanent state of surprise. 'You don't recognise me, do you?' he asked as they met in the discreetly quiet Boulevard Café in Westwood.

Shaking her head Helen sat in the offered chair and felt a bewildered unreality settle about her. That morning she had woken on a yacht alongside the quay in Guadeloupe, nine or so hours later she had been transported across a continent and felt her mind had been lost somewhere in transit.

'I was one of the dive leaders that day,' Wesley was saying. 'Jesus – what a day! The worst of my life.' Helen watched the raw-boned young man shifting his gaze randomly between herself and Jeffrey before addressing her directly. 'They lied to you,' he said.

'Exactly what happened?' asked Jeffrey.

Wesley shifted uneasily in his seat and looked almost grateful to be interrupted by the girl that came to take their order. Uninterested in the food Helen settled for coffee while Wesley, his appetite belying his thin build, ordered several complicated sandwiches which seemed, to Helen, to take ages to detail.

Finally turning back to the point Wesley went on. 'I was working at the dive school only to make some money during the summer, you understand?'

'Get to the point,' Jeffrey urged.

'Right! Well that day we had a rush of business. Too many people – too little equipment. The boss told me to check out some of the older stuff and see what could be used to meet the shortfall. I found a couple of usable items but we were still a couple of sets short and I told him there was no way we could stretch. He took over from me and pulled out this old air tank – a real museum piece – you know, steel and all, which they don't make any more – today's air tanks are in aluminium. Anyway, they told me to issue it. I protested that there were signs of corrosion around the valve but he told me he'd used worse in the past and if I wanted to keep working there I'd better do as he asked.' Wesley paused and glanced at Helen. 'It was your husband got the short straw.'

Helen, feeling slightly sick, stayed silent as Jeffrey pressed for more detail. 'They knowingly gave him a faulty air tank?'

Wesley looked even more uncomfortable. 'Well . . . yes, but . . .'

'"But" what?'

'Corrosion usually works from the inside out which makes it hard to see . . .'

'So how did you know it was there?'

'From the general state of the tank and the valve. It

hadn't been maintained in God knows how long. You could say I was making an educated guess.'

'But if you could, they could, too. They should have known?'

Wesley nodded. 'They should never have issued that tank.'

'So what do you think happened down there?'

'I *know* what happened. Anybody with half an eye could see what happened.'

'Which was what?'

'The tank must have been knocked against something on the wreck they were diving on. The knock caused the tank valve to blow off . . .' Wesley glanced awkwardly at Helen '. . . it crushed the back of his skull.'

Helen felt as if a great weight was crushing her as she sat there and when Jeffrey reached out a hand to hers she held on to it as if to a lifeline.

'So he died instantly?'

Wesley nodded. 'The story about him getting trapped and his air running out – they made that up to try and get off the hook. They thought a law suit for negligence would bankrupt them so they told me and everyone else to keep their mouths shut.' Welsey's huge eyes peered at Helen. 'I'm sorry, ma'am, but it's been bothering me ever since. I'm glad to, finally, tell the truth.'

Jeffrey was relentless. 'And the truth is that nobody – not Helen – or anyone else on God's earth could have made any difference by being there?'

Wesley shook his head. 'The only difference it would have made would have been that this lady – excuse me ma'am – would have seen her husband die.'

'And you'll sign an *affidavit* to that effect?'

Wesley was still nodding agreement when Helen shot to her feet. 'No!' she cried. 'Please – just get me out of here!'

Wesley, looking confused, got to his feet as Jeffrey put an arm round the distressed Helen and, telling

526

Wesley he would be in touch the next day, led Helen from the café and into the waiting limousine.

Sobbing uncontrollably Helen sat huddled in the capacious rear of the car and she heard Jeffrey directing the driver to the Bel Air Hotel.

Gathering every last ounce of strength left in her Helen, unwilling to look directly at him, spoke. 'Jeffrey . . . I want a separate room tonight.'

Jeffrey renewed his comforting embrace. 'Is that a good idea, darling? You really want to be alone?'

'I *won't* be alone,' she told him in set, determined, tones. 'There's things I have to tell Kenneth.'

Jeffrey nodded his understanding and sat back in his seat as they rode to the hotel in silence.

Helen usually preferred the fast facility of the shower to the bath but, this night, felt in need of a long contemplative soak.

Eyes closed, she consciously prepared herself for the night ahead. She had never subscribed to any formal religions – finding worthy values in them all, she lived in an ethical supermarket – taking this item from there and that from another place and vaguely imagining herself one day arriving at a spiritual check-out, fully provided for what may lie ahead.

Her belief in the spiritual survival after death was based more on optimism than conviction – an attitude she thought totally rational since atheism – a total rejection of all gods and the hereafter – required a bravery she didn't possess. The atheists were brave since, if *they* were proved wrong, they had much more to lose than the mistaken believer.

What, then, did she hope for in the coming night's communion?

Her belief in the survival of the spirit after death being tenuous, her one firm conviction was in the spirituality of the living and that spiritual survival, as much during life as after death, if any, depended on the

527

discovery of the true self, and it was that which she sought tonight.

When she was at a pre-pubertal age and still prepared to believe 'grown-ups' were the font of all wisdom, she had been much affected by a remark made to her by Aunt May. Visits from Aunt May, considered by her mother to be of the 'shameful' side of the family, were rare but one day, walking a wintry Eastbourne promenade, Aunt May had uttered words that, these many years later, were still locked into her consciousness. Aunt May had said: 'To get by in life you have to lie. Everybody does it. Tell them what's good for them to know, tell them any damn thing you want but never, *never* lie to yourself. Do that and you're lost!'

Aunt May lay with her tonight in this Bel Air bathroom. She may not, this night, summon the shade of Kenneth, but was convinced she could, with application, find herself.

Determined to confront herself in the best possible light Helen rose from the bath and after drying herself, oiled her body, applied some lip-gloss and a touch of mascara, brushed out her hair and went naked into the darkened bedroom and spread herself, offering up every orifice, on the top covers of the bed.

Unable to immediately face the agony of Kenneth's death she, with a conscious sense of cowardice, began with Millie's telephone call.

'You'll have to start going out sometime. Either that or join a religious order.'

It had been the appalling prospect of facing a positive philosophical choice, as much as anything, that had led her to Millie's pre-Christmas party and the meeting with Jeffrey.

Jeffrey, she now saw, was a man carrying almost as much guilt as herself. Could it have been the mutual need of expiation that had established their first bonding?

Both had unconsciously recognised the other's need;

Jeffrey had given her the physical pain with which she had sought to obliterate – or, as she now recognised, disguise – the spiritual catharsis of loss.

That Kenneth had gone and she remained were facts beyond denial. Kenneth, she reasoned, had the certainty of death while she was left with the bewilderment of life. Kenneth had gone where she could not follow and all the grieving in the world would not change that so, in one sense, the choice was simple. Life and death.

Since there was no life without the living of it, it would seem she had simply to accept the facts and go forward bravely. Which brought her to what might be the crux – who, or what, was she?

Aunt May's homily haunted her as she reviewed the people and events of the past weeks. To which of them had she shown her true self?

First, foremost and central to everything, there was Jeffrey. She had no doubt in her mind that she had stood spiritually naked before him and that his judgement mattered the most to her since it was, among all living people, the most informed.

At that time of their meeting she had been spiritually numb and ready to greet any feeling or stimulation as better than the emotional void into which Kenneth's death had plunged her.

Jeffrey had served her need instead of exploiting it.

More, he had assiduously sought out Wesley Pike and shown her that her guilt was baseless. In doing that he risked the core of their relationship. So what had motivated him? He had already spoken of love but where lay the border between love and lust?

Was it marked by shame?

Where lay the boundary between what was done in lust and that given in love? Were both, indistinguishable to a dispassionate observer from Outer Space, marked on the one hand by the shame of lust and on the other by exaltation of love? If so, had she felt shame?

Most certainly not before Jeffrey. With Qito? With

Madame Victoria, with Carla . . . ? This last gave her pause. The image of Carla excited her beyond reason. With Carla she had discovered that lust recognises no gender frontier. Everything she had done since meeting Jeffrey had been directed by him until her precipitous flight from Paris.

The two pilots on the plane, the nervous novice stewardess, her joyous submission to Carla and the excitement of Tsai. The fisherman on the island. These had been lust-led ideas of her own but they did not shame her, so where now lay that elusive no man's land between lust and love?

Lust simply demanded gratification while love took its time and brought with it the onus of trust. Could Jeffrey trust her? Did those excursions from his trust make her unworthy of his love? If so why then had he forgiven her?

She was confused by an inextricable link between the image of the flaring, exciting Carla, exulting in the joy of sexual domination, and Jeffrey. Where was the connection?

It was then that she drew a crystalline clear image of Jeffrey's eyes as he had looked on Carla. At the time she had jealously considered that, in that moment at least, he had desired Carla before herself. Now, quite suddenly, the pattern was resolved and she knew exactly what Jeffrey, but more importantly, she, wanted of herself.

It was as if a great weight had been lifted from her as she understood that while Jeffrey had relieved her of an oppressive guilt, his own remained.

She now knew that, relieved of her own guilt, she had within her hands the power to grant him the gift of shame!

The coming day could not now dawn too soon!

530

Chapter Twenty

At Helen's insistence she and Jeffrey met the following morning on the neutral ground of the hotel's coffee shop.

Jeffrey, smiling anxiously, rose to greet her as she made her, deliberately delayed, entrance. He waited warily as she consciously took her time over ordering her breakfast, but couldn't contain himself the moment the waitress had left them. 'Well?' he asked. 'Did you come to any conclusions?'

'Several,' she said lightly. 'I had a good long talk with myself and feel confident that I now know what I want.'

'Do your plans include me?'

Helen felt her spirits soar. She knew precisely what agonies Jeffrey must have suffered in the night and found herself content to continue teasing him. 'Possibly,' she finally allowed.

Jeffrey visibly flinched. 'Just "possibly"?'

'Perhaps "conditionally" would have been a better word.'

Anxiously nodding he insisted, 'So what do I have to do?'

At that moment the waitress returned with piled plates of toast, scrambled eggs and overflowing glasses of the juices she had ordered. Helen, sitting back, considered the interruption perfectly timed and let Jeffrey watch with frustration as she deliberately fussed over the cream and sugar pots.

Finally, she relented enough to allow herself to smile brightly into his apprehensive face. 'The first thing you have to know is that I've changed.'

'"Changed" . . . ?'

'Very much so.'

'In what way?'

'Difficult to define,' she said, consciously enigmatic.

'Try,' he urged.

'No. It's impossible to put into words.'

'Then how am I to find out?'

'In time.'

'How long a time? For Christ's sake, Helen, the past night has been a purgatory for me. I did some thinking too. I love you. Also I want to marry you.'

'Which "me"?' she asked. 'The compliant little sex-slave? If so I'm afraid you might be disappointed.'

'I *never* thought of you like that,' he protested. 'I never *treated* you like that. I thought what I was doing was providing the shock treatment you needed.'

Nodding, she allowed him his point. 'And you did it remarkably well, but there are questions arising.'

'Anything you want to know about me . . . anything.'

'There is one point – the answer to which could be crucial.' She looked directly into his eyes and made an interval of silence as she bit greedily into her buttered toast. Carefully dabbing the crumbs from her lips, she went on: 'How did you come to know Madame Victoria?'

Jeffrey's expression went from astonishment to caution as he absorbed this most unexpected question. 'I don't understand . . .' he murmured defensively.

'My understanding of that estimable establishment was that it catered to men seeking a certain form of physical domination. I was merely curious as to how you came to be such a welcome guest there.'

Watching him closely Helen was, for a moment, afraid Jeffrey was about to retreat into blustering denial and was pleased when her faith in his honesty was justified by seeing him relax, for the first time that morning, and smile.

'You've found me out,' he finally said.

'Have I?' she asked, pretending uncertainty. 'In what way – *exactly*?'

'I'll answer you the same way you answered me: "It's difficult to put into words".'

Sitting back into the banquette Helen allowed him to bathe in the brilliance of her smile. 'Then it seems we are left with the necessity of practical demonstration.'

'What does that mean – *exactly*?'

'Do you remember the first time you took me to your place?' Seeing Jeffrey warily silent, she went on. 'We were lying under the sun lamps in the conservatory. You said you wanted to "worship" me?' She waited until she had Jeffrey's answering nod before adding, 'Well, I now intend you shall have your chance.'

After a moment of considered silence Jeffrey nodded. 'There's nothing in the world I want more than that chance.'

'Good!' she said breezily. 'In that case I shall need the morning alone. I have some shopping to do. What do you say to us meeting back here in time for lunch?'

'Can't I come with you?' he pleaded.

'No,' she said firmly.

Nodding, Jeffrey rose with her. 'Whatever it is you want,' he said anxiously, 'they can deliver to the hotel and charge it to my account.'

'Thank you,' she smiled, allowed him a cheek-pecking kiss and was turning away when he caught her.

'You didn't answer when I asked you to marry me.'

'We've time to discuss that, surely,' she smiled.

'No we haven't. I wanted us to get married today.'

'"Today"? Is that possible?'

'Not in California, but in Nevada we could. I was

533

hoping we'd take a plane to Las Vegas. They leave every half hour.'

'Then there's no need to decide before lunch is there?' she asked. 'Meanwhile I have my shopping to do.'

Jeffrey nodded before her implacably pussy-cat smile. 'You certainly seem to have your priorities straightened out.'

'Along with much else – as you will shortly discover. Until lunch, darling . . .' she called as she moved away from Jeffrey's imploring – and undeniably tempting – gaze.

Lunch was a meal taken in fraught silence. The boxes containing Helen's various purchases arrived one after the other and Jeffrey was constantly interrupted by requests for his signature.

One of the names of the stores to which Helen had given her custom caught his eye. 'Leather Bound?' he asked, looking up from the debit slip to her challenging eyes.

Helen dismissed his concern with a shrug of her shoulders. 'A whim of mine,' she smiled.

Jeffrey had signed and then picked at the meal in which neither was particularly interested. 'So when am I to know what's expected of me?' he finally asked.

'I'm surprised you haven't already guessed,' she answered in deliberately syrupy tones.

'My imagination is running riot but I haven't dared to come to any conclusion.'

Deciding that the time had come to relent a little she reached across the table to take his hand and asked, 'Do the words: "Love, honour and *obey*" have any meaning for you?'

'They do,' he answered throatily. 'The question is: who is to obey who?'

'If you haven't understood that . . .' she said '. . . then you haven't been listening.'

It seemed Jeffrey was having difficulty with his throat

as he asked: 'When am I to be allowed to "under-stand"?'

Rising from the table Helen motioned him to stay where he was. 'I shall be in my room. One hour from now you may call me there.' Smiling, she leaned down and kissed his cheek. 'Bye, darling,' she called as she breezily turned away.

Jeffrey stood naked in the very centre of Helen's room and knew that he was in the only place in the entire world he wished to be.

Helen's instructions on the telephone had been crystal clear.

'In fifteen minutes you will come to my room. The door will be ajar. Just inside the door you will find a small lobby where you may strip. Naked you will forward into the room and wait for me. Be warned that I shall consider anything less than a manifestly full arousal a personal insult.'

The latter part of her instruction had worried Jeffrey but, in the event, he awaited her knowing that he had never before known such an overwhelming excitement. His anticipation of what might be to come was heightened by the transformation Helen had wrought in the hotel room. The furnishings and fixtures were almost identical to those of his own room but Helen had managed to completely alter the ambience.

With the afternoon sun completely eliminated by the heavy drapes the room's only illumination came from two candles – widely dispersed – which rendered a solemn ritualistic air.

His nerves, already tense and jangling, were sent into a state of near panic when he heard her voice cut through the dimly lit room.

'Don't turn,' she rapped. 'Stay exactly as you are until I tell you otherwise.'

Rigid now Jeffrey waited, every fibre vibrant with anticipation. His ears tingling with the soft sounds of movement behind him and his nose filled with the heavy musky perfume she wore, Jeffrey inwardly begged for some sight of her.

When next she spoke she was close to his shoulder. 'I intend asking much of you,' she sighed into his ear. 'A great deal more than you ever demanded of me. Do you understand?'

His throat closed, Jeffrey could only nod.

'You will find that a woman can be far more pitiless than any man would know how to be.' Jeffrey heard the slight sounds of Helen moving away from him and tensely waited until she spoke again. 'In a moment you will turn and see the results of my morning's shopping. It is on your reaction that our entire future depends. If you understand – nod.'

Jeffrey's immediate assenting nod sent Helen's confidence soaring. In truth she was almost as nervous as Jeffrey was excited and had to take a very deep breath before speaking again. 'You may now turn and look on me,' she said softly.

Hesitating a moment as he fervently prayed that he was not about to be disappointed or made ridiculous, Jeffrey turned and thought for a moment he saw, not Helen but a vision conjured out of his most fervent imaginings.

She stood tall in six-inch heels of closely fitted black leather boots, fishnets supported by eight garter straps suspended from the base of a scarlet leather basque corset, cut high over her hips, and rising over a tightly cinched waist to the breasts which were barely covered by a frill of black lace. About her throat was a collar, such as he had last seen on Carla, while on her face she wore a half-mask above which her hair was swept upwards to be caught by a glittering Spanish comb.

Aware that he was simply staring dumbfounded while Helen challengingly waited for his reaction, he allowed his weakened legs to speak for him as he sank to a kneeling position before her.

With a light delighted laugh Helen came forward to loom over him, legs spread, and letting him see the leather riding stick she had in her hands. Her question was superfluous but she insisted anyway. 'Do you approve?' she asked.

For answer Jeffrey let out a gurgle of excitement as he leaned forward to kiss her boots.

'I take it you do,' she told him, turning away in a deliberately dismissive gesture only too aware of the electric shock-waves travelling up her arm, emanating from her tight grip about the riding stick. 'Get on your feet,' she told him and didn't turn to look at him until the tiny sounds of his moving to obey subsided.

Still with her back turned, she spoke again. 'I shall not tie you for your whipping since to do so would be to imply that I might be afraid of your reaction.' Now turning to him, relieved to see he was even more aroused than previously, she went on. 'I am not,' she told him as she advanced on his now trembling figure. 'However, now, and for the last time you have the opportunity to dissent and leave. There will be no further opportunities for you so to do, so I suggest you give your answer very careful consideration.'

Finding voice for the first time since coming into her presence, Jeffrey spoke with assertive force. 'You're more than I hoped – everything I ever dreamed about.'

Finding his answer pleasing, she smiled. 'And everything that went before was simply instruction in what you really wanted?'

Jeffrey nodded. 'As I said earlier – you have found me out.'

Elated, it was Helen's turn for the affirmative nod. 'I trust you will find I proved an apt and attentive pupil.'

'Do you still want to marry me?' Helen asked as she lay on the bed while Jeffrey, obeying her instructions, furrowed with his tongue between her thighs.

'More than ever,' he breathed.

'Very well,' she said. 'You have my permission to make the arrangements.'

An air taxi brought them to a Las Vegas already brazenly lit by its night neon. The ceremony, with a minimum of attention to fussy detail, was conducted in a place called the 'Wee Kirk o' the Heather' after which the happy couple retired to the honeymoon suite of a ludicrously over-decorated Casino Hotel.

There, Helen confronted her new husband.

'Tonight you will do something – in full view of all the diners in the club restaurant – which you and I have never before dared. I want your sworn oath that you will not disappoint me – no matter what.'

His throat working nervously, Jeffrey felt bold enough to protest. 'There's no question that I'll do whatever you tell me,' he breathed. 'But I would ask you to remember that the people that come to Las Vegas are not as sophisticated as some cities. There might be trouble if it's too explicit.'

Helen smiled. 'It is *very* extreme.' she smiled. 'But you will obey – no matter what?'

Filled with apprehension he felt he had no other option but to agree.

Together, he dressed in a black-tie tuxedo, she in a flowing newly purchased evening gown, they made a striking entrance into the almost filled to capacity club room. Conducted to a table which seemed to have been carved from a jungle clearing they were seated and served aperitifs.

Enjoying making him wait, Helen sipped at her drink and commented on the big-band dance music playing in the background. 'The orchestra is very good, don't you think?' she asked of the tense Jeffrey.

'Excellent,' he said.

Helen sat back and appeared to be devoting her attention entirely to the music for some time before speaking again. 'It's time, darling,' she said. 'Time to test how far you dare to trust me.'

Even in the roseate glow of the table lamp Helen saw how suddenly he paled. 'Look,' he said as he rose to accompany her towards the dance floor. 'I'm going to go through with it no matter what – just bear in mind what I said. These people are not the sophisticated kind we might meet in Paris or London.'

Pausing on the edge of the sparsely populated dance floor Helen smiled. 'But you will do whatever it is I ask of you?'

Nervously, Jeffrey nodded. 'What is it I have to do?' he asked, his words made almost inaudible by apprehension.

'As I told you – something you and I have never done before. Can't you imagine what that might be?'

Shaking his head Jeffrey prepared himself for the worst.

'What you are going to do – now, instantly, and before all these people – without regard to the consequences is . . .' she let the sentence hang for some moments and enjoyed his stricken anticipation before going on '. . . *dance* with me.'

And dance they did.

Elena's Conquest
Lisette Allen

Summer, 1070 AD

Chapter One

With a rebellious little sigh, Elena put down her basket on the dusty flagstones. It was still only half-full. But the day was so hot; far too hot to be gathering herbs for old Sister Winifred's medicinal salves!

Overhead, the sun burned down from a cloudless blue summer sky, its heat trapped within the mellow stone walls of the little herb garden. Elena heard the chapel bell tolling noon, its silvery chimes hanging heavy in the still air. White doves murmured sleepily in the eaves. The dark, thick forest that surrounded the convent was silent, as if waiting for something to happen.

But nothing ever did happen here at this remote little convent of Linby, lost in the northern wilds between the hills and the sea – this place where Elena had spent nearly all her life. And their very remoteness, Sister Winifred would remind her severely, was why they were safe – why their impoverished, tiny community had survived, when all around them the king's soldiers were wreaking savage punishment for the great Saxon uprising last winter. Elena had heard murmurs of terrible happenings, rumours of harsh bloodshed, like the rustling of the leaves in the forest before a storm. She'd heard that at Thoresfield, the great Norman stronghold to the south, the king had installed the notorious Aimery le Sabrenn as commander of the garrison. At the very mention of his name, the nuns crossed themselves, as if to ward off evil.

But nothing had changed here at Linby, except that perhaps food was harder to come by than ever, and people were more fearful, more wary of strangers. Just occasionally, they had visitors; travellers who stopped for a night or two with the old priest, Father Wulfstan; mysterious, hungry-looking men who rested and moved on quickly. Otherwise, here in the little convent, they were shut off from the world. And this, thought Elena, with a sudden pang, was to be her life, for ever.

There were some travellers staying with the priest at the moment. Elena knew, because yesterday she'd been ordered to take some of the nuns' meagre rye loaves over to the priest's little cottage. She'd not gone inside; the priest's slatternly housekeeper had taken the bread from her quickly, then given her a bundle of tallow candles that the priest wanted taking to the chapel, and bade her be gone.

Elena had turned slowly back along the path to the convent – and then, through the trees, she'd seen the man. He was coming towards her, heading purposefully for the priest's house; tall and fair-haired, holding himself proudly in spite of his shabby clothes. Elena's heart skipped a beat; Sister Winifred had told her sternly that she must never, ever talk to Father Wulfstan's visitors. But this man, who was perhaps not much older than herself, was blocking her path! Catching her breath, she dipped clumsily to one side to avoid him; the tallow candles slipped from her basket and scattered on the ground.

The man bent swiftly to gather them up, while Elena stood by helplessly, her face burning with confusion. He placed the candles carefully in her basket, and said,

'They are undamaged. I'm sorry if I startled you – you are from the convent?'

'Yes – I must take these candles to the chapel.'

He still barred her way, assessing her carefully, taking in the long white veil that had slipped askew as usual over her thick blonde hair, and the shabby grey gown that concealed her slender figure. 'So,' the tall man said, 'they've shut you up here? With only those old nuns for company? What have you done to deserve such punishment?'

Elena, startled by his direct question, couldn't bear to be disloyal to the kindly nuns. 'The sisters have been good to me! My parents died of the fever when I was but a child – I was left with nothing, so they took me in, gave me a home.'

She was uneasily aware all the time of his eyes burning into her. Vivid blue eyes, that burned with fire in his tanned, masculine face. Her heart thudded uncomfortably. How different he was to the men she was used to; the worn, kindly old priest, the haggard peasants who scraped a living from the forest clearing. Something stirred restlessly within her as she gazed helplessly up at this tall, golden-haired Saxon. She caught a glimpse of smooth, sunburned skin at the base of his throat, where his tunic lay open, and she felt her mouth go dry.

'You are too beautiful,' he was saying softly, 'to be locked away here. Yes, beautiful. Don't you realise it? Has no-one ever told you?'

'I – I know that it is wicked to be vain,' stammered Elena.

'Vain?' smiled the disturbing man. 'It is not vain to know that you are beautiful, it is God's gift!' He lifted one hand and softly touched her blushing cheek. 'You should not let them shut you away. Those nuns are like old carrion crows, preying on your youth and innocence.'

In the distance, through the trees, Elena caught sight

of Sister Winifred looking out anxiously for her. 'I must go!' she blurted out desperately.

The golden-haired man had shrugged, and watched her with narrowed, thoughtful eyes as she hurried back to the convent in confusion.

That encounter had made Elena strangely restless. Locked away here, he said. Yes, she was! And he had told her she was beautiful; but surely, he himself was beautiful, with his vibrant, masculine features, and his strong body so tautly muscled beneath his shabby clothing! Last night, she had dreamed strange, disturbing dreams that were shadowy and dark. She often had dreams, but the nuns told her that it was wrong, and she must forget them.

This time, she dreamed that she was lost, alone in the forest, and a man riding by saw her and came slowly towards her. She knew it was sinful of her; but instead of running away she found herself drawn towards him, as if under a spell. He held out his arms, and she felt her heart fill with happiness. But as she ran into his embrace and looked up into his face, expecting to see the tanned Saxon features of Father Wulfstan's nameless guest, she felt a terrible, deadly chill strike into her heart. *The man who held her was one of the king's soldiers . . .*

Even now, here in the familiar safety of the little walled garden, she felt a strange tightening in her stomach as she remembered the alien horseman of her dream. Her rough linen shift chafed suddenly at her breasts; her hand moved instinctively to adjust her gown, and she discovered, with a little, juddering shock, that her nipples were swollen and hard. She snatched away her fingers as if they had been burned, aware that her breathing had become shallow and ragged.

The nuns had always instructed her that it was the work of the devil himself to even think about – let alone touch – your own flesh. Elena always tried to accept

548

their rulings without question. But her dream had unsettled her, and she knew, without a doubt, that it would return.

Her lips felt full and slightly swollen; she moistened them and tried hard to fight down the strange yearning that filled her tender body. It was the heat, she told herself desperately, that made her feel so restless. Oh, but she was wicked. Perhaps too wicked to become a nun! She must do penance for her sinfulness, for feeling this aching dissatisfaction with her fate when all around her people were suffering so much as a result of King William's punishment of the rebels.

But even as she resolved to make her confession to Father Wulfstan, she knew, with a quiet feeling of despair, that she would never forget the dark, unknown stranger in her dream.

The familiar, everyday sound of the chapel bell broke into her anguished thoughts. Elena jumped from the stone bench and picked up her wicker-basket hastily. She would be late for the service! How quickly this last hour had gone!

Then she realised that something was wrong. The chapel bell was not tolling the hour steadily and calmly, as usual. Instead, it was being pealed in panic, almost desperation, over and over. A cracked, uneven sound. Elena froze to the spot, suddenly cold in the sunlight. In disbelief, she heard the sound of horses' hooves; of people running; people shouting; doors slamming.

'The Normans! God help us, the Normans are upon us – ,The hoarse cry broke off, and somewhere a woman's high-pitched voice lifted in a scream. The doves rose clamouring from beneath the eaves. Iron-shod hooves clattered on the cobbles of the courtyard; harsh foreign voices cursed aloud. Elena heard the sound of steel being drawn, and smelled the stink of burning thatch. Trapped by fire or slaughtered by Norman steel – how many others had died like this?

Her heart hammering wildly, Elena ran out of the

little walled garden and stopped, transfixed by terror. There were mounted soldiers in the courtyard – rough men-at-arms in stained leather jerkins. Aimery le Sabrenn's soldiers had found them at last! And one of them had his swordpoint at the old priest's throat. Poor Father Wulfstan, who'd herded the terrified nuns indoors, and run out of the little chapel to face *this* .

The soldier was threatening the priest in a low, menacing voice. 'The rebels, old priest – the Saxon rebels. We know you harbour them on their travels, give them shelter. Where have you hidden them? Tell us, or it will be the worse for you, you old fool!'

Elena listened in anguish. *The rebels*. Father Wulfstan's mysterious visitors, who came and went with such secrecy – the tall Saxon who had spoken to her yesterday . . .

In a flash Elena understood it all. The soldiers from the great stronghold of Thoresfield had come here because Father Wulfstan was sheltering Saxon rebels! She let out a little cry of despair and one of the horsemen, on hearing her voice, wheeled round to face her. His horse, startled, reared up, and its great forequarters plunged down towards her.

A sudden blinding pain seared Elena's senses as a flailing hoof caught her on the side of her head. She called out in terror, and then the blackness engulfed her.

Darkness fell early in the forest that night. It was still hot and sultry, with the threat of thunder hanging in the air. The light of burning torches, held on high by the men who rode slowly on horseback, cast grotesque shadows on the wavering line of figures that tramped with bowed heads southwards along the forest track. Now and then, someone slipped or stumbled, jerking at the line of coarse rope that bound each one tautly by the wrists. Whenever this happened, the lash of a horseman's whip would hiss through the air, and

550

everyone would tense involuntarily as they waited for the scream. Afterwards, the silence would be strangely intense.

Back at the rear of the roped line, someone missed a step, slipping on the sodden leaf mould. A mounted guard, his flaming torch held high, cursed and moved his big horse back towards the offender.

'God damn these Saxon rebels,' he muttered. 'More trouble than they're worth . . .' Then he saw who had fallen, and smiled slowly.

The prisoner, who was desperately scrambling up before he could reach her, was female. The flickering light from his torch danced mockingly over the tangled fair curls that tumbled to her shoulders. The plain grey gown, that clung to her slender figure, was stained with mud from her fall. She was one of the little prisoners they'd taken from the convent – the convent that sheltered those cursed Saxon rebels.

His thin lips curled suddenly, and he leaned across the high pommel of his saddle, his dark Norman face keen with sudden anticipation.

'Pick your feet up, convent brat!' His voice was silky and slow as he fingered the leather whip in his belt. 'Or I'll give you reason enough to move . . .'

The Saxon prisoner looked up in sharp fear as she was dragged along by the thick hemp rope. Already, he could see, her fragile wrists had been rubbed raw.

Blood of Christ, he breathed to himself, but this one was a little beauty. Her features were delicate and regular, her wide, terrified eyes a dark, sultry blue such as he'd never seen before, and her small pink mouth was full and ripe. Even the drab grey of the hideous convent gown couldn't conceal the high swell of those rounded little breasts. He moistened his lips. A nun? A disguise, most like. Yet more evidence of the rebels' cunning ways.

She said, in a low, broken French, 'I pray your forgiveness, sire. There was a branch across the path.'

The Norman gave a harsh laugh. So she knew their language! An educated bitch! 'Save your prayers, little sister,' he jeered, his white teeth gleaming in his coarsely handsome face. 'You'll need all the prayers you can think of where you're going – to the stronghold of Aimery le Sabrenn, lord of Thoresfield!'

He saw how the wench shuddered and briefly touched the crude wooden cross that hung on a thong of leather at her breasts. So, she'd heard of the Breton lord Aimery. The devil himself. She knew what she was in for.

He felt a sudden, urgent need for this fair-haired Saxon maid. His eyes narrowed as he rode alongside her, and he licked his dry mouth, feeling the familiar ache in his loins, the tightening. Damn le Sabrenn, he thought suddenly. Hadn't their fine lord started out as a Breton mercenary, no better than the rest of them? Would he miss one of these Saxon sluts that they'd picked up along with the rebels? Why, with a bit of luck, he wouldn't even know she was missing! Surreptitiously he adjusted his constricting breeches, stroking himself briefly as he did so, like a secret promise. Later, perhaps. Later, he would show this little slut what a real man was made of.

He rode back to his place at the front of the procession, his smoking torch held high. The image of the blonde wench from the convent inflamed his blood.

Elena watched him ride off with a strange, sick feeling in the pit of her stomach. She couldn't forget the way he'd looked at her, with that hungry light in his dark eyes. She swallowed down the nausea that suddenly shook her, and struggled to keep walking, though she didn't know how much longer she could go on. The rope had rubbed the skin from her wrists. Her thin leather shoes were almost worn through, and her tender feet were cut and bruised.

Was it worth going on? Shouldn't she just refuse, and lie there? If she did, they would cut her free of the rope, and then they'd flog her. Already on this nightmare journey she'd seen strong men quail at the floggings. Yet could it be worse than where they were going? To the vile stronghold of the Breton lord Aimery le Sabrenn, William the Conqueror's notorious commander.

Even at their remote little convent, she'd heard of him. The nuns whispered of unspeakable happenings, of some strange, dark evil that Elena could only guess at. They said that he had personal reason to hate all Saxons with a hard, relentless fury.

The twisted black branches of the forest reached out to grip her, like fingers tearing at her face. An owl cried and swooped low in front of her. Elena whimpered softly in her fear.

Her head still throbbed dully from where the plunging horse's hoof had struck her. When she had at last recovered consciousness, she had found herself lying in a cart, on filthy, soiled straw, along with other prisoners who were too weak to walk. The jogging motion of the cart along the rutted forest track had made her feel sick; the stench of the other prisoners, all sick or badly wounded, made her senses swim. When the man who was guarding them sloped off into the bushes to relieve himself, she had slipped from the back of the cart and tried to run.

She hadn't got far. Sneeringly, they had told her that if she was well enough to run, she was well enough to walk. Roped into line with the rest of the prisoners, she began her long walk into captivity, south to the stronghold of Thoresfield. They told her that she was a serf now, the property of Aimery le Sabrenn, great lord and friend of the king, persecutor of Saxons. This surely was her punishment for her rebellious, restless thoughts. 'Oh, sweet Mary, blessed Mother of God,' Elena muttered in despair. 'Help me in my hour of need . . .' A sob broke in her throat. 'Help me. *Please* . . .'

* * *

It was almost midnight when at last the commander of the guards ordered them to halt in a small, grassy clearing near a half-ruined hovel. As soon as the ropes were untied a man tried to run off into the trees. The other captives watched in despairing apathy as a guard on horseback quickly pursued him and dealt him such a vicious blow with the heel of his whip that he slumped unconscious to the ground. He lay where he fell in the darkness beyond the circle of torchlight, because nobody dared to go and help him. Elena watched it all in horror, her tender heart torn with pity for the poor man.

After that, the guards moved round on foot, tossing out hunks of coarse dry bread and passing round leather skins of brackish water.

The water went quickly, because the night was still oppressively hot; and by the time the waterskin reached Elena, it was almost empty. She took a small sip to wash the dust from her throat, and then, looking round quickly to make sure no-one was looking, she hid it beneath the folds of her grey dress. Then she moved silently towards the edge of the clearing, searching in the darkness of the overhanging trees for the fallen man.

She found him. He was conscious now, but his face was almost grey in the shadows, and a trickle of blood ran from his forehead, darkening his long fair hair. With a gasp of horror, Elena recognised him as the man who had spoken to her only yesterday as she hurried back from the priest's house. One of Father Wulfstan's guests – one of the rebels! She swallowed down her sudden, sharp distress at seeing him here, like this.

He looked up, dazed, at the slim, beautiful girl in the grey dress who knelt beside him. 'It's you . . . the girl from the convent . . .'

'Here is some water,' Elena whispered. 'Please drink it.'

The Saxon managed to raise himself carefully on one

554

elbow, though he grimaced with the pain. She held the waterskin to his parched lips and he swallowed feebly. Then he lay back on the ground.

'I have brought this upon you,' he muttered. 'And now you're going to the devil's lair. God help you, sweet maid.'

Again, Elena felt that tight constriction round her heart at the mention of Aimery le Sabrenn. The devil's lair? 'W . . . what do you mean?' she faltered.

The man's head twisted round in alarm. 'Hush! Be silent – ' Too late, Elena heard the crunching of boots through the undergrowth behind her. As she whirled round, a cry on her lips, a rough hand caught at her shoulder.

The Saxon man struggled to raise himself from the ground. 'Let her go, damn you! Vile Norman scum—'

The guard silenced him with a swift blow to the stomach that had him doubled up. Then he turned to the girl; and Elena realised, with a shudder of fear, that he was the mounted guard who'd spoken to her earlier and watched her in such a disturbing way.

'Well, well,' he said softly. 'The little convent brat. Like to explain what you were doing here, would you? With *him*?'

Elena struggled to free herself, but his strong hands dug into her shoulders. He was big and muscular, with a dark, floridly handsome face, and she could smell the wine he'd been drinking.

'I brought him water!' she retorted defiantly, hoping he wouldn't notice how her voice shook in secret fear. 'Poor man – he was injured! I couldn't just leave him there!'

His calloused thumbs were fondling her shoulders through the thin material of her gown. He seemed to be breathing strangely, and something in his hot, dark gaze really frightened her. 'A soft little heart, eh?' he said, grinning slowly. 'By Christ, but I've heard all about you convent brats. Desperate for it, are you, sweetheart? Well, I've got good news for you – no need to make do with a filthy Saxon rebel – '

'I don't know what you're talking about! Let me go, please, you're hurting me . . .' But before she could even scream, the soldier's eager mouth had come down thickly on hers, his hot, rasping tongue capturing the inner tenderness of her lips. In desperation she struggled to push him off, but her anguished efforts seemed to excite him all the more. He clutched her helpless body hard against his; she whimpered beneath his fierce kiss and struggled again, but his hands pinioned her already sore wrists with iron strength.

'Here's one juicy little prize our fine lord Aimery won't get to first!' the soldier muttered thickly. Then he reached for the neck of her dress, and ripped at the coarse grey wool; it parted easily, as did her white linen shift beneath it. He went very still then, and his grip slackened involuntarily as he gazed with hungry avid eyes at Elena's small white breasts.

With a cry of alarm, Elena tried to turn and run, but he caught her and threw her roughly to the ground, pinning her down with the weight of his heavily-muscled body even as she kicked and struggled wildly beneath him.

'Oh, my little beauty,' he muttered as he gazed at her soft nakedness. 'My little dove . . .' And he moistened his thin, curling lips as he kneeled in homage over her prostrate form.

He bent low over her, to kiss her again; she jerked her head to one side in an effort to escape, but he'd got her pinned down, his hands holding her wrists against the ground on either side of her head, while his leather-clad thighs straddled hers. He gazed with lascivious eyes at the blue-veined whiteness of her innocent breasts; then, with a sudden groan, he plunged his head down and started to lick at her tender nipples with his hot, wet mouth.

Elena felt her body arch in spasm. She was fighting

556

him wildly, wrenching herself from side to side beneath him. 'Get off me! You brute – '

'You can stop pretending now, wench,' the soldier chuckled. 'The women back at the camp beg me for this, just as you would if I stopped now! Such lovely little breasts; so perfect, so white, my sweetheart . . .'

Still Elena fought on, though she was all but over-powered by the maleness of him, by the harsh threat of his powerfully muscled shoulders, his demanding mouth. Sweet heaven . . .'

She tried to kick him. With a harsh oath, the man swiftly pushed both her hands together on the ground behind her head, so that he had one hand free. As Elena felt her strength failing, she watched with wide, horror-stricken eyes as he fumbled with his leather tunic, pulling it up somehow and reaching under it. He seemed to be stroking and rubbing feverishly at himself, while his eyes began to glaze over with satisfaction.

'Ah, my little Saxon,' he sighed, 'I've been longing for this since first I laid eyes on you.'

Elena squeezed her eyes shut tightly and prayed for this nightmare to end. It must be a nightmare, mustn't it? With this hateful man, muttering and trembling above her.

She opened her eyes again to make one last, desperate plea. 'You must let me go. You must!'

The words died on her lips. Because what met her eyes was a rigid, swollen shaft of flesh. The soldier gripped it in his hand, seeming to stroke it in some private ecstasy as he gazed adoringly at her naked breasts. Seeing how her eyes opened in horror, he went very still, watching her, letting her get the full impact of his swollen penis. 'Not seen one of these before, my little nun?' he whispered softly, cajolingly. 'There's many a fine lady like yourself begged me for a sight of this, I can tell you, so take a good look . . .' He rubbed his hand slowly, luxuriantly, along the rigid shaft and a drop of clear moisture gleamed and dropped, glistening, on to her tender breast. He bent, adoringly, to lick it off her skin.

Elena screamed, but the sound was choked in her dry throat as the man lunged forwards and covered her mouth with a hot, devouring kiss. Darkness engulfed her. And then, in the stifling stillness of that forest clearing, there was a sudden, alien sound – a harsh, whistling crack – and the man above her let out a sharp cry of pain.

For a second, he arched rigid above Elena. Then he slumped to the ground, moaning and whimpering, while Elena hugged her arms round her bruised body, numb with shame and despair. Dear God, what was happening now?

Then she saw. In the shadows was a group of men, and the one at the front carried a whip. Even as she watched, he raised his hand in a cold, calculating gesture, and the whip cracked out again, cutting with deadly accuracy into the man at her side. The soldier let out a thin sob and doubled up.

The man with the whip stroked the lash softly, as if it were a friend. Elena, dragging herself to her feet, gazed at her rescuer in helpless fascination. Tall and wide-shouldered, he wore a leather gambeson, with soft deerskin boots encasing his strong legs, and a grey woollen cloak slung across his shoulders. As she watched, he turned and spoke to the men in the shadows.

'Take him back to the camp. Tie him up, and wait there for me.'

The men did his bidding silently, dragging the whimpering guard away towards the fires of the soldiers' camp. Elena was alone with the man who stroked the whip.

Chapter Two

*H*er heart thudding sickly, her dark blue eyes wide with despairing defiance, Elena gazed silently up at this new threat. Then, she almost stopped breathing.

Something happened to her when she met this man's scrutiny – she felt a shock of recognition, as if she knew him already. Yet how could she? Certainly, she would never have forgotten him – no one could. His eyes were a pale silver-grey, like ice. Cold, and yet they burned into her. With a little gasp, she felt his face imprint itself for ever on her mind; the thick, tawny hair, so unlike the severely-cropped cuts of his fellow soldiers; the high-bridged, arrogant nose; the harsh jutting cheekbones. And down one lean cheek ran a terrible scar. White and ridged, it drew up the corner of his thin mouth and gave him a perpetual, menacing smile. The most chilling smile she had ever seen. Elena shivered, and bit into her soft lower lip to stop herself from crying out when she saw it.

He studied her with cold scorn. 'I thought,' he said, in a low cool voice that sent tremors through her exhausted body, 'that you Saxon vermin would be too weary tonight for such entertainments. Obviously I was wrong. You must be truly desperate to degrade yourself with a common soldier like Mauger there.'

Elena pulled her torn gown across her breasts, and lifted her small head proudly.

'You think,' she breathed in quiet defiance, 'that I *wanted* him to do what he did? My lord, I would rather he had killed me!'

The scarred man's eyes narrowed. Why, Elena wondered desperately, had she called him 'my lord'? The words had slipped out by mistake; yet there was something about this man that commanded obedience and respect, even from her. She suddenly realised that he was staring at the little wooden crucifix on its leather thong, a pathetic reminder of her former status.

Abruptly, he reached out with the handle of his whip and touched the cross, playing with it. 'Such sweet defiance,' he mocked silkily, 'from a Saxon rebel. No wonder poor Mauger was inflamed. You tried to tell him you were in holy orders, did you, wench? I hope he considers you worth it.'

Elena almost cried out at the injustice of his words. 'He knew!' she choked out. 'He knew that I was from the convent!'

'The convent that was a nest of rebels?'

'I am no rebel!' Elena's voice broke. 'Though if this is the kind of treatment I can expect, then I wish I had fought along with them! I would rather be killed than treated like this!'

She gazed up at him, quivering with anguish. His eyes were as cold as the harsh steel of the sword he wore thrust in his belt. His face was hard and impassive. With an idle gesture, he moved the handle of his whip away from the crucifix, and jerked it at the torn material of her gown. It fell apart, exposing her breasts. He flicked lightly at one nipple; it stiffened involuntarily, tugging at the soft flesh of her breast, and Elena caught her breath, her hands helpless at her sides at this fresh humiliation.

'So you are still claiming to be a nun?' He sounded almost bored. Elena felt the blood rise in her cheeks as

560

he made light, circling motions on her tender skin with his whip.

'A novice, sire,' she faltered out. 'I was destined to take my vows next month.'

'And how old are you, little novice?'

'They tell me I was born in the sixth year of King Edward's reign – oh!'

He was thoughtfully feathering her nipple with the tip of his whip. She gasped, and felt a hot, churning sensation in her stomach. Her rosy flesh jutted out with a strange yearning and she felt weak and dizzy. What refined game was this? What was wrong with her? Her breasts swelled and throbbed as he toyed with them so casually. The blood rushed to her face. She wanted to feel his hand there. She wanted him to hold her. *His hands looked strong and firm, and cool . . .*

She shuddered, and he dropped the whip, bored. She clutched the material high to her throat, and tried desperately to regain control of her body.

The man was speaking to her, saying, 'Then you are two and twenty, and according to your account, which I take leave to doubt, a complete innocent. That man Mauger – did he violate you?'

Elena's face flamed. 'His very touch was violation, my lord!'

His face twisted mockingly. 'I can see I shall have to be more precise. Are you still the virgin you claim to be?'

'I am! How dare you doubt it?'

His mouth twisted cynically. 'Well, we shall see. And in the meantime, Mauger will get a flogging he won't forget.'

Elena's head jerked up at that. A man – a Norman – was being punished because he'd dared to assault her, a Saxon prisoner?

Seeing her surprise, the man went on silkily, 'You misunderstand, little Saxon. He is not being punished out of deference to your feelings but because he dared

561

to defile my personal property.' He paused; a sudden shaft of moonlight through the trees caught at his strong, hard profile and glinted on the tawny streaks in his thick dark hair. 'You see, I am Aimery le Sabrenn, lord of Thoresfield, the man who owns you. Ah, I see from your face that you are acquainted with my name. Learn the rules well, little nun, many don't get a second chance. No-one tampers with my personal property. No-one.'

Elena gazed up at him with despairing eyes. She'd known. Somehow, she'd known as she set eyes on him who he was. It was as if the last of her breath had been knocked from her body.

Meanwhile, the Breton's hypnotic silver eyes narrowed almost to blackness as he inspected his young captive's anguished face. It was a face of delicate, almost breathtaking fragility. Her skin was so pure and pale that it looked as if it would bruise at the lightest touch. Her deep blue eyes, fringed by thick, soft lashes, gazed helplessly up at him, still wide with despairing defiance. Her long blonde curls, totally disordered in her struggle with the arrogant fool Mauger, shimmered like a silver halo in the moonlight. He remembered her small, perfect breasts, and how she'd trembled as his whip brushed their rosy, nubile tips.

This Saxon maid was beautiful, and spirited. Isobel would like her.

At the thought of this new acquisition in Isobel's power, some distant, half-forgotten emotion stirred within him, as he considered how Isobel would make her suffer. His face hardened, and he pushed the thought away without any difficulty. She was a Saxon – a rebel, in spite of her denials. She deserved what she was about to get. They all did. And if she was determined to keep up this pretence of innocence, then she would serve the lady Isobel's purpose very well.

He smiled and Elena, on seeing that chilling smile, felt her greatest fear yet.

Aimery le Sabrenn took the Saxon girl by the wrist. She felt fragile, like some helpless bird. She didn't struggle. It was almost as if she'd given up as she followed helplessly in his shadow, back towards the firelit circle where his men were gathered. He'd unpinned his grey cloak and given it to her, to hide her shame; he didn't want any more trouble from his men tonight. She'd kept her eyes lowered as he fastened it around her. She looked dazed with weariness and despair; yet there was still defiance there, he knew, even in her silence.

Aimery wondered briefly to himself what would have happened if he hadn't been with his men that night. No doubt the girl would have suffered badly at the hands of Mauger and his friends. He knew, because he'd seen it happen before. She was Saxon, she deserved her fate. Nevertheless, he was angry with his men for attacking the tiny convent, even if it had been harbouring rebels. And, strangely, he was glad he'd been in time to save the Saxon girl from Mauger's crude attentions.

He glanced down at the girl's white face. Her pretence of being a nun was quite disarming. Whatever her story, he knew, from cold experience, that she would be sweet when he finally took her, sweet and tantalising, with that slender figure and beguiling though feigned innocence. Also, if Aimery's judgement was not at fault, her responses would be more than satisfactory once he and Isobel had trained her properly. There was no denying how her dark blue eyes had flown open, and her soft lips parted in a gasp, as he teased her tender little breasts with his whip. She had a lot to learn but he would teach her with care, and then would wait patiently, even indifferently, until she was ready.

His men-at-arms, lolling around the fire with their wineskins, jumped to their feet when he suddenly appeared at the edge of the clearing with the Saxon girl stumbling at his heels. Aimery le Sabrenn smiled to himself, feeling the taut scar pulling at his cheek. They were afraid of him. Good. That was how it should be.

One solitary figure moved slowly out of the shadows towards him. A man not quite as tall as Aimery, but burlier and more thickset, with a face and arms as dark as night, and a gleaming, curved sword at his belt. Elena stifled a little sob of fear as Aimery thrust her towards the man; he saw how she trembled but still held herself straight and proud. He was pleased to see this fresh evidence of her courage; she would need it.

'I want this girl put in chains, away from the rest of the serfs, Hamet,' Aimery said softly to the Saracen, his servant. 'For her own safekeeping. I will see to the punishment of the guard, Mauger. Keep the men away from her.'

The big Saracen looked at the trembling Elena keenly. 'She is beautiful, lord,' he said, in a foreign, sing-song voice. 'She is for you?'

'For the lady Isobel,' said Aimery. A wintry smile twisted his mouth. 'Do you think she will like her present?'

Hamet's black eyes gleamed. 'Oh, yes, lord,' he said softly. 'The girl is a Saxon – and untried?'

'So she claims. Whatever the case, we will soon teach her – Isobel especially.'

The black servant nodded, his eyes devouring Aimery's captive. He swallowed hard. Aimery saw it, and laughed shortly. 'You will have your turn, Hamet. But remember, Isobel as ever, is the tutor.'

Hamet nodded eagerly and went for the chains. When he came back with them, the girl cried out in protest but Aimery just nodded to his servant, who began to fasten the cold shackles around her wrists and ankles with powerful yet strangely gentle fingers. As he fastened her arms, the borrowed grey cloak slipped by accident from her shoulders, revealing her small, creamy breasts. The Saracen froze in his task, and Elena gave a low moan of protest as his hungry black eyes fastened on her vulnerable flesh. His big hand jerked slowly towards her tempting breasts, but his master's voice stopped him like a sword in the back.

'Lay one finger on her before I give the word,' said Aimery, watching impassively with folded arms, 'and, friend though you are, you will die. Very slowly, I assure you. Now, fasten the cloak around her, and get on with your task.'

As Hamet worked on her chains, the thunderstorm that had threatened for so long rolled down from the hills. Lightning played on the horizon; low rumbles of distant thunder menaced the still air. Heavy drops of rain were already pattering on the thick canopy of leaves overhead as Hamet fastened the last of Elena's shackles. Then he swung her easily up in his strong arms and, at his lord's command, carried her to the shelter of the half-ruined woodcutter's cottage that lay at the edge of the clearing, where he had already placed his master's things for the night. Aimery followed, and indicated that Hamet should take the girl into a small thatched outhouse that leaned against the main building. As Hamet lowered her to her feet inside the crude hovel, Elena struggled to hold herself upright, with a last burst of desperate defiance.

'I beg you, sire, if you have any justice in you at all, then you will let me go! I was not one of the rebels, I swear. What possible use can I be to you? Let me go back to the convent where I belong!'

The Breton watched her oddly, his hands on his hips. His harsh face, twisted by the scar, was suddenly lit up by a gleam of lightning. She shivered at the look in his cold, glittering eyes.

'The convent is no more,' he said softly. Elena cried out in anguish. He went on quickly, 'The nuns were spared, they will find refuge elsewhere. But you are no nun, Elena, and contrary to your own belief, you will learn to be a good deal of use to me, I think. You see, at my stronghold of Thoresfield you will have a new mistress – the lady Isobel. She will train you in your new tasks and Hamet, my faithful servant, will help you to learn. There is much you need to know.'

Elena's face jerked wildly from one to the other. They were smiling at each other as if they shared some dark secret. Wild with sudden fear, she twisted in her chains, but the shackles cut into her soft skin. She stumbled to the ground, and the Breton's grey cloak twisted around her body. Aimery knelt to restrain her struggles. She trembled at his touch, feeling a sudden wild heat blaze through her as his palms grazed her shoulders. His hands were almost gentle . . .

'Lie still,' he said in his low, compelling voice, 'and learn to accept what you cannot change. That will be your first lesson for tonight.' He stood up and said abruptly to his servant, 'Guard her well, Hamet. I'll be back soon, when I've arranged Mauger's punishment.' Then he was gone. Elena lay still, her heart thudding, because for one wild moment, a moment of utter madness, she had wanted the Breton to hold her in his arms.

Hamet sat cross-legged with his broad back against the turf walls of the half-ruined outhouse, watching the helpless girl. A tear glistened on her pale cheek, but she glared at him defiantly. Hamet was sorry for her; she must be so frightened, yet she was full of courage; few people spoke up against the lord Aimery. He wanted to help her, but Aimery had told him not to touch her, and Aimery was his master, the person who had rescued him years ago from a stinking dungeon in Messina, where the Normans were fighting the Moors. Hamet had sworn to devote the rest of his life to the Breton. Le Sabrenn, they had called him then, even his enemies, when he was a lowly mercenary living by his sword – Aimery the swordsman.

'Don't touch her,' Aimery had said. Hamet didn't. But the aching in his loins intensified as he drank in those soft curves wrapped in his master's cloak. He

566

remembered that glimpse of beautiful white flesh, and softly stroked himself beneath his tunic, his dark face intent. 'It's all right, little Saxon girl,' he murmured in his own language. 'It's all right. I won't touch you. I won't harm you.'

The rain thudded on the thatched roof and the thunder rumbled across the forest. He watched until she was asleep, her slight body released at last from fear and tension. The storm had moved on. Hamet got up quietly and went across to where she was lying. He moved the cloak, just a little, and then adjusted her torn dress so that one small breast was revealed, its pink tip soft and innocent in sleep. Then he sat down again at her side and reached beneath his clothing for his already stiff penis. Slowly, ecstatically, he began to bring himself towards orgasm, whispering endearments as he gazed at the sleeping girl.

She was so sweet, so pretty, with her curling fair hair and her creamy skin. Once, he stopped what he was doing to reach out and touch her tender little nipple, but she shuddered in her sleep and he stopped, in case she woke. He sighed and thought of what the lady Isobel would do with her, what she would let him, Hamet, do with her if he was patient. His member jerked and stiffened anew at the thought. He closed his eyes, rocking softly and crooning to himself, as his feverish hands brought his erect penis to a shuddering climax at last.

When the throes of his ejaculation were over, he still stroked his dark flesh gently, lovingly. He was happy now. And so would this gentle girl be. He, Hamet, would make her happy.

Carefully he rearranged the sleeping girl's cloak. Then he sat by the door to wait patiently for his master.

Back at the stronghold of Thoresfield, in one of the candlelit upper chambers, Isobel de Morency also waited for Aimery le Sabrenn, only with rather less

567

patience than Hamet the Saracen. Weary with pacing up and down her room, she moved yet again to the window and pushed aside the piece of oiled hide that curtained the narrow embrasure. Then she looked out into the courtyard below, drinking in the warm evening air, as if it could settle the restless craving in her blood.

There was the usual activity for this time of night. Sentries, sullen in the sultry night air, were posted around the palisade that surrounded the stronghold and its outbuildings; smoking torches fixed into iron holders gave a shadowy light for some late travellers arriving from the south. Grooms rushed to hold their dusty horses, and two off-duty young soldiers lounging against the armoury wall looked up with idle curiousity from their game of dice. Then one of the soldiers saw Isobel, up at her window, and his gaze, frankly admiring, warmed her. She watched him appraisingly for a moment, then turned away petulantly. No. Too coarse, too common. Oh, when would Aimery be back?

Isobel was wrenched by a sudden, hungry longing. He'd only left yesterday, riding into the wild country to the north, because there had been reports of rebel activity again. Only yesterday, but already it seemed too long! What did other women do during these long, hot summer evenings when their menfolk were away? Embroidery, she supposed, or some insipid music-making on their shrill lutes. Isobel's full, ripe lips curled in scorn. She smoothed her beautiful silk gown round her hips, and fingered the circlet of pearls round her neck. Aimery had bought them for her in France, from a merchant who travelled regularly to Constantinople for silks and spices and precious stones.

It was so hot, even at this late hour! Perhaps there would be a thunderstorm soon, and she would be able to watch the lightning playing above the dark line of the forest that surrounded them – anything to relieve the monotony of this place without Aimery. Sighing fretfully, Isobel flung herself across the white linen sheets of her wide bed and reached for the jug of white wine that her maid had left for her. She poured a refreshing draught into her silver goblet and remembered when she had first met Aimery.

It was nearly five years ago now. Her old, nearly impotent husband, the Baron de Morency, had hired a band of Breton mercenaries to fight in some petty skirmish on the borders of his land. Aimery le Sabrenn, illegitimate son of a poor Breton knight and a French serving maid, was the leader of those mercenaries. As soon as she saw him, Isobel wanted him, badly.

She sipped luxuriantly at her wine, still cool from the dark cellars beneath the hall. Aimery had it imported specially from France for her, knowing how she couldn't bear the sour English ale. She stretched languourously and leaned back against the soft pillows that were filled with goose down. Aimery le Sabrenn, the swordsman, his own men had called him admiringly. She remembered how the Breton had first looked at her, cool and challenging, as she sat beside her husband at the high table. Her ripe breasts tingled pleasantly beneath the silk of her green gown at the memory. Thoughtfully she unlaced the fastening of her bodice and slipped her hand inside her white chemise, coaxing both her darkening nipples into a pleasurable stiffness with her fingertips. Already, the sweet wine was starting to course warmly through her blood.

There was a knock at the door, and her maid came in. 'Was there anything else you wanted, my lady?'

Isobel's slanting green eyes spat venom at the interruption. 'Nothing. Go away! And, Alys, if you disturb me once more – ' Alys beat a hasty retreat as Isobel sank back onto her bed. The candle flame, disturbed by the draught from the door, flickered crazily on the tapestries that adorned the bare stone walls. Isobel closed her eyes.

If she couldn't be with Aimery, she resolved silently,

she'd rather be alone with her desire on this hot, sultry night.

Her jewelled fingers fluttered slightly on the soft swell of her breasts. Oh, Aimery. She remembered their first night together, and parted her warm thighs softly beneath the rustling folds of her silk gown.

It had been hot, then, too; a velvety night in late summer. Isobel had found out from her maid that Aimery was alone in one of the guard rooms, attending to his armour. Isobel had pulled a hooded mantle over her thin chemise and run from her chamber under cover of darkness. The Breton was there, as her maid had said. As she entered the dark little room, he'd had his back to her, but she could see that he was polishing his long sword by the light of a guttering tallow candle. Isobel had stood very still, enchanted by the sight of him. He'd removed his soldier's leather tunic because the night was so hot and was wearing only his cloth leggings and deerskin boots. Isobel felt her heart thudding painfully as she drank in the wide-shouldered beauty of his body in the candlelight; the tanned, heavily-muscled yet graceful torso laced with silver sword scars; the lean hips, the long, powerful thighs. She wanted to run her fingertips over every inch of his warm, exciting flesh.

Even now, at the memory of that first night, her lips parted in a soft little groan. Her fingers trailed along her open thighs, gently caressing the smooth flesh above her silken hose, reaching up carefully to touch those tender, private parts that she knew would be swollen and moist already. She ran her small, pointed tongue over her lips.

When Aimery had turned round to see who his visitor was, Isobel had thrown back her hood, so that a mass of glossy black hair spilled out over her shoulders. The Breton had smiled, his strange grey eyes glittering, and Isobel had stopped breathing, because he was so beautiful. He'd said nothing – that smile had been enough.

He'd walked slowly towards her and removed her cloak. Slipping her white chmise from her shoulders, he let it fall unheeded to the floor. Then he bent his head to take each of her ripe breasts in his mouth, feasting on their luxuriance, laving and suckling with his tongue as she thrust them more and more urgently towards him.

Her breasts tingled anew at the memory. As she sprawled on the bed, her fingers stroked her tender clitoris with increasing urgency. Suddenly, she cupped the pulsing mound of her femininity with her cool palm, feeling how engorged the flesh was. It wasn't enough – oh, it wasn't enough! She needed something thick, and firm, and satisfying . . .

Her eyes heavy with desire, Isobel slid impatiently from her lonely bed and searched purposefully in the carved wooden coffer that contained her robes. At last, with a little sigh of satisfaction, she drew out an object wrapped in soft chamois skin. Slowly she unwrapped it, and drew out a long, coiled whip. Smiling, Isobel poured some scented oil from a small glass phial into her hand, then ran her palm up and down the long leather handle until it was slick and moist. Then she curled herself back on the bed, resting her shoulders against the pillows. Her tongue glistened between her white teeth as she parted her legs and began to slowly and sensuously stroke her pouting vaginal lips with the firm leather shaft. It glided sweetly across her already-moist flesh; her cheeks became softly flushed and she uttered a little sigh of contentment.

She remembered, then, how Aimery had barricaded the wooden door of the guardhouse. How he had spread her discarded cloak over the straw-covered floor, and lowered her naked body upon it. Isobel, already quivering with uncontrollable desire, had reached out desperately for him as he crouched over her in the candlelight. She'd covered the rippling muscles of his chest with kisses, run her hands wonderingly over the

571

iron hardness of his forearms; and when he released his manhood from the constriction of his clothes, she'd gasped and felt the blood burn in her cheeks. She'd let out a little cry, and rubbed her soft thighs against the coarse silk of his body, begging wordlessly for his embrace.

At first he'd teased her, rubbing tantalisingly at her yearning entrance with his throbbing phallus, until she'd pleaded with him for mercy. Then, her pleas had become little guttural cries of delight as he at last impaled her, slowly easing the whole of that wonderful length into her quivering, juicy hips, only pausing to let her feel it properly and grip it deep within her hungry loins. He toyed with her then, sliding the pulsing shaft slowly out again so that Isobel had cried out with loss; only to thrust it back in, oh so deeply, as she clutched at his shoulders and gasped out as the approaching ecstasy built up inside her like an unstoppable flood.

She'd climaxed quickly, too quickly that first time, because she found the merest touch of him so exciting. She still did.

Now, alone on her bed, her breath coming in short, agonised gasps, she guided the thick leather handle of the whip longingly into her yearning vulva. Her inner muscles clutched with relief at the slick, hard shaft; the trailing lash tickled tantalisingly along the soft flesh of her inner thigh. Her straying fingers coaxed her sweetly engorged clitoris, as she imagined Aimery plunging himself deep within her, filling her, satisfying her . . .

Isobel rolled convulsively onto her side, her hips thrusting desperately against the long, solid shaft, as her whole body went into spasm. With furious fingers she slid the leather whip hungrily into herself, over and over again, as waves of pleasure engulfed her shuddering body. Aimery, oh Aimery.

She lay back exhausted on the damp linen sheets, her legs splayed, the smooth leather disappointingly cold

572

and unresponsive within her still pulsing vagina. Frowning, she soothed her aching breasts.

It wasn't enough. Nothing was enough, without him.

When Aimery had left France for England with William of Normandy's motley, land-hungry army, Isobel had decided to leave her husband and follow him. Society had disowned her, but she cared nothing for that, as long as she could have Aimery.

Then, at Hastings, when the battle hung in the balance, Aimery had caught Duke William's attention by rallying the mercenary cavalry on the left flank as they hovered on the brink of retreat. When the duke was unhorsed, and the cry went up that he was dead, it was Aimery and his men who swung to surround him, standing firm against the wild onslaught of the Saxon shire-levies as they thundered down the hill towards the French army.

Duke William, now King of England, had not forgotten him.

Was it really only yesterday that Aimery had left the castle? Already it seemed so long. He'd taken his troop of soldiers northwards, after the Saxon rebels who were rumoured to be still in league with the Danish fleet that hovered off the English coast. Isobel had known better than to protest at his absence. After all, hadn't her lover been rewarded with lands and wealth in order to defend this northern outpost for his king, this isolated stronghold, Thoresfield, that guarded the ever-dangerous route between London and York? Isobel understood that Aimery was first and foremost a soldier, who had sworn allegiance to King William of England. But how would she survive without him? No-one compared, as a lover or a man, with Aimery le Sabrenn.

At least she had his return to look forward to. Rearranging her sadly crumpled gown, Isobel stretched lazily across the bed to pour herself some more wine, cheering up at the prospect. Perhaps her lord would bring back some captives, some young Saxon women,

573

for his own pleasure. And for his own bitter, secret revenge, which only Isobel knew about.

She moistened her lips, freshly aroused at the prospect of training new prisoners. As she moved she felt the whip handle, still satisfyingly firm, nudging at her yielding thighs. What she needed was warm, hard flesh.

Isobel gave a rueful sigh and creased her smooth forehead in a frown.

It was no good. She would have to find someone else for her pleasure tonight. Her eyes half-closed, she began to make plans.

Chapter Three

*I*n the woodcutter's cottage in the heart of the forest, Elena, utterly exhausted, slept. As she slept, she dreamed her dream again; only now it was vivid, almost real. The tall man on horseback dismounted, and came slowly, purposefully towards her; she ran gladly towards him, longing for his embrace, but she could not see his shadowed face, and she wanted to, so much . . .

She woke an hour later with an instinctive cry of fear as she glimpsed the big Saracen still watching her from his place by the door. He had fixed a smoking torch into the hard earth, and it cast grotesque shadows around the little hovel. With his dark skin and exotic features, he frightened her almost as much as his cold, scarred master. She tried to move her limbs, and bit her lip as the iron fetters reminded her of her captivity. The Saracen, seeing her awake, slid softly to his feet and padded across the damp earthen floor towards her.

She shrank back from him instinctively, but he held out his hand in a soothing gesture. 'The lord Aimery says that the chains can be removed now. If you promise not to run.' His voice was soft and curiously rhythmic, almost – kind. Kind? She must be losing her mind – how could these men, her enemies, be kind?

She said, in a low voice devoid of emotion, 'I promise not to run.'

What was the point in trying to escape? Even if she managed to get away from here, the forest was not her friend. These wild northern wastes of England were full of starving outlaws, fleeing from the recent destruction wrought by King William and his commanders on the northern rebels. If she tried to flee, she would starve, or suffer an unknown fate at the hands of desperate Saxon runaways.

And, Aimery le Sabrenn had promised that she wouldn't be hurt. Elena knew it was madness, but somehow, she trusted him.

The big Saracen was surprisingly gentle as he released her from the chains. The huge, sinewy muscles of his forearms glistened, and he frowned in concentration as he undid the locks. He smelled musky and masculine; Elena had never seen a man with skin of such a dark, sunburned hue, though she had heard of such people. She blushed to think of his flesh being such a strange colour, every part of him.

'You must not be afraid, Saxon girl,' he said suddenly. 'But you must do as my master bids. In every way –'

Then he broke off, as a tall, forbidding shadow filled the doorway and Aimery le Sabrenn himself entered the little hovel.

Elena looked up at the man who held her captive, and felt strangely weak. He was tall and powerful in the knee-length leather tunic that emphasized his broad shoulders and was drawn tight over lean hips by a wide, buckled belt. In the sombre shadows cast by the torch, his face looked bleaker, harder than ever, with those strange light eyes a startling contrast to his dark, rain-streaked hair. In his cold gaze, there was a weariness, a hint of harshness that made Elena shiver uncontrollably. He was not so much older than her – he could not be more than thirty – yet somehow he looked so

576

experienced, so bitter. Elena felt the muscles of her taut stomach contract painfully as his eyes raked her.

'Well, my little Saxon,' he said, almost lazily. 'You'll be pleased to learn that the guard who assaulted you is about to be punished. Naturally, you are to witness his punishment.'

'No!' gasped Elena. 'No – I could not bear to—'

The man's face twisted, and the pale scar lifted his cruel mouth in a mocking smile. 'It was not a question,' he said softly. 'Hamet, bring her to the clearing.'

The rain had stopped, though the forest still dripped damply around them. The man, Mauger, was already roped to a tree, his back laid bare for the whip. The Breton's men stood in a silent circle round him, waiting. Aimery took his position, and nodded to the sergeant, chief of his men-at-arms, who stepped forward. In his hand the sergeant held a thickly plaited leather quirt. Aimery reached for Elena, and held her wrist so that she had no choice but to watch. His lean, strong fingers burned into her delicate veined skin.

At first, Mauger was silent, though his sturdy, muscular body shook each time the whip seared his taut flesh. Elena turned her head away, revolted, as the leather quirt continued to mark its red weals on the soldier's broad back. Aimery saw her turn and gripped her small chin between his finger and thumb.

'You will look,' he commanded. 'This man is being punished for you.'

'No! You can't make me! I – I'll shut my eyes – '

'Every time you do that,' said the Breton softly, 'I'll add ten strokes to the man's punishment. Now – look.'

Elena thought she would faint. Aimery held her by the shoulders now, forcing her to witness the punishment. When at last he called out, 'Stop – it is enough,' she turned to swallow dryly, her throat agonised.

He waited one moment, then turned her tear-stained face up to meet his.

577

'You did not like that, little Saxon?'

'No!' she choked out. 'It – it was vile.'

He stroked one lean finger down her white cheek. 'Then you will have to be more careful about your complaints in future, won't you? You will have to grow up, little Elena. We are soldiers, in hostile territory, and discipline must be maintained at all times. The man's punishment was not severe. He is a good soldier, and we need him. But he has learned his lesson. As for you – you must learn to enjoy these little games we play . . .'

Games? Elena was dumbstruck. Meanwhile Hamet, at his master's shoulder, was watching avidly. 'Shall we begin now, lord, with her training? I have put your things under shelter, in the woodcutter's hut – it is quite private there – '

The Breton still held Elena by her shoulders, and was watching her carefully, his grey eyes narrowed in speculation. Elena felt herself tremble beneath his gaze. 'No, Hamet,' Aimery said at last. 'We will savour her education properly. Once we are at the castle, the lady Isobel will prepare her most thoroughly. It will be worth the wait, I assure you.'

Hamet's shoulders drooped with disappointment; Aimery said dryly, 'I see you have little patience tonight, my friend. Why not fetch a willing girl from among the captives?'

Hamet nodded eagerly. 'Yes, lord. And the Saxon girl – she will watch?'

Aimery frowned impatiently. 'No, I told you before. She will begin her education at the castle. Put her back in her chains and fetch yourself a girl.'

Elena, barely understanding their exchanged words but sensing the threat in them, began to struggle as the cold fetters were fastened carefully round her tender limbs once more. Aimery le Sabrenn said, 'You are foolish, little Saxon. Unless you submit to my orders, I cannot guarantee your safety. Would you rather be out

578

there alone with the other slaves, at the mercy of men such as Mauger?'

Elena sagged in Hamet's arms, forced to acknowledge the truth of his cold words. Aimery watched as Hamet carried the girl gently back to her shelter, and his lip curled in scorn. His heart was filled with renewed bitterness against the Saxons.

The girl, Elena, with her pretence of fragility and innocence, disturbed him. He told himself that her facade was all a cunning mask. She'd probably incited that fool Mauger, and no doubt she would cause yet more trouble before he was finished with her.

Hamet came back promptly, his teeth gleaming whitely in the darkness. He was trailing a Saxon redhead behind him, one of the rebels they'd swept in from the woods, who somehow managed to look voluptuous in spite of her ragged gown. Her eyes widened when she saw to whom she had been brought; she moistened her ripe lips as she assessed Aimery's strong, handsome figure.

'You wanted me, my lord?' she whispered.

Aimery let a cold smile twist his features. 'Of that I'm not sure,' he replied. 'But perhaps you can persuade me.' And he led the way purposefully across the clearing to the woodcutter's cottage, where Hamet had placed his things in the main room. A dim lantern flared shakily in one corner, casting flickering shadows on the sagging roof and earthen floor. Aimery leaned his back against the coarse flint wall, and folded his arms across his chest. On the other side of that wall lay the chained Saxon girl, in the little outhouse. Pushing the image of her frightened yet defiant face from his mind, he turned his cold gaze on the voluptuous redhead.

'Amuse me,' he said.

The redhead, gazing after him hungrily, nodded. Then she turned to Hamet.

She swayed sinuously towards the Saracen, pouting her mouth provocatively at the open delight in his face.

579

With one swift movement she slipped her ragged dress from her shoulders, to reveal full, luscious breasts with a dusting of freckles across the creamy skin. Hamet caught his breath. 'Oh, yes,' he sighed.

He lunged towards her, but with one finger at her mouth she stopped him, and indicated that he should lower himself to the ground. He did so, lying on his back on the uneven floor, with his big hands pillowing his head. Already his eyes were glazed in anticipation, and his white smile showed his pleasure.

The girl, breathing heavily, dropped to one side and bent over his hips. With nimble fingers she pushed back his tunic and felt for the ties of his leggings, eagerly pulling them away. When the Saracen's fully erect penis sprang into freedom, quivering with tension, she let out a little moan at the sight and stroked it with feverish fingers. Then she let her full breasts hang over it and teased the glistening dark knob with her nipples, each in turn, sighing at the pleasure it was giving her. Hamet moaned aloud, and the redhead glanced across at the Breton provocatively. Aimery, still leaning against the wall, watched the interplay of black and white flesh in the light of the lantern with a kind of languid detachment and made no move to join them.

Then the redhead bobbed down, her flickering pink tongue darting snake-like at the dark, swollen glans. She licked the bead of moisture from its tip, and swirled the tip of her tongue round its sensitive ridge. Hamet jerked convulsively. He reached out to grab at her breasts, his fingers clutching at the sweet, creamy flesh, and his hips arched to thrust his rigid penis full into her mouth.

She flinched at first, but forced herself to relax, and took as much as she could into herself, using her tongue to suck and caress as the big Saracen jerked and moaned beneath her. She was aware, all the time, of the Breton lord watching her. Now, there was the one she really wanted. She felt her own juices flowing, her flesh

580

tightening in anticipation at what she hoped would come next. Meanwhile, she used all her skill on the Saracen, cupping his balls gently in her hand, feeling the wrinkled skin tauten and quiver until at last, with a great cry of release, he pumped himself into her soft, moist mouth. She did her best to hold him in there while he bucked, but it was hard, because he was so big. She sucked him and swallowed, hard, until at last his violent spasms began to subside.

Then he lay back with a groan, the satisfaction glazing his face, and the redhead turned with a coy smile to Aimery. 'Your turn, my lord?'

He was already unbuckling his belt. She watched, her small pink tongue flickering between her lips in hot anticipation as she appreciated his wide-shouldered, sinewy body. She knew, somehow, that this man would be the very essence of cool, powerful masculinity.

'Turn round,' he bit out curtly.

Disappointed, she dragged her gaze from his gauntly handsome face. Then she felt his hands pushing her roughly into place, on all fours. So *this* was how he liked it. She was sorry, because she would like to have seen that chillingly scarred face in the throes of sexual ecstasy. Perhaps, if she performed to his satisfaction, the Breton lord would summon her again. This was better than living as a runaway in the forest, scratching for food and shelter!

He was pushing her full skirts up round her waist. His cool, sensitive hands were on her flaring buttocks, feeling for the cleft; stroking, probing. She shuddered and involuntarily arched herself towards him, still wet and excited from the Saracen's attentions. The Saracen was watching her avidly from the shadows; she heard his master snap a sharp command to him, and the servant slid beneath the girl to suckle with his full lips at her tender nipples, making her quiver with delight.

Then she gasped aloud, as the Breton parted the wet lips of her swollen vulva with skilful fingers and thrust

581

his manhood in to the hilt. Once sheathed in her moist softness, he stopped moving, and held himself very still.

'Oh!' The redhead could not stop herself from crying out at the pleasure of it. The shaft of his penis seemed exquisitely long and smooth, and it filled her to the point of delirium. His refusal to move drove her wild; she waited as long as she could, raptly drinking in the pleasure of feeling him deep inside her; then, with a groan, she started to writhe along the hard, wonderful length that filled her, while the Saracen licked at her dangling breasts with hot, darting strokes of his stiffened tongue.

'Stop.' Aimery's low, masterful voice whispered in her ear. She couldn't stop, but continued to massage herself along his shaft, quivering in her mounting ecstasy.

Aimery's fingers clasped her buttocks, stilling her. 'I told you to stop. You were ordered not to move,' he repeated, in a calm voice that nevertheless chilled her heated blood. 'You will not move again until I give you permission – do you understand me?'

She swallowed hard, and nodded. Her left breast was on fire where the Saracen was licking her with his big, agile tongue, softly rasping at her burning nipple, sending dark, fiery pleasures arrowing down to her abdomen.

Aimery started to withdraw his penis very, very slowly. She wanted to cry out loud to him to thrust it within her aching flesh again; her hips quivered threateningly with her need.

'I said – *don't move* . . .'

She nodded dumbly and bit her lips hard as he slid himself slowly into her clutching vagina again. So beautiful, so firm, so strong . . .

It was no good. She gave a harsh cry of need and worked herself feverishly against him, the black man's hungry lips at her nipple driving her on into a delirious vortex of pleasure that was conscious only of his thrusting manhood deep within her. She writhed her hips in desperate abandon, and rubbed her swollen, aching breasts against the Saracen's face.

The Breton withdrew, leaving her cold and empty. She was still.

Then, coldly and deliberately, he re-entered her and began to drive himself to his own orgasm within her, his thrusts increasing with devastating impulsion, while she struggled to restrain her own pleasure. The Breton said nothing; all she could hear was the harshness of his breathing as he gripped her by the waist and drove his engorged manhood into her soft flesh. At last he gave a final fierce lunge, and she quivered involuntarily, unable to reject the wild pleasure as his long penis quivered and spasmed in the very heart of her body. With a high-pitched cry, she writhed against him, gripping at him, rubbing herself up and down the delicious shaft as her own inevitable orgasm convulsed her feverish body.

He withdrew, and began to adjust his clothing, watching impassively as the voluptuous redhead lay in damp exhaustion on the floor. Hamet, excited by the scene he had just witnessed, was erect again and straddling her prone body, he began to slide his throbbing member into her open mouth once more. The girl quailed momentarily, but the Saracen circled her damp lips with the glans of his penis, and the feel of his silken skin excited her so much that she willingly took him in. Hamet, throwing back his head in triumph, pumped himself with long, deep strokes into her mouth, spurting into her. The girl rolled over onto her side, sated and exhausted.

Aimery touched her disdainfully with his foot. 'You can go now,' he said, barely troubling to mask the scorn in his voice.

She sat up, clutching her torn clothing to her body. She gazed up at him lasciviously. Damn him, with that fascinating scar and long, lithe body. In spite of his coldness, she still ached for him.

'My lord.' She reached out a beseeching hand. 'If you wish, I will warm your bed for the full night – '

He gestured her hand away. The hunger in her face disappointed him. There was no pleasure in it when they were so eager. 'She can go now, Hamet,' he said shortly.

She called back over her shoulder as the Saracen led her out of the hut. 'Send for me, my lord! My name is Morwith . . .'

The Saracen escorted her without a word back to the slave lines. She lay down to sleep with the rest of the serfs, and quivered with reawakened desire as she remembered the sweet feel of the Breton's manhood deep within her heated body.

She'd heard that Aimery le Sabrenn was like no other man, and now she knew it was true. Stirring feverishly, she reached down between her legs and stroked herself, moaning his name in the darkness as she shuddered towards climax once more.

Perhaps, thought Morwith longingly, her chance would come again – at the castle.

Elena lay awake in the outhouse, restless and disturbed. The chains were only a light restraint but, however hard she tried, she couldn't get comfortable. She could still hear the occasional rumble of thunder in the distance; the night was hot and oppressive.

Then, she heard the sounds, muffled by the dense stone wall. A woman's voice, first; then she recognised the Saracen's deep, velvety chuckle, and his master's harsh voice giving orders. Then silence; she thought they had gone, or perhaps slept.

Elena felt the breath catch in her throat when the woman started to moan. Little animal noises; a man's harsh grunt; then the woman's voice, crying out, over and over again, small, thin, high-pitched – as though she was somewhere beyond pain, beyond pleasure. Oh, what was happening? More punishments? More – *games*?

The muffled noises seemed to go on forever. Elena listened, fascinated in spite of herself, the blood burning in her cheeks, until the last sounds died away. Her pulse still beating wildly, she huddled up in her corner against the crude turf walls. Then she stopped breathing, as the rickety wooden door was pulled open from the outside and a gaunt shadow filled the entrance.

It was Aimery le Sabrenn. Elena stared speechlessly up at him, her heart thudding wildly as he stood there gazing down at her. She felt her throat go dry, not with fear, but with something else; some emotion she didn't recognise.

He watched her for a moment then said, 'I have brought you bread and wine. You must be hungry. Afterwards, you must sleep. We have a long journey tomorrow.'

As Elena watched, her blue eyes wide with unspoken questions, he put the wineskin down beside her, along with a manchet loaf wrapped in a white linen napkin. Then he was gone once more, like a shadow, and Elena lay trembling in the darkness, his lean, scarred face imprinted forever on her mind.

She knew now why she thought she had recognised him, why he had seemed so familiar; the way he walked, the way he moved, everything about his lithe, muscular figure. Aimery le Sabrenn, Breton lord of Thoresfield, was just like the man in her dream!

Elena squeezed her eyes shut against the sudden, dizzying sensation that swept through her body.

And she had wanted him to stay . . .

Chapter Four

*I*sobel said scornfully, 'I saw her from the window as you rode into the courtyard. She looks too young. And, my dear, so innocent!'

Aimery, who had been pacing the private chamber that Isobel had furnished as her bower, turned suddenly. 'She is twenty-two. And as for innocence – I thought, Isobel, that was what you wanted.'

Isobel stepped softly across the rush matting towards him and stroked his cheek where the thin scar split it, the hard ridge of tissue almost silver in the flickering light of the candles fixed to the walls. 'I thought that was what *you* wanted, Aimery my love. For your revenge.'

She pressed her supple body against him, running her hands up his brown, sinewed forearms, and pressing little, nibbling kisses against the smooth muscle of his chest, where she'd parted his tunic. That wicked Saxon blade had scarred his beautiful face, but he was still as exciting, as dangerous as ever, especially now that he was as rich and powerful as any woman could desire, basking as he did in the king's favour. As she caressed him, her coiled tongue was hot and enticing; Aimery pushed her away before his own desire should flare too openly. Isobel was worried at this hint of rejection, though she was too clever to show it. She wondered if perhaps he had heard about her visitor last night.

'She's ideal for our purpose,' he said curtly. 'She claims she was a novice in a convent – a convent that was harbouring rebels. She's yours to train, Isobel.'

'And yours to reward, my lord,' murmured Isobel de Morency. A hungry green light gleamed in her eyes. 'Shall I go to her now?'

Aimery nodded curtly. 'Yes. And send Hamet to me.'

He didn't need Isobel to remind him about revenge. The bleak anger rose in his throat as he remembered.

Last year, while garrisoned in York, Aimery's younger brother Hugh had taken a beautiful Saxon woman as his mistress. A golden witch. She'd ensnared Aimery too, persuading him to keep their mutual passion a secret from his unsuspecting brother. Aimery had despised himself, and worshipped her, even forgetting Isobel for a while.

The woman had led them into a trap – both of them. She'd been working for the Saxon rebels, all the time. When York was taken by the Saxon army, Hugh had died in captivity, while Aimery had escaped, scarred for life by the cruel sword that had split his cheek in two.

Since then, Aimery had vowed that the Saxons would pay for the death of his brother. It was his own personal mission of revenge; of which King William, who had entrusted him with this northern outpost, knew nothing.

Elena lay back, dazed, in the warm, scented water of the bath tub they'd brought for her. Her freshly washed hair, spread like damp silk around her white shoulders, gleamed in the soft candlelight. She didn't understand any of it.

She had spent the remainder of the journey to the

castle on the back of a horse; a quiet palfrey, roped to one of the guards, who'd been so respectful that he'd scarcely even dared to look at her.

They'd reached Aimery's stronghold of Thoresfield at dusk. Originally a wealthy thane's stone manor house, it had been strengthened in haste by the Normans last year in order to guard the dangerous route north, and to protect its garrison from the rebels and bands of outlaws who haunted the vast forest. It had become notorious. As the convoy of captives was led through the wide gates, Elena heard the ragged line of slaves whisper in fear; then the roped wretches were driven into the torchlit courtyard of the castle by burly guards, and driven off to the thatched hovels that lay clustered within the palisade.

Once, she caught sight of the Saxon man, whom she'd tried to help in the forest – the man who'd stayed with Father Wulfstan. She felt her heart give a little lurch as the blond Saxon man turned to smile at her, and she was glad he'd survived.

Then Elena waited breathlessly in the courtyard, deafened by the shouts of the soldiers and the jangling of horses' harness, her heart beating wildly. This was to be her home.

She'd expected to be lined up with the other serfs, but instead they'd brought her in here, into the very heart of the stronghold. Through the huge, raftered hall they led her, with its great fire forever burning at one end; up the stairs, along the gallery past the Breton's living quarters into this room, which she was told would be hers.

After the bare meanness of the little convent, even this tiny chamber was luxury. The maidservant who awaited her had helped her off with her ragged clothes, exclaiming with pity over her torn, bruised feet and her chafed wrists where the chains had been. Then she helped her to step into the wooden tub.

Elena, still dazed by everything that had happened,

lay back when the maid had gone, and revelled in the sweetly-scented soap and the delicious sensation of warm water lapping at her skin. She had never had a hot bath before. At the convent they washed every morning using buckets of cold water from the spring, and harsh soap made from wood-ash and lye. This was bliss. The small but private room was hung with tapestries, had a fire burning in one corner, and a hide curtain to the window. There was a narrow bed, covered with wolfskins as blankets, and real wax candles on the walls, not the crude, foul-smelling tallow they used at the convent.

She frowned and bit her lip. Perhaps everyone was wrong. Perhaps Aimery le Sabrenn was truly a kind man, who intended to help her. After all, hadn't he punished that evil man, Mauger, for attacking her?

She shuddered suddenly, remembering how they'd left his limp, beaten body roped to the tree. Aimery le Sabrenn – kind? She must be in danger of losing her wits! She swallowed hard, thrusting the Breton lord's disturbing image from her mind, and began to soap herself, luxuriating in the warm water. Her body was bruised and aching from the long ride. Exploratively she ran her fingers along her calves and up along her smooth, slender thighs. Her small breasts lay buoyantly just above the surface of the water; she soaped them carefully, and lapped the soothing water over their tender tips.

Suddenly, she remembered the puzzling noises that the unseen woman had made last night in the darkness, and frowned. At the same time, strangely, her nipples tingled and darkened, and as she touched one inquisitively, a pleasurable little shock arrowed down towards her flat stomach. She caught her breath and did it again. A vague, yearning ache flooded slowly through her relaxed limbs, and the warm blood rose in her cheeks.

She bit at her lower lip thoughtfully, and stroked her swelling breast. The Breton's low, compelling voice

echoed in her brain: *'You have much to learn, little Saxon
. . .'* With a blush of shame, she snatched her hand
away.

At the convent, they'd been told it was a sin to touch
their bodies. The younger ones slept in dormitories with
older nuns to keep an eye on them, and they had to
sleep with their hands above the coarse blankets or they
were beaten.

Closing her eyes, Elena lay back, and her hands
wandered down to her inner thigh. They were so
bruised from the long ride. Perhaps if she stroked them
a little, it would soothe them. Her palm, by accident,
grazed the soft mound between her legs. Her body
quivered and jumped. She did it again, her eyes wide
open with surprise. Her little triangle of womanly hair
was light golden, like soft down; she fingered it, and
her hand slipped lower, exploring the strange, folded
flesh in that secret place. She caught something with
the tip of her finger – it felt like a tiny, sensitive bud –
and a sudden, delicious sensation flared, spreading a
melting heat into her stomach. She snatched her hand
away quickly, but her cheeks flamed, and a little pulse
beat wildly in her soft throat.

She jumped with shock, sending ripples of water over
the edge of the tub, as the door that divided her room
from the gallery was pushed aside and a woman glided
in.

Elena thought that she was the most beautiful woman
she had ever seen in her life. She was small and slender,
with glossy dark hair and perfect, creamy skin, and a
kind smile. She wore a green silk gown that matched
her wonderful, dark-lashed eyes; it was girdled to fit
her body tightly, pushing up her small, rounded
breasts, while the skirt flared out in rich swathes from
her hips to brush the ground.

She was carrying a silver goblet in her hands. On
seeing Elena's blush of surprise, she came softly

590

towards her and knelt at he side, with a rustle of silk and perfume.

'My dear,' she said, in a low voice, 'don't be afraid of me, I beg you! My name is Isobel, and I've come to look after you. You poor thing, what a dreadful ordeal you must have suffered! How I feel for you . . .'

Elena tried to sit up, but the lady put out one exquisite jewelled hand, restraining her. 'There is no cause for alarm! Lie back – relax.' By accident, it seemed, her little fingers brushed Elena's exposed breasts. Elena let out a tiny gasp; the woman heard it, and smiled to herself.

'Here,' she said, holding out the goblet. 'Drink this. It has medicinal properties. You will find it soothes you, relaxes you.'

Elena, forgetting to be ashamed of her nakedness at those soothing words, gazed hypnotised into the woman's spellbinding green eyes, took the goblet and drank deeply. It was delicious, tasting of honey and sunshine, and strange, exotic fruits. Almost immediately her body was filled with a flooding sensation of languor. She gave a blissful little sigh and leaned back against the side of the tub, her eyes closed.

A smile flickered round Isobel's mouth as she studied her carefully by the light of the glimmering candles. Aimery was right. The girl was astonishingly beautiful for a Saxon peasant, with that sweet, heart-shaped face, and the full, curved lips, and the glorious golden hair that cascaded round her shoulders and curled into little tendrils where it was damp.

And her breasts! High and firm, they darkened deliciously into tiny rosebud crests. She was young, surely untouched. Isobel licked her lips and drew in her breath sharply. The girl stirred and her eyes flew open.

'Let me take the goblet,' Isobel said soothingly, taking the vessel from the girl's nerveless hands. 'And then let me finish washing you, my dear. You must be so tired – '

And, before the girl could protest, she picked up the

scented soap and the washing cloth, and began, with light, circling strokes, to lave at her shoulders.

Elena felt light, as if she were floating. She felt exquisitely calm and carefree after that wonderful healing drink. This woman, so beautiful and kind, was truly her friend.

Isobel's busy hands worked carefully at first, so as not to disturb her. She washed her shoulders and arms with gentle thoroughness, as a maid would have done.

But then, her white hands soft with soap, she slid her fingers round Elena's ribcage, and slipped them upwards to caress her soft, virginal breasts.

Elena gasped, and went rigid. Her eyes, which had been slowly closing with the heady effect of the wine, flew open in alarm.

Isobel said softly, 'Relax, my dear. Let me bathe you properly. You have no need to be ashamed of your beautiful body. After all, you are a lady of the castle, are you not? And this is what fine ladies do to one another.'

Elena nodded dumbly, because she couldn't speak. Isobel was kneading her nipples so slowly and exquisitely that the pleasure melted her and set up hot, churning sensations in her belly. She felt her breasts swelling and tugging, aching for some nameless release. Oh, what was happening to her? Her breath was coming rapidly and she could feel her cheeks burning with shame. She had to escape, and yet she didn't want this beautiful lady to stop. Her jutting nipples danced beneath Isobel's soapy caresses, and she felt a sweet, blissful ache in the soft, secret flesh between her legs. She suddenly thought of Aimery the Breton and quivered, as if his scornful eyes were watching her coldly. Her mouth went dry, and she felt herself ache for Isobel's cool hands to continue their work, to soothe her throbbing breasts, to –

Isobel stopped. She had watched the young Saxon slave's sweet, tormented little face, watched as her lips parted tremulously and her thighs rubbed against one another in an effort to sooth the exquisite need. She was thrusting her breasts involuntarily towards Isobel, trying to find those cool palms again. Definitely time to stop, decided Isobel, before she took her beyond the brink. Aimery would be angry if she went any further.

Isobel sighed. It was quite obvious that this stupid, naive girl was totally ignorant about her own body – had never even pleasured herself, brought herself to a feeble, solitary orgasm. How angry Aimery would be if he missed her first one.

Isobel was aware that she had probably overdone the wine too. She prayed that the girl would stay awake long enough for their purposes.

Reluctantly, Isobel de Morency got to her feet. The girl watched her, obviously shaken. Her vivid blue eyes were hazed with sexual longing.

'Come along, my dear,' said Isobel a trifle sharply. 'Time to join the lord Aimery.' Isobel was excited herself now at the thought of Aimery waiting for them. She called the maidservant, and watched as Alys dressed the sweetly-scented Saxon slave girl in a silk chemise, fine stockings that were gartered above the knee, and a pretty dark blue gown of softest wool that matched her eyes. The bodice was laced at the front, like Isobel's, and the finishing touch was a lovely silver girdle tied round her waist. Then Alys helped Elena to buckle on some dainty little shoes of dark red leather, and finally brushed out her long golden hair and let it hang loosely, a shimmering gauze around her shoulders.

Isobel, surveying the bewildered Elena in her new finery, suddenly didn't feel quite so pleased with Aimery's latest acquisition. The girl was truly beautiful, more beautiful than perhaps Isobel had realised at first. Her skin was ivory-pale and delicate, not like the nut-brown hue of the other Saxon serfs. And she was young – several years younger than Isobel de Morency.

Isobel frowned. But she could cope with it, couldn't

she? Aimery needed her – she inflamed his blood. No other woman could satisfy him, because he grew bored with their adoration and their desperate, clinging ways. Whereas Isobel was useful to him, because she understood his need to use and humiliate these stupid Saxon girls who became his slaves. For that was all the wench was – a slave – and she'd be reminded of that soon enough. Isobel would see to that.

Only once had she lost him for a while, and that was to that Saxon witch, Madelin, who'd all but destroyed him.

'You look quite lovely, my dear Elena,' Isobel said graciously. Elena overwhelmed by her new finery, smiled shyly up at her, and Isobel took her by the hand.

Aimery was waiting for them in his private chamber. Usually he ate in the great hall below, with his soldiers and retainers, but tonight he'd had food brought upstairs so he could dine alone. He'd almost finished, and the remains of the feast – roast fowl, succulent venison, white manchet bread and pork with honeyed apples – lay about the table.

He dismissed the waiting manservant when Isobel came in with Elena, and stood up. 'Be seated at the table,' he said courteously to Elena, extending one firm, well-shaped hand. 'And take what you want to eat.'

Elena gazed up at him, speechless. Aimery le Sabrenn, the vile beast of rumour, at whose very name the elderly nuns used to cross themselves, was actually smiling at her. And as he smiled she realised, with a little jolt that made her heart pound, that in spite of the cruel scar he was the most devastatingly handsome man she had ever seen. His smile made her feel faint as his thin lips twisted. She sat down suddenly in the chair he indicated and stared at the table, her senses swimming. Isobel sat down too, opposite Elena.

'There is spiced venison here, or perhaps you would

prefer the chicken?' the Breton offered graciously, pushing a dish towards her.

'Thank you, my lord,' muttered Elena, not able to meet his eyes. 'But I am not hungry.'

'Some wine, then?' He thrust a goblet towards her. Elena grabbed at it and drank thirstily, because her mouth was suddenly burning dry. She put it down when it was empty, and closed her eyes as the sweet liquid trickled down her throat.

When she opened them, something had happened. Aimery had sat down again at Isobel's side; and she, Elena, might as well not have been in the room. Most of the candles had been snuffed out; only two remained alight, glimmering from their iron sconces on the wall. Shadows leaped from the log fire, bringing to life the hazy, mysterious figures on the tapestries that adorned the bare flint walls. Her head swam. Aimery and the lady Isobel weren't even touching. But there was something about the way they *looked* at each other . . .

Elena felt her pulse racing, her blood pounding thickly with the wine she'd drunk. She gazed in horrified fascination, unable to tear her eyes away as she saw how the Breton was dipping the sweet red grapes in his wine and dropping them, very slowly, between Isobel's red lips. The lady accepted them with pleasure, gazing all the time into his strange silver eyes; then, as he slowly inserted yet another grape, she nipped at his hand with her perfect white teeth, and caught his flesh between her lips, and sucked and sucked. Aimery smiled slowly, and Elena watched in dazed disbelief as the tiny tip of Isobel's tongue caressed her lord's lean, sun-browned finger.

Elena caught her breath and leaned forward in her chair, her limbs strangely on fire. The soft silk of her chemise tantalised her scented flesh. She clenched her hands.

Isobel looked at her and smiled. Then she gazed into Aimery's eyes again and slowly, very slowly, she

595

unlaced the bodice of her beautiful green dress and slipped it down to expose her white, perfect breasts. They gleamed with the milky whiteness of pearls in the soft candlelight.

Aimery dipped his finger in the wine. Completely ignoring the wide-eyed, trembling Saxon girl, he circled his moist finger round each of Isobel's nipples in turn, totally absorbed his his task. Darker and larger than Elena's, the delicate buds of erectile tissue stood out proudly to meet his sensuous caress. Aimery paused, watching, then reached out both his hands to cup her full breasts together. Isobel shuddered. Then, as Elena watched, hypnotised, the Breton lowered his head as if in homage, and took each of her breasts in turn into his worshipping mouth. Elena could see his sensual, curved tongue licking and circling the quivering flesh. She saw how Isobel threw her head back, her eyes closed, her breath coming in short, ragged pants as she gripped his shoulders with a sudden, fierce hunger.

Elena felt wave after wave of hot, shameful emotion washing over her helpless body. She knew that she should turn and run. But she couldn't move. She felt her own heated blood surge and pulse as Aimery's mouth devoured the lady Isobel's tender breasts. An almost unbearable ache was rising down at the pit of her taut stomach, and her own swollen breasts seemed to be thrusting against the confines of her tight bodice, the turgid nipples hot and painful. Oh, she thought, with a sudden flood of shame, how cool the Breton's cruel mouth would be against her own burning flesh! He was teasing Isobel now, his firm hands lightly spanning her waist; she could see how his tongue was darting and flicking at her thrusting, creamy breasts, while Isobel writhed and panted in his embrace. Elena gripped the edge of the table, and a tiny moan of longing escaped from her parted lips.

They both heard her. Aimery stopped his exquisite torment of his lady; raising his head, he turned slowly towards Elena, and smiled his slow, crooked smile. Isobel lay back in her chair panting, her lovely face flushed and contorted, her body still quivering. As if – as if he had hurt her. But he hadn't, surely? Elena's small face twisted in bewilderment.

Aimery stood up. He lifted the lady Isobel easily in his strong arms and carried her across to a fur-covered bed in the far corner of his chamber. Then he came back towards Elena. She shrank back in her chair, appalled, yet unable to take her eyes from him. He knelt before her on the rush matting, so that his face was at the same height as hers, and let one hand rest lightly on her thigh. He was so masculine, so beautiful in his lithe strength.

'Well, my little Saxon rebel,' he said, his low, cool voice sending renewed tremors through her. 'Did you enjoy that?'

Elena clenched her hands in confusion. 'No! How could I?'

'Then why,' he said, leaning forward, 'did you watch it so avidly?'

She shook her head in desperation, her eyes transfixed by the hard, clear lines of his face. Oh, if only she hadn't drunk that wine! Her brain, like her limbs, was hot and fevered. 'I had no choice!' she whispered.

His strong, capable hands were touching her gown. She caught her breath in horrified excitement. 'But you enjoyed it,' he went on relentlessly. 'Was it because you wanted me to do the same to you, little convent girl? Is that how you and your sweet friends pleasured one another at your nunnery, your nest of rebels? Like this?'

'No! I – oh, please!' Her voice broke off in a gasp of pleasure, because his hands had slipped her silk chemise under her aching breasts so that the taut fabric thrust them provocatively upwards. He began to stroke them, gently. Little arrows of impossible rapture seared Elena's quivering flesh. She gasped and thrust against his big, cool palms, rubbing the tautened globes desperately against his caress. His silver eyes narrowed as he watched her; deliberately his thumbs found her stiffened nipples, and rubbed them tantalisingly. Shafts of hot and cold sensation burned through her. She closed her eyes and shuddered as his hands slipped round her back.

Then a new, impossibly delicious sensation engulfed her trembling flesh. If he hadn't been supporting her, she would have collapsed, because all of a sudden her small breasts felt wet, and hot, and so deliciously sensitive that she was moaning aloud. He was licking her, savouring her with his mouth, in the same exquisite way that he'd tormented the lady Isobel. His long, stiffened tongue rasped slowly, softly to and fro across her engorged nipples, flicking at them, then sucking moistly. Waves of excitement convulsed her flesh; she clenched her legs together, and was suddenly aware of a shameful wetness seeping from her most secret parts.

Oh, could such dreadful things really happen? This must be the work of the very devil, and she would be damned forever for enjoying it . . .

She threw herself back, pushing her quivering flesh hard against his strong sensual mouth, gasping aloud as his teeth nipped deliciously and his firm lips suckled and caressed. Rippling tides of ecstasy washed in mounting waves through her shaking body; she reached out mindlessly to clutch at his wide, strong shoulders, pulling him towards her, pressing his hard-boned face down against her sensitised flesh in an agony of wanting yet more.

In a deliberately calculated move, he stood up, and she sagged helplessly in her chair, gazing up at him with wide, imploring eyes.

'Please,' she whispered, clasping her hands across her still quivering, blue-veined nakedness. 'Oh, please, my lord – '

He stood towering above her, his hands on his hips. The expression on his dark, brooding face was unreadable; the white scar seemed livid in the hard-boned masculinity of his face.

'What did you want me to do next, Elena?' he said in a soft voice that sent shivers through her. 'What did you want me to do to that pretty little nun's body of yours?'

Elena shook her head numbly. 'I don't know, my lord,' she whispered. 'I only know that – I didn't want you to stop – '

He smiled a slow, harsh smile. 'You didn't know, did you?' he said softly, taking her by the shoulders. 'You really have no idea . . .' He turned to Isobel, who was leaning forward, her eyes hungry, on the bed. 'We have a lot to teach her, you see, Isobel. Let us hope that she learns well.'

He let go of her, and she fell in a shaking heap on the ground, burying her head in her arms. Aimery went to the door of his room to open it, and Hamet came in.

'Restrain her,' Aimery said curtly to the Saracen. 'She wishes to partake in our games.' Then he went back to the table and poured himself more wine. He watched impassively as Hamet led the dazed Elena across the room to a darkened alcove and, raising her slender wrists, shackled her carefully to some chains that protruded from the cold stones of the outer wall. Elena's blood was racing wildly at this new degredation. Her bodice was still undone, and she was aware of the big Saracen's hungry black eyes eagerly devouring her nakedness. Her arms were dragged up above her head by the chains, so that her breasts were lifted high. She felt sick with excitement when they began to tingle and burn in anticipation as Aimery le Sabrenn strolled languidly towards her with a full goblet of wine in his hand.

His mouth tightened in mockery as he registered her stiffening nipples. Elena bowed her head in submission. Then, with one hand, he raised her small chin and pushed the goblet against her lips.

599

'Drink,' he said, almost unkindly. 'Drink it all down, Saxon girl.'

He trickled it down her throat, and she drank thirstily. A lot of it was spilt; she felt it running down her chin, down her throat and across her burning breasts, tormenting her with its coolness. The Breton lord smiled, and reached out to flick the drops away; her body jerked towards him, in automatic reaction. 'Later,' he said softly. 'But first, we must continue with your education.'

He pointed towards the bed. Elena's eyes jerked wide open.

On top of the big, fur-covered bed, the lady Isobel was lying moaning as the big Saracen crouched on top of her. At first, Elena thought that he was attacking her. Then she heard Isobel's low gurgle of delight, and realised that Hamet had pulled Isobels's skirts up around her waist, and she wasn't fighting him. Elena could see how his loose mouth suckled at her exposed breasts, while all the time he was fumbling with his own clothing, throwing his tunic and leggings to the ground and exposing his huge, glistening dark limbs.

Elena closed her eyes in disbelief. The wine swam round in her fevered blood. Aimery raised her head upright again. 'Look,' he commanded. 'You wish to learn? This is your lesson.'

Elena forced her eyes open and watched in dismay. The Saracen's huge male member was fully exposed as it jerked upright between his muscular black thighs. It looked so swollen and massive to Elena that she gasped aloud. She watched, rigid with apprehension, as he seemed to part the lady Isobel's tender thighs and thrust his obscene protuberance against her quivering hips. Elena felt faint; yet at the same time she felt a strange, stirring excitement deep within herself.

She bit her lip as she saw how the big black penis slid into Isobel's private parts, and then withdrew again, glistening with moisture, while a lewd expression of

600

delight contorted the man's face. Surely, Isobel would protest at the intrusion? But no – she was crying out softly, happily, and clutching at the man's shoulders, lifting her swollen breasts into his greedy mouth as he slid that giant shaft into her arching hips yet again.

Elena jerked her head away, feeling that she could watch no more. But there was no escape that way. Aimery, who had been watching her, reached up to her chains, and somehow, by a little ratchet device, shortened them an inch or so, stretching her arms even higher. It was bearable, but made her only too aware of his power over her.

'A warning,' the Breton said softly. 'They can be tightened much, much more. Now, watch.'

Nodding in dumb acquiescence, Elena watched as the little tableau was played out in the flickering, smoky light of the candles. On the bed, the Saracen was now kneeling upright, his swollen member twitching upwards against his belly. The lady Isobel, her slender legs in their silken hose spread apart and an expression of avid delight on her face, began slowly to lower herself onto it, making little squealing noises as she impaled herself. Then she writhed up and down on the slippery shaft; slowly at first, but then, as Hamet's stiffened tongue darted to and fro and guzzled at her pouting breasts, she began to move faster and faster, wriggling in her delight, as the Saracen clutched her to him and thrust himself hard within her. Her gown had ridden up to expose her plump white buttocks. 'Oh, yes,' Isobel was muttering. 'Oh, please . . .

And Elena felt her own lips echoing those lewd animal noises. Because Aimery, still at her side, had put his arm round her straining shoulders, and was rubbing and stroking carefully at her breasts, still tautly upthrust by the tight chemise, his fingers reawakening the heady, exciting delirium that had gripped her before. He was watching the panting couple on the bed with a little smile on his face; still fingering Elena's breasts

601

voluptuously, he whispered in her ear, 'You like this? I wonder, what do you want next, my little nun?'

Panting, Elena felt the hot, wet liquid seeping down between her thighs. Her whole body burned; she was suddenly aware that this powerful man was reaching down to some deep, dark fire in her own soul that she hadn't realised existed, that the nuns had falsely shielded her from all these years. Her loins twitched and jumped instinctively as she watched the lady Isobel bringing herself close to the very extremity of pleasure. She moistened her burning lips. 'I want – oh, I want – '

His thumb and forefinger gently gripped her nipple, pulling at it; she writhed rapturously against the wall, her shadowy blue eyes heavy with desire. Isobel had almost lifted herself off the man completely; Elena could see the huge, dark pillar of flesh rising from the man's thighs. She saw the expression of glazed rapture that contorted Isobel's face as she carefully slid herself down onto him again.

'What do you want, Elena? Tell me,' came Aimery le Sabrenn's husky voice in her ear.

Isobel was squealing in her pleasure, writhing with little jerking spasms on the hard flesh that impaled her, throwing her head back and thrusting her breasts into the man's mouth. Then she stopped, suddenly, her eyes wide open, and began to moan in a strange, high pitched voice, holding herself rigid as Hamet gently pumped upwards, his big hands on her back, his tongue licking hungrily at her straining nipples. Isobel's delirious cries of pleasure echoed round the candlelit room. Elena couldn't tear her eyes away from the woman's spasming body.

'What do you want?' repeated Aimery relentlessly.

Elena wetted her dry lips, and felt the wine swirling around her heated body. 'I want – to feel a man inside me – like that – ' She broke off with a moan, seeing how Isobel, her face gleaming with sweat, had collapsed at

602

last onto the man's body. 'Oh, God help me! It must be a sin! To want that.'

Aimery, on seeing how the girl couldn't tear her face away from the couple on the bed as Hamet continued to thrust very gently at Isobel's still twitching body, let his mouth twist in a mocking smile. 'No sin,' he said. 'But bodily love between man and woman. You will learn to enjoy it, little Saxon. You will learn to satisfy *me*.'

Elena shuddered, gazing up at his strong, hard body, his lean, scarred face. The thought of doing that, with him . . . The blood rushed to her face, and she felt weak with longing. Dear God. *She wanted Aimery le Sabrenn* . . .

'But first,' he went on carefully, 'you must learn to know yourself – to know your own secret desires.'

Her body quivered involuntarily as he stroked her tender breasts. 'You're learning well, little Saxon,' he said softly. 'But you are not ready for me. Not yet.'

He looked across at the bed. Isobel lay curled in the furs, her eyes closed. Hamet crouched over her, and Elena saw with a shock that he was still fully erect, his massive male member twitching as he waited for his master's instructions. He was looking, hopefully, at *her* – Elena bit back a gasp.

Aimery heard it, and laughed. 'She's not for you, Hamet,' he said to his servant. 'Not yet. Finish with Isobel, then we'll proceed.'

Hamet nodded in obedience, though he still looked at the chained, writhing girl with longing. He turned back to Isobel, and her prone figure fluttered with reawakened pleasure as he rubbed his swollen member across her breasts and swiftly, with one big, practised hand, brought himself to his extremity. He threw his head back and gave a bark of delight as his seed spurted forth; then he rubbed the creamy liquid gently into her soft, trembling flesh with the velvety glans, muttering strange little crooning sounds to himself.

603

Elena had never before been witness to a man in the throes of his climax. Her face was transfixed in an expression of shock and amazement as she watched the virile, white substance jet forth from the dark nest of his private parts.

This alarming spectacle left Elena in a state of confusion; she had never seen anything like it before. But she didn't close her eyes, and she didn't turn her head away. She felt compelled to watch every second of the explicit moment, and yet she knew that she was observing something which should have been a private act. This knowledge filled her with a feeling of utmost shame. She, an innocent convent girl, was being made to relish the role of a voyeur. Her face flushed at the very thought and she lowered her gaze to the floor, knowing that her ordeal was far from over.

Aimery watched impassively, his hands still fondling Elena's breasts until she sagged in her chains with the unbearable ache of unsatisfied desire.

When Hamet's huge erection had subsided at last, Aimery commanded, 'Isobel. Over here.'

Languidly, like a cat, Isobel rose from the bed and pulled her gown together, a faint flush still staining her cheeks. Hamet too tied up his leggings, and sat cross-legged on the bed, watching Elena intently.

Isobel swayed across the room towards her lord. 'What is your command, my lord?' she said softly.

He glanced with a certain distaste at her swollen lips, her glittering eyes and disordered hair. 'You will attend to the girl,' he said tersely. 'She is obviously untried and ignorant. You will pleasure her gently, as women do. Hamet, come and help.'

Then he reached out, casually, and ripped Elena's gown apart from the waist downwards, exposing her slender legs and her quivering lower abdomen.

Elena gasped aloud. But then the sound of protest died in her throat, because now Hamet had joined his master, and the two men were bending to caress her breasts with their silken mouths. She shuddered with sudden, fierce pleasure as the hot, voluptuous sensation engulfed her chained body. They took one breast each, stroking and licking until she thought she would explode with rapture.

Then she froze, and the men stopped too. Something else was happening. Isobel was kneeling between her legs, stroking her thighs above her gartered stockings. She was pulling aside Elena's ripped gown, and fingering her gently in her most private parts, where she was already melting.

'No – please, no,' begged Elena.

Isobel smiled, gazing at her prisoner's exposed, quivering flesh. Then, before Elena could cry out again, she plunged her head forwards, and started to lick at her most secret place – that place which the nuns said it was a mortal sin even to touch.

The sweet, rasping feel of Isobel's darting tongue, combined with the powerful suckling of the Breton and his servant on each sensitive breast, was too much. Wave after wave of sensation flooded her yearning body, the most wonderful feeling she had ever known.

Then suddenly Isobel's cunning tongue stopped licking, and pushed up, hard and hot and wet, into her inner opening. Elena cried aloud and then shuddered wildly, because the sensation of all three tongues, thrusting and caressing and biting, filled her with a burning pleasure so intense and so unlike anything she had known before. Her brain was flooded with a hot, dark redness and she pushed herself down, jerking against Isobel's pointed wonderful tongue as it circled tenderly inside her pulsing vagina. The men's mouths were caressing her softly, tenderly now as her helpless body shuddered into an exquisite orgasm. Isobel, with a final effort, pushed her tongue hard up inside the climaxing girl so she could grip as it in her final throes of delight. With little whimpers, Elena subsided into the Breton's strong arms.

At Aimery's terse command, Hamet unlocked her from the wall and carried her to the little chamber where she had taken her bath. He slid her torn gown from her sleepy, sated body, and rolled down her silk hose with an expression of rapture. Then he laid her on the narrow bed and covered her with a soft woollen blanket, finally brushing her hair almost tenderly from her flushed face. The Saxon girl didn't open her eyes. He gazed down lovingly at her prone, fragile figure, remembering the luscious taste of her sweet little breasts and the melting cries she'd made as they pleasured her.

The big Saracen thought longingly of the next stage in her education.

Chapter Five

*A*imery's desire, so long restrained, burned hot and hard at his loins. Isobel, watching him, caught her red lips between her teeth and beckoned him across to the bed. But Aimery hesitated, because Isobel was too openly eager for him. The moistness of her excited body was too predictable. Once, when he'd first known her, she was refined and deliciously tantalising. But now . . . He remembered her shameless coupling with Hamet, and frowned.

She sensed his distaste, because she knew him so well. She thought for a moment, then urged in a low voice, 'Aimery, my lord. Tie me up.'

He raised a mocking eyebrow. 'Like the girl?'

She couldn't stop her tongue sliding across her lips in delicious anticipation. 'Oh, yes. Like the girl . . .'

She was already moaning softly as he shackled her arms to the wall.

Aimery felt his excitement surge again. Not troubling to undress, he reached beneath her silk chemise to grip at the hot mound that was the core of her feminity. Down there, she was dark and luxuriant.

The little nun, he'd noted, had a soft triangle of curls, that barely covered her tender flesh.

He thrust up her fine clothing around her hips, glimpsing the soft skin of Isobel's white thighs above her stockings. Her legs parted readily for him and she groaned eagerly as his hands brushed her moist vulva. He unlaced his hose to release his throbbing erection from the constriction of his clothing, and thrust into her without preliminaries. Once his penis was sheathed in her velvety grip, he brushed with his thumb at her exposed clitoris, and she closed her eyes and made soft little noises of pleasure. He realised, with a frown of irritation, that she was trying to imitate the innocent, astonished cries of the Saxon girl.

For once, Aimery had to admit that he had been wrong about the girl. She did indeed seem to be a true innocent, as she claimed – either that, or exceptionally clever. Like Madelin.

Aimery wondered, suddenly, what the Saxon girl would be like when she first felt a man deep within her. He tried to imagine the look of quivering surprise that would transfix her features before the pleasure took over her senses. Had Isobel ever been that innocent? She probably couldn't even remember her first man, he thought grimly.

Isobel, unaware of his thoughts, shuddered with delight as she felt Aimery's wonderful length impale her helpless body over and over again. She wanted to cry out in despair each time he withdrew, leaving her aching with loss. But then she would feel the shuddering, mounting arousal, and her vaginal walls would grip feverishly as he slid slowly back in. It was always wonderful with Aimery le Sabrenn – she would never tire of him. He could sustain his erection for ever, it seemed, he exerted an icy control that was possessed by no other man she had ever known. Any other man, by now, after what had happened tonight, would have been panting with excitement, totally beyond control. Even Hamet, well-trained though he was, was a little too excitable. But Aimery – oh, Aimery was a man . . .

His hands kneaded her trembling breasts as his penis slowly did its magical work. She writhed against him to stimulate her clitoris, the dark pleasure flooding her body, drawing in harsh breaths as her excitement mounted. She wanted to clutch him to her, to undress his wonderful body and stroke his smooth flesh, but she couldn't because she was trapped by the chains. She wriggled in exquisite torment as he thrust himself hard within her and moved his hand down to stroke her engorged clitoris with the pad of his thumb while keeping himself completely still and solid inside her body. Isobel moaned aloud for release, her cheeks flushed with delight. This, this was the blissful part, where Aimery could keep her lingering on that exquisite brink with a finesse that no other man possessed.

'Please,' she begged, with a harsh guttural sound. 'Oh, I beg you – please – '

Slowly he withdrew from her, leaving her empty. She groaned out his name as he stood back and smiled at her. 'Shall I leave you like that, Isobel?' He seemed calmly unaware of his stiff penis twitching hungrily towards hers. 'I have a fancy for a little wine . . .' And deliberately he turned his back towards her and walked towards the flagon on the table.

Isobel spat after his retreating figure. 'Dear God, Aimery! You vile beast! You can't leave me like this!' In her extremity she writhed in her chains, trying desperately to rub her legs together to stimulate her fevered body. 'Bastard,' she moaned to herself. 'You bastard – I hate you – '

Aimery, having refreshed his thirst, came sauntering back and swung her round to face him. 'I thought you, enjoyed being tormented, Isobel,' he said calmly. 'It seemed quite an exquisite game to me, to arouse you so and then leave you chained up, so that even your busy little fingers can't assuage the ache down there.'

He mockingly rubbed the tip of his powerful penis against her throbbing vulva. She gasped and thrust out at him, grasping at the heady sensation. 'Oh, Aimery. My lord, I beg you, have mercy on me.'

He smiled that chilling smile that she knew so well, then shrugged, and coldly sheathed himself within her. She came immediately, jumping and bucking in her chains, her face contorted as the shattering explosions of delight ripped through her yearning body. Aimery leaned his hands against the wall above her shoulders and thrust into her with unbelievable strength.

It took him some time to spend himself within her, and by the time he had finished his breathing was ragged. Isobel, completley sated, let her limp body hang in the shackles and savoured every moment of his wonderful, quivering manhood as he reached his climax deep within her. So, she thought, with an exhausted triumph, even for her masterful Breton lord, the strain of holding on for so long took its toll. She kept very still, wanting him to stay inside her. This was the only time she felt he was really hers.

At last, without saying anything or even looking at her, he withdrew, and turned to straighten his disordered clothing. Then he released her from the shackles.

Isobel swayed against him, her silk gown rumpled and torn, her body weak with wonderfully sated desire. 'If you wish it, Aimery,' she murmered, 'I will spend the night with you.'

He shrugged her off almost impatiently. 'Not tonight, Isobel. Go and wear yourself out with Hamet if you must. I need some peace.'

Isobel was frightened at his outright rejection. That Saxon girl had something to do with it, she was sure.

Pretending not to care that he wanted her to go, she said lightly, 'I'm surprised, my lord, that you've given the little Saxon slut a room up here. She should be bedding down with the serfs in the yard, surely? I thought you wanted to humiliate her – treating her like a lady will hardly do that.'

610

Aimery's mouth tightened. He said, 'What I do with her is up to me. But I'd remind you that humiliation is all the worse when it is unexpected.'

Isobel frowned and bit her lip. Was he talking about the girl, or about her, Isobel? Feeling a sudden unease, she turned to go.

She paused at the door of the Saxon slut's chamber. To let her sleep, even for one night, in the lord's private quarters was a grave mistake. Tomorrow, she herself would have to remind the girl that she was nothing but a slave. She was smiling a little at the prospect by the time she reached her own luxurious chamber. She wondered whether to send for the inexhaustible Hamet, just to spite Aimery, but decided against it. Hamet was too faithful to his master, like some big dog. He told Aimery everything.

Thinking hard, Isobel nibbled at her white finger and in the end sent her servant Alys to fetch Pierre, the young serf from the kitchens. Pierre was strong, willing, handsome enough, and a simpleton. According to the housekeeper, he wasn't much use for anything, except carrying sacks of grain and turning the iron spits in the kitchen. But Isobel had found another use for him. As well as being simple he was also mute, which meant that he'd never tell anybody anything. Desperate for physical satisfaction, she'd summoned him to her room last night in a moment of inspiration. His eager, if clumsy willingness to pleasure her in every way she could think of was a marvellous physical relief, and a vivid if somewhat startling contrast to Aimery's sophisticated refinements.

By the time he arrived in her chamber, the young man's eyes were already glazed with anticipated pleasure, and his mouth was slack. Isobel could see the bluge of his excited genitals beneath the thin cloth of his homespun tunic; he rubbed at himself surreptitiously as she shut the door. Isobel felt a frown crease

611

her smooth forehead. Pierre was handsome and muscular, but so lacking in any sort of finesse.

Suddenly repelled at the thought of his clumsy attentions, she slapped at his masturbating hand and his face fell.

'Not now, you stupid fool,' she hissed angrily. 'But listen, you can please me very much, if you do exactly as I say. You know we have some new slaves at the castle?'

He nodded eagerly.

'Well,' said Isobel, 'one of them has already seen you, Pierre, and heard about you, and she is very excited at the thought of meeting you – properly. She can see what a big, fine man you are. And she says – she says, Pierre, that she would like to kiss you. In that very special way. You know?'

Beads of sweat stood out on Pierre's downy upper lip. He nodded hard, almost shaking in his excitement.

'Tomorrow,' went on Isobel languidly, 'I will take you to her. She will kiss you and caress you just as you like it, and I will be there to watch. Oh, she might protest a little at first, because that's what she enjoys. But you can do what you like with her, I promise you.' Isobel smiled thoughtfully and touched her own breasts with light fingers. 'Do you know,' she went on, 'at the thought of it, I could almost take a fancy to your services after all . . .'

The serf's hungry eyes, brown and faithful like some adoring dog, widened in anticipation. He gazed with open lust at her full, perfect figure. Then Isobel remembered Aimery. No. After her lord's masterful lovemaking, she was deliciously replete. A shame to spoil it with this crude wretch. But all the same, she felt like some entertainment.

A little smile pulled at her mouth as she started to unfasten her clothes. 'Alys!' she called out impatiently.

She knew that Alys would be outside the door, listening. 'Keeping watch,' Alys called it, when really the maid was just pleasuring herself by listening to the sounds that emerged when her mistress had visitors. Isobel had actually caught her rubbing frantically at herself one night, when she was entertaining Hamet. Poor Alys was small and ugly. She was almost thirty, and no man wanted her because of her badly pocked skin. Isobel took great pleasure in occasionally providing her with what she wanted more than anything.

As the maidservant hurried into the room, Isobel said in a bored voice, 'I'm going to bed, Alys. But first I want you to let Pierre pleasure you. Do exactly as he says, will you? And don't make too much noise.'

Pierre's face fell a little as he absorbed what Isobel was saying. But his penis was painfully rampant after hearing what was in store for tomorrow, and at least he would be pleasing his mistress.

Alys' ugly face had lit up immediately. Isobel reclined on her fur-covered bed, propped up by feather cushions, and watched the little scene with amusement as Pierre turned to the maid and indicated by gesticulation that he wanted to take her animal fashion, on all fours. A good idea, thought Isobel approvingly, then he doesn't have to watch her face. She sipped with relish at her wine, and made them move around so could see Pierre's swollen, twitching member and tight balls as he rucked up the woman's woollen skirt and felt hungrily for her coarse outer lips.

Isobel reached down and played with herself gently as Pierre thrust his rampant penis between the woman's buttocks and Alys squealed in ecstasy. Pierre withdrew slowly, and Isobel chuckled softly as the glistening shaft came back into her interested view. Really, it was grotesquely ugly, swollen and purple with a strange, upward curve to it. Not that Alys seemed to mind. Pierre impaled her again, and the two of them worked with desperate enthusiasm towards orgasm, bucking eagerly away like dogs in the courtyard. No finesse, sighed Isobel, finding her own engorged clitoris and stroking it tenderly. No style.

The woman came first, crying and moaning with delight. Then Pierre huffed towards his own climax with long, shuddering strokes that took him some time. Isobel was excited by the strength of him, almost wishing that she'd taken him herself, and she brought herself to a pleasantly satisfying little orgasm as she thought of that hot, desperate length of male flesh within her own quivering vagina.

Then she ordered them both quickly out of her sight, because she'd had enough. She blew out the candle, and began to think happily of what the next day would bring.

Alone in his chamber, Aimery le Sabrenn, former penniless mercenary and now lord of Thoresfield, sat restlessly in his carved oak chair toying with his wine goblet.

Something was troubling him, and he knew what it was. He wanted the Saxon girl, badly.

He poured himself some more wine from the flagon, and drank it slowly. A single candle flickered smokily on the wall above his head. He stroked the tight scar on his cheek, which was hurting him more than usual.

The girl, Elena, filled his mind. He told himself that she was a rebel, no doubt responsible for the death of countless of his comrades in arms – a golden Saxon maid, to be enjoyed and cast aside, like the rest. Since his infatuation with Madelin – Madelin, who'd betrayed his brother – he'd humiliated many of them.

Madelin had made the mistake of thinking that she still had some power over him, even after she'd betrayed himself and his brother to the Saxon rebels. When Aimery escaped from the rebels and tracked Madelin down at last, she'd pretended to be sorry about it all and actually welcomed him into her vile bed. She'd even cried over his terribly scarred face, because he

614

used to be so handsome. Aimery had aroused her to her usual state of greedy lust, and then, when she was panting like a bitch on heat, he left her there, with just his bitter, ringing words of accusation for company. At least she still had her worthless life, though his brother Hugh had not been so lucky. The Saxons had tortured him, and castrated him, so that he was glad to die at last.

Aimery's hands tightened round the goblet, remembering. After Madelin, he'd fought the rebels so fiercely that even his own men feared him. And ever since that time, he and his mistress Isobel, had made a game of revenge, by selecting suitable young Saxon girls and making them plead for the pleasure he could bring them, before discarding them. Isobel always had plenty of ideas for their games – no doubt she had plans for Elena.

But, and Aimery frowned, there was something different about the convent girl. She might be one of the rebels, but even so he was strangely aware that he'd never encountered such beauty and innocence before. Soon, the innocence would be destroyed – they'd started on that process this evening. Soon she'd be as eager as any of them for sexual pleasure. She'd sidle up to him hopefully, as Isobel did, and when he grew tired of her she'd turn to other men for satisfaction, like the ever-willing Hamet or that young fool Pierre. Isobel thought Aimery didn't know about Pierre last night, but Aimery had spies everywhere. Since Madelin, he'd trusted no-one.

Aimery felt a sudden craving to know this girl in her innocence before she was changed for ever. He wanted to explore her sweetness for himself, with no-one else watching. He wanted to kiss those firm, sweet young breasts, and feel her yield to his thrusting manhood with all the passion he guessed she was capable of, until she was trembling at the very brink of ecstasy . . .

His mouth twisted mockingly at his fantasy. The little

nun had cast a spell on him. All right, so he wanted to
try her out. Nothing wrong with that. After all, she was
his slave. Afterwards, he promised himself, he and
Isobel would begin her training in full.

Elena had drifted into sleep, but it was a sleep tormented by her disturbed dreams. She was back in the
bleak little dormitory of the convent; the cold moonlight
shone in through the high, narrow window, casting its
silvery gleam on the familiar flint walls and flagged
floor. Wrapped in her coarse woollen blanket, she felt
unbearably, achingly alone.

Then, still in her dream, someone gently touched her
shoulder. She moaned and stirred in her sleep, and saw
a wide-shouldered, tall figure standing over her little
wooden bed, a man with a harsh face that was cruelly
scarred. Aimery le Sabrenn. The shadowy horseman of
her dreams. He was standing over her, slowly removing
his clothes, and Elena cried out his name in soft disbelief. What was he doing here, in the convent? In her
dream she felt no fear, only wonder, because she'd
never seen anything so beautiful in her life.

In the smoky candlelight, his naked body was hard
and strong, and marked by old sword scars that only
accentuated the muscled smoothness of his skin. His
hips were lean, his thighs heavily muscled, and his
pulsing manhood was jerking upwards from that dark,
mysterious cradle of soft curling hair, waiting for her,
wanting her. With a soft cry of need, Elena reached out
to him, and he was beside her on her small bed, cradling
her to him, pushing back her long golden hair and
closing her tear-stained eyes with his kisses. His cool,
flat palms slid beneath her silk chemise to caress her
small breasts; she moaned with soft delight and nuzzled
against the smooth, muscled wall of his chest, a sweet,
undefinable longing tugging painfully at the very pit of
her stomach. Her dream had never been so clear, so
sweet before. She never wanted to wake.

'Slowly, *caran*,' his voice came cool in her ear. 'We have all night remember? And you have so much to learn, little Elena, before the dawn . . .'

'*Caran*,' she repeated wonderingly. 'Please – what does it mean?'

He smiled softly, playing with her hair. 'In my own language, the language of Brittainy, it means *beloved one*.'

Elena gazed wordlessly up at him, her eyes soft with desire. She reached out to touch the cruel scar that split his cheek, and felt the tense ridge of white skin against the tip of her finger.

The feel of it brought her to her senses. That face. That scar. *That voice*. Dear God, this was no dream!

With a cry of alarm, Elena wrenched herself back into reality. She was not in the convent, but in Aimery le Sabrenn's castle! And she was in the Breton's naked arms . . .

'No!' she cried out. 'No!'

But it was too late. Already, she was his prisoner. His hands continued their gentle stimulation, and he was still smiling at her. Her heart turned over. Heaven help her, but she *wanted* to be here like this! He had imprisoned her with some dark, potent magic, and she couldn't have torn herself away, even if she'd wanted to.

His erect manhood stirred heavily against her soft belly, sending strange, liquid sensations flooding through her helpless body. She let out a little, quivering moan and arched against him so that she could feel the rasping hardness of his long, muscular thighs against her own trembling legs. To lie in his arms, like this, to breathe in the warm masculine scent of him, was indescribable bliss. With a little shock, she realised that *this* was what she had always longed for, in her wistful daydreamings at the convent.

'You want me?' he whispered softly, his tongue flicking her earlobe, his hands slipping her chemise

617

from her shoulders. 'You were dreaming of me? Tell me, *caran.*'

She shook her head helplessly, her blood already fevered. 'Yes, I was dreaming. I often dream.'

'You have the sight?'

'No!' How often had the nuns warned her not to tell anybody about her strange premonitions? 'No . . . But this *must* be a dream.'

In answer she felt his skilful hand slide down to her private woman's place, where her flesh churned, soft and melting. 'No dream,' he said, 'but a reality. Elena, let me teach you.'

She caught her breath as he parted her moist lips and stroked, very gently with the pad of his thumb. He found her little bud of pleasure, and stroked it lightly so as not to over-stimulate her tender sex; Elena gasped aloud and went rigid, her eyes dark with sensation. 'Wh – what are you doing?'

His voice came softly out of the darkness. 'This, my little Saxon maid, is the heart of all your bodily delight, the tiny bud that flowers into sweet passion. You have never given pleasure to youself?'

She gasped again, because as his thumb stroked she felt the sweet, melting yearning spiralling like flames through her helpless body. She shuddered in his arms, realising that even if she had the choice she could not leave him now.

He bent his head to suck gently at the pink, tender tips of her breasts, and she writhed in rapture as the sensations poured through her. He raised his head to gaze at her. 'Your first lesson,' he went on softly, 'is to learn that it is not wicked, but wonderful, to pleasure one another so. As the lady Isobel pleasured you tonight. You enjoyed it, didn't you? The way her hot little tongue flicked at you – like this – and like this – '

Before Elena could speak, he had moved down the bed, and parted her unresisting thighs. Dear God. His head was lowering to her belly; she felt the hot warmth of his tongue at her navel, and then it was sliding down her flat abdomen to slip between her lips and stab gently at that unbelievable pleasure place, just as Isobel had done earlier, only Aimery's moist, silken tongue was so firm, so fulfilling. She moaned, and writhed against his wonderful, rasping mouth.

He lifted his head to gaze at her, and his teeth gleamed whitely in the darkness as he smiled. 'You liked that, Saxon girl?'

Her body arched violently against him in reply, desperate for release. He could feel the waves of urgent desire spasming through her. 'Not yet, little one,' he murmered warningly. 'Not yet. You want to learn, do you not, about this wonderful instrument of pleasure?'

He reached to take her small, trembling hand and enfolded it round the throbbing shaft of his manhood.

Eleanor gasped aloud at the hot feel of it in her fingers. It was huge and velvety soft, beautiful to touch, yet so full of pulsing power. Would the lord Aimery do to her, now, what the terrifying Saracen had done to the lady Isobel? How could she ever take it within herself? Such a huge, swollen thing – almost like another limb – surely it was not natural! And yet she ached desperately to feel its silken caress inside her secret parts.

She snatched her hand away, trembling with confusion.

Aimery gave a low chuckle, and said, 'You will learn soon enough, *caran*, to worship my instrument of love. And, whether you realise it or not, you are more than ready to pay homage . . .'

His wonderful, teasing hands slid down once more between her moist thighs. He ran a finger up and down her quivering flesh, caressing that wonderful point of pleasure with his circling thumb, until Elena was crying aloud with pleasure and thrusting her swollen breasts against the hard, muscular wall of his chest.

'Ready, little one?' he whispered. And he arched himself above her.

Elena stopped breathing when she felt the velvety smooth head of his penis stroking between her lips. There was no room for him! There couldn't be room! And yet, that swollen glans caressing her own engorged, melting entrance was a feeling so exquisite that she wanted it to go on for ever.

'Surrender to me,' he was whispering in her ear. 'Give in to me, Elena. Do you not desire me?'

'Oh, yes. Nothing more . . .'

With a husky groan of satisfaction, he thrust gently into her melting flesh.

And then, something happened. Elena felt the long shaft slip inside her, between her throbbing lips, and slide slowly up, into the very heart of her. There was a sudden, sharp pain that made her cry out, but the Breton kissed her mouth, and she forgot it in the wonder of feeling his manhood moving so slowly, so masterfully within her.

She lay back, breathless, her eyes wide open. He caressed her parted mouth with his skilful tongue, and then he began to thrust, gently.

It was the most wonderful thing Elena had ever known – beyond her dreams, even. Aimery was sending wave after wave of hypnotic pleasure flooding through her with each slow stroke. Once, he paused, and gazed down into her transparent, wide-eyed face; she gasped and clutched him to her, running her fingers up and down his muscular back. 'Don't stop,' she pleaded. 'Oh, please don't stop – '

For answer, he lowered his head to suckle at her aching breasts. Then she moaned with pleasure and instinctively coiled her slender legs round his thighs as he slid his hard length deep within her again. He continued to lick her breasts, sucking hard at the taut nipples, and Elena cried out with a new fever of delight as his hand moved down to touch her engorged clitoris, very gently. Her blood was on fire, her breath was coming in short, ragged gasps as wave after wave of rapture engulfed her dazed body.

'*Oh!*' She gave a long, shuddering cry and bucked wildly against him as her senses exploded in a shimmering orgasm of pleasure. 'Oh, dear sweet Christ . . .' He continued to move gently within her, his lips flickering at her jutting nipples, and she gripped his penis fiercely with her inner muscles, clenching at the wonderful, hard length of him with wild sensuality. She cried out, again and again, as he used all his skill to prolong her ecstasy. Then, as her strange little animal cries subsided, he lifted himself high above her, so that she could see the engorged shaft wet with her own juices in the darkness, and he plunged into her, over and over, driving himself to his own fierce, shuddering release. Elena quivered with renewed orgasm at the feel of his hot release within her. She held his sated body tight in her arms, glorying in the feel of his hard nakedness, her body still warm with delight.

Aimery was shaken as he lay there in the darkness. It was a long time, almost longer than he could remember, since he'd taken such pleasure in conventional lovemaking. She was truly innocent, just as she had claimed. Perhaps, too, her claim that she knew nothing at all about the Saxon rebels who visited the convent was true as well.

He reflected with some surprise that normally, a clinging, innocent girl such as this one would bore him out of his mind, and he'd turn away in disgust to find more sophisticated pleasures. Yet the Saxon girl's rapture had moved him strangely as he watched her exquisite face light up the darkness.

Not part of his plan, he reminded himself. His plan was to coldly arouse her, as he'd aroused others; to make her hunger desperately for him, then reject her. Remember Hugh's death – remember Madelin. Wasn't this girl tainted with the same Saxon blood?

He withdrew sharply from the girl's innocent, tender embrace and stood up. Elena looked up, bewildered, and saw how harsh his scarred face was in the shaft of moonlight that glanced through the shutter. She felt suddenly cold. 'My lord . . .'

Aimery reached for his clothes. He said, flatly, 'Not bad for a first time. But you still have a lot to learn. Isobel will teach you some new tricks.'

She shrank back as if he'd struck her. 'No! Not Isobel!' She put out one trembling hand. 'My lord – I only want you!'

Again, Aimery le Sabrenn felt that stupid wrench at the heart he knew he no longer possessed. He buckled his belt over his tunic and said abruptly, 'Isobel; Hamet; you will submit, Elena, to whoever I decide will teach you. Remember that you're nothing but a slave. You will do exactly as I say.'

The girl gazed up at him from the bed, her soft face dazed with misery. 'I am your slave, lord,' she whispered. 'I will do whatever you command. Only – will you come to my room again – like you did tonight?'

Aimery's mouth twisted as he glanced down at her. Her little breasts were adorable, her sweet face still flushed by that intense, fevered orgasm. Damn it, but if he stayed any longer he'd be making love to her again in a few moments.

'Perhaps,' he forced out coldly. 'But not for some time. As I said, you have much to learn.'

As her dark blue eyes clouded over in sudden pain, Aimery turned and swiftly left the room.

Elena lay on the cold little bed and hugged her aching body. She was racked with an empty sensation of loss at the memory of the sweet, dark pleasure the Breton lord had bestowed on her. Already, she yearned for him again.

She'd given herself, body and soul, to Aimery le Sabrenn, and she knew that she'd do anything, anything, to persuade him to return and pleasure her again in his powerful, exquisite way. And she knew, she was sure, that he desired her.

She had much to learn, she knew. But he was all that she wanted; and if this was to be a contest, then she resolved that she would win him.

Isobel, who had heard Aimery go to Elena's chamber and had suffered a violent hour of intense jealousy as the stupid girl gasped away her virginity, heard her lord return to his own room at last. Only one hour, and he had had enough of her.

Isobel cheered up immediately, and revised her plans for tomorrow. Pierre would be a part of them, of course. But what else? With a sudden smile of pleasure, she remembered the little wooden chest where she kept her most precious possessions. She found the key and unlocked it, and fingered thoughtfully through its contents. At last, she withdrew a wonderfully carved piece of ivory that had once been brought to her by a traveller from the Mediterranean lands. It was shaped like a man's phallus, of more than generous proportions, and was designed, with careful carvings and protuberances, to stimulate a woman's pleasure zones; though not all women were capable of taking the huge shaft within themselves, especially not virginal Saxons. By the time Isobel and Pierre had finished with her, the girl wouldn't even *want* Aimery to touch her again for, oh, a good while.

Isobel fondled the instrument, rubbing it gently against her still tingling breasts until her nipples peaked and strained against the fabric of her shift. She smiled, imagining the Saxon slut's innocent face when confronted with this formidable weapon. Would Isobel show it to her first? Or would she wait for Pierre to finish with the girl, and then . . .

Her green eyes gleaming with anticipation, Isobel kissed the ivory phallus and locked it away in its box. Then she went to bed, and laid her plans for tomorrow.

Chapter Six

*E*arlier that same night, soon after the slave convoy had arrived at the castle, Morwith, the young, redheaded Saxon woman, had been herded into a low, thatched hovel along with the other female serfs. Disconsolately, she lay in the darkness on her crude, straw-filled pallet with just a rough blanket for cover, and turned her back on the other women. After all, she Morwith, was different. Hadn't she, in the most delightful way possible, entertained the lord of Thoresfield and his Saracen servant on the way here?

A Saxon reeve, who'd been here in the days before Hastings when Thoresfield had been no more than a fortified manor house, had brought the women food: dry bread, and stale cheese. Morwith had caught his arm before he left, and said haughtily, 'I think there must be some mistake. You see, I shouldn't be in here, with the others. I wish to speak to the lord Aimery.'

The man had laughed sneeringly. 'They all say that,' he mocked. 'Will I do instead, wench?'

Morwith was disappointed that a mistake had been made, and that she'd been put in this hovel. But she was confident that the lord of Thoresfield would send for her, in his own good time. Since the sacking of York last winter, she'd lived with a band of homeless Saxon outlaws in the forest, and was used to looking after herself. She would wait, and watch for her chance.

While the other women tossed and muttered in exhausted sleep, Morwith lay awake, her pale blue eyes glittering, her ripe body in its tattered chemise feeling unbearably warm and restless in the stuffy air of the windowless hovel.

She remembered every minute of that wonderful encounter in the half-ruined hut in the forest. The Saracen's muscular, gleaming body and dusky skin; the lord Aimery's coldly handsome face as he looked on impassively. She'd serviced the Saracen well, hadn't she? Used all her practised skill to tease him with her warm tongue; taken him smoothly into her willing mouth, huge though he was, while cupping and stroking the heavy pouch of his testicles until he had groaned aloud in ecstasy.

The Breton lord could hardly have failed to be aroused. But he'd taken her silently, impersonally, so Morwith had not been able to witness his powerful release.

She stirred restlessly on her scratchy pallet and her hand closed round her aching breast as she relived that sublime moment when the Breton's wonderful, iron-hard shaft had slipped slowly inside her juicy love-passage from behind. Oh, she'd never known such masterful, exquisite pleasure. While the Saracen's eager mouth had suckled her dangling breasts, each slow, muscular thrust of the Breton's phallus had built up the waves of sensation shamelessly quivering through her body, until the final orgasm had washed through her in warm floods.

She gave a little moan and cupped her aching vulva with her cool palm, feeling how it pulsed moistly, hungrily, at the memory of the Breton's darkly satisfying manhood. She would have him again, the Breton lord. Her chance would come, and she would take it.

She stroked her clitoris, rubbing quickly with her fingers, imagining the Breton's long penis soothing her hungry flesh. She spasmed quietly, biting on her lip to stop herself crying out.

Morwith slept at last.

Early the next morning, Elena woke with a start. She sat up jerkily, feeling frightened and confused. Then the sounds of the castle courtyard came floating up through her narrow window, and she remembered. The early morning sunlight danced across her bed. Somewhere, a distant bell tolled.

The hour of prime. At the convent, the nuns would be filing into the little chapel for the first service.

No. The convent no longer existed. That life was over.

Elena slid from her rumpled bed, her skin golden in the sunlight, and ran her hands dreamily through her tousled blonde hair. Her naked flesh was warm and sensitive; her breasts softly flushed. Had last night really happened? Or was it all a dream? The colour rose in her cheeks as she remembered. Walking slowly to the window, she pushed the oiled hide shutter to one side and peeped out.

It was all true. She was really here, in the very heart of Aimery le Sabrenn's northern stronghold. The courtyard below was already a hive of early morning activity, full of bustle and noise. Servants from the kitchen were hurrying across to the bakehouse carrying trays of warm, scented bread; young squires frowned in concentration as they carefully polished their masters' armour on the trestles set up outside the guardhouse; a groom was leading a big warhorse from the stables, while some female serfs giggled and gossiped as they scattered grain to the hens.

Aimery's castle. Aimery's people. And last night, Aimery le Sabrenn had taken her in his arms . . .

Elena breathed in deeply, the sunshine warm on her

face and her bare shoulders. This was to be her new life. There was no going back now. She knew that, and accepted it willingly. Her heart stirring in that knowledge, like a challenge, she turned to pick up her silk chemise from the floor, where the lord Aimery had cast it so carelessly last night. She held the soft fabric to her cheek.

Suddenly, the door opened. Elena looked up, startled, as the lady Isobel glided in; she looked exquisite in her beautiful green silk gown, with her dark hair coiled smoothly at the nape of her neck. Over her arm was a folded garment of rough homespun wool.

'My dear,' she purred, 'I trust that you slept well after our little *entertainment* last night?'

Elena, conscious of Isobel's slanting green eyes flickering with interest over her vulnerable, naked body, clasped the silk chemise she'd just picked up close to her breasts and said quietly, 'Thank you, my lady. I slept well.'

Isobel's words were kind enough, but there was something cold, assessing, in her eyes. Elena shivered suddenly, in spite of the warmth of the room.

Isobel's eyes rested on the beautiful silk chemise Elena was holding, and her mouth curled in amusement. 'As for today,' she went on briskly, 'I'm sure you understand, Elena, that as a serf you are expected to earn your keep. Edith, the housekeeper, is expecting you in the kitchens this morning. Here – I have brought you suitable clothing.' And she pressed a coarse serf's tunic into Elena's hands.

Elena's blue eys widened; she could not stop her gaze wandering to the beautiful gown she had worn the night before, lying on the oak chest at the foot of her bed. 'The – the kitchens?' she stammered out in confusion. 'But last night my lord Aimery said – '

Isobel's eyes snapped with annoyance, and she arched her exquisitely shaped dark eyebrows. 'Oh, dear. I do hope you're not going to be difficult, Elena.

Naturally, I am informing you of Lord Aimery's specific commands, however could you think otherwise?'

Elena swallowed down the sudden ache in her throat. Last night she'd been too eager, too open. She'd repelled him. 'If it is my lord Aimery's wish,' she said in a low voice, 'then of course I will obey.'

Isobel smiled, satisfied. So, this was the way to subjugate the girl! My lord Aimery's wish. What an innocent little fool she was! Lord Aimery, in fact, knew nothing at all about all this, as he had ridden out on the dawn patrol with his men and would not be back till this evening. But how was the Saxon slut to know?

In fact, Isobel had felt a desperately fierce pang of jealousy as she'd entered the room and seen the unclothed girl standing there as if she was in a dream. The sunlight had played magically on her high, perfect breasts, on her slender hips and long legs; on that soft golden fleece at the top of her thighs and the clouds of glorious silken hair cascading round her shoulders.

Isobel vowed anew in that moment that she would subjugate this girl herself, if Aimery would not.

Elena was slowly lifting the rough woollen tunic over her head when Isobel reached out languidly to stroke the exposed, taut skin of her abdomen. Elena gasped and froze; Isobel, with a smile, trailed her fingers towards the juncture of the girl's thighs, where the soft gold hair curled so delicately.

'My dear,' she murmered, 'just like gold silk! So delicate. Quite, quite charming. But you really do need educating, don't you? So sadly lacking in any refinement. And Aimery really does not care, you know, for unsophisticated women.' Isobel's thumb brushed tantalisingly at the top of Elena's secret place, stroking the pleasure bud, pinching the outer lips swiftly, then withdrawing her hand. Elena gasped and flushed at the sudden burst of pleasure that assailed her, and Isobel laughed at the girl's consternation.

'So,' she went on, 'the lord Aimery has given me

something for you. A little gift, if you like. He made it quite clear that he wished you to wear this special garment.'

Elena, her spine tingling with unease, said suddenly, 'Where is lord Aimery?'

'Gone out with his men. He then has to escort a convoy from Lincoln through his territory, so he will not be back for some time. But he left this for you, my dear. Here – let me show you.' And, reaching into the recessed folds of her skirt, she drew out what looked to Elena like a small leather belt.

Elena, still naked, clutched the serf's tunic to her defenceless body, and shivered with apprehension. There was something sinister about the belt that Isobel dangled teasingly before her, with its buckles and straps. 'I would rather not wear it,' she whispered.

Isobel, watching her, felt a renewed surge of hatred. This girl was fresh, young, innocent. *And Aimery had gone to her room last night* . . .

'Oh, dear,' chided Isobel in her sweetest tones. 'Disobedience already! I shall have to tell Aimery – he will be most disappointed in you –'

She saw how the girl's face became drained of blood. She was obviously terrified of Aimery's disapproval. Poor girl, she was besotted, like all the others before her. And therefore well on the way to her downfall . . .

'So, of course,' Isobel went on brightly, 'you will wear the belt, won't you, my dear? Here, let me help you.'

'It is the lord Aimery's wish?' said the girl quietly.

'Of course.'

The girl bit her lip and nodded mutely. With a secret smile of satisfaction, Isobel helped her into the little belt that was one of her own favourite devices. Elena had to step into it because, although the main strap was buckled round her waist, there was a further piece of leather that pulled up tightly between her legs, cradling the soft mound of her femininity, narrowing at the back to slip between the rounded cheeks of her bottom.

629

Elena gasped at the unfamiliar feel of the cold leather against her outer flesh lips. 'It is too tight!'

'Nonsense!' retorted Isobel briskly as she nimbly tightened the big buckle at Elena's small waist, thus drawing up the strap between her legs even further. 'This is how it is meant to be worn. You will soon be perfectly used to it. It is quite customary for favoured female slaves, I assure you!'

She let her fingers trail along the firm leather that pressed against the girl's delicious femininity, secretly revelling in the exquisite combination of soft, tempting flesh and dark, thick leather. The girl, with her stupid, innate modesty, recoiled with a shudder from her touch; but Isobel knew that already the cunningly-made love belt would be doing its work. Because where it pressed against Elena's pink folds it was slightly ridged, so that it would exert gentle yet persistent pleasure on her tender flesh lips. It would eventually part them, chafing against her sweet pleasure zones with every step she took, preparing her for the entertainment that Isobel had in mind for the afternoon.

Already, Isobel could see that the girl was breathing raggedly with the secret combination of shame and promised pleasure. Isobel smiled. 'The lord Aimery will be most pleased to know that you are obeying him,' she lied softly. 'Now I will send my maid Alys, to take you down to the kitchens.'

And with that, the lady Isobel left the room.

Elena stood very still after she had gone, trying desperately to order her reeling thoughts. She would run away from Thoresfield! She would not suffer this humiliation!

Pulling on her coarse woollen gown, she moved purposefully towards the door. The castle gates were open. No-one would notice yet another serf heading off towards the fields.

Suddenly, as she moved, the ridged leather slipped up between her flesh lips and rubbed with heart-

stopping sweetness at her secret parts. The delicious
warmth, the novel feeling of constriction, flooded her
belly, and she felt her nipples tingle suddenly where
the woollen gown chafed them.

She remembered Aimery's dark embrace; her body's
awakening in his arms. Already, the leather belt was
moist between her legs. She moved again, tentatively,
towards the door; the leather rubbed softly against that
very heart of her pleasure, nudging at the little bud that
the Breton had caressed so sweetly last night. Maybe
tonight he would come to her again.

Elena knew then that she would not, could not run
away. She knew that a day of exquisite torment lay
ahead, like a challenge – a challenge issued by the lady
Isobel. She drew a deep breath and turned back into
her room, to await her next orders.

She would rise to that challenge, and win.

Beyond the castle, in the great south field that bordered
the encroaching forest, Morwith was growing hot, tired
and rebellious. Since daybreak, when they had
meagrely broken their fast on bread and weak ale, she
and the other serfs had been working their way up and
down the field gathering armfuls of the hay, newly
mown by the lines of men with scythes. The midday
sun burned into her face; the sweat gleamed on her
arms; the blades of grass tickled her legs unbearably.
Everyone else passively accepted the barked orders of
the Saxon reeve and his men, and trudged obediently
across to the big cart with armfuls of grass. But Morwith, who knew she was different, felt the irritation
boiling up inside. Somehow, she would find a way to
get to the lord Aimery! He, surely, would not expect
her to labour like this, to sleep in a hovel with the other
women! There must be some mistake.

'You, there!' The reeve called out sharply to her. She
swung round defiantly, pushing her hair from her face.
'You, who think yourself too good to be a serf – yes,

you, the red-headed wench! Go to the kitchens, and fetch more ale for the mowers. And be quick about it!'

Glad at least to escape from the backbreaking work for a while, Morwith bit back her retort and hurried across the fields towards the castle's gates. At the kitchen, they gave her a big earthernware jug and told her to help herself from the ale cask in the store room. She found her way there slowly, taking her time; it was shadowy and dark in the cask-filled store room, and cool out of the heat of the sun. She filled the jug with the creamy, fragrant ale and took a long drink of it herself. It slid down her parched throat like nectar. She drank more, then set down the heavy jug and went to stand in the doorway, running her hands through her thick red curls.

'You are in trouble, lady?'

The soft, dark voice broke into her thoughts. She turned with a gasp of alarm; someone was coming along the side of the storeroom towards her. The dark-skinned man, Hamet – the Breton's servant.

Morwith stammered, trying to collect her thoughts, 'I – I was but resting for a moment, sir. They sent me for ale. Ale for the reapers.'

He nodded, his arms folded across his burly chest, watching her. He wore a sleeveless leather tunic; his hugely muscled shoulders glistened with perspitation in the midday heat. Did he remember her from that night in the forest? Surely – surely he did. He had taken such pleasure in her. Morwith's heart beat furiously. Now. Now was her chance. Hamet the Saracen was the lord Aimery's personal servant. If she could find favour with him, then surely he would take her to his master again.

Morwith moved slowly and thought fast. Picking up the heavy jug, she gave the Saracen a shy smile and moved to go past him. Suddenly, she swayed and lost her balance; the jug crashed to the floor, and the big

Saracen caught her quickly, his hands steadying her waist. 'Lady, you, are not well?'

Morwith swayed hungrily against him, feeling her loose bodice slipping from her shoulders. 'No,' she whispered, gazing up at him hungrily and moistening her full lips. 'I am not well. But you can make me feel better. So much better . . .'

Slowly, tantalisingly, she reached up to run light, provocative fingers over his strong arms. Then she licked her forefinger and touched his lips, half-closing her eyes. With a harsh foreign oath, Hamet crushed her to him and devoured her mouth. Morwith leaned back, panting, against the cold stone wall of the store room. 'Oh, yes,' she gasped through his kiss. 'Please . . .'

Her eyes opened wide in lascivious delight as Hamet cupped and lifted her ripe breasts, freeing them completely from her ragged gown. Then he ran his hungry tongue greedily across her pouting flesh, lapping and sucking at her turgid nipples. Eagerly, Morwith reached for his belt, but Hamet anticipated her. Swiftly he untied the lacing at the top of his leggings, and freed his huge erection. It sprang out, quivering with tension, already fully rigid.

Morwith gasped and coloured at the sight of the dusky, throbbing shaft as it reared towards her. 'So magnificent,' she breathed huskily, reaching with trembling fingers to stroke its satin length. 'My lord, you are truly a stallion.'

With a throaty groan of delight, Hamet reached to pull up Morwith's full skirts. She was wearing nothing underneath; the plump, freckled flesh of her inviting thighs drove him insane. Devouring her luscious mouth, Hamet lifted her in his arms to prop her against the wall, supporting almost all of her weight while he thrust eagerly against her.

Morwith, breathless with excitement, arched her own moist, pouting secret flesh towards the Saracen's lunging hips, wrapping her thighs tightly round him as he held her off the ground. Hamet prodded blindly, at last finding the quivering entrance to her love-channel. With a sigh of satisfaction, the Saracen slid up inside her.

Morwith gasped, her arms clutching convulsively at his leather-clad shoulders. Her hungry flesh was a riot of delight as he licked and suckled her pouting breasts. Oh, the feel of his massive penis, gliding so slickly in and out of her greedy flesh! She felt herself rising inexorably to a shuddering, delicious climax as he serviced her; felt him thrust his hips powerfully towards his own release, his penis jerking and spasming within her luscious, grateful body.

The pleasure washed over her, again and again. Simple, crude and wonderful. Sated, she clung to him still, licking the smooth dark skin of his cheek, caressing his soft earlobe. Slowly she felt his subsiding manhood slip out of her and nuzzle her damp thighs.

'Good,' she murmered. 'So good.' Gently she unwrapped herself from him, smoothing down her crumpled skirt. 'Hamet, you like me, do you not?'

He groaned in acknowledgement, swiftly lacing up his leggings. 'Lady, with you, the pleasure is wonderful.'

'Then,' whispered Morwith, 'why do I not come to you again? You sleep within the castle itself, do you not? Near to the lord Aimery?'

Hamet visibly hesitated. 'I do. But – '

'Send for me,' she whispered. 'Your master need not know. Send for me, Hamet, and I will be yours, all yours, for the night!' She reached up to kiss him languorously. He began to harden again, against her belly; she released him with a soft laugh of delight and whispered, 'Now, go quickly, before we are seen. And remember – this is our secret.'

At a tiny window overlooking the courtyard, the lady Isobel de Morency, who had seen everything, moved

634

away with a smile of satisfaction playing around her full lips.

When Isobel had first caught sight of the redheaded Saxon serf talking to Hamet, distracting him from his duties as Aimery's deputy, she'd frowned, and been on the point of sending someone down to chastise her.

But then, as Isobel saw how swiftly the lascivious hunger took over their bodies, she felt her own excitement rise. Hamet was so straightforward in his pleasures, and so undeniably well-endowed. And the redheaded slut, who must be new to the castle, how ripe and voluptuous she was as she took her greedy pleasuring from the big Saracen! No innocent she; why, she positively crowed with delight as Hamet slid his willing shaft up into her juicy flesh. What a contrast to the pale, virginal convent girl, who would be slaving away in the kitchens, no doubt tormented by the belt that would be chafing so deliciously between her slender thighs! Surely, the redhead would be more suited to Aimery's needs?

Isobel felt pleasantly aroused from watching the little scene in the courtyard. Smiling to herself, she revised her plans – just a little.

Later that afternoon, Isobel lounged back on her fur-covered bed, sipping from a silver goblet filled with sweet, heady wine. 'You see,' she was explaining, 'I need a very *special* kind of servant . . .'

Morwith stood in front of her, hands clasped together, head meekly bowed. She'd just enjoyed a luxurious bath, a blissful experience for her, and she'd been given an old but serviceable woollen gown of Isobel's to wear instead of her serf's tunic. Her glorious red hair, newly washed, hung in silky tendrils around her shoulders. She looked the picture of meekness; but Isobel, having seen her antics with Hamet earlier, was not deceived.

Thoughtfully, Isobel poured herself more wine and

inspected her new prize. The young woman had a lovely figure, voluptuous yet firm, with full breasts and swelling hips. A trifle plump, perhaps, but all femininity.

Isobel ran her finger round the rim of her goblet and stretched her legs languorously beneath her silk gown. Leaning back against the soft down-filled pillows that were piled up behind her, she went on casually, 'You know, I take it, that you are in the stronghold of Aimery le Sabrenn?'

The woman seemed to flush slightly; then nodded.

Isobel continued, 'My lord Aimery, like all great and powerful men, needs his relaxation, Morwith. He likes me to arrange certain little – entertainments for him. I wonder if you understand?'

There was certainly now no mistaking the brightness in the redhead's pale blue eyes. Isobel slid languidly from the bed, still holding her wine, and walked over to her. Morwith's gown, a little too tight, strained provocatively across her chest; Isobel ran a slow hand across the woman's constrained breasts, felt the instant hardening of her nipples, heard her sharply indrawn breath.

'Are you a good servant, Morwith?' Isobel said softly. 'Are you going to be truly obedient to your lord?'

The Saxon woman moistened her lips eagerly. 'Oh, yes, my lady,' she breathed.

Isobel's hand whipped up and struck her hard across the cheek. Morwith bit back a cry and staggered back, her flesh glowing red where Isobel's hand had caught her.

'You lie to me!' You are far from obedient! I saw you earlier today, out in the courtyard with the Saracen! Who gave you permission to pleasure yourself so vilely, to distract my lord's servant from his duties? You will be punished, Morwith!'

The young woman sank to her knees, trembling. 'My

lady, I crave your pardon. I humbly beg your forgiveness. Please, please don't send me away!'

Isobel watched her thoughtfully, a little smile playing at the corners of her lips. Morwith, on seeing that smile, shivered and felt a sudden dark excitement leap in her breast. Isobel said very quietly, 'You will most certainly be punished. Remove your gown, and abase yourself.'

Morwith, still kneeling, her eyes lowered, slowly lifted the woollen gown over her head, then her cotton chemise. She crouched naked before the lady Isobel, her red hair sweeping her pouting breasts, her plumply rounded thighs splayed just a little so that Isobel could glimpse the secret flesh veiled by the tightly curling red hair. Her flesh was creamy white, dusted with light freckles like a sprinkling of gold dust.

Isobel licked her lips and said, huskily, 'You are ready, then, for your punishment?'

Morwith lifted her pale, glittering eyes. 'My lady,' she whispered. 'Only tell me how can I do sufficient penance for my dreadful sins?'

Isobel laughed aloud. Without bothering to reply, she eased herself onto her bed and leaned against her pillows. Then she drew her silk gown up above her stockinged thighs, and whispered, 'Pleasure me.'

Morwith could not belive her luck. Her heart pounded. First the encounter with the Saracen, and now, for some reason, the lady of Thoresfield; this beautiful, sophisticated woman who was lucky enough to be Aimery the Breton's mistress, had singled her out!

Entertainment, she had said. Entertainment for the lord Aimery . . .

Keeping her head low, so that the lady Isobel would not see the lascivious gleam in her eyes, Morwith said meekly, 'Anything you say, my lady.' Then, with a slow, wicked smile, she walked to the foot of the bed and climbed up between Isobel's parted thighs.

With a little groan, Isobel reached out for the Saxon woman's dangling breasts. They were heavy and full,

637

with large, dark brown nipples that already jutted fiercely. Isobel leaned forward to suckle hungrily, stroking the turgid flesh with her fingertips, then she leaned back against her pillows, her eyes closed dreamily. 'Kiss me, Morwith. Kiss me, down there.'

Breathless with excitement, Morwith stroked softly at Isobel's thighs above her gartered stockings, parting them still further. The sunlight from the narrow window fell across the bed; she could feel it warm on her back, though Isobel was in the shadows beneath her. Now she could see the lady's most secret place; the softly curling dark hair, the crinkled flesh lips; such a luxuriant contrast to the white smooth skin of Isobel's belly and thighs! Morwith, already excited by Isobel's urgent suckling of her breasts, felt the heat begin to churn in her own loins. Hungrily she dipped her head between Isobel's thighs and licked softly, parting the dark outer folds with her gently exploring tongue.

This, to Morwith, was new; the pleasuring of a female, the feel of the moist, wrinkled folds of flesh against her tongue. But she knew only too well what she herself enjoyed; knew how the tongue's soft, teasing delicacy could be a most delicious replacement for a man's rigid phallus. Delicately she drew her tongue between the soft labia that were already engorged with desire. If this was how fine ladies lived, then she, Morwith, would be a fine lady!

Gliding her tongue steadily up the smooth pink slit, Morwith's pointed tongue at last found Isobel's sweet bud of desire, already enlarged and sensitive. Careful not to abuse it, knowing how easily a harsh touch could kill pleasure. Morwith let her tongue circle the quivering stem, caressing it tantalisingly. Isobel threw her head back and clutched at Morwith's heavy breasts with desperate fingers. 'Kiss me. Oh, your tongue is so sweet, Morwith. Let me feel your tongue, deep inside – oh, yes, yes!'

With a little smile, Morwith drew her sensuous

mouth in a swirling caress round Isobel's tender flesh. Then, pointing and stiffening her ready tongue, she glided lightly up and down between Isobel's inner flesh lips and thrust it gently, teasingly in and out of the entrance to Isobel's juicy love channel.

Isobel groaned aloud and jerked her hips desperately towards Morwith's teasing mouth. Morwith gave a low chuckle and continued to slide her tongue up and down, but more firmly now; lightly swirling Isobel's engorged pleasure bud, then gliding down to thrust slickly inside her, to satisfy her. So close now – so close . . .

Her tongue glanced, then flickered on the shaft of Isobel's swollen clitoris. Isobel's body arched violently into the air, her buttocks tight and straining in her extremity. Morwith, taking a deep breath, stuck her tongue as far as she could inside the other woman's love passage, making little jabbing motions to simulate a man's phallus, using all her skill to satisfy her new mistress.

Iosbel exploded, uttering fierce little cries. She spasmed again and again against Morwith's busy mouth, almost throwing her off the bed, then she collapsed, sated with exquisite pleasure.

Slowly, Morwith slipped from the bed, the coverlet of wolf pelts exciting her own heated, sensitised skin as the fur brushed her belly and thighs. She kneeled on the floor at the foot of the bed, her heart beating wildly. Unbearably excited herself, her own secret flesh was moist and slick and hungry. She bowed her head, submissive but hopeful.

After some moments of utter stillness, Isobel stirred and drew herself up, stretching in lazy contentment. Her cat-like green eyes regarded the kneeling, naked serf thoughtfully.

'You show some promise, Morwith.'

Morwith looked up, her eyes bright, her body flushed with her own eager desire. 'My lady?'

Isobel chuckled as she surveyed the wet pink flesh between Morwith's parted thighs. How the woman begged, wordlessly, to be pleasured! But she would have to wait. 'You must learn patience, Morwith, if you are to progress. I can see that you are all too eager for your own satisfaction.'

Morwith licked her lips, her eyes pleading. Isobel slid from the bed and smoothed her silk gown so that her skirts fell in rich swathes to the ground.

'But first,' Isobel went on calmly, 'you must help me in another task. You seem to have forgotten, Morwith, that we have someone else to punish.'

Morwith's eyes widened. 'My lady, if I can help in any way – '

Isobel poured herself more wine, and drank contentedly. Aimery would not be back for a long, long time. Which was as well, because there was so much she had to do. She went on, 'You can help me indeed. You see, we must punish Hamet the Saracen for neglecting his duties, and for serving you so lasciviously. Don't you agree, Morwith?'

Morwith gulped and nodded, her heart pounding with excitement.

The hot afternoon sun beat down relentlessly on the procession of wagons and horses travelling slowly northwards along the sandy track. The clumsy wooden wheels of the baggage carts kept embedding themselves in the ruts; the drivers cursed impatiently, whipping on the plodding horses, sweating and grumbling in the baking heat.

Aimery le Sabrenn rode at the head of the armed escort, watchful and wary. Here, at least, bracken and thorn scrub replaced the dense oak forest to the west, making visibility better and Saxon ambush less likely.

Though if the Saxons knew that the twelve baggage wagons contained arms and provisions for the isolated garrison at York, Aimery had no doubt that they would attack, and kill.

'My lord, a horseman! Coming down the track – about a mile away – '

Aimery nodded acknowledgement at the hurried warning from the sergeant-at-arms, his hand tightening briefly on his sword. He reined in his big black destrier, aware once more of the sun's heat burning through his chainmail hauberk, and ordered his men to halt. Another wagon was stuck anyway; at least a dozen of his men were heaving and grunting at the wheel where it was embedded in a deep, sandy rut.

He could see the horseman himself, could see the glint of armour through the cloud of rising dust. Leaning back against the high cantle of his saddle, Aimery pushed his hand through his dust-streaked hair and silently gestured to his men to fan out around the convoy, all of them warily scanning the bracken wastes that surrounded them. Perhaps the horseman brought news of battle. He was aware of a swift, unusual regret, that his return to Thoresfield might be delayed. The fair-haired Saxon girl had haunted his thoughts all day.

'One of de Ferrers' knights, my lord, by my reckoning,' muttered the sergeant at his side.

The horseman rode up in a cloud of dust, pushing back his helmet from his sweat-streaked face.

'My lord Aimery?' he gasped.

Aimery pushed his horse forward, but there was no need; his air of natural authority had already identified him. 'You have a message for me?' he said quietly.

'Aye, my lord. You are shortly to be relieved of your escort duties, by a convoy of Henri de Ferrers' men travelling northwards to York for garrison duties. They will converge with you shortly, my lord, at the next crossroads. They carry all the necessary papers, by your leave . . .'

Aimery turned round to his silent, waiting men. 'It

looks,' he said, 'as if we shall be returning to Thoresfield earlier than planned.'

His men grinned and relaxed. 'That's good news, sir,' said the sergeant. Escort duty was never popular, with the constant fear of ambush and the possibility of scrappy, isolated fighting in the outlaw-ridden forest, though Aimery knew that his men would follow him to hell and back if he asked them.

Aimery smiled back at the burly sergeant, his scar twisting his firm mouth. 'Good news indeed,' he replied softly, half to himself.

He found that he was thinking of the girl again. Remembering her soft, tender body in his arms last night, he grew hard. He gritted his teeth silently against the harsh, burning desire that leaped through his body.

Chapter Seven

Throughout that day, Elena had struggled to do her work alongside the other serfs. She knew, without being told, that she was hopeless at it. She could barely carry the heavy trays of dough to the bakehouse; the great cauldron of stew that she was ordered to stir burned and stuck to the sides of the pot; and as for plucking chickens, the other serfs took the half-feathered birds from her in disgust when they saw how little progress she made. Everything about the busy, bustling place confused her; people shouted and scolded, and try as she might, she succeeded at nothing.

And all the time, the love belt chafed insistently at her flesh, filling her bewildered body with unfamiliar sensations, like a secret caress. A reminder that she was a prisoner. Every minute of the day, the lord of Thoresfield's scarred, beautiful face haunted her mind; the look of tenderness in his steel-grey eyes as he murmured, 'We have all night, *caran* . . .'

She struggled on alone, because Isobel had told her it was Aimery's command, and only once did someone try to help her.

She was carrying two pails of milk across the yard, for the cheese-making. The wooden pails were so heavy, she was afraid of dropping them; but she did not dare to put them down. The sun burned down on her and her arms ached as she struggled on.

Then someone came up behind her, and took the pails from her, swinging them easily into this own strong hands. 'Let me take those,' a strangely familiar, male voice said quietly. 'Just follow me across the yard – don't trouble to express you thanks, or people will notice us.'

Elena gasped as she gazed up into the man's face.

The tall, golden-haired Saxon – the rebel. The man she had met coming from Father Wulfstan's house. The man she had taken water to, that night in the forest, the night she had first seen Aimery. 'You!' she whispered, gazing up at him as he stopped outside the kitchen.

He put down the heavy, frothing buckets. 'My name is Leofwin,' he said quietly. 'I am a serf. A prisoner here, like you. But, lady, if you need help of any kind, then summon me. I will do anything I can to help you.'

Elena felt her breath catch in her throat. Even in the ragged tunic of a serf this man was breathtakingly handsome, with his tanned, muscular body gleaming with perspiration in the heat of the day, and his sun-streaked mane of hair. And the way he looked at her, so tenderly, with those fathomless blue eyes . . .

Elena suddenly felt the tight love belt rub between her thighs, and a hot, liquid, churning sensation in her stomach. She knew instinctively that this man Leofwin would hate Aimery le Sabrenn with a burning hatred; would want to kill him, for what he had done to her last night.

From inside the kitchen, someone called out, 'Hey, you there! With the milk! Are you, going to be all day?'

Hurriedly Elena picked up the heavy pails and struggled to haul them inside, while the Saxon, watching her with his hands on his hips, said quietly, 'Remember me if ever you need a friend.'

* * *

644

In the afternoon, after a meagre lunch of rye bread and weak ale, Alys, the lady Isobel's maid, showed Elena how to wash the fine household linens in buttermilk, then peg them out in the sun to bleach them dry.

'You are lucky, Elena,' sighed poor, pockmarked Alys, suddenly stopping her work and regarding the slender blonde Saxon girl with envy. 'It won't be long before one of the men chooses you for his own. No such chance for me!' And Alys squeezed fiercely at the linen sheet she was dousing in the big tub of buttermilk.

Elena, her heart wrung with pity in spite of her own suffering, said quickly, 'You may well meet some good man who will wish to marry you, Alys. Looks should not be so important!'

'It's all vey well for you to say that, when you are so beautiful!' sighed Alys. 'It won't be long before one of lord Aimery's fine knights takes you for himself, I'll be bound.'

Elena remembered Aimery in her bed last night, and a slow blush stained her cheeks. As she knelt to peg out the linen, the leather belt tightened at the soft flesh between her legs, sending little arrows of desire burning through her belly and breasts. How long would she be kept in this exquisite torment?

Someone shouted across the yard at her. 'You! The new girl! The lady Isobel wants you up in her room. Make haste!'

Elena paled, and felt suddenly dizzy as she stood up. Alys said laconically,

'Better hurry, then, girl. My lady doesn't like to be kept waiting.' Elena bit her lip and set off towards the castle; Alys watched her go enviously.

Alys knew what the summons from Isobel meant. She knew what kind of things were in store for the beautiful blonde Saxon girl, and envied her wildly.

Elena blinked, disorientated, as she was shown into the lady Isobel's chamber.

645

The hide shutters had been drawn across the window embrasures, blocking out the sunlight. The heat from a brazier in the corner was intense. Two candles burned in silver holders placed on an oak coffer, their flames casting glimmering, unreal shadows around the tapestry-clad room. At first, accustomed as she was to the dazzling sunshine outside, she felt blinded.

Then she began to see. And what she saw made her want to turn, and run.

Isobel reclined in a carved wooden chair in the corner. Even in this claustrophobic darkness she looked as cool and elegant as ever, with her beautiful green silk gown and coiled black hair. Taking no notice of Elena, she continued to gaze at a little tableau in the opposite corner of the room, and a hazy smile played round her full red lips. Elena followed her gaze, and the breath caught in her throat.

In the near-darkness, Hamet, Aimery's servant, was kneeling on the floor. He wore leggings, but his gleaming dark torso was completely naked. His hands were tied behind his back to an iron ring in the wall, and he was blindfolded.

In front of him, with her back to Elena, was a redheaded woman wearing nothing but a strange, tight bodice made of black leather. She was leaning over the Saracen, dangling her large ripe breasts lewdly in his face, as he strained hungrily up towards her. Apart from the laced bodice, which thrust up her breasts and emphasised the curvaceous flesh of her rounded bottom, she wore nothing.

Elena leaned back against the closed door, feeling suddenly faint. Isobel glanced across at her, and laughed. She had plenty of time, to punish this stupid Saxon girl and get rid of her before Aimery got back.

'You are just in time, little Elena,' she said caressingly. 'Just in time to witness Hamet's punishment. Hamet, you see, has disobeyed me. He is now paying

646

the price of his disobedience, and you, Elena, are to take part in his punishment.'

Elena felt her throat go dry. 'No! I – '

Isobel went on briskly, 'My dear Elena, I thought you understood. This is what the lord Aimery wishes; what the lord Aimery commands. And you want to please him, don't you?'

Elena was breathing shakily. The door behind her was unlocked. She was not in chains. She knew she should turn and run from this decadent, shadowy chamber, with all its dark promise. But the love belt squeezed gently, insistently at her fevered flesh, and just the mention of the Breton's name was enough to set her blood on fire. The redhead in the corner, oblivious to everything but the powerful man imprisoned beneath her, continued to torment him by rubbing her creamy breasts against his face. Elena felt the dark hunger in her secret places burn more fiercely than ever. She moistened her lips and whispered steadily, 'Yes. I wish to please the lord Aimery.'

Isobel nodded her satisfaction, and leaned forward. 'Then let me explain. Hamet here has behaved badly, with Morwith, the Saxon slave who torments him so with her lascivious body. He ravished her, serviced her crudely in the yard as if she were some animal on heat; drove his massive member into her quivering flesh.'

Hamet, in the corner, let out a soft moan of despair at her crude words. Isobel stood up, and Elena saw that in one hand she carried a small leather whip, its lash trailing on the ground as she walked slowly across the dimly lit room towards the imprisoned Saracen. Morwith saw her coming and stepped silently back into the shadows; Elena saw, with a jarring shock, that the red-gold hair at the juncture of her plump thighs was slick with moisture.

Isobel stood in front of Hamet, who gazed blindly up at his lady. He let out another moan as Isobel trailed

647

her whip across his broad chest and let the lash dangle across the swelling bulge at his crotch.

'And Morwith too,' Isobel went on, turning suddenly on the redhead. 'Your punishment is not yet complete. Slut, I remember your face – how you enjoyed every wicked second as Hamet's rampant shaft slid up inside you. I saw you as you flung your head back in ecstasy! I heard you squeal with pleasure as you felt him impale you!'

The redhaired Saxon woman hung her head, but her nipples were dark and turgid above her leather bodice, and her pale blue eyes glittered with repressed excitement. 'My lady,' she whispered, 'I deserve further punishment. I wish to do penance.'

'Then,' said Isobel sternly, 'you must prepare yourself. Go and lie down on the bed. And Elena, who has been brought here to join in your punishment, will carry out that punishment. Come here, Elena.'

Elena stood immobile by the door as Morwith sprawled back luxuriantly on the fur-covered bed. She couldn't move. The heated blood coursed through her trembling body; the taut love belt pressed more tightly than ever, riding high between the soft pink folds of flesh at the top of her thighs. She knew that she couldn't bear this exquisite torment for much longer, and that even to move would send ripples of pleasure coursing through her body.

'Come here, Elena, dear,' repeated Isobel sweetly, fondling the handle of her whip, 'or the lord Aimery will be greatly displeased with you!'

Drugged with her own dark desires, her abdomen strangely heavy, her breasts tingling, Elena moved towards Isobel slowly, as if in a dream. Isobel smiled.

'Look, Elena,' she whispered, 'see how hungry Morwith is for love. Look at her sweet, ripe body, that drives Hamet to such torment!' Swiftly, Isobel opened up the chest by her bed, and drew out a length of fine silk cord. 'Here, Elena,' she said, 'she is yours. Tie her wrists to the bed. See, how she writhes, longing for her punishment!'

Elena stood hesitantly, her dark blue eyes wide with uncertainty. Isobel said softly, 'Now, we don't want to have to tell the lord Aimery how disobedient you are, Elena, do we? Why, he might even send you away! And you don't want that, do you, my sweet Elena? You don't wish to leave, never to see Aimery again?'

Swallowing hard, Elena shook her head. She was completely in this woman's power. Because Isobel knew she would do anything, anything, to obey Aimery's wishes.

Taking the rope numbly from Isobel's outstretched hands, she silently bound the redhead's wrists to the wooden frame of the bed, as Isobel indicated. While she worked, the musky heat of Morwith's voluptuous body reached up to her, inflaming her even more. With a little shock, she saw the wet pink flesh of her woman's parts protruding excitedly from the nest of red hair between her thighs, waiting desperately for a man's touch. Elena thought of Aimery's mysterious, proud phallus, and it was like a dark shaft through her soul, possessing her.

Isobel watched contentedly. Good. The fair-haired convent girl was learning obedience at last. The leather belt would be driving her to distraction by now. No doubt she was eagerly awaiting her own reward. Perhaps she even had illusions that Aimery would come to her again.

By the time Isobel had finished with her, Aimery wouldn't even want to set eyes on her, ever again. Isobel sighed with satisfaction at the way her plans were working out.

She suddenly became aware of Hamet, kneeling blindfolded and chained at her side. Poor Hamet, already he was breathing raggedly with suppresssed excitement. And Isobel, fondly imagaining how his rampant penis would spring out when freed from the constrictions of his clothing, decided that some speed was now necesary, before he was driven to extremity.

'Poor Hamet,' she said softly. 'Can't you picture Morwith as she writhes on the bed, longing for you to fill her with your hungry flesh? But her wish is not to be fulfilled, Hamet. You see, you are going to have to wait, and listen, as Morwith is pleasured by Elena.

Isobel saw, with satisfaction, how the blood drained from the Saxon girl's face. She reached, again, into the chest. 'With this.'

And she pushed her prized possession into the trembling girl's hands – the ivory phallus – so beautifully designed for a woman's extremity of pleasure, so thick and long and cunningly carved. Morwith, on seeing its size, gave a little squeal of delight; Isobel pushed impatiently at Elena.

'Use it, Elena. Use it. Do I have to explain how? Pleasure her. You see how eager she is, how she spreads her legs and writhes towards the ivory? Pleasure her, Elena, and your lord will reward you well!'

Elena shook her head helplessly, the ivory phallus cold and heavy in her hands. 'I – I cannot. I do not know how.'

Isobel frowned impatiently, her slanting eyes becoming dark emerald slits. 'Aimery will be displeased, Elena, you realise that? Very well, we shall have to show you; and soon, very soon, you will feel the kiss of the ivory yourself. But first, poor Morwith. See what torment she is in. And Hamet too.'

Taking the phallus from Elena's nerveless hands, Isobel moved across to the bed, where Morwith sprawled, her knees raised, her legs wide apart. Carelessly Isobel ran her hands over the tight leather bodice, over Morwith's full, pendulous breasts. Then, without preliminaries, she thrust the giant phallus deep into Morwith's hungry, moist entrance. Morwith cried out, and squirmed her hips in delight, ravished by the cold, rough feel of the ivory's protuberances sliding deep within her. Isobel, holding it firm and still as Morwith writhed around it, looked scornfully across at Elena. 'Go and sit down,' she hissed out. 'Watch, and learn. Then perhaps next time the lord Aimery is foolish enough to visit your bed, he will not find you quite so totally incompetent!'

Shaking and humiliated, Elena did as she was told. Everything she saw, everything she heard, made her yearn unbearably for the hypnotic presence of Aimery le Sabrenn. As she sat down, she felt the shaming moisture seeping from between her legs, dampening the leather strap that tormented her so with its promise of pleasure. She wriggled on the chair, but that only made it worse.

'Watch, I said!' hissed Isobel.

Slowly, the lady of Morency was working the ivory phallus in and out of the bound woman on the bed, while Morwith twisted against her ropes, groaning her pleasure, her stretched flesh lips clutching obscenely at the creamy shaft. Hamet listened avidly, breathing harshly as he knelt in his dark corner, the bulge at his groin sufficient indication of his huge arousal. Glancing across at him, Isobel moved suddenly away from the bed, taking the phallus with her, slick and wet with Morwith's love juices. The redhead moaned her disappointment, rubbing her thighs together to ease the fierce ache. 'Remember your punishment, Morwith,' said Isobel coldly. 'It is not over yet.'

And as Morwith writhed helplessly on the bed, Isobel walked across to Hamet. 'Here. Smell, taste these juices; feel how she longs for you, Saracen.' She thrust the big phallus at Hamet's open mouth; avidly the blindfolded prisoner licked and sucked and tasted. 'Are you sorry now for your greedy lust?'

'Yes, oh, yes, my lady!' Hamet groaned in despair as Isobel kneeled to probe at his concealed erection with the cold ivory.

'You will not pleasure the redhead again, so lewdly, so publicly, without my permission?'

'No, I swear, never!'

'And do you want to watch now, while I pleasure her with this?'

Hamet gasped, nodding his head. With a few deft movements. Isobel ripped the woollen blindfold from his eyes. Then she unlaced his leggings.

His dark phallus sprang out, immense and straining, quivering against his taut belly with excitement. Already a clear drop of moisture gleamed at the swollen tip. Elena, hypnotised, felt a spasm of almost unbearable excitement shudder through her loins. Shutting her eyes, she fought for control. Isobel moved purposefully across to the bed and once more slid the huge ivory phallus into Morwith's hungry flesh, sliding the cool, ridged shaft teasingly in and out, twisting it so that its protuberances pulled at her swollen lips, rubbing at her hot, throbbing clitoris. Morwith, shuddering as the ecstasy built up inside her desperate body, turned her head and glimpsed the pinioned Saracen's huge, dusky erection rearing up helplessly from his loins. In that instant, she imagined wildly that it was Hamet's throbbing penis that she gripped so tightly within herself; that it was the Saracen himself who thrust his rampant, hardened shaft within her.

It was enough to take her over the brink. With strange, delirious little cries, she clutched at the ivory phallus with her inner muscles, and was convulsed in wave after wave of blinding pleasure, squirming about the bed as Isobel, frowning in concentration, pushed the ivory deep within her spasming flesh.

Hamet, watching avidly, was unable to control his body any longer at the lascivious sight. His hands still tied behind his back, he clenched his buttocks tight and let out a wild cry of abandon as jet after jet of milky white semen began to spurt from his throbbing penis.

Isobel waited silently for their climaxes to subside.

Then she turned slowly to view the white-faced, anguished girl in the chair. 'Now, Elena,' she said silkily, 'I think it's your turn. Don't you?'

Elena, her whole body now throbbing with the torment of desire after the pleasure she had witnessed, shuddered in refusal. She longed unbearably for her burning flesh to be assuaged – but not so shamelessly, not in front of them all!

Isobel, seeing her shake her head, frowned. So, it was not going to be as easy as she thought! Swiftly releasing Hamet from his chains, she ordered him abruptly to dress and depart. She'd decided that Hamet was too loyal to his master to witness what she had in mind. Morwith watched silently, curled on the big bed in the shadows, as Isobel turned back to Elena.

'You would refuse my orders?' she queried in surprise. 'You would displease the lord Aimery? You mean to say that you do not wish for his favours, do not wish him to visit you shortly?'

Elena's head jerked upwards, her delicate face suddenly flooded with colour again. Aimery. All she wanted on this earth was for Aimery to come to her, to release her from this sweet torment. 'He is coming here? Soon?' she whispered.

'Oh, indeed,' lied Isobel. 'And how do you think he will wish to find you, my dear? Ready and waiting, of course.' She lowered her voice. 'Now remove your gown and lie upon the bed.'

And then Isobel had the satisfaction of watching, as the trembling Saxon girl, whose innocent beauty she so hated, started despairingly to lift the coarse serf's gown she wore above her head. Isobel noted avidly where the rough fabric had scratched the girl's small, tender breasts, which were such a contrast to Morwith's freckled voluptuousness; saw where the tightly buckled belt cut into her tiny waist; saw how the leather between her thighs was moist with her sweet juices.

Elena started to unbuckle the tormenting belt with shaking fingers.

'Oh, no,' said Isobel swiftly. 'Not yet. First, you must make a promise. Do you swear to submit to whatever the lord Aimery wishes? To – anything?'

Elena moistened her lips. 'Yes, I swear it.'

Nodding, Isobel jerked the belt upwards; the tautening of the strap still higher between her legs sent waves of dark pleasure through Elena, like a secret promise. *Oh, Aimery . . .*

'Lie on the bed,' soothed Isobel in her ear. 'Let Morwith tie you up, and Aimery shall come to you!'

Blindly, Elena did as she was told, and Morwith moved in.

Morwith had watched the unfolding scene with interest, and a certain amount of pity. The girl Elena was a Saxon, like herself; and Morwith could see that she was on fire, tormented by her own longings, yet afraid to give in. Gently, Morwith started to fasten the silken cords round Elena's blue-veined, slender wrists and ankles.

'Don't be afraid,' she whispered in Elena's ear. 'Such pleasure in store, Elena, I will teach you!'

There was a soft knock on the door. Isobel went to answer it impatiently, and came over to the bed. 'Bind her mouth with this,' she instructed curtly, handing Morwith the black cloth that had been used to blindfold Hamet. 'We don't want her crying out and making a stupid fuss. Morwith, you know what to do, I'll be back very shortly.' She turned and left the room, slamming the door behind her. Morwith smiled to herself.

Carefully, she knelt up on the bed beside the frightened Saxon girl, stroking her inner wrist gently. 'Don't worry, I won't do anything to hurt you,' she whispered. 'Believe me, there is only pleasure in store. Were you taken prisoner by the Normans, like me?'

Elena shifted in anguish on the bed, terribly aware of the sensuous wolf pelts caressing her buttocks and the

654

back of her thighs, of the pleasure that seared through her threateningly as her bonds tightened. She nodded her head desperately.

Morwith had a sudden inspiration. 'I know, you are from the convent!'

That explained so much – why this girl was so ripely feminine, so ready for love, and yet knew so little! On a sudden impulse, she reached out to stroke Elena's firm, lovely young breasts, noticing how the sudden spasm of pleasure shot through the girl's helpless body. 'Submit to me,' she whispered. 'Submit while I prepare you for Aimery's love, and you will find everything so much the sweeter! Listen, isn't this better than being out in the hot fields gathering hay, or slaving in the kitchens? Elena, you and I can be friends. Such friends! Let me show you what your body longs for . . .'

One of the candles guttered and went out. The room was almost in darkness, hot and oppressive. Carefully moving down to Elena's hips, Morwith stroked the leather belt. Then her fingers slipped downwards, parting the girl's tender, swollen lips, so that the pink flesh protruded in moist silken folds on either side of the taut strap. Then she dipped her head and started to lick softly, caressing the oversensitised flesh, curling her tongue beneath the thick leather, lapping up the sweet moisture that trickled down her secret cleft.

Elena went rigid with shock. Then, as the other woman continued so gently with her wonderful tonguing, she gave a muffled groan, and closed her eyes helplessly as the warm, soothing pleasure washed over her. Her belly tightened and her breasts throbbed unbearably as Morwith's long tongue licked so sweetly up and down her love channel. She arched her hips; the leather band pressed against her throbbing bud of pleasure, chafing at it, driving her almost to the brink of which she'd so long despaired.

She didn't hear the door open; neither did Morwith. But they both heard Isobel's voice, as she said, approv-

655

ingly, 'Well, well. Morwith, you exceed your duties, I think. It seems as if we have arrived just in time.'

Elena, warm and flushed with shameful pleasure, jerked her head round to the door. *Aimery. Isobel had brought Aimery to her, as she had promised . . .*

Her eyes widened in shock.

Not Aimery, but a strong, muscular young serf whom she'd seen working in the kitchens. Isobel drew him forwards into the dark, heated room. 'Let me introduce you both,' she said huskily, 'to Pierre.'

The young serf's brown eyes had lit up with disbelieving pleasure as he saw the two beautiful women on the bed. He stumbled eagerly forward; Isobel stopped him with the lash of her tongue.

'Not yet, Pierre! First, you must show us that you are ready! Remember?'

Nodding avidly, Pierre started to fumble eagerly with his clothing. Elena, suddenly all too aware of her extreme vulnerability, struggled in her bonds, and felt her heated flesh growing cold. Surely – surely Isobel did not intend this youth for her? Morwith was crouching very still on the bed, watching and waiting. She said, almost accusingly, 'You told the girl that Aimery would be coming here.'

'In a while,' Isobel replied. 'In the meantime, we have a special treat for our convent girl. Dear me, Pierre, you are a little slow tonight. Would you like some encouragement?'

The handsome, strapping youth nodded fiercely, his hands still fumbling beneath his shabby tunic. Isobel glanced across at the bed and caught the look of blind rebellion on Elena's face.

'Oh, dear, Elena,' she sighed. 'And I thought you were so eager to learn, to carry out my lord Aimery's wishes!'

Elena squeezed her eyes shut. Aimery wished this? On her? After the tenderness he had shown her last night? No, she would not believe it! She struggled, trying to free herself again; Isobel watched her, her face hardening.

This was going to be more difficult than she thought. And yet, Pierre was an essential part of her plan. Elena must be desperate for pleasure by now after her day of torment, truly desperate for the feel of a strong man inside her hungry flesh. Surely, once she glimpsed Pierre's exceptional appendage, she would be begging for it, pleading wildly for him to pleasure her, to drive himself within her! And then – then, she could tell Aimery how his precious little Saxon slave had degraded herself with a common serf, a simpleton, and he would turn from the girl in utter disgust. Isobel turned her attention to the expectant redhead.

'Now, Morwith. As you can see, Pierre is a little shy, but he is truly, exquisitiely well-endowed. Encourage him a little, will you? You will find yourself well rewarded, I promise.'

Morwith glanced anxiously at Elena's white, despairing face. Then, obediently, she got up from the bed and swayed sensuously across the room to the muscular young serf, her breasts jutting proudly above her tight leather bodice. As she reached him, she sank to her knees and slowly began to unfasten the belt that supported his thonged trousers. 'Show me,' she smiled softly up at him. 'Show me, Pierre, what a man you are.' And she reached inside his clothes, licking her lips.

Pierre gasped, and clutched at her mane of red curls. Carefully, happily, Morwith drew out his already thickened penis, and cradled it between her palms, watching enraptured as the engorged shaft stiffened and grew. The lady Isobel was right. It was of exceptional proportions, long and solid, with an endearing curve towards the end that made it appear proud and eager to do service. Pierre was quivering with excitement, his penis jerking desperately towards her soft lips. Taking pity on him, Morwith stuck out her pink tongue and circled him lasciviously, licking slowly round the edge of the swollen purple glans, pushing back the foreskin and mouthing him delicately until he gasped with delight.

Isobel, seeing the perspiration standing out on Pierre's forehead, broke in swiftly. No, not yet. He must save himself for the convent girl, who trembled in her bonds as she gazed at Pierre's huge, glistening purple erection. 'Stop, Morwith. That is enough.'

Obediently but reluctantly, Morwith withdrew her mouth from Pierre's penis, so that it swung free, pointing blindly into the empty air. Pierre's face fell; his big hand moved swiftly to soothe his engorged shaft, sliding up and down in smooth, powerful strokes while his eyes closed in rapture.

'Stop that, Pierre!' cried out Isobel sharply. Pierre's hand fell swiftly to his side; he hung his head. Isobel went on, more gently, 'Now for that special treat I promised you yesterday, remember? A young Saxon girl, who is most eager to try out your splendid equipment – are you not, my dear Elena?'

Already the serf had turned eagerly towards her naked body on the bed, a grin of anticipation spreading across his blandly handsome features, his purple protuberance jutting out in excitement. Elena wrenched wildly at the silken cords that bound her wrists and ankles. *No*, Aimery could not want this for her. He could not!

Morwith, seeing what was happening, crouched quickly by her side. 'You'll enjoy it, Elena!' she whispered urgently. 'Don't be afraid! See what a man he is – see his fine instrument of pleasure – oh, don't your love juices flow for him? Don't you long to feel him inside you?'

Isobel, overhearing, chuckled in agreement. 'How right you are, Morwith! Pierre, get on with it. The girl is ready and waiting. All this protest is just part of some silly game that she likes to play. Take her, Pierre – she is yours.'

With a grunt, Pierre knelt on the bed between Elena's spread thighs. Eagerly he bent over her and began to struggle with the buckle that fastened her love belt, his huge purple member quivering and straining as he worked. Licking his lips, he drank in greedily the sight of those moist pink flesh lips protruding so sweetly from her soft golden fleece, longing to thrust himself in that honeyed passage.

The door to the chamber flew open suddenly, letting in a draught of fresh air and daylight. Pierre kneeled up, blinking.

Aimery le Sabrenn, lord of Thoresfield, stood outlined in the doorway, and in the shadows his scarred face was black with rage.

Chapter Eight

A imery slammed the door shut. The draught blew out the final candle, throwing the room into complete darkness except for the glowing brazier in the corner.

Isobel moved quickly to relight the candles. 'Why, my lord! We did not expect you back so soon, but you are most welcome. We were preparing a little entertainment for you . . .'

Aimery's strong mouth curved in the dangerous smile that always sent a shiver of fear through even his closest friends. His tense, powerful figure dominated the room; it was as if everyone had stopped breathing, waiting for his reply. He still wore his leather gambeson, though he had removed his armour. The heat and dust of the long hours in the saddle were with him still, streaking his tawny hair. His eyes were like cold steel as he surveyed the still figures on the bed in the corner. Elena, lying helpless in her bonds, shivered when she saw the icy scorn in his glance.

He hadn't known. He hadn't wanted all this for her. Isobel had lied. And now, thinking that she'd willingly submitted to this degradation, he despised her with all his heart. She had lost before the game had even begun. Isobel had won.

Pierre, bemused and more than a little frightened by the lord of Thoresfield's presence, slid from the bed and backed into the shadows, his erection drooping quickly.

'So,' grated the Breton to Isobel. 'This is how you spend your afternoons when I am absent?'

Isobel moved swiftly towards him. 'It was all for you, my lord!' She ran her dainty hand down his muscular shoulder, gazing up with rapt emerald eyes into his tired, harsh face.

'And the girl?'

'You mean Elena? Why,' said Isobel, thinking quickly, 'your new acquisition has been most willing to join in with everything, my lord! She has displayed a touching eagerness, you wil be delighted with her progress! So enthusiastic, so passionate! Hamet, Morwith, Pierre – she has enjoyed them all!'

Aimery le Sabrenn felt suddenly sick. The dark bitterness rose in his soul. Once more he'd been mistaken, deceived. As he'd been deceived by the Saxon, Madelin . . .

Abruptly, he crossed to the chair and sat down, pouring himself a full goblet of wine from the silver jug resting on the nearby table. He drank it down and poured again. He felt a sudden, wild rage that transmuted itself into a hardening lust, a familiar tightening at his loins. So, they'd all pleasured the Saxon girl. Very well, then he, too, would take his pleasure from her, before throwing her out – off his property, his land, his demesne.

Elena had given up struggling. She was gagged still, and even if she were not, she knew, from the look on the Breton lord's face, that there was no point in trying to deny what Isobel had just told him. He would not believe her. He looked so tired, so bitter; and she burned desperately with longing for him.

Isobel, not sure which direction things were taking, said quickly, 'My lord, you are weary. I will dismiss

661

these others, send for food, and you and I can spend some time alone.'

Aimery's face twisted cynically. 'What, Isobel – send them all away, when it seems that I have missed most of the entertainment already? Surely you can exercise your imagination and share a little of your diversion with me?'

Isobel, uncertain of the strangely harsh tone in his voice, felt suddenly uneasy. 'My lord – what is your will?'

Aimery let his black, bitter glance scald them all. His gaze alighted on the bewildered Pierre, who hovered, still hopeful of pleasure, in the shadows. 'What about him?' Aimery grated out. 'Your new favourite looks disappointed, Isobel. Have I interrupted him? Let him choose his pleasure – presumably he had finshed with the slut on the bed. Let me see him try the other one, the redhead!'

At this, Pierre brightened considerably; so did Morwith, who had been kneeling in stillness, breasts pouting, naked thighs just slightly apart, hoping desperately that she would catch the Breton's attention. Now was her chance! If she performed well, the Breton might take her himself.

Shivering at the very thought, Morwith moved voluptuously to crouch on all fours, her heavy, brown-nippled breasts dangling, her full buttocks wide and plump beneath the leather corset. Pierre, his erection suddenly jerking into life again, kneeled joyfully behind her, feeling for her juicy cleft, and with a soft hiss of delight thrust himself deep within her ripe, glistening folds. Morwith groaned aloud in ecstasy as his long, thick shaft possessed and filled her silky inner flesh. 'What a fine lad you are, Pierre,' she muttered in encouragement. 'Let me feel all of it, all of it – ah, yes, that's it.'

Meanwhile, Isobel kneeled hopefully beside her lord and let her fingers rest on his strongly-muscled thigh.

He ignored her and drank more wine, seeking oblivion, of the body and the mind. He was strongly aroused by the crude coupling going on in the shadows, and felt once more the urgent need for his own release. Not with Isobel. Not with the redheaded Saxon, whom he remembered from that midnight journey through the forest. She was doing all this for him, he knew, casting sideways glances at him through lascivious eyes. Dismissing her, his eyes strayed to the bed.

Elena lay very still, her eyes to the wall, the black cloth still fastened crudely round her mouth. Her beautiful blonde hair cascaded in disarray over her slender shoulders; her small, firm breasts rose and fell slightly with every breath she took, the rosy nipples tender and sweet. Her legs were drawn apart by the cords at her ankles; he could see the tender pink flesh of her femininity peeping out from either side of the tight leather belt. How many of them had used her today. Which of them had she enjoyed most?

Last night, he had thought she was different. But now he knew that she was just like all the rest.

He could feel his penis rearing up against his belly, hot and hungry. 'Untie the girl,' he rapped out to Isobel at his side. Isobel got up slowly, slanting a look of venomous hatred at the fair-haired Saxon bound to the bed. Pierre and Morwith were by now totally engrossed in their copulation; the young male serf kneeled above her, his muscular hips pumping away enthusiastically, while Morwith's face flushed with delight as Pierre's satisfying length of iron-hard flesh worked vigorously up and down her moist love channel.

Elena, freed by the coldly furious Isobel, the gag removed from her mouth, got to her feet and stood with her head held high.

'Come here,' said Aimery flatly, and she obeyed slowly, still not looking at him.

Blood of Christ, but she was beautiful, swore Aimery silently. Her wide, vulnerable eyes were dark sapphire pools in her pale, delicately shaped face; her glorious hair framed her head and shoulders like moondust. Her body was slender and graceful. Even in that tight leather belt, which must have been driving her into a frenzy of lust all day, she looked so pure, so untouched. Surely . . .

Isobel, crackling with jealousy, said with a light laugh, 'You will find dear Elena somewhat exhausted, my lord. She has such enthusiasm for our little games! Spare her your attentions as well, my lord, the poor girl can barely stand, so sated is she with pleasure.'

Elena's head jerked at that. She looked as if she were about to speak and gazed almost imploringly at Aimery le Sabrenn, her fathomless blue eyes dark with some kind of pain, then she changed her mind and lowered her eyes, her full lower lip trembling with passion.

So, she was ashamed. Aimery's empty stomach curdled suddenly on the strong wine he'd been drinking so freely. He said in a low, venomous voice, 'You mistake me, my lady Isobel. The girl is to give me pleasure, not to take it for herself. Obviously, you are taking her training very seriously. I wish to see the results so far.'

Elena stood before him with her hands clasped and her head bowed, so that her golden hair almost obscured her face. Her whole body burned for this man. His mere presence melted her; his voice, harsh though it was, sent impossible arrows of desire quivering through her helpless, naked flesh. He despised her so utterly, that she knew he would scorn anything at all that she tried to say in her defence. Would he take her word instead of Isobel's? Never.

Behind her, Pierre and Morwith reached their noisy climax, bucking wildly in each other's arms before collapsing, sweaty and sated, onto the floor. Aimery waited till they were still, then bit out roughly, 'Very well, then, Elena. Show me what you have learned.'

Elena gazed up at him, bewildered; Isobel gave her a

little shove, and hissed in her ear, 'Pleasure him, you fool! Have you learned nothing all day? Kneel, and pleasure your lord!'

With sudden realisation, Elena fell to her knees. Pleasure him. As Morwith had pleasured Pierre, when he first entered that hateful room.

Her cheeks flooded with colour now, Elena bowed her head so that her swathes of golden hair hung like a silk curtain across the Breton's strongly muscled thighs and brushed the tops of his leather boots. With trembling fingers, she reached for the lacings that fastened his woollen hose. Oh, if only men's clothing were not such a mystery to her! Unintentionally, as she fumbled beneath his leather tunic, she brushed the Breton's heated groin, saw his strong hands suddenly tighten on the arms of the chair. Her throat went dry. His bare forearms were tanned and sinewed, the skin covered with fine, sun-bleached hairs that she longed to kiss . . . She was this man's slave, she acknowledged hopelessly, in more ways than one.

As she knelt on the ground before him, the leather belt pressed in again on her soft, moist flesh. Already this afternoon, Morwith's sweet mouth had aroused her almost to breaking point. Now, with the Breton so near, she felt the drugged desire build up almost unbearably. She tried to hold herself very still, so that the leather strap would not slide any further between her swollen lips, but already her breathing was short and ragged.

Isobel's sneering laugh mocked her as she struggled with the stubborn laces. Then she found the opening, and her fingers shook as she caught a glimpse of smooth, taut thigh, darkly covered with soft, secret hairs. And then – between his thighs was that thickly curling pelt, from which grew his mysterious phallus, already thickened and stirring with life . . .

Forgetting her anguish, she gazed silently at its beauty, her breath catching in her throat. This was the heart, the dark, masculine core of this man who dominated her every thought.

From behind her, Isobel hissed, 'Go on, you little fool. Don't just stare!' She was aware of Morwith and Pierre, too, watching avidly from the shadows behind her. She panicked. What was she supposed to do?

Suddenly, she remembered how Morwith had taken Pierre's manhood in her mouth, when he first entered the room. She had been horrified then by the act, by the redhead's blatant sexuality. But this was different.

Elena felt herself filling up with an exquisite, yearning tenderness. No-one else in the room mattered, no-one else existed, except for Aimery. She leaned forward gently, to press tiny, delicate kisses on the warm flesh that stirred so strongly between the Breton's powerful thighs. As she did so, the root thickened still more, nudging her, caressing her parted lips. Elena kissed it again, carefully, along the now rigid shaft. Her heart thudded slowly as she felt the veined silken skin pulsing, tautening, lengthening. It was so beautiful, so warm and full of life.

Dimly, she heard Isobel exclaim impatiently, 'My lord, would you rather I gave you satisfaction instead? Clearly the girl has much to learn yet!'

Aimery, not taking his eyes from the girl's bowed head, said coldly, 'Isobel, your interruptions annoy me. Can't you find something, or someone else, to occupy your time? Another crude kitchen serf, perhaps?'

Isobel gasped aloud, as if he'd struck her. With a swirl of her silken gown, she turned and left the room, slamming the door behind her. Pierre, watching the kneeling Saxon girl as she paid homage to her Breton lord, was stirring with excitement again; Morwith too watched with moist, open lips.

Elena was oblivious to them all. All except her lord, Aimery. This suddenly seemed to be the only way she could express her love for this proud, bitter man, and her whole body hungered to serve him. All her yearning self, all her pulsing flesh, so exquisitely tormented during that long day, centred on her slow, deliberate caresses. His penis stood proudly erect now, straining at the flat, hard muscle of his belly; with a little gasp at the sight, almost frightened by it, she leaned forward on impulse and rubbed her small breasts, one by one, against the throbbing, silky glans.

The feel of his strong phallus against her tender, rosy nipples excited her unbearably. Sweet flames of sensation burned through her flesh, to meet in a molten blaze at the pit of her abdomen. Oh, to feel that massive pillar of flesh deep within her, caressing her, filling her!

Aimery groaned aloud at the unexpected delight of her breasts against his fevered phallus. Reaching out blindly, he clutched at her mane of hair and pulled her face down close to his throbbing erection. Shyly yet defiantly, Elena parted her lips and kissed him there, softly running her small tongue around the ridge that encircled the swollen glans. Then, drawing a deep breath, she took him in her mouth, sliding her moist lips down the straining shaft as far as she could, sensing rather than hearing the Breton's harsh gasp of pleasure.

He tasted exquisite. Warm, silken, aromatic – the very essence of masculinity. Knowing that she could take no more of that imposing shaft into her mouth, she instinctively gripped the base of his phallus with her hand, and continued to run her soft mouth up and down up and down the rigid flesh, shuddering with pleasure herself as he gasped and clutched at her shoulders.

Suddenly, Elena, her blood pulsing by now with almost unbearable excitement, felt the Breton's taut hips go very tense and still. With exquisite sensitivity, she continued to lick and suck, pouring her whole heart into her caresses; his strong hands moved to cup her breasts, his palms working deliberately to and fro across her stiffened nipples. Conscious of her own surging rapture, Elena gasped and felt the leather belt rub more tightly than ever against her secret parts. She thrust her

667

breasts against Aimery's cool hands, rubbing the swollen globes desperately, dipping her head to pleasure him more fiercely than ever.

Then, the Breton suddenly withdrew. She feared she'd displeased him, but he soothed her, stroking her hair, restoring her confidence. At the same time his fingers squeezed her heated breasts, kneading and pinching her engorged nipples; the leather belt seemed to press harder between her moist inner lips, rubbing unbearably against her clitoris; until at last, with a wild shudder of ecstasy, Elena's racked body arched and exploded, all her senses obliterated by the shimmering waves of pleasure that rolled through her exquisitely-tormented nerve endings.

Still dazed with sensation, she felt an overpowering urge to bring him to the same plateau of rapture. Pushing her hair back from her flushed face, she leaned forward to draw her tongue tip around the sensitive glans of his urgently throbbing phallus, taking as much as she could into the soft cavern of her mouth, while with her hand she stroked and gripped the base of his rigid shaft. She felt a wonderful sense of power as he started to thrust strongly, uncontrollably within her mouth, and when his first spurt of semen shot out, she felt her body ripple in renewed orgasm. Dazed with the pleasure of it, she continued to suck and swallow the salty, exquisite emissions as his penis jerked powerfully at the back of her throat.

At long last he was still, and she felt the rigid shaft begin to soften within her mouth. She kissed it tenderly and knelt before him, her head bowed in silent homage. Surely, he would realise now what he meant to her. Tears of emotion welled in her eyes, making them translucent.

She felt his hand cupping her chin. He raised her head gently, compelling her to look up at him. His scarred, handsome face was stern and expressionless, the grey eyes cold. Yet behind it all, she knew, she was triumphantly sure, that there was some tenderness for her! He had sensed her own approaching release and urged her towards it, with infinite skill, even though he was so close to his own climax of passion.

Then suddenly, Aimery le Sabrenn saw the unshed tears of emotion in Elena's eyes, and stood up so abruptly that Elena almost fell.

'My lady Isobel has failed in her tuition,' he grated out sharply. 'You are not supposed to shed tears, Elena. Even if I am the person you hate most in all the world.'

'My lord!' she stammered out, shocked. 'I – '

'Enough.' He cut her short. 'From now on, you can take your pleasure with the rest of Isobel's rabble – presumably they please you more!' Swiftly, in less time than it took to blink an eye, he fastened his clothes and left the room. Elena drew a deep, shuddering breath of despair and gripped at the legs of the chair he had just left, fighting back the sharp pain that seared her. He had misunderstood. She would go after him.

From behind her, Morwith said softly, 'Dear me. You've got a lot to learn, haven't you? A lot they didn't teach you at the convent.'

Elena whirled round. Pierre, sated, was asleep on the floor; Morwith was watching her with a strange light in her pale eyes. 'Was I so bad then?' Elena whispered brokenly.

Morwith frowned. In fact, she'd been wildly jealous of the Saxon girl's exquisitely natural, sensual caresses, and she'd seen, only too well, the effect they'd had on the Breton.

But she wasn't going to tell her that, because Morwith wanted Aimery too, and she hoped that she might be able to turn this incident to her own advantage. 'Not bad,' the redhead conceded grudgingly. 'Not bad – for a first time. But I'd be very, very surprised if he came back for more. I'll tell you what, I'll give you lessons sometime.'

Pierre stirred in his sleep, and emitted a gentle snore.

Elena went slowly over to the bed and started pulling on her serf's tunic, her heart unbearably heavy. Suddenly, she wanted more than anything to be out of this room, away from the heavy, overloaded atmosphere. 'Thank you, Morwith,' she said. 'I will remember your offer.'

Then she went back to her own little room further along the gallery and lay on her bed, the despair washing over her.

In the great raftered hall, brightly lit by scores of smoking wax candles set in iron sconces on the walls, the evening meal was drawing to a close. Knights, men-at-arms, stewards and reeves relaxed noisily at the trestle tables set up through the length of the hall; shouting for more ale from the serving wenches, telling bawdy stories, picking at bones and mopping up the last morsels of juicy gravy with slabs of manchet bread. In front of the great log fire that always burned, day and night, several shaggy hunting hounds sprawled on the freshly-strewn rushes, gnawing contentedly at the half-finished scraps that had been thrown to them.

Only at the high table, raised on its dais at the end of the room, was the company subdued. Aimery le Sabrenn, lord of Thoresfield, was in a dangerous mood, and even his friends, the loyal knights who had campaigned with him in the old days in France and Sicily, were wary. One by one they left, to see to their horses, or their armour, or to join the cheerier company in the body of the hall as stories were told and dice were rolled. Aimery watched them go, stirring himself briefly to rap out some brief, curt orders to the sergeant-at-arms who was responsible for the night watch. Then he poured himself more wine and gazed into the smouldering logs of the fire. Even when his favourite deerhound came loping up to him and nuzzled hopefully at his hands, Aimery barely noticed him, and his face remained set and hard.

670

The girl obsessed him. With what pleasure Isobel had told him how the Saxon girl had enjoyed her tuition! Hamet, Aimery could almost forgive; but to think of her with that coarse serf, Pierre, was too much.

Why had he hoped she'd be different? Was it because of last night, when she'd surrendered so sweetly to him in her room? A fresh stab of bitterness coursed through his blood. Perhaps she wasn't even a virgin. Last night, he would have sworn, as he sheathed himself so deeply within her tender flesh, that she'd not known a man before. But perhaps she was especially cunning, like Madelin. Perhaps it was one of the tricks she'd learned, while servicing the rebels who stayed at that rat-hole of a convent, to look and sound innocent – as if it was her first time, every time.

Even this afternoon in Isobel's oppressive chamber, when the girl had taken him in her mouth, she'd seemed exquisitely innocent, yet so tender and loving that he thought he'd never known such pleasure.

At least, he should be grateful that her tears of revulsion had given her away in time. She'd not been able to conceal them. Aimery had no doubt that she'd reached a shattering plateau of pleasure herself – her shuddering climax was no pretence – but then, when she came to her senses and remembered who she was with, she hadn't been able to hide her true feelings.

He was her enemy, her people's enemy, and he was also hideously scarred. He thought he'd got used to that, but perhaps he hadn't.

Madelin. Madelin, the Saxon witch who'd killed his brother, was the one who'd scarred his face and embittered his soul

He drank more wine, remembering. The flames in the fire died down; a log settled, sending sparks flying. The noise and merriment of his soldiers at the lines of trestle tables seemed suddenly very far away.

Madelin, the young widow of a Saxon cloth merchant, lived in a house in York, while the brothers were garrisoned there under the command of William fitz Osbern. Hugh, who was in love with her, had been slightly injured in a skirmish with Saxon rebels and was confined to York castle. That night he asked his older brother to visit Gudrumgate, where Madelin lived, to tell her.

Madelin's maid, thinking perhaps in the darkness that Aimery was his brother, sent him straight upstairs to Madelin's chamber. When Aimery opened the door and went in, he realised the mistake; but by then, it was too late.

Madelin, the golden witch, lay on the bed, with a tall candle burning on the table beside her. It was a small, shabby room, but he didn't notice that. He only noticed her.

She was waiting for his brother. She was sitting up against her pillows, the cool linen sheet just touching her hips. Otherwise, she was naked. The candlelight turned her pale, smooth skin to gold, its incandescent flame shimmering on her wonderfully full, pouting breasts, on the glistening fair hair that hung in swathes round her shoulders. Her shadowed eyes were violet, her mouth was wide and full; and she smiled as she said huskily, 'Welcome, Aimery le Sabrenn.'

Aimery felt the heat scorching through him and said harshly, 'My lady, there has been some mistake. I come with an apology from my younger brother, Hugh.'

She sat forward then, so that the sheet fell back and he saw the smooth curve of her raised, silken thigh.

'No mistake,' she said softly. 'I have been waiting for you, Aimery le Sabrenn, since the day I saw you ride into York.'

Aimery still felt sick when he remembered how quickly he had betrayed his brother.

She sat up, the Saxon witch, in her soft bed, and slowly spread her raised knees, so he could see the smooth, completely hairless folds of flesh that framed her femininity. Then, still gazing at him with those

672

drowsy, violet eyes, she'd put one hand on her full breasts, caressing it softly until the scarlet nipple grew heavy and turgid. With her other hand, she reached down to her thighs, and started to stroke herself, playing with delicate fingers at her naked love mound and making little soft noises of longing at the back of her throat while she gazed at the man standing motionless by her bedroom door. With a slow shudder, she dipped her index finger between her lower lips, inserting it carefully into the moist pink flesh, then she drew it out and sucked at it, rapturously, with her mouth.

'Aimery,' she murmured. 'Oh, Aimery.'

Aimery the Breton was no saint. At his first sight of her, his penis had reared up, darkly massive, chafing against the thick belt that girded his tunic.

Freeing his phallus from his leggings with abrupt, jerky movements, he pulled her spread legs to the edge of the bed and took her standing up, planting his hands on either side of her reclining shoulders and sheathing himself up to the hilt in her soft, juicy love passage. Madelin seeemed to almost faint with pleasure as he slid his stiff rod between her legs; she dragged her fingers lasciviously across his broad, muscled shoulders, crying out huskily and arching fiercely against him as he lowered his head to suckle at her full breasts. She felt so good. Shuddering, Aimery bent over her, his feet still firmly planted on the ground, taking his weight with his arms. Slowly he slid his massively erect member in and out of those hairless, pouting lips, savouring her moist, delicious wantonness.

'Oh, Aimery,' she whispered. 'I have dreamed of this, since first I saw you. Fill me, fill me to the brim.'

Suddenly she wrapped her supple legs around his hips, clutching him to her; and Aimery, driving his engorged penis deep within her hot, pulsing flesh, reached a fast, shuddering climax deep within her as she writhed and bucked against his spasming body.

They lay entwined on the bed, slick with sweat, dark

with shame. Aimery drew away at last, and started to tell her that this must never happen again. She had gazed up at him with those wonderful violet eyes, her face soft and drowsy, and nodded.

'Oh course,' she murmured. 'Whatever you say, Aimery le Sabrenn.' Then she'd knelt above him, and positioned herself carefully, her tongue between her pearly teeth, so that those wonderful, scarlet-tipped breasts stroked heavily against his somnolent penis. With a life of its own, it began to stir thickly again. She knelt lower to take his testicles in her mouth, sucking at the rough, tautening globes one by one, nipping and licking at the coarse flesh until his phallus reared jerkily again, its powerful length all too ready for her soft, enticing flesh.

'Take me like this, Aimery,' she'd whispered, swiftly turning so she was on all fours, her secret flesh wet and glistening between the ripe roundness of her bottom cheeks. 'Take me, drive yurself into me, with your wonderful shaft. Yes, oh yes . . .'

Aimery had left the house in Gudrumgate two hours later, degraded and bewitched. He told his brother Hugh that he'd delivered his message; and from that night on, the intimacy, the trust between the two brothers had gone for ever.

He remembered it all now, only too clearly, as he sat in the great raftered hall; surrounded by all his men, and yet alone.

Since Madelin, he'd hated all Saxon women, and hated himself as well, for betraying Hugh.

Seeing that his goblet was empty, and the jug beside it, Aimery beckoned for more wine, and looked up to see that it was Hamet the Saracen who brought it to him. Hamet had been missing at the evening meal and Aimery had assumed that it was because the Saracen was ashamed to see his master, after what he had done with the Saxon girl.

Hamet started to fill his goblet from the jug, but

Aimery gestured curtly for him to stop. 'Leave me the jug. I'll pour.'

Hamet hesitated a moment, then sat down carefully on the bench at his master's side. 'I think,' said the big Saracen in his soft, musical voice, 'that you have perhaps had enough, my lord.'

Aimery's face twisted sardonically. 'I shall be the judge of that, I think. Where have you been this evening, Hamet? Sleeping off the afternoon's excesses in your room?'

Hamet's face shadowed in puzzlement at his master's bitter tone. 'My lord? I have been out on patrol, with a dozen men-at-arms – we left before your return. There were reports, this afternoon, of a band of armed rebels, down near the river. That is what I wished to speak to you about. We found no Saxons, but there were hoofprints, a good number of them, down by the ford. If your lordship thinks fit, perhaps we should mount extra guards tonight.'

Aimery frowned, forcing the potent wine fumes from his brain. 'I appreciate your excess of zeal, my friend. But if it's because you feel guilty about the Saxon girl this afternoon – '

Hamet looked down at his big hands. 'Then the lady Isobel has told you,' he said humbly. 'I apologise, my lord, for temporarily neglecting my duties. But the girl waylaid me, around noon. She was wanton and eager – I swear, it was all over in a few minutes!'

Aimery felt the bleak anger rise within him. God's blood – wanton and eager! His fist clenched. If Hamet had not been his friend of many years, he would have struck him down to the rush-strewn floor in that instant.

'It seems,' Aimery said, with a voice like splintered ice, 'that she deceived us all last night. Either she has learned very quickly, or her feigned innocence was all a pretence.'

Hamet's head jerked up at that, his dark eyes

675

puzzled. 'My lord – last night? I swear to you, I did not even see the redheaded Saxon woman last night!'

It was the Breton's turn to look surprised. 'A redhead? This – coupling you spoke of this afternoon – I gathered it was with the convent girl, Elena . . .'

Hamet's heavy brow cleared in relief. 'Why, no, my lord! The Saxon I spoke of was the redhead, Morwith. You might remember her from the woodcutter's cottage, on our way here!' He coughed awkwardly. 'I came across her in one of the outhouses at noon. She recognised me, and . . . and . . .'

Aimery le Sabrenn was watching him strangely. 'Then the fair-haired girl, Elena. The one who was in my room last night. You are telling me that you have had no contact with her today?'

Again, Hamet cleared his throat in embarrassment. 'My lord, the lady Isobel arranged for myself and Morwith to be punished for our misdemeanour. The girl you speak of was brought in, to watch. But she took no part in any of it, my lord!'

'She was there willingly?'

'I think not, my lord. Though,' and Hamet added this hastily, on seeing the Breton's expression, 'as far as I saw, she was not touched or harmed in any way; but merely made to witness our chastisement.'

With an oath, Aimery was on his feet. The wine jug on the table went crashing to the floor with the violence of his movement.

Hamet, confused, said, 'My lord. The extra patrol I mentioned?'

'Speak to the sergeant-at-arms,' called Aimery over his shoulders as he left the table. 'Tell him what you think fit.' Then he was gone, taking the stairs up to the sleeping chambers two at a time. Hamet, totally perplexed, turned back to ruefully survey the spilled wine.

Elena sat on the edge of her small bed in the darkness, thinking still of Aimery. At every encounter with the

Breton lord, she needed him more and more. Yet he despised her, openly.

She clenched her hands in her lap, trying to think coolly and calmly. Later tonight, she would try to escape from the castle. She didn't think she could bear to see the Breton again, to be so flayed by his cold scorn. She knew that she must leave, before he destroyed her completely.

The door to her room started to open, slowly. Her throat dry with fear, Elena leaped to her feet. *Aimery* . . .

Chapter Nine

The Breton shut the door very deliberately behind him, and stood there, watching her. Elena, standing by the bed, felt herself trembling. His strange silver eyes blazed with light above his hard, jutting cheekbones; his strong, curved mouth, so cruelly twisted by the long white scar that slashed his cheek, was compressed in a thin hard line. Her heart hammered against her ribs, because he looked so *angry*.

Aimery said, in a low voice that seemed to her to be filled with menace, 'So, Elena. Tell me exactly what happened this afternoon.'

Elena moistened her dry lips. Somehow she stammered out her reply, forcing herself to look up into his stern, compelling face.

'The lady Isobel summoned me. I – I was working in the courtyard, bleaching the linen – '

Aimery bit out an oath. 'You were bleaching linen?'

He looked wildly angry. Elena, frightened and confused, said defiantly, 'Yes, my lord! I worked in the kitchens all morning, and in the afternoon, I washed linen, as you commanded! Was it not your will?'

Aimery said softly, dangerously, 'Go on. Tell me more. You were summoned inside, by the lady Isobel. And then?'

Elena bit her lip; the colour blazed in her cheeks. 'They were punishing him,' she whispered. 'Your servant – Hamet. Isobel and Morwith were punishing him. Then Morwith, too, was punished . . .' Her voice trailed away helplessly as she remembered the ivory phallus that gave Morwith such pleasure, remembered the Saracen in his extremity, his pulsing phallus spurting seed across the room.

Aimery was saying quietly, 'And you helped with their punishment?'

'I – I secured Morwith to the bed.' Her voice was scarcely discernible. She added, again with that note of desperate defiance, 'The lady Isobel told me that it was your will, my lord!'

'And the love belt that you wore? Your own bondage? You submitted willingly to all that?'

'Yes – because it was what you wanted! Wasn't it?'

Aimery ran his hand wearily through his thick hair. 'And you were so frightened of me that you would submit to anything Isobel said?'

'Not – not *frightened* of you, my lord,' Elena whispered.

A throbbing silence hung in the darkened room. Aimery suddenly realised how very tired he was. The girl stood before him in the darkness like a flame, pale and golden, shimmering with beauty and a quiet strength that defied him, defied all of them. He said, heavily, 'The lady Isobel told me that you joined in willingly with the others this afternoon – with their games. That you encouraged them to pleasure you. Was this true?'

The girl's face went white; he noticed how she clasped her hands rigidly at her side. 'No, my lord!'

'Then why, in the name of Christ, did you not deny it earlier?'

Elena gazed up at him, her dark blue eyes burning with some emotion he could not name. 'How could I?

679

When I had been told that the lady Isobel was merely carrying out your commands?'

His commands. The girl was right. More right than she would ever know. His commands, to choose a vulnerable Saxon slave from the latest batch of newcomers, to pleasure her, humiliate her, destroy her. His own revenge, for Madelin. His own soul, dark with a hatred that needed to feed on innocence.

With a bleak gesture of despair, Aimery le Sabrenn turned to the door. 'I will give orders, Elena, that you are not to work in the kitchens any more. And you may leave the castle tomorrow, if you wish. You are no longer a serf. You are free.'

Her incredible blue eyes widened with emotion at his words; numbly, still gazing at him, she whispered, 'My lord, as you wish!' Aimery, somehow expecting more reaction, paused with his hand on the door.

'One last thing. This afternoon, in Isobel's room. I would have you know that it was not my intention to grieve you so.'

The girl's face jerked upwards. '*Grieve* me?'

'Your tears. I did not mean to cause you such distress.'

She took a step towards him. 'My lord. Those tears – they were not caused by distress, but because I felt so completely unable to express how I felt . . .'

Aimery had gone very still. 'And how do you feel?'

Elena took a deep, steadying breath. 'All my life,' she said softly, 'I have been a captive, of sorts – in the convent. I was not unhappy, or ill-treated. But nevertheless, I was captive; I had no choice, nowhere else to go. Here, in your castle, I find myself a prisoner again. And now you offer me my freedom. But,' and her clear voice sank to the merest whisper, 'I do not want to leave, my lord. All I want in life is to be yours. In whatever way you wish.'

In three strides, Aimery le Sabrenn had covered the ground between them and caught her slender figure in his arms. She gazed up at him silently, her delicate face pale, her eyes dazed with helpless love.

'Elena,' he muttered as his strong hands gripped her shoulders. 'Oh, Elena. I thought, this afternoon, that you hated me. I thought I repelled you.'

Steadily she reached up her hand to smooth back his hair, and drew one delicate finger down the white ridge of scar tissue. 'My lord,' she said simply, 'at the convent, I used to dream. You are all I ever dreamed of – and more.'

Slowly, she began to lift her tunic over her head. Then, as Aimery gazed mesmerised at her slender, graceful figure, she sank to her knees and reached beneath his tunic for the lacings that fastened his hose. As her fingers did their work, she continued to gaze up at him, her face radiant. 'You will find me your most willing slave, my lord,' she whispered. 'Command me – I am yours.'

His penis was already thick, hanging lengthily down his inner thigh. With gentle little caresses, she bent to run her pointed tongue lovingly round its tip, kissing the swelling shaft until it sprang rapidly into a magnificent erection, jerking hungrily towards her soft, moist mouth. Aimery groaned aloud with pleasure, his hands clutching at her shoulders; she heard it, and caught her breath. She longed to feel him within her. But she was his slave; she was obedient to his commands.

Gently, he moved her head away. She looked up at him, dismayed. 'I do not please you, my lord? I know I have much to learn . . .'

He laughed, a soft, smoky laugh. 'Caran, you are exquisite, all that a man could desire. But I would pleasure you too. Come, let me show you . . .' Slowly, he too sank to his knees, with his shoulders back against the wall, facing her. He too, pulled his tunic over his head, and Elena gasped with pleasure at the sight of the thick, rippling muscle that ridged his chest and shoulders. He bent to kiss her mouth, tenderly; she responded wildly, clasping at his back, running her fingers over his smoothly-tanned skin, fingering the old sword scars that adorned his soldier's body with burning pity, conscious all the time of his proudly erect phallus jutting up from his loins, like a dark, thrilling promise of delight.

'Spread yourself, Elena,' he whispered softly, 'Kneel astride me – I will support you. Spread your thighs, and let me slip into you, like this, ah . . .' With a gasp, Elena did as he said, straddling his strong, bent thighs. He eased himself into her, gently at first, inch by inch, rocking slightly to ease his entry into her tight, slick passage, trying his best not to hurt her with his massive erection.

Elena threw her head back, gasping with pleasure, rubbing her small breasts against his hard chest. All day, she had longed for this, and now it was unbelievably exquisite, to feel his thick, strong penis sliding up into her, totally within her control. She quickly discovered that if she raised herself so that the long shaft was almost free of her, and then slid slowly down again, clutching with her inner muscles, Aimery's face darkened with rapture; and her own pleasure mounted in relentless waves as the solid rod of his phallus filled her plump, tender flesh.

Then Aimery's fingers slid down to her little pleasure bud and softly stroked. With delicious little cries of pleasure, she closed her eyes and rode him, up and down, faster and faster, her jutting nipples grinding against his chest, until at last she exploded in a cataclysm of rapture, quivering and clutching with her inner muscles at that hot pillar of flesh that filled her so deliciously. Holding her tightly, Aimery pumped with his strong thighs to find his own driving release, spurting up within her; then she slumped against him, murmuring his name, knowing a moment of perfect peace as his lips gently kissed her tangled hair.

Then suddenly, somewhere out in the darkness of a

castle courtyard, a horn blared shrilly. Elena, her senses lulled by pleasure, barely heard it, thinking that it signalled the change of watch as usual. But then she realised that Aimery, still enfolding her in his arms, had become suddenly tense.

The horn brayed again, nearer now, a raucous, searing sound from beneath the window. Elena, still dazed with love, murmured in sleepy protest as Aimery moved into action. Carefully but swiftly, he lifted her up, laying her on her cold little bed, and began to dress himself.

'*Caran*, I must go. No time to explain.'

Elena lay shivering, suddenly cold. 'The horn, Aimery, what does it mean?'

He was buckling on his sword belt. 'It's the alarm. It could mean that the Saxons are about to attack.' He bent to kiss the top of her head. 'Wait for me, little one. I will be back.'

Then he was gone, the door slamming shut behind him. Shivering with premonition, Elena pulled the linen sheet from the bed around her shoulders, and tiptoed on bare feet to her little window.

The courtyard below was ablaze with the light of torches and lanterns. Men ran to and fro in a purposeful melee, seizing arms and horses, shouting barked orders to grooms and squires. The great gates of the palisade were already being swung open; the first mounted band was preparing to ride out into the darkness of the night, to face the enemy.

And the enemy, she knew, would be the Saxons, her own kind. She shivered suddenly.

Aimery plunged down the stairs to the hall below, where all was in a state of uproar. His faithful squire stood silently ready, holding out his armour and his sword. Hamet was already buckling on his own sword-belt.

'Scouts we sent out earlier have spotted a large band

683

of rebel Saxons moving through the forest from the east,' Hamet told Aimery grimly. 'Planning, no doubt, to surround Thoresfield and take us by surprise.'

Aimery nodded, making for the door. 'Leave twenty men-at-arms to guard the castle.'

A soldier came running in up the steps to the main door, and stood panting in front of the Breton. 'Sire, there are rumours that the Saxon serfs are planning to escape tonight, to join the rebels!'

Aimery gritted his teeth. 'Then impound them. Lock all the Saxons securely away until our return.'

'Sir!' The soldier acknowledged the command, and ran off towards the armoury. Aimery made for the stables, where his big black warhorse was ready for him, and sprang into the high saddle. With a harsh shout of command, his sword held high, he led his knights out through the wide-open gates, their horses' hooves trampling the beaten earth, their weapons glinting in the smoky torchlight.

Isobel watched them go, her heart burning with venom. She knew, because her spy Alys had just told her, that Aimery had been in the Saxon girl's room when the alarm sounded. Now was her chance to get her revenge, and put paid to the troublesome convent girl for good.

Elena too watched Aimery le Sabrenn ride out through the gates at the head of his men. Silently she watched the band of horsemen gradually disappear into the darkness of the night; saw the flickering light of their torches as they crossed the river by the ford and plunged into the dense silence of the great forest. Shivering, she turned away forlornly from the window and pulled on her serf's tunic.

There was a sudden loud hammering at her door. Bewildered, she hurried to open it. At once, two burly manservants shoved their way in, wrenched her hands behind her back, and started pushing her out of the room.

'No!' She tried to struggle out of their grasp. 'There must be some mistake!'

'No mistake,' growled one man. 'All rebel Saxon scum to be locked away until the lord Aimery returns. Are you saying you're not a Saxon, wench?'

'Yes! I'm Saxon but – '

'All Saxons,' repeated the other man grimly. That was what the lady Isobel had told him a moment ago, wasn't it? Especially, she pointed out, the little Saxon in the top chamber. She'd made a point of mentioning her, said she was to be locked in the dungeons along with the other women.

The men half-pushed, half-dragged their captive down the stairs and winding passages to the stone cellars beneath the castle. They opened up a dark doorway and roughly pushed her through; she stumbled down the stone steps and fell heavily on the straw-covered floor. Behind her, the door thudded shut, and she heard the chilling sound of the heavy bolt being slid into place.

Slowly, her head aching from her fall, she opened her eyes. There were other people, women, in here with her; she could hear their soft whispers as they crouched against the walls in the darkness.

'Here, take some of this,' said a sympathetic voice in her ear. 'It's only stale water, but it's all you'll get down here.'

Elena looked up jerkily, her cheeks smeared with dirt and tears, and recognised the plump, pretty face of Joan, one of the kitchen serfs, bending over her in the darkness.

'M – my thanks,' Elena stammered out, drawing a deep breath to steady herself and taking the proffered wooden beaker in her trembling hands. Then she tried to withdraw into the shadows, but Joan rocked back on her heels, and studied her with interest.

'Why,' she said, 'it's the new girl! You were working in the kitchens this morning, weren't you? You were the one who couldn't pluck chickens to save you life! And then you disappeared – what happened to you?'

The others, all young fair-haired Saxon women, had crowded around now in a circle on the straw, avidly curious about this newcomer. One of them chuckled huskily at Joan's question. 'Perhaps Aimery le Sabrenn carried her off to his chamber!'

Elena caught her breath *Did they know?*.

'What, her?' laughed one of the others scornfully, tossing back her thick golden braids. 'That little waif? She's from a convent, isn't she? A lot of good she'd be to the lord Aimery! Why, she wouldn't know what to do with a man like him! Now, if it was me . . .' And she whispered something in another girl's ear that had them both rippling with laughter.

Elena blushed and clasped her hands tightly in her lap.

'That redhead, Morwith,' another of the girls was muttering, 'she boasts that she lay with the lord Aimery on their journey here!'

'Ah, she's a stuck-up piece, that Morwith,' scoffed another, sprawling back in the dry, heaped-up straw. 'Lying again, no doubt. Anyway, why isn't she here with us? She's a Saxon serf, isn't she?'

'Lying or not, she described it all in perfect detail! Apparently,' and the speaker lowered her teasing voice, so the others crowded in close to listen, 'apparently, our fine lord is most exquisitely equipped. It's not only his sword that he has skill in wielding, they say!' She gurgled with laughter. 'Oh, what wouldn't I give for just one hour of his fine company?'

'Stop, stop, I can't bear it!' sighed another girl, tossing back her long hair. 'Gytha, how can you talk of such impossible delights, when we're locked up down here, with only each other for company?'

Suddenly, she whirled round on Elena. 'And what

about you, little convent girl? I saw you, blushing away in the darkness. Bet you don't even know what we're talking about, do you?'

'Yes, what was it like in the convent?' challenged Gytha, laying her hand on Elena's shoulder. 'Did you lie awake, little nun, dreaming of some fine man coming to your lonely bed?'

'Or,' whispered another one, rubbing close up to Elena's side, 'did you enjoy yourself with your friends? Did you pretend that you had a man to pleasure you?'

Suddenly they were all giggling, teasing, touching. One of them clutched laughingly at her tunic; it ripped, and they sighed with pleasure as her small white breasts were revealed to their avid gaze.

'No,' begged Elena, flushed with shame. 'No, I beg you—'

But they took no notice. The woman Gytha bent her head swiftly to suckle at the rosy crest; it pouted and stiffened beneath her teasing lips. 'Imagine,' she whispered hungrily, 'that it's the lord Aimery pleasuring you. Oh, just imagine little nun, that he's preparing to enter you with his great thick penis, getting ready to slide it into that hot, juicy little nest between your thighs . . .'

Elena felt the wild, dark pleasure rise in her just at the sound of his name. The women, sensing her shameful excitement, moved in on her quickly; two of them held her thighs apart, while Gytha gently ran her hands up beneath her tunic. Elena gasped as the exploring little finger caught tantasingly at the secret folds of flesh between her thighs; she twisted and turned, but there was no escape, and Gytha's cunning finger sliding up into her yearning, moistened flesh was so delicious that she let a soft moan escape from her parted lips.

Gytha gave a secret smile of satisfaction, and held up the finger that glistened with Elena's love juices. 'Such a sweet, hot little love mound, girls,' she whispered gleefully. She used two more fingers to stroke Elena's

687

flesh lips, parting them softly and rubbing with gentle insistence so that the flesh around her swollen clitoris was stretched and pulled. 'Our little nun is more than ready, it seems, ready to feel a strong man slide his thick shaft inside her, to feel him pleasure her until she squeals for mercy. Is this what you did at the convent? All of you using your eager little fingers, to give yourselves pleasure? Girls, let's show her that we can do the same!'

Instantly two of them bent to her pointed little breasts, suckling and licking at her exquisitely sensitised nipples as Elena writhed helplessly beneath them. The dark pleasure flooded her; she was terrified that she was going to climax hotly beneath their teasing fingers and hot busy mouths. Slowly, she was being drawn into a whirling vortex of sensation that it was impossible to resist –

'Stop!' hissed Gytha suddenly. 'Someone's coming!'

Elena was abandoned. She rolled over into the shadows, clutching her torn tunic across her breasts, her whole body aching with wild, unsatisfied desire. The other girls, suddenly silent, flew apart and shrank back into the shadows against the bare stone walls.

The bolt grated back slowly, ominously, and everyone held their breath. The door opened, and the light of a torch fixed at the top of the stairwell flooded in, temporarily blinding them. A soldier was coming warily down the few steps into the cellar, carrying a stone pitcher of water and a big wooden platter piled high with coarse rye loaves.

Suddenly, someone darted up to the door and slammed it shut, blocking out the light so that they were plunged into pitch darkness again. Within seconds, the soldier, tripped up by a slender ankle, was on his back in the straw, with the water and bread scattered to the four corners of the cell; two of the girls had seized his wrists, while two more straddled his muscular thighs, pinning him down. He opened his mouth to yell, but Gytha had already whipped the sharp dagger from his belt, and now she held it to his throat.

'Keep very still, soldier,' she said throatily, her blue eyes dancing in the shadows. 'I rather think you're the answer to our prayers.'

The French soldier, who was young and darkly handsome and understood barely one word of Saxon, lay very still.

Then, one of the girls who sat astride his thighs started to slowly lift her ragged dress above her head. He watched, hypnotised, and swallowed thickly, aware that even in the midst of his terror his eager phallus was stirring between his imprisoned thighs. Cursed Saxon witches, he muttered silently to himself. What devilment were they planning?

Then another girl, laughing softly, reached beneath his leather tunic and unlaced his leggings. With soft, busy little fingers, she released his genitals, cupping his hairy balls and giving a little gasp of pleasure as she felt how his penis had already thickened. He continued to struggle instinctively, his eyes on the sharp knife; he almost choked with fear as his own dagger pricked at his vulnerable throat.

'What is your name?' someone whispered throatily in his ear. 'Your name, soldier.'

Struggling to comprehend, he muttered, 'Henri.'

'Well, then, Henri,' said the voice smoothly, 'lie still, and watch.'

The girl who had removed her tunic leaned forward, and the young soldier groaned aloud as her full, ripe breasts brushed across his loins. His penis jerked upwards from its bush of black hair, yearning to savour those rosy nipples; the girls surrounding him gave soft murmurs of delight at the generous length of his throbbing erection, and watched avidly.

'Who's first?' whispered one, licking her lips.

'Take turns,' commanded Gytha softly. 'Isn't that fair, soldier?'

Needing no encouragement, the naked Saxon girl who was so busy rubbing her hardened nipples against the soldier's swollen glans moved swiftly to straddle his hips, and lowered herself, licking her lips, onto the swollen red shaft. She closed her eyes with delight as he slid up her and threw her head back, wriggling in a delirium of sensation as the thick, engorged penis hungrily filled her aching flesh.

The others watched avidly, enviously. Gytha murmured, 'We must make the most of this, girls. This fine young fellow will earn his keep tonight.'

And, pulling her own tunic deliberately over her head, caressing her own flushed breasts, she crouched above the soldier's head to face the girl who was riding his hips, her secret flesh poised above his mouth.

'Lick me, Henri,' she whispered. 'Lick me. Push your fine, hard tongue up into me – ah, yes, that's it – ' On the verge of spasming already, she leaned forward to grasp the other girl's breasts in her cupped hands, pinching at her nipples, so the other girl cried aloud and rode herself harder and harder on the imprisoned man's rigid shaft.

Elena, hot with shame, was unable to tear her eyes away, aware that she was almost on the brink of explosion herself, her love-channel slick with juices, crying out for satisfaction. She could see the thick base of the soldier's rigid penis as the excited woman slid up and down his shaft; the thought of feeling that long, hot stem sliding within her own juicy passage made her feel faint with desire. At the same time, she could see how the solider lapped avidly at Gytha's moist vulva, licking and tasting greedily, sliding along her inner lips and thrusting high into her swollen pink flesh.

Suddenly, with groans of ecstasy, the three of them began to explode; the two girls writhing their hips as they clutched hungrily at the young man beneath them, while the soldier pumped deliriously hard with his penis, at the same time swirling and licking at Gytha's wetness with his mouth. With a great cry, the soldier, feeling his seed gathering relentlessly, arched his hips as his climax overtook him in spasms and he thrust hungrily into the juicy loins of the Saxon girl above him.

Exhausted, sated, the three of them stretched out alongside one another's bodies, still licking and caressing softly, as the afterwaves of orgasm melted deliciously through their contented bodies. The other girls watched in envious silence.

Gytha got up first, her eyes glittering brightly in the shadows. 'Whose turn next?' she whispered softly.

The young soldier, lying back with his eyes closed, caught the gist of what she was saying and gave a weak groan of protest. Gytha smiled wickedly at him, admiring his fine, muscular body. 'That's only the start, soldier,' she grinned. 'You're here to service us all – you realise that?'

Henri shook his head, not understanding, but he smiled. Gytha's eyes darted intently round the room, until they rested on Elena, still curled in her corner. 'Well, well. I think I have just the thing for you, Henri. How does an innocent convent girl take your fancy? Joan, you others, hold her down.'

With a scandalised cry of rebellion, Elena tried to wriggle into the shadows. But there was nowhere to run. Laughing huskily, the four girls held her down, just as they'd pinioned the soldier, and pulled her ripped tunic apart once more so that her quivering breasts were exposed. Gytha, standing over her with her hands on her hips, gave a slow smile of satisfaction.

'Now, my handsome young friend Henri,' she said softly. 'On your knees before her. See how her flesh burns for you! See how the little convent girl yearns for a real man's caress! Bow down before her – taste her – kiss her – '

Henri understood not one word, but he did understand what he was meant to do. Eagerly he kneeled

691

between Elena's spread legs, and she wrenched her head aside, closing her eyes in shame.

But then, as she began to feel his slow, rasping tongue wriggling along the folds of her secret flesh, the hot tide of pleasure began to build up inside her like an unstoppable flood. His touch was exquisite. Skilfully, he drew his long, pointed tongue up and down the entrance to her inflamed love channel, sliding lingeringly along the moist plump flesh, flicking at the pleasure bud at the end of each stroke, until she cried aloud with the sweetness of it. The girls who pinned down her arms were licking moistly at her distended nipples until she squirmed with pleasure; still she fought desperately to hold back, because she couldn't bear the thought of these women witnessing her shameful delight in this degradation.

Then the young soldier slowly slid his stiffened tongue up inside her, gently thrusting against her pulsing inner walls. At the same time, the two girls nipped and sucked at her swollen breasts, drawing out her aching nipples with their teeth; and Elena, lost in a haze of voluptuous sensation, crashed into a violent frenzy of rapture, writhing her hips against the man's delicious tongue, and rubbing her breasts against her tormentors' sweet mouths.

In endless waves, the exquisite pleasure washed over her and slowly receded. The girls smiled down at her, pleased with themselves, and looked round for their next entertainment.

The soldier had enjoyed Elena's cries of rapture, and was fully erect again. The girls on seeing his proud, handsome appendage thrusting out so eagerly, squabbled fiercely over him. They ended up in a confused tussle in the corner; until three of them crouched over on all fours in a row, desperately thrust their juicy, naked hips towards him, openly parting their moist flesh lips with eager fingers. Henri, taking his time and thoroughly enjoying himself, crouched on his knees to fondle their plump bottoms and to service each one of them briefly; then he withdrew, and moved on. Each girl panted breathlessly with excitement as her turn approached; each girl savoured every second as his glistening red phallus drove passionately into her hungry flesh; then moaned in despair as he withdrew and moved on with a grin. Every eye was on his long, jutting penis, every eye watched enviously as he lingered at last with the third girl, who convulsed into orgasm the minute his rampant shaft slid up her tight, aching love channel. Her little gasps of pleasure were too much for the soldier. They all watched avidly as he clutched at her plump hips, pumping hard into her until, with a groan of shattering delight, he spasmed into her quivering flesh, the sweat glistening on his ecstatic face.

'Hush! Someone's coming!' hissed Gytha.

They all froze. They could hear heavy footsteps coming down the stairwell beyond the wooden door. The soldier Henri, exhausted though he was, sprang to his feet in alarm and pulled down his leather jerkin; the women rearranged their rumpled tunics and shrank back into the shadows, completely silent. Elena felt as if everyone must be able to hear the heavy pounding of her own heart. She had watched, transfixed, as the young soldier drove the three women to distraction, her own body still awash with delicious sensation. Oh, if only it had been Aimery, she yearned silently.

Rusty hinges grated, and the door slowly opened. The light from a lantern poured into the dark, airless dungeon.

A captain of the guard stood outlined in the doorway, his sword drawn, his grim face menacing.

'Henri!' he grated out. 'They have been looking for you this past half hour. Your turn for the night watch, lad, or had you forgotten? A good job someone remembered you were due to take bread and water to these sluts.'

693

The young soldier Henri, his face admirably straight, said, 'I stumbled and fell down the steps, sir.' He gestured apologetically at the scattered loaves, the spilled pitcher of water. 'Gave myself a knock on the head. These girls were – most helpful, sir.'

Someone stifled a giggle; the captain raised his lantern and scoured the shadows suspiciously. They all gazed back at him, wide eyes innocent. Meanwhile, Henri had bent to pick up his fallen dagger.

'Move yourself, then, lad!' said the captain gruffly. 'Your turn at the gate!'

'Sir!' said Henri smartly, and hurried through the door and up the stairs. The captain turned one last time to glare at the women. Damned Saxons, he muttered to himself. All the same, a good-looking young bunch. And the air in here was strangely heavy and scented, musky, almost as if – as if . . .

Shaking his head, he followed Henri out of the cell and slammed the door.

Back in the darkness, the girls collapsed with laughter, and huddled in a circle to relive the delightful ordeal of their all-too-willing prisoner. Someone gathered up the scattered rye loaves that Henri had brought, and they devoured them greedily. Then Joan sat back suddenly, and sighed. 'I wonder how much longer we'll be shut up in here?'

Gytha said curtly, 'You heard the orders when they rounded us up. All Saxon serfs are to be locked away until Aimery le Sabrenn returns.'

'Perhaps,' murmured someone longingly out of the darkness, 'the lord Aimery himself will visit us . . .'

'Then we could kidnap *him*!' murmured another girl excitedly. 'Oh, every time I see him riding out through the castle gates, I go hot and cold all over. That face, that voice, that body! I tell you, the things I'd do to him, if the lord Aimery were my prisoner!'

Gytha said sharply, 'Best steer clear of him if you've any sense.'

Elena, kneeling at Joan's side, almost stopped breathing. 'Why?'

'Because, little convent girl, I've heard stories. About the Breton.' She looked around the hushed circle, seeing how their pretty young faces watched her avidly. 'I've been here longer than any of you. And, believe me, I've heard tales of how the Breton likes to amuse himself.' She paused; the silence was absolute.

'Our fine lord Aimery,' she went on softly, 'has a liking for Saxon girls.' Someone gave a murmur of excitement. 'Yes, girls like you. Any of you. He picks on a pretty serf, and takes her upstairs, to his private chamber. Lavishes her with fine clothes, wines from his own cellar, the finest, most delicate food. And nights of exquisite pleasure. Unimaginable pleasure.'

'How do you know all this, Gytha?' someone whispered eagerly.

'I heard it with my own ears from the lady Isobel's maid, Alys. You know how she's always eavesdropping, spying at keyholes. Poor Alys, she's so desperate for a man, she'd tell us any secret, if we find a sturdy Saxon to service her. She told us – ' and again her voice dropped – 'that's it's the Breton's twisted idea of entertainment to choose himself an innocent Saxon girl, one who's new to the estate, then he drives her mad with devilish pleasure, and when she's quite besotted, demented with longing for him, he casts her out again. Back onto the dungheaps, where he reckons all we Saxons belong.'

It seemed suddenly cold in their dark cell. 'But why?' someone faltered. 'Why would he do that, when he can have his pick of anyone?'

Gytha shrugged grimly. 'I've heard it said that he hates all Saxons – especially women – with a deep, poisonous hatred. There's something hidden in his past, that's burned into his very soul.'

The others sat in silence, absorbing what they'd just heard.

Elena, glad of the near-darkness, was clenching her knuckles until her nails dug into her palms. *No.* She wouldn't believe it. He had called her *caran* – his beloved. She wouldn't believe it. She was different!

But wasn't what Gytha spoke of happening to her already? Already the powerful Breton lord dominated her every thought, her body, her soul. Even at the height of sensual pleasure bestowed on her by the soldier, Henri, it was Aimery's name that rose to her lips. And, if what Gytha said was true, then it explained why she was imprisoned down here, at Aimery's command.

'Are you all right, Elena?' Joan, who'd been watching her, put a friendly hand on her shoulder. Elena pushed her tousled hair back from her white face.

'I'm tired, that's all.' She tried to smile.

'Then sleep,' said Joan soothingly. 'We're friends, you know.'

Elena nodded silently, and curled up in a corner on the straw. Someone covered her with a tattered cloak, and she slept through the night, exhausted.

She awoke with a start. It was morning. The daylight flooded down the stairwell through the open door of their cell. She was aware of lots of noise and confusion, with armed guards standing by the doorway hustling the women out.

Elena scrambled to her feet; Joan reached out to grab her hand, pulling her urgently towards freedom. But at the last moment, two of the guards seized Elena roughly and pushed her back into the cell so that she stumbled and fell.

'Let her go, you oafs!' said Joan sharply. 'Isn't she to be freed, like the rest of us?'

'That one stays,' said the guard warningly. 'You'd argue with the lord Aimery's orders, would you, wench?'

Joan was pushed, protesting, out of the cell. The guards followed and the door was locked.

Elena lay on the straw in the corner, her arms wrapped around her shivering body. 'The lord Aimery's orders?'

Gytha had been right about the Breton, but her warning had come too late for Elena. Already, her punishment was beginning.

Morwith should have been locked up with the other women. In fact, she'd been rounded up with the rest of the Saxon serfs when the order for their restraint first came through; but she'd quickly pointed out to the guard the error of his ways. In fact, she'd whispered in his ear and the young guard, confused and excited, had promised to take her to the guardroom instead, to keep her safe while the alarm was on.

Two other guards were rolling dice at the roughly-hewn oak table as she was shown into the barely furnished guardroom that lodged by the main gates to the castle. The candles flickered as the door opened; the soldiers looked up from their game, and grinned slowly as the young guard ushered in his prize.

Morwith returned their challenging stares with a slow smile, tossing back her thick red curls, and smoothing her plain woollen gown tightly over her voluptuous hips.

One of the seated soldiers said slowly, 'Tell you what. We'll play dice for her.'

'What a good idea,' said Morwith, moistening her lips as she surveyed them. They were all young, all sturdily built and sternly attractive, with their leather gambesons and sunburned faces framed by close-cropped dark hair. Her own excitement surged. 'Just as long as you *all* win . . .

The soldier who'd brought her in, the youngest of the three, gulped noisily. With a wicked smile, Morwith untied the girdle at her waist and pulled her long gown over her head, dropping it on the hard earth floor. Then she slipped out of her cotton chemise and stood provocatively before them, clad only in a pair of Isobel's silk hose, that were gartered with silk ribbon around her plump, freckled thighs. She clasped her hands demurely across her ripe mound, where the red-golden hair so tantalisingly outlined her sex. In doing so, her upper arms squeezed her full breasts up and together, so that the large brown nipples, already stiffening, pouted hungrily.

She felt the heated excitement licking like tongues of fire at her belly, here in this bare guardroom, with three fine soldiers and all the trappings of war, the armour and the weapons, scattered about the room. This was the kind of power she'd only dreamed of, when she was a shabby, homeless outcast in the forest!

All three of them – why not?

'Well, lads,' said one of the guards thickly, scarcely able to tear his eyes from Morwith's glorious body. 'Looks like we've got ourselves a tasty, willing morsel for tonight. Which one of us first?' and they began to roll the dice with feverish haste.

A straw pallet intended for the use of off-duty soldiers lay in the shadowy corner of the guardroom. Morwith swayed tantalisingly across the room towards it and sprawled languorously on her back, her hands behind her head, watching the three intent soldiers as they played by the light of the candle. 'Come on, then,' she murmured provocatively. 'Show me what you can do.'

With a cry of triumph as the dice settled, one of the soldiers jumped to his feet. Swiftly he unfastened his belt and loosened his leggings. He had no time for any further preparation, and Morwith soon saw why; he already sported a huge erection. Her eyes widened with joy as he kneeled eagerly between her parted legs and, frowning with concentration, gripped at his throbbing member.

'Ah, soldier,' she breathed, drawing up her knees to

display her ripe, moist flesh. 'That's a beauty! Stick it up me – oh yes, yes!' She wrapped her legs eagerly round his muscular hips, and her words were lost in a delighted cry of pleasure as he slid his engorged shaft up her juicy love passage and began pumping eagerly away.

And now the second soldier had won his game of dice; he pulled down his leggings swiftly, and his angry red penis reared up from his loins, searching blindly for an orifice. Morwith's mouth, gasping with pleasure as the first soldier made his deep, searching thrusts, was open and tempting; with a groan he kneeled astride her face and thrust himself within that velvety opening, feeling her soft lips adjust instantly to receive the swollen glans, her insolent tongue darting, licking, sucking as hard as she could.

The third soldier, the youngest and the one who'd brought her here in the first place, stood watching enviously, his hand pumping despairingly at his own slim, pulsing shaft as he watched.

Then he noticed the first man's buttocks, tight and muscular as he drove himself in and out of the Saxon wench. He saw the man's heavy balls dangling between his thighs; saw the shadowy curls of hair that outlined the dark mysterious crevice between his bottom cheeks; caught a glimpse of the tightly puckered brown hole that he knew would be pulsing with excitement.

Eagerly, the young soldier spat into his hand, and rubbed the moisture over his ravening penis. Then he knelt behind the other man, smoothing his hands lovingly over those muscular bottom-cheeks, parting them, rubbing his finger along the dark, hairy crease and poking his forefinger exploratively into the tightly collared hole.

Then, swiftly, he pushed himself into the tiny aperture, groaning aloud with delight as the narrow anal rim caressed his hot, angry phallus. The other man shouted aloud as he felt the intrusion; gasped with excitement, and began, almost immediately, to climax into the redhead with harsh, spasming jerks. The young soldier who impaled him was also carried over the brink, his own orgasm washing over him in hot, flooding waves; while at Morwith's head, the man who occupied her mouth let her wonderful, silky lips suck him into a rapture so extreme that he cried aloud in delight as his seed gushed into her throat.

As for Morwith, she had never known anything like it. Three virile, splendidly-equipped, muscular men, all writhing in ecstasy above her, within her. She arched her hips convulsively as the ripples of exquisite sensation coursed through her body and exploded in a blinding torrent of pleasure.

Slowly, grinning somewhat sheepishly, the men withdrew and got to their feet. Morwith lay on the pallet, flushed and sated, her red hair billowing about her shoulders and her eyes drowsy with delight.

'Gentlemen,' she said softly, 'consider me your prisoner for the night. Another game of dice? Only this time, I'll join in . . .'

Chapter Ten

*I*t was late afternoon when the lady Isobel de Morency, flanked by guards, stood expectantly in the sunbaked castle courtyard. She had come to witness a punishment.

The sergeant-at-arms pointed brusquely to where a man was fettered on his knees against the stable wall.

'That's the man, my lady. Just some Saxon clod, a serf. My men caught him trying to escape from the armoury where he'd been locked in with the rest of the rabble. An informer warned us – said he intended to escape and join the rebel army. He's been in chains all day, without food or drink and now, by your leave, my lady, he'll be flogged, as an example to the rest of the rabble.'

Isobel nodded, her green eyes narrowing as she surveyed the prisoner kneeling on the hard cobbles, trapped in the full glare of the hot summer sun. Without water to ease his thirst, he would be suffering. She felt a pleasurable pulse beat in her white throat.

She'd known he was Saxon by the striking colour of his ragged, shoulder-length blond hair. He looked young and muscular, a fine figure despite his ragged breeches. Out here in the dusty courtyard there was no

701

relief from the sun and his bronzed back glistened with sweat. Moistening her full lips, Isobel drank in the subtle interplay of taut muscle and assessed the stretched tendons and corded sinews of his powerful, imprisoned arms as he knelt there in his humiliation, his hips upthrust into the air.

Isobel smiled to herself. Suddenly, life didn't seem quite so tedious. Walking slowly across the yard, the guards following, she stopped in front of the bowed prisoner. Then she reached out for the sergeant-at-arms' leather quirt, and trailed the lash of the whip softly across the serf's broad shoulders.

The man shuddered briefly, then looked up at her in silent defiance.

Isobel's eyes widened, taking in the regular, tanned features; the strong, square jaw shadowed with blond stubble; the proud yet sensitive mouth and the vivid blue Saxon eyes that were filled with a natural arrogance, even in this hopeless subjugation. A find indeed.

'They tell me,' she said softly, 'that you were trying to run. What a coward you are. What is your name?'

The proud Saxon moistened his parched lips and grated out, 'I am no coward, lady. And my name is Leofwin.'

'Well, Leofwin. You may know that I am in charge of this castle while my lord Aimery is absent. And it is my duty to see to your punishment.'

'May your precious lord Aimery rot in hell,' said Leofwin the Saxon, slowly and clearly. A gasp went up from the guards at Isobel's shoulders; she held up her hand to restrain them.

'Have a care, my fine Saxon,' she said silkily. 'Remember that it is up to me to determine the severity of your punishment.'

His eyes flickered with lazy scorn. 'Do what you will. You can think of nothing new.'

Isobel's eyes danced. 'Oh,' she murmured, 'you would be surprised. I can think of lots of things,

702

Leofwin.' She turned suddenly to the sergeant at her side. 'Take off his clothing.'

Leofwin's head jerked up at that and he gritted his teeth as the sergeant ripped at the ragged breeches that were his last vestige of modesty. Leofwin closed his eyes briefly, as if bracing himself, as his nakedness was revealed.

Isobel gazed with pleasure at the heavy pouch of his balls hanging amidst the blond nest of hair between his legs, at the long, thick phallus that lay prone between his powerfully muscled thighs. Raising the whip, she drew the tip of its lash gently along his buttocks, thrust into prominence by the posture that the fetters forced on him. Then she let the lash dangle between his cheeks, drawing the leather up slowly. The man Leofwin bit his lip to stifle a groan, and Isobel saw, with delight, how his phallus was beginning to stir into life. The soldiers, gathered around, were grinning openly at her subtle torment of the prisoner. Isobel turned again to the sergeant. 'Encourage him,' she said pleasantly. 'Our poor guest seems a little – reluctant – to entertain us.'

With a grin, the sergeant thrust out his big fist and bent down to grip Leofwin's swelling shaft. Swiftly he pumped up and down a few times, drawing back the foreskin so the smooth glans was revealed. The other men murmured in appreciation as the Saxon's tumescent member throbbed and grew to impressive proportions, jerking up against his belly as the sergeant gave it a last, appreciative rub and reluctantly let go. Leofwin had closed his eyes; his mouth was set in a gaunt rictus of mingled shame and pleasure. Isobel, watching with rapt pleasure, brought the whip sharply down across his tautly-muscled buttocks and Leofwin groaned aloud as his now rampant penis jerked hungrily into thin air.

Isobel said, 'So, my proud Leofwin. Do you still consider that we can think of nothing new to torment you?' She picked up the man's discarded clothing and tossed it at the sergeant. 'Make him decent again, and have him taken down to the lower dungeon. In chains.'

'But my lady, the girl is still down there, as you commanded.'

'You heard me!' Isobel snapped dangerously. 'Do it – now!' As her men started to unfasten the stocks, she fingered the whip softly, with pleasure.

Elena, lying on the straw in the corner of the dark cell, looked up with a start. She heard footsteps; someone was coming down the stone steps outside. Perhaps they brought bread and water again. Or perhaps Aimery was back? No. She swallowed hard at the ache in her throat. Hadn't she heard, with her own ears, that it was Aimery who'd ordered her to be kept in solitary confinement down here? Gytha's words had haunted her all day, *He hates all Saxons – especially women – with a deep, poisonous hatred.'*

The bolt was rasped back. The door was flung open; the sudden light from the stairwell all but blinded her. A man in ragged breeches, with his arms chained behind his back, was kicked and shoved down the stairs; he fell, and the two guards behind him started to pull him up roughly. Behind them stood the lady Isobel de Morency who carried a gleaming torch, which she stuck into a cresset fixed to the wall.

The prisoner was pulled to his feet and held upright by the guards, his arms still in chains. He spat out a harsh Saxon oath at his captors; Elena, pulling herself to her feet, stared into his familiar face.

Leofwin. Leofwin, the captured rebel, with his gaunt, proud features and his blazing blue eyes.

Her own eyes widened in distress at his humiliation. He caught her gaze and shook his head very slightly, as if to say, 'No. Don't talk now. Don't let them know that you know me.'

Isobel, her hands on her hips, was saying with silky relish, 'We've brought a friend for you, my little Elena.

One of your own kind, to keep you company down here. You Saxons are used to wallowing in filth, aren't you? I should think this cell is quite luxurious for you both!'

Leofwin jerked himself free, sending his guards flying; they scrambled to get a grip at his chains and wrestled him, still struggling, to his knees.

Elena, unable to bear any more, launched herself towards Isobel. 'Leave him alone! What harm has he done? Why should he be punished like this?'

Instead of answering her, Isobel turned towards the guards. 'Get out,' she told them.

'But my lady – '

'I can deal with them. Both of them. Get out.'

The guards reluctantly obeyed, closing the heavy door behind them. Isobel turned towards the still kneeling Leofwin. 'Well, my fine Saxon, it seems as if you have found yourself a little champion here. A soft heart, hasn't she, our little convent girl? A pity, though, that she's a slut.'

Elena whitened. 'No. I beg you . . .'

Isobel advanced slowly on her, her silk gown rustling against the straw scattered on the floor, the flames of the torch bringing the fine fabric to life. 'Oh, yes, a slut. Tell Leofwin here, convent girl, how you let the Breton ravish you – how you welcomed him into your lonely bed on your very first night here, and moaned aloud with pleasure – go on, tell him!'

Leofwin looked up at her steadily. 'It's all right, Elena. I know she's lying.'

Elena hung her head, feeling sick. Isobel chuckled.

'No lies, my fine Leofwin! Why, she couldn't wait for it, could you, Elena? Show him – show him that tender, luscious body that you allowed lord Aimery to use as a plaything!'

'No,' whispered Elena. 'No . . .'

Isobel moved meaningfully towards the kneeling Leofwin, and Elena saw that she was carrying a small but lethal whip, which she trailed lightly across his bronzed, muscular shoulders.

'Show him, Elena. Or he will suffer. I mean it.'

Her heart thudding with shame, Elena slipped her ragged tunic from her shoulders and stood very still, her cheeks burning with silent degradation in that dark prison cell. The torchlight flickered on her soft skin, on her high, pouting breasts, on the shadowy triangle of soft golden hair at the apex of her slender thighs. Isobel jerked Leofwin's face upwards with the handle of her whip. 'Look,' she commanded exultantly. 'Isn't she pretty? A pity my lord Aimery tired of her so quickly, but then he gets his fill of these eager, insipid Saxon wenches – '

Leofwin looked, but it was as if his eyes did not see. The strained sinews of his powerful torso gleamed in the half-light; his handsome face was bleak as he said quietly, 'I'll take no part in your games, lady.'

'No?' Isobel laughed, and moved suddenly to crouch on the straw at his side, heedless of her fine gown. 'Well, my proud Saxon. What have we here?'

And she reached out delicately, to cup the Saxon's groin. With a low chuckle of satisfaction, she brushed her fingers along his ragged breeches, then reached for the opening, ripping it apart.

Between the man's powerfully-muscled thighs, his phallus, so recently erect, was again stirring helplessly. Isobel stroked it gently, lasciviously, with light, teasing fingertips, then moved her hand carefully to cradle the heavy bag of his testicles in her smooth palm. The Saxon groaned aloud in despair and closed his eyes; Elena stood frozen, watching, equally trapped by Isobel's power.

Isobel continued to stroke lightly, relentlessly at Leofwin's hardening flesh until the long, thick shaft reared high against the man's flat, muscled belly, throbbing angrily.

'Such a fine big weapon,' murmured Isobel huskily

as she stroked the silken skin with her fingertips. 'How I wish I had time to savour it fully.'

Elena's head jerked up. The lady Isobel was about to leave? Then this humiliation, for both of them, was about to end?

Isobel, rising slowly to her feet, caught the sudden flare of hope in the naked Saxon girl's haunted blue eyes. 'As for you, my dear Elena,' she went on softly, 'you, I am happy to say, will have all the time in the world. He is yours. My present to you. Use him well, won't you?'

Elena said, with quiet scorn, 'I will do nothing of the sort.'

Isobel arched her dark eyebrows mockingly. 'Still defiant, my dear?' Then she gazed thoughtfully down at the helpless Leofwin's still massively rigid penis, and trailed the tip of her lash along the velvety, purple glans. Leofwin shuddered in spite of himself at the subtle promise of pain.

'If you do not obey my orders, Elena,' said Isobel silkily, 'then this man will be punished. By me, personally.' Elena rubbed her hand across her eyes in fresh despair, Leofwin clenched his jaw. 'Do as I command,' continued Isobel sweetly, 'and you will both be rewarded by your own gratification. Is it so very much to ask? A satisfactory – more than satisfactory, I should think – mutual pleasuring?'

She started to walk towards the door, and at the top of the stairs she turned round. 'By the way, don't think to deceive me. I assure you, I have very reliable ways of knowing whether or not my orders have been obeyed.'

Then she was gone, the heavy door bolted behind her.

Elena sank to her knees, and wrapped the torn tunic forlornly round herself to hide her shame. How Leofwin must despise her. How she despised herself.

* * *

Isobel climbed the stone stairs quickly, and went down a long, dark passage at the back of the great hall. No-one was around to see her; the castle seemed strangely deserted in Aimery's absence. Using one of the keys fastened to her girdle, she opened a recessed door and went quickly inside, shutting it behind her. Good; Alys had prepared everything, as she asked.

The room was small but luxuriously furnished, with silk hangings covering the bare stone walls and rush matting on the floor. There was a low bed and a carved wooden chest and, because there were no windows, the room was lit by two wax candles in wall holders.

Isobel went purposefully over to the far side of the room and knelt down on the floor, lifting up the edge of the matting.

Yes. This was the place. Below her was a crack in the wooden floorboards, that had been cunningly, secretly enlarged to form a spyhole into the room below. Pillowing her cheek on her arm, she gazed through the crack. The glowing torch she'd left for them lit the scene perfectly. She was directly above the cell where the chained prisoner Leofwin was locked up with the insipid Saxon girl. How virginal she looked, with her pale golden hair and girlish figure! How, oh how could Aimery be so besotted with her?

And what, she suddenly thought, would the Breton say if he knew what she, Isobel, had done?

Frowning angrily, Isobel turned her gaze on Leofwin. She felt herself soften and melt as she gazed on his proud, handsome face, his mane of fair hair, his heavily-muscled torso that gleamed so enticingly in the flickering light. She'd have him later, perhaps. She made herself a secret promise. Then, filled with eager anticipation, she settled down to watch.

Still kneeling in the straw of the cell below the castle, Elena lifted her pale face and pushed back her tangled blonde hair. 'Leofwin,' she said quietly, 'I would do

708

anything to save you from punishment. But I must tell you that everything the lady Isobel said was true. I have no excuses to make. I – I understand that you will have nothing but scorn for me, will not want to touch me . . .'

She tried to keep her voice steady, but it broke slightly at the end. Leofwin, who had listened in silence, said huskily, 'Elena. Come here.' Puzzled, she moved slowly across towards him and knelt on the straw to gaze anxiously up into his face.

Leofwin, taking a deep breath, drank in the sight of her; the pale gold, tousled hair framing that lovely, innocent face; those dark blue, anguished eyes and the small rosebud mouth. Even in her rags, he realised, she was still the loveliest girl he had ever seen.

Softly, he said, 'Elena. You are beautiful, and your body longs for pleasure – the pleasure that only a man can give you. There is nothing wrong with that. But did you know that Aimery le Sabrenn bears a personal hatred for all Saxon women?'

She nodded, the sudden pain clouding her eyes. 'I know now. But why, Leofwin? I had heard that most of King William's commanders were stern, but fair, that the king himself is anxious for peace between Normans and Saxons. Why does the lord Aimery hate us so?'

'I have heard that he was once betrayed by a beautiful Saxon lady, with whom he was in love – betrayed by her to the rebels. He escaped, but was scarred for life. That, it seems, is the reason for his cruel vengeance.'

She tried to look calm and sensible as she nodded again, but he saw the tears glitter suddenly in her translucent blue eyes. 'Oh, Elena,' he groaned out suddenly, 'that you should suffer so. Elena, kiss me . . .'

With a little gasp, she suddenly flung her arms around his neck, running her hands through his thick, tangled mane of hair. He was pressing hot, burning kisses against her cheek; finding her lips, his mouth devoured her, his tongue thrusting and probing, and she responded dizzily. Her torn tunic slipped unnoticed from her shoulders; her soft breasts nuzzled the hard, ridged muscle of his broad chest, teasing his brown nipples into hardness, until his breathing became harsh and ragged. He strained at the chains that shackled his hands behind his back, but he was cruelly pinioned still. Elena, seeing his silent struggle, bent to kiss his straining shoulder muscles, to lave the hard buds of his nipples with her small tender tongue.

'See, Elena,' he grated out hoarsely. 'See what you do to me . . .'

With a little gasp she looked down, and saw how his penis, darkly-engorged, had reared anew from his ragged breeches. The blood pounded dizzily in her temples at the throbbing masculinity of it. With a soft moan, she reached to caress its magnificence softly with her fingertips; it quivered, jerking towards her eagerly. Her flesh was on fire for this proud, beautiful Saxon man; already she could feel a melting in her loins, a soft ache in her secret parts, a sweet yearning not properly assuaged by the girls' caresses and the French soldier's lascivious kiss. She wanted him; oh, she wanted this man, to take him within her yearning, quivering flesh . . .

With a little whimper, she kneeled upright, her hand gripping and stroking at the long, bone-hard phallus, as she thrust her breasts eagerly into his mouth.

He lapped hungrily, wickedly, laving her heated nipples with cooling saliva, sucking on them with deeply satisfying caresses that made her throw her head back in blissful arousal, her hand still clasping the strong silken shaft of his penis. 'Oh, Leofwin, please . . .'

'Turn round,' he muttered huskily. 'Turn round, my Saxon princess. On your knees. Ah, yes, that's it . . .'

In a drugged haze of desire, she turned to do his bidding, and Leofwin sighed aloud as her slender yet rounded buttocks were presented to his hungry gaze. By the light of the glimmering torch, he could see her pouting sex between her bottom cheeks, could see the moist pink flesh, so hungry for him. He narrowed his eyes and leaned forward, his rampant penis searching hungrily for her entrance.

His chains made it difficult; but she thrust her hips wantonly towards him, driven wild by the merest touch of that huge throbbing glans against her secret places. Leofwin, his wildly-excited member almost out of control, aimed as carefully as he could, sliding his long, thick shaft between her thighs, rubbing higher and higher against her soft pink folds, hearing her little sighs of eagerness, until at last he found her.

Slowly, catching his breath, he slid his rampant rod between her silken flesh lips and into her tender, hot love passage. He was wild to thrust deep within her, to the very hilt; but he was careful not to hurt her, knowing the power of his fully erect member.

Elena trembled in an agony of delight. Crouching on all fours, her swollen breasts dangling free; she laid her cheek on her arm and cried out softly in her pleasure as the big Saxon entered her from behind. Her whole body was on fire as that deliciously long shaft slid into her hungry love channel, stroking her, driving her slowly to the very edge of rapture. Surely – surely, she couldn't take any more! But still, he filled her with his gentle but powerful thrusts, and waves of delicious heat began to spread upwards into her belly, into her breasts. She moaned, and thrust against him finding his rhythm, feeling herself exquisitely impaled on that hot, hard length of male flesh. 'Please,' she groaned, 'please, Leofwin . . .'

The torch glimmered smokily on the wall above them. She closed her eyes, shivering with exquisite pleasure, hearing Leofwin's harsh breathing above her, picturing his magnificent, naked body crouching above her with his arms chained behind his back, servicing her, driving his wonderful penis slowly in and out of her juicy, clutching flesh. She was so near. And yet, and yet . . .

711

'Touch yourself, my princess,' murmured Leofwin huskily in her ear. 'Your sweet little pleasure bud – it longs for release. Touch yourself, gently.'

In a daze, she did what he said, finding with a shock that the little pinnacle of flesh was hotly aroused and exposed. Carefully, she touched it, while Leofwin paused in his movements, leaving his swollen penis nudging hungrily at her inflamed entrance. The sensation sent a violent spasm coursing through her; carefully she touched again, and began to rub, slowly, along her own exquisitely sensitised little shaft.

'You are ready?' murmured Leofwin gently.

'Oh, yes! Leofwin – I beg you please – '

He gave a throaty chuckle that drove her wild. 'Very well, my princess. Then you shall have it – all . . .' He plunged into her, with solid, powerful thrusts that sent wonderful sensations coursing through her blood. Elena cried out in rapture, panting greedily as she worked herself against him; softly she touched her pleasure bud, and the exquisite sensations built up and exploded shatteringly over and over as his huge penis continued to slide juicily inside her quivering, convulsing flesh. She cried aloud, throwing back her head as the orgasm engulfed her and her inner muscles spasmed around his iron-hard shaft.

Leofwin himself was driven over the brink by her ecstasy. Moaning her name, he jerked powerfully within her, crashing over the edge of rapture. They both collapsed, still damply entwined in the straw.

And in that moment Elena, physically replete, felt a dark shadow pass over her. Her mind was suddenly filled with the memory of a scarred, handsome face, softened by love, and a huskily accented voice that seemed to haunt her every moment.

The torch gave a final glimmer and died. Elena knew, in that moment, that Aimery le Sabrenn had made her his slave for ever.

Chapter Eleven

With an exclamation of impatience, Isobel rolled away from the spyhole and crouched, panting with desire, on the rush matting of her little secret room. What she had seen – the big chained Saxon so thoroughly pleasuring Aimery's virginal little convent bitch – had aroused her unbelievably; she was so wet, so quivering with juices that she had to have somebody, and quickly.

She heard a low, muffled cough outside the door. Her brow darkened. A spy – someone spying on her! Swiftly, she moved across the room to fling open the door, and Pierre almost fell into the room.

Isobel chuckled softly. Of course. Pierre, who followed her everywhere like a faithful big dog. She had neglected him a little lately – remiss of her, especially as he was so young and handsome . . .

She relocked the door carefully; Pierre gazed at her eagerly, with hope flaring in his faithful brown eyes.

Isobel moved deliberately across to the low bed and lay back on it luxuriantly. Then, very slowly, she lifted her silk skirts to her waist, and spread her stockinged thighs. She watched Pierre all the time, saw him jump with excitement, imagined the lovely, swelling bulge at his groin. Shuddering with anticipated pleasure, she reached down to touch her moist nether lips. Her pleasure bud was already hot and throbbing. She slid one finger around it, lovingly, raising her knees higher and letting them fall apart so Pierre could see all her crinkled, hairy lushness; the serf's eyes were wide with longing.

'You see how I need you, Pierre?' Isobel whispered softly. 'You see how I need a good, stout man like you to pleasure me? But I've not quite decided yet, Pierre. Show me – show me what you can do, and then I'll decide . . .'

And lasciviously she continued to stroke her deliciously-engorged clitoris, safe in the knowledge that the dumb serf would never be able to tell anyone of the lady of Morency's crude preferences.

Nodding eagerly at her invitation, Pierre unlaced his leggings and pulled out his already-rampant phallus. Isobel eyed it with mock severity, pursing her lips. 'Not bad,' she said critically, 'but I'm a little disappointed in you, Pierre.'

Crestfallen, the youth gripped his engagingly curved penis with his hand and started working it quickly, hissing between his teeth, his eyes fastened on Isobel. The swollen purple knob glistened and throbbed angrily; he watched her in an agony of desire, as the red tide of frustration built up inside.

Lazily, Isobel, still reclining on the bed, reached to undo the lacing of her fine gown, lifting her full breasts from the confines of her chemise and squeezing them together, played lazily with her hardened pink nipples, as though Pierre did not exist.

It was too much. The sweat stood out in beads on Pierre's broad forehead; his balls were tight and aching. His hand suddenly dropped to his side; his huge shaft reared upwards with a life of its own, jerking hungrily towards the woman on the bed.

'Come on, Pierre. You can do better than that – '

714

With a gasp, Pierre rushed across the room, his penis rearing threateningly. Violently, he flung himself between Isobel's parted legs, trapping her hands above her head, knocking the breath from her. Then, nudging her open thighs still further apart, he thrust his throbbing manhood desperately into her wet glistening flesh. Isobel made a sharp cry of protest; but her words quickly became soft moans as Pierre's thick, pulsing shaft slid so deliciously into her aching love passage and began to ravish her.

'Pierre,' she gasped aloud. 'How dare you, you wicked boy . . .'

For answer, he shuddered and leaned into her still further, driving himself into her juicy moistness with all his power, relishing every moment as his engorged penis filled her wildly clutching vagina. She locked her ankles around his back, and came almost immediately, bucking with ecstasy as his wild thrusts continued. Then, as she spasmed and relaxed, Pierre, muttering wordlessly to himself in his extremity, withdrew his long, slippery shaft and began to rub it excitedly across Isobel's flushed, pouting breasts.

Isobel moaned aloud, shuddering in renewed orgasm as his swollen, silky glans caressed her incredibly sensitised nipples. Gripping and caressing the proud stem of his manhood, Pierre crouched over her greedily, rubbing his penis first against one breast, then against the other, his eyes closed in ecstasy. At last, with swift, jerking movements of his strong hand, he drove himself to the brink; and Isobel watched, wide-eyed, as his proud member quivered in ecstasy and his seed spurted out in milky jets all over her white breasts.

With a sigh of contentment, he bent to lick it off greedily, guzzling like a child at her nipples, his subsiding manhood still deliciously hot against her smooth belly.

Isobel lay back, utterly sated as his strong, rough tongue trailed across her flesh, the afterwash of pleasure still trickling gently through her. She closed her eyes, smiling contentedly.

Then she jerked upright, almost throwing Pierre to the ground.

Someone was knocking, lightly but insistently, on the door. A voice – Alys' voice – could be heard, low and urgent. 'My lady. My lady Isobel. Messengers have arrived! They say that the lord Aimery won't be returning to Thoresfield till tomorrow at the earliest. I thought you ought to know.'

Isobel got up, hurriedly rearranging her rumpled gown, tying up her laces with trembling fingers. She flung open the door.

'Damn you, Alys,' she muttered viciously, 'must you follow me everywhere? Go, and prepare my bath – and a fresh gown. And not a word of this to anyone, you understand? Or I'll beat you with my own hands . . .'

Alys, who had not failed to see the bemused Pierre sprawled on the bed, swung round and marched off, her face red and angry. One of these days, her ladyship would go too far. One of these days, she, Alys, would cease to act as Isobel's faithful spy – and then, it would be interesting to see what happened at Thoresfield, she told herself grimly.

Elena sat on the edge of the bed in the upper chamber of the castle – the very room where she had spent her first night in the Breton's arms. It was almost dark, but wax candles had been lit against the soft dusk; a flagon of sweet wine, together with spiced chicken, soft manchet bread and honeyed grapes had been set out carefully on the little table.

She clasped her hands anxiously in her lap, feeling utterly bewildered.

She'd spent another night in the cell, with Leofwin sleeping beside her, and during all the long day that followed, they'd talked quietly of the past.

She'd been resigned to yet another night of impris-

716

onment when two guards had come down to her dark cell, about an hour ago, and dragged her up here. She'd had no time to bid a proper farewell to her fellow-prisoner, Leofwin, but he'd managed to whisper to her in their own tongue as the guards waited impatiently for her by the open cell door. 'Soon, I'll escape from here. And you shall come with me!'

For one last moment, she lifted her wistful face towards him. Oh, if only she could escape! But she was a true prisoner here, a prisoner of her heart. She couldn't tell him that, though she thought he had guessed. Since that first wild coupling, he hadn't attemped to make love to her again.

She gave him a swift, brave smile and followed the guards, wondering fearfully what lay in store for her now.

In her wildest dreams, she wouldn't have guessed aright. What lay in store was luxury, just as she had experienced on her first night here. Isobel's attendant, Alys, waited quietly on her; here, in this now-familiar room, she was bathed and anointed with scented oils, and clothed in stockings and a chemise of finest cream silk. Her gown too was silk, in palest blue; it had a long, closely-fitting sleeves and a flowing skirt that clung to her waist and then flared out around her slender hips. Her tiny waist was further emphasised by an exquisite silver girdle that trailed almost to the floor; and as a finishing touch Alys helped her into a pair of dainty red leather shoes that fastened at the side with little buttons. Then, with the utmost care, Alys brushed out her newly-washed hair, gleaming softly gold, and braided it loosely, coiling it with ribbon at the nape of her slender neck.

Elena, dazed and bewildered, gazed unseeing at her own reflection in the silver mirror Alys had silently handed to her. 'Why, Alys?' she whispered. 'Why all this finery?'

'I only do as I'm bid,' said Alys shortly, turning to leave.

She was interrupted by a sudden cacophony of noise from the courtyard outside the window. Men were shouting, running, barking out orders; there was the unmistakable sound of horses' iron-shod hooves on the cobbles.

Elena, her breath stopped short in her throat, faltered out, 'What is it, Alys? What's happening?'

Alys paused by the door. 'The lord Aimery and his men have returned.'

'Has he – has he defeated the rebels?'

'Doesn't he always?' Alys started to open the door, and hesitated. 'Best get out of here, my lady, while you can. You're too good and beautiful for this evil place . . .' She looked as if she would say more, then pressed her lips together suddenly and hurried out, slamming the door behind her.

Elena's heart was hammering. She flew to the window, and looked out.

Far beyond the estate, the great forest that surrounded Aimery's lands was in ominous darkness. But the castle and its courtyard were a blaze of light and activity. The night air was cool on Elena's flushed cheek as she gazed down. Mounted knights, still on horseback, milled around, pushing back their stern helmets, while eager squires carrying wavering lanterns rushed to do their bidding. The cold, silvery moonlight glimmered on harsh Norman faces, on chain-mail hauberks and the glinting steel of swords. Grooms hung to the big destriers' reins as the victorious knights dismounted, and Elena leaned from the window, longing for just a glimpse of Aimery le Sabrenn. Perhaps her captivity in the cells had been a mistake. Perhaps . . .

The door opened slowly, and Isobel de Morency walked in, and Elena knew that all her stupid hopes were in vain.

Isobel, her enemy, shut the door behind her, and

718

smiled. It was not a friendly smile. She was exquisitely dressed, in an opulent silk gown of madder-red, embroidered with gold thread. Her raven black hair was concealed by a thin white veil, secured by a delicate golden circlet on the crown of her head; and her slanting green eyes glittered with suppressed excitement.

Elena knew now that this woman hated her. She stood very still, her back to the window, and waited.

Isobel said, 'Well, my little convent girl. So you know now that the lord Aimery has returned.'

Elena bowed her head briefly in acknowledgement and resumed her quietly defiant stance, her hands clenched at her sides.

'So,' went on Isobel, walking further into the room, 'the game begins afresh. A word of warning, however. I would rather – *much* rather – that the lord Aimery did not know about the time you spent below, in the cells. It was, you see, purely for your own safety. As a Saxon, you might otherwise have suffered reprisals from the other inhabitants of the castle.'

Elena's heart thudded slowly in understanding, her eyes meeting Isobel's malevolent gaze in renewed scorn. So, her imprisonment was not Aimery's order! He knew nothing of it! A sudden wild hope blazed through her.

Isobel paused by the table where the food had been set out. Picking up a honeyed grape, she placed it delicately on her tongue, licking her dainty fingers one by one. 'But,' she went on silkily, 'if, my dear Elena, you should take it into your silly head to complain, why, then, I shall have to tell Aimery about your ardent coupling with the prisoner Leofwin. Rather – bestial, my dear, wouldn't you say? And you did appear to enjoy it so much . . .'

Renewed despair washed over Elena in numbing waves. How did Isobel know so much? The cruel Frenchwoman was toying with her, manipulating her, and Elena felt suddenly quite helpless again in her evil

719

toils. As steadily as she could, she said in a low voice, 'You know very well, my lady, that I did what I did in order to save the man Leofwin from the punishment you threatened.'

Isobel laughed and took another grape, savouring its plump, juicy sweetness. 'Whose word do we have for that, my dear? Yours? Rather a feeble excuse, I would have thought, for such enthusiastic copulation! Do you really expect Aimery to believe you?'

Elena sagged back against the stone window ledge, her eyes wide and dark in her white face. Isobel laughed softly, lapping up her distress.

'Tonight, Elena, we will play the game more subtly than ever, you and I. And remember, there can only be one winner.'

She turned to go, and shut the door softly behind her.

Outside, on the landing, the smile vanished from Isobel's face. She was, for the first time since Madelin, seriously worried.

The girl was breathtakingly beautiful, and quietly brave. Isobel would gladly have left her for yet another night in that dark cell, but she feared Aimery's anger too much. Better play safe for the moment. Have her bathed, fed and clothed in luxurious garments while Isobel made her next decision – the best time to tell Aimery how the innocent convent girl, with whom he had become so besotted, had been rutting on the soiled straw of the prison cell with a virile Saxon rebel.

Isobel knew from experience that Aimery was always grimly ready for sexual release when he got back from the tension of battle. He would be on edge, covered in sweat and dust, physically honed, wanting plenty of activity. She, Isobel, would be waiting for him.

Aimery le Sabrenn strode into the hall at the head of his men, his armour glinting in the spurting light from the cressets, his hair streaked with sweat where he had removed his helmet.

The floor had been freshly strewn with herb-scented rushes. The serfs, busy setting up the trestle tables for the evening meal, stood back in deference and gazed in awe at their Breton lord. Tales of the recent battle against the Saxon rebels were already flying round the castle; the bravery and strength of Aimery le Sabrenn needed no embroidery.

Hamet, at his master's side as always, said in his soft, rich voice, 'My lord. Shall I order wine to be brought to the high table?'

Aimery hesitated. 'In a while – though see that the men are served with everything they want. First, I shall go and change.'

Hamet nodded. 'My lord.' He watched thoughtfully as Aimery le Sabrenn, showing no outward signs of the tiredness that must grip him after two days and nights in the saddle and some of the bloodiest skirmishing the Saracen had yet seen against these native rebels, made purposefully for the stairs that led to the sleeping chambers.

For two days and nights, as he swept through the forest with his men, Aimery had thought of the girl. The scent of her hair, the caress of her silken skin, had stayed with him. The way she had sunk to her knees and whispered, 'You are all I ever dreamed of, my lord.' Words that were followed, so sweetly, by her little cries of love. She was innocent, yet so instinctively, wildly sensual – all that a man dreamed of.

If Isobel had obeyed his instructions, the girl would have been well taken care of in his absence. Already he felt the hard ache at his loins, the tightening of desire at the pit of his belly. Later, he promised himself. Later . . .

His face set, he headed for his own room, fully intending to summon his squire to remove his armour, and then to go down and feast with his men. But on his way along the gallery, he saw a soft line of light beneath the door of the small chamber that the Saxon girl used. He stopped, and pushed open the door, quietly.

Elena, lying curled on her bed in silent despair after Isobel's visit, spun round. The Breton stood in the shadowy doorway; his harsh, gaunt face was unreadable.

Elena's thoughts whirled giddily. What had Isobel told him? Had she told him about Leofwin? And, whatever happened, she must remember what they'd all told her about him. That he was using her, intent on destroying her because of his poisonous hatred for all Saxon women. She crouched on her narrow bed, trembling.

He said, simply, 'Caran,' and held out his arms, drawing her to him.

He kissed her deeply, hungrily; his hands roving over her face, her breasts, her slender hips. Elena, in disbelief, wrapped her hands round his wide shoulders, shuddering at the kiss of steel, running her fingers through his mane of tawny hair. He still loved her. Nothing had changed – everyone was wrong.

With a soft murmur of impatience, the Breton unlaced her gown and chemise, barely allowing the filmy silk to slip to the floor before bending to kiss her small white breasts. Then he unbraided her hair, combing it sensually with his fingers so that it glittered around her face and shoulders. Elena shuddered with desire, her soft, naked body clamped against the cold chain-mail of his hauberk. Aimery gave an oath of impatience at his own hampered body; lifting her up and swinging her gently onto the bed, he quickly unbuckled his armour, and threw off the long linen undershirt that he wore beneath it.

Elena watched him from the shadows, her heart hammering passionately as his muscled torso gleamed in the golden candlelight. He was so strong, so beautiful. He sat on the edge of the bed, swiftly pulling off his dusty boots and leggings; she leaned towards him, and caressed his shoulder gently.

A laugh rasped in his dry throat. 'Ah *caran*. See what you do to me . . .' He took her small hand within his own sword-calloused palm and ran it slowly up the rough silk of his steel-muscled thigh to close over the hot, throbbing bulge of his genitals.

Elena gasped, the spasms of pleasure running through her, as she felt his powerful penis quiver and surge beneath her trembling fingers. Catching her lower lip between her teeth, she stroked again experimentally, loving the soft, silken feel of his inner thigh, the rough coarseness of his heavy testicles, and then the pulsing, almost frightening strength of that mysterious phallus, the very core of him, rearing up massively now against his flat, darkly-fleeced abdomen. Already, she felt a burning need to feel that magnificent male strength within her. Instinctively she bent her head to lick at the swollen purple glans, to catch its velvety rim between her soft lips while her hand cupped his testicles.

Aimery groaned aloud, his fingers kneading her hardening nipples. 'Little one, how quickly you learn. Your mouth is so sweet. And now, it is my turn . . .'

With swift, powerful movements, he lifted her unresisting body across the bed and crouched between her tender, outspread thighs. Then he bent his head and started to lap at the soft, moist folds of her secret flesh.

Elena drew up her knees in ecstasy, stroking and clutching at his thick hair as his strong tongue darted fiercely at her quivering bud of pleasure then slid down tantalisingly to probe at her honeyed entrance, thrusting and caressing until she moaned aloud, almost at the very brink. Her eyes opened wide in momentary disappointment when he suddenly pulled himself up beside her, enfolded her in his arms, and rolled onto his back.

'Ride me now,' he whispered. 'Take me into yourself, Elena. Make me your prisoner.'

As he guided her astride his hips, she shuddered in delirious excitement at her sudden sense of power over him. She saw his soft, lazy smile as her eyes widened in surprise at this new, blissful sensation. Gently, experimentally, she wriggled above him, feeling his hugely thrusting penis desperately trying to gain entry; then, as she poised carefully above it and felt the swollen glans just start to slide between her hungry flesh lips, she gasped aloud in pleasure.

Carefully, she lowered herself inch by inch. Surely – surely, it was too much! Surely this hot pillar of flesh would never fit inside her own tight, aching entrance!

Aimery reached up slowly with his strong brown hands, his silvery-grey eyes strangely intent. Gently he began to roll and twist her jutting rosy nipples. The pleasure shot darkly through to her abdomen, like hot tongues of flame; she rose with a soft cry, and sank down again onto his beautifully engorged shaft, gripping tightly with her silken sheath as waves of almost unbearable pleasure washed through her.

He filled her now. Her whole being was nothing but glorious sensation. Languidly, teasingly, he continued to play with her aching breasts, driving her to delirium as she slid herself up and down on his magnificently solid penis, feeling it fill her, posess her, as she gripped tighter and tighter, driving herself relentlessly to glorious ecstasy.

Smiling softly into her dazed eyes, Aimery reached deliberately to stroke her engorged, exposed clitoris with the pad of his thumb. '*Oh . . .*' Elena threw her head back with a wild cry, tossing back her mass of golden hair in abandon as the molten pleasure seared her; the Breton's face tautened as he clutched fiercely at her juicy buttocks and pumped himself into her, spending himself within her just as her own fierce, rapturous orgasm racked her quivering body.

She collapsed onto his chest, her breasts and hair

caressing him, the waves of delight still washing over her as he gently kissed her face, her hands, her hair.

A candle guttered and went out. She was suddenly aware of the raucous sound of men feasting in the great hall below. Another world; the world where Aimery belonged. A dark shadow passed over her heart. Her face suddenly troubled, she raised her head to gaze down at him, pushing back his tousled hair with her fingers and gently caressing his lean, scarred cheek.

'I want to remember you like this,' she said quietly.

He took her finger and nibbled it gently between his lips, sending little pleasure messages through her still-heated body. 'You talk, *caran*, as if we are to be separated,' he said softly. 'Another premonition? Have you so little confidence in me?'

He cradled her gently in his arms. Elena felt his solid warmth, and tried desperately to fight away her fear, telling herself that all her doubts were a nightmare and this was the reality. She pressed her cheek against his warm chest and listened to the sound of his slow, steady heartbeat.

Exhausted after two nights without sleep, Aimery's breathing grew slow, and he fell asleep, still holding her tightly.

Chapter Twelve

*I*t was Alys who accidentally let slip to the lady Isobel that Aimery le Sabrenn had not joined his men for the evening meal. Isobel, pacing her room in an agony of tension, whirled round on her unfortunate maid. 'Then where is he, you fool?'

Alys, her pocked face stricken with sudden fear as she realised her mistake, backed instinctively towards the door. 'He – he is with the Saxon girl, my lady! He went to her room immediately on his return, more than an hour ago. Nobody dares disturb them . . .'

Isobel strode across the chamber and struck her servant hard on the cheek. 'You're lying! Stupid slut, you're making this up.'

Alys back whimpering to the door. 'No, my lady! I swear! They all know about it, down below in the hall. Hamet has told them to begin the feast without him.'

'Get out,' said Isobel dangerously. 'You've already said too much. Get out of my sight. No – wait! One thing you can do for me – find out where Morwith is. And send her to me immediately!'

Shaking with almost uncontrollable anger, Isobel waited for Alys' footsteps to die away down the corridor. So, Aimery, instead of celebrating his victory over the Saxons with his men, was in the chamber of the little Saxon slut, pleasuring her, making her gasp and writhe in sluttish ecstasy!

Like molten iron ready to be forged, Isobel's anger cooled and hardened. Quietly, she tiptoed down the back stairs, the stairs used by the house serfs to bring hot water and food to the upper storey of the stronghold. She had her ring of keys fastened to her girdle. Purposefully she went down the dark, echoing stone steps that led to the dungeon where the Saxon rebel Leofwin was still imprisoned.

She didn't realise that Alys, still burning from the blow to her cheek, was watching her every move.

Hamet, though he'd given the order for the feasting to begin, was also missing from the high table, like his master. He'd removed his armour, to wash and change. Then he'd gone outside in the darkness to the stables, to check that the horses were all right. He lingered for a while enjoying the dark peace out there, the scented smell of the hay and the horses' contented whickering.

He knew without being told that his master had gone straight to the beautiful Saxon girl's room. In his fierce loyalty to his master, he was instinctively worried, because he knew that the lady Isobel hated Elena and would stop at nothing to destroy her.

He went back out into the courtyard, checking that the guards were alert and in position inside the palisade. Then, a muffled giggle from the shadows caught his attention, and he whirled round, his sword drawn.

It was the Saxon redhead Morwith, watching him from the darkness behind the stable wall.

'It's not your sword I'm after, my lord Hamet,' she murmured huskily. Hamet grinned, his teeth white in the darkness, and strode towards her, catching her up in his burly arms.

* * *

727

It was there that Alys found them, her attention caught by the soft rasp of indrawn breath and the rustling of clothes as she edged round the corner of the stables. She caught her breath as the cold moonlight shone on the two figures coupled together, oblivious of everything.

Hamet had caught Morwith up in his big arms, supporting her so that her shoulders rested gently back against the stable wall. While she, her skirts rucked up shamefully around her waist, had wrapped her legs tightly round the Saracen's hips, locking her ankles together; he was thrusting into her eagerly, his face nuzzling at her generous breasts, while she flung her head back and groaned in delight.

The Saracen's loose-fitting hose gaped at the crotch; Alys gasped and felt the blood burn hotly in her cheeks as she glimpsed the base of his powerful, thick shaft, ramming so eagerly up into the lady Morwith's lascivious flesh, while his heavy balls bounced up and down with exertion. Oh, Morwith was so lucky! If only she, Alys, could feel that huge, dusky penis driving into her own love-starved flesh, ravishing her so sweetly!

Biting her lip in anguish, Alys pressed herself into the shadows. Avidly, her hand slipped down to her own heated love mound; it was juicy, desperate. Pulling up her full skirts impatiently, she pressed with her busy fingers, working away hotly at her swollen nether lips. Oh, to feel the Saracen inside her, pumping fiercely away, his mouth guzzling greedily at her own aching breasts . . .

Then the Saracen drew his penis slowly out of Morwith, so that the tormented Alys could see almost all of its slippery black length. Alys bit her lip in an agony of desire as he drove it back in with a hoarse cry of triumph and proceeded to jerk quickly to his climax, his muscular hips thrusting madly, while Morwith bucked and spasmed in his arms, her heels drumming excitedly against his waist. It was too much for Alys. Groaning aloud, squeezing her hard nipples tightly with her free hand, she rubbed fiercely at her clitoris with her fingers, spasming in solitary delight, her secret flesh pulsing and twitching hungrily as she reached her lonely orgasm.

The inevitable disappointment coursed through her. She wanted a man inside her; a man's hard, strong flesh, so she could clutch at him with her churning love passage and savour every delicious moment until the last spasm died away.

Her mouth thinning in disappointment, she let her skirts drop, and waited for the two of them to recover from the violence of their copulation and make themselves decent.

That Morwith was nothing but a slut. Alys had heard, indeed the whole castle had heard how she'd spent the whole night with three of the guards. But because she had a bonny, unmarked face and a plump figure, the men were round her like flies to a honeypot.

Her feet dragging, Alys stepped forward out of the dark shadows. 'You, Morwith! The lady Isobel wants you,' she called out sullenly.

Morwith spun round. 'Spying again?' she taunted. 'I suppose it's the nearest you'll ever get to the real thing, Alys!'

Her mouth pressed tight, Alys headed back to the hall, not waiting to see whether or not the redhead followed.

Her plans complete, Isobel de Morency glided along the gallery and gazed down into the great candlelit hall below.

The feast to celebrate the return of Aimery's soldiers and the rout of the Saxon rebels was in full swing. Serfs rushed from the hot kitchens carrying platter after platter of hot, spicily-scented food: boars head with chervil, venison, roast heron and haunches of pork in cinnamon, accompanied by jugs of strong wine and ale for the jubilant men lining the trestle tables in the body of the hall.

With a pang of bitterness, Isobel observed that Aimery le Sabrenn had condescended to join his men at last. Seated there at the high table in a fine grey woollen mantle, surrounded by his loyal knights, he looked magnificent, a natural leader of men as he rose to his feet and drank to the health of King William of England. A man to worship with his proudly handsome face and his beautiful, battle-hardened body.

And he'd just come from the little Saxon's slut's bed . . .

Isobel's long fingernails dug into her smooth palms as she watched and waited in the shadows. Her patience was stretched almost to breaking point as the feasting and drinking went on interminably and Aimery, though finished with the food, went on talking and drinking with his soldiers. Hadn't she known him when he was an impoverished, land-hungry mercenary? Hadn't she helped him rise this high? And yet he'd not bothered to come and see her, his lady.

The poison gathered in her blood, festering. Stepping at last out of the darkness, she walked along the gallery and glided down the stairs into the great hall, her red silk skirts rustling. There was a satisfying silence as men turned and gaped. They at least knew how beautiful, how desirable she was even if the Breton didn't!

Swallowing down her icy anger, she walked proudly up to the high table, her head held high. 'My lord,' she said in clear, melodious tones, 'I crave a moment of your time.'

Silence fell at the high table. Aimery said, 'Now? Here?'

Isobel held herself steady. 'In private, if you please.'

Aimery hesitated, his face unreadable. Then with a slight bow of his head, he said, 'My time is all yours, my lady Isobel.'

Liar, burned Isobel. *Liar!* But she kept a smooth, calm

730

smile on her face as she turned to go back upstairs, with Aimery behind her.

To Aimery, Isobel's chamber seemed dark and oppressively hot after the space and airiness of the great hall. He suddenly became aware that he'd drunk a lot of wine – too much. As he followed Isobel inside, it took him some moments to adjust to the shadowy darkness, relieved only by a single tall candle in a silver holder. Isobel's hand lay lightly on his sinewed brown forearm; his nostrils were assailed by a musky eastern perfume. He was aware suddenly of impending danger, of some obscure evil.

Then he saw them. In the dark corner. The redhead, the Saxon serf called Morwith, crouched on all fours; her bottom cheeks pouting obscenely from beneath her ragged tunic. And kneeling behind her, shafting her vigorously, was a big blond Saxon, clad only in ragged breeches, with his hands shackled behind his back. Morwith the redhead was writhing in pleasure, eagerly thrusting her buttocks at the grunting, sweating man as he thrust his penis deep within her.

Aimery, his mouth set tight, swung round towards the door, suddenly realising that he was in no mood for Isobel's tricks tonight. But Isobel barred his way, her back to the door, a strange, excited gleam in her dangerous green eyes. 'Wait, my lord! There is more . . .'

'Of that,' said Aimery acidly, 'I've no doubt. But you'll excuse me, lady, from your entertainments this evening.'

Isobel's eyes darkened almost to points of blackness. 'Even if I tell you,' she hissed, 'that the scene in the corner was enacted only yesterday by your little convent slut, Elena, and a Saxon prisoner?'

Aimery felt the blood drain from his hard-boned face. 'God's blood, but you jest, lady. Let me pass. Your games no longer amuse me.'

Isobel's eyes spat venom. 'It's the truth! Are you so

731

unwilling to hear it? I saw them myself – saw the Saxon scum, pleasuring one another – just like these two! It's the truth, my lord – ask her! Bring your little slut in, and ask her!'

Aimery felt the bile rising in his throat. Madelin. Just like Madelin.

'Ask her,' went on Isobel softly in his ear. 'Force her to watch this pair in their open lust, and see if she can deny it. One thing more, my lord. The man with whom she copulated so eagerly was a Saxon rebel – a traitor. She is a danger to you and your men, conspiring wickedly against you.'

Madelin and Elena. Elena and Madelin. The past churned up in the dark, wine-soaked recesses of Aimery's agonised brain. He had been making wild, abandoned love to Madelin when the Saxons came and captured him, just as she had planned. The witch had stood over him, still naked and moist from his love as her Saxon compatriots struck him to the ground, tied him with ropes, kicked him. She'd stood over him, with a smile on her beautiful face, and a long sword in her hand . . .

'You really thought I loved you, didn't you, Breton?' she had taunted him softly. 'Such pride, such self-delusion.' It was then that she had slashed at his face. 'Take him away.'

Now, the fierce, devouring anger burned white-hot in his brain. 'Very well, then,' he grated out to the waiting Isobel. 'Fetch her.'

He sat blindly in the carved chair, gripping at its arms for support, while she was gone. The couple on the floor were bucking wildly towards climax; he felt his own phallus rearing hot and hard in cynical desire, pushing against his leather belt. He knew he had already drunk too much wine; but he reached out to fill Isobel's goblet from the half-full jug at his side, and drank it all down, hoping for numbing release.

* * *

732

Elena was asleep, dreaming of Aimery when Isobel came in. The soft smile died on her lips when she saw who was shaking her awake.

'The lord Aimery wishes to see you – slut,' breathed Isobel, with a fierce triumph burning in her eyes. 'Go, he is waiting in my room.' Trembling with a nameless fear, Elena clothed herself and left the room. Isobel watched her go, then moved back to the girl's still warm bed, slipping something quickly between the sheets.

As soon as Elena entered Isobel's room, the room that she hated, she saw Aimery, and as he looked at her the expression in his cold, slate-grey eyes was enough to fill her with despair. Isobel followed behind her, and shut the door; it was then that she became aware of the couple on the floor, entwined around one another, damply exhausted; Morwith the redhead, and a big blond serf, clad only in ragged breeches, with his hands chained behind his back.

'Leofwin!' she gasped out, her hand to her mouth.

Isobel's chuckle warned her what she had done. The Saxon on the floor turned round to look at her, grinning. He looked like Leofwin, but he wasn't. The sick dread rose through her limbs, numbing her. Aimery said nothing, but watched her from his chair with cold, fathomless eyes. She started to tremble.

Isobel said, rapturously, 'So you recognised the little scene they have just enacted for my lord's entertainment! You thought he was Leofwin, didn't you, this fine Saxon who has just serviced Morwith so delightfully? With his mane of blond hair, and the shackles on his wrists, I can quite understand your mistake. Because, only yesterday, you were lying on the floor, pleasurably sated, just like Morwith here . . .'

Elena took a step forward, her hands clenched to whiteness, 'No – no!'

Isobel hissed, 'Do you dare to deny it? That you coupled, like those two in the corner, with the Saxon rebel Leofwin, while my lord Aimery was away?'

733

Elena hung her head in bitter despair, her long golden hair sweeping her pale cheeks. Defeat. Isobel had defeated her.

At last, Aimery spoke, and his voice was like the slither of steel through her naked heart. 'Your only hope,' he said expressionlessly, 'is to convince me that you were forced against you will.'

Brokenly, Elena shook her head. No, she was not forced. At least, not physically. She had been told that Leofwin would be beaten if she refused to comply – but how could she prove it? And at the time, she had felt so alone, so bereft. But all the time that Leofwin was making love to her, it was Aimery – Aimery, with his dark, bitter soul and his wonderful prowess – that she was dreaming of . . .

She swallowed down the searing ache that threatened to choke her and said, in quiet despair, 'No, my lord. I – I was not forced.'

The silence hung ominously heavy in the airless room. Even Morwith and her partner, whom Isobel had summoned because he looked so like Leofwin, had subsided into stillness, watching and waiting.

Isobel, scenting success within her grasp, said smoothly, 'One more thing, my lord Aimery – bad news, I fear. I learned a short while ago that the prisoner we talk of, the Saxon rebel Leofwin, escaped a short while ago from his cell. While you were feasting just now with your men, someone stole down to the dungeons and released him.' She shook her head in mock concern. 'You will, I think, find the key hidden in the convent girl's room.'

Aimery was on his feet; Elena whirled to face Isobel, her dark blue eyes shadowed with despairing denial. 'No! That is a lie!'

Aimery gripped Elena's shoulders and twisted her round to face him, hurting her. His white-ridged scar made his expression dark and menacing. 'Be very careful, Elena. That man, Leofwin, is a dangerous ringleader. If what Isobel says is true – '

'It isn't!' she whispered, gazing up into his wintry face. 'She's lying, I swear it! How can you believe her?'

'Why don't you come with me, my lord?' said Isobel silkily, turning to leave the room.

Aimery followed her, dragging Elena behind him, his fingers bruising her wrist.

Glancing behind to make sure he could see, Isobel entered Elena's small room and triumphantly drew back the sheet of her narrow bed. There, starkly black against the white linen, lay a big iron key.

'Look – the key to the dungeons,' said Isobel, shaking her head sadly. 'Do you need any more proof, my lord?'

With casual, biter strength, Aimery flung Elena across the bed. She lay there stunned, the breath knocked from her body.

'Do what you will with her, Isobel,' said Aimery le Sabrenn curtly. 'She's all yours.'

The moonlight gleamed softly on the deserted courtyard, on the dark granaries and low-roofed stables where the horses whinnied restlessly.

Elena, taking a deep breath, forced herself to watch a tiny wisp of straw that fluttered uncertainly across the cobbles, lifted now and then by the warm night breeze. Perhaps, if she watched it very carefully, if she concentrated on its light, delicate dance with every fibre of her being, then she might forget the overwhelming horror of what was happening to her.

About an hour ago, two of Isobel's guards had tied her up here with her back against the palisade. They'd stripped her first, at Isobel's orders; Isobel had looked on, her face so full of savage triumph that Elena hoped she would choke on it.

It was Isobel who ordered the men to lift their trembling prisoner's arms, so that her breasts were raised high, her rosy nipples hardening already in the soft kiss of the night air; Isobel who told them to plant her feet widely apart before securing her ankles with leather straps, so Elena knew, with burning shame, that all her pale golden fleece was exposed; even the tender pink flesh that peeped from between her thighs.

She's all yours, Aimery had said with cold scorn to Isobel. His words of utter contempt still rang in her ears. At first she'd tried to struggle, but the guards had tightened the straps that bound her wrists and ankles, dragging her feet yet further apart. One of the men had surreptitiously brushed his big, calloused hand high between her legs, drawing in his breath in appreciation; Elena felt the shame flood through her body, and leaned back against the palisade in numb despair.

Isobel watched her enemy's degradation in silent joy. 'Beg,' she said softly. 'Beg for forgiveness, Saxon girl; promise me that you'll crawl to me on your knees, and then I might – just – consider releasing you!'

Elena shook her head wildly, her long hair sweeping her naked shoulders. 'Never!' she whispered. 'You know I didn't free the Saxon! I would rather see you in hell, than apologise for something I've not done!'

Isobel's face tightened, her features sculpted to ivory by the moolight. She turned to the guards. 'See that the girl is not actually harmed,' she said curtly. 'Otherwise – ' She shrugged her shoulders expressively and moved to go back into the hall. To Aimery.

Elena watched her depart and hated her with a wild, bitter passion, because it was better to feel this hatred than to feel the aching void which overwhelmed her when she thought of Aimery.

She whirled round suddenly in alarm, her bonds tugging at her wrists and ankles. In the pools of darkness that lay between the outbuildings, she could see men coming, sidling up in the shadows. Word had got round, and the scum of the estate was gathering, like a den of rats, to gaze on her punishment.

Her naked flesh burned. Her exposed breasts

throbbed, her rosy nipples tingled as the soft night air caressed them. And between her legs, at the pit of her abdomen, she was aware of a pulsing ache of shame, the dark pain of utter degradation.

She held her head high and proud, trying her best not to see them, but their appreciative mutters drifted across the hushed courtyard. Her guards stood on either side of her, grinning broadly in anticipation.

'See what we have here, lads!' one of them called encouragingly to the silent furtive onlookers. 'What'll you give us for a closer peek at this fine slave, eh?' He reached out with his rough hands and cupped her breast in his palm; Elena shuddered and wrenched her head to one side. 'Just look at these proud beauties,' he went on, rubbing her nipple with his thumb, 'good enough for the lord Aimery himself!'

Someone lurched forward out of the shadows, but the other guard pounced on him and drove him back.

'No touching, now! But you can have your fill of watching. See, if I spread these lovely legs a little further for you, you can see that sweet pink flesh, all parted and melting . . .'

Dazed with shame, Elena tried not to listen any more. Their hot, greedy looks; their casually filthy comments as they gazed lecherously at her vulnerable body and pawed secretly at their swelling erections. It was all far worse than any physical abuse.

She was squeezing her eyes shut in desperation, trying to block out their leering faces, when suddenly, silence fell. The men in the shadows melted away, like the vermin they were, as a tall, familiar figure brushed them aside.

'What is the meaning of this outrage?'

Elena's head jerked upwards, her heart beating. That deep, velvety voice was so familiar. Hamet, the Saracen – Aimery's servant. *Aimery had sent for her.*

Even as the thought flashed through her mind, she knew she was wrong.

But nevertheless Hamet pushed the remaining stragglers aside scornfully and walked up to her, his dark face full of concern. 'Elena – what is happening?'

'The – the lady Isobel's orders, sire!' stuttered the guard at her side, quailing beneath Hamet's icy anger. 'This lass here, she helped a Saxon rebel to escape, and the lord Aimery himself commanded her to be punished. She's not actually been harmed, sire!'

'Then see,' said Hamet, 'that she is not.' In a swift, sinuous movement, he pulled his woollen cloak from his shoulders and wrapped it gently round Elena's trembling, bound figure. She lifted her dazed blue eyes to him in mute appeal, but he frowned and shook his head sadly.

'I have no power to countermand my master's orders,' he said quietly. 'Or the lady Isobel's, for that matter. But,' and he turned once more to the guards, 'if you let any of that – that scum out there come near her again, or touch her yourselves, then you will answer to me, personally. Do you understand?'

'Sire!' The guards stood rigidly to attention as Hamet turned, reluctantly, and headed back towards the hall.

Elena sagged in her bonds, half-sleeping, half-waking, throughout the short midsummer hours of darkness. Thoughts of Aimery came to her like a nightmare now, not a dream. How could he? How could he let this happen to her?

Dawn broke early, revealing itself in pink and golden streaks above the dark line of the forest. Alys hovered warily outside the kitchens, on the pretext of fetching hot water for her mistress. She'd heard and seen everything, and ranted silently against them all. It was too much! They way the lady Isobel had treated her, Alys; the way that slut Morwith had laughed at her so openly for her plainness! And now, they were making that sweet girl, Elena, suffer unbearably.

Alys looked across the courtyard and shivered. It was

cold in this early grey light. The girl was pinioned there
still, her head bowed, the Saracen's big cloak wrapped
tightly round her slender figure. The watch had
changed twice during the night; two young, yawning
men-at-arms were with her now, plainly bored and
weary since Hamet had warned them all against any
sport with their prisoner. That Hamet might be a
heathen, but he was the only decent one amongst them
all.

Alys shifted the bundle in her arms, lifted her chin
resolutely, and set off across the deserted courtyard
towards them. Now was the time. As she'd calculated,
the big gates were just about to be dragged open, in
readiness for the dawn patrol to ride out.

The guards watched warily when they saw Alys
coming. She was well known as a troublemaker, only
too ready to carry spiteful tales back to her mistress.

'You're to set her free,' said Alys briefly. 'And then
you can go.'

'But – '

'Quickly, damn you! You want me to tell the lady
Isobel that you dispute her commands? Be off with you!'

Worried, they did as she said. The girl almost fell
when her limbs were freed, but she struggled to lean
against the palisade. Her small face was white and
drawn. The guards hesitated still; Alys snapped, 'Go
on, you great brutes!' and watched until they were out
of sight. Then she turned urgently back to Elena.

'Now's your chance to escape!' she hissed, thrusting
the bundle towards her. 'Here are some clothes, and a
little food. Head for the forest – get away from this evil
place while you can. Quickly, they'll be closing the gate
again soon!'

The girl took the bundle, but she looked dazed and
uncertain, her eyes wandering longingly towards the
great hall. God help her, thought Alys, but the sweet
maid is still in love with the Breton. After what he's
done to her . . .

'Go, for pity's sake!' she pleaded. 'Don't you realise that Isobel will never, ever let you have him? That between them, they'll destroy you?'

As if waking from a long dream, the girl tightened her grip on the little bundle and took a deep, shuddering breath. Then she hurried towards the beckoning gates, not looking back.

Alys watched her go as the first pale rays of dawn spread tentatively across the castle courtyard. She should have done more. She should have told the lord Aimery about the key, and told him who it really was who set the dangerous Saxon rebel free.

But she didn't dare. Not yet. She was too frightened of Isobel.

Chapter Thirteen

*I*t was the shrill birds of the forest that woke her as they clamoured in alarm above her head, their wings beating in panic against the suffocating canopy of the high trees. Someone was coming!

Elena leaped to her feet in alarm, her throat dry. It was late afternoon and the sun was still hot as it slanted through the dusty branches. She'd not meant to fall asleep, but this soft, grassy bank beside the trickling stream had been so tempting, the sun so warm, that she'd lain down on the mossy turf and slept in utter exhaustion.

All day, she'd wandered deeper into the trackless forest, driven by nothing other than the wild, instinctive urge to get as far away as she could from the domain of Aimery le Sabrenn. Now, she was alone, and frightened, and completely lost. And she could hear the echoing sound of voices, male voices, and heavy footsteps crackling through the undergrowth nearby.

She cowered behind the trunk of a great gnarled oak, her heart hammering wildly. Outlaws. Brigands! Or perhaps Isobel de Morency had ordered the soldiers to follow her, to kill her.

Holding her breath in panic, she pressed herself into

the shadows as three young men came into sight, laughing and talking to each other. They paused to drink at the stream; she thought for one wild moment that they'd pass by without seeing her. But suddenly one of them, getting to his feet, spotted her and called out, 'Look – over there! A girl!'

She tried to run, but in her state of exhaustion she was no match for their nimble feet. They caught her easily, gripping her wrists, staring curiously down at her and asking questions all at once. 'Who are you? Where are you going? Why are you all on your own in the forest?'

The knowledge swept over her that they were Saxons – men of her own race. In sudden blind inspiration, Elena stammered out, 'I'm looking for Leofwin. Please, do you know him?'

The name was like a magic talisman, Smiling in wonder, the young men stepped back, releasing her.

'Leofwin?' said one, his grin wide and friendly in his sunburned face. 'Know him? Lass, if you're a friend of his, then you're a friend of ours! Come with us!'

Considerately adjusting their energetic pace to her weary limbs, the three young Saxons led her along the winding paths of the forest, until at last they came to a sun-dappled clearing set between stately oaks. The same stream ran more deeply here between rocky boulders, emptying itself just beyond the clearing into a deep, limpid pool fringed with ferns. The stream's banks were edged by soft, rabbit-nibbled turf that was like velvet to Elena's bruised and aching feet.

In the shade of the trees were some low turf shelters, built carefully to merge into the undergrowth. In front of them a young woman was tending a simmering cauldron over an open fire; she looked up questioningly as the men led Elena into the clearing.

'This is our home,' said the young, suntanned man who'd first spoken to her. He gestured proudly round the clearing, as if it were some nobleman's estate. 'My name is Gyrth – I'll introduce you to the others later. But first things first. You must eat, and rest!'

The young woman, who was plumply pretty with thick blonde curls, brought her over a wooden bowl full of hot, delicious rabbit stew, and smiled at her shyly. Elena ate hungrily, suddenly realising how long it was since she'd had a proper meal. The sun was starting to set behind the tops of the great trees, but its rays still warmed the clearing, mottling the mossy turf with soft shadows.

She felt safe, and at peace, as long as she tried not to remember about Aimery.

What was he doing now? Was he thinking of her?

She put her bowl to one side, suddenly no longer hungry. By now the others had gathered round her companionably; the woman and the young men, with their own bowls of food.

'You have come far?' The pretty woman, Freya, handed her a beaker of clear water from the stream. 'Forgive me for prying, but you look so gently-born, and so tired. No lady should wander on her own through the forest!'

Elena hesitated, knowing she could never tell them everything. 'I – I was captured from a convent, and held as a serf at Thoresfield.' She clasped her fingers tightly round the wooden beaker. 'Leofwin was kind to me there. I thought perhaps he might help me again'.

'So you too escaped from Thoresfield!' breathed Freya, leaning forward. 'When Leofwin reached us last night, he said that the place is full of evil; that he wants to go back there and raze it to the ground, and kill its Breton lord! Oh, did you suffer greatly there?'

'Leave her alone, woman!' said Gyrth sharply, seeing the tears that sparkled suddenly in Elena's blue eyes. 'Isn't it enough that she was the Breton's prisoner?'

Elena bowed her head. 'If you and Leofwin will but shelter me for a while,' she whispered, 'until I find somewhere elsc to go – '

743

'How do we know she's not a spy?' broke in a venomous voice. 'Sent by the Breton to track down Leofwin and bring the soldiers down on us?'

Elena looked up, startled. A girl had just joined them, standing with her hands on her hips at the edge of the circle. Vividly pretty, with a suntanned, elfin face, she wore her silver-blonde hair cropped short like a soldiers', and wore a boy's tunic that only emphasized the soft curves of her slender figure. A murmur of protest ran through the rest of them at her challenging words.

'Leave her be, Sahild!' said Gyrth shortly. 'Leofwin himself will be here to identify her soon enough.'

'Don't be so sure of that, Gyrth! I still think she's a spy!'

Elena shrank instinctively from the venom in the girl, Sahild's, blue eyes. Freya meanwhile, seized Elena's hands and held them up angrily. 'Look! Look at these rope marks on the poor girl's wrists! She's been bound, Sahild, bound and punished! Would the Breton really do that to his spy?'

Sahild glared. 'Just don't blame me if the soldiers do follow her here!' And she flounced off into the trees.

Quickly Freya put her arm round Elena's trembling shoulder. 'Take no notice of Sahild – she's always wary of newcomers. You see, we've all suffered at the hands of the Normans, and we value our refuge here so highly.' She touched Elena's wrists gently. 'You poor thing. How you must have suffered. Leofwin will be so pleased that you've found us.'

'Will Leofwin be here soon?' Was it her imagination, or did a strange, expectant hush fall over them all at her question?

'Soon,' said Freya softly. 'Very soon.'

After their meal, Elena helped Freya to clear away. Sahild seemed to have disappeared, for which she was glad. With Freya, she took the wooden platters down to the stream to wash them; Freya chatted companionably, soothing her secret fears. When they got back to the clearing the men, taking advantage of the evening sunshine, had got out their bows for archery practice; and Elena, sinking down onto a mossy stone, watched them entranced, her chin clasped in her hands.

They were good, she could see. Even though they laughed and joked as they waited their turn, their concentration was intense. Two of the men looked so alike that she kept confusing them; they must be brothers, she decided, both bronzed and handsome in their soft leather tunics and boots, with long, wayward blond hair bleached by the sun.

Just then, one of the brothers glanced across the clearing towards her. Catching her eye, he grinned and winked; she smiled back shyly.

'Hands off, convent girl,' hissed a voice at her shoulder. Elena whirled round to see Sahild standing behind her; the beautiful outlaw girl dropped to her knees to face her, her eyes malicious. 'If you're looking for a man, you should have stayed with Aimery le Sabrenn. They say he's incomparable as a lover. What a pity you didn't wait to find out!'

Elena took a deep breath as Aimery's name jolted through her. Then she said, steadily, 'You don't like me being here. I'm sorry, for I mean you no harm. Leofwin is my friend.'

The girl's mouth twisted in a slow smile. 'Then you can help us kill the Breton,' she said softly. 'You'll enjoy that, won't you, seeing as you hate him so much?' And, without waiting for a reply, she went quickly across the clearing to join the men in their archery practice.

Elena watched her, dazed by her venom. Just then Gyrth, who had been watching from a distance, sauntered over to sit beside her, his bow across his knees.

'I'm out of the contest,' he said ruefully. 'Mind if I join you?'

Still shaky from Sahild's hissed words, Elena forced a smile. 'Of course not! I don't know how you can decide on a winner – you all look so good to me. Especially those two, the ones who look so like each other.'

The twins, you mean? Wulf and Osric. Yes, they're the best we've got. And Sahild is as good as any man with her bow.' Gyrth frowned a little into the setting sun, his hands clasped loosely on his knees. 'But we need to be even better. You know, some say that it was because of William's archers – the Bretons, the Flemings, the men of Maine and Poitou – that we lost the day at Hastings. They fired high above our shield wall, and killed King Harold. But some day soon, we'll drive the Frenchmen out!'

Elena suddenly remembered that night when a band of mail-clad knights, with Aimery le Sabrenn at their head, had ridden out menacingly into the blackness of the night to hunt down rebels such as these. How could Leofwin, Gyrth and these men, however brave, hope to defy the might of King William's armies? She shivered suddenly; Gyrth laid his hand gently on her shoulder.

'Why don't you rest for a while? You look exhausted. And Elena, take no notice of Sahild! She doesn't speak for the rest of us, you know!'

Elena nodded, trying to smile. 'Where are the rest of your womenfolk?'

He shrugged wryly. 'You've met them. Freya and Sahild, that's it.'

'And Leofwin? When will he be back?'

He hesitated, just like Freya did when she asked the same question. Again, the air of mystery. 'You'll see him soon enough,' he said finally. 'Now, you must rest. I'll fetch Freya to attend to you.'

Suddenly, Elena realised how very tired she was. Freya took her to an empty hut; she longed to curl up on the straw pallet in the corner, but first she decided to go down to the stream to wash the dust of her journey away.

The sun was setting at last behind the trees as she scrambled down the bank towards the water's edge.

Then she stopped, frozen. Further downstream, where the water eddied into the deep, limpid pool fringed by overhanging alders, two people were already bathing. A girl and a young man. And the girl was Sahild.

As they rose gasping and laughing from the clear water, the droplets streaming from their naked bodies, Elena saw that the man was one of the twins she'd admired earlier. She wondered if he was the one who'd grinned at her. Then he emerged further from the water; and she saw, with a shock that brought the blood coursing to her cheeks, that he was already hugely erect, and the suntanned, crop-headed girl was fondling his penis happily, whispering endearments in his ear and rubbing her small, pointed breasts against his muscled chest.

With a husky laugh, the man lifted the girl in his arms and carried her to the soft, grassy bank on the other side of the stream, laying her down eagerly. Then he cupped her slim, boyish buttocks with his hands and eased his pulsing erection deep within her, groaning aloud in ecstasy as Sahild clasped him to her.

Elena gasped aloud as she saw the second brother move out of the shadows, smiling. He, too, was naked; he crouched lazily beside them, fondling his own ravening penis, waiting patiently.

Elena tore her eyes away and hurried back upstream to wash herself, splashing her burning cheeks with the cool water. Thoroughly shaken by the shameless pleasuring she'd seen, she walked quickly back to the hut Freya had shown her and curled up on the straw pallet, closing her eyes and shutting her mind to everything except sleep.

With sleep came her dreams. She saw a faceless figure, a knight, lying bound and helpless in the centre of the clearing. Instead of the sunlit, friendly forest scene she'd been part of today, everything was dark and sinister; the trees reached out gnarled black fingers

747

in silent threat, and the bound man was surrounded by a ring of fierce, menacing figures, who gathered round him with knives in their hands, ready to plunge them into his helpless body. Elena tried to cry out, to stop them, but her throat was closed up with fear. She ran to the man and threw herself across him, to protect him from the knives; he turned to look at her, and his strange, silver-grey eyes were filled with hatred. '*Aimery,*' she whispered, agonised. '*Oh, Aimery. No . . .*'

She woke up. It was pitch black in the little hut. Her heart raced wildly, and her eyes were still wet with tears from her dream. She pulled herself up, and buried her burning face in her hands.

Just then, the door to the hut opened softly, and Freya stepped inside. 'So you're awake. Good.' There was a hint of suppressed excitement in her carefully controlled voice.

Elena jumped to her feet. 'Leofwin – he's here?'

'Yes – ' Again, Elena noticed the slight hesitation. 'You must follow me.'

The clearing was deserted. It was a warm, sultry night and to Elena the air seemed almost oppressive as Freya led the way deeper through the trees into the blackness of the forest. High above them, an owl hooted softly and Elena jumped, her heart hammering.

She saw the ring of lights first. Small fires, flickering eerily like will o' the wisps through the tangled trunks of the forest. Then she saw the people, sitting cross-legged in a circle round the fires, their heads bowed as if in prayer. Only they weren't praying but murmuring, chanting low, mysterious words to themselves as if they were in another world.

Elena felt the shock juddering through her at the unreality of the scene. Were these really the same people who inhabited that sunlit, peaceful clearing? Yes, there they were. Garth, Freya, Sahild and the twins, the other men.

But tonight, here in this mysterious moonlit glade,

hemmed in by ancient, gnarled oak trees, everyone seemed different – frighteningly so. And in the centre of the ring, dully illuminated by the low, flickering fires, was a huge, flat slab of stone, cold and grey and ominous.

Elena whirled round to flee, her throat dry with fear. She realised now. The nuns had spoken in hushed whispers about the old religion, the gods of ancient Britain, surviving still in the darkly remote forests and the wild northern hills. Sickened, she remembered morbid rumours of rites and magic, of stern, cruel priests and human sacrifices. *This was a sacred grove* . . .

Freya's hand closed round her wrist, preventing her escape. Her voice was low and hypnotic. 'Sit here, Elena, beside me,' she whispered. 'And don't be afraid. Remember, Leofwin will be here soon.'

Helplessly, Elena sank to her knees in the circle. Where else could she go? The soft droning of muttered voices throbbed in her head. Someone leaned forward, breaking the tight circle to throw a scattering of dried herbs on the tiny fires. The pungent smoke assailed her nostrils like incense, sweet and heady. She was aware of the girl Sahild watching her coldly and felt another pang of fear; but Freya's fingers stroked her wrist soothingly, and as she breathed deeply she felt strangely calmed.

Someone was passing her a brimming bowl. She drank obediently, finding it to be rich, honey-sweet mead. The potent liquid hit her stomach almost instantly, making her limbs warm and melting. She held the big bowl wonderingly. It seemed to be made of silver and was carved with strange inscriptions: bulls' heads, birds, spoked circles, and a single crude engraving of a tiny, ithyphallic man, his lewd penis rising to his shoulders.

Her eyes widened at the startling obscenity, yet she was unable to draw her eyes from it, until at last someone gently prised the bowl out of her hands and she let it go, reluctantly. From across the circle, one of the twins smiled at her mysteriously; she smiled shakily back, dazzled by the sudden warmth of his smile, feeling dizzy and unreal.

Something was about to happen in the forest that night, and she felt wildly, terribly excited. The image of the tiny silver man and his enormous member seemed to dance mockingly before her eyes in the darkness; she suddenly realised that she was hot and moist, and her pleasure bud was pulsing hungrily.

A tall man stepped silently out from behind the dense, shadowy oaks. An intense hush fell suddenly over the kneeling circle. The man wore a long, dark cloak and Elena saw with a shock that a mask covered his face; a strange, sinister mask made of bronze with black, staring eyeholes. Elena shuddered in nameless fear as the man started to speak in low, vibrant tones. 'The time has come,' he said softly. Surely his voice was familiar? Yet it was so muffled by the mouthless mask and her senses were swimming, from the scented smoke fumes and the mead.

A murmur of excitement ran through the circle at his words, and he held out his hand commandingly for silence. 'Which of you is the chosen one?'

There was a deathly silence. Shivers of fear ran up and down Elena's spine. Then Freya stood up slowly. Her face looked strange, and her eyes glittered unnaturally. 'Here, master,' she whispered. 'It is I. I am to be first.'

'And who have you chosen as your menfolk?'

'The brothers, my lord – Wulf and Osric!'

The two young men, the twins with their lithe, muscled bodies and long, sun-streaked hair, got to their feet, their heads high and proud. They looked as if they were in a trance; Elena gazed and gazed at them, hypnotised by their youthful, masculine beauty. This could not be real.

A soft breeze moaned through the trees, wafting the sweet smoke from the fires all around the clearing.

'Summon your men, Freya,' said the tall masked man in a low voice. 'And prepare for the final sacrifice.'

Sacrifice! Sweet Jesus . . . Half-forgotten tales of grim rituals, of live burial and hideous impalement, tore through Elena's subconscious mind. She leaped to her feet.

'I – I must go!' she stammered out in confusion. 'I should not be here.'

Sahild laughed unpleasantly. 'The little convent girl doesn't approve of our ceremony. I told you she wouldn't!'

But the men on either side of Elena pulled her gently down. 'Stay,' they whispered soothingly in her ear.'There is nothing to fear. All you will witness is pleasure. Stay, and watch!'

They gave her more mead to drink; the little ithyphallic man grinned up at her, mocking her, and she felt the languorous warmth of the potent honey drink seep meltingly through her veins. When she looked up again, the two men, Wulf and Osric, were standing on either side of Freya, undressing her with deliberate care. When she was completely naked they bowed in silent homage before her. Elena watched, her throat dry. But she had thought that Freya was Gyrth's woman! And Wulf and Osric, she'd seen them earlier, with Sahild! Yet Gyrth was smiling, and Sahild too looked spellbound.

Slowly the twins caressed the naked woman, kissing and licking every inch of her plump, golden flesh. One of the brothers reached for the half-empty bowl of mead and trickled some of it over her full breasts; then they each took a brown nipple in their mouths, licking and sucking the sweet, sticky liquid over her breasts, while caressing and stroking her with their hands.

Freya stood very still, her eyes half-shut in rapture, for as long as she could bear it. Then she sank to her

751

knees with a sigh, and her eyes closed. Raptly, the men slipped their own clothes to the ground, while everyone in the circle gazed in silence. Elena could hardly breathe. The two men stood there in blond, muscular beauty, their magnificent twin phalluses rearing proudly over the kneeling Freya's fair curls. Then, with tender care, they lifted her in their strong arms and laid her on the cold, waiting stone.

Elena felt the low, aching pressure building up relentlessly in her loins. Her breasts swelled and throbbed; little tongues of desire arrowed to her abdomen, setting her flesh on fire. She moistened her lips at the powerful eroticism of the moonlit scene unfolding before her as Freya writhed voluptuously on the grey stone slab, the secret flesh between her thighs already plump and glistening.

The two men stood at her head and feet, naked, muscular, beautiful. Wulf bent to kiss her, thrusting his tongue deep within her swollen mouth. Then, with a soft smile that turned Elena's heart over, he started to rub his engorged phallus against her nipples, and Freya groaned aloud, her legs threshing with desire.

Gently, Osric grasped her thighs, parting them widely so that everyone could see the wet, shiny folds that emerged from her golden fleece. 'Please,' she was murmuring hotly. 'Oh, please . . .'

Osric grasped his thick, solid penis with his right hand and dipped it purposefully towards her throbbing vulva. But instead of entering her, and giving her what she craved so much, he rubbed the velvety glans gently round her entrance, just brushing against her hungry pleasure bud. The touch of his swollen, massive member drove her to distraction; she gasped aloud, her breath coming short and fast, and began thrusting her hips wildly against him.

The masked man stepped forward. 'Enough. She is ready.'

And, with a nod to the twins, who stood obediently

aside, he took his place at the edge of the raised stone dais. He lifted Freya's legs gently, bending her knees and pulling her towards him so that her quivering plump buttocks rested almost on the edge of the stone. Then he parted his long cloak slightly, so that his enormous phallus reared forth, dark and mysterious, as if it had a pulsing life of its own.

Meanwhile, Wulf and Osric stood at Freya's shoulders. Matching each other's movements, smiling conspiratorially at one another, they began to gently rub one another's pulsing shafts, pushing them downwards to brush against Freya's hard brown nipples. Freya moaned and arched her hips desperately, making little animal sounds of pleasure in the back of her throat.

The masked man gripped his penis, stroked gently with it at her hot vulva, and thrust himself in up to the hilt.

Elena felt her own hot, wild excitement racing through her body. Her own secret parts were wet and slick as the mysterious masked man slowly withdrew his magnificent length, now shining wet with Freya's juices, and drove himself in, again and again, while the twins masturbated one another with loving care over Freya's plump breasts.

Freya was beside herself with rapture, gripping and writhing at the masked man's deliciously satisfying penis. She came quickly, racked by an intense, voracious orgasm, as the faceless man thrust firmly into her, his hands resting on either side of her on the big stone slab. With wicked grins of delight, the twins pumped each other to a state of frenzy, shooting their milky sperm in ecstatic spasms across the girl's breasts, rubbing their shafts lasciviously in the pooling liquid and letting their heavy balls drag along her silky flesh until all of her upper body gleamed with their deliciously mingled seed.

Freya lay sprawled on the stone, sated and flushed,

her blonde hair spread out in thick curls around her shoulders.

The masked man let the cloak fall over himself, and drew back into the shadows.

'The first sacrifice,' he said softly. 'Who is next?'

Elena was so aroused that she ached. Her blood coursed through her veins like fire; her breasts burned to be touched, while the flesh between her thighs was swollen and damp. The mead pulsed through her in dizzying waves.

'Next?' repeated the masked man. She couldn't see his eyes through the black holes of the mask, but she knew he was looking straight at her.

Sahild stood up eagerly; the masked man shook his head, still watching Elena. Wulf and Osric, at a nod from the man, walked slowly towards her; Elena stood up shakily.

'Yes,' she breathed. 'Oh, yes! *I* am next . . .'

Chapter Fourteen

With gentle fingers, the twin brothers divested Elena of her clothes and lifted her carefully onto the stone slab, stroking her, soothing her. They turned her over, face down, so that her throbbing breasts kissed the cold stone. Catching her breath in delight, Elena rubbed her hardening nipples against its flat surface.

The brothers were moving down her body, kissing her with delicious feathery strokes, but it was the faceless man she was thinking of, waiting there in the shadows, ready to thrust his hugely powerful shaft into the aching void at the pit of her belly.

'Raise yourself.' One of them – Wulf, or was it Osric – was muttering in her ear. She twisted her head and saw that he had a tiny, arrow-shaped scar at the base of his tanned throat. 'Raise your hips, beautiful Elena – yes, that's right . . .'

Blindly she did as she was told, thrusting her quivering buttocks into the air, not caring about her shame, about the watching silent circle drinking in her white, firm flesh, the dark bottom cleft, the pink, glistening lips that twitched and trembled hungrily. Oh, please, she begged silently, let it be soon!

Wulf – or was it Osric – was pouring scented oil into his palms from a phial. Then he began to stroke and pull at her dangling nipples, lengthening the dark teats, sending exquisite shafts of pleasure through her sensitised body. And the other twin was softly parting her buttocks, and licking slowly; starting at the top of her crease and sliding down with his wicked tongue.

'No!' gasped Elena. 'No – '

'Hush,' murmured a twin in her ear. 'Nothing but pleasure, little one, I promise you.'

Someone in the circle began the low, murmuring chant again; rhythmic, throbbing, exciting. And a darting tongue had found her tight, secret hole. Even while the twin's fingers played with her hot, juicy nether lips, sliding lightly past the little bud that quivered and strained for more, his tongue plunged into that shameful rear entrance, swirling, licking, thrusting. Elena moaned aloud as the dark pleasure swept through her, feeling the moisture gather and slip over the twin's big hand as he rubbed his knuckles up and down her churning vulva and pressed his tongue so deliciously deep within her hidden passage.

Elena caught her breath and went very still as the unfamiliar sensations gathered in her womb and she hovered on the very brink of ecstasy, ready to crash over the edge.

'Stop,' muttered one of the brothers thickly, abondoning the small breasts he was teasing so deliciously with his oil-softened hands. 'Stop, damn you, Osric. Can't you see she's almost there?'

Elena wanted to cry out in loss as their hands abandoned her. She couldn't bear it, for these two beautiful men to leave her, when she was on the brink of such wickedly ecstatic pleasure . . . 'Please!' she moaned, biting on her lip in her anguish.

Then cool hands stroked her buttocks, parting them, soothing them. Elena sighed, burying her head in her arms, and felt the trickle of warm oil running down her crease. The gentle but persistent nudging began again at her tight rear entrance; thinking it was Osric's tongue, she smiled rapturously and thrust towards him.

With a shock, she realised it wasn't his tongue, but the velvety head of an engorged penis that was trying to enter her there. Like a blind animal; stubborn, persistent, prodding. No, she protested silently. It was too big!

Then a hand stroked her softly between her flesh lips, finding the hard bud of pleasure and caressing it, very lightly. Elena shuddered, and gasped aloud as fresh waves of desire racked her body. At the same moment, she felt the engorged phallus slipping through her dark rear hole, sliding deep within her, filling her to bursting and sending a heavy, aching pleasure throbbing through her taut abdomen.

She went very still with the shock of it, almost afraid to move with this huge, pulsing shaft so deep inside her. The crowd was still murmuring its insistent, almost demonic chant; she felt the watchers' rising excitement, breathed in the heavy scent of the aromatic flames, like incense numbing her brain, heightening every sensation to a level of wild eroticism.

The beautiful brothers, Wulf and Osric, were standing by her shoulders. Opening her pleasure-hazed eyes, she saw that they were fully erect again, their penises pulsing with glorious life, their testicles tight and hard. They smiled down at her kindly in the shadows and bent to kiss her shoulders, reaching underneath her crouching body to caress and tease her dangling breasts with sweetly pinching fingers.

And, behind her, the masked man who had so shamefully, so lewdly taken her secret entrance was starting to move.

Elena cried out as she felt the huge, hard shaft slide relentlessly between her silken walls. A twin bent to kiss her, smothering her cry; she responded wildly as he thrust his tongue deep within her mouth. The masked man's penis was fully in her now; she realised with a numbing shock that she could feel the rough, hairy skin of his balls dangling against her tender bottom cheeks. And his hand was still sliding up and down her juicy vulva, teasing and stroking that aching cleft.

The dark waves of pleasure built up relentlessly. Lifting her head, Elena let out a long, low moan. The man behind her, responding to her needs, began to drive his shaft in and out in long, pulsing strokes that penetrated deeply; at the same time he lightly stroked the shaft of her straining pleasure bud, while the two brothers cupped and fondled her oiled, tingling breasts. Clutching blindly at the wonderful phallus that pleasured her so dispassionately, Elena felt her whole body come to a trembling standstill; felt the huge, cataclysmic orgasm rack her quivering flesh in wave after wave of rapture mingled with an agonised sense of shame as the mysterious man behind her gripped her buttocks fiercely and drove himself to his own wild climax. She heard him grunt harshly deep in his throat as he jerked and spasmed deep within that forbidden passage.

Melting in the afterglow of forbidden pleasure, Elena collasped limply on the cool stone slab, aware of the hot, hungry eyes from the firelit circle watching her avidly, longing to share in her rapturous release. The twins continued to caress her gently, their own huge erections almost weeping with tormented desire as they stroked her lovely, flushed breasts. Gently, they turned Elena round and lifted her shoulders so that she was sitting up on the stone, blinking dizzily into the firelit shadows.

The masked man stood before her, at the foot of the stone slab. As she'd always known, it was he who'd pleasured her in that wonderful, shameful way. But who was he? His cloak still covered his tall, powerful body, but as she gazed up at him, desperately trying to frame her question, he slowly took off the bronze mask.

She gasped, 'Leofwin!'

Gently, Leofwin the Saxon wrapped her in his cloak and carried her back to the clearing, laying her gently on a soft straw pallet in his own shelter.

'My Saxon princess,' he said tenderly. 'You're safe now.'

So Elena became one of the outlaws. During the next few days, she learned how to snare rabbits and skin them; how to mend the rough, homespun clothing; and how to make bread for them all, by heating large flat stones in the fire and placing round cakes of unleavened rye dough on the surface until they were cooked. Freya helped her to learn, and was always kind and friendly. But Sahild watched her with narrowed eyes, and hardly ever spoke to her.

At night, Elena slept in Leofwin's arms. He was a strong, tender lover, and there was no hint of the mysterious, almost sinister rites that had marked her first night in the forest. She felt safe, and shut her mind to the past, trying not to think of Aimery the Breton.

Then, early one evening in the soft shadows of dusk, she was going down to the pool to bathe the heat of the day from her limbs when she saw something in the bushes that made her freeze. A man, sprawled on the ground with Sahild.

All the men had gone out hunting for the day, except for Leofwin, who had injured his ankle slightly in an expedition the day before. But – what was Leofwin doing with Sahild?

It soon became obvious.

Leofwin was sprawled back on the mossy turf, his eyes closed in ecstasy, his legs spread wide. Sahild was crouched over his hips, her back to Elena. She shifted slightly, giving Elena a clearer vision; and what she saw made her senses swim. Because Leofwin's huge penis, darkly, erect, was rearing up from his disarrayed clothes, and Sahild was sucking and licking him enthusiastically, diving her lips over his flesh, gripping the base of his thick shaft and making strange little moaning noises in the back of her throat. Leofwin, who had made passionate love to her only last night.

Feeling sick with betrayal, Elena whirled round to go, and almost fell into the arms of Wulf, who stood behind her. His strong hands fastened round her shoulders. 'Wait,' he said.

Elena's hands pummelled frantically at his broad chest. 'Let me go!' she whispered blindly. 'Damn you, Wulf – let me go!'

He held on to her, ignoring her wild struggles. 'Listen, Elena,' he said, in a low, urgent voice. 'Leofwin loves you. We all love you. This is the way we live in the forest. Didn't you realise, after that first night?'

She stopped struggling, and stared blankly up at him. That dark, erotic ceremony on her first night here. She'd tried to push it to the back of her mind. Pretended it had never happened, would never happen again. *This is the way we live in the forest.*

Her heart thudded as she gazed up at him. He was so young, only about her age – so handsome and carefree and kind. That first night, she'd seen him and his brother making love to Sahild down by the stream, and then they'd both caressed her, so beautifully, while the masked Leofwin stood waiting in the shadows.

Already aroused by the sight of Leofwin's depravity, Elena felt moist and hot; her stomach churned. With his sun-streaked blond hair and his laughing blue eyes set wide apart in his suntanned face, he set her pulse racing in a way he shouldn't.

His hands had slipped now from her shoulders to her breasts. Lightly, still gazing into her eyes, he caressed her tender nipples until they peaked and thrust beneath her tunic. She trembled suddenly with wanting him.

He was smiling down at her, his palms rubbing flatly

along her breasts, sending whirling, fiery sensations through her body. 'You called me Wulf,' he said softly. 'How did you know it was me, and not my brother?'

Hypnotised by his gaze, she whispered, 'The little mark – the white scar at the base of your throat, shaped like an arrowhead. I noticed it on the first night, when – when –'

'When Osric and I made love to you?' His hands had slipped round the back of her waist; he held her very close, so she could feel the hot, hard arousal at his loins.

'Yes.'

'And did you enjoy it? I wonder, which one of us did you want the most?' He put his head teasingly on one side, lifting his eyebrows so engagingly that Elena found herself smiling breathlessly in response.

'Both of you,' she whispered, her heart racing. 'Oh, both of you.'

He laughed in response, his teeth gleaming whitely in his suntanned face. 'You should have said – you. You, Wulf! Just you! – For that, I fear, I shall have to punish you, sweet Elena. When the time comes . . .' He smiled, a smile full of secret promise. Suddenly she realised that she didn't mind now about Leofwin and Sahild. *This is the way we live.*

Her body tingled with excitement; Wulf drew her closer, his breath warm on her cheek.

Then they jumped apart as the mingled sound of heavy footsteps and raised, excited voices came crashing through the forest towards them. Gyrth and his men were back from their expedition. Reluctantly Wulf led Elena towards them. 'Good hunting?' he enquired laconically.

'Good hunting indeed!' Gyrth clapped him on the back, scarcely able to restrain his excitement. 'A Norman baggage train, no less! Wine, wheat, even some gold. All on its way to York, where they'll miss it sorely!' He gestured proudly towards the two laden pack ponies that the other men were starting to unload. 'We've brought back as much as we could. This calls for a feast! Where's Leofwin?'

'I'll fetch him,' said Wulf diplomatically, flashing a reassuring smile at Elena.

That night they sat down to a feast of roasted venison and fine wheat cakes that Freya had baked. The men were drinking the heady French wine they'd captured; Elena only sipped at it, but already she could feel it pulsing warmly through her blood. The outlaws were quaffing it down as if it were ale, recounting again and again how they'd ambushed the Norman supply wagons on their way north from Lincoln.

The shadows lengthened, and tiny bats swooped in the trees overhead. The fire crackled hypnotically, and the smell of the venison filled the air with its savoury perfume.

Sahild too was drinking like a man. Her eyes gleamed jealously in the light of the fire as she listened to their stories; she leaned forward intently and said, 'I should have been with you, Gyrth! Why didn't you take me? I'd have killed them all!' She licked her lips. 'After I'd made them suffer, of course.'

Elena shivered at the girl's quiet venom. Leofwin, who had pulled her down beside him as if the episode with Sahild had never existed, put his arm round her, and she was glad to lean into his quiet strength. But Elena knew that Leofwin too was under the influence of the wine, and inflamed by his men's success. As if a kind of subtle blood lust gripped them all, they sat in their shadowy circle round the fire, watching Sahild with baited breath.

Wulf said softly, 'How? How would you make them suffer, Sahild?'

Kneeling upright, conscious that she had everyone's attention, Sahild drew out the dagger she always carried at her belt. The moon sparkled down on her cropped silver hair and her beautiful elfin face. Her wide blue

762

eyes seemed dazed by her own dark imagination. Slowly, she inverted the dagger and began to stroke its thick, ribbed pommel between her thighs. Elena gasped aloud; everyone else had gone very still.

Sahild rolled over luxuriously onto her back, and raised her knees. She wore a soft leather tunic, and deerskin boots that clung to her calves; her lithe, sun-tanned legs were bare. As her tunic fell back over her hips, they saw that she wore nothing beneath her tunic; her pink secret flesh glistened damply between her slim thighs. Her eyes closing in rapture, she gently positioned the rounded hilt of the dagger between her silken flesh lips, and slid the metal slowly in, her face flushing with pleasure.

Osric leaned over her, watching raptly. 'Is that how you'd torment the Normans, Sahild? Don't you think they might – enjoy it?'

She slanted a wicked grin up at him. Her breathing was short and shallow. 'I'd say – can you do as well as this soldier? Can you fill me with a shaft as solid as this steel? Can you – oh!'

Suddenly she broke off as Freya, who'd been watching avidly in the shadows, jumped up and moved swiftly to crouch over her friend. With nimble fingers, Freya took the dagger's hilt in her own hand and started to pleasure Sahild gently, rubbing the hilt between Sahild's parted legs, while Sahild moaned and writhed on the soft grass. She pulled her tunic high above her head; greedily Freya dipped her head and began to suck and lick at the girl's suntanned, pointed little breasts. She circled the nipples lasciviously with her tongue, while still sliding the rounded metal pommel sleekly in and out of her pink, juicy love channel. Sahild began to moan and whimper, on the verge of explosion; while the men sat round silently in a circle, their hungry expressions lit up by the flickering fire as they waited.

Elena, overwhelmed by the erotic tension, jumped

up suddenly, freeing herself from Leofwin's imprisoning arm, and ran blindly away from the lewd scene. She found herself down by the little stream; breathing hard in the gathering darkness, she crouched down to bathe her burning face in the cool water.

She heard soft footsteps coming up behind her. She felt strong hands on her shoulders, firm fingers that crept round from behind to stroke her breasts, caressing her stiffening nipples. She whirled round, the blood hot in her face. '*Wulf!*'

He smiled softly in the darkness, and she melted. His hands slid round her waist, pulling her up to his hard, muscular body; he bent his head and kissed her deeply, languorously, his sensitive tongue stroking and probing round the soft silken flesh of her mouth.

Elena pushed at his chest, gasping for breath. 'No – we shouldn't – Leofwin . . .'

Wulf smiled again. 'Leofwin sent me,' he said.

'And me,' added Osric, emerging out of the shadows.

She glanced wildly from one to the other. Already they were lifting their tunics over their heads, unfastening their hose from around their slim, muscular hips, so that she could glimpse their dark, erect phalluses. She backed away, trembling with excitement. 'No! Someone might see us!'

'The others,' said Osric calmly, 'will be totally occupied with Freya and Sahild by now.'

'But we,' said Wulf softly, stepping forward to remove Elena's clothes, 'are for you, sweet Elena.'

She gasped and shuddered as her gown slipped to the floor and she felt Wulf's hot, silken penis rubbing against her belly. He bent to kiss her again, and she clung to him weakly, feeling the hard, rippling strength of his beautiful, suntanned body, the long strength of his heavy, shapely legs. And now Osric was behind her, lifting her long hair and kissing her shoulders, while his own engorged shaft rubbed tenderly at her bottom cheeks, nuzzling between her thighs.

Already she was pulsing wet, aching with excitement, her clitoris quivering. Gently they laid her on the soft turf, and kneeled, one on either side of her, their faces amused and tender. With both hands, she grasped their twin penises in delight, caressing and stroking those two magnificent pillars of flesh that waited to do her homage, reaching up to take each one's tip in her mouth, swallowing and licking greedily while the hot hunger churned in her loins.

It was almost dark. She could see the wicked gleam in their dancing blue eyes as they looked at one another and nodded. Then one of them – she thought it was Wulf, but she couldn't be sure – kneeled between her legs, facing her, and lifted her hips gently. He licked his finger and ran it moistly down her slippery cleft, up and down, sliding teasingly past her twitching pleasure bud; she moaned aloud, and he gave a secret smile as he gripped his massively erect shaft and slid it slowly into her. She shouted aloud at the pleasure, gripping hungrily at the hot flesh that nudged its way in, possessing her so beautifully.

Then the other twin – Osric? – crouched astride her head, facing his brother, so that the musky, masculine scent of him excited her nostrils, and her whole vision was filled by the coarse, velvety flesh of his balls and the veined underside of his throbbing penis. Gently, he lowered himself over her, caressing and pinching her breasts with his fingers; until, with a little gasp, she felt his hairy sac kiss her soft lips, and instinctively she began to lick and caress him there with her tongue.

All her flesh, all her senses quivered in reaction to the two men pleasuring her. Wulf's fine penis drove deeply into her; Osric's fingers tugged and tweaked at her nipples, his balls exciting her soft lips. When Wulf's finger slid once more across her hungry clitoris, she moaned aloud, and heard her high, delirious cry of ecstasy echoing round the trees as he slowly, deliberately pumped himself into her and wickedly teased that tight, hard little bud, while Osric squeezed her nipples, tenderly.

She threw herself into the air, spasming wildly, as the pleasure exploded in white-hot shafts through her tense, yearning body. Wulf drove himself into her fiercely, his taut hips jerking, until at last, with a husky groan, he shuddered to his own delicious release, his penis pulsing wetly within her.

'Now me,' said Osric softly, his ravening member jutting hungrily into the empty air.

He was still crouching astride Elena, though careful not to lean his full weight on her. Now, he lowered himself again, rubbing his thick, hairy sac against her lips; she opened her moist mouth as wide as she could, to suck and caress at the coarse skin. He gasped with dark pleasure, throwing his head back; Wulf leaned forward with a wicked grin and took his twin's engorged phallus in his mouth. He swept his lips down hard over the silken, throbbing flesh, licking fiercely at the sensitive glans; then, just at Elena felt Osric's balls tighten and quiver in pre-orgasmic tension, Wulf lifted his head away.

Osric groaned aloud as his hot semen began to spurt into the air; he pushed his testicles hard against Elena's soft mouth, and she shivered with renewed pleasure as she felt the milky liquid surge through him and spatter on her heated nipples.

Then the twins kneeled gently on either side of her and began to lick up Osric's sticky seed from her flushed breasts. She lay back dazed with pleasure as the two brothers, their faces exquisitely tender and handsome in the moonlight, caressed and stroked her sated flesh, murmuring her name in adoration as they did so.

They bathed themselves in the moonlit stream, giggling and whispering. Then they headed back towards the clearing, Elena still light-headed with wine and lovemaking.

The fire was burning low. The others reclined in a

circle around it, murmuring in low, hazy voices. From the disarray of their clothing, Elena guessed, blushing, that they too had all been busy pleasuring one another; Gyrth and Freya were still together, kissing languorously. Elena wondered hazily who Leofwin had been with. Did it matter? It certainly didn't seem to when he saw her at the edge of the clearing, and reached out his hand to her with a gentle smile. She went to sit with him, settling contentedly in the crook of his shoulder.

They were talking, telling stories about battles and the old times, before the Normans came. Elena listened, fascinated.

Then Sahild sat up. The twins had settled on either side of her. She was still drinking wine, and her eyes were unnaturally bright. Her tunic had slipped over one shoulder, exposing one high, small breast; she leaned forward, her hands clasping her knees. 'When I first came to the forest,' she began huskily, 'before I met up with you all, something strange happened to me.'

Wulf laughed easily, fondling her bare, suntanned shoulder. 'Is this another figment of your over-vivid imagination, sweetheart?'

She shrugged him off. 'No! Listen, and I'll tell you! It happened in high summer, around the time of the feast of Lughnasad. I'd been wandering through the forest for days, living off what I could find. I was tired and hungry. Then I found the stone – our stone! It was past midnight . . .'

Elena felt the prickles of unease racing up and down her spine. The sacrificial stone, in the sacred grove.

'It was hot,' continued Sahild. She spoke in a low, breathless whisper; she had everyone's rapt attention now. 'I was restless, uneasy. I laid on the cold stone, letting it cool my burning skin. Then, suddenly, I knew that someone else was in the grove with me!

'I jumped up, and a man stepped forward. A big man, wearing a bronze mask of a bull, with dark slits

767

for eyes and great, protruding horns. He wore a crude leather tunic, and was very powerful, with wide shoulders and a great, muscular chest. I shivered as I gazed up at him. He was so strong, so incredibly virile, so mysterious. I wanted to run but I found I couldn't move.

"*Who are you?*" I whispered.

'He said nothing. But he lifted me, and turned me, forcing me to crouch on all fours on the cold stone slab. My heart was thudding so fiercely I thought it would burst.

'Then, my bull-man kneeled up on the slab behind me and, tearing off my clothing, began to ravish me. And, oh – ' Sahild shuddered deliciously at the memory – 'never, never have I known anything like it! Up and up his wonderful shaft slid into me, never-ending. I thought I would die of pleasure! With his weapon as magnificent as any bull's pizzle, he filled me to bursting, and then began to take me wildly, riding up and down, gripping and pawing at my quivering buttocks.'

'Did he say anything?' asked Freya enviously.

'No, but I could hear him grunting, panting deeply, like some big animal in the shadows behind me. I was so filled with dark excitement that I cried out, over and over again, as he drove himself into ecstasy and spent himself deep, deep within me.' She sighed wistfully.

'I tell you, he drained every last drop of pleasure from my body with his magnificent penis. Short, juicy caresses that made me melt; long, satisfying thrusts that made me cry out in delight – oh, if only I could have seen him properly as he serviced me! I still dream of it now – how his shaft must have looked, so thick, so angry, so wet with my love juices as he pumped himself between my cheeks.

'When at last he slid himself slowly out of me, I slumped face down on the slab, exhausted. And when I turned round, he'd gone! Vanished, into the blackness of the forest . . .' Her voice trailed reluctantly away.

Everyone hung onto the echo of her words, rapt and aroused again.

Only Elena shivered, disturbed by Sahild's strange tale.

In the silence, the dark presence of the forest pressed in around them. She was only too aware again of the mysterious, supernatural forces, the old magic, that underlaid the lives of all these people.

Freya was listening open-mouthed, her eyes glazed with excitement and longing.

'It sounds,' she said, laughing a little shakily, 'like one of the stories they tell about Aimery le Sabrenn! I've heard that the Breton is a truly magnificent lover.'

Elena felt the shock jar through her at Aimery's name. Leofwin's arm tightened protectively around her. 'It's all right, princess,' he murmured soothingly. 'You're safe from him here.' Aloud, to the others, he said, 'Who knows? You might have the chance to find out for yourselves soon.'

Freya turned on him, her eyes wide with excitement. 'What do you mean?'

Gyrth said, with a grin of triumph: 'He means, my sweet, that we found out today from one of our Norman prisoners that the Breton will be travelling to Lincoln shortly, for a meeting with the king's justiciars. If we can get him away from his men, he'll be ours. To do with as we wish.'

A hush fell over the ring of faces. Sahild fondled her dagger. 'How will he die?' she whispered.

'We'll take pleasure in deciding that when the time comes,' said Leofwin chillingly. 'And in letting him know a long time in advance, so he can dwell on the prospect.'

Elena went tense in his arms, her face drained of blood. Leofwin looked anxiously down at her.

'Something is wrong. Elena?'

'No! No, I'm just so tired. Will you all forgive me if I go to bed?'

Leofwin touched her hand affectionately. 'Of course. It's late. I'll join you shortly.'

Sahild watched her go, narrow-eyed.

Elena was asleep by the time Leofwin joined her. She tossed and muttered, dreaming again of the ring of dark, malicious faces around the captive knight in the clearing. 'Aimery,' she groaned aloud. 'Oh, Aimery.'

Leofwin turned restlessly in his sleep and held her close, not hearing what she said.

But Sahild, wandering restlessly outside in the darkness, heard the convent girl cry out the Breton's name and froze outside the hut, her breath an indrawn hiss of discovery.

Elena was down by the stream one evening, fetching water, when she heard the men get back. They'd been gone all day – hunting, Leofwin had told her. She was glad they'd returned before nightfall, because the wild forest still frightened her without Leofwin's arms around her.

It was late summer, and the nights were drawing in. Already, the gibbous moon hung palely overhead, and a nightjar let out its eerie cry, making her jump. She picked up her heavy wooden pail and hurried back to the clearing.

It seemed the hunting had gone well, because the men were in high spirits as they stood in a circle gazing down at their prize. Leofwin saw her coming through the trees; his face lit up as he reached out for her, but his eyes were strangely cold, cruel, almost.

'See what we have here, princess,' he said softly. 'A fine day's hunting.'

Elena, bewildered by his mysterious air, stepped forward into the circle of men and looked down.

An unconscious man lay bound on the mossy turf. A soldier. Stripped of his chain-mail and helmet, he lay limp and defenceless in his linen tunic, his arms trussed behind his back, his legs tightly bound. She couldn't see his face, but his hair was thick and tawny, and streaked with blood.

She let out a low cry.

'Recognise him?' said Leofwin with grim satisfaction. 'Aimery the Breton – ours at last! We got him away from his companions on the road to Lincoln, though he still put up a damned stubborn fight.'

Elena whispered, 'Is – is he dead?'

Leofwin laughed shortly. 'Not yet. I promised the others we'd have some fun with him before he breathes his last.' He pushed at Aimery's shoulder with his booted foot, turning him onto his side; Elena's heart lurched sickly as she saw the familiar, strong-boned face, the silvery scar, the dried blood on his forehead. His eyes were closed, with shadows under them like bruises; and she saw that his leg was gashed, the blood seeping through his woollen hose. She dug her finger-nails into her palms to stop herself crying out loud and said, as steadily as she could,

'The King would give a fine ransom for him. Lord Aimery saved his life once, in battle.'

Gyrth smiled chillingly. 'Don't worry, they'll give us gold for his body. When we've finished with him.'

'That's right.' Sahild stepped forward, her face a cold mask of triumph. 'And Elena will want to join in with his punishment. She'll want to see him beg aloud, and plead for death, won't you, Elena? Won't you?'

Elena felt the bile rise in her throat. Blindly, she stammered out, 'I must go. I've left things down by the stream – '

She got to the water's edge just in time. She leaned over the bank and retched helplessly. They were going to kill Aimery, and she realised that she couldn't bear it.

When she got back, her pale face outwardly composed and calm, the outlaws were drinking and celebrating. Their laughter was wine-soaked and coarse; they talked determinedly of vengeance. Suddenly to

Elena her summer idyll seemed a summer lie. Even the twins, of whom she'd grown so fond, had a hard, cruel light in their eyes. They all hated Aimery so much.

She forced herself to take her usual place in their circle beside Leofwin, and said quietly, 'Where is he?'

Sahild said scornfully, 'Where he should be. Bound to the old oak by the stone – ready for us. Though we hardly needed to bother to tie him up. With that leg injury he won't get far.'

Leofwin said, 'It's nothing serious. Tonight he'll stay where he is, and tomorrow we'll feed him, restore him to some semblance of strength. Then – we'll begin.'

His calm words chilled Elena to the bone. She bowed her head, her eyes dark with distress, and pretended to drink the mead they offered her in celebration.

The injured, helpless Aimery le Sabrenn was to be their next sacrifice.

Sahild watched the convent girl with cold scorn. How she despised her. She'd come amongst them uninvited, with her innocent blue eyes and soft feminine ways, and cast her spell over the menfolk until they were all besotted with her.

No-one had listened to Sahild when she warned them that the convent girl was a spy. They wouldn't listen to her now – she knew better than to try. But she, Sahild, had heard the girl moan out the Breton's name in her sleep; she'd watched her face go pale every time he was mentioned, and had followed her secretly as she went down to the stream to be sick.

Sahild thought she knew how to deal with her. She caught Freya's hand quietly in the darkness. 'Freya. You know those stories you mentioned about the Breton?'

Freya nodded avidly. 'Yes. Oh, yes!'

'Then let's,' said Sahild, 'find out if they are true.'

Chapter Fifteen

*A*imery stirred and groaned as consciousness returned. His head hammered painfully from the blow that had finally felled him. He remembered, with a brief grimace at his own stupidity, how the Saxons who waited in ambush on the road to Lincoln, had lured him away from his men, yelling to him that they had Hamet and were about to kill him.

A trick, of course. He realised it the instant before the blow that felled him, when he saw the Saracen galloping wildly towards him – too late.

He shifted his limbs experimentally; his leg throbbed damnably where a sword had caught him a glancing blow. Fortunately the wound was superficial, but it was enough to slow him down. Not that he'd get away tonight, with these leather thongs round his wrists and ankles, strapping him to the tree.

Judging by the position of the moon and stars, it was well past midnight. There was a curious raised stone slab in the middle of the shadowy clearing; he thought wryly of pagan ceremonies, of tales of human sacrifice. Then he shut his eyes and tried to empty his mind, as he'd taught himself to do during the long night before a battle. Waiting for dawn, possibly for death.

He was brought back to reality by the sound of whispered giggles. He opened his eyes, startled, and saw two women approaching him stealthily in the darkness. One was plumply pretty, with curling blonde hair; while the other was slender and boyish, with her silver hair cropped short like a soldier's around her elfin face.

'There!' whispered the plump one. 'I told you he'd be awake!'

They stood in front of him, assessing him. 'Greetings, Breton,' said the short-haired one softly. 'My name is Sahild. And this is Freya. We've come to get better acquainted with you.'

Saxon witches, thought Aimery to himself.

Freya was saying, nervously, 'What if Leofwin finds out we're here? Won't he be angry?'

'He won't even know.' Sahild laughed chillingly.

Aimery listened grimly, his face expressionless. They talked of Leofwin – the Saxon leader Elena had helped to escape. Her beautiful face still haunted him, damn her.

Then he braced himself, expecting death, because the Saxon elf-witch Sahild had drawn a wicked knife from her belt, and was holding the point at his throat.

She smiled, chillingly. Then to his surprise she started to cut at his tunic, ripping the linen away from his chest, slashing at the lacings of his hose so that they fell in tatters round his leather boots, fragments of fabric clinging to the dried blood on his leg.

Then she went very still, the knife still poised in her hand, while Freya edged up close to his other side, her eyes wide.

'Oh,' Freya sighed happily, 'It's true, what they say! He's so beautiful!'

And with eager fingers she began to stroke his pinioned shoulders, running her palms over the ridged muscle of his bronzed chest, sliding down to the flat plane of his stomach where the dark, silky mat of hair arrowed down to his groin. His phallus hung long and thick between his iron-hard thighs.

Aimery's eyes glittered. 'I suppose,' he said calmly, 'that it's a long time since you've seen a real man.'

The girl Sahild whipped the point of her blade to his neck, nicking his throat. 'So you speak Saxon, do you? Arrogant scum!' She turned to the other girl, who was stroking the rough silk of his heavily muscled legs with rapt attention. 'Time to teach the Breton some manners, Freya!'

Freya whispered keenly, 'What are we going to do?'

'We're going to humiliate him,' said Sahild. She smiled, and Aimery felt a shiver of unease ripple down his spine. Already his phallus was stirring though he fought hard for control.

Then the two blonde Saxon witches began to undress in front of him, and he groaned inwardly.

'See here, Breton,' Sahild was whispering. She was slim-ipped and boyish, apart from her pointed breasts. 'Wouldn't you like a taste of this?' And she stood in front of him with her hands on her hips, dressed only in her soft deerskin boots, her body firm and lithe in the moonlight.

His lip curled. 'Saxon slut,' he said. 'You think you can interest me?'

Sahild gasped, then she reached out to grip his heavy testicles, laughing softly. She twisted hard. 'I know I can interest you,' she said. 'Animal. Animal.'

Freya gave a little cry of delight, wriggling her plump breasts. 'Look at him, Sahild! Oh, look!' She was gasping in pleasure as the Breton's heavy phallus stirred into life. The blood pulsed along the thick, veined shaft that prodded hungrily against Sahild's cool hands as she caressed and squeezed his big, velvety sac.

Aimery shut his eyes, trying to fight his helpless arousal with all his iron strength; but the girl's cool hands were too much. He clenched his fists tightly in their bonds and waited, resigned, knowing that he was fully erect.

Freya's eyes widened as she gazed on the massive shaft that reared so powerfully from the pinioned Breton's loins. 'Oh, Sahild,' she whispered, licking her lips. 'Please – can I?' And she reached to touch.

'One moment,' said Sahild sternly. 'We're going to make the most of this, you and I.'

It was then that Aimery saw that she'd brought ropes with her. She was clever and resourceful, this elf-witch – he'd give her that. With nimble fingers, she retied him at the wrists with a long loop of rope, which she secured to the tree. Then she cut his old bonds, and forced him to slide down and kneel on the ground with his back against the tree trunk, his arms stretched taut above his head. He resisted, every inch of the way; but she held the knife to his throat menacingly.

'Fight any more, Breton, and you're dead. Now for the real test. You think you can defy us. We know you can't.' She moistened her lips salaciously, running her narrowed eyes over his bronzed, naked flesh. 'We're going to pleasure you, Freya and I. And every time you give in to us – every time you climax – we shall punish you.'

The kneeling prisoner laughed bitterly. 'You'll be disappointed then.' His erection had subsided during his struggles; he felt coldly unaroused.

'Oh,' said Sahild, 'I don't think so. Freya – he's yours.'

With a little sigh of pleasure Freya sank to her knees beside the Breton and rubbed her palms against his hardening nipples; then she thrust out her ripe breasts, grinding their soft flesh against him. She then bent to touch his long, lazy phallus where it lay along his bent thigh; Aimery fought silently for control, and won.

Sahild broke in. 'It seems you have a certain amount of restraint, my fine lord Aimery. Either that, or you've got a problem. Let's find out what really excites you, shall we?'

'Not you,' drawled Aimery, 'that's for sure.'

She hissed in anger. Turning her back on him, she went over to her discarded clothes, and came back with her leather belt and another, unfamiliar object that gleamed in the moonlight. She handed the belt to the crestfallen Freya. Then she held out her hands, to show him what she carried.

It was a thick bone, he realised with a shock; sun-bleached and pale, from some animal in the forest. At least, he hoped it was an animal, he thought wryly. As long as his arm from wrist to elbow, it had been carved and polished into the familiar, obscene shape of a man's phallus, the knob at either end ground down and rounded smoothly.

Sahild stood in front of him, her booted feet planted firmly apart, so he was looking up at her slender brown thighs. Gazing down at her captive defiantly, she gripped the thick bone phallus and slowly, licking her lips, began to slide the smooth, rounded head up between the pink, glistening lips that peeped from between her golden fleece. 'Oh,' she murmured lasciviously, 'that's good. So good.'

Aimery said, 'Is that what you use when your man can't get it up?'

She stopped, her face frozen with malice. Then she said, 'Hit him, Freya – with the belt. Hit him hard.'

Obediently Freya unfolded the belt and drew it down hard across his bent thighs, inches from his somnolent penis. Aimery jerked in his bonds and bit his lip; she hit him again, her face intent. Sahild drew the obscene bone phallus from her damp vulva and rubbed its glistening tip across her small pointed breasts, her lips parted in pleasure as she drank in the Breton's humiliation.

'Watch,' she said, 'watch and enjoy. You want me really, don't you? You wish it was you, ramming up me like this . . .' She stood almost astride him now, her vulva inches from his face; he could smell the musky, animal scent of her. She slid the bone phallus up inside herself again, her face glazed with ecstasy, and drove herself swiftly to orgasm, shuddering and heaving as the sweet pleasure racked her body.

Aimery's penis jerked hungrily, rearing up towards her, and he shut his eyes. Sahild gazed with pleasure at his darkly massive erection. 'Do you still want to tell me, Breton, that you don't find me exciting?'

He forced a cold smile. 'Is that the best you can do? I've seen old whores on the streets of Rouen that put up a better show.'

Sahild's eyes went very pale, and her eyes glittered. 'Oh, you'll be sorry for that, you bastard. Very sorry. Freya, do what you want with him. Afterwards, we'll punish him properly.'

With a rapturous sigh, the plump girl positioned her legs on either side of the kneeling prisoner, and squatted astride his lips. Her eyes half-closed already in rapture, she parted her swollen sex lips with loving care and rubbed her cleft juicily along the velvety tip of his hungry phallus, moaning softly to herself.

Aimery clenched his teeth.

Shuddering, Freya slid down on the full length of his penis, gasping with delight, caressing her bouncing breasts with fevered fingers. 'Oh, Sahild,' she whispered. 'I don't think I can last very long! He's so deep inside me, so strong and cool. I've never known anything like it – '

'Ride him, then,' said Sahild sharply. 'Take him with you to the brink. Make him spend himself inside you! I want to see him groan.'

And Freya did as she was told, bouncing up and down in delirious ecstasy, her love passage tight and juicy around the Breton's massive shaft.

Aimery fought his own climax dispassionately. The girl would climax very soon; he could tell by the wild twitching of her hungry inner flesh; and he was nowhere near. He watched with narrowed eyes as she

trembled on the brink and ground herself wildly against
him, gasping and muttering in the delicious throes of
orgasm.

She collapsed against his chest, dazed with pleasure.
Her weight hurt his leg, and he closed his eyes. At last
she eased herself off him, still flushed and trembling. He
was ramrod straight, his mouth set in a thin, hard line.

'Is that it?' he enquired with quiet scorn.

Sahild was still fingering her thick bone phallus,
stroking her lips with it. 'No, it isn't,' she said softly.

They rearranged his bonds roughly so that he was
forced to turn around on his knees and face the tree; his
arms clasped round its trunk, his cheek rasped by the
rough bark. His naked hips were forced into exposure.
Sahild knelt behind him and slowly ran her hand over
his tight, muscular buttocks. Then she licked her forefinger and slid it down the dark, hairy crease between
his cheeks. She felt the little puckered hole tighten in
shame; heard the hiss of the Breton's indrawn breath as
he pressed his face against the tree.

'So,' she said. 'That's what you like, is it, Breton?'
She lifted the bone phallus and gripped its cool length
lovingly.

Elena couldn't sleep, for thinking about Aimery.
Tomorrow the Saxons were going to kill him – slowly.
Her dark longing for him burned in her blood, as it had
from the first moment she met him. She couldn't bear
to think of his suffering.

Holding her breath, she eased herself from the sleeping Leofwin's arms. He snored gently and turned over
in his sleep, still sodden with wine. Silently she slipped
into her tunic and crept out of the hut.

Sahild whirled round, hearing light footsteps coming
through the trees. Quick as a flash, she slipped into the
blackness at the edge of the clearing, dragging Freya
with her.

As the covent girl drew near, Sahild pounced on her, smothering her cries by putting her hand over her mouth and holding the knife to her throat.

'One word, convent girl, and you're dead! What are you doing here?'

'I couldn't sleep.'

'You'll never sleep again, if you breathe a word of this to the others. Worried about your Breton, were you?'

Elena tried to fight down her panic. 'I – I don't know what you mean, Sahild!'

'I may not know everything,' said Sahild grimly. 'But I've been watching you, and I'd hazard a guess that you and the Breton were lovers! And I still think you're a spy. Coming to set him free, were you?'

Elena tried desperately to order her thoughts as the knife pricked at her throat. If Sahild ever guessed how she felt about Aimery . . .

'What are you two doing here, then?' she challenged, trying to sound cool and calm. 'Perhaps *you've* come to set him free!'

Sahild chuckled, relaxing her grip. 'Oh, no. You can see what we've been doing. Look!'

And she thrust Elena forward to the edge of the clearing, where she could see Aimery, bound and naked, his face pressed to the tree so he could see nothing.

Elena's heart pounded painfully as Sahild dragged her across to the prisoner. 'Now's your chance to prove that you're really one of us, convent girl. Otherwise I'll tell Leofwin that you're a spy! Here – take this, and use it on him!'

And she thrust the long bone phallus into Elena's trembling hand. 'What do you want me to do?' Elena whispered between white lips.

'What do you think?' hissed Sahild scornfully. She pushed Elena onto her knees behind the Breton. 'Shove it up his arse, of course – go on. Go on. Slide it behind

780

his tight cheeks – push – that's it! Go on, make him whine for mercy!'

And Elena, quivering with shame yet wildly excited at what she was being forced to do, gripped the thick phallus in her palm. She slid its rounded end tentatively up and down the tight crease between the Breton's cheeks; then, finding the brown, puckered little hole, she pushed blindly.

Aimery swore aloud in Breton, struggling to twist his head to see who was inflicting this new torment; but the ropes caught him, restraining him. Freya kneeled low by his hips, excitedly watching his straining phallus as it pulsed into erection again. 'Oh, he likes it, he likes it!'

Elena slid it in deeply, surprised at how easily it went in, feeling him clutch instinctively at its cool length with his rectal muscles. The pleasure and shame swept over her at his proud helplessness.

'Again!' hissed Sahild. 'Drive it in and out now – quickly – that's it! See how he quivers and throbs!' She leaned against the tree, next to the Breton's head, and whispered viciously in his ear. 'You like it really, don't you, my fine lord Aimery? You're nothing but a base-born mercenary, aren't you? And it shows!'

'You like feeling that cool shaft sliding deep inside your tight arse – filling you – fucking you. That's what you're used to, a slim young soldier's eager cock shoved up inside you! I can see your balls twitching and tightening. Any moment now, you'll be grovelling, pleading for more, before your hot seed shoots out. Then, if you're very lucky, we'll start again.'

Aimery gritted his teeth, his eyes closed. 'Anything you say. Just as long as I don't have to do it with you, Saxon whore.'

Sahild spat on him. It landed on his scarred cheek. She spat again; then she reached for her belt, and struck him across his broad, sweat-streaked brown shoulders so that he shook in his bonds.

781

Elena, hotly aroused herself, saw how his proud penis reared and jerked against his smooth belly; saw how his heavy balls tightened against his body. Oh, how she longed to soothe him in his extremity, to bring him the wild comfort of pleasure in the midst of his degradation! With frenzied fingers, she drove the bone phallus swiftly in and out of that pulsing rear entrance; Aimery let out a great groan, and strained against his bonds until she thought they would break.

His climax shook them all with its ferocity. His buttocks clenched tightly round the slippery bone phallus, almost dragging it from her grasp; his whole body shuddered, and the sperm jetted from his penis in great spurts, time and time again, until the soft earth beneath the tree was pooled with the milky fluid. Elena felt her own pleasure bud quiver hotly, wishing desperately that he was driving himself into her, instead. She leaned forward, greedily rubbing her hot breasts against his hard buttocks; her nipples hardened and peaked, and she felt the moisture gathering between her legs, longing for him.

Gently, so as not to hurt his still pulsing rectum, Elena withdrew the phallus, and pressed its length against her cleft, rolling it gently between her legs. It was enough. She climaxed silently but ferociously, the hot pleasure waves crashing over her as the shaft of hard bone soothed her throbbing little bud of flesh.

Sahild rolled up her belt, and nodded at her approvingly. 'You did well there, Elena. You earned your pleasure.'

Still dazed from orgasm, Elena nodded blindly, not realising what had happened.

Then, she heard the hiss of Aimery's indrawn breath, and she realised what Sahild had done. Aimery knew, now, who it was who had degraded him. He'd heard her name.

She froze in anguish. He knew. What could she do? If he let them know, let Sahild know what had existed between them, then she was lost, and all her plans were in vain. Sahild would drag her back, and denounce her to the others.

He was straining to turn his head, to see his tormentor, but his bonds stopped him. But she heard his voice, and it was dark with scorn. '*Saxon scum.*'

Then he sagged in his bonds, lapsing into semi-consciousness.

Sahild and Freya got dressed, chattering companionably as if nothing much had happened. Then they linked arms with Elena, not seeming to notice how pale and quiet she was, and wandered slowly back.

'What a wonderful evening,' sighed Freya rapturously. 'But what will they do with him tomorrow?'

Sahild shrugged. 'Whatever happens, they'll make sure that it's good sport for us.' She turned companionably to Elena. 'You did well tonight – really humiliated him. Maybe they'll let you help tomorrow.'

Elena, feeling sick and dazed, tried to smile. 'Maybe,' she acknowledged shakily.

They left Elena outside Leofwin's hut. She pushed the hide door aside and tiptoed in. She had already decided what she must do.

Leofwin was still asleep. Thank goodness he had drunk so much wine. Taking a deep breath, she went over to where his discarded clothes lay in a heap, and picked up his tunic and his knife. Then she crept out again; dawn was starting to break coldly in the east. After checking that Sahild and Freya were nowhere in sight, she plunged back towards the sinister grove, her heart beating wildly.

Aimery le Sabrenn was still slumped against the broad oak to which he was bound, his eyes closed, his face stubbled and shadowed with utter exhaustion.

Swallowing hard, Elena drew close to him, the knife gleaming in her hand. 'Aimery,' she whispered.

He looked up tiredly and saw the knife. 'So you've come to kill me now, have you?'

783

She flinched. 'No! I've come to set you free!'

His steely grey eyes narrowed in scorn. He grated out, 'What game is this?'

'No game, I swear!' Her small face grimly determined, she started to saw through the rope that bound his wrists. 'Aimery – I didn't want to hurt you, earlier. But I thought that if I didn't join in, the others would suspect!'

The knife sliced through the thick rope; one of his hands was free. She started on another cord; Sahild had been thorough.

Aimery said, his voice hard with scorn: 'You expect me to believe all this? What does your lover, Leofwin, think of your nocturnal wanderings?'

She caught her breath. 'He doesn't know. Quickly – oh, quickly! They'll be awake soon.'

Her knife severed the last strand of rope. He got slowly to his feet, testing his injured leg; he seemed big and naked and muscular in the grey light of sunrise. Elena shivered and pushed the clothing she'd brought towards his hands. 'Here – put these on! And go, please go. Don't you realise that they're going to kill you?'

'The thought had crossed my mind.'

Swiftly he pulled on Leofwin's tunic. He buckled the belt and looked at her suddenly, his familiar grey eyes burning into her. 'I thought you would be glad at my death.'

She gazed up at him, drinking in those strong, proud features; the cynically curved, beautiful mouth; the lean, stubborn jaw darkened now by stubble. Her small fists clenched round the knife; she burned for him, remembering the dark, glorious pleasure he'd revealed to her with his powerful body. 'Would I be here now if I wanted you dead?' she whispered in a low voice. He hesitated, suddenly uncertain.

'Please, please go, Aimery!' Daylight was spreading its cold light across the forest – someone might come, any moment now.

Too late! She moaned aloud at the sound of crashing footsteps plunging through the forest towards them. She whirled round. There – at the other side of the clearing: Gyrth, Leofwin, and Sahild! All heavily armed.

'There she is!' shouted Sahild triumphantly. 'See, she's cut him free – she's a spy – I knew it!' She raised her bow and took aim.

Before she could even cry out, Elena felt Aimery grab her. He held her in front of his body like a shield; then he snatched the knife from her nerveless hands and held the blade tight against her throat.

'Move any closer,' he called out ominously to the outlaws, 'and I'll kill her. Shoot, and *you'll* kill her.'

Sahild pulled her bowstring taut. 'Then I'll kill her, Breton, never fear! She's a spy, a traitor to her kind! After that, I'll kill you – you won't get far, with that leg!'

Elena, trapped tightly against Aimery's powerful body, saw Sahild's arrow aimed straight at her heart.

Then Leofwin moved. Before Sahild could release her bowstring, he swung his arm fiercely, knocking her over; then he turned to glare in helpless impotence at his enemy. 'Let her go, Breton!'

Aimery smiled chillingly, the white scar pulling at his mouth. 'Oh, no. I'm taking her with me, Leofwin. If you try to follow me, I'll kill her – slowly.'

Leofwin lurched forward blindly; Gyrth grabbed him and used all his strength to hold him back. 'Let her go, Leofwin – she's not worth it.'

Sahild, lying winded on the ground, gasped out, 'Fools! You should have let me kill them both!'

Swinging Elena round, Aimery pinioned her arms behind her back, gripping both her slender wrists in one strong hand. Then, the knife gripped ready in his other palm, he pushed her into the darkness of the forest, away from the clearing, away from the helpless outlaws. 'Move,' he hissed. 'Move, damn you!'

Chapter Seventeen

The serfs toiled in the fields, wearily gathering in the last gleanings of the wheat harvest. Hard-faced reeves moved amongst them with whips. 'Faster, faster!' All eyes were on the heavy rain clouds piling up above the bleak moors to the west.

Elena worked blindly, beyond weariness. Last night, when they got back to Thoresfield, she'd been herded in with the other serfs, and at dawn she was sent to the fields with them. At least she'd not been thrown in the dungeons and flogged, as other runaways were. Or handed over to Isobel.

She shivered as the cold wind blew across the field and the first heavy raindrops started to fall from the leaden sky. Her back ached with stooping, and her fingers were raw from the stubble, but she scarcely noticed.

It all seemed like a dream now, yesterday's flight through the forest with Aimery. They'd sped breathlessly along the secret, grassy tracks beneath the trees, further and further from Leofwin and the outlaws. Aimery's injured leg dragged slightly, but otherwise his lean, hard body seemed untouched by his ordeal. He never once let go of her arm.

As the day wore on, the canopy of trees grew less dense, and the huge, mossy oaks started to give way to birch and bracken. It was then that Aimery stopped at last, breathing hard. Elena swayed for support against a tree, almost sobbing with fatigue.

He said, 'We're almost at the boundary of the forest. You can go back now. I don't need a hostage any more.'

'You know I can never go back.' Elena forced her voice to be steady. 'You know they'd kill me. For helping you to escape.'

His mouth thinned, pulling at his scar. 'I'm sure you can find some way to redeem yourself. Why did you do it?'

Her dark, fathomless blue eyes met his cold grey ones. 'Because I didn't want you to die,' she said in a low voice.

His lips curled in scorn. He gripped her chin, forcing her to look up at him again as she trembled at the touch of his lean brown fingers. 'You're full of tricks, little Elena, aren't you? Such fine excuses. How you enjoyed humiliating me with your friends!'

She shuddered, remembering the bone phallus and her own fierce, shameful excitement at this proud man's degradation. 'I had to do it – don't you see? Or they'd have suspected me, and then I wouldn't have been able to free you!'

'So clever,' he murmured coldly. 'So subtle, so ingenious . . .'

Slowly he ran his fingertips through her hair, lifting it and letting it fall like golden silk. Then he took her face in his hands and kissed her fiercely, the stubble of his jaw rasping at her soft cheek. The tears burned in her eyes.

He let her go, so suddenly that she almost fell. 'Someone's coming,' he said.

It was the soldiers, led by Hamet, who'd been scouring the forest ever since Aimery's capture.

Now she was back at Thoresfield, a forgotten serf. And she'd just heard from the other serfs that Aimery was leaving for the south, to join his king.

Isobel was in the hall, attending to a visitor – Godric, a Saxon thane who lived on a small neighbouring estate. He'd managed to hold on to his property by feigning illness when King Harold's summons to battle arrived, and then by vowing immediate allegiance to the victorious William. He was well aware that the lord Aimery utterly despised him, and he was glad to have audience with the lady Isobel instead.

'I need more workers, my lady,' he was explaining. 'The summer fever took so many of my serfs, and I've still half the harvest to get in and the threshing to be done. I heard that the lord Aimery was leaving shortly, and I thought maybe you'd be wanting rid of a few workers, before the winter sets in.'

Isobel was thinking hard. Aimery was out riding, inspecting his lands for a final inventory before he left. Now – now was her chance.

She hadn't been able to conceal her dismay when the little Saxon slut was brought back to Thoresfield on the back of Hamet's horse. And Aimery hadn't even punished her for running away! When Isobel had suggested that the girl be flogged, he told her curtly to mind her own business. The girl was still at large, even if she was out in the fields; still a threat to her, until she and Aimery were safely away from Thoresfield.

'Do you want women as well?' she asked Godric thoughtfully.

He grinned. 'If they're willing wenches, yes. If they're pretty, and will satisfy a few of the male slaves, then that's even better.'

'I know one who's just right for you,' said Isobel, her eyes gleaming. 'She's young, and extremely pretty – and she knows a lot of tricks. You'll probably want to try her out yourself before you hand her over to your men for their sport. You can have her for five pieces of gold.'

The man licked his fleshy lips. 'My lady. How can I thank you?'

'Just take her. Quickly.' Before Aimery gets back, she added silently to herself.

When Aimery and Hamet finally rode into the court-yard, the rain was falling steadily from an overcast sky. They'd been talking of the long journey to London, then perhaps to Normandy where William was again involved in defending his lands against the troublesome Fulk of Anjou. When they got to the stables, Aimery dismounted quickly and led his big black horse inside, dismissing the groom and starting to unfasten the girth himself, as the rain pounded on the rye straw thatch overhead. Hamet followed him into the hay-scented warmth, checked that they were alone, and said hesitantly,

'About the girl, my lord. Be careful that you don't judge her too harshly.'

Aimery carried on unbuckling the saddle, his expression forbidding. 'Of whom, friend Hamet, are you talking?'

Hamet stood his ground. 'Elena, my lord.'

Aimery turned round to face him. 'She came here as a rebel spy. She set the rebel leader free, then ran off to join him and lived with him in the forest. And you think I judged her harshly? She's alive, isn't she?'

'You told me that it was the girl who freed you.'

Aimery turned to stroke his horse's thick black mane. He remembered the forest, remembered the three Saxon witches who'd degraded him until he broke. He remembered how he'd felt when he realised that one of them was Elena. He said, 'There are other things I've not told you, Hamet. Believe me, the girl's escaped lightly.'

Hamet bowed his dark head and said no more.

Aimery pushed past him into the wet courtyard. 'I've decided I'm leaving tonight. Prepare an escort, will you?'

Alys crouched in the shadows by the steps that led up to the hall. The heavy rain streamed down from the eaves, turning her mousy hair into straggling rats' tails and soaking her clothes. But she didn't care. She had to see the lord Aimery! She had to!

This afternoon, while he was out, they'd made sport of her again – the lady Isobel, with her minions, Morwith and Pierre. Isobel had called her up to her room, and told her that she had a new beauty salve that would make a woman wildly desirable to any man if she rubbed it into her most private parts. She'd given Alys a phial of it; Alys had rushed away and smeared it carefully where Isobel had suggested, on her nipples, between her legs.

Then, the ointment had started to tingle and burn, driving her into a frenzy of desire. The lady Isobel had called Alys back into her room, and made her watch while Morwith was serviced crudely on the floor by the virile Pierre. Alys was driven mad by lust as she watched, longing to feel Pierre's great thick penis cooling her own burning flesh; while Isobel had laughed at her. Laughed at her!

Alys had rushed off to wash away the tormenting salve in icy cold water, her heart burning with rage. And then, she'd seen the girl, Elena, roped and driven away with some other serfs by that brute Godric. She'd heard Isobel tell him to take them quickly, before Aimery returned.

Now, Alys waited in the pouring rain, her heart pounding, as Aimery's tall, familiar figure emerged from the stables and came towards the steps. If Isobel knew what Alys was about to tell him, that it was the lady de Morency who had freed the dangerous Saxon

790

rebel, then hidden the key to the dungeons under the girl's pillow, then Isobel would kill her.

'My lord Aimery.'

'Yes?' He stopped mid-stride, his scarred face dangerous as the bedraggled woman stepped in front of him. 'My lord – I have something that I must tell you! Please – can we go somewhere private?'

Godric cursed as the rain poured down and turned the track to muddy sludge. Damn it, he'd be lucky to get home before nightfall with these sullen slaves. And the girl that Isobel had been so anxious for him to take – the pretty blonde one with the big blue eyes – she was giving him more trouble than the rest put together! While his surly reeve kept an eye on the rest of his purchases, he'd roped the blonde girl to his saddle, so she had to almost run to keep up, and he could keep an eye on her just by turning his head. But she was still a damned nuisance, arguing and complaining.

He reined in his horse, swearing vividly, and turned round in the saddle. She'd stopped yet again, her feet planted firmly in the mud, her head raised proudly even though he could see that she was white with tiredness.

'I won't go any further! You can't make me!'

'Can't I indeed!' He unfurled the vicious plaited whip he carried. 'We'll soon see about that, you stubborn wench.'

He broke off in surprise as he heard the thunder of a galloping horse's hooves pounding down the muddy track towards them. He squinted through the rain impatiently, and gasped in surprise.

Aimery. Aimery the Breton. Looking as black as thunder . . .

Godric watched stupefied as the big Breton soldier, his cloak dripping wet, pulled up his huge black horse beside the girl. Then he drew a knife from his belt, and started to cut her free.

791

'Hey!' Godric called out. 'My lord, I paid good money for that girl! Gave it to the lady Isobel, before witnesses. Ten pieces of gold.'

'Five,' replied the Breton curtly, and flung the money towards him so that it landed in the mud. Then he carried on slicing through the rope. The girl, Godric noted, looked dazed.

'My lord!' said Godric fussily. 'I don't, as it happens, choose to sell her back to you! I particularly singled her out – after all, she'll be no use to you once you've left Thoresfield! The lady Isobel told me she was very skilled, with lots of tricks. A clever little whore, she said – '

Aimery stopped then. He came up to the man, Godric, in three powerful strides; pulled him off his horse, and hit him so hard on the chin that he landed on his back in the squelching mud.

Then he picked up the girl in his arms and set her on his big horse. Swinging up in the saddle behind her, he held her tightly in his arms and swung his horse back towards Thoresfield.

Aimery the Breton carried her through the courtyard, where his men, preparing for the imminent journey south, looked on in silent amazement; then through the hall and up to his room, where he slammed the door shut.

He laid his burden carefully on the thick wolfskin pelts that covered his big bed, then went to put more logs on the fire, kicking at the embers with his booted foot to get the flames leaping higher.

Elena struggled to sit up, her soaking tunic clinging to her skin. Her teeth were chattering with the cold. 'W – why did you come after me?' she whispered.

'Because I didn't damn well know you'd gone!' He stood with his back to the flames, towering over her, his face dangerously angry. But, she realised with a little thud of her heart, *not with her* . . . When he looked down at her, his grey eyes burned not with anger, but with tenderness.

She swallowed hard, fighting down the painful hope, and pushed the soaked tendril of hair from her pale cheeks. Then she began to shiver, uncontrollably.

Aimery le Sabrenn cursed under his breath, and strode towards her. Swiftly he peeled her soaked garments from her chilled skin; then he fetched a warm woollen cloak from the coffer by the bed and wrapped her in it. He pulled the luxurious wolfskin cover from the bed and laid it on the floor before the fire. Then he picked her up in his arms as if she weighed no more than a feather, and laid her down on it.

Elena shivered more than ever, but not just with the cold. It was the way he looked at her – the way those hard, steely grey eyes burned into her.

She lay curled on the thick fur, wrapped in his cloak, the flames leaping and dancing in the darkening room, the rain pounding down outside the window. The cloak he'd wrapped her in slid apart; he bent to kiss her exposed breasts, his mouth burning hot against her cold skin. The fierce pleasure knifed through her.

He stood up, his face darkly intent, and started to remove his own clothes. She gazed up at him silently, drinking in his wide-shouldered, masculine beauty; his long, heavily-muscled legs covered with silky dark hair; his proud, mysterious phallus, which stirred already with life against his inner thigh.

He knelt to lie beside her, naked, and took her in his arms. His body was gloriously strong and warm against her own cold, trembling flesh. He pressed her close to him, silently covering her face with kisses; she wondered if she was dreaming. This must be a dream. And he was leaving tonight.

His hands roved across her back and her hips, warming her, melting her. When he knelt to kiss her secret flesh, she shuddered with desire, tangling her fingers wantonly in his thick damp hair; his tongue was hot and wonderful as it slid languorously between her lips, driving her into a frenzy of molten desire. She reached out to clutch at his massively erect penis, stroking its silken length with silent rapture, tenderly caressing the velvety sac of his scrotum, feeling him pulse and quicken beneath her fingers.

He entered her quickly, his own desire burning hard at his loins; but then he pleasured her slowly, withdrawing almost to the brink and then sliding in again, filling her, caressing her, until she writhed her hips deliriously against the fur-covered floor and wrapped her ankles tightly around his strong thighs. He held her wrists to the ground on either side of her head, pinioning her gently, and bent to kiss her breasts, teasing and drawing out her rosy teats until she gasped with longing, her hips thrusting blindly towards him, her face flushed.

He smiled softly, and began to plunge his massive shaft deep within her, faster and faster, every powerful stroke driving her quivering bud of pleasure into a rapturous orgy of need, until she exploded in a shimmering frenzy, clutching blindly with her moist inner flesh at the wonderful phallus that filled her so exquisitely. Then he drove himself to his own powerful climax, jerking strongly within her still-pulsing flesh. and collapsed beside her, damp with perspiration.

Elena lay sated in his arms, her eyes closed. She didn't want this moment, this languorous, perfect peace, ever to end.

But reality pressed in. Outside the window, below in the great hall, she could hear the sounds of Aimery's knights, preparing to leave.

The pain sliced through her. He was leaving, and taking Isobel with him. Oh, why hadn't he just let her go with that man Godric, instead of bringing her back to remind her that there could never, ever be another man to compare with him?

She twisted her head away; he leaned up on one

elbow, the firelight warm on his face, and touched her eyelashes gently. 'Elena. Why are you crying, Elena?'

His voice was husky and tender, and it twisted her heart. She fought back her tears furiously and sat up, clutching his warm cloak around her naked shoulders and staring blindly into the fire. 'Why did you bring me back, Aimery?'

'Isn't that obvious, *caran*?'

Caran. Beloved . . . Her heart thumped wildly, making her dizzy. She whispered, 'No, it isn't obvious. I don't understand.'

He sat up beside her and clasped her in his arms so that her cheek was against his shoulder. 'I've been wrong, Elena – about a lot of things. Chiefly, I failed to realise just how much Isobel hated you.'

Elena, hardly daring to breathe, whispered, 'I thought it was *you* who hated me.'

'Never. Oh, never.' He drew her towards him, and tenderly kissed her hair. 'Elena – if the rebels had caught you, they would have killed you for helping me to escape. Why did you do it?'

'I – I couldn't bear it. They were going to kill you, Aimery.'

'I'm a soldier. I've faced death – and worse – many times.'

Her voice was low. 'I've told you – I couldn't bear it.'

He was silent; she read it as coldness. Someone, one of his men, thumped on the door outside and called out, 'My lord! The men are ready, and your horse is saddled up!'

'I'll be with you shortly.' But still, he didn't move.

He was leaving her – any minute, he was leaving her. Elena swallowed down the agonising ache in her throat and forced her voice to be clear and cool. 'What will happen to me when you go to join the king?'

His hands tightened round her shoulders. '*Caran*. You're going to join me, of course.'

The blood pounded dizzily in her head. 'But – Isobel?'

795

'Isobel,' he said softly, 'leaves at dawn tomorrow – by herself. Where she goes, I don't particularly care.'

He stood up slowly, still holding her, and she clung to him, unable to stop trembling now.

'I'll send for you, *caran*. Hamet is staying here for a while – he'll take care of you. As soon as I know where the king is posting me, I'll send for you.'

'Are you going to fight? In France?'

'Most likely. The king has need of me there.'

'But you might be killed.'

'It's my occupation, Elena. My life.' He smiled down at her anxious face. There was another, harsher knock on the door. 'My lord Aimery! Your men await you!'

Aimery said, 'I must go.' She lifted her face to him proudly, her eyes shining for him. 'At least, now,' she said softly, 'I know what love is.'

He kissed her with infinite tenderness, a promise of future passion; then he left the room.

She went to the window, in a trance, and gazed out into the sullen grey drizzle of the courtyard. She watched him mount his black horse, pull its strong head round towards the open gates, and set off at the head of his men.

He turned round once and looked up at the window where she stood. He raised his hand in silent salute, and rode out of the gates, heading south to fight for his king.